I0822090

Illustrated by Toby Briles

The Chimera

THE CHIMERA JOURNALS

BOOK ONE – THE SERPENT
INTO THE ABYSS

by Robert E. Balsley, Jr.

Illustrations by Toby Briles and Maps by
Dana De La Woods

Trient Press
3375 S Rainbow Blvd #81710, SMB 13135
Las Vegas,NV 89180

Ordering Information:
Quantity sales. Special discounts are available on quantity purchases by corporations, associations, and others. For details, contact the publisher at the address above.
Orders by U.S. trade bookstores and wholesalers. Please contact Trient Press: Tel: (775) 996-3844; or visit www.trientpress.com.
Printed in the United States of America Publisher's Cataloging-in-Publication data
Robert E. Balsley, Jr.
A title of a book :
THE CHIMERA JOURNALS
BOOK ONE – THE SERPENT
INTO THE ABYSS

ISBN Hardcover : 979-8-88990-146-4
Paperback : 979-8-88990-147-1
E-book: 979-8-88990-148-8

THE CHIMERA JOURNALS

Book One – The Serpent: Into the Abyss
Book Two – The Dragon (Forthcoming)
Book Three – The Lion (Forthcoming)
Book Four – The Goat (Forthcoming)

DEDICATION

Ecclesiastes 3:1-8: "There is a time for everything, and a season for every activity under heaven: a time to be born and a time to die, a time to plant and a time to uproot, a time to kill and a time to heal, a time to tear down and a time to build, a time to weep and a time to laugh, a time to mourn and a time to dance."

This book is dedicated to my mother in Heaven.
Love you, mom!

Books by Robert E. Balsley, Jr.

Published by Trient Press

The Salvation of Innocence
(Book One of the Bridge of Magic Trilogy)

The Struggle for Innocence
(Book Two of the Bridge of Magic Trilogy)

The Loss of Innocence
(Book Three of the Bridge of Magic Trilogy)

Stanley and Aloysius
(Short Story from "Rising from the Ashes—Stories to Warm the Heart and Settle the Mind")

The Lycanthropy Chronicles—Beginnings
(Novella at no cost available from bridgeofmagicnovel@gmail.com)

TABLE OF CONTENTS

PREFACE

What Has Gone Before:

War had come to the elvan island of InnisRos. With the bulk of the InnisRos army up north, marching to battle Father Goram and his allies at Calmacil Clearing—a battle concocted and put into motion by the Abyssian demon Nightshade and her mortal accomplice, Mordecai—the Dark Elves from the Svartalfheim, led by Nightshade's father, Aikanáro, invaded the island of the elves in the south. Nightshade's theft of the Ak-Séregon Stone, a strong magical relic which made it possible to move from world to world, universe to universe, and dimension to dimension, made this possible.

With most of the elvan army in the north, the Dark Elves conquered the capital city of Taranthi with ease. They subjugated its people and fortified the city into a dark elf stronghold before marching north to capture the rest of the island. Aikanáro's plan was to secure InnisRos and then move across the ocean to the mainland to gather human allies, either by treaty or by force. But conquering the world of Aster was only one piece of the puzzle which made up his ambition. His ultimate goal was the elvan home world, the Alfheim, which he hoped to seize with the armies of two worlds at his back.

To prevent any interference of Aikanáro's plan by InnisRos's human allies on the mainland, Nightshade kidnapped the princess and heir to the Draugen Pesta realm... a land of giant warriors known by the humans as the Black Death... and forced the king of that nation to bring his armies across the Greater Boreskyre Mountains, where they allied themselves with the mercenary cities of Madeira and Hebron. Together, the giants and their human collaborators marched southward to threaten the powerful sorcerer stronghold of Havendale. Nightshade had designed this excursion to draw the human armies of the mainland eastward to fight their own war. This threat would negate any willingness by the humans to come to the aid of InnisRos.

The plan was working to perfection until the one thing Aikanáro couldn't foresee became reality... Nightshade's conversion from the forces of the Dark to those of the Light. This unexpected complication led to the death of the traitor Mordecai at the hands of Nightshade and to the eventual downfall and destruction of Aikanáro and his fearsome black dragon. With the demon overlord destroyed and his daughter converted to the Light, the InnisRos Calmacil Clearing defenders, now allied with the InnisRos army, routed the Dark Elves. Nightshade returned the Draugen Pesta princess to her father. Without this impetus, the incursion into the human lands fizzled away as the Draugen Pesta returned to their homes across the Greater Boreskyre Mountains. Without them, the mercenaries from Madeira and Hebron had no choice but to return home as well.

But the defeat of Aikanáro and his army came at a steep cost, the most serious of which was the kidnapping of InnisRos's Queen Lessien Arntuile and Father Goram's wife, Autumn. Aikanáro had spirited both away from the battlefield and sent them to the Abyss, to be held unharmed, as a bargaining chip. But neither Father Goram nor Nightshade would accept anything other than the overlord's death. Aikanáro, in an ultimate act of defiance before his destruction at the hands of Father Goram, released his demon guards upon the two captives. As a result, Autumn was brutally raped before both were released to the horrors of the Abyss.

Father Goram, Nightshade, and Calmacil Clearing's military leader, the knight Landross, sought Michael, the leader of the B'nai Elohim, guardians of the Abyss, for help. Michael agreed, but only to provide a safe passage from Aster to the Abyss. The B'nai Elohim would take no part if the hunt for the two mortals. After making preparations for the security of both InnisRos and Calmacil Clearing, the three traveled to the Abyss to locate and retrieve Queen Lessien and Autumn.

As the war to secure InnisRos from the Dark Elves raged on, deep underground and beneath the human lands, a primeval race of beings known as the sylph—amorphous creatures created by the older gods to act as guardians over a newly created Aster—awoke from a forced comatose slumber with one goal in mind, the continuation of their ambition to destroy all life on Aster. This awakening was foretold by the Maelstrom Prophecy of the black dragons, who lived in caverns beneath the surface of the world. The dragons, in response to this ancient prophecy, considered it their sacred duty, their destiny, to battle the sylph uprising and stop them from reaching the surface. But the sylph were too many and too powerful. They destroyed all but two of the black dragons in the confrontation—Erika, a black dragon priestess, and a scholar, Jörmungander, the youngest of the black dragon race. A third black dragon, the cleric Solveig, also survived, though not in a physical sense. Killed by the sylph, she remained behind as a ghost.

Together with Max, a ghost who was a rogue when alive, Elbedreth, the only sylph not involved in the rebellion, and Azriel, a dwarf-sylph hybrid, they destroyed the sylph and prevented the extinction of all life on the surface of Aster. The discovery of the cavern of the Johari occurred during this world-saving event.

Map of the Abyss
Kor Prefecture

Book One – The Serpent: Into the Abyss

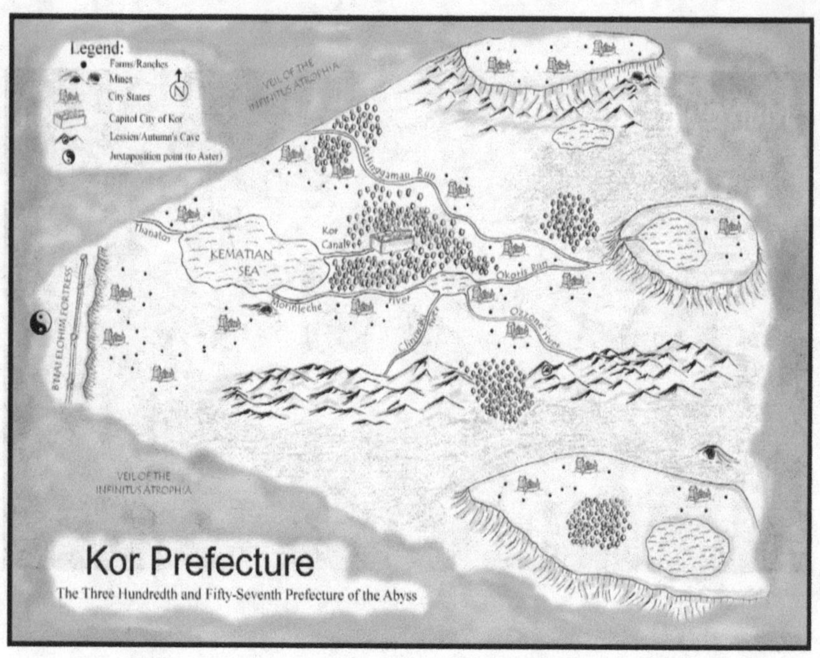

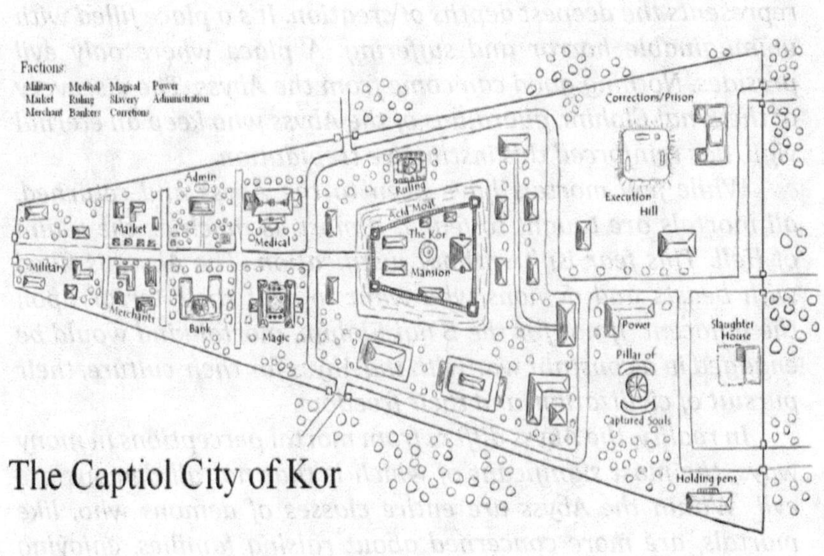
Factions:
Military Market Merchant
Medical Ruling Bankers
Magical Slavery Corretions
Power Administration
Admin
Market
Military
Merchants
Bank
Magic
Medical
Ruling
Acid Moat
The Kor
Mansion
Corrections/Prison
Execution Hill
Slaughter House
Power
Pillar of Captured Souls
Holding pens
The Captiol City of Kor

FORWARD

From the Mia Pragmateía Gia Ti Daimonología Tis Avyssou
(A Treatise on Abyss Demonology):

The Abyss: *From a mortal perspective, the Abyss represents the deepest depths of creation. It's a place filled with unimaginable horror and suffering. A place where only evil presides. Nothing good can come from the Abyss. The discovery of the B'nai Elohim, guardians of the Abyss who keep an eternal vigil, has reinforced this instinctive trepidation.*

While few mortals have been to the Abyss and returned, all mortals are taught to fear it almost as much as the realm of Hell. This fear isn't without justification. The Abyss is filled with beasts and demons who want to visit their terror upon the innocent. If not for the B'nai Elohim, mortal kind would be engaged in a constant war with the Abyss for their culture, their pursuit of civilization, and their freedom.

In reality, the Abyss differs from mortal perceptions in many ways, the most significant of which is that not all demons are evil. Within the Abyss are entire classes of demons who, like mortals, are more concerned about raising families, enjoying life, and working hard so that future generations can have a better existence. Most demons within the Abyss love as much, or more, than they hate.

But Abyssian demons are an occupied population. They're occupied by demon overlords who rule with brutality and use vast armies to maintain control. However, if a leader were to emerge—a leader who is strong and sought independence from the evilness that permeated the Abyss and suffocated its people—most demons in the Abyss would follow for the opportunity to experience freedom.

The Physical: *For clarity, envision the Abyss as a vast sphere* *of islands. (This is an oversimplification. Each layer exists within its own reality and universe. There is no physical commonality except for shape, size, organizational structure, and demon composition.)*

The Abyss comprises several thousand separate and distinct layers. Each layer is called a "Prefecture" by its denizens. Each Prefecture has a Juxtaposition Point between the Abyss and its own, distinct counterpoint in the mortal realm. The Juxtaposition Point, closely guarded by the B'nai Elohim, is the magic that the guardians use to locate and close magical doorways from the Abyss to the mortal realm. (Key to the Juxtaposition Point's existence is the Johari, which resides in the mortal universe. The Johari is a live being whose life force powers the Juxtaposition Point.) Without the Juxtaposition Point, Abyssian armies would overrun the B'nai Elohim. And without the B'nai Elohim, those same armies would engulf the mortal worlds. The physical size of a Prefecture is equivalent to the size of the world on the other side of the Juxtaposition Point.

Prefecture Leadership: *Each Prefecture carries the name of the demon lord sitting on the Living Throne—a gigantic diamond chair infused with the souls of the previous rulers and attuned to the current demon lord leader. The demon lord absorbs the metaphysical power of the souls and uses it to control the inhabitants of his own Prefecture. The stronger the souls, the longer a demon lord will rule. But the souls do not give their power without a struggle. While the demon lord uses the power of souls to his advantage, the souls resist. They wage this battle every second of the demon lord's existence until the time comes when the demon lord is too old or too weak to fight. Then his soul becomes trapped in the Living Throne, and the process repeats itself with a new demon lord. The current demon lord leader of the Abyss layer connected to Aster is Kor (formally Gog, formally Oleth, formally Blith, formally Noth, and so on).*

Prefecture Organizational Structure: *A demon lord rules each Prefecture. A demon overlord rules each city state (the number varies from Prefecture to Prefecture). Every demon overlord commands one hundred demon underlords, who in-turn command one thousand minor demons. Each city state maintains an army comprising twenty thousand demons specifically bred to be warriors. There are one hundred thousand inhabitants within the city limits of each state. Several thousand additional demons inhabit the smaller towns, farms, and ranches that surround each city state.*

Prefecture Geography: *Each Prefecture has a capital city where the demon lord lives and rules. The capital city is twice the size of the other city states and is always in the center of the Prefecture landmass. Around each city state are the farms and ranches that provide food and other goods to the city state. Each city state maintains a number of merchants and craftsman as well as other the workers—food laborers, waste management, entertainment, construction, administrative—needed to run a successful city-based society.*

Prefecture Borders: *The Veil of the Infinitus Atrophia surrounds each Prefecture. Any demon crossing into the Veil becomes lost. No one has ever returned to bear witness, but demon lore describes it as a place of infinite size where demons roam for eternity, searching for, but never finding, a way out. Early in Prefecture history, during the reign of Demon Lord Dalren, the Veil was used to punish almost as regularly as Execution Hill.*

The B'nai Elohim: *One thousand B'nai Elohim warriors guard each Prefecture. Michael commands the B'nai Elohim guarding the Kor Prefecture. It's their responsibility to keep demons from escaping into the mortal realm... in this case, Aster.*

That's their only obligation. They do not interfere in Prefecture politics, nor do they try to rectify the brutality visited upon the ordinary inhabitants of Kor by their demon masters.

Factions in the Capital City of Kor: *Each faction represents a segment of Kor society and defends its own interests against the larger interests of the Kor throne. Each individual city state mirrors these factions. The greatest of these factions is the Ruling Faction—the demons that serve Kor directly and, as a result, have his ear. But its ascendency isn't always the reality. The Military and Magical are two other powerful factions that regularly challenge the Ruling Faction.*

Military Faction: *Forty thousand minor demons with an underlord demon command structure. They're responsible for city defense, which includes maintaining order and carrying out Kor's instructions within a one hundred-mile radius surrounding the city.*

Market Faction: *A large, open market where farmers sell fruits and vegetables. Though run by an underlord, it's debatable whether this is a true Faction... except during times of famine, which is rare in the Abyss.*

Merchant's Faction: *Retailers with non-food items offered for sale (clothing, jewelry, housewares, farm equipment). This Faction, like the Market Faction, has little power.*

Administration Faction: *The city's civil servants who oversee the management of Prefecture business (trade policy, minor disputes, pay, census, management, improvement of Prefecture physical property such as roads and grounds, sewage, and trash removal among others). This is the Prefecture's entire bureaucracy and overseen by an overlord.*

Bankers Faction: *The financial district of the Prefecture. The peasant class of the Abyss depends upon the economics of trade, barter, and money. But between the capital city of Kor and the other city states, or between individual city states, only the monetary system is used in all transactions and/or negotiations. This includes trade, taxes, and purchases of goods and services. The demons employed by Kor and the other city states are paid with Prefecture currency, and all purchases made within the city states require currency.*

Kor Prefecture Currency:

Kor (Round coin made from platinum.) The largest currency coin in the Kor Prefecture.

Kronie (Eight-sided coin made from cobalt.) Ten Kronies equal one Kor.

Remadie (Four-sided chromium coin.) Ten Remadies equal one Kronie.

Shecale (Three-sided zinc coin.) Ten Shecales equal one Remadie.

Medical Faction: *The hospitals and medical buildings where demon clerics treat injuries of the ruling class and city workers. These services are not available to the common folk both inside or outside city limits.*

Magical Faction: *Schools, laboratories, and residences of all Prefecture sorcerers and sorceresses. The Magical Faction controls everything regarding magic and its use. With few exceptions, only overlords and sorcerers or sorceresses can invoke magic.*

Ruling Faction: *The residence of Demon Lord Kor, current ruler of the Prefecture. This also includes the residences of Kor*

Prefecture's overlord ambassadors and staff. (The overlords stay in their city state unless called to the capital. In most instances, their ambassadors handle business for their overlord.)

Corrections/Slavery Factions: *These Factions work together under one overlord. They control the prison and slave pens. There's no attempt to rehabilitate prisoners. If they survive their treatment in the prison system, they're banished from the capital city for life on pain of death if they should ever return. Demons accused of minor offenses such as pick-pocketing, stealing of items worth less than one Kor, disorderly conduct, and the like, can choose to serve their sentence as indentured servants. Only a few slaves exist at any one time, but those made slaves are used to maintain Execution Hill and The Pillar of Lost Souls (preparing the Hill and Pillar for executions, removing bodies and body parts, cleaning blood and excrement, keeping the holding pens and slaughter house clean). Executions carried out on Execution Hill are reserved for special circumstance prisoners (i.e.–those Kor wants put to death), traitors, those accused of murder, attempted murder, or overthrow of a superior. An overlord who makes all life and death decisions runs this Faction. (Kor, or anyone who speaks in his name, has overruling authority.)*

Power Faction: *This Faction never vies for Kor's approval and support, nor does it compete with the other factions. It doesn't have to. It's the one Faction that all the other Factions leave alone. Here lies the Pillar of Captured Souls, which keeps the Veil of the Infinitus Atrophia from closing in and swallowing the entire Prefecture. As its name suggests, the Pillar of Captured Souls is a huge, swirling pillar of dark energy which generates its power from the consumption of physical and spiritual bodies fed into it. Two overlords oversee the operation of the Power Faction and report directly to the Demon Lord Kor.*

Prefecture Weather: *The weather of the Kor Prefecture is hot and humid with frequent powerful lightning storms and rain showers. There is no "sky" like those found on worlds in the mortal realm. Instead, it's covered by dangerous-looking clouds that go up several miles. Beyond the clouds is a continuation of the Veil of the Infinitus Atrophia. There is no true day or night in the Prefecture. Instead, a semi-dark illumination prevails for roughly half of every twenty-four-hour period. This allows the inhabitants to maintain a day/night cycle. The atmosphere is breathable for mortals, but not without difficulty... at least until enough time has passed to adjust, usually within a few days.*

Prefecture Animals and Fauna: *Many of the same animal and plant species found on Aster are also found in the Abyss, with two notable exceptions to physical appearance. While the Kor Prefecture has common animals such as dogs, cats, horses, and the like, they are larger and walk on six or twelve legs instead of four. And like most worlds, the Kor Prefecture has animals, insects, and fauna that are unique to it alone and not found anywhere else in the multiverse. The primary source of meat is the field strider, an animal similar to a cow on Aster. They are, however, larger, more dangerous, and have vicious dispositions. Meat of a calf field strider is considered a delicacy by the Prefecture hierarchy and banned for consumption by the peasant class.*

Illustrated by Toby Briles

The B'nai Elohim

CHAPTER ONE

The Abyss

Demon Lord Kor sat on the Living Throne in the main audience chamber and listened to his advisors, the Faction leaders, argue. It was something they did far too often. But at the present moment, he wasn't interested in putting a stop to it. There were far too many more interesting and exciting things to think about instead—primarily his newest concubine. One of his overlords, Valafar, who was currently vying for the open overlord position in the city state of Kolhapoor, gave her as a gift. Kor encouraged his underlings to offer bribes, but he never doled out favors based on that alone. With this female, however, Kor might be more obliged than usual. She was beautiful! Her alluring dance was like nothing he'd ever seen before!

A commotion at the chamber doors brought Kor out of his reverie. Everyone's attention, including Kor's, turned to the guards as they brutally refused the entrance of an obvious courier. The demon looked close to death even before his guards went to work on him.

"Let him approach!" the souls in his throne screamed in unison. Kor was used to hearing their advice in his head, but never had they been this insistent.

The demon lord raised a hand. "Show the messenger in."

Two of Kor's personal bodyguards retrieved the messenger from the door guards, dragged him across the chamber to the *Living Throne,* and threw him to the floor in front of the dais. The messenger prostrated himself before Kor while the council members watched as this new interruption played itself out.

"My Lord, I've information smuggled from the mortal world."

"Indeed!" Kor declared. "Or else you wouldn't risk kissing

the *Pillar* by coming to me unannounced."

"No, My Lord," the messenger replied. He kept his face plastered against the floor.

Kor clapped his hands. "Bring me a chair... and drink."

The guards had the messenger sitting on a chair with a gem-encrusted mug of mulled, spiced wine within seconds. He didn't try to drink—not without permission.

"Go ahead, drink," Kor insisted. "Then tell me your name."

The messenger nodded and sipped the wine. It seemed to bring a little life back into him. "Imdugud, My Lord."

Kor considered. The demon before him had the body of an eagle with a head of a lion... one of many demon mixes that populated the lower echelon of demon hierarchy. It surprised him that someone of such low stature would be counted upon to deliver an important communication.

"First things first," Kor said. "Who sent you?"

Imdugud shook his head. "I don't know, My Lord. I only saw him long enough to be handed the message. He told me to get it to you as quickly as possible... that my life depended upon it."

"Give me the message."

Imdugud produced a small crystal from an unnoticeable pouch buried in the feathers of his wing.

Kor had one of his guards retrieve the crystal and held it up to the light. There was definitely a message scroll inside, and the magic of the crystal would reveal it soon enough. Kor tucked the crystal in a pocket of his robe. "I'll read this in the privacy of my quarters."

The council members sighed in frustration.

"Now, Imdugud, I need the rest of your story."

The minor demon looked confused. "I beg your pardon, My Lord?"

"Oh, come on!" Kor hissed. "There has to be more to the story. For instance, why would you be chosen to deliver a message of importance? Something as significant as you say... if you're to be believed... isn't just handed over to a random messenger. There has to be an element of trust involved."

"My Lord?"

"I need provenance, Imdugud."

"My Lord?"

"Who are you working with?" Kor thundered.

Imdugud looked around at all the faces staring at him—faces that were waiting for an answer. He never actually believed he'd be able to keep what he was part of from the demon lord, though he had hoped that providence might intercede. "So be it," he whispered.

"What was that?" Kor asked. "I didn't quite hear."

"I belong to the Order of the Talisman, My Lord."

Everyone around the chamber laughed.

"Silence!" Kor barked as he glared at Imdugud. "I ordered that sect disbanded because the Talisman doesn't exist."

"The Talisman exists, My Lord! Just not here on Kor."

The admission caused Kor to pause. "Then... you mean on Aster?"

Imdugud nodded.

"How could you know?" Kor questioned. "Nothing gets past the *B'nai Elohim* and into the mortal realm!"

"We did, My Lord," Imdugud said. "A doorway to Aster. The *B'nai Elohim* shut it down within seconds and killed most of those involved... but it was opened long enough to deduce the Talisman's location on Aster."

Kor and everyone in the chamber waited expectedly.

"Well?"

"That's all I know, My Lord. But it's in the message."

Kor sat back on his throne. "*Read the message!*" the souls in the *Living Throne* cackled. *"Destroy the Talisman and the B'nai Elohim will become vulnerable. Aster will be ours!"*

Kor stood. "This meeting of the council is adjourned." He

motioned for one of his guards. "Send Imdugud to the *Pillar*," he whispered.

When Kor entered his luxurious apartment in the palace, a handful of minor demons who were always at his beck and call met him. One held in his hand a goblet of farim, a strong drink fermented from the roots of the foxglove plant. Kor grabbed the goblet and drained its contents, then took a platter of toasted meat rolls and cheese from another.

"Where's Emprusa," Kor asked.

"Upstairs awaiting your pleasure, My Lord."

Kor nodded. He didn't need to be told where upstairs she was. He knew he'd find her in his bedroom. "You may carry on with your duties."

The minor demons bowed in unison.

"I'll not need any of you until morning," Kor said as he mounted the stairs.

When Kor entered his bedroom, he saw Emprusa lying in his enormous bed, dressed in a seductive nightgown and holding two goblets of wine. Her two horns were painted indigo, Kor's favorite color, and she smelled of perfumed leatherleaf bittersweet. She had allowed her waist-length red hair to flow freely, framing both sides of her head and going down her back.

"I understand you had a bit of excitement during your council meeting," Emprusa remarked.

Kor laughed. "You miss nothing, do you?"

"That's why I'm your favorite concubine," the female demon replied. "Here, drink. Then you can tell me all about it."

Kor accepted the wine and sat on the edge of the bed. "The same old boring details. Some days, I wish I could squash a coup attempt. Killing always relieves my boredom."

"You don't need an excuse to do that, My Lord," Emprusa purred.

The demon lord sighed. "Killing without cause makes me seem… weak. Like I can't solve my problems using my intellect alone. True… I want to be feared. But I also want respect."

"You have it, My Lord."

Kor let out a quick burst of laughter. "That's not what the souls tell me."

Emprusa kissed the side of Kor's neck. "They just want you to join them," she muttered.

Kor closed his eyes. He liked the feel of Emprusa's lips on his neck. "They'll not have me for a long time, my love." He let Emprusa continue for a few more seconds before he got down to business. "More wine," he ordered as he handed her his goblet.

While she did as he commanded, he pulled out the message crystal and activated it. The message appeared in the air before him.

"Looks like gibberish to me," Emprusa said as she handed Kor his wine and sat down on the bed next to him. "Is it some kind of code?"

Kor shook his head. "Not code… coordinates. The messenger who brought this to me said they'd found the location of the Talisman."

"I thought the Talisman didn't exist."

"As did I," Kor said. "Apparently we were wrong."

"Who found it?"

"The Order of the Talisman," Kor replied.

Emprusa frowned. "Didn't you order them disbanded?"

"I'll send them to Execution Hill later," Kor replied impatiently. "Right now, I need their help to figure out where these coordinates lead to. All I got from the messenger was it's on Aster."

"On Aster?" Emprusa asked. "How's that even possible?

And how'd they know?"

"How'd they know the Talisman's on Aster?" Kor repeated. "They couldn't without some damn fine sorcery. And if they figured that out, maybe they figured out a way around the *B'nai Elohim*. I always thought you couldn't do one without the other. But Nightshade and her father, Aikanáro, did... so I know it's possible." Kor took a sip from his wine goblet as he thought. "I need to find the Order's sorcerers to see if they actually know a way around the *B'nai Elohim* safeguards," he announced to Emprusa a few moments later. "If any of them are still alive, that is."

"So you need the help of an organization that you ordered disbanded. How's that going to play out with the Faction leaders... particularly with the Military Faction? They might see your change of heart as a vulnerability."

Kor shook his head. "No. Azazael knows about the Talisman and its potential to end the B'nai Elohim. Plus, I'll have the support of the Magical Faction. Lilitu will have her sorcerers drooling over the idea of learning a new spell. I don't need anyone else."

"Except for the Order of the Talisman," Emprusa pointed out.

Kor sighed. "Except for them," he said as he reached for a meat roll and bit into one. "*Cold*," he thought.

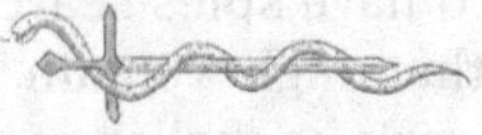

It was later that same day back in Kor's audience chamber. Besides his guards, the only other demons in the chamber were Azazael and Lilitu. Kor shook his head. The *Living Throne* was cranky and all its complaining was giving him a headache. The Prefecture leader decided he'd had enough of the nagging and went over to sit with the two Faction leaders.

"Azazael, I want your warriors to find the Order of the Talisman… or what's left of it," Kor commanded. "And I don't want anyone hurt. Understood?"

Azazael nodded. "Though it's a pity," he added.

"And us?" Lilitu asked.

Kor studied the Magical Faction leader. She was beautiful, as are all succubi. Though he considered her an ally, she was still dangerous. In the Abyss, power was everything, and allies are unreliable, though Kor felt good about Lilitu's loyalty. Without him, she'd still be an under lord in one of the border cities.

"The Order has apparently found a way to open a portal between here and Aster… a new portal that isn't guarded by the *B'nai Elohim*," Kor explained. "If they can do it, so can your Faction sorcerers. Find me a new portal."

"Why not wait for Azazael to find the Order survivors?" Lilitu asked. "Wouldn't it be easier to get the information out of them instead of trying to develop the spell from scratch?"

Azazael snorted. "There might not be any Order sorcerers left to find! How long do you think the *B'nai Elohim* would allow their safeguards, once discovered, to be breached? And I assure you that a breach would have been found in short order. They're not dullards… and they can be quite efficient, and brutal, if the situation calls for it. If I were Michael and found out about this, I'd butcher as many of the Order as I could get my hands on. Then I'd have spies searching high and low for any Order members that might remain. Opening up portals to Aster is a profoundly serious challenge to their authority. Hell, it threatens their entire existence!"

Kor nodded. "Azazael's right. But it goes much deeper than that. Right now, Michael's probably thinking we're developing the portal magic just to escape the Abyss, which is partially true. But it's not the complete picture."

Both Azazael and Lilitu looked at Kor for a few moments.

"The Talisman!" Lilitu guessed. "You believe it exists!"

"I do now," Kor said. "And I have the coordinates of its location on Aster. It was in the message delivered during our council meeting."

Azazael laughed. "Delicious!"

"The destruction of the *B'nai Elohim* and complete, unrestricted access to Aster!" Lilitu declared.

"Or so the legend goes," Kor added. "If true, all we have to do is get a few agents through a portal and onto Aster to find and destroy the Talisman. Once we do that, then it's bye-bye *B'nai Elohim* and hello Aster!"

All three demons erupted into maniacal laughter.

Kor dismissed Lilitu. "Any news on that other thing?" he asked Azazael after the Magical Faction had left the chamber.

Azazael shook his head. "Not since our last private conversation. We're getting close, however. From your fixer, we know the dates and times when the rebellion leaders meet. Now we only have to get the location. Then we cut off the head. The rest will fade into the background quickly enough."

"I don't want Belladonna killed," Kor ordered. "I have a special punishment lined up for that one. The Pillar's too easy a death."

Azazael nodded. "I understand, My Lord."

"How are things going with our mobilization?" Kor then asked.

"We're ready to march," Azazael replied. "The city armies should also be ready within the week."

Kor nodded. "Thought as much."

"Should I light a fire under their asses?" Azazael inquired.

"I can't move until I have the spell… and I need the Order to get that. But…" Kor paused, thinking. "I guess it never hurts to rile people up now and them. You know, just to keep them on their toes. Go ahead… and don't spare the Pillar. Every army needs an occasional culling to get rid of the deadweight."

Azazael grinned.

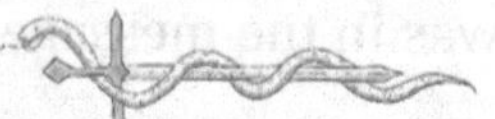

Michael watched as the demon was being interviewed. He was the last of several demons who had opened a doorway to Aster. They had killed the others who preferred death over capture. Pity. Michael would have liked to have a few others to question for verification.

"How many others know the spell used to open the doorway?" Gabrielle asked the cowering demon. Gabrielle was Michael's chief interrogator and his second-in-command. She was intelligent, cunning, decisive, and unrelenting. But perhaps her greatest quality was her ability to read a demon and trick it into making admissions, sometimes without the demon realizing it.

The demon shook his head as he continued to stare at the floor. Gabrielle grabbed a tuff of hair and raised his head. The demon looked at her with wide, fright-filled eyes, but remained silent. She let go of the hair and turned to Michael. "Let's speak outside, shall we?"

Michael nodded, opened the door to the adjoining room, and let Gabrielle pass through. He closed the door behind him and turned to his chief interrogator.

Gabrielle shook her head. "He's been a tough nut to crack. But there was a little fruit still left on the tree."

Michael sat on the floor. The *B'nai Elohim* have no need of chairs. They curl their four legs and sit on the floor using thick carpets or large pillows as a buffer. "Explain."

"I didn't get the spell they'll use to create the doorway," Gabrielle said as she sat on the floor as well. "I don't even think he knows it."

"So, nothing more than a common demon."

Gabrielle shook her head. "He's more than that… but he's

not a sorcerer. From what I could glean, he's like a mid-level manager... somewhere in between an under lord and a minor demon."

"That's odd," Michael remarked.

"Not within his particular group," Gabriella said. "He belongs to what he calls the Order of the Talisman."

"Never heard of it."

Gabriella raised an eyebrow. "Michael, the Talisman is the Johari. At least that's what demons call her."

"Hmmm... that puts a different light on the matter," Michael observed.

"Yes, it..." Gabriella said before a raised hand by Michael cut her off.

"Let me think about this for a moment."

Gabriella, exasperated, ignored Michael's demand for silence. "Isn't it obvious, Michael? If they've found her, they'll try to destroy her. We can't let that happen. The Johari not only gives us our invulnerabilities and power, but she also controls the Juxtaposition Point, through which we know when a demon opens a dimensional doorway to the mortals. Without her keeping the Juxtaposition Point functional, we'd never know when a demon attempted a crossing into Aster. Without her, we couldn't do our job. The demons would have us chasing our tails and mortal kind would be lost as a result."

"It goes deeper than that, Gabriella," Michael said. "We understand this layer of the Abyss we guard isn't the only one. There's an untold number of layers. Our brethren guard each from demon access to their adjoining mortal world. And each of those mortal worlds has a Johari-type being working in concert with their own *B'nai Elohim*."

"What're you implying?" Gabriella asked.

"If a similar situation had developed on another of those layers, I'd have known about it," Michael responded.

"You're in contact with the other layers of the Abyss?"

Gabriella questioned.

Michael nodded. "With the other leaders of the *B'nai Elohim*... yes. But only in emergencies that might affect us all. I've heard nothing for millennia... so this threat's new. And..."

"Spit it out," Gabriella said.

"Though there's been no evidence, I've little doubt the demons can do the same as us," Michael answered.

"You mean talk to each other inter-dimensionally?"

"Exactly, Gabriella," Michael replied. "So there's really nothing to stop them from transmitting their doorway spell to their comrades in the other layers, as well as any other information they may have regarding the Johari. And if they do that..."

"If they do that... if our demons can destroy our Johari... the other demons will destroy their Johari's throughout the multiverse. Then all the mortal worlds are free for the picking and there's nothing the *B'nai Elohim* can do to stop it short of a bloody war... a bloody war we would probably lose and which would devastate all the mortal worlds." Gabriella understood Michael's concern.

Michael shook his head. "Close, but not quite, Gabriella. There'd be bloody wars, all right. But the Johari, as you said, is the magic that maintains the Juxtaposition Point between the Abyss and the worlds of the mortals. Without her... without the Juxtaposition Point... both of the dimensions will come into alignment, meaning they'd phase into one singular reality. We control the demon's entry into the mortal dimension because we control the juxtaposition. If we lose that bottleneck, the demons won't even need a special doorway spell. They'll simply overrun us in no time with far simpler magic."

"What's next?" Gabriella asked after a long pause.

Michael considered. "I think it's safe to release our demon friend back into the Abyss. Give him a warning about trying this sort of thing again... but make it more threatening this time. Then have one of our spies follow him. Maybe we'll get lucky. Oh, and stop by and tell our guests I'll be with them as soon as I can."

Gabriella nodded. "You?"

Michael shrugged. "They need to be warned... which I should do myself."

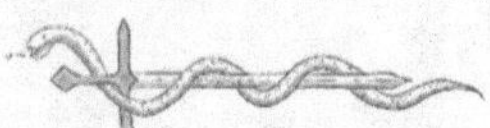

Father Goram, Nightshade, and Landross were sitting in Michael's study and library, a comfortable, enormous room that made them feel small by comparison. The four Qénsharma had been safely secured in a backpack that Nightshade carried. By unanimous consent, the three kept the presence of the Qénsharma secret. Michael had been about to give them a stern lecture about the dangers of the Abyss when he was called away unexpectedly. That was three hours ago.

Landross was pacing. "I'm starting to feel a bit put off by this whole situation! Why the wait? Doesn't Michael understand the importance of our quest?"

"Sure he does," Nightshade said. "Something else is going on."

"You saw it too," Father Goram commented.

Nightshade nodded. "Michael didn't bother to hide his reaction when he was pulled aside. Whatever it was, he looked... concerned."

"That's putting it mildly," Father Goram remarked.

Landross stopped pacing. "You don't think whatever it was will prevent our search, do you?"

Father Goram shook his head. "No, my boy. But it may put a wrinkle in it."

"Particularly if we're asked to help with whatever it is," Nightshade added.

Landross sat back down. "By the gods," he whispered.

Shortly thereafter, Gabriella stopped by to give assurances that Michael would be back soon and to ask if they needed anything, which they declined. After she had left, the three were even more concerned.

"The *B'nai Elohim* don't hide their emotions very well," Nightshade concluded.

"Aye," Landross said. "Even I could see she was scared."

Michael made his way to his study, where Father Goram, Nightshade, and Landross waited. Though he had many other important things on his mind, he was uncomfortable making them wait so long. Although unavoidable, he understood the importance of their own search and figured they'd be angry by the delay… as well as the favor he was going to ask. Soon he'd learn he was right on both counts.

Michael open the door to the study and was confronted with an angry knight. Father Goram and Nightshade were sitting on a pile of decorative pillows. Though the two remained calm, Michael saw from the look in their eyes that they weren't overjoyed, either.

"What the hell, Michael," Landross demanded. "My queen and Father Goram's wife are lost somewhere in the Abyss, and you play games with our time! By the gods! They're lost, hurt, and confused… probably ready to give up hope… and here we sit, awaiting your favor! I repeat. What the hell, Michael!"

"Landross!" Father Goram warned.

Michael shook his head. "No. I deserved that." He went over to a decanter and goblets on his gigantic desk and poured himself a goblet of a gold-colored liquid. "Want some?"

"We're wasting time," Landross barked.

Father Goram decided he could use a drink. "What is it?"

"Ambrosia," Nightshade said. "It's quite good. I'll have one."

"I thought mortals couldn't drink it," Landross commented.

Nightshade laughed. "I'm surprised anyone still gives credence to that old wives' tale."

Landross whirled on Nightshade with fire in his eyes, "Listen to me, you..."

"Stop it, Landross!" Father Goram snapped.

"But, Horatio..."

Father Goram shook his head to end further discussion. "As for you, Nightshade... quit baiting him!"

Nightshade nodded.

"That's better," Father Goram said. "We'll each have one, Michael."

Landross sniffed his but didn't taste it until he watched Father Goram and Nightshade take a sip from their goblets. His sip turned into a goblet-draining gulp. He coughed as the sweet-tasting liquid turned into fire on the way down to his belly. Once there, an incredible warmth radiated throughout his body. He felt revitalized. It was as if he'd just woken from a deep night's sleep.

"Damn, that's good!" Landross declared. "How come we don't have this on Aster?"

"The plants needed to make ambrosia only grow in the Abyss," Nightshade answered. "Even here, they're exceedingly rare. Furthermore, the *B'nai Elohim* are the only ones who know the secret recipe to brew it. That's the real reason demons don't overthrow Michael and his band of merry tyrants... their ability to make ambrosia."

Michael snorted. "If only that were the case. We'd keep the demons here so high on it they'd never want to leave!"

"It's time to get serious," Father Goram scolded. "Michael, let's address the real reason you were called away and how it's going to affect us."

Michael set his goblet down and looked at each of the three. "Obviously, I understand the importance of your search."

"Are you sure?" Landross asked. Even with the goblet of ambrosia spreading warmth and serenity in his belly, he hadn't lost sight of the mission... or the fact that his queen and Autumn could be, at this very moment, suffering at the hands of demons.

"You wouldn't be allowed here if I wasn't," Michael snapped. "What happened to your loved ones, however, is unconnected to a more recent, and dangerous, situation we just now learned about. It's a problem that involves not only the *B'nai Elohim,* but all the mortal races on your own world."

"We're listening," Nightshade said.

"Does the word 'Johari' mean anything to you?" Michael asked.

Father Goram shook his head. "Can't say that I've heard of it. Nightshade? Landross?"

Both shook their head as well.

"Not surprising," Michael said. "The Johari is our most closely guarded secret. She's a living being buried deep in the depths of Astor. The old gods created and placed her there. Like the sylph."

"Kristen talked to me about the sylph," Father Goram commented. "She met one."

"Elbedreth," the *B'nai Elohim* leader remarked.

Father Goram nodded. "Until I talked to my daughter, I didn't know they existed, either. I don't think any of us surface dwellers knew."

"The old gods created the sylph to guard a young Astor from any threat to evolving life," Michael explained. "However, during the development of Aster, the sylph changed. They broke with the old gods and killed new life, considering Astor to be theirs alone."

"They defied the old gods?" Landross asked.

Michael nodded. "And for that, the old gods put the sylphs into a permanent hibernation... all except for Elbedreth. She alone stayed true to her calling."

"What a lonely life," Nightshade remarked.

"Her loneliness was remedied by the improbable turning of the dwarf Azriel into sylph," Father Goram stated. "At least according to Kristen. It's a long story. Please continue, Michael."

"The Johari is like the sylph in that the old gods created her for a specific purpose." Michael looked at the three. "That purpose is to keep two dimensions... the mortal and the demon... from being on the same plane of existence."

Landross shook his head. "I thought we already were on the same plane, and the only reason demons don't overrun us is because of you *B'nai Elohim* fellows?"

"No, Landross," Michael replied. "Far from it. There are hundreds of thousands of demons in this part of the Abyss. There's only a thousand of us."

"Before you go any further, what do you mean this part of the Abyss?" Landross asked.

"There's more than what you can see, Landross," Nightshade answered. "We're in what's called a 'Prefecture' of the Abyss. Hundreds, thousands, perhaps billions of these Prefecture's make up the entire Abyss. Each of these are connected to its own physical world. Some of them are in other dimensions or other universes."

Michael nodded. "Correct, Nightshade. Where there's a physical world with life, there's a corresponding Prefecture. But that doesn't mean the Abyss and the mortal world it's connected to are in the same dimension. As you said, most times it's just the opposite."

"That's something our scholars have hypothesized for generations," Father Goram remarked. "It makes sense."

Landross frowned. "Maybe to you. To me it's mind blowing gobbledygook. All I know is that a person can summon a demon from whatever dimension using a simple ritual spell."

"It's not as straightforward as that," Nightshade said.

"Special preparations are required, sacrifices made, symbols drawn to prevent the demon from killing you, and something to trade or barter... something the demon wants in return for its service to you."

"You'd know about that, wouldn't you," Landross observed.

"Let's not start that again," Father Goram ordered.

Landross remained defiant but nodded. He'd need more evidence of Nightshade's benign motives before he'd trust and accept her.

Michael looked at the burly knight and saw doubt about Nightshade's allegiance still remained. "Landross, you have my word. Nightshade has left her demon life behind."

Landross shook his head. "I also have Father Goram's word. Perhaps I'm just not as trusting... or forgiving... of all the evil she's done."

Father Goram sighed. "We went over this before we even came here. Should Michael send you back?"

"Certainly not!"

"Then straighten the hell up, Landross!" Father Goram snapped. "We don't have time for all your nagging little doubts."

Michael pointed a finger and Landross froze. "Will you be able to keep him under control?" he asked Father Goram. "When you're out there, you'll need to trust each other completely, or you'll never find your queen and wife... or help me."

It was Nightshade who answered. "He'll come around. Finding his queen means more to him than life itself."

Michael nodded and released Landross from the spell. "You heard," Michael said. "Nightshade says you'll be fine. Is she right?"

Landross looked at the *B'nai Elohim* leader and nodded.

Michael continued as if nothing had happened. "Though this Prefecture of the Abyss is in a different dimension, it's connected to your world at a place we call the Juxtaposition

Point, or, if you will, the corridor between your world and the Abyss. My people guard this point. And while there's nothing we can do about a mortal summoning a demon, we stop demons from going over to your world on their own. The only reason their numbers don't overrun us is because the Juxtaposition Point funnels everything down to a defensible position. Without that..." Michael shrugged.

"Without that, your thousand wouldn't stand a chance against the overwhelming numbers of demons," Landross said. "That I understand clearly enough."

Michael nodded. "This is where the Johari comes in. If she were to be destroyed, there'd be no Juxtaposition Point."

"But if demons can't get past you..." Father Goram began but stopped. Suddenly, he understood what concerned Michael and his brethren. "They've figured it out, haven't they. They figured out how to get to the Johari... where she's located and how to get past the Juxtaposition Point."

Michael nodded. "We monitor and locate all demon created doorways and shut them down quickly enough to prevent their successful use. We can do that because those spells must go through the Juxtaposition Point. According to my sources, however, there are rumors of a powerful spell which allows them to by-pass the Juxtaposition Point. This means they can transition from anywhere in the Abyss to Aster and we can't stop it. But that's not our only fear."

"I imagine not," Father Goram said. "Those spells, though a breakthrough, are only going to be available to powerful demon sorcerers. Unfortunately, the more powerful the sorcerer, the harder it's going to be to track down and eliminate them because of the wards and protections they can cast. Am I right?"

Michael nodded.

"So that's going to take time... time you don't have."

Michael nodded again. "We know the demons have

discovered the location of the Johari… or the Talisman, as they call it… on Aster. They also know what the Johari does and how important it is to the survival of Aster and the *B'nai Elohim*. Combine that with knowledge of the spell needed to create a doorway from the Abyss to Aster which bypasses the Juxtaposition Point, and they've the means by which they can send an… an assassination squad, for want of a better term… to destroy the Johari and eliminate the Juxtaposition Point. As you said, we don't have a lot of time to counter their plans."

"So without this Johari, the Juxtaposition Point ceases to exist," Landross remarked. "And if they neutralize the Juxtaposition Point, they'll overrun Aster in short order."

"That's where we stand," Michael concluded. "Like I said, I've contacts beyond the gates, but I don't think they'll learn anything useful… at least not in time to stop the threat to the Johari."

"How can we be of help?" Father Goram asked. "We know nothing about the Abyss… except…" The priest looked over at Nightshade.

Nightshade smiled and nodded. "He really only needs me."

Michael concurred. "It's not that a high priest and a knight won't be helpful, but Nightshade is the key."

Father Goram looked between Michael and Nightshade. "One of you care to clue me in?"

Nightshade sighed. "Horatio, besides knowing the Abyss, I think Michael's referring to my twin sister. Her name's Belladonna. But Michael, I don't see how she'd be any help. She's always been disinterested in anything other than her own comfort. Harmless… and useless."

Michael laughed. "I can tell you've been away for a while. From what I've learned, your sister is using your late father's wealth to finance the resistance movement taking place among the ordinary populace against Kor and the ruling class. She may have more knowledge about Kor's plans than I do. And the resistance movement can certainly provide a distraction to Kor... perhaps even enough to delay the attack on the Johari. Even a day could be the difference."

Nightshade snorted. "You sure you're talking about the right Belladonna?"

Michael shook his head. "No question about it. I'd like you to reconnect and use her contacts to get the information I need."

"Belladonna?" Nightshade whispered. "My sister?" She looked at Michael. "The Abyss has truly gone crazy!"

CHAPTER TWO

The Abyss

Belladonna was in a primitive cave with two mortal females. She knew her demon form might be frightening and wouldn't help build trust, so she'd taken on the appearance of a mortal female, though her eyes maintained the same blackish hue of her demonic form. Lessien, the self-proclaimed queen of the island nation of InnisRos in the mortal world of Aster, was doing what she could to make the other female comfortable. The other, the one Lessien called Autumn, stared at everything—yet nothing at all. An underlord demon had raped her and she was now carrying the living result of that forced union within her body. Belladonna could only imagine the trauma Autumn had suffered.

"Have you ever seen anything like this?" Lessien asked.

Forced out of her reverie, Belladonna shook her head. "No. I'm surprised she even survived. Underlords aren't noted for their gentility."

Autumn lay in a make-shift bed of leaves and soft furs provided by Belladonna. Lessien gently tucked in a fur being used as a blanket. Even the heat of the Abyss didn't stop the cold shivers Autumn was experiencing.

"She almost didn't," Lessien said. "I couldn't stop the bleeding and thought a merciful death was imminent. The gods forgive me, I was praying for one. Then, for no reason, it stopped and Autumn stabilized... except for the shivering. That and she won't wake. And now, the demon child inside her grows at an alarming rate."

"I've talked to local midwives and none have ever heard of the like," Belladonna said. "Nor do they know what we can expect. They gave me pain-killing herbs, but in her state, I don't think she needs them. That, and we don't know their effect on a mortal. They might be powerful enough to kill without knowing the correct dosage."

Lessien sat back against a wall. The magical sword, *Ah-HritVakha*, lay next to her only hand. Her magical cloak, the *Mantle of the Sovereign*, was loosely draped over her shoulders. She'd endure the extra heat for the comfort it gave her.

"It's still unbelievable to me that there's such a thing as peasant demons," Lessien remarked. "Especially peasant demons willing to help a mortal. Yes, Verfax helped me. I paid him to do so. Greed's commonplace... even in the Abyss. But peasant demons?"

Belladonna sat on the other side of the recumbent Autumn. "In the few days we've known each other, we've avoided all kinds of conversations. You, because of your concern for Autumn... though I also suspect you're too frightened to want the truth... at least the truth as you fear it to be. As for me, I need your help and don't want to risk turning you away. But it's been long enough. We need to get a few things out into the open. It's time to be truthful with each other."

Lessien laughed. "You're a demon! How can I trust any demon to be truthful?"

"That's one thing we need to discuss," Belladonna stated. "The reason the peasants are so willing to help is because their good folk who are being ruled by evil overlords. All contact the mortal world has had with demons are those who hate you... those that want to tear the flesh from your bones... those who want another people to subjugate. That's not who all of us are, however."

"Your sister was one of those!" Lessien hissed. "She... she and your own father were responsible for the invasion of the Dark Elf army on my own kingdom!"

"Yet in the end she helped to defeat them," Belladonna countered. "You yourself said so."

Lessien didn't respond. It was the truth. One of Father Goram's crystal dragons said as much to Autumn before they were kidnapped and sent to the Abyss.

"Lessien, my father was an overlord and evil to the core. But that's not me, nor is it Nightshade."

"Then why, Belladonna?" Lessien asked. "Why did Nightshade help your father?"

Belladonna shook her head. "I can't say for sure. She was always father's most favored, and I believe he corrupted her spirit… though there was another whom she loved growing up that might have offset some of that. I also believe the time she spent with your people helped her to regain her perspective."

Lessien sighed. "You could be right. It seems Father Goram trusts her, as does the goddess Althaya. Only the gods know how much my perspective has been altered over the last year. People change… and there's no point in trying to reason it out. Sometimes it just is. Sometimes you're forced to take a deep breath and accept your new reality."

Belladonna smiled. "Wise. Anything else would be a waste of time."

Both demon and queen looked over as Autumn moaned. It was the first sound from her since the rape.

"Perhaps she's finally coming out of it." Lessien said.

Belladonna shook her head and pointed towards Autumn. "I'm not so sure. Look!"

Lessien looked to where Belladonna indicated and saw a fresh stream of blood coming from between Autumn's legs. "It's too early! A miscarriage?"

"We're dealing with something that rarely ever happens, at least here in the Abyss," Belladonna replied as she moved to investigate. "We're clueless about…"

Autumn let out a high-pitched, pain-filled scream. "Get it out of me!"

An hour later, Autumn gave birth to a perfectly developed,

though small, baby boy. The only difference between the child and a normal elvan baby was the eyes. They glowed with the golds, browns, and reds of a summer sunset on Aster. The child didn't cry or protest in any manner as Lessien cut the umbilical cord and cleaned him. Afterwards, the InnisRos queen wrapped the child in a light fur and laid him on Autumn's chest before she and Belladonna retreated to another part of the cave to discuss their next move. The baby, secure in the warmth of his mother's body, went to sleep. Autumn, though withdrawn, raised both arms to cuddle her newborn.

"The child's going to die if he doesn't get nutrition," Belladonna said. "And clearly Autumn's body hasn't had time to adjust."

Lessien shook her head and sighed. "Maybe that would be for the best."

Belladonna drew back, surprised. "Even in the Abyss, we value our young! How could you say such a thing!?"

"What?" Lessien answered back. "You didn't hear the part where I told you how that baby came to be? Do you think Autumn, if she ever comes back to us, is going to want that constant reminder?"

"There're many families here in the Abyss who'd be grateful for a child to raise," Belladonna argued. "Heritage or manner of conception notwithstanding. And, I suspect, there'd be just as many on Aster."

"Wanting a demon spawn?" Lessien retorted, though she wasn't as sure about it as she once was. Remarkably, Belladonna, a being she'd been taught since childhood was evil, argued for the life of the child. She felt guilty.

Belladonna jerked back as if Lessien had slapped her. "I'm demon spawn!"

Lessien cringed. She'd just insulted the only friend she had in the Abyss. "I'm sorry. I didn't mean it that way."

Belladonna stared at Lessien for a few seconds and then

shrugged. "I guess I don't blame you for feeling that way about demons. We've caused quite a bit of trouble for you on Aster. But that's only part of the picture, as you'll soon see. So save your apologies until the time comes when you'll really mean them."

The InnisRos queen nodded.

"I think we should let Autumn decide the fate of her baby… if, as you've already stated, she returns from her stupor," Belladonna said. "Since your friend can't nurse, we need to find someone who can."

Lessien frowned. "You mean a wet-nurse? Here?"

"Correct. And I know where there's one."

Minor Demon Appearance, General: Humanoid with pale blue skin tones, long white hair, blue eyes, and small, antler-like horns growing from the top of their heads. Males stand between six and seven feet tall, while females are only slightly smaller at six feet on average.

From the Mia Pragmateía Gia Ti Daimonología Tis Avyssou (A Treatise on Abyss Demonology)

After bedding down the kids for the night, Hodya joined her husband, Ekrah, in the main room for a relaxing cup of javah, a bitter, hot brew that served as coffee in the Abyss. Their six-legged dog, Gleep, lay on a hide between the two minor demons as both sipped javah and rocked their chairs back and forth. A small fire burned in the stone hearth… not enough to provide much heat, something the Abyss had an abundance of, but instead for ambiance. Staring into the dancing flames, smelling the aroma of burning wood, and hearing the occasional "pop" of the fire had a calming effect on both demons. After a long day of raising four kids and tending a small herd of field striders—twelve-legged cow-like creatures with the claws and stinger of a scorpion and a nasty temperament—the couple used the silence of the evening to discuss the day's events.

"How's Jezan?" Ekrah asked.

Hodya sighed. "I can't get her fever down. We may have to take her to a healer."

"Harrumph!" her husband exclaimed. "He's nothing but a quack! And his prices are outrageous! Three shecales for a simple diagnosis. And who knows how much for the actual treatment. Then there's the medicine he'll prescribe. Nothing but snake oil."

"I know, but what else can we do?" Hodya sighed. "I wish mom were still with us."

"So do I," Ekrah replied. "She was a decent type... really loved the kids."

Both rocked, sipped javah, and watched the fire for a few silent moments before Ekrah broke the stillness. "Tomorrow Gleep and I will go to the east pasture and cut out one of the field striders to sell. The one I have in mind should fetch us at least five kronies."

"Are you sure?" Hodya asked.

Ekrah nodded. "Unless Jezan's fever breaks overnight."

Gleep awoke from his light slumber, raised his head, and looked at the front door. He didn't growl or act concerned—only on the alert. Both Hodya and Ekrah, warned by Gleep's actions, looked at the front door just as there was a light, almost imperceptible knock.

"I wonder who that could be at this hour," Ekrah said as he went to answer the door.

"Gleep doesn't seem too alarmed," Hodya remarked.

Ekrah opened the front door a crack and looked out before

opening it all the way. "Belladonna!" he exclaimed. "It's so good to see… Mortals? Mortals!"

Belladonna, followed by two female mortals, one of which carried a baby, wasted no time entering the simple farmhouse. "I'll explain, but first we need to get in out of the night."

"You weren't followed, were you?" Hodya asked as she went over to join her husband. Gleep got up and sniffed Lessien and Autumn. Satisfied, he lay back down.

Belladonna shook her head. "I don't think so. Argomon's watching my back. He'd either warn me or take matters into his own hands if I were."

"He's a good sort," Hodya said. "You need to keep him close."

"Always," Belladonna replied. "I need a favor, Hodya."

Hodya nodded. "A young one to wet-nurse, by the look of it. Give the child to me."

Lessien handed the child to the female demon. She didn't think she had any choice but to trust Belladonna, and it was obvious Hodya had just given birth within the last fortnight.

Hodya's eyes opened in surprise when she unwrapped the baby's swaddle. "It's…"

"He," Lessien protested.

Hodya looked at the mortal queen and nodded. "He's mortal. How…"

The baby opened his eyes.

The demon wife stared. Glowing eyes of golds, browns, and reds looked back. "No… not just a mortal. That's quite obvious when you look into his eyes." She opened her bodice and offered a breast. The baby accepted without hesitation.

Hodya sat back down on her rocker. "What's his name?"

"We haven't given him one," Belladonna replied.

"He has to have a name," Hodya said. "A good name that matches his demon-mortal heritage."

"No!" Autumn suddenly exclaimed. "Not demon!"

Lessien and Belladonna walked Autumn to Ekrah's rocking chair. Autumn had already collapsed back into her withdrawn state by the time they eased her down.

"She's the mother?" Ekrah asked.

Belladonna nodded. "The child's a product of rape... by one of my father's underlords."

"And it's not the only time she's been raped," Lessien said. "The first time was about a year ago on Aster. From what I was told, it was a savage gang rape."

"Were the fiends caught and held responsible?" Hodya asked. There was anger in her voice.

Lessien nodded. "On Aster... yes. They've paid for their crimes."

"The underlord who did this, however, is still free and I doubt will ever be made to answer for his assault," Belladonna added.

Gleep raised his head and snarled. Everyone went silent. Within moments, there were several timed soft raps on the door.

"It's okay," Belladonna recognized the code and reassured them. "It's only Argomon."

"Any problems?" Belladonna asked when Argomon was let in by Ekrah.

Argomon, like Belladonna, has, as do all underlords and overlords of the Abyss, two personas that he could use at will. One is his natural demon form while the other is that of a huge and powerfully built human male with glowing red eyes. Also like Belladonna, and in deference to the mortal females, he had chosen the latter.

He shook his head in answer to Belladonna's question. "No one was interested. Thought I'd come in to see how things were going... and maybe trouble Ekrah for a mug of javah. It's been a long day."

Lessien had taken up a position between Autumn and the

newcomer. Even with Belladonna's reassurances, she didn't wish to take anything for granted in the Abyss.

"Rest easy, mortal queen," Argomon said. "I've no hunger for your flesh… at least not today." He winked at Belladonna.

Lessien drew *Ah-HritVakha* and laid the blade across her stubbed arm. It glowed with power, as did her *Mantle of the Sovereign*. "That's a good thing, Argomon. You'd not live long enough to have that taste."

Everyone in the room looked at Lessien, then Argomon. Belladonna shook her head. But Argomon paid her no heed. Instead, he roared out in laughter so hard he doubled over.

"My… my… my little queen!" he exclaimed between guffaws.

"Hush!" Hodya warned. "You'll wake up the children!"

Argomon put a hand over his mouth. "Sorry," he mumbled from behind it. Then he addressed Lessien. "I've little doubt that demon-sticker you're holding could do its job, but you looked so damned…"

"That's enough, Argomon!" Belladonna ordered.

"As you wish, Belle," he said. Then he bowed to the Lessien. "My little queen," he said before turning to Ekrah. "Lead me to the javah."

As Argomon left the room with Ekrah, Lessien smiled. "He's right. I guess I did look kind of ridiculous. Sorry for the over-reaction."

Belladonna shook her head. "I'd have done the same if our positions were reversed. He's a bit…"

"A bit much?" Hodya interjected as she put the baby she was nursing over her shoulder to burp. "I'd say he is. But Lessien, for all his irreverence, he has a good heart. Oh, I know it might be hard for a mortal to believe, but the Abyss isn't like the stories you've been told. We have terrible… unbelievably terrible… demons. But we have good and righteous demons as well. Demons who long for freedom as much as any mortal.

Demons who'd be willing to reach out a hand of peace and cooperation to the mortal world."

"Burp!"

Hodya smiled. "That's a good boy. We need to give him a name."

Belladonna agreed. "The sooner the better."

Lessien sighed. "That should be Autumn's responsibility. I don't know why it's so important to decide right now."

"There's power in a name," Belladonna said. "At least here in the Abyss. Unnamed children have no rights... not even a right to live. If he's discovered by the authorities unnamed, they'll feed him to the *Pillar*."

Lessien frowned. "The *Pillar*?"

"I'll explain later," Belladonna replied.

"Why is there power in a name?"

"A true name is registered and accepted by the Abyss itself," Hodya said. "This isn't just a place where we live. It's the place where we belong. It's a part of our soul."

"I don't want this child to have anything to do with the Abyss," Lessien protested.

"It's too late," Belladonna said.

Lessien took the child from Hodya. "Can he survive in the mortal world?"

Belladonna nodded. "Yes... though the nature of his existence on Aster makes that problematic for reasons we'll discuss later. But you must understand, he can't leave the Abyss without a name. He'll die during the transition."

Lessien looked first at Autumn and then at the child she held in her arms. She didn't want to take the naming right away from her friend, but who knew if or when Autumn would ever come out of her funk? And if she waited, what effect might that have on the baby? She had to assume Belladonna was correct in her assertion it might doom the child in the Abyss.

"Is there some type of ceremony involved?" Lessien asked

Belladonna.

Belladonna nodded. "There is. The overlord demons add a lot of pomp and circumstance, but the procedure itself is quite simple. Hodya!"

"Certainly, overlord."

Lessien frowned. "You're an overlord demon?"

Belladonna nodded. "Argomon and Nightshade as well. I escaped the life father had planned... as did Nightshade from what you've told me, though I imagine there's much for which she must answer."

"There is," Lessien answered. "Father Goram has taken responsibility for her training, however, and her penance. There's no better on Aster to rein her in and keep her there."

Hodya returned. "Here you go, overlord."

"What's that?" Lessien asked.

Belladonna held up the object Hodya had just given her. It was a sheathed knife. The bone handle bore flecks of gold all around with semi-precious gems inserted along the length of both sides. The demon overlord removed the sheath to reveal a gleaming silver blade. Magical runes had been etched into both sides.

"The silver must mix with the blood of the one being named," Belladonna offered. "You must cut the child enough to draw blood. Then drive the knife into the dirt of the Abyss while chanting an incantation."

As the queen of InnisRos, Lessien understood ceremony and the impact it had on people. But she also knew many ceremonies are more than just "pomp and circumstance," as Belladonna had put it. Some were actual rituals that required magic not only to get a desired outcome but also to seal a compact between two parties. In this case, the child and the Abyss. But Lessien wanted more. She also wanted that same compact between the child and Aster... and she thought she knew how to get it.

She handed the child to Hodya and drew *Ah-HritVakha*. "If I use this instead?"

Belladonna raised an eyebrow. "Interesting! But yes... I believe that would work, though there might be unforeseen consequences using the sword."

"I'm willing to take that risk," Lessien said. "My sword will bond him to Aster as well as the Abyss."

"Or so you hope," Belladonna remarked.

The InnisRos queen nodded.

"Very well," Belladonna agreed. "There's an incantation you must memorize. It's in two parts... one you speak as you're cutting the child, and the other as you drive your bloodied sword into the earth of the Abyss." The demon overlord paused. "Again I ask... are you sure you want to use the sword?"

"I am."

"Then remember this, mortal queen," Belladonna instructed.

"Darah ayah, malam Stygian.
Darah ibu, terbakar terang.

Bergabung bersama, menjadikan anak Jurang.
Bergabung dengan bumi, untuk kebahagiaan terikat." [1 2]

With coaching from Hodya and Belladonna, Lessien practiced the phrases until she had memorized the exact wording and inflections. By now everyone in the Ekrah and Hodya household, including the children... Belladonna had used magic to heal Jezan of her fever... and Argomon was watching as Lessien rehearsed the incantation. When she was ready, everyone moved outside the house to stand on the dirt of the Abyss. The light of the Abyssian day was just breaking. They surrounded Lessien, the unconscious Autumn who was propped up with her back against the base of a tree, and

Autumn's child.

Belladonna, holding the baby, presented his arm. "Use the tip of your sword to cut the palm after speaking the first invocation. Mind you, only a small amount of blood is required. After you've done that, let the child's blood drip to the ground as you speak the second part. Then drive the sword into the ground as hard as you can."

Lessien looked at Autumn and was surprised to see her eyes were open and looking back. Autumn held Lessien's stare for a few seconds before she nodded. Lessien smiled. Perhaps her friend was returning? But her happiness turned to horror as she watched Autumn close her eyes and take her last breath.

"*No*!" Lessien screamed in her mind as she watched Hodya move to Autumn.

Hodya listened to Autumn's heart. She raised her head, looked at Lessien, and shook it. The gentle demon female crossed Autumn's lifeless arms and straightened her clothes. She used her fingers to comb through Autumn's long hair. "You should look your best, my dear, for the naming ceremony of your son."

Lessien hesitated as grief filled her heart.

"I'm sorry for your loss, Lessien," Belladonna said. "But this is important for the child. You must begin."

Lessien took a deep breath to choke back her tears and spoke the first part of the invocation. The wording and intonation were perfect. There were still tears in Lessien's eyes as she pulled *Ah-HritVakha* from its scabbard. She whirled and brought the tip of the sword across the child's hand. The baby didn't flinch or cry out.

InnisRos's queen then voiced the second part. As she did so, multi-colored lightning moved up and down her sword, crackling with power. After she finished the invocation, she drove the sword into the dirt of the Abyss.

"I name you Martin Goram," she bellowed. Lightning from

her sword shot up into the bleak skies of the Abyss, piercing the grayness with ease. A tremendous clap of thunder which stunned everyone rang down upon the land, followed by absolute silence.

"Damn!" Argomon whispered.

"The Abyss will never release this child to Aster," Belladonna thought.

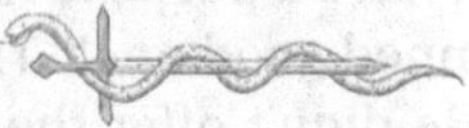

On the other side of the Abyss, the Taumaru leader Uraxas heard the crack of thunder that announced the arrival of the bastard child, the cambion.

"Xerxes has arrived," Uraxas said to himself. "The prophecy has been fulfilled and the Taumaru will have their champion. Our days of being outcast are over."

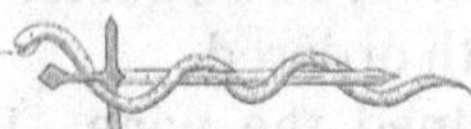

The demon overlord ruler of the city-state of Uz Urreth, Trolgroth, reclined in his bed while two females fed him his morning meal even though it was mid-day. The overlord had a long night overseeing the torture of a few unguilded peasants for various offenses like theft, trespassing, and lying to a city watchman. Afterwards, they were sent to the capital to be executed. The peasants actual guilt was irrelevant. Getting his quota to Kor and the Pillar was all that mattered.

The overlord decided he'd had enough to eat and waved the females away as he settled into his bed to drift back into sleep. Without warning, there was a commotion outside his bedroom doors. Trolgroth heard angry muttering coming from the guards. The voice that answered them was none other than Kor's Magical Faction representative, the sorcerer Droth-Toxol.

"What's he doing here?" Trolgroth said to the empty room. The two females had left through a secret passage.

"Trolgroth!" Droth-Toxol called from the other side of the room doors.

"Let him in," Trolgroth thundered as he got out of bed to pour himself a goblet of wine.

Droth-Toxol walked through the now open doors and bowed to Trolgroth. "I have a purpose for being here."

"It better be a damned good one!" Trolgroth said as he sat in his favorite chair. He didn't offer the sorcerer a seat of his own.

"Thunder, Trolgroth. Close by."

The overlord looked at Droth-Toxol. The Abyss Prefecture of Kor had its share of lightning storms accompanied by thunder, so Trolgroth knew there must be something special about this particular thunder to bring the sorcerer to his bedchamber. He offered Droth-Toxol a chair and a goblet of wine.

"Explain," Trolgroth ordered.

The sorcerer drained the wine. "It was magical... and unsanctioned."

"Have you reported this to your superiors?"

Droth-Toxol nodded. "Of course I did! It was unsanctioned, remember!"

Trolgroth frowned. "I could send you to the Pillar for taking that tone with me."

The sorcerer didn't budge from his mindset.

"*And no wonder,*" Trolgroth thought. Droth-Toxol's boss was Lilitu, the Magic Faction leader. And Lilitu had Kor's ear. "But you're lucky," the city overlord said aloud. "I just reached my quota. Tell me, sorcerer, just what the hell does Lilitu want me to do about this... this unsanctioned magic!"

"She asks that you seek the source and eliminate it."

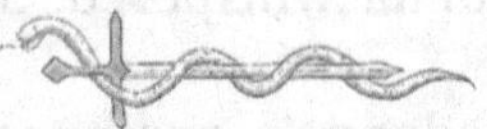

Lessien sat next to the dead body of Autumn. She leaned forward and closed her eyes while her emotions spiraled downward into a deep depression. Dark thoughts came in rapid-fire succession as she mourned for her dead friend. She couldn't deny them. Nor could she hide from them. Everything she'd been through because of Mordecai's maneuvering—the false accusation of murder against her, the civil war he started which set her island kingdom on fire, his alliance with Abyssian demons to bring about the dark elf invasion, and her own suicide attempt—already weighed heavily upon her soul. And now this.

Lessien clutched her chest and wailed. Her heart hurt so much she didn't think it'd ever recover. Autumn! Her anchor. Her safe harbor against the storm of life. The one person she trusted enough to reveal her innermost secrets and thoughts. The only person she knew who saw her as a person and not just the queen. Even her own sister, Nefertari, didn't have the same claim on Lessien's spirit as Autumn.

But as much as she loved Autumn, Father Goram loved her so much more. She was the yin to his yang. They were opposites in their outlook on life, yet perfectly suited for each other. Lessien loved the priest as well and knew he'd be devastated. First Mary McKenna and now Autumn. And Lessien would have to be the one to tell him. She'd have to endure his stare of disappointment and anger at her for not keeping Autumn safe. Then his tears would come, followed by his need to seek revenge. The priest she knew wouldn't allow himself to be comforted. Nor would he accept help in his quest to seek justice and find peace with his loss. Lessien's greatest fear, even more so than death, was that she'd not only lost Autumn, but Father Goram as well.

"Lessien," Belladonna whispered. She had knelt next to Lessien unnoticed.

Lessien felt Belladonna's presence and heard her call out, but it sounded as if an enormous gulf of space separated them. She looked in the voice's direction, but it took her a few moments to bring herself back from her inward ruminations.

"I'm okay," Lessien said.

Belladonna took Lessien's good hand. "We both know that's not entirely correct."

Lessien didn't respond as she looked at Autumn's face. For the first time since the abduction, it looked peaceful.

"We need to make a few decisions," Belladonna said. "The magic of your sword will bring unwanted attention, I fear."

"I'm surprised it did that," the InnisRos queen replied. "I'm sorry."

Belladonna shook her head. "It was reacting to your emotions. You'd just lost your friend, so I'm not surprised."

"That wasn't it," Lessien responded. "At least not entirely. *Ah-HritVakha* and I know each other well enough to control those types of outbreaks. No… it had something to do with the child. My sword was welcoming it."

"I don't understand."

Lessien frowned. "Neither do I. At least not entirely. It's as if *Ah-HritVakha* sensed something significant about the child… that he was more than just the bastard offspring of a demon and a mortal."

"What do you mean?" Belladonna asked.

"The sword doesn't talk to me… at least not exactly," Lessien answered. "It picks up on my emotions and reacts accordingly. When I first received it, I didn't understand how to manage it. It would feed off my feelings, particularly my rage, and react… usually by trying to convince me to release its bloodlust against my enemies. I can't tell you the number of times someone, mostly Autumn's husband, Father Goram, told me to 'control my damn sword,' as he would say. But this..." Lessien shook her head. "I just don't know, except to say that the child has a part to play in something... and the sword knows it. *Ah-HritVakha* was not only welcoming the child but also acknowledging him."

"Which means we need to protect him," Argomon said as he joined the two.

"I already plan on doing that," Lessien remarked. "He's Autumn's son and named after my father."

Belladonna nodded. "You belong back on Aster, and only the *B'nai Elohim* can do that. We're going to them as soon as you and the child..."

"Martin," Lessien interjected. "We should start calling him by his rightful name."

"Martin," Belladonna acknowledged. "As soon as you and Martin are ready to travel. I need their help as well."

"You want to leave the Abyss yourself?"

"No." Belladonna looked over at Argomon, who nodded. "I'm part of a resistance to the demon overlords here in the Abyss. For decades we've been building our strength, stockpiling weapons, training sorcerers, and developing plans to take this Prefecture of the Abyss away from Kor and his followers. When the time comes, we need to guarantee the B'nai Elohim won't interfere, or, despite their reluctance towards our internal affairs, possibly even help us."

"That would be good for Aster, don't you think?" Argomon interjected. "Both our peoples could live our lives in peace. And who knows? Perhaps we could establish diplomatic relations... or even introduce trade between us."

Lessien almost laughed. But when she looked at the two, she understood how serious they were. "Is there even a chance you'd be successful?"

Belladonna shrugged her shoulders. "Who knows? But we're prepared to die trying. The people of the Abyss value their freedom as much as yours."

The InnisRos queen studied the two as she thought of the possibilities. "*True, we have our own problems,*" she thought. "*But demon overlords have caused much suffering to my people and Aster. If we could end that...*"

Finally, Lessien nodded. "Very well. And maybe I can also help. If the *B'nai Elohim* were to be inclined, I have an entire army that would like nothing more than to bash in some demon heads."

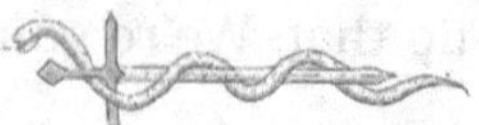

Trolgroth relaxed in his wooden, fur-lined throne. Its back raised up twenty feet and was intricately carved into the visage of Lord Kor clutching the body of a dead B'nai Elohim warrior. The sentiment was wishful thinking to most, but no one dared voice that error in the carving least they be forced to Kiss the *Pillar*.

"Where the hell is he?" Trolgroth roared as he stood and paced. His guards, the only other demons in the receiving hall, didn't flinch. They remained at attention and kept their stony gaze directed forward.

The double-doors to the receiving hall opened and Korzidok, Trolgroth's second-in-command, entered while dragging a pathetic minor demon behind him. Korzidok approached his liege and forced the unfortunate to kneel before Trolgroth. The minor demon had a longish, slimy body with arms and legs and a flickering, forked tongue.

"What's this?" the demon overlord asked as he stood. "Why is this wretch cluttering up my hall?"

"This one calls himself Verax, My Lord," Korzidok replied. "He was seen in the market flashing around this."

Trolgroth took the gold trinket Korzidok held out in his hand.

"Gold!" Trolgroth exclaimed. "And not like any design I've ever seen. Worth a small fortune. And illegal. But how would something this valuable come to be in this one's possession?" Trolgroth pushed the prostrate minor demon with his foot.

"I've yet to put that question to him," Korzidok said. "I thought you'd want to have first crack."

Trolgroth frowned. "Why? Because it's gold? Because the design's unusual? That means nothing. He obviously took it from someone. He's a simple thief. What could he possibly have to tell me that's the least bit significant? Send him to the Pillar and be done with it! You have more important things to do!"

"It's not just the unusual design of the gold trinket he was flaunting," Korzidok replied. "It's also who he's been seen with."

Trolgroth looked at Verax. "Alright, Korzidok. Who?"

"Belladonna."

The demon overlord sat back down on his throne. "Now you have my complete attention."

The prostrate Verax raised his head. "My Lord... My Lord... I'll tell you everything!" Pleassse don't sssend me to the *Pillar*, I beg you!"

Trolgroth laughed. "That was easy. Tell me everything you know and I'll consider leniency."

"I didn't sssteal the gold," the minor demon answered. "It wasss given to me."

"By whom and why?" Trolgroth asked.

"Mortalsss, My Lord," the minor demon responded.

"Mortals? Here in the Abyss?"

Verax nodded. "Yesss! Two female mortalsss. In a cave to the sssouth. They paid me with that gold trinket to get them food and drink. They alssso wanted information... information about the *B'nai Elohim*. I... I... I wasss too afraid to asssk around for sssuch a thing. Ssso I went to sssee Belladonna."

"You know Belladonna?" Trolgroth asked.

"It would seem everyone in the market square knows Belladonna," Korzidok answered for Verax. "She's like a good Samaritan... always helping and sometimes even hiding folks from your *Pillar* roundups. You get regular reports about her activities."

"I don't look at those things," Trolgroth snapped. "That's why I have underlords... to keep me appraised about the important things."

"Then I suggest you have a long talk with those underlords," Korzidok remarked. "Or do you wish for me to do that?"

Trolgroth waved his hand. "I'll see to it. You've got other things to do."

Korzidok nodded. "Continue, Verax," he ordered.

"I took Belladonna to the cave with the mortalsss," Verax replied. "Then I wasss dismisssssed."

"Can you take Korzidok there?" Trolgroth asked.

"Yesss, My Lord."

"Good. Korzidok, it's possible the unsanctioned magic we spoke of earlier and this sighting of mortals are related. Take as many warriors as you think you'll need and investigate this cave of Verax's. I doubt the mortals are still there, so stop at any farms or ranches along the way and question as many of them as you see fit. No one's going to forget hearing strange thunder or seeing mortals... especially if they're traveling with Belladonna."

Korzidok nodded.

"Oh, and on your way out, send my chamberlain to me. It's about time I do something about Belladonna. Kor may have favored her father, Aikanáro, but he's dead. She's been using her status as his daughter to annoy me for far too long."

"Yes, My Lord," Korzidok said as he bowed. "And Verax?"

Trolgroth looked at the pitiful minor demon. "When he's done his part, give him a few shecales and turn him loose."

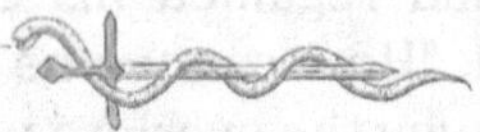

Gleep barked a desperate warning as he ran to the door. Jezan, laying in a large bassinet with Martin, began crying while the other three young children ran to stand behind Hodya, who was putting together the family's evening meal. Martin didn't respond to the commotion and remained silent. There was little that upset the cambion, and loud, sudden noises weren't one of them.

"What now?" Ekrah said as he walked to the door. "Quiet, Gleep! We know someone's here."

"Honey..." Hodya cautioned.

Ekrah didn't respond to his wife as he opened the door. "It's dinnertime! Can't this wait?"

On the other side of the open door was a demon overlord and several demon underlords surrounding a pitiful looking, much smaller demon. "No, rancher, it can't."

Complete silence settled over the house. Even Gleep, sensing the power radiating from the overlord, quit barking, though he stayed beside his master and remained alert.

"May I enter?" Korzidok said as he stepped through the threshold. His companions and their captive remained outside next to the doorway.

"Umm..." Ekrah muttered as the overlord walked past him.

Hodya recovered from the intrusion faster than her husband. "Please, My Lord, have a seat," she said as she scooted the children back into their own room. "Would you like something to eat? We were just about..."

"To sit down for dinner," Korzidok interrupted. "Yes, I know. Your husband said as much. No, my palate's a bit more refined for whatever you'll be serving. But I thank you for the offer. I will, however, accept a chair."

Hodya nodded and pointed to an empty chair.

By now Ekrah had regained his composure enough to address the overlord. "How can we be of service, My Lord?" He thought he knew why the overlord was here—Belladonna, Argomon, and the two mortals. His eyes briefly shifted to the fireplace mantel, where the ashes of Autumn were resting in a crude, wooden urn.

Korzidok noticed the momentary tilt of Ekrah's eyes and made a mental note. "There've been reports of an unusual weather event which occurred in the area around here. Specifically, the singular crack of thunder unrelated to a storm. Our sorcerers tell us this odd thunder may have resulted from illegal magic usage."

Ekrah registered no surprise, but Korzidok, aided by the magic he wielded during interviews, heard a sudden increase in Ekrah's heartbeat. "*Interesting*," the overlord thought. He stood and walked around the main room of the ranch house. He looked in the bassinet and saw one child. "Tell me, rancher, how many field striders do you tend?"

Ekrah looked confused. "My Lord?"

"Field striders," Korzidok repeated. "How many?"

"I only have a small herd… usually three dozen, sometimes less if the market's good," Ekrah replied. "Or if we need to butcher one or two for ourselves or our neighbors."

The overlord nodded. "I imagine it takes a lot of hard, dangerous work to manage your herd."

"Gleep and I get along okay."

"And I can see your wife certainly has her hands full with four children."

"Yes…" Ekrah replied. "*Where's this going?*" he wondered. "*And why four? Didn't he see two children in the bassinet?*"

Korzidok had stopped in front of the fireplace and was looking at everything on the mantel, particularly the urn. Then he whirled on Ekrah. "I was just thinking how terrible, and difficult, things would be for your family if something were to happen to you. Something like a freak accident… or a debilitating disease."

"We'd get help from the neighbors, My Lord," Hodya said. She'd picked up Jezan and rocked her back and forth to calm her. Martin was quiet as usual. "*The overlord said four children and didn't seem surprised when I only picked up Jezan,*" she thought, much the same as her husband. "*It's as if he only expected one baby to be there. He doesn't see Martin*!"

The overlord smiled. "Of course they would, providing they didn't have their own problems to deal with."

Suddenly, the line of questioning made sense. And the implications were terrifying. "What do you want, My Lord?" Ekrah asked.

Korzidok returned to his chair, satisfied he'd made his point. "I want you to do what's best for your family and neighbors. I want you to save yourself from the Pillar. Did you hear the thunder?"

Ekrah nodded. "Yes, My Lord. We heard the thunder."

"Ekrah!" Hodya exclaimed.

Ekrah held up his hand as he looked at his wife. "The overlord needs to know. It's our duty to Kor."

"Yes it is," Korzidok affirmed. "Go on."

Ekrah nodded. "As soon as I heard the thunder, I knew right off it wasn't from an electrical storm. It had an unfamiliar sound to it… almost like… well, it didn't rumble like ordinary thunder. It was more of a short 'snap.' Like the crack of a whip, but much louder. You remember, right Hodya? Well, old Gleep and I went outside right away. But we didn't see a thing. Nothing out of the ordinary. Well, except for…"

Ekrah paused. Korzidok looked at the rancher suspiciously. His heartbeat remained steady and there were no other telltales in his eyes or on his face, but it still didn't feel right. "Continue."

"Off in the distance, I thought I saw several figures running into a stand of trees to the south." Ekrah shook his head. "Whoever they were, they sure were in a hurry. Now that I think upon it, there's an old base camp built for climbers on the other side of those trees. Used to be lots of folks would go up there to explore the caves at the lower elevations." Ekrah nodded. "Yep. That's where they were heading. I'm sure of it."

"Caves, you say," Korzidok commented.

"Oh, yes sir, My Lord," Hodya interjected. "We've taken the kids up there several times… well, not since the little one came… but several times to explore."

Ekrah concurred. "Nothing dangerous up there except for an occasional fanged panda or horned sheep. And even if you run across one…"

"Yes, yes… I'm familiar with both," the demon lord interrupted. "And that's it? That's all you saw out of the ordinary?"

"Yes, My Lord," the rancher replied. "The field striders were making trouble because of the thunder and Gleep and I had our hands full calming them down. I was too busy to notice anything other than that."

Korzidok looked at the rancher and his wife. From an open doorway to an apparent bedroom, he saw three small heads peeking out at him. The overlord stood and headed towards the front door. "Thank you, citizens, for your time and the information."

"Yes, My Lord," both said as the stranger opened the door.

The overlord suddenly stopped and turned before stepping outside. "Oh, and citizens. If you should see those figures again, you'll let me know, correct? It'll go so much easier if you do. Do you understand?"

"Absolutely, My Lord."

Outside, Korzidok's underlords looked at him. He shook his head and led them south to the trees Ekrah said the strangers had gone. Once under their canopy, he stopped.

"He's a smooth one, he is," Korzidok said. "Both him and his wife. And they know more than their saying. Brazzuroth, I want you to stay here and keep an eye out on the ranch. If anything out of the ordinary happens, come and get me at once. Don't engage! Right now, I need information more than I need dead underlords… or ranchers."

Brazzuroth snickered.

Korzidok smacked the insubordinate demon across the face. "There's more danger out here than you could ever imagine! Just follow orders. As for the rest of you, follow Verax and me."

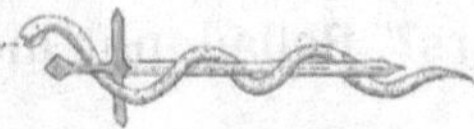

Belladonna knocked lightly on the door. On the other side, Gleep nudged the arm of a drowsing Ekrah to wake him. Hodya and the kids, including Martin, were asleep. The three older children were in their own room while Hodya and the two babies were in the master bedroom.

"Huh?" Ekrah said as he rubbed his eyes and took a swig of his unfinished wine to cleanse his mouth. "What now, you mangy mutt?"

"Ekrah!" Belladonna whispered through the barred and locked door. "Let us in!"

Ekrah took another sip of wine, swished, and spit the mouthful into the fireplace and walked over to the door, scratching his belly and yawning. "I'm coming," he grumbled. "Just hold your horses."

Belladonna, Argomon, and Lessien crowded through the doorway as soon as it was clear. Each carried a backpack of purchased supplies and several full waterskins, which they deposited in a corner by the door. Ekrah closed and relocked the door before turning to his guests. Right away, he noticed they were agitated. Each looked around the room as if they thought something, or someone, might be lying in wait.

"No one but us four," Ekrah said as he went to the stove to warm up some javah.

"Woof!"

"Oh, and Gleep. Now try to be quiet. Everyone else is asleep."

Belladonna looked at the rancher. "You had visitors?"

Ekrah nodded before he took a seat at the kitchen table. "The javah should be ready soon."

"I'll have wine, if you don't mind," Argomon said as he grabbed a bottle from Ekrah's wine cabinet and a cup.

Everyone joined Ekrah around the table.

"So you had visitors?" Belladonna inquired for the second time.

"We did, but that was a few hours ago," Ekrah replied. "How did you know?"

"There was an underlord watching from the trees just to your south," Belladonna replied. "Lessien took care of him with her sword. It was quite impressive."

"I've been well trained," Lessien remarked. "From someone I hope to see again. Besides, the sword did most of the work."

"Don't sell yourself short," Argomon commented. "I've seen worse from actual sword masters."

"Let's get back on point, shall we?" Belladonna reminded everyone. "Your visitor, Ekrah?"

"An overlord," Ekrah replied. "I believe his name is Korzidok. He didn't mention it to me, but I've seen him once or twice in Uz Urreth after bringing my field striders to market. He's usually there to pick out a calf for the city overlord's dinner, so he's well known by most of the ranchers in the area."

Argomon whistled. "That's Trolgroth's number one," he said.

Ekrah shook his head. "I wouldn't know. He came here looking for the source of the thunder that came from that sword of yours, queen, during the naming ceremony. He threatened me, my family, and damn near every farm or ranch around us."

"What did you tell him?" Belladonna demanded. Her attitude had taken a serious turn.

The tone of Belladonna's voice angered Ekrah. He'd known her and Argomon for years and he trusted them. And he believed they trusted him. But Hodya had cautioned him several times that someone from the peasant class can never truly know an overlord and the motives that drove them. Ekrah took a deep breath to calm himself before answering.

"I said I heard the thunder and saw figures moving into the trees south of here," Ekrah responded. "I told him I only got a passing glance… that before I could take a more active interest, my field striders started acting up because of the thunder and I had to calm them down. Then I told him of the old camp at the base of the mountains and of the caves up there."

"We're very familiar with those caves," Lessien mentioned.

Ekrah nodded. "I sent them there. I didn't know they were going to have an underlord stand watch, but I suppose that makes sense."

Belladonna smiled. "You did good, Ekrah."

Though it felt good to have the overlord compliment him, there was one thing that worried Ekrah about the underlord watcher and his ultimate demise. He began to hem and haw.

"Spit it out, my good fellow," Argomon said.

"Belladonna, I did what I did because you've helped my family…"

"As well as all the other families around here," Hodya added. She'd just come out from her bedroom and sat next to Lessien.

Ekrah nodded. "Yes. And we're grateful. But when Korzidok comes back and sees his dead underlord, he's going to blame me. Hiding the body won't matter, either. He might even take it out on our friends as well. The *Pillar* never seems to have enough victims, guild standing or not."

"Good point," Belladonna mumbled as she considered.

"I think I have an idea," Argomon announced. "But it's going to mean sacrificing one of your calves."

Ekrah shook his head. "Field striders only breed once a year. And even then, the mother's more likely as not to devour the calf herself. I got to get the two separated from the rest of the herd and moved to another corral. Then I need to make sure the mother accepts her calf and knows how to nurse, especially if the young'un's her first. After that..."

"Calm down, Ekrah," Argomon cautioned. The rancher had been getting more and more animated as he explained the problems he had to deal with. "Unless someone has a better idea, it's either that or go into hiding to save your family."

"And what about the other families?" Hodya mentioned. "Can they go into hiding as well?"

"Running's not the answer," Ekrah said.

"Then we're back to the calf," Argomon stated.

Ekrah shook his head. "I'd rather lose a full-grown field strider. There has to be another answer."

"Can an underlord cut out an adult field strider from the herd?" Belladonna asked.

Hodya laughed. "It takes Ekrah, Gleep, and me to do that. And we know what we're doing. One demon, even an underlord, wouldn't stand a chance."

"How about a mother and her calf?" Argomon inquired. "You said you keep them in separate corrals, didn't you? At least until the mother has acknowledged the calf?"

Ekrah shook his head. "You're correct. But right now, all my calves have been accepted and in one corral with their mothers. Like all females, the adults bond together to protect their young. You kill one, you have to kill them all. No underlord would even attempt such a fool-hardy thing."

"I think I know where you're going with this, Argomon," Belladonna weighed in. "You're thinking of putting the body in the corral with a dead calf to make it look like the underlord was trying to get a free meal and was caught by the mother."

"Or maybe he wanted to present the meat to Korzidok," Argomon said. "Field strider calf meat is a delicacy reserved for overlords only... and kissing your superior's butt is an underlord specialty. Either scenario seems believable... and more importantly... sellable."

"Perhaps we don't have to kill a calf to achieve the same result," Belladonna remarked. "What if we threw the body into the corral with the calves and their mothers? Would that be enough to induce the mothers to sting it?"

"More than enough," Hodya stated. "And with that much poison in him, his body would blow up until it burst apart. He'd hardly be recognizable. Other injuries would be hard to distinguish without close examination."

"What terrible creatures," Lessien commented.

Ekrah shrugged. "They can be. But like the rest of us, they're a product of their environment... though they're docile enough if you know how to handle them. Even Gleep can round up a small-sized herd."

"And field strider meat is one of the major staples in the Prefecture," Hodya added. "The overlords have little respect for life... but they do like their supper."

"That's right," Ekrah agreed. "And how we prepare their supper, just like how we dress the meat for edible consumption, are closely guarded guild secrets. No one but ranchers and butchers knows it. The overlords are forced to respect us as a result... well, as much as us peasant folk can be respected. Those of us protected by the guilds are somewhat safe from the *Pillar*... or their other execution methods. We have our ancestors to thank for that. As I said, we're a product of our environment."

Lessien shook her head. "Unbelievable!"

Hodya patted Lessien's hand. "This shouldn't surprise you, my dear. Most societies, no matter how different, are still the same in many ways ... even down to the boogieman we use to scare our little ones. Just last week I told the kids if they didn't go to sleep, the queen of InnisRos was going to come to them and pull out their horns. That was before I knew you, of course."

Lessien drew back. "You..." Then she smiled as everyone around the table laughed.

"Oh, before I forget," Hodya said suddenly. "The overlord, as he was questioning us, roamed around the room. He looked into the bassinet but made no mention of Martin. I thought that was odd."

Ekrah nodded. "He mentioned only four children. I've thought about this for most of the evening since. For whatever reason, I don't think he saw Martin."

Lessien shrugged. "Perhaps he made an assumption?"

"Overlords don't make assumptions," Belladonna stated. "Or they'd not be overlords. That is strange indeed."

"A mystery to be solved later," Argomon said. "We need to get out of here before Korzidok returns. C'mon, Ekrah. Let's go take care of that body."

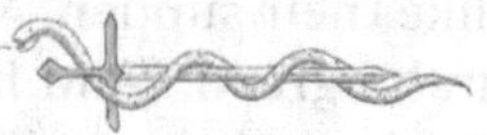

"Any luck, Korzidok?" Trolgroth asked. He was having dinner—succulent field strider calf covered with black sauce, steamed entrails, potatoes, and the fruit of the Bristly Kenaf Gallberry Tree—in his private dining room.

"Verax was telling the truth," Korzidok said. "He led us right to the cave and there were signs the mortals had been there... including quite a bit of blood."

"Had been?"

Korzidok shrugged. "You didn't really think we'd find them, did you? Not with Belladonna involved."

Trolgroth sighed. "I had hoped. What else of interest?"

"I lost an underlord," Korzidok replied.

Trolgroth took a sip of spiced lager. "Go on."

"We came upon a ranch which I believed to be near the source of the thunder," Korzidok answered. "It was located just before the foothills of the mountains where we found the cave. The rancher told me he'd heard the thunder, went out to investigate, and saw several figures heading into a stand of trees in front of the foothills."

"This rancher didn't bother to investigate, right?" Trolgroth assumed.

Korzidok nodded. "The thunder riled up his herd of field striders. Unsurprisingly, calming them took precedence. His story made sense. Even so, I thought he was hiding something, though I couldn't pin it down. I suppose I could have used force..."

"No," the overlord leader said. "You did the right thing. I've already got enough problems with the Rancher's Guild. Another complaint and I'd probably have to go see Kor. Never stepping into the capital again would be too soon for me. Continue."

"I left an underlord, Brazzuroth, to watch the ranch while I investigated the mountain caves. When I got back, I discovered the underlord's body in a corral of field striders... females with their calves. They had stung him multiple times... to the point he was barely recognizable."

"Why would he do something so stupid?" Trolgroth wondered. "Did the rancher know anything about it?"

"No. The rancher, who seemed just as surprised as I, suggested that Brazzuroth wanted to pull out a calf." Korzidok paused. "Actually, I've been wondering about that... and it makes sense. Brazzuroth was never the smartest of my underlords, but he was the most corrupt. I can see him going after a calf to sell on the black market."

Trolgroth nodded. "Or perhaps he wanted to give me a gift to gain favor. Either way, it sounds plausible."

Korzidok agreed. "That's what I thought."

"Conclusions?"

Trolgroth's second-in-command sat for the first time. He picked up a three-pronged fork and hovered over the steamed entrails. When Trolgroth nodded, he helped himself. "That we have mortals in our midst, one possibly wounded, is undeniable. If the rumors are correct, this is possibly Aikanáro's doing, which means they're important. It also looks as if they were involved with the thunder… and Belladonna is connected."

"Most likely," Trolgroth replied. Black sauce was running down his chin. "My guess is they're running as fast as they can to the *B'nai Elohim*."

"No doubt you're correct. We know Belladonna's involved with the resistance. So I supposed she might also seek refuge with one of their local cells. Not too many other places she can go to save her skin."

Trolgroth laughed as he leaned away from the table.

Korzidok frowned. "What's so funny?"

"Kor's fixer infiltrated the resistance with a few of his spies," Trolgroth answered. "While you were gone, I learned that his people had rounded up most of the leaders and forced them to talk… after a little persuasion, of course. While most of the resistance had been congregating around the capital, we had a few here. They've been captured or killed… at least those we could find. The *Pillar's* going to feed well for the next few months. As for Belladonna and the mortals… I doubt there're any cells close by she can run to… at least any still operating. Put out an alert for her between here and the *B'nai Elohim's* fortress. Oh, and after you've done that, prepare the army to march."

"What?"

"We're ordered to rendezvous east of here along with the armies of the other cities," Trolgroth answered. "It appears Kor's going to do it again."

"You mean..."

"Yeah. He's going to move on the *B'nai Elohim*."

Korzidok shook his head. "If we've learned anything, it's that their fortress is impenetrable."

Trolgroth nodded. "Kor knows that." The overlord leader of Uz Urreth stopped talking while he tapped the tips of his talons on the arm of his chair. "He's got something else planned."

CHAPTER THREE

The Abyss

"That's it!" the sorcerer exclaimed. He turned to his assistant. "Mozzen, be a splendid fellow and run along to Lilitu. Tell her I found the formula."

Mozzen ran out the door of his master's workroom.

Gizgoluch looked at the hastily scribbled scroll. "Don't need those damn Order of the Talisman sorcerers telling me how to do my job. Just one last check."

The sorcerer picked up the scroll and studied the incantation while checking the magic. Everything looked good. Gizgoluch took a deep breath.

"Mawar merah,
Violets adalah biru.

Buka pintu,
Jadi saya boleh lalui." [3]

The magic of the spell coalesced at a point in front of the sorcerer and five feet up from the floor. The point moved outwards on all sides until it became a spinning ten foot diameter circle. Gizgoluch smiled. "*Perfect!*" he thought as he used his talons to further manipulate the magic.

"Wait until Lilitu sees..."

Gizgoluch didn't finish. A powerful arm reached through the doorway and grabbed the surprised sorcerer. It raised the helpless demon up and crashed him back to the floor. It did this several times until nothing remained of Gizgoluch except a crushed, lumpy corpse. The B'nai Elohim guardian leaned in through the doorway, looked around, and grabbed the scroll. By the time Lilitu and Mozzen reached Gizgoluch's workroom, the magical doorway had collapsed. What was left of the sorcerer's body had stopped quivering, and there was no sign of the magical scroll.

"Damn!" Lilitu cursed. Then she looked at Mozzen, who had gone to a corner to cower. "Get this mess cleaned this up!"

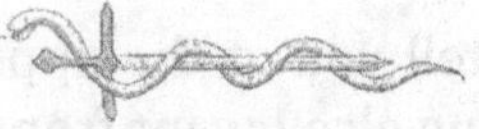

"There you are!" Kor called from down the hallway.

Lilitu stopped. She wasn't ready to tell her master about Gizgoluch's failure, but now she had little choice. She turned. "My Lord."

"I heard some disturbing news about your Faction's latest attempt to open a doorway to Aster. Another abject failure. Is this true?"

Lilitu nodded, though she wondered how Kor already knew. It wasn't Mozzen. He didn't have the time since he was busy dying. Maybe that weasel, Mozzen? "Unfortunately, that's correct. The fool used the spell before I checked its veracity. Considering the condition of his body, I've little doubt that a guardian intercepted the magic and once again proved to us why attempting such a thing is futile and so dangerous to our health."

"Do you still have his version of the spell?" Kor asked.

Lilitu shook her head. "His work scroll was gone. As usual, the guardian took it. Besides, it doesn't matter. From the look of things, I'd say it was no better than what we already have. The *B'nai Elohim* can still read us like a book."

"The Order says they've discovered an answer to that," Kor remarked. "Once we find them, I'll have the means to destroy the Talisman and free the Abyss of the *B'nai Elohim* once and for all."

"So you don't want us to continue our search for a doorway spell?"

"By all means, keep working on it," Kor replied. "Just in

case we can't find what spell the Order's developed… or my information about them is incorrect. But don't put too many resources on it. I've other ideas about what we can do, so I don't want you to waste time."

Lilitu frowned.

Kor smiled. "I'll tell you at the appropriate moment. For now, there's something else I want from you."

"I'm yours to command."

"Of course you are," the overlord leader said as he laughed. "At least as long as I command the *Pillar*."

The Magic Faction leader remained silent.

Kor became serious. "Tell me, Lilitu. Are you able to make it so a non-sorcerer can invoke the magic of a scroll?"

"No, My Lord," Lilitu answered. "There're secrets we'll never divulge to anyone without the gift."

"Figured as much," Kor responded. "But I had to ask. Due diligence and all that."

"Where's this going, My Lord," Lilitu inquired.

"I want your Faction to prepare several hundred doorway scrolls," Kor said. "A thousand if you can get it done. And if I were you, I'd assigned them to your most expendable sorcerers."

Things began to make sense. "You're going to draw out the guardians, aren't you? You're going to use my sorcerers as a diversion for something larger."

Kor smiled.

"You're planning an all-out attack on the *B'nai Elohim's* fortress?" Lilitu guessed. "And you want my sorcerers to act as bait? What if they don't fall for your distraction? And even if they do, any guardians my sorcerers draw away will only be gone for a few minutes… not long enough to weaken their defenses for any sustained period."

"You're smart, Lilitu," Kor stated. "Sometimes I forget just how smart you are."

"I'm a sorceress," Lilitu said, as if that explained everything. "Then figure it out!"

The Faction leader could only draw one conclusion. "Everything's a distraction!"

Kor smiled again. "You have one week to get ready. I want daily status reports. I'll leave it to you to handle the logistics."

"This is going to cost my Faction heavily."

"Best start recruiting," Kor said.

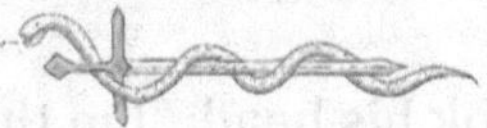

Azazael sipped javah as he watched the demon he'd been following eat an early morning breakfast in a small tavern overflowing with patrons. Four of his underlords were also watching from different locations within the building. Outside, eight more of his warriors surrounded the tavern. His quarry, a demon sorcerer named Bezrameth, was rumored to be part of the Order of the Talisman.

As Azazael watched, he got glimpses of what was underneath the richly designed hooded robe Bezrameth wore. It was a rare mixture of bone and leathery skin. The sorcerer was a monstrosity, even by demon standards. That made Azazael even more cautious.

Azazael determined that a direct approach was the safest way to eliminate the possibility of a risky apprehension. Put all the cards on the table so everyone knew where they stood. Most times, this eliminated costly misunderstandings all around. He picked up his mug of javah and went over to Bezrameth's table and sat down opposite of him.

"Don't be alarmed," Azazael said.

The Order sorcerer smiled, though it was hard to distinguish on the face of a skeleton. "You took your time contacting me, Azazael. I was wondering if I needed to send up a fireball announcing my location and desire to talk?"

Azazael was taken aback but knew better than to show it.

"And I know of your team both inside and outside," Bezrameth continued. "You have me surrounded and at your mercy." He spoke that last with amusement. "But I appreciate your directness."

Azazael cleared his throat. "Then you understand why I'm here."

"Indeed, I do," Bezrameth answered. "I'm the one who sent the message to Kor about the Talisman."

"I thought..."

The sorcerer shook his head. "I'm the leader of the Order. I have the doorway spell our liege requires."

Azazael nodded to his underlords, who stood and surrounded the table. Bezrameth tapped a finger on the table several times and all four froze in place, helpless to do anything other than listen and observe. "But I have demands," the sorcerer added.

"One doesn't put demands on Kor!" Azazael retorted. "Not unless you've a wish to Kiss the Pillar!"

Bezrameth laughed. "I've heard Kor can be a reasonable fellow. I've something he wants and he can give me something that I want."

"You want to be the Magic Faction leader?" Azazael remarked. "I think Lilitu might have something..."

"Don't be silly," Bezrameth snapped. "I don't fear Lilitu, but I sure as hell don't want to be tied down to her responsibilities."

"Then what?" Azazael asked.

Bezrameth lowered the hood of his robe to expose two black-filled eyes surrounded by gleaming bone. "Kor's going to destroy the Talisman, right? He's going to use my spell to send an assassin team to Aster."

The Military Faction leader nodded. "That's why you sent the coordinates, correct?"

Bezrameth smiled. It was one of the creepiest things

Azazael had ever seen.

"I want to go with them," the sorcerer said. "I want to be the one to destroy the Talisman. Afterwards, I want to be granted the governorship of Aster once we've conquered the mortals."

"You want to be given a world to rule?" Azazael was dumbfounded.

Bezrameth didn't back down. "Just a little tradeoff. What I have is worth it in the long run."

"Kor could force the information out of you!"

"Oh, Azazael!" Bezrameth snorted. "You think you'll break me that easily?"

"Well… Lilitu has ways…"

This time the Order sorcerer chuckled. "I bet she does. But consider this."

Bezrameth began an incantation and a few moments later, the four underlords who had been frozen in place disappeared.

"Where…" Azazael began.

"To the *Veil of the Infinitus Atrophia*," Bezrameth answered. "They're not coming back. A steep price to pay for your skepticism of my abilities, no doubt. But one that was necessary. Now, are you going to take me to Kor?"

As both stood to leave the tavern, Azazael kept thinking over and over, "*I'll be kissing the Pillar myself after Kor's done with me!*"

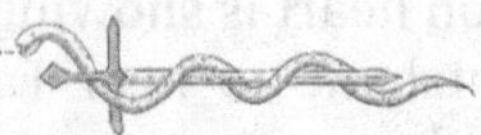

Father Goram, Nightshade, and Landross were in the courtyard of the B'nai Elohim fortress waiting for the gigantic gates to open. Gabriella was there as well, and all of them were awaiting Michael. The guards wouldn't open the fortress gates without his specific order.

Nightshade checked on the Qénsharma. They were awake

but appeared satisfied enough with their current situation.

And though she couldn't communicate with them like Eric the Black or one of his associates, she had a sense for what they were feeling. They knew they were back in the Abyss, and that seemed to satisfy them. Nightshade didn't know yet how she was going to use them, but she was determined to set them free once they'd concluded their mission.

Father Goram approached and looked over Nightshade's shoulder as she was looking at the beasts. "You figured out how you're going to use those little beggars?"

Nightshade shook her head. "Not yet. But I've decided to release them once we're ready to go home."

The high priest nodded. "I suppose that's for the best. Eric the Black might not appreciate it, but he'll get over it soon enough."

"I don't think we're going to see that sorcerer on Aster anymore," Nightshade said. "He appears to be somewhat infatuated with the Alfheim's queen."

"Noticed that too, did you?"

Nightshade nodded. "Once they get their friends back, I believe he'll stay with her. It's amazing how much control the heart of a mortal has over rational consideration."

Father Goram chuckled. It was the first time he'd laughed since the abduction of Autumn and Lessien. "You're a mortal now, as well. And though you may not be ready to admit it, your cold, black demon heart is showing signs of life."

It delighted Nightshade to hear Father's Goram's light-hearted banter. "It was happening even before Michael induced the change in me. I thought it was a weakness."

"We'll need to separate," Father Goram, back to business, commented. "We have two different tasks now."

Nightshade nodded.

"I don't want you out there beyond these walls without backup," Father Goram continued. "You're my student and I'm responsible not only for your training but for your safety as well."

Nightshade closed the backpack containing the Qénsharma and looked at the priest. "I know the Abyss as well as you know InnisRos. Besides, I've got allies… and I also have my little friends here to help if needed. You and Landross… particularly Landross… will be the ones in real danger."

Father Goram said nothing.

"Remember our discussions regarding the Abyss," Nightshade said. "You'll find plenty willing to help if you're prepared to accept them."

"I'm more concerned about our armored friend over there," Father Goram replied as he looked at Landross, who was involved in a discussion with Gabriella.

Nightshade shook her head. "I wouldn't be. Regardless of his rigidity, he has a kind heart and a keen sense of right and wrong. When he's introduced to the ordinary demon… the farmer, the rancher, the craftsman… he'll understand. I suspect it'll make him that much more determined… not only to rescue the queen and your Autumn… but also to help the peasant class in any way he can. I can envision him coming back and leading his knights against the ruling overlords, though it'd be a futile effort."

"If it's as you say, he'd care little about the uselessness of it at all," Father Goram countered. "He'd do what he believes to be his duty… and die if necessary. People like Landross and his knights are a rare breed. But it won't come to that. His first duty is to his queen."

"And his love," Nightshade added.

Father Goram nodded. "There's Michael!"

The *B'nai Elohim* looked worried and somewhat distracted. Landross broke off his conversation with Gabriella and met Michael. Father Goram didn't think now was a good time for the knight to annoy the guardian. To his surprise, however,

Landross didn't engage Michael, but just fell in beside him as he walked to join Father Goram and Nightshade.

"What's wrong?" Nightshade asked. She recognized Michael's apprehension by his stride and the look on his face.

"I've lost contact with my informants," Michael answered. "That's never happened before… at least not with all of them at the same time."

"The demons are planning something," Father Goram surmised.

"It's worse than that," Nightshade said. "If they've compromised your contacts, it also means any information you may have already received from them might be compromised as well."

Michael nodded. "That's exactly what it means. If my intelligence has been wrong…"

"You're not going to try to stop us, are you?" Landross asked Michael. "Because if you are…"

"No, knight!" Michael said. "Just the opposite. I need you out there. I need whatever information you can gleam from the peasants. As for you Nightshade, it's even more important you contact Belladonna. If my resources have been compromised, then so have hers. She needs to be warned."

Father Goram shook his head. "This changes things, Nightshade. Things just got much more dangerous. You're staying with us. Whatever needs to be done, we'll do it together."

Nightshade nodded as she shouldered her backpack. "Will you give Belladonna sanctuary?" she asked Michael.

"Of course," he responded. "As well as any of her followers." Michael looked at the massive double-gate and nodded. They began to open slowly.

"Finding her out there will be like finding a needle in a haystack," Landross said as he stared into the Abyss.

"I'll find her… or she'll find me," Nightshade replied as she walked forward through the gates.

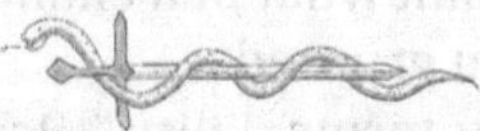

Bezrameth inspected the small room Azazael had led him into. Compared to the rest of Kor's lavish palace, it was spartan—plain with uncomfortable chairs, blank and dreary-colored walls, no artwork to speak of, and a cold, stone floor. The only thing of actual interest was the single door into the room. Made of teak, it had elaborate runes which encompassed not only the door but the door frame as well. Bezrameth could feel the magic radiating from the symbols that were obviously designed to keep a sorcerer from leaving without permission. The Order sorcerer wasn't worried, however. He had something Kor wanted badly... something Bezrameth wasn't inclined to give away for free. And he was strong enough to resist any magic they might throw at him to induce cooperation. A succubus entered the room without preamble.

"You must be Lilitu, the Magic Faction overlord," Bezrameth said.

"Indeed," Lilitu answered. "And you're Bezrameth, leader of the Order of the Talisman and outlawed sorcerer."

Bezrameth smiled. "Outlawed? Or just wanted for the information only I hold? Information that will allow Kor to do an end-run around the dreaded *B'nai Elohim* and occupy the mortal world of Aster?"

"That's what I'm here to determine," Lilitu replied.

"Ahhh... here to test my mettle, then."

Lilitu shook her head. "More like here to test the veracity of your claim. Azazael told us of the four underlords you sent away..."

"To the *Veil,*" Bezrameth interrupted. "Gone forever."

"So you say," Lilitu snapped. "There's no way to actually authenticate it."

"I could send you there? You might find them. Getting back, of course, would be somewhat of a challenge."

"Harrumph!" Lilitu grunted.

"I told Azazael my terms, Lilitu," Bezrameth said. "That's the only way Kor will get the doorway spell from me."

"Kor might be agreeable… if you have what you say you do," Lilitu replied. "As we've already established, I'm here to make sure you have the goods."

Bezrameth studied Kor's top sorcerer. She was a beauty, that much was certain. And intelligent. Kor wouldn't have her as his Magic Faction leader otherwise. Maybe he could persuade her to rule Aster at his side? What a dynamic pair the two would make! Forget the threat of Aster's gods, old or new. For the Black Magic the two could wield against their followers would keep them at bay. Even the new goddess of Aster, Esmeralda, wouldn't move against them as long as they had her empaths under their control. Evil has one advantage over good—the willingness to sacrifice everything and everyone to achieve a goal. The lives of innocents mean nothing.

Lilitu broke Bezrameth's musings. "My own sorcerers are working on the solution, even as we speak. We may not even need you or your so-called breakthrough."

Bezrameth laughed long and hard. It took a few minutes before he could control himself. Wiping tears out of his eyes, he said, "Is… is that a fact?"

Lilitu said nothing. She understood the improbability of her sorcerers finding the correct spell as much as Bezrameth did. Only to her, it wasn't a laughing matter. Kor had expectations, which meant her position as the Magic Faction leader was on unstable ground if she didn't come through for him.

"Get me parchment, quill, and ink," Bezrameth requested. "And a table."

Lilitu opened the door and had a brief conversation with one of the two guards outside in the hallway. "I'm glad you decided to cooperate," she said after closing the door.

"My cooperation only goes so far, Lilitu," the Order sorcerer said. "You get a small part of the invocation. Enough so you can confirm its authenticity. But not enough to allow you to deduce the rest."

Lilitu nodded. "That's all Kor asks."

The door opened and two underlords brought in a small table, parchment, quill and ink, and a tray of field strider meat cakes and wine.

Bezrameth set the table next to a chair and placed the parchment, quill, and ink on it. Then he looked at the food and wine.

"Help yourself," Lilitu said as she grabbed a meat pie and poured wine for herself.

"*It's the least they can do since they disturbed my breakfast,*" Bezrameth thought as he downed two meat pies and a mug of wine.

"So," Lilitu said after giving the Bezrameth time to finish eating. "Are you ready to get down to business?"

Bezrameth swallowed the last of his meat pie and nodded. "How much do you know about mathematics?"

"Mathematics?" Lilitu said as she tapped her chin with an elaborately painted talon. "Enough to know that its basic premise closely relates to magical spell creation and functionality. That it deals with the logic of shape, quantity, and arrangement. Mathematical formulas prove specific outcomes by placing components in the proper order to reach a desired result. You don't have to understand mathematics to craft a spell. But you have to know how it relates with regard to spell development."

"Correct!" Bezrameth agreed. "Spell enchantments lay the groundwork for the gathering, control, and manipulation of magic. Similar to a mathematical equation, each spell stanza, or verse, represents a specific component of the spell. Putting the stanzas together is a matter of understanding the desired outcome, figuring out the proper sequence, developing the words of power, and putting them into the correct order with the proper cadence and tonal inflection."

Lilitu held up her hand. "Enough! It's hard. I get that."

The Order sorcerer shook his head. "Hard! You think it's only hard? Madam, some spells are damn near impossible to create! When crafting a doorway spell of this magnitude, there are many things to take into consideration when building the proper mathematics. I needed to consider its beginning and endpoints, the physical size, the length of space it must transverse, the number of dimensions, or universes, it must pierce as well as their resistance to the spell, and so forth."

"Their resistance?"

"Lilitu, not every dimension or universe is magic rich," Bezrameth scolded, as if the Magic Faction leader were a student. "Then there're the variables! I had to make allowances for the *Veil*, the *B'nai Elohim*, the Juxtaposition Point, the specific location point on Aster, the time it must stay open, etcetera."

"Just how large is this enchantment?" Lilitu asked. By "large" she wasn't only referring to just the number of stanza's, but also to the number of necessary components and the physical elements required by the casting sorcerer.

Bezrameth knew what Lilitu was asking. But he wasn't going to admit he'd taken care of all the other aspects within the spell itself. All a sorcerer had to do was read the spell out loud in the proper cadence—easy enough for most.

"Most of the information is for my eyes only," Bezrameth replied. "You don't get that much. But the spell length is forty-seven stanzas."

Lilitu didn't react. "Fine. I guess I couldn't expect more. Show me."

Bezrameth bent over the small table, loaded the quill with

ink, and wrote. "This is stanza twenty-one... but it should be enough to give you the proof you seek," he said when finished.

"B'nai Elohim, penjaga takdir,

Kelewatan kesedaran mereka, jadi kebimbangan akan reda." 4

Lilitu read the stanza and knew it was for real. In effect, what it did was remove, at least temporarily, the *B'nai Elohim*'s ability to sense a new magical doorway when it opened.

"Brilliant," Lilitu remarked. "Yes, I believe you have the goods. Wait here while I get Kor."

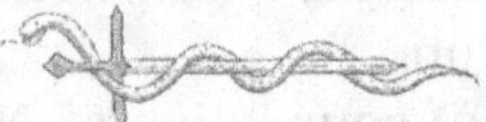

It didn't take long before Father Goram, Nightshade, and Landross ventured onto a demon farm. Around them were fields of reds, oranges, and browns. The crop looked like the oats and barley grown on InnisRos and the mainland.

"You'd be amazed at the many similarities between the Abyss and Aster," Nightshade remarked. "The food grown and eaten here is also safe for all of Aster's races. It goes both ways. We won't go hungry... nor would demons go hungry on Aster."

"Demons eat children!" Landross exclaimed. "Elf flesh... human flesh... dwarf flesh!"

Nightshade remained calm. "Not by choice. Oh, there's no doubt some demon overlords and underlords enjoy the taste..."

Landross shook his head. "It's more than the demon upper-class! All demons have acquired the taste of flesh!"

"Is that from your books, scrolls, and manuscripts?" Nightshade asked. "What makes you think any mortal can write accurately about demon behavior? Most inhabitants of the Abyss would retch at even the thought of eating flesh."

The knight choose to remain silent.

"The fact is the few demons who bypass the *B'nai Elohim* via summoning and make it to Aster are overlords, underlords, or warriors. None of the common folk have any actual interest in leaving their homes in the Abyss. Nor are they ever summoned. Think of it. You're an Asterian sorcerer who wants to bring a powerful demon to Aster. Are you going to call for a peasant? Maybe... if all you want is someone to clean your house or make your dinner."

Nightshade stopped walking and watched a six-legged grasshopper jump and fly from one stalk to another. Unlike grasshoppers on Aster, however, it wasn't interested in eating any part of the crop. Instead, it attacked a much smaller insect that was eating the crop.

"Landross, think of your knights," Nightshade continued. "Lessien once called them a boy's club... drinking, eating, carousing together... and doing competitive things to 'one-up' each other. The same things happen here, particularly within the overlord community. Yes, they've developed a taste for flesh. Part of that's because they have no choice. It's what you'd call the 'price of admission' into their club. It allows them to keep their standing within their group. And before you ask, I'm as put off by it as the peasants."

Father Goram spoke for the first time. "You need to keep an open mind, Landross. Our written knowledge of the Abyss pales compared to what Nightshade has in her head."

"Aye, Horatio," Landross replied. "She's *from* here!" He ripped off the top part of a single stalk of barley and put the end in his mouth. What he saw next caused his mouth to open and the stalk to fall out.

On the dirt road they traveled, a herd of three dozen field striders appeared over a hill in front of them. Four dogs, six-legged and twice the size of dogs on Aster, ran along both sides of the herd, barking and keeping the herd in line. A rancher followed.

"By the gods!" Landross exclaimed. "Are those your cows?"

"Very good, my knight friend," Nightshade responded. "In the Abyss, they're called field striders. Field striders provide most of the meat that feeds the population of the Abyss. The females are milked, and the meat of the calves is a delicacy reserved for the ruling class… though ranchers rarely ever follow that edict. The problem comes if they're caught, but even then, with a bribe of meat, they can coax officials to look the other way."

"They don't look too friendly," Landross observed.

Nightshade nodded. "They're dangerous and should be given a wide berth… at least by those of us who don't raise them. A decent rancher with one or two excellent working dogs can control them well enough."

"Do all of your animals have six or twelve legs?" Father Goram asked.

"Generally speaking," Nightshade answered. "On most of them, the two front legs can act as primitive arms, which helps them in a fight. Fortunately, that doesn't apply to field striders. They're dangerous enough with that stinger."

As the three, well off the road, observed the herd pass, one dog, a youngster by the size of it, ventured too close and took several stings before it could disengage. The remaining three dogs kept the herd moving while the rancher bent down to inspect his injured animal. He shook his head and returned to driving the herd. As he passed Father Goram, Nightshade, and Landross, he stopped.

"Never seen mortals before," the rancher said. "Best stay out of sight of the overlords… begging your pardon, ma'am."

"No harm intended, I'm sure," Nightshade answered. "We'll do what we can."

The rancher then took a good, long look at the female overlord. "Haven't I…" but he shook his head before he finished.

"Never mind. Herbie probably won't make it, the damn fool dog. Wish I could, but I don't have time to stop. Normally I'd have put him out of his misery, but I saw you and thought maybe you can help. If you heal him, he's yours. He's young and inexperienced, but a good worker... you won't be sorry. If not, I'd ask you to bury him. He deserves at least that much."

Father Goram nodded. "We'll see to it."

The rancher tipped his hat. "Appreciate it, stranger. And remember. Keep away from the overlords!"

Father Goram and Nightshade watched as the herd disappeared down the road. Landross had gone over to the stricken dog.

"Curious," Father Goram pondered aloud. "He didn't appear too concerned about Landross and me other than to issue a warning regarding the overlords."

"Abyssian culture conditions the common folk to accept things as they are," Nightshade said. "Particularly when there's an overlord involved. But don't think you and Landross won't be the topic of at least one conversation tonight around the dinner table or in the local pub."

"And you," the priest added. "He seemed to know you."

"That much I doubt," Nightshade replied. "Unless he mixed me up with my sister."

Father Goram nodded. "Probably."

"Horatio!" Landross called. "Herbie needs your help!"

"Coming, my boy."

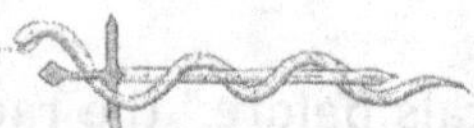

Kor needed more persuading than Lilitu, but in the end, Bezrameth convinced him he was telling the truth.

"Azazael has informed me the price for your help is Aster," Kor remarked.

"That's correct," Bezrameth replied. "Well, not in the

respect that I want to own it. Nothing can take that privilege away from the great Kor. But I'd like to be named its governor."

"Why?" Kor asked. "Surely there's something else that interests you?" Kor looked at Lilitu. "For instance, the Magic Faction."

Lilitu knew better than to object. Though an overlord and Faction leader, she wasn't immune from kissing the *Pillar* if Kor demanded it.

Bezrameth laughed. "Lilitu can keep her job. I've no interest in being an administrator."

Lilitu choked back an angry response.

"Aster is a magic rich world," Bezrameth continued. If he noticed Lilitu's flash of anger, he didn't react to it. "It has millions of peasants I can use for my experiments."

"You have those here," Kor pointed out.

Bezrameth shook his head. "You ever tried to fill out the paperwork involved for that? Kor, your Administration Faction makes it damned near impossible. Then you need to contend with the guilds. And once you cross those two hurdles, you need permission from Lilitu's Magic Faction to do the experiment. It boggles the mind!"

Kor shrugged. "Rules are rules. Only I can break or change them... which I'm not willing to do. I'm far from ready to join the souls in that damned Living Throne, something they'll demand if I show weakness."

"And if you destroy the *B'nai Elohim*?" Emprusa asked from the doorway. "If you do that, the souls will never dare challenge or call you to them again. Everyone will hail you as the greatest overlord of all time. It'll seal your destiny for eternity."

"What are you doing here?" Kor asked his concubine. "Better yet, how did you find me? This is supposed to be a secret meeting."

"I have my sources," Emprusa answered. "You know that."

"This is none of your concern," Kor snapped back.

Emprusa sat in a chair next to Kor. "Is it not, My Lord? You don't expect me to watch while you vacillate on the greatest opportunity an overlord's ever had, do you?"

"She's not wrong," Azazael said.

"I'd be ruling Aster in your name," Bezrameth added.

Kor looked at Lilitu. "And you?"

The Magic Faction leader looked at Bezrameth. It'd be worth it just to have him gone. "I don't see how you can pass up the opportunity."

"Now's the time, My Lord," Emprusa said. "Destroying the Talisman is the key to getting the *B'nai Elohim* off our backs... and it gives us Aster. Don't let Bezrameth's demands stop you. It's worth the price he's asking."

"So it would seem," Kor agreed. "Alright, Bezrameth. You can have Aster as your little playground. Azazael, I want to see your plans to distract the *B'nai Elohim* in writing. As soon as Lilitu has her sorcerers ready, I want to go. There's no sense wasting time. The longer we wait, the worse the odds for success get."

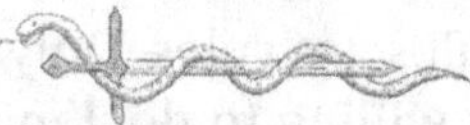

Michael nodded at Gabriella, who was standing in the doorway to his study awaiting permission to enter. "News?" he asked as he returned to the mountain of administrative paperwork on his desk.

"Not really," Gabriella replied. "Just something that's troubling me."

"Go on."

"Well, there's been a sudden increase of doorways being opened by demon sorcerers," Gabriella answered. "Opened and closed fast enough that we've no time to respond."

Michael looked up from the daily reports he was reading.

The *B'nai Elohim* leader had learned long ago to trust his second-in-command's nagging feelings. "You have my full attention."

Gabriella nodded. "I went to the source. It wasn't easy... as I said, the doorways were being closed as soon as they opened. But we managed to bring in two. They got sloppy."

"Two?"

"One for the story and the other for verification," Gabriella replied.

Michael waited.

"We didn't get much. But what we got confirmed my suspicions. The doorways being opened and closed are in preparation for something much larger. Exactly what they didn't know. But that's not too surprising, considering. They're low level sorcerers... apprentices at best."

"I know you, Gabriella," Michael said with a smile. "You wouldn't be here unless you've already drawn a few conclusions."

"I have indeed, Michael. I believe they're getting ready to deploy a spell which will bypass us... probably to get to the Johari. The simple doorway spells are meant to distract us from the real thing... something much larger... something we've never seen before. What we're seeing now is a test before the real diversion."

Michael shook his head. "The spell signatures won't be the same. We won't have any trouble distinguishing between the two, and I'm sure they understand that."

"But we must respond to each, regardless! If they flood us with a few hundred doorway spells, we won't have the numbers on our side!"

"Understood," Michael said as he stared into space, thinking. "Except it's unlikely they have enough of the spells... or the sorcerers... to take on all of us. There's got to be more to it."

Both Michael and Gabriella remained quiet for a few minutes.

Michael looked at Gabriella. “There’s only one other possibility. They’re going to launch a full-scale attack on our fortress before inundating us with diversionary doorway spells. That would explain reports of a military buildup just before our sources went quiet. Combined, the two would drain our manpower to the extent we’d never see the more powerful spell they’ll be using until it’s too late.”

“That has to be it,” Gabriella agreed.

“Kor’s not stupid,” Michael added. “And he’s ruthless. I’ve no doubt he’d risk half his army and sorcerers for a chance at the Johari. And the numbers are on his side.”

“That also explains why we’ve heard nothing from our contacts,” Gabriella concluded. “Kor’s put a lid on all outgoing intelligence because he’s getting ready to move. Michael, we need more troops to defend our fortress.”

Michael nodded. “What did you do with the two sorcerers you questioned?”

Gabriella frowned. “Same thing we always do with demon sorcerers casting doorway spells to Aster. Banged the life out of them and returned their bodies back to where we got them. Why?”

“I only want to make sure nothing’s out of the ordinary,” Michael replied. “No point giving Kor any hint that we’re doing things differently or suspect things are off-kilter.”

Gabriella concurred. “Makes sense. Any idea how we’re going to stop this?”

Michael smiled. “We need more troops, right? I think I know where we can get them.”

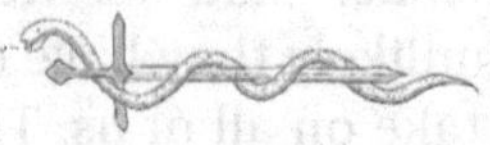

Landross and Herbie bonded at once. Other than appearance and size, the young demon dog didn't seem much different from dogs on Aster—loving, goofy, loyal, accepting, and sometimes a delightful pain in the arse. Father Goram, Queen Lessien, and Kristen had their wolves, and now Landross had his very own six-legged demon dog. He soon discovered he'd not give up Herbie for an entire pack of Ajax's.

It was dusk of the third day since leaving the *B'nai Elohim* fortress. The only inhabitants they'd come across during that time were the rancher and his field striders. There were no wandering squads of demon warriors to avoid. No overlords or underlords to bother them. No incredible monsters to threaten their existence. Just the heat and a landscape, though alien in color and design, that spoke of relative peace.

"This isn't Hell, Landross," Nightshade once said to the knight when he commented on the lack of conflict. "The Abyss is a world much like Aster. Poles apart yet the same because it has a populace doing their best to survive, raise families, and contribute to their society as best they can. Outside the cities are plenty of good demons."

"Inside the cities?" Father Goram asked.

"In some respects, it's a completely different story," Nightshade answered. "There, the overlords rule with an iron fist and have an army to back them up. It's not unusual to see squads of warriors roaming the streets looking for lawbreakers, particularly towards the end of the month. If you fall out of line... if you so much as spit on the sidewalk... you'll find yourself heading to the capital to Kiss the *Pillar*. Sometimes even the guilds can't prevent it depending upon the seriousness of the crime. Every city has a monthly quota. It's evil... but it's a structured evil. And many would argue a necessary evil when you consider keeping the *Pillar* strong is a matter of life or death for everyone in the Abyss."

"But on the other side of that, city life can be quite

peaceful... peaceful for everyone except those in power. Those can find it to be very cutthroat. Most of the overlords in the cities are too busy watching their backs to pay much attention to the populace under their rule, leaving that to their underlords... though underlords run their own power-grabbing schemes. It's so cutthroat some might say it's more dangerous for an overlord or underlord than a peasant to live in a city. The peasants have a saying... 'A threatened overlord is a blind overlord. And all overlords are blind.' It's true in many respects. Guarding your back from treachery leaves little time to monitor the peasants. Besides, as your people are fond of saying, they know what side their bread's buttered on. The demon peasants are their only source of food, clothes, labor, and the luxury items they crave. Again, the one true danger the peasants face, those caught breaking the law or not under guild protection, isn't justice meted out by an overlord. It's the *Pillar*... particularly if the monthly quota is lacking."

"That sounds rather ominous," Landross said as he threw a log for Herbie to fetch. It didn't take him long to teach this new game to the demon dog—a game Herbie discovered he loved to play. "Why hasn't anyone destroyed this *Pillar*?"

Nightshade almost laughed at the naivety of the question but caught herself. Landross had no way of knowing why the *Pillar* was so important. "As I said, that would have disastrous consequences."

Landross nodded. "Yes... it means life or death for the Abyss. But why is that?"

"As much as the Abyss is similar to Aster, geographically it's completely different," Nightshade answered. "Abyssian boundaries aren't defined by black space or the stars in the sky, but rather a shroud of nothingness. We call it the *Veil of the Infinitus Atrophia*. If you go in there, that's it. You're either dead or so lost you can't find your way. No one whose entered has ever come back out. Our sorcerers have speculated someone can wander in the void until the body wastes away. The *Pillar of Captured Souls* is the means by which the Abyss keeps the Veil from collapsing."

Father Goram sighed. "Let me guess. This 'Pillar' is powered by the death of Abyssian inhabitants."

Nightshade nodded. "Informally we call it '*Kissing the Pillar,*' and anyone with a soul can power it. This includes your people living on Aster. It requires a specific number of deaths each month to keep the *Veil* from collapsing. Only Kor knows what that number is, and each city has a target goal to reach. Usually it's lawbreakers… but not always. Guild members are somewhat exempt from this… this… peasant tax, if you will, unless it's the end of the month. Then all bets are off. The guilds declare the last two days of each month a holiday. This is so their members can stay off streets roamed by squads of *Pillar* collectors."

"You mentioned guilds before," Landross said.

"Another story, Sir Knight," Nightshade responded. "Another time. Look!"

They had just crested a hill. In front lay a valley. Spread out below them were three large cities surrounded by numerous farms and ranches. Past the cities was an enormous body of water to the north and mountain ranges to the south.

"How do we find Autumn and Lessien in a place so large… so populated?" Father Goram exclaimed.

"We do that by expanding the number searching for them," Nightshade remarked as she looked over at the priest. "I have contacts."

Zerzoroch looked down from the second-floor balcony at the full amphitheater below. He knew it was dangerous to call in all his resistance leaders at one time, but matters had taken a turn for the worse and he needed to disseminate vital information to as many people as possible… and he had little time to do it.

"Any chance Kor knows about this?" he asked his fellow resistance leader, a normal enough looking demon except for the spikes that ran along his back.

Drorikan shook his head. "Kor's too busy planning something else right now."

Zerzoroch nodded. "I've heard the same rumors. That's why I've taken the chance to call the cell leaders here."

"What of Belladonna," Drorikan asked. "I don't see her."

Zerzoroch returned his gaze back into the amphitheater. "Neither do I. And I haven't heard from her…" He stopped as he caught sight of a commotion below. It appeared his cell leaders were fighting each other.

"What the hell!" he cried out. "Drorikan…"

The double-edged blade of a shagoth, a demon dagger with several downward-curved nodules running along the primary blade, slashed across Zerzoroch's throat. Blue blood gushed out and ran down the front of the dead demon's tunic as he fell to the floor, the head attached to the body by only a thin piece of flesh.

Overlord Drorikan looked below as he wiped his dagger's blade on the tunic of the dead Zerzoroch. The resistance leaders were giving an excellent account of themselves, but their situation soon became untenable as warrior demons sent by Kor's fixer reinforced his own people who'd been planted in the resistance. Most of the surprised resistance leaders died fighting, but there were enough left alive to interrogate. The resistance in the city was, for all intents and purposes, defeated.

A winged demon flew up and landed on the balcony. "We'll have things wrapped up soon, Overlord."

Drorikan nodded. "Any reports on Belladonna?"

"She's not here."

The overlord leaned against the balcony and looked down at the little pockets of fighting still ongoing. "Too bad," he whispered before turning back to the winged demon. "What's your name?"

"Gorgraath, Overlord."

"Well, Gorgraath, be sure to remind your colleagues that Belladonna's to be taken unharmed if she's found," Drorikan warned. "Those are the fixer's instructions. If she's hurt, the one responsible won't Kiss the *Pillar*. Nor can he expect a date on Execution Hill. He'll be mine… and I can guarantee it'll take him a thousand years to die."

Gorgraath blanched and nodded. "As you will, Overlord."

"Carry on!"

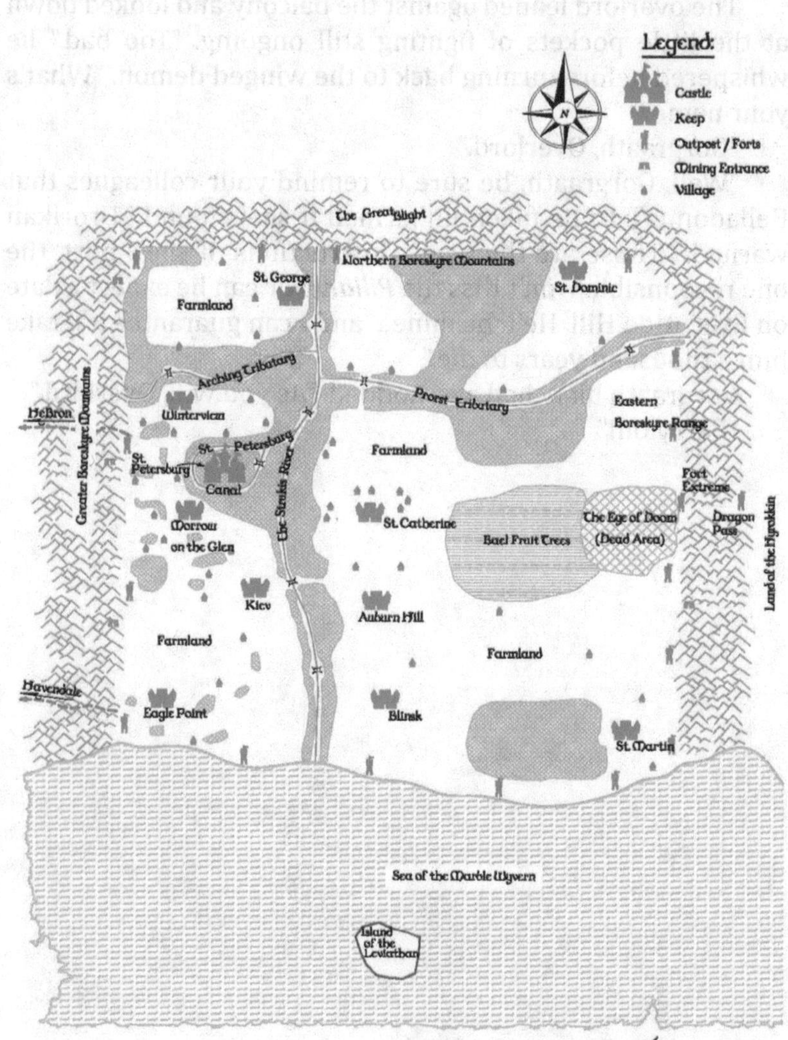

Draugen Pesta

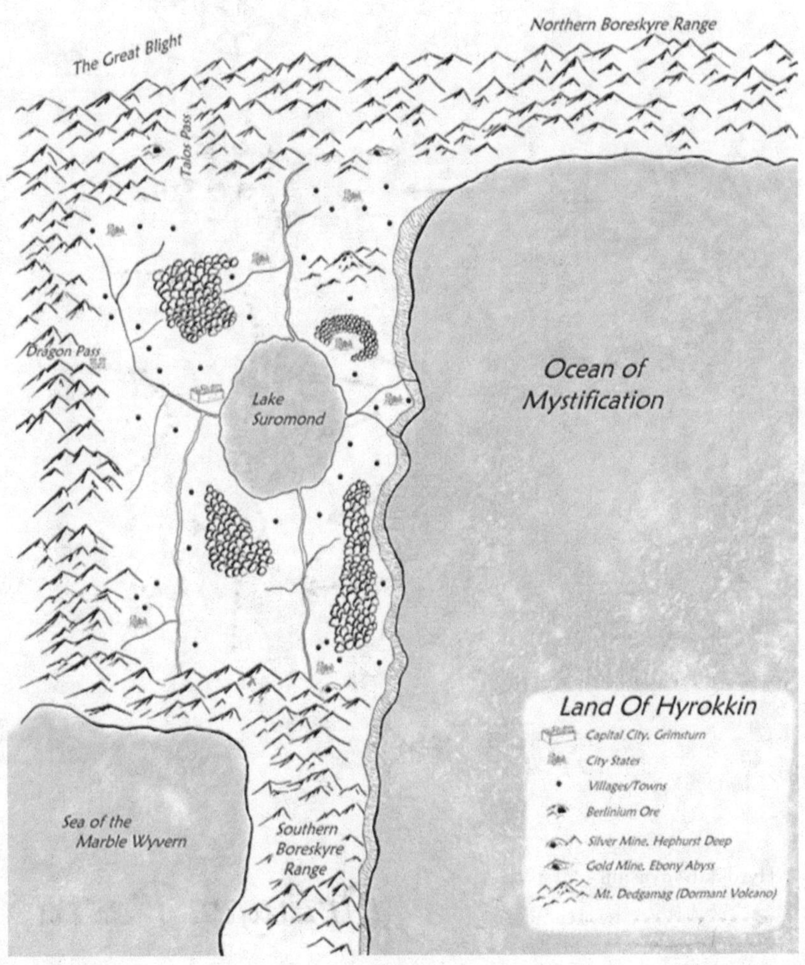
Northern Boreskyre Range
The Great Blight
Talos Pass
Dragon Pass
Lake
Suromond
Ocean of
Mystification
Sea of the
Marble Wyvern
Southern
Boreskyre
Range
Land Of Hyrokkin
Capital City, Grimsturn
City States
Villages/Towns
Berlinium Ore
Silver Mine, Hephurst Deep
Gold Mine, Ebony Abyss
Mt. Dedgamag (Dormant Volcano)

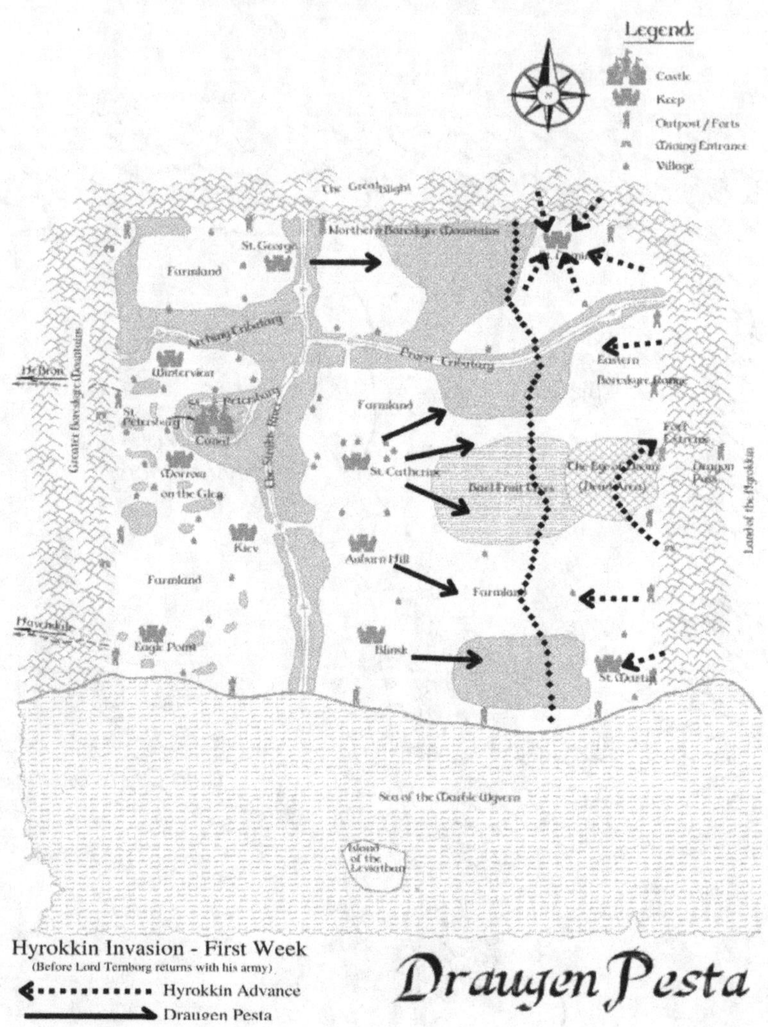
Legend:
Castle
Keep
Outpost / Forts
Village
Farmland
St. George
Farmland
St. Catherine
Kiev
Farmland
Auburn Hill
Eagle Point
Eastern
Hyrokkin Invasion - First Week
(Before Lord Temborg returns with his army)
Hyrokkin Advance
Draugen Pesta
Draugen Pesta

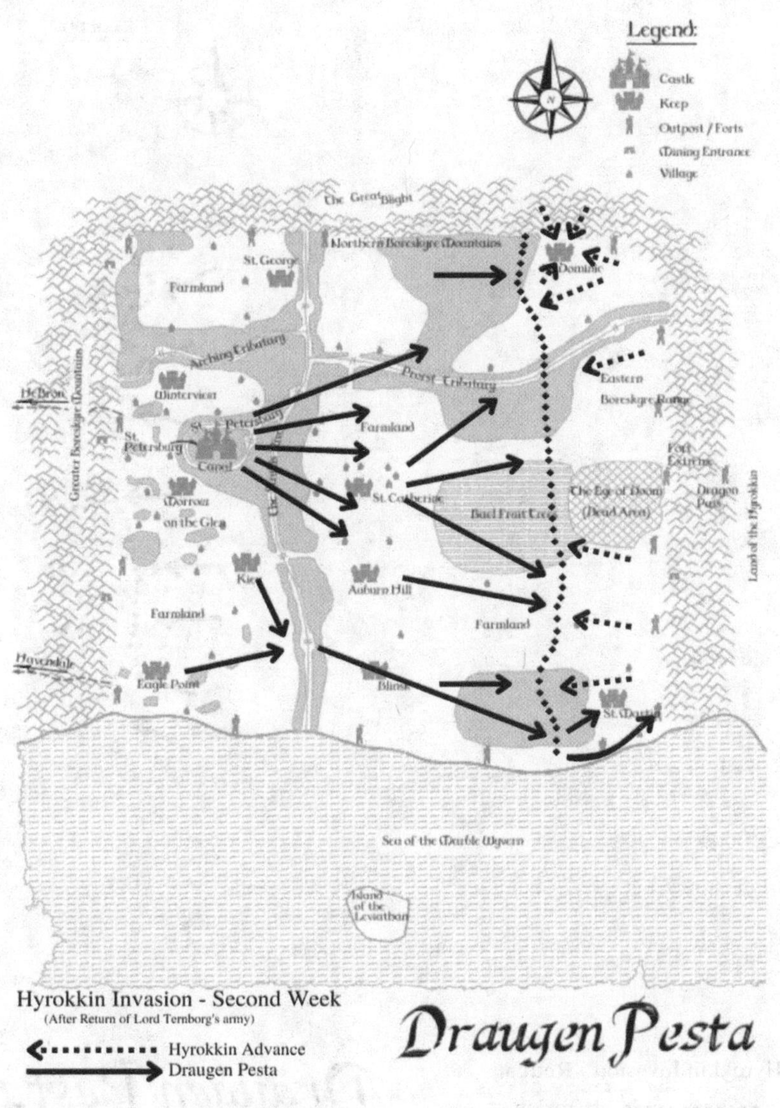
Legend:
Castle
Keep
Outpost / Forts
Mining Entrance
Village
The Great Blight
Northern Boreskyre Mountains
St. George
Farmland
Arching Tributary
Priest Tributary
Wintervian
Hebron
Greater Boreskyre Mountains
St. Petersburg
St. Petersburg
Canal
Farmland
Eastern
Boreskyre Range
Morrow
on the Glen
The Eye of Doom
(Dead Area)
Dragon
Pass
Land of the Hyrokkin
Auburn Hill
Farmland
Farmland
Havendale
Eagle Point
Sea of the Marble Wyvern
Island
of the
Leviathan
Hyrokkin Invasion - Second Week
(After Return of Lord Ternborg's army)
Hyrokkin Advance
Draugen Pesta
Draugen Pesta

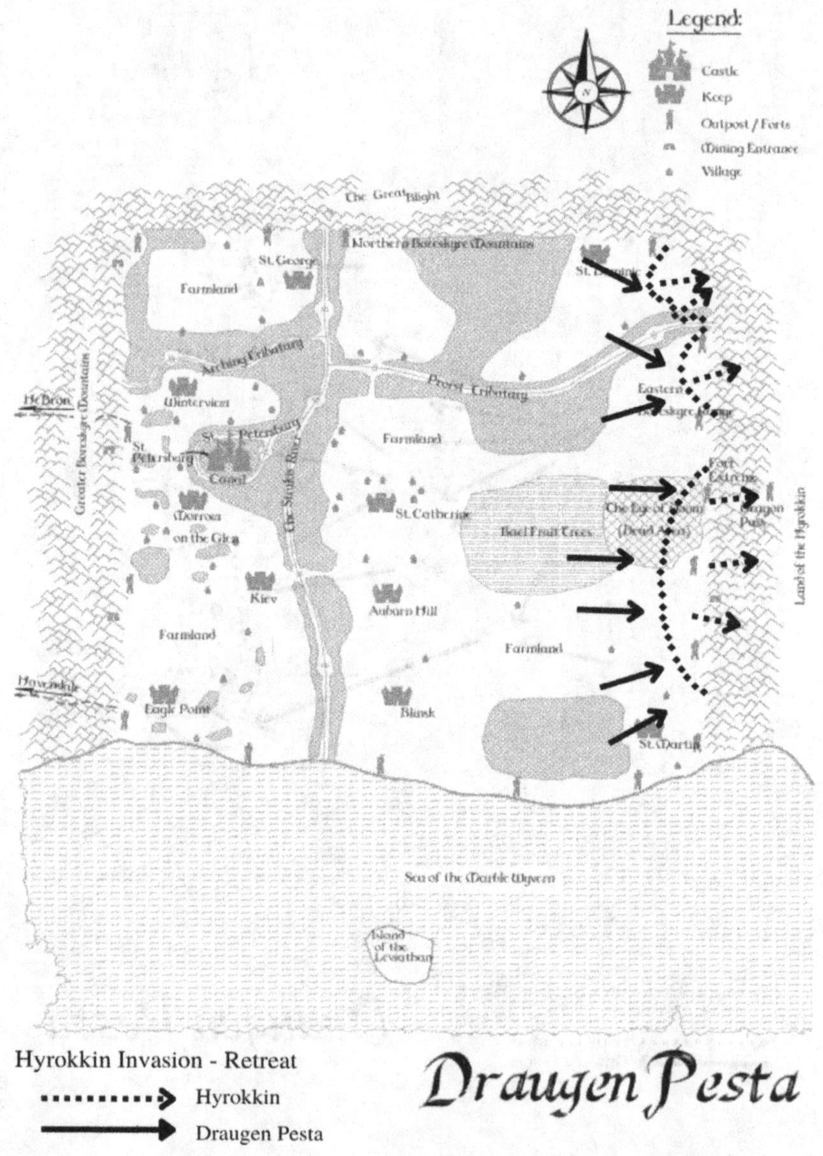
Legend:
Castle
Keep
Outpost / Forts
Mining Entrance
Village
The Great Blight
St. George
Farmland
Arching Tributary
Frost Tributary
Farmland
St. Petersburg
Canal
St. Catherine
Bad Fruit Trees
Kiev
Auburn Hill
Farmland
Farmland
Eagle Point
Blinsk
Land of the Hyrokkin
Sea of the Marble Wyvern
Island of the Leviathan
Hyrokkin Invasion - Retreat
Hyrokkin
Draugen Pesta
Draugen Pesta

CHAPTER FOUR

Aster - Draugan Pesta and the Hyrokkin Empire

The Hyrokkin commander, Theronius, studied the situational map from atop Fort Extreme, the captured Draugan Pesta fortress on the western end of Dragon Pass. His tactical position had become untenable and his army was in retreat along the entire front. The defeat had been so decisive he doubted he'd have a fifth of his army left alive to bring back home.

Things couldn't have gone any better for the first ten days. The old tunnels under the Eastern Boreskyre Mountains, the ones the dwarves had first excavated and then collapsed hundreds of years ago, had been cleared of debris, reinforced, and used by Hyrokkin troopers to invade Draugen Pesta. The Draugen Pesta army, half of which was with their king west of the Greater Boreskyre Mountains, was taken by complete surprise. Within hours, Hyrokkin forces had taken Fort Extreme and the city of Saint Martin in the south. To the north, St. Dominic, a larger and better fortified city, was surrounded and put under siege. By the end of the first week, the Hyrokkin had extended their front line almost two hundred miles westward. A fifth of Draugen Pesta was under Hyrrokin control.

The Draugen Pesta military units defending the eastern border were butchered, though as many Hyrokkin troopers had also died in the fight. Civilians, those not killed resisting, were rounded up and sent through Dragon Pass to begin their new lives as slaves. Full storage bins of oats, barley, and corn were emptied and fruit trees picked clean. Soon, an endless trail of crop-ladened wagons and livestock was heading back to the Hyrokkin homeland.

But Theronius always knew the raid was doomed from the beginning. The Draugen Pesta were too powerful to allow the incursion to stand, even with half their army away. His leaders knew it as well… and they weren't wrong. But the Draugen Pesta's weakened defenses made the lure of new slaves and a bounty of food and livestock too tempting to ignore.

The unexpected return of the rest of Draugen Pesta's army from the western campaign, and their subsequent addition to the battle, resulted in a full retreat of Hyrokkin forces along the entire front. Theronius's only option was to retreat and try to save as much of his force as possible, something that was becoming harder to do by the hour.

"Look, commander!"

Theronius looked away from the map and in the direction his spotter pointed. What he saw sent chills down his spine. On the other side of the field which separated the base of the fort and a forest stood an imposing figure. It could be none other than the Draugen Pesta king surrounded by a large contingent of the First Phalanx. Next to the king was a smaller figure, a female, who looked even more dangerous. Both figures stared at the Hyrokkin commander on top of Fort Extreme. With a flick of the king's hand, commanders shouted orders and the Draugen Pesta warriors, getting ready to overrun the Hyrokkin line, ceased their advance and took up defensive positions. The Draugen Pesta king and his queen moved out of their bodyguard protection and into the open field.

"Hail the fort!" the king called.

"Come to gloat!" Theronius yelled back.

"I take no pleasure in death! I'm Ternborg, king of Draugen Pesta. You have invaded my nation, killed or enslaved my subjects, and stolen our crops and livestock. I give you one chance to surrender unconditionally and return that which is Draugen Pesta's or suffer the consequences!"

The Hyrokkin commander looked at several archers. They shook their heads. "Not even one of you can make the shot?" he asked.

"They're almost out of range," one replied. "It's possible, but it'd have to be a perfect shot, given the wind and the distance. None of us are that skilled."

"Just send a damn volley!" Theronius screamed.

Six arrows flew from the top of Fort Extreme and towards Lord Ternborg and his queen, Sofia. Neither of the two flinched as the arrows came closer. When they landed, four were ten yards short, while the other two came within five yards. None of the arrows were online to strike, even if the distance was right. In response, a dozen heavy ballista bolts rose out of the forest and fell on Fort Extreme's battlements, killing eight Hyrokkin.

"So I suppose that's your answer?" Lord Ternborg called out.

"Hyrokkin would rather die than surrender!" Theronius screamed. Spittle flew from his lips.

Lord Ternborg was about to answer when Sofia grabbed his arm. "Look! Something's happening up there!"

The Draugen Pesta king took a spyglass from his belt and focused it on the fort's battlements. He saw several Hyrokkin restraining another. A few seconds later, a body flew out into open space, screaming as it fell to the ground. The thud as it landed carried across the field. The figure didn't move.

"We accept your terms," a different voice called out.

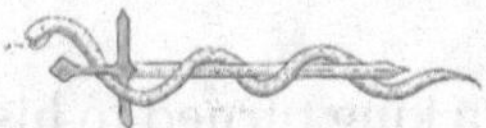

Lord Ternborg, Sofia, his command staff, and members of the First Phalanx met the new Hyrokkin commander in a hastily erected tent at the base of Fort Extreme. Draugen Pesta warriors had re-taken control of the fort and closed Dragon Pass. The body of Theronius was removed and prepared for return to his homeland. The official narrative was he'd been killed in combat.

"Your name?" Sofia asked the Hyrokkin commander.

The centaur snorted. "I don't answer..."

"You'll show my wife respect," Lord Ternborg snapped. "And make no mistake... she's as dangerous as any one of my bodyguards. Maybe even more so. Now answer her!"

"Baledon, My Lord," the Hyrokkin answered.

Lord Ternborg shook his head. "Not to me. To her."

Baledon bowed his head to the Draugen Pesta king before he addressed Sofia. "My name is Baledon, My Lady."

"Thank you, Baledon," Sofia said. "Are you authorized to speak for your queen?"

The centaur shook his head. "I wouldn't think so. Most of my countrymen will consider me a traitor once they find out I didn't fight to the death."

"So why didn't you?" Lord Ternborg asked.

"I've always viewed things from a different... perspective," Baledon replied. "As do any Hyrokkin you've managed to capture. Unlike many of our fellow Hyrokkin warriors, death isn't something we cherish."

"Are there any scenarios in which your queen will return our people?" Sofia queried.

"None whatsoever," Baledon answered. "The generals will never give her that option."

Without saying a word, Lord Ternborg, followed by Sofia, his adjutants, and most of the First Phalanx bodyguard, left the tent.

The Draugen Pesta king turned to his theater commander, General Anatoli Valeryevich. "Split the prisoners and send half to Saint Martin and the other to Saint Dominic. Have them put into work parties to clean-up and repair the damage they're armies did to both cities. We can release them afterwards. Also, make sure those tunnels they used to go under the Eastern Boreskyre's are secured. Get teams in them to shore up weaknesses that might cause a collapse. We might need them later."

"Is there anything else, Your Grace?"

Lord Ternborg shook his head. "Not for now. But use your own initiative. Do what you think best."

General Valeryevich saluted and left, bellowing orders to his own staff. Lord Ternborg took Sofia aside. Though she was his queen, her cunning and strategically orientated mind also made her his best general. "We need to get our people back one way or the other. Right now the army is spread along a broad front. Collect what you can and bring them to the pass. I want to be ready to invade if we must."

"You?"

Lord Ternborg hugged his wife and kissed her on the forehead. "I'm going to try a little diplomacy first."

"The Hyrokkin don't understand the meaning of the word," Sofia replied.

"After what we just did to their invasion force, they might not have a choice," Lord Ternborg remarked.

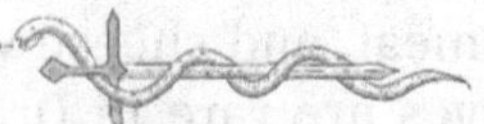

Daphnia, alongside her wolf-friend, Adimar, son of the immortal wolf, Fenrisúlfr, strode the streets and back alleys of Saint Petersburg. At her insistence, none of her Phalanx warriors accompanied the two, though several followed behind and out of sight, reasoning that was the only way to follow both the king's and the princess's orders. Adimar had sensed their presence but didn't pay them much heed. He understood the necessity, even though he was capable of protecting his young friend by himself. There are advantages to being the son of a half-god.

As usual, whenever Daphnia went amongst the common folk, well-wishers surrounded her and inundated her with gifts—things such as warm meat pies, fresh fruit, bakery goods of different kinds, as well as bracelets, necklaces, and toys. Daphnia particularly enjoyed receiving books. She always insisted upon giving fair payment—to everyone. She wouldn't shortchange them. These people were hers, and she was theirs. Despite her young age, she understood that.

"I wonder when mother and father are going to come home?" Daphnia asked Adimar.

The gigantic wolf gently nudged her with his snout. He didn't have an answer but made sure she knew she wasn't alone.

"We should make peace with the Hyrokkin," the princess continued. "Too many die on both sides when we war against each other."

"Begging yer pardon, Your Grace?" an unknown voice said.

Daphnia looked around. She'd been so intent with her own thoughts, she stopped paying attention to her surroundings, relying on Adimar to keep her from strolling into harm's way instead. The person who had addressed her, a dwarf, was sitting at a table outside a small café. He was enjoying a quiet, cold lunch of bread, meat, and cheese with a mug of wine to wash it down. Dwarves are rare in Draugen Pesta. Daphnia thought he was probably a descendant of the original dwarves who were slaves to the Hyrokkin many centuries ago. The few who escaped had made their homes in Draugen Pesta and now their progeny were citizens of the nation of giants.

"My apologies, sir," Daphnia responded. "I was talking to my wolf... well... I guess thinking out loud would be more appropriate. I didn't mean to disturb your meal."

"Ye didn't, mah wee bonny lassie," the dwarf replied. "Please, hae a seat 'n' rest yer bones a minute. Ah kin order ye food if ye wish?"

Daphnia looked at Adimar. He wasn't alarmed by the stranger, and she was tired from walking. "Alright, sir. But just something to drink, please. I get enough free food whenever I go out, so I'm not hungry even in the slightest."

The dwarf caught the attention of a waiter and motioned. "A gless of..."

"Water," Daphnia said.

"Right away, Your Grace," the waiter replied as he hurried back inside the building.

"Jarsus Blackmantle at yer service, Princess," the dwarf said after the waiter had left.

Daphnia nodded and offered her hand. Instead of shaking it, the dwarf brought the back of her hand up to his mouth and lightly brushed his lips across it.

"My, but aren't you the gentleman," the princess said. She couldn't hide the red flush that briefly appeared on her face.

Jarsus smiled. "Ye be a Princess, ur ye nae? Thare ur protocols."

Daphnia shook her head. "I don't much stand for... for..."

"Protocols, Your Grace."

"Yes, that," Daphnia answered. "Neither do my mother and father. They say everything must be earned... that special treatment, demanded by rank alone, separates a king or queen from their people. Father says that, in Draugen Pesta, the king and the people are one and the same."

Jarsus nodded. "Draugen Pesta, o' a' th' lands, is unique in that belief," he said. "It's mibbie th' reason ah choose tae bide among th' giants. An' lassie, if true be kent, Draugen Pesta offers a' a dwarf lik' me cuid waant. Mountains oan three sides 'n' bonny land wi' civilized cities in atween. 'N' th' vino ye mak' fae th' fruit o' th' sapphire rose canna be duplicated anywhere oan th' mainland."

"What do you do, Mister..."

The dwarf held up a hand to stop Daphnia. "Please... ca' me Jarsus, lassie."

"Only if you'll call me Daphnia."

Jarsus looked at the young girl and nodded. "Aye. Daphnia

it is. As fur mah vocation, ah dabble in mony things... bit I'm paid by th' university tae teach."

"A learned dwarf!" Daphnia exclaimed.

"Does that surprise ye?" Jarsus asked.

"Oh no, Mister... I mean, Jarsus," Daphnia answered back. "It's just all the teachers father and mother have for me are... are..."

"Bloody dunderheided idiots?"

"I was going to say arrogant."

"That too," the dwarf replied as he lit a pipe.

The aroma of tobacco floated through the air around the small table where they sat. Adimar raised his head and sniffed, then settled back down. Daphnia decided she approved of the cherry-vanilla fragrance.

"You don't appear to be like them," the princess continued. "Teachers, that is. Not dwarves. Heaven knows I don't ever talk to many dwarves. Well, in fact, you're my first and I never thought... Oh, dear! I'm running my mouth, aren't I?"

"Jis a pucklie. Bit ah hiv plenty o time an patience."

"Patience?" the princess snorted. "A dwarf? Now that's funny! I've heard that..." Daphnia stopped. "Oh, Jarsus, I'm so sorry!"

The dwarf smiled. "Aat anely goes tae show fit lacking yer education has been."

Daphnia looked at Jarsus. "You talk to me as if I'm an adult. To all my teachers, I'm just a child to be ordered about. Adimar's chased more than a few away because of it. Now father has to pay triple the price. And even then it's getting harder to find someone 'of caliber,' as he says."

Jarsus exhaled pipe smoke. "Ye ur a bairn, Daphnia. That canna be denied. 'N' as sic, there's muckle ye need tae learn aboot th' world... aboot history... aboot richt 'n' wrong. Ah ainlie ken yer faither by reputation... 'n' that he's mah king. Bit ah suspect neither he nor yer mither hae let thair wee bonnie lassie wallow aboot in a pigsty o' ignorance. Sae a child... aye. Bit nae an ordinar child. Yer teachers shuid be honored tae instruct ye."

Daphnia sighed and sipped her water. "One day I might have to be queen."

"Only if th' fowk decide it shuid be so," Jarsus commented. "That's anither thing ah lik' aboot this country... though it's a monarchy, th' fowk hae a say in who'll leid 'em. Tae be queen ye mist be worthy."

"I know," the princess replied. "It scares me."

"Ye be ready, lassie, shuid th' time come," Jarsus concluded.

Daphnia suddenly had an idea. "Jarsus, I was wondering... that is... ah..."

"Speak yer mynd, lassie," the dwarf said as he smiled behind his pipe.

Daphnia reached over and petted Adimar for reassurance. "Well, I know we just met and all, but, if mother and father are agreeable, do you think you could give me lessons? You teach at the university, so experience won't be a problem."

"Lassie..."

"Now hear me out, Jarsus. You know I don't like my teachers... those that are still around, that is. They spend more time telling me what they think I should do as a princess than teaching me the lessons I need. Stand up straight... don't talk with your mouth full... get that wolf out of here... that sort of thing. I want... I need... someone who'll actually talk about the real world. I need to know the 'how's' and 'why's' of things."

Jarsus tapped the tobacco out of the bowl of his pipe before putting it away in his vest pocket. Then he raised his hand to signal the waiter. "My check, Ivan."

"You're not just going to walk away, are you?" Daphnia said.

"Princess, please bring yer monstrosity alang 'n' follow me," Jarsus replied as he paid the waiter. "I've something tae show ye."

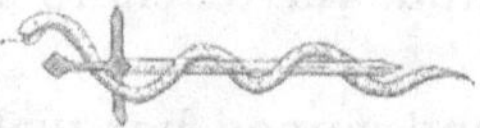

The centaur queen, Thesonia, awaited her generals in her audience chamber. She'd heard from various sources that her army, after they'd successfully breached the Draugen Pesta defenses and occupied a fifth of the kingdom, was now in full retreat. Thesonia wasn't surprised. It was a long shot even if everything had gone according to the Army's extensive planning and preparations… which it didn't.

The invasion of the Draugen Pesta homeland had been planned for decades. The dwarven underpasses through the mountains, a remnant of an attempted invasion several centuries ago and essential for success, had been cleared and shored up. Hundreds of Army wargames were conducted to iron out the details and work out the kinks. But that's as far as it went. The kings and queens preceding Thesonia's rule never made another attempt, believing, rightfully so, that even a surprise attack wouldn't be enough to further Hyrokkin interests. The giants were just too strong.

But the Hyrokkin Empire, primarily an agricultural economy, had been suffering through a three-year long drought. Thesonia knew from reports she'd received through her agricultural advisors that current crop production levels wouldn't sustain the general population. With no trading partners to rely upon, they'd be starving within a fortnight. A starving populace was likely to take their discontent out on those in authority… most likely by a rebellion that she'd be compelled to suppress at a significant loss of life. To eliminate that possibility, she needed to find food. So she reluctantly gave her generals permission to invade when Lord Ternborg took half his country's army west. Gamble taken, gamble lost.

The double doors to her audience chamber opened and

her three top generals strode in. The clapping of their hooves on the stone floor echoed throughout the room until they stopped in front of the throne. Each bowed. None would speak until given permission.

"Report, General Darrasius," Thesonia ordered.

"Yes, Your Grace!" the general responded. "Our raid..."

Thesonia interrupted. "So that's what you're calling it? A raid? Three weeks ago you called it an invasion followed by an occupation."

"Well..."

"And now we've been humiliated by the giants," Thesonia continued. "We've been driven back while losing most of our army."

"We managed to capture and send back two hundred carts and wagons full of fruits and vegetables as well as several hundred cows," General Darrasius mentioned. "In that sense, we were successful."

"I saw those two hundred carts and wagons," Thesonia barked. "How long do you think that'll last? Even with the additional food and livestock, we'll still be starving in a matter of weeks? You were supposed to *hold* the land. You assured me you could for several months... long enough to feed our people and restock our bins."

"That devil Ternborg came back earlier than expected," General Cephandros, silent until now, pointed out.

"You didn't consider that in all your planning?!" the queen barked.

"Of course we did, Your Grace," General Darrasius said. "You saw the plans. You witnessed our war-gaming." The general shrugged. "They counterattacked with a savagery none of us expected... or experienced from them in the past."

"Of course they did!" Thesonia exclaimed. "They were fighting for their homeland! They were exacting revenge for what we did to their people!" The queen calmed and looked at the three generals. "But you have a point... and I can't really blame you since I approved the attack, knowing the possibility of defeat existed. Alright, is there anything else you care to mention... like perhaps the prisoners you brought back?"

"Slaves, Your Grace," General Darrasius said. "For the fields."

"You mean more mouths to feed," Thesonia snapped. "And what good will they be in fields that are withered and thirsty for water? Have you looked up, lately? All you'll see are those new cloud-like creatures floating across the sun-scorched sky without a care in the world... and they're not sending any rain our way."

"But the prophets..."

"Bugger the prophets!" Thesonia screamed. "We treat them as if they're half-gods, yet the only thing they do is flummox us with words no one understands. And we let them... blindly believing! We're fools!"

"That's blasphemy!" General Cephandros warned.

"It's the truth!" the queen replied. "They eat better than any of us while they sit around a great round table spouting nonsensical predictions about this and that, cross their arms over their chest, and expect us to bow down and glorify their greatness."

"They said rain is coming!"

"Of course it is!" Thesonia said. "It always does, eventually. Drought's been coming and going for generations. It's nothing new. The only question is, when will it end? Have the prophets given us that little piece of information?"

The generals remained silent.

"Have they!"

The queen looked at the three and sighed. "They haven't," she hissed. "They haven't because they don't know. But admitting that exposes them for the charlatans they really are. Perhaps I should ask them how many of us will still be alive when the rain *does* come."

General Darrasius changed the subject. "Do you wish for us to release the prisoners?"

Thesonia considered the question for a few moments, then shook her head. "No. Keep them comfortable the best you can. Ternborg will want them back. Maybe we can use them as a bargaining chip for more food. Hell, if we're lucky he'll invade and make us all *his* prisoners. At least then we'll get fed."

The three generals thought the queen was breaking under the pressure.

Thesonia smiled at their confusion. "You're dismissed."

As the generals were filing out of the audience chamber, a messenger came through the door in the opposite direction. The messenger was breathing hard from exertion.

"Your Grace," he said between breaths. "In the pass... something..."

The generals had stopped their departure and turned to look at the messenger. "Spit it out!" General Darrasius ordered.

Thesonia held up a hand. "Let him catch his breath, General."

"Your Grace," the messenger said. "The Draugen Pesta king is in Eagle Pass."

"What!" the three generals shouted at the same time.

"Calm yourself, gentlemen," the queen ordered. "What's your name?" she asked the messenger.

"Nikandras, Your Grace."

"Thank you for bringing this to me, Nikandras," Thesonia replied. "Have any of our people approached?"

Nikandras shook his head. "No. He brought a few of his bodyguard..."

"The First Phalanx," General Cephandros said.

The messenger bobbed his head. "I guess that's them. They look terrifying. No one dares approach."

Thesonia already knew the answer to her next question

but asked it anyway. "What's he doing?"

"He's just waiting at the half-way mark," Nikandras answered.

Thesonia nodded. "He wants to parley for the prisoners. Very well, Nikandras. Go to the kitchens. They'll feed and give you a place to rest. Then you can return to your unit."

As the messenger left the room, the third general, Telistos, spoke for the first time. "We can assassinate him, Your Grace."

Thesonia shook her head and sighed. "General Darrasius, why have you promoted this idiot?"

"Ahhh... I... ahhh..."

Thesonia wondered why this was the best Hyrokkin had to offer. "Never mind. I'll meet Ternborg myself... alone." She clapped her hands to signal her personal retainers.

"You... you can't do that, Your Grace," General Darrasius sputtered. "It's too dangerous!"

The queen frowned and then had a short, private discussion with her chief lady-in-waiting before she returned her attention back to the generals.

"Here's how it's going to be, boys," Thesonia began. "This drought, and our subsequent disastrous invasion into Draugen Pesta because of it, has forced me to take a hard look at our history of self-isolation, belligerency to all races, particularly the Draugen Pesta, and our penchant for lying, stealing, cheating, and general unsuitableness in a world of civilized societies."

General Darrasius coughed. "You're talking about your own people!"

"Have you ever been among the people, General?" the queen snapped. "Has any of the ruling elite? It's not the ordinary people of Hyrokkin I'm speaking of. I'm talking about you, me, the ruling elite, and everyone else who keeps supporting our past policies. Our warriors die following orders and now our people are about to die of starvation. And meanwhile we're a pariah to the rest of the world. That has to stop!"

"How dare you for even thinking about reversing our history!" General Telistos screamed as he drew his sword. "You're a traitor to all Hyrokkin kind! Our past kings and queens will see you in Hell!"

General Telistos took one step towards the queen and then dropped dead with a dozen arrows sprouting out from his front, back, and torso. Twelve female centaur warriors then stepped out from behind well-hidden doors spaced around the throne room. Their arrows were now trained on the two remaining generals, who backed away a step and kept their hands well away from their own swords.

Thesonia sighed. "I'm sorry it had to come to this. But sometimes a bit of culling is necessary if you want to move forward."

"He made a good point," General Cephandros said. He kept his voice as steady and nonthreatening as possible.

"No... no he didn't," Thesonia countered. "Think, gentlemen! What did we just do? We attacked Draugen Pesta because we're on the verge of starving from this damn drought. And how did our attack turn out? Nothing but death... on both sides. For what? A few days of food?"

The two generals looked at each other. "Hard times demand..."

"Not any longer!" the queen shouted. "I'm going to change that, damnit! Again I ask you to think! What if we were allies with the giants? Then all we'd need to do is ask for help during hard times or drought. Why would we want it any other way?"

As Thesonia looked at the generals, she wasn't sure they understood. And perhaps that was asking too much, considering the history of the Hyrokkin Empire and the education of the military elite. They could be dangerous to her new plans of peace and prosperity for her people. "You're dismissed."

After the generals had left the audience chamber, the leader of the twelve female warriors entered the room. "I thought for a moment we were going to be forced into killing all three," she said. "Not that my Shield Maidens would have minded. We don't trust your generals."

"You might still get your wish, Galissa," Thesonia replied. "Do you understand what I proposed to them?"

"I do, Your Grace."

"It's a radical idea which goes against the normal Hyrokkin mindset. Are you still with me?"

Galissa nodded. "Until our deaths."

Thesonia nodded. "Have a few of your spies watch the generals. They won't take this lying down."

"Anything else?"

"Get servants in here to clean up the mess left by General Telistos's untimely demise. He attempted regicide, so have him buried in an unmarked grave. If any of his family gives you or the servants any trouble, tell them they can join him if they choose."

Drakogeus made his way along a secret trail above Dragon Pass. It was slow, dangerous going, but he'd climbed it several times before and was well familiar with all its pitfalls and hazards. As he worked his way to the ambush point, his mind wandered to the job they commanded him to do… kill a sovereign. He didn't like his orders, but his commander quelled any reservations he may have had by assuring him it was both necessary and lawful. He was told the new king would be grateful for his service… enough to set aside a small, permanent stipend and assure he'd eat well despite the famine that was descending over Hyrokkin. They always give loyalists special privileges over peasants.

The assassin arrived at his destination. He studied the pass below him. Sitting on horses were the Draugen Pesta devils. In the center was their king. Though the wind howled as it sped through the pass, he could still hear the faint banter between the king and his party—relaxed and familiar. The king treated his guards as if they were old friends, and they treated him the same, though their deference to him was still obvious. There was no question each one was ready to sacrifice his or her life to protect the king.

Drakogeus was glad the Draugen Pesta king wasn't the target. Even from his perch one hundred feet above, he could see a familiarity in the giants actions that made him long for the same camaraderie allowed by their king.

Movement from the Hyrokkin direction of the pass caught his attention. The queen and her personal bodyguard were cautiously moving towards the Draugen Pesta, whose king rode through the circle of his bodyguards and waited in front.

Drakogeus propped his crossbow up on a few rocks and aimed it at the queen. But as he did so, several nagging thoughts raced through his mind. He was told the queen planned to betray Hyrokkin, that she intended to allow her kingdom to be occupied by their ancient enemy. He gently squeezed the trigger. But before he let the bolt fly, the consequences of this one action suddenly became dreadfully clear. *"If I kill the queen, the generals will blame Draugen Pesta and we'll go to war... a war we're not prepared to fight... a war that we can't win. How many more must die for the generals? The people have suffered enough!"* Suddenly Drakogeus felt it was the generals who were the real traitors. He set aside his learned hatred of the Draugen Pesta and the planned betrayal of his queen. He took his finger off the trigger.

Drakogeus lifted the crossbow. "I can't do it," he said to the air. "It's time to stop the bloodshed. I must warn the queen of her general's deception. But how?"

After a few moments of consideration, Drakogeus decided upon a risky course of action. An assassination attempt would at least put her on guard. He once again trained his crossbow on the queen and fired. The bolt flew through the wind and grazed the queen's arm before burying itself into the ground. Within moments, the queen's Shield Maidens had her surrounded with shields held up to protect against another attack.

The king of the giants pointed upwards and several arrows were released with deadly accuracy. But by the time they had reached their mark, the assassin had already disappeared.

Lord Ternborg caught just a glimpse of the crossbow bolt as it streaked towards the Hyrokkin queen. He pointed at where he thought the origination point might be, and several of his guards released their own arrows. Though the arrows arrived where he had pointed, it was impossible to tell from his vantage point if they had hit their target, or if there was even a target to hit.

"Should we go help?" the First Phalanx commander, General Angelica Gagarin, asked.

Lord Ternborg shook his head. "We'd be encroaching on their part of the pass. Even if it were to help, the Hyrokkin might still consider it an act of war."

Angelica snorted. "As if they hadn't already declared war on us!"

"I know it makes little sense, Angelica," Lord Ternborg responded. "But right now, I don't want to push things. They still have our people as hostages. If we make the wrong move, it could lead to a death sentence for them. Let's see what happens."

As Lord Ternborg answered his general, the Hyrokkin

queen appeared from behind the shield wall her bodyguard had hastily built after the crossbow shot. Slowly, and with dignity, she continued her journey to the middle of the pass. Lord Ternborg, along with multiple pairs of eyes from his bodyguards, scanned the rocks above the pass for any hint of another attack. When the queen and her retinue approached to within five feet, Lord Ternborg dismounted his horse. He beat his armored chest with an arm and bowed. The Hyrokkin queen, in her people's way, bent her two front legs in return.

"It looks as if you had some trouble, Thesonia," Lord Ternborg said. "Do you need my healer to attend to your wound?"

"That won't be necessary, Ternborg," Thesonia replied. "It's just a scratch. An injury from an errant shot by one of the many people I have watching over me in the mountains on both sides of this pass. I've little doubt it was just a case of nerves and won't happen again."

Lord Ternborg knew she was lying but didn't take offense. It was part of the game played between two opposing sovereigns. "Or maybe I was the target? Perhaps whomever it was needs a quick lesson in Hyrokkin physiology. We don't look at all alike."

Thesonia smiled. She understood what had happened well enough. Her generals had just tried to assassinate her. If it had been successful, they'd blame the Draugen Pesta and use it as an excuse to continue hostilities... or at the very least garner some type of favor using the captured Draugen Pesta as hostages. Despite the wind that howled through the pass, she doubted the miss was accidental, which meant somewhere there was an assassin who saw through the treachery and gave her a warning.

"I have a proposal, Ternborg," Thesonia said.

"Ahh... a talk," Lord Ternborg observed. "And perhaps a negotiation for the people you kidnapped?"

Thesonia grimaced and nodded.

Lord Ternborg turned to General Gagarin. "Let's get an awning put up so we can get out of the sun."

"That won't be necessary, Ternborg," Thesonia said. "This won't take that long."

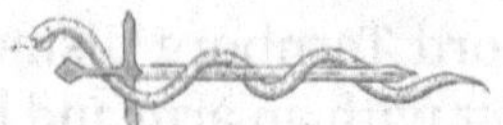

With an army of thirty-thousand mounted warriors at her back, Sofia approached Dragon Pass from the west. An additional twenty thousand warriors waited at the tunnels for the sappers to finish stabilizing the support beams. If an attack was going to happen, those coming through the tunnels would go first. Sofia knew the Hyrokkin expected that, but it remained her best option. She needed to draw as many of the depleted Hyrokkin army away from Dragon Pass as possible or else they'd bog her down in the pass. She'd still get through because she had the larger force, but the number of causalities would be high. That was something she didn't want to see.

The commander of Sofia's scouts rode up to the queen from the east. "Report, Captain," Sofia ordered.

"We've contacted Lord Ternborg's guards," Raisa Stanislav replied.

"Did you speak with my husband?"

The rider shook her head. "He's in the pass."

"In the pass?" Sofia wondered out loud. "What the hell is he doing there?" she asked.

"Meeting with the Hyrokkin queen, Your Grace," Captain Stanislav answered.

Sofia was about to release a string of invectives before she caught herself. *"Of course he is,"* she thought. *"He'd much rather be a diplomat than a warrior!"*

"Anything else, Raisa?" Sofia asked.

"Only that the First Phalanx warriors at the fort have their hackles up because they'd been left behind to, in their own words, 'Fiddle fart around with nothing better to do then spit into the wind.' No one trusts the Hyrokkin, and our king has put himself into a dangerous position once again."

Sofia groaned. "If you can tell me how to talk him out of doing that, Raisa, I'll make you a general!"

Raisa laughed. "You're no different."

"I guess not. You may return to your post."

"Very well, Your Grace."

"Oh, and Raisa," Sofia said before the scout could bound away. "We should be there by dusk. Tell the First Phalanx that if anything happens to my husband, they'll answer to me."

"If anything should happen to our king, I doubt the First Phalanx will leave much of Hyrokkin standing," Raisa retorted. "Right before falling on their own swords."

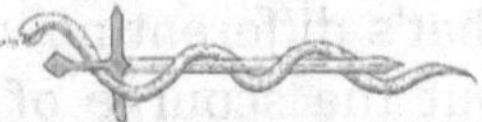

"Say your piece, Thesonia," Lord Ternborg said.

"I'm tired, Ternborg," Thesonia replied. "Tired of constant war... tired of reading casualty reports... tired of the grip my military generals have on my people."

"That's none of my concern," the Draugen Pesta king stated. "Besides, your words ring false in light of your recent invasion into my lands. An invasion that needlessly wasted the lives of both our people. An invasion which has put many of my people into enslavement. You must know I'll not let that stand."

Thesonia shook her head. "Desperation, Ternborg. Desperation born from a drought that threatens to starve thousands of *my* people. It was a maneuver planned and executed because you took half your army west across the Greater Boreskyre's. I only wanted to bring back crops to feed my people and a few of your farmers to help drought-proof my lands once and for all."

"Hyrokkin's been through drought many times before," Lord Ternborg countered. "We all have."

"But we've never learned the lessons you have," Thesonia replied. "We're a stoic, warlike race who'd rather muscle through drought than admit things such as farming, land management, and planning ahead are just as important as having a sharp blade."

"Why are things different now?" Lord Ternborg asked.

Thesonia looked at the Draugen Pesta king. His face remained hard. He was suspicious… and rightfully so, considering the history between both nations. This wouldn't be easy. But she was determined to take the first step to alter that history, and Hyrokkin's future. Her success relied upon the giant's king, however. If she didn't win him over, nothing would change.

"What's different now is that I'm queen," the centaur leader answered. "What's different now is that I see a future for my people without the scourge of war always hanging over us. What's different now is that I've the courage to ask for something no other centaur leader would have ever considered."

"Which is?"

"I just attacked his country," she thought. *"How do I get him to believe my sincerity?"* Thesonia took a deep breath. "First, let me begin by apologizing for our raid. My generals brought the proposal to me and I approved it. As the Hyrokkin queen, I alone bear the responsibility and will submit myself to your judgment. Second, we'll immediately return your people and the goods we stole. Finally, we'll pay reparations."

Lord Ternborg nodded. "That's a good start, though you can keep the goods. Consider it a gift from my people to yours. Now, what is it you want?"

"I need your help. I want peace."

Lord Ternborg shook his head in sadness. "All you ever had

to do was ask."

Daphnia caught her breath as she stared into the library of Jarsus Blackmantle. Except it wasn't just a library, though there were enough books, tomes, and scrolls to fill a decent sized one. It was also an apothecary laboratory filled with beakers, strange-shaped glasses, flasks, test tubes, and tongs on a gigantic workbench. Behind that were shelves of different bottled items—roots, bark, leaves, flasks of blood, dried animal parts, and hundreds of other things Daphnia couldn't identify.

Laying in front of a massive fireplace was the largest bear she'd ever seen. But as she studied it, she saw that it wasn't really a bear, though that was the only word that fit its description. Nor was it from this world, at least not to the best of her knowledge. The bear had multi-colored fur—blue, white, gray, and brown—with shiny blue eyes and what appeared to be magical runes tattooed into its back and sides. The teeth made the bear look ferocious, but Daphnia felt a calming reassurance emanating from its mind. It didn't move. Instead, it just stared as Daphnia, Adimar, and Jarsus entered the room. The hackles of Adimar rose, but Daphnia reached up and placed a calming hand on the wolf's side.

"The bear is an unexpected surprise," Daphnia commented. "Well... all of it is."

"Daphnia, I'd lik' ye tae meet Sienna," Jarsus said. "I've awready talked tae her aboot baith o' ye. She asks me tae gie ye her greeting."

"I didn't hear anything," Daphnia said before putting a couple of things together. "But then again, you talk with her 8 through your mind, don't you?"

Jarsus smiled. "Perceptive! We hae a mynd link. Bit how...

"I think she used her mind to calm me when I walked

into the room."

Jarsus nodded. "Yes, ah suppose she did. It's something she'd dae. 'N' she kin talk tae ye if she wants. Ah reckon she doesn't wantae overwhelm you."

Sienna got up and lumbered over to sit next to Jarsus. She was larger than Adimar by about a fourth. The wolf paced back and forth in front of Daphnia. His warning growl was low and almost imperceptible. Sienna watched but didn't respond.

Daphnia reacted to this new situation with the aplomb her parents had trained into her. "You're a sorcerer and the bear… Sienna… is your familiar?"

Jarsus smiled. "Only partially correct, lassie. A'm a sorcerer o' sorts, bit Sienna's far fae a familiar. She's mony times mair important tae me than a mere familiar. We've buckit th'gither fur decades. She's saved mah lee countless times 'n' I've saved hers. Wur like… weel, ah guess ye cuid say wur lik' ye 'n' that wolf o' yer's."

"I love Adimar," Daphnia said without hesitation. "He's the only real friend I got."

"And noo ye hae twa mair mukkers if ye wur tae accept us," Jarsus said as he smiled. "And if ah wur tae become yer teacher, this wull be th' classroom… nae th' palace."

Now over the surprise of Sienna, Daphnia began a closer inspection of the room. She'd never seen anything like it. The books, tomes, and scrolls covered everything from history, science, mathematics, and all the other normal disciplines to magic, folklore, superstition, mysticism, and the paranormal. The workbench contained beakers and flasks of oddly colored liquids, including a few which released steam as she watched. Several of them gave off a faint, noxious odor, but nothing too noticeable. Behind the bench were shelves and shelves of glass bottles containing all sorts of things. As Daphnia looked, she came across one jar that made her eyes widen.

"That jar says it contains stalks of the dreamvine!" Daphnia exclaimed. "That doesn't exist!"

"It does beyond th' Northern Boreskyre's," Jarsus replied. "It's native tae th' stoatin Blight 'n' thrives several feet underground. Kind o' lik' a tree root wi'oot th' tree. In th' cauld it's relatively harmless. Bit whin warmed 'n' mixed wi' th' correct ingredients, it kin either be th' cruelest drug in nature or th' maist pleasant. A dichotomy, actually... bit baith ends o' this spectrum leid tae th' identical conclusion. Death."

Daphnia was silent as she continued to look over the workshop and library. Jarsus let her, though he closely watched. But she never allowed her curiosity to overcome her caution. As her eyes glided over the countless shelves of books, she suddenly stopped and moved closer. Three books had caught her attention. She tentatively ran her fingers along each cracked, well-worn spine. Then she looked back at Jarsus, who nodded. She slid the first book out of its place on the shelf with extreme care. Printed on the outside cover was something indecipherable. She ran her fingers over the strange letters: "Флорентина Ковалевская."

"I don't recognize this writing," Daphnia said as she showed the book to Jarsus.

The dwarf looked at the script. "Interesting ye shuid be attracted tae this particular book... weel, actually, it's a ledger. Th' writing's in a dialect that's hundreds o' years auld 'n' na langer used except by scholars 'n' historians. It reads 'The *Florentina Kovalevsky.*' It's th' name o' a ship. Whit ye haud in yer hauns is th' foremaist volume o' th' ship captain's ledger."

"A voyage history?" Daphnia asked.

"Ye be a clever lassie," Jarsus replied.

Daphnia opened the ledger and looked at the title page. "The captain was Pyotr Sharapov?" The princess paused. "That name sounds familiar. It seems to me father once mentioned him. He... there was a tragedy of some kind."

Jarsus nodded. "Aye, lassie. One o' oor mair visionary

kings... Koshkin... paid one o' th' wealthy merchant families oan th' mainland coast tae build a couple o' ships fur a lang journey. Huge 's'ips thay be. Bigger 'en anythin' oan th' ocean at th' time... 'n' perhaps since. They ships wur manned by Draugen Pesta 'n' led by Captain Sharapov. Thay flought the baoot west tae explore th' waters beyond InnisRos."

Daphnia was hooked. She wanted to know everything about the voyage. "What'd they find?"

"Hard tae figure out," Jarsus responded. "Lassie, we hae th' ledgers, bit that's a.' Na one returned alive fae th' voyage."

"I don't understand. If that's the case, how'd you get the ledgers?"

"Aboot ten years efter th' ships left, a lifeboat crewed by three decomposing bodies wis found by pirates operatin west o' InnisRos," the dwarf explained. "The pirates wur later captured by th' InnisRos navy. Thare wis na doubt th' lifeboat 'n' sailors belonged tae th' *Florentina Kovalevsky*, sae th' lifeboat, bodies, 'n' ledgers wur returned tae Draugen Pesta."

Daphnia, by now completely enthralled by the story, asked, "Did the king send anyone else to see what had happened?"

Jarsus shook his head. "New king... freish priorities. Ye hae tae ken th' cost o' sic an expedition. Draugen Pesta's hud few kings in tis history willing tae explore tae sic an extent... 'n' expense. 'Twas a' buried intae oor history books lik' sae mony ither hings 'n' left alone. Thare is one ither thing, though. Something that kin hae scared th' king away."

Jarsus pulled the third volume off the bookshelf and opened it up towards the end. "Look at this," he said as he pointed towards several hastily scribble words on the last page. 'Остерегайтесь забвения... конец всему!' It means, 'Beware th' oblivion... th' end o' a' things!' At th' time 'twas considered th' ravings o' a madman."

Daphnia looked at the dwarf. "Do you?"

"I don't ken. Th' afore king wis kind enough tae len me

thae fur as lang as ah wanted thaim. Bit nothing kin pure be resolved wi'oot anither expedition. Ah shelved th' project, sae tae speak, 'til ah kin raise enough funds tae finance mah ain expedition. 'N' that's how come ah dabble in a' th' hings ye see here."

"Will you teach me about this and everything else I need for my education?" Daphnia asked. "I'm sure mother and father won't mind me taking my lessons here. And maybe I can talk father into helping with the funding for another expedition."

"Let's nae git ahead o' ourselves, lassie," Jarsus said.

Inwardly Jarsus smiled. His run-in with the princess hadn't been an accident. He believed if he could earn her trust, it might give him access to her father. Just one chance to explain to the king the danger he believed was coming out of the west was all Jarsus felt he needed. That meeting, he hoped, would secure him the funding he needed to mount his planned expedition. To that end he'd been keeping tabs on Daphnia as she walked the streets of Saint Petersburg each day, interacting with the citizens while letting them become familiar both with her and her gigantic wolf.

But the more he watched, the more impressed he became with her natural ability to set people at ease. Whenever she met someone for the first time, they saw her as the princess she was and responded with the deference due her rank. But by the time she'd left them, most considered her a friend as well. Did she realize how valuable that relationship with ordinary citizens was going to be someday if she ever ascended to the throne? Jarsus figured she probably did, though that wasn't foremost in her dealings with them. When he finally introduced himself, he no longer considered her just a means to an end. She was everything he'd wish for in a daughter—caring and respectful of other people, fair-minded, easy to approach, intelligent, aware of her status as a princess but unwilling to use that to her own ends. Sure, she was young.

But Jarsus had a good idea of the person she'd be as an adult.

"Of course I'll teach ye," Jarsus said. "But it kin ainlie be efter mah daily obligation tae mah students at th' university... 'n' wi' th' allowed o' yer mither 'n' faither. Whin ye be ready, ah usually tak' mah breakfast 'n' tea at that café we met at earlier. Ye kin fin' me either there... or 'ere wi' Sienna."

"I'm sure they'll approve," Daphnia said. "Can we start now?"

Jarsus studied the youngster and wished his university students were as thirsty for knowledge as the princess appeared to be. "Where wid ye lik' tae begin?"

"The lost voyage!" Daphnia replied.

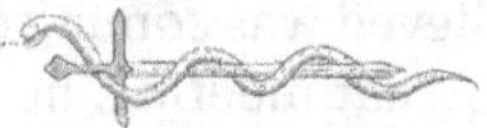

With the Hyrokkin queen leading, the Draugen Pesta army had little trouble ending what little resistance the rogue army generals could muster. After the disastrous invasion of Draugen Pesta, most of the Hyrokkin warriors had little taste for more of the same, particularly since their queen ordered them to cease and desist. The Hyrokkin executed the generals involved in the assassination attempt for treason and the attempted murder of a sovereign. Drakogeus, the assassin who warned the queen with an errant crossbow bolt, was the star witness at the trial.

The Hyrokkin Empire returned the Draugen Pesta captives unharmed in exchange for their own prisoners taken during the hostilities. As part of the new peace accords, the Hyrokkin queen agreed to steep monetary reparations to compensate the families of those killed during the Hyrokkin's "illegal incursion"... the new diplomatic term for "invasion" written into the peace accords. Thesonia claimed it would give her "cover" in the historical record. Lord Ternborg didn't care, just as long as peace between the two nations was realized and preserved for future generations.

Trade between the two became a real thing, and soon supplies were flowing from Draugen Pesta to Hyrokkin. The centaur nation, though it didn't have enough foodstuffs to battle the drought, had a substantial treasury. Both sides benefitted from the arrangement.

Though an uneasy peace settled over the two nations, not everyone on the Hyrokkin side of the mountains adapted to it. A warrior race by nature, many of the combatants who fought for the rogue generals but later accepted parole and laid down their weapons, broke the conditions of their agreement and led several uprisings which had to be subdued by force. Thesonia had given them one chance for redemption—one chance only. Those that escaped execution were driven underground with the hopes that one day they would become strong enough to challenge the queen once again.

When Daphnia asked permission to study with Jarsus Blackmantle, Lord Ternborg didn't hesitate to give his consent. He didn't know the dwarf in person but had heard enough about him through Jarsus's colleagues and students at the university to understand he had a brilliant mind and was one of the better instructors, if not the best. Even the dwarf's insistence upon tutoring Daphnia at his home located in the backstreets of Saint Petersburg did little to dampen the king's enthusiasm. He had little concern for her safety... no one was going to threaten his daughter with Adimar at her side. The wolf was only a little smaller than a Draugen Pesta calvary horse, and, at least according to Nightshade, the son of Fenrisúlfr, the wolf demigod. He also knew from his spies that the common folks of the city adored his daughter. They'd watch over her as much as the wolf would. Even so, as extra insurance, Lord Ternborg had two warriors from his First Phalanx tag along whenever she left the palace.

Not long after his employment tutoring Daphnia began, Jarsus Blackmantle approached Lord Ternborg with his fears of an unknown danger that might rise up from beyond the ocean west of InnisRos. As proof of his concerns, the dwarf showed the king and queen the ledgers and the message scribbled at the end of the third. He then explained the circumstances of the voyage and the subsequent return of the ledgers. Lord Ternborg promised the dwarf he'd consider the matter.

In the end, Lord Ternborg decided Jarsus Blackmantle might be on to something. Not long after his meeting with the dwarf, the king sent inquiries to the ocean-trading merchants on the western coast of the mainland requesting the feasibility of such a trip, would they be willing to build or rent a ship capable of making the voyage, and the expected expense. He didn't know if he'd commission the trip, but wanted to be prepared.

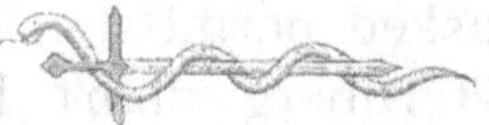

Lord Ternborg had just spent most of the day with his exchequer. Numbers, percentages, long and short-term gains, investments, money circulation, and other facts and figures he scarcely understood flowed through his mind like water cascading downhill—fast and uncontrolled. It was enough to give him a sizable headache. As he entered the palace and saw the looks of terror on the faces of the servants, he had the distinct feeling his headache was about to expand exponentially.

"Where's Sofia?" he asked the nearest servant, a girl of only seventeen, as he handed her his cloak.

"Your Grace… um…"

"Spit it out, girl!" Lord Ternborg snapped. "I've had a long day and I'm not in the mood to play guessing games!"

The servant nodded. “Her Grace is in the audience room, Lord Ternborg. She’s with… she’s with…”

By now, several other servants had gathered around.

“She’s with a Doom Warrior, Your Grace,” one of the other servants said. “A magnificent creature he is, too.”

“He gives me the heebee jeebees,” another said.

Lord Ternborg shook his head. “Why now of all days?” he said to himself.

“I beg your pardon, Your Grace?”

“Nothing,” Lord Ternborg replied. “You may return to your duties.” The Draugen Pesta king turned away but paused and turned back. “Oh, and Miss…” he said to the servant who clutched his cloak.

“Maiya, Your Grace.”

Lord Ternborg nodded. “I apologize for shouting at you, Maiya.”

Maiya’s eyes grew large as she shook her head vigorously. “Unnecessary, Your Grace!” she exclaimed.

“My mother would disagree,” the king responded. “As do I. Now run along.”

Lord Ternborg continued his walk to the audience chamber. His head was pounding. It came as no surprise that, when the guards opened the double-doors, he saw his wife was conversing with Michael of the *B’nai Elohim*, the Doom Warrior Maiya and the others had mentioned.

“There you are!” Sofia exclaimed.

Lord Ternborg kissed his wife on the forehead. “Duties, my love. Did you call Michael?” he asked.

“I came of my own volition,” Michael replied to the king’s question.

“For once, it’s the *B’nai Elohim* who need our help,” Sofia blurted out.

Lord Ternborg walked to a nearby table that held various decanters of wine and liquor and poured himself a stiff drink of whiskey. “Get me a headache powder,” he called out to the guards at the doorway after he downed a second glass. “I’m damn sure going to need it.”

CHAPTER FIVE

The Abyss

Lessien, holding the baby Martin, Belladonna, and Argomon approached the amphitheater under the cover of darkness. It was quiet. Too quiet. Belladonna knew they'd missed the meetings by a full day, but there still should've been one or two agents to meet and get them to a safe-house. Zerzoroch, the local resistance leader, had guaranteed it.

"Something's not right." Argomon stated the obvious.

Belladonna surveyed their immediate surroundings for any sign of a trap. Seeing none, she led them to an abandoned building on one of the backstreets that surrounded the amphitheater. Inside the sparsely furnished building and under a dilapidated rug on the floor was a barely perceptible latch to a trapdoor. When opened, it revealed a small underground safe-room complete with a light source, dried fruit, and fresh, running water. After climbing down the ladder, Lessien sat on a simple wooden chair. Belladonna and Argomon, holding Martin, followed.

"You and the baby will be safe enough here, Lessien," Belladonna said after Argomon handed the baby to the queen. "Argomon and I are going to scout the amphitheater to see what's going on."

"I'm afraid I know what's going on," Argomon said. "They've discovered and broken the resistance here."

"We don't know that," Belladonna replied. "We need to find out for sure."

"Be careful," Lessien whispered as the two climbed back up the ladder. As they lowered the trapdoor back into place, Lessien looked down at Martin in her lap.

"Why don't you ever make a sound?" she asked.

The baby stared back at the queen with wide eyes. In those

eyes was a hint of something that shouldn't be there. It wasn't evil, that much she understood. Nor was it malice towards her. What she thought she was seeing was an awareness—an intelligence—that no baby should have. It was unnatural and frightening.

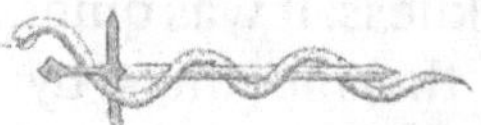

Belladonna and Argomon stealthily approached the entrance to the amphitheater. Upon first impression, there didn't appear to be anything amiss. But the two demon overlords weren't looking for that. Instead, they concentrated on the little telltale things… those things that, though at first glance were insignificant, would confirm their suspicions. Argomon found one such piece of evidence at the base of a small bush near a side entrance. It was fresh blood.

"We're walking into a trap," Argomon whispered as he showed Belladonna his discovery. "They're good at covering their tracks… but I'm better at finding them."

Belladonna shook her head. "That could be anything. A stray animal caught on one of these thorns… or anybody passing by."

"There's no blood on any of the thorns," Argomon said. "Nor does any part of this plant appear disturbed. Look at the blood drop."

Belladonna took a closer look. "I see it… splatter pattern?"

"Exactly," Argomon agreed. "See the pointed end of the bloodstain going towards the bush? This blood came from outside the bush overhang and was heading towards the trunk when it hit the ground." Argomon saw several more going in the same direction.

"That's pretty flimsy," Belladonna remarked.

Argomon used a knife to scrap the surface of the ground away in a straight line from the bush over to the side entrance of the amphitheater. It wasn't long before he uncovered other traces of blood... a large amount by the time he'd finished. "It seems a bit more plausible now, doesn't it? Someone who'd been bloodied was running in the bush's direction, probably trying to escape. It's also obvious someone else tried to hide the evidence. And I'd wager we'll find more blood inside."

Belladonna closed her eyes and whispered, "Damn it!"

"I bet they're also rounding up the resistance in the other cities," Argomon said. "These type of operations are always coordinated. We'll have no help getting to the *B'nai Elohim*."

"Years of work for nothing," Belladonna thought. *"So many lives lost."*

"Who do you think it was?"

"What?"

"The traitor," Argomon answered.

"Why does there have to be a traitor?" Belladonna asked. "Maybe Kor's overlord in this city just got lucky... or we got sloppy." But deep down, she knew she was grasping at straws. "Let's go," she grumbled. "I've seen enough."

"I don't think you're going anywhere, Belladonna," a demon underlord said as he and two dozen warriors came around one end of the amphitheater.

"Gorgraath, you son of a demon whore," Argomon screamed.

The demon smiled. "So good to see you too, Argomon," he said. "Drorikan sends his best wishes. Take them!"

"Run," Argomon bellowed to Belladonna as he ran to attack Gorgraath and the other demons.

As much as Belladonna hated to leave her friend, she understood it was the only alternative left to her. She couldn't leave Lessien and the child on their own. She conjured a *Fire Storm* spell and centered it in the middle of Gorgraath's demons. That was all the help she could give Argomon before she fled. As she dodged behind a small building a few yards away, she heard swords clashing and spells exploding.

Belladonna leaned against the side of the building and studied her surroundings. The building where she had hidden Lessien and the baby was a few streets away. Though the nearest street appeared to be deserted, she overheard movement from several different directions.

"Damn it!" she thought. *"I've walked into it this time!"*

"You there!" a voice shouted from behind her.

Belladonna invoked and sent several magical missiles of power at the demon. He clutched his chest and dropped dead. But his warning shout and the explosions of the magic against his flesh would be hard to ignore. Belladonna ran, using buildings, trees, and magic for cover. She chose a path away from Lessien. Once she evaded her pursuers, she'd circle back, though the chances of escaping the city before daybreak dwindled with every passing minute.

During the next two hours, she was able to elude detection with one exception. It happened when she turned the corner of a building and came face to face with a small patrol of six demons. Though alone, she was still a demon overlord. After a brief struggle, she left six corpses smoldering on the street. She hadn't come through the exchange unscathed, however. She suffered a right shoulder separation and her arm now hung uselessly at her side. The pain was bad enough. But it also meant there weren't many magical spells she could conjure since the injury prevented use of her right hand to manipulate the energies of the ley lines overhead.

It was close to dawn by the time Belladonna had worked her way back to the safe-house. The threat of demon patrols diminished as the night wore on... and those she had come across she was able to avoid. From across the street of the safe-house, she sat and observed the building and its immediate surroundings for half an hour before she decided it was safe enough to go inside. She took one last look around as she opened the door. Argomon was sitting on a chair, smiling. Standing next to him was Drorikan, First Overlord of Uz Urreth. Two underlords, hidden behind the door, slammed it into Belladonna. The force of the blow knocked her backwards and to the ground just outside the building. Other demons materialized from all around and surrounded her. The two underlords pulled her to her feet and one of them tied her arms behind her with rope. Belladonna cried out in pain, but her right arm mercifully slipped back into its socket as they were manhandling her.

"Not so rough!" Argomon demanded.

Drorikan looked at Argomon. "A soft spot?" he asked.

Argomon had stopped smiling. "Do as I say," he said.

The city overlord looked into the eyes of Argomon and saw death. "Bring her in… but gently," he ordered.

Belladonna was shoved back into the building by a hard push on her back. She stumbled but maintained her balance and stayed on her feet. The last thing she wanted to do was fall on her face in front of her enemies. Argomon snarled and encircled the offending demon with a whirlpool of white-hot plasma. It died screaming.

"Anyone else care to defy me?" Argomon asked.

"Do you think treating me with care is going to make it better between us?" Belladonna asked. "To think I came to care for you! Why did you betray us, Argomon?!"

The overlord sighed. "You don't honestly believe your little resistance movement stood a chance against Kor, do you?"

"Given time, yes," Belladonna replied. "The people back it."

Drorikan grunted. "The people!"

Argomon stood and moved to face Belladonna. "The resistance was doomed from the beginning. It was always just a matter of time before Kor destroyed it." The overlord shrugged. "An inevitable conclusion."

"Being given the city of Zhaarmoth by Kor as payment

helped in that conclusion, I'd wager," Drorikan commented. He and the rest of the demons in the room hooted with raucous laughter.

Argomon's face remained still and calm. That Drorikan's comment didn't amuse him was plain to see, however. The city overlord cringed and ordered silence.

"Belle, come with me. I can give you your freedom… and a city to rule," Argomon said.

"And what will it cost me, Argomon?" Belladonna retorted. "What pound of flesh does Kor insist upon for my freedom? What treachery saves me from Execution Hill?"

"Tell us where Lessien and the child are," Argomon answered.

The question took Belladonna off guard, though she hid it well. Argomon knew exactly where they were. Perhaps he's playing a game and trying to lead Drorikan away? For a brief second Belladonna thought Argomon was still on her side. His next comment extinguished any such hope.

Argomon looked at the trapdoor in the safe-house's floor. "She's not where we left her." Then he nodded to Drorikan, who bent over and raised the hatch. "See for yourself."

Belladonna walked over and peered inside. There was no sign of Lessien or the baby. She smiled. "I know no more about this than you."

"You're lying!" Drorikan screamed as he slapped Belladonna across the face.

"Drorikan!" Argomon snapped. "Need I remind you once again of the nature of our relationship? Disobey me again and your days of being the First Overlord to Trolgroth are numbered." To Belladonna he said, "Your last chance, Belle."

In his eyes Belladonna saw none of the amusement or caring that was his trademark. Instead, they were cold and calculating. "How could I have been so blind?" she whispered.

Argomon turned to Drorikan. "I'll take her to Kor. He can

deal with her. While I'm gone, I recommend you leave no stone unturned in your search for the mortal and the child."

Drorikan looked uncomfortable as he watched Argomon, Belladonna, and several of his demon guards leave.

"Your orders?" an underlord inquired.

"Find the mortal, you damned idiot!" Drorikan screamed as he slammed shut the trapdoor.

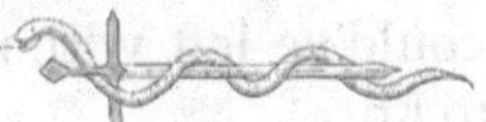

Lessien, with Martin sleeping in her lap, dosed off as well. Footsteps above brought her awake. She looked down at Martin and saw him staring back.

"Shhh!" she whispered to the baby before realizing the futility of such a gesture.

Above she heard voices. One of them she recognized as Argomon's, but the other was male as well. That seemed curious. Why wasn't the second voice Belladonna's? Perhaps it was one of the resistance members they'd gone to contact at the amphitheater?

"It's okay, Lessien," Argomon said from above.

Lessien heard the trapdoor being opened and saw Argomon and another demon's face peering down. Both were looking around as if they were trying to locate her, though she and Martin sat in plain view.

Confused, she started to get up when the newcomer exclaimed, "Well! Where is she?"

"I've no idea," Argomon said as he began to descend the ladder.

Lessien didn't know what was going on, but her instincts told her to keep quiet. That Argomon had betrayed her, and Belladonna, seemed likely. And why couldn't he see her? Had Belladonna placed a spell on the two of them before she left? Was Argomon still on their side and covering for her? Lessien shrugged. How she escaped detection was a mystery she'd delve into later. Right now, she needed to be more concerned about escaping the demons above.

Argomon reached the floor of the safe-room and looked around. When his gaze swept over her, there was no flash of recognition in his eyes. He really hadn't seen her.

"She must have left," Argomon called out.

"How!" Drorikan asked. "I've had this place watched. There's no way she could've left without being noticed. If I don't get this mortal to Kor..."

"Shut up, Drorikan!" Argomon shouted.

Lessien saw the demon Drorikan getting ready to respond when she heard a third voice call out. "She's coming, My Lord!"

Argomon sprinted up the ladder and closed the trapdoor.

Lessien looked at Martin. "Did you do that?" she whispered as she placed a hand on his chest. "Did you hide us?"

To Lessien's surprise, the baby cooed and grabbed one of Lessien's fingers. The InnisRos queen looked into the child's remarkable eyes, smiled, and kissed him on the forehead.

What Lessien heard next confirmed her suspicions about Argomon. First, there was a commotion followed by a scream of pain. Lessien recognized the voice. Belladonna! The InnisRos queen felt both relief and fear. Belladonna hadn't betrayed her like Argomon. But with Belladonna now a prisoner, she wouldn't be of any help. Lessien and the child were on their own.

There was the mumbling of voices. Lessien recognized Belladonna, Argomon, and the demon overlord Argomon called Drorikan. Suddenly, the trapdoor opened again. Belladonna looked into the safe-room and, as did Argomon's, her eyes went past the two without a trace of recognition.

With the trapdoor now open, Lessien could clearly hear everything being said. Argomon was taking Belladonna to Kor, and Drorikan was to continue the search for her and the baby in the city. The trapdoor slammed shut, but Martin didn't react to the sudden sound.

"Think we should try to rescue Aunt Belladonna?" Lessien whispered to the child. "*Ah-HritVakha* is dying for a taste of demon blood."

Martin looked at her. Except for his eyes, he looked like any other elvan baby. But Lessien now knew different. *"What other special abilities does he have?"* she wondered.

Lessien grabbed the skin of field strider milk Hodya had given her. "Let's got you fed before we make any more decisions."

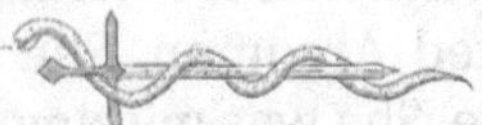

"It was smart to get Lessien and Martin away from the safe-house," Argomon said. They were waiting to take a barge up the Ozzon River and then they'd cross the Grimfail Reservoir. The capital city of Kor was only a couple of days further through Pelwater Forest.

Belladonna shook her head. "I had nothing to do with it. Actually, I've been thinking you're the one who orchestrated the whole thing. Playing tricks. Not too surprising since our entire relationship has been a deception."

"You honestly had nothing to do with their disappearance?"

"Again, no!" Belladonna exclaimed.

"Interesting," Argomon remarked.

"Really?" Belladonna replied. "That's all you have to say about it? You instigated this... this disaster! And now Lessien and the baby's become just two more of your victims. She won't last a day on the run from Drorikan and his goons."

"We'll see," Argomon answered. "Belle, join with me. Together we can..."

"Forget about it!" Belladonna responded. "I want nothing to do with you!"

"Why are you playing it this way?" Argomon asked. "Once Kor has his hands on you, there'll be no way to keep any remaining secrets you still might have. Afterwards, the best you can hope for is a quick death… though Kor's set on sending you to Execution Hill. I can hide you."

"Or you could just let me go!" Belladonna countered. She looked at her former partner. "What about Drorikan, his underlords, and his warriors? They know that I'm with you. And how do you hide someone like me from Kor?"

"Don't worry about Drorikan or any of his bunch," Argomon answered. "They understand the situation and know I can silence them. Permanently. As for Kor… leave him to me."

Belladonna studied Argomon. She had the same feeling back in the safe-house. She was missing something important. "Who are you?"

"Who do you want me to be?" Argomon responded.

"What kind of answer is that?"

"The only one you're going to get… at least for now. Ah, our barge is ready." Argomon turned to the warriors Drorikan had provided. "You're discharged. Go back to your lord."

Since Belladonna's hands were still secured behind her back, Argomon helped her into the barge and had her sit down towards the front with her back against a pallet of crates. He then left to have a brief discussion with the barge owner-operator. He returned and settled next to his captive.

"I'm going to take a quick nap," Argomon said as he made himself comfortable. "Don't try to escape or I'll also gag and blindfold you. And please consider my proposal."

Belladonna watched the dreary, dark scenery of the Abyss as the barge made its way up the Ozzon River. Field strider ranches and farms with fields of crops dominated the landscape. This was the part of the Abyss she was trying to free. Unless she did something about it, however, freedom would now have to wait for another generation. But what could she do? Even if she was able to escape her captivity, the resistance movement she'd spent years building and nurturing had been infiltrated and destroyed. Belladonna closed her eyes.

"Wake up," Argomon said as he gently shook Belladonna. "We're at the Grimfail. I've already secured passage for the crossing."

Belladonna realized she'd fallen asleep for at least several hours. "You left me alone?"

"No," Argomon said as he helped her to stand. "See those burly bargemen?"

"I'm an overlord," Belladonna said.

"An overlord who's not interested in harming the innocent," Argomon replied. He knew Belladonna well. "We'll have our own cabin on the ship. It won't be spacious, but it'll keep us dry. The captain says there's a weather front moving in."

"Why not wait until it passes?"

Argomon shook his head. "That might take several days. Besides, the captain has assured me it won't be a problem. His ship's built well enough to survive any storm thrown at it."

"Even so, why take the risk?" Belladonna asked.

Argomon ignored the question.

Belladonna fumed. "Eager to get me to Kor? You can't even be your own person! Nothing but a Kor sycophant!"

Argomon didn't respond to Belladonna's outrage. He gave her a slight push in the back. "Move."

The two left the barge and crossed the docks to a medium-sized, two-masted ship. It flew the flag of Kor, and the captain and crew wore Kor livery. They treated Argomon with every courtesy as they escorted him and Belladonna below decks to a luxurious cabin.

"Not spacious?" Belladonna commented as she sat on the edge of an enormous bed with a plume-filled mattress. "Treated with deference and put into opulent quarters. No...

not a sycophant. Something much more important."

Argomon shrugged. "The captain owes me a favor or two."

"Based on what I just saw, and these accommodations, it's more than just a favor or two."

"I spend a lot of time and money harvesting allies. You know that."

Belladonna stared at her overlord companion.

Argomon sighed. "I saved the captain's sister from the *Pillar*, for which he's eternally grateful. It's a long story."

"I bet," Belladonna remarked.

Argomon changed the subject. "Belle, I can get you away from Kor. I have the means to do that. All you have to do is say yes."

"Who are you?"

Argomon studied his prisoner. His real identity was a state secret. He couldn't do his job if it weren't. And as it now stood, Belladonna was an enemy of the state, and one of the last persons he should tell. But she was also someone he'd fallen in love with. Someone he very much wanted to return his affection. And though it appeared he was going to turn Belladonna over to Kor for the city of Zhaarmoth, there was no truth to it… just the opposite. Oh, he still wanted the city, but not at Belladonna's expense. It was his hope that he could have both. But if they were to have any chance of a life together, she needed to know the truth. So he decided to take the risk.

"My name's not Argomon. That's only one of a number of aliases I use. My real name's Braz'galar."

Belladonna laughed. "No. Seriously, who are you?"

Braz'galar made no comment.

"You can't be!" Belladonna exclaimed. "Saying you're him doesn't make it so!"

"What do you know about him?"

"He's Kor's fixer… and the second most powerful overlord in the Abyss," Belladonna replied. "That Braz'galar's next in line to rule should Kor ever decide to join his predecessors in the *Living Throne*."

Braz'galar nodded. "That's about all that anyone... anyone other than Kor and his favorite concubine... knows."

"Still..."

"Tell me, Belle," Braz'galar said. "What's more important to Kor than weeding out and destroying all resistance to his rule? Nothing. It's a threat to his authority. It doesn't matter if it's your resistance, a city overlord, or even a Faction leader. If he knows about it, he'll do everything in his power to overcome it with overwhelming force. Who do you think he'd put on the job to do that?"

Belladonna sighed and started to believe. "Alright... I'll grant you that. But why didn't you just kill me in the beginning, like you had done to most of the other resistance leaders? You had plenty of opportunities."

Braz'galar shook his head. "That was never the plan. Though you are... were... an integral part of the resistance, killing you wouldn't solve the problem. There are too many cells in too many cities, not to mention the ones in the rural areas. We needed to neutralize the leaders, which we have. By doing that, we... I... hope everyone else involved would walk away. That'd lead to far fewer casualties... and it'd keep families together. Kor may want to go scorched earth, but I understand that's the last thing he should do. As for you, Kor wanted you turned back into an ally. This was before your family failed with that ridiculous plot to take over Aster. Before then, Kor thought highly of Aikanáro."

"And now?"

"And now the resistance has been crushed and Kor's moved on to other priorities... other things to occupy his time. And mine. He still wants you... but not to win back. He wants you for Execution Hill, though he's given me the latitude to kill you on my own if I so wish. Payment for a job well done. Either way, you're supposed to die."

"So I join you or die horribly on Execution Hill?" Belladonna inquired.

"I won't allow that, Belle."

"Then let me go!"

Braz'galar frowned. "That's out of the question as well. Your only chance to survive is with me. Look... I hope we can work together to build a new resistance. I spent a lot of time infiltrating yours and know where you went..."

"Getting to know us before you betrayed us?"

"Your resistance never had a chance," Braz'galar snapped. "Can't you understand that?! Kor's in his prime and he's too strong. As long as he remains so, none of the Factions are going to waver. Believe me, Belle, if you're to have any hope at all of defeating Kor, you must have at least a few of the Faction leaders on your side. But that only happens if Kor displays weakness."

Belladonna shook her head. "You helped me recruit! You helped me build the resistance!"

Braz'galar nodded. "I had to gain your confidence. But that was in the beginning. Later..."

"Later you believed?" Belladonna spat. "You expect me to accept that! You handed us over to be slaughtered!"

"Yes, I betrayed the resistance!" Braz'galar shouted back. "But not because Kor wanted it. Don't you see? If I allowed you to go on, Kor would've stopped you on his terms and not mine. I destroyed the leadership but left the people alive. Kor's inclined to wipe out whole towns as an example. He wouldn't stop until he not only defeated you and the rest of your leadership, but all of your sympathizers as well. You yourself showed me how big that following is amongst the regular folks."

"We could have prevailed," Belladonna insisted.

"I said it once and I'll say it again... you didn't stand a

chance!"

"The *B'nai Elohim* would've helped," Belladonna said. "I was trying to get to them, if you recall."

Braz'galar sighed. "They won't help. Not in something like a revolution. Internal politics is off limits. The only thing that concerns them is keeping us on our side of the Juxtaposition Point."

"I've heard their leader, Michael, isn't as rigid as many believe."

"You can't be that naïve, can you? A civil war amongst us demons helps them. It means no one will try to breach the boundary... neither during or for a long time thereafter. Kor will be too concerned with shoring up his power and removing the radicals before making any more serious attempts to get to the mortal world."

Though Belladonna didn't want to admit it, Braz'galar was making sense.

"Belle, I turned the resistance in because in my judgment it caused fewer deaths. Kor would've sent thousands of innocents to Kiss the *Pillar*." Braz'galar shook his head. "As improbable as it may seem, you've shown me a different way. You've shown me that folks like Ekrah and Hodya are not only necessary to the Abyss's future, but they're also just good people... as are the other peasants you've introduced me too. I didn't want to be responsible for their deaths."

"Is that where you draw the line between who you kill and who you don't," Belladonna barked. "Many of those leaders were 'just good people' as well!"

"I'm sorry it had to come to that," Braz'galar repeated. "It was the only way."

"Maybe dying for the cause of freedom might be preferable to slavery!" Belladonna countered.

"And if that cause is still alive?" Braz'galar asked.

Belladonna frowned.

"Drorikan was right about one thing," Braz'galar replied. "Kor has offered me the city of Zhaarmoth… and I intend to claim that prize." Braz'galar withheld the fact that his operatives had already removed Kor's overlord and his loyalists from the city hierarchy and replaced them with his own. "And from there, we can build a new resistance."

Belladonna shook her head. "You just said the resistance wouldn't work."

"Not this one," Braz'galar responded. "But a new one… one we can build together… one that'll have a much better chance at success. Zhaarmoth is the second largest city in the Prefecture. We'll have resources you couldn't even dream about. It's isolated…"

"I don't need a geography lesson," Belladonna snapped. "The other cities will still be loyal to Kor."

"Don't underestimate me," Braz'galar said in response. "I've lived my life as Kor's fixer… his right-hand demon… his most trusted associate. This has allowed me to form relationships, gain allies, and collect favors from a good number of overlords and other demons with interesting and specific skill sets. And don't overestimate Kor's popularity amongst those he rules outside of the capital. Overlords, with few exceptions, are cruel, dispassionate beasts who seek power and power alone. Most of them feel Kor stands in their way. Again, if Kor shows the slightest weakness…"

"And you?"

Braz'galar shrugged. "I suppose… though I've always liked the excitement and challenges working as Kor's fixer has brought me. I've never had a strong desire to lead a city. Being on my own has only reinforced that. Then I met you."

Belladonna raised an eyebrow. "I don't understand."

"As I said, you've helped me realize things… things I've always suspected but never really thought about." Braz'galar got up and poured two goblets of wine and handed Belladonna one before he continued. "I've never paid much attention to the simple denizens of our native land… the ranchers, the farmers, the makers of goods, and all the others… that we depend upon to put food on the table, make the robes and tunics we wear on our backs, build the houses that shelter us, and do all the other things essential to the maintenance of a civilization. And while the guilds have become powerful enough to speak for the peasants and shield them from too much harm… to all the overlords and underlords, including me for most of my life, peasants are just background people. Nothing but parts of the landscape like the rocks, trees, and mountains. They're not important… only to be controlled and used. With your help, whether or not you choose to believe me, I've come to see the peasants as equals. Indeed, even better than the overlords and underlords who rule them."

Belladonna snickered. "You're correct. I find it hard to believe you!"

"I don't blame you… especially after what I've done to destroy your resistance." Braz'galar drained the rest of his wine. "I realize what I ask is hard to digest. Nor do you have a reason now to trust me. But I do want to build a new movement to destroy Kor. Our ways go back to the dawn of time. And from a purely logical sense, it works… except it's filled with hate and cruelty. It's a system that places no value on life unless that life belongs to the elite. But what I've learned from this assignment… from you, Belle… is that every life has meaning and we should respect it."

Belladonna wouldn't relent. "Nice speech. Or maybe the truth is you're the next in line to succeed Kor and want to overthrow him so you can take his place on the *Living Throne*. And I'm just a means of getting you closer to what you want."

Braz'galar heaved a sigh of frustration. "Belle, I've explained everything as clearly as I can. Your dream isn't dead. But you need me to succeed… and I need you. Take one last chance on me."

Instead of answering, Belladonna turned to peer out a porthole. "A nasty storm's brewing."

"There's one other thing I think you should know," Braz'galar said. He suddenly felt like a young demon again as he summoned the courage to open up his soul.

Belladonna continued to look out the porthole. The forming storm continued to build as broad strokes of lightning added to its intensity. Several waterspouts formed. "What?"

"I'm in love with you." Braz'galar's voice broke slightly, though he covered it with ease.

"Ha!" Belladonna exclaimed as she whirled around. Then she looked more closely into Braz'galar's eyes and saw he was telling her the truth. Several days ago, she may have returned the declaration. But now? "You do, don't you. How am I supposed to..." Belladonna paused. "And if I refuse?"

"Even if you refuse I'm going to build a new resistance. Belle, I want you by my side, though I won't force you. But with or without you, I'm determined to get it done."

Belladonna looked back out of the porthole. The storm had continued to build, and the ship's present course had them going straight into it. "How good's the captain of this ship?" she asked.

"Huh?"

Belladonna shook her head. "Never mind," she said as she continued to look out of the porthole.

The ship suddenly bucked up and threw both to the floor. A loud "crack" followed. The splintering of wood and screams of sailors filled the air. Neither Belladonna nor Braz'galar had a chance to gather their wits before a second explosion, stronger than the first, struck. Everything glowed as electricity surrounded the ship and invaded every nook and cranny. It knocked both unconscious. They were unaware of the rain pouring down upon them through the massive hole in the deck above.

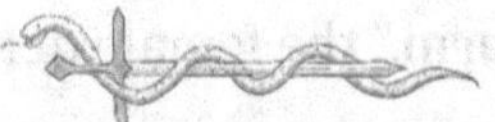

As Lessien fed Martin, she kept her ears open to the sounds coming from above. After Belladonna and Argomon had left, she listened as the other overlord screamed orders to his minions. Seconds later, it became quiet. Lessien was about to get up when the trapdoor suddenly opened again. The overlord, Drorikan, looked into the safe-room.

"Damn mortal female!" he shrieked. Spittle splashed to the floor at the base of the ladder. "You'll not get away from me! I'll find you and have my way with you before sending you to Kor!"

The trapdoor was once again slammed down and another door banged shut. Lessien and Martin were alone once again.

InnisRos's queen waited a few hours before she decided it was safe enough to leave. She built a soft bed with her *Mantle of the Sovereign* to lay Martin in and climbed the ladder, hoping the trapdoor wasn't locked. It opened, and Lessien looked around. The single-room building was empty. Lessien descended back down, gathered her meager supplies, picked up Martin in her cloak, and climbed back up the ladder. She set the child in a corner and returned to the trapdoor to close it. As she did so, the outside door opened. Lessien stood and turned to face her adversary as she drew *Ah-HritVakha* out of its sheath. It came out singing its willingness to draw demon blood.

The female demon stopped short of entering when she considered the glowing sword pointed at her throat. Behind the demon, Lessien heard the growl of an animal. Lessien moved over to stand in front of Martin, who was watching her intently.

"Do that thing you do," Lessien whispered to the child.

"Make us invisible!"

Martin grinned and cooed.

"I mean you no harm," the female demon announced. "But, you *are* trespassing."

Lessien studied the demon. She was dressed in a white robe with blue teardrop fashioned stones going down the front. White leather gauntlets covered the top part of her hands and went up to the elbow. Each gauntlet had a row of four gold triangles along the length. Embedded in each triangle was a large ruby. Her robe was tied at the waist by a red leather belt. Long white hair, gathered together by a white scarf that covered her forehead and the top of her head, ran over the cloak's hood and down to the lower back. Her face was exquisite. The only thing that screamed demon were the two rows of horns, partially covered by the scarf, that ran down both sides of the back of her head. In her hand she carried a wickedly curved trident which looked as if it'd been used often.

The beast that stood behind the female demon was as ugly as she was beautiful. It had an elongated snout that was like a wolf. In its mouth were double rows of teeth. Two horns which curved forward came out of each side of the face. A series of three pointed, bony protrusions covered its head. The creature stood five-feet tall at the shoulders, was hairless, well-muscled, and it's skin appeared to resemble rawhide. Each paw ended in four six-inch long talons that churned dirt, or chipped stone floors, as the creature walked. Its tail whipped back and forth. Along its back ran four rows of two-foot high spikes.

Lessien didn't know how much of a threat these two represented, but that the demon talked to her and hadn't immediately attacked gave her something to latch on to. She decided communication might be best… at least for the time being.

"I didn't mean to trespass," Lessien said as she re-sheathed her sword. "I needed a quiet and safe place... a refuge... so my baby could sleep. This place, especially with the bonus of a cellar, suited me. I intended no harm."

As Lessien was talking, the creature ambled over to her. The InnisRos queen tensed.

"Don't be alarmed," the strange demon said. "He'll not hurt you. Unless, of course..."

"I understand."

Lessien endured the sniffing for a few seconds, then decided Martin might be safer in her arms. She slowly turned and picked up the child still wrapped in the *Mantle of the Sovereign*. The creature continued to sniff her the entire time.

"Yesper perceives something," the demon said. "That's why he's so interested."

"I... Finley and Razor!" Lessien exclaimed as thoughts of her loyal dire wolves came to mind. "They're my animals friends like..."

"Yesper?"

"Yes. Like Yesper. But it's been weeks since I've been around them."

The demon shook her head. "Your animal friends are not what Yesper senses. It's the smell of Aster... and of a mortal."

Lessien shook her head. "Somehow I don't think you needed Yesper to tell you that."

"True enough." The female demon called to Yesper, who dutifully complied. "You're Lessien Arntuile, queen of the elvan island nation of InnisRos on Aster. There was another with you... a mortal priestess called Autumn Goram. But no mention of a child. Please explain."

"So your information isn't completely foolproof," Lessien replied. The demon's knowledge of her was surprisingly detailed. There was no way this was a chance meeting. Lessien didn't know the intentions of this female demon, but she wasn't going to back down. She was a mortal, yes, and a stranger in a strange land. But she was also a queen. If her life or freedom were to be forfeit, that's how she'd handle it—head held high and fearless. "I'll not answer questions until I know to whom I'm addressing?"

The demon smiled. "Proud and defiant. I was told you were that… plus much more. That's good, because we're going to need your talents if I'm to get you back."

Lessien frowned. "Back?" Then she shook her head. "More to the point, who told you about me?"

"The *B'nai Elohim*," the demon replied. "And the 'back' is to Aster. The island of InnisRos needs her queen."

Lessien stared. "You know the *B'nai Elohim*? Just who are you?"

The demon bowed her head to the queen. "Laylah, Fifth Consort to the great Lord Kor, the Supreme Potentate of the Kor Prefecture, Warden of the *Living Throne*, Noble and Illustrious Purveyor to the *Pillar of Captured Souls*, Peer of the Realm, blah, blah, blah. But in my spare time, I spy for the *B'nai Elohim*."

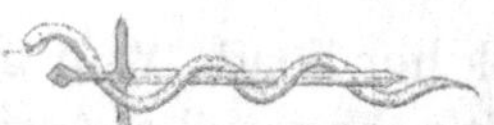

Braz'galar regained consciousness lying in several inches of water. It took a few seconds for him to shake the confusion out of his mind. He looked through the new hole in the deck above and saw the electrical storm had passed. Next, he looked around the stateroom and noticed Belladonna on the other side of the cabin. The force of the lightning strike had thrown her against a wall and left her in a sitting position. *"At least she didn't drown,"* he thought. Still, she was motionless and Braz'galar's heart lurched when he considered she might be dead.

The demon overlord moved to Belladonna's side and breathed a sigh of relief when he found signs of life. Her respiration was slow, steady, and her heart was beating strongly. As he had his ear on her chest to listen to her heart, he caught a slight odor of burnt flesh. The source was a deep burn on the palm of her left hand. Further inspection led to the discovery of another serious burn on the bottom of her right foot. The boot she'd been wearing was in tatters.

"She's been hit by a bolt," Braz'galar thought.

He looked around the room for something to bandage the two wounds. Everything suitable had been drenched with rainwater. "At least it's clean," he said aloud as he pulled the sheet off the bed and, using his boot knife, cut it into strips. Braz'galar squeezed as much water out of the strips as his strength could muster and wrapped both wounds. While he dressed Belladonna's foot, he noticed the water in the room was rising. The ship was sinking.

"Let's get you out of here," Braz'galar said as he shouldered Belladonna's limp body and stood.

Apart from the rushing of water from somewhere below decks, it was quiet in the hallway outside the stateroom doors. There wasn't a crewman to be seen. As Braz'galar mounted the steep steps to the main deck, the one thought that kept running through his mind was, *"Ghost ship!"*

On deck, the sight that welcomed Braz'galar was complete and absolute destruction. Dead sailors littered the deck, their burned and charred bodies still smoldering. Here and there were black outlines on the deck planking of sailors who'd been disintegrated. The sails were torn to pieces, and the masts, though still in place, had been blackened by the lightning. Braz'galar looked up at the quarterdeck. He saw the captain hanging over the railing... at least he believed it was the captain. What little that was left of his tunic was the right copper color.

A sudden, muffled "crack" sounded from below. Braz'galar knew that sound. Breaking timber! He looked and spotted a five-person skiff which still looked seaworthy. He carried the still unconscious Belladonna over to it and gently laid her on the deck of the ship. He took the thick, waterproof leather cover off the top and stowed it away in the skiff. Everything else they'd need—dried food supplies to last several days, oars, a medical kit, fresh water, and two ten-foot long spears to goad underwater threats away from the boat—was already there.

Braz'galar picked Belladonna up and placed her in the skiff. Then he worked the wenches to move it over the side of the ship, which by now was listing to starboard and sinking much faster, before he climbed in. The skiff was on the port side of the ship, so if he didn't get it into the water and away soon, the skiff would either hit the side of the ship as she rolled or be too close and suctioned under.

Braz'galar had sailed on enough ships to know where the emergency release was on the wench. They'd hit the water hard, but he deemed it their only chance. He braced Belladonna with his own body as best as he could before working the release. The skiff dropped in freefall for a couple brief seconds before it landed on the water. The force of the impact rocked the skiff and its two passengers, but other than losing one of the oars, which Braz'galar retrieved, none were the worse for wear.

Braz'galar wasted little time rowing the skiff away from its parent craft. He stopped at a safe distance to rest and watch the ship's death throes. By then, half of it was already underwater. He heard two loud "snaps" as first the mainmast and then the mizzenmast broke and fell into the water. A few seconds later, only the stern of the ship was visible as it went horizontal and began its dive to the bottom of the reservoir. It slipped quietly into the water and disappeared beneath the waves, carrying its dead crew to a watery grave… or most likely into the stomach of an underwater denizen. In the end,

Braz'galar thought it was all rather anti-climactic. And sad. Not that the demons who crewed the ship deserved any sympathy or consideration. They were the same as the other demons in Kor's army, cruel and bloodthirsty. They deserved to die. But the ship itself was majestic, fashioned from wood by skilled shipwrights who put their heart and souls into their work. It didn't deserve its fate.

Braz'galar frowned. *"Funny I should care more for the beauty of an inanimate object than the beauty of creation,"* he thought. "*When did I get so maudlin? It was just a ship!"* Even so, as he watched the rudder, the last visible part of the ship, disappear, he felt a slight pang of loss and regret. The overlord shook his head to clear the idea from his mind.

As the water slapped against the sides of the skiff, Braz'galar, caught alone with his thoughts, let his mind wander to the problems at hand. He estimated they were about halfway across the reservoir when the storm hit. He could either return to look for Lessien and the child or continue on to the capital to claim Zhaarmoth. If the latter, he'd spin a story concerning Belladonna, if the demon lord still cared, and take Kor's payment. After that, he'd be free to take Belladonna and leave for Zhaarmoth to plan a new resistance. On the other hand, Belladonna would want to go back to rescue Lessien and the child first. And with good reason. Any mortal on the run in the Abyss would never survive more than a few days, especially while being hunted in a city. That Lessien has endured as long as she has speaks highly of her abilities. But that wouldn't last. And for all he knew, she may already be in the hands of the city overlord. In the end, even though Braz'galar liked the brash mortal queen and wished to see her safe, it was more important to claim his city from Kor. Unfortunately, that wouldn't please Belladonna.

"Maybe I can do both!" Braz'galar thought as he patted his tunic and robes until he found what he needed... a

communications crystal, one of the few things the Abyss had copied for use from the mortals. They were rare. Kor and each of his city overlords had one. Braz'galar made sure his more important contacts had one as well. The ability to communicate with his people was one of the many things that made him so good at his job. *"Time to call in a favor."*

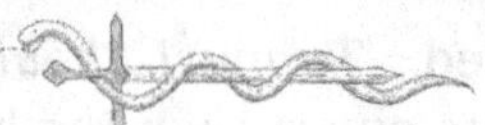

"For the last time, I didn't know he was under guild protection!"

The demon speaking was having a rough time of it. He was caught earlier in the day chomping on the unattached leg of a street urchin. His kind, though repeatedly warned, continued their destructive behavior of cannibalism, roaming the backstreets and alleys of cities at night in search of what they describe as "fresh meat." Their food preference was any young demon who didn't have a guild affiliation. Of course, no system is perfect, and the aforementioned leg came from a guild protected pickpocket who was at the wrong place and time.

"Ignorance isn't an excuse!" another demon, the one conducting the interrogation, replied.

The captured demon was a seven foot tall, hideous mass of pus and putrid excretions with twelve tentacled arms, two thick legs, and a gaping maw right in the center of the main body. The interrogator stood at an imposing nine feet tall and took the form of a human male. Underneath the floor-length robes, which were his only attire, was a perfectly chiseled and powerful body. Physically, no demon in the Abyss could match him for sheer strength. His entire body was hairless and colored a deep, rich indigo. The only break in color was his eyes—lavender, which glowed garnet whenever he grew angry. So far, the eyes hadn't changed color.

"Please, yer honor! I was *so* hungry!"

The interrogator shook his head. "Look... what's your name?"

"Iggok, yer honor," the demon prisoner replied. "Of the Mith Zoruuss Iggoks."

"You're a long way from home, aren't you?"

A pus pocket exploded from near the prisoner's mouth. "That backwards, dirt-water town! A demon could starve hunting there. The meat supply's much better..."

"Much better here in Khass Maazzus?" Associate Interrogator Kazrallan interrupted. This demon was from the same species as the Chief Interrogator, though not as imposing. Associate Interrogator Kazrallan was also female. "How much longer are you going to listen to this dribble, Zachariah?"

Chief Interrogator Zachariah looked from his assistant to the prisoner. Iggok was a disgusting beast, but he couldn't help what he was or the proclivities of his kind. And while the death of the youth was regrettable, the problem wasn't so much what had happened, but instead that the victim had guild protection, and the city thieves' guild had lodged a complaint. Otherwise, Zachariah would simply ban Iggok from ever entering the city again.

"Well, Zachariah?" Kazrallan asked.

"I swear, yer honor, I'll ask to see a guild card next time!" Iggok added.

Zachariah laughed at the sight of Iggok asking to see a guild card before taking a chunk out of his next meal. Then he laughed even harder at the ridiculousness of it all. As he laughed, he realized something else. "So this is what my life has come to," he said aloud.

"What was that?" inquired Kazrallan.

Zachariah shook his head. "Nothing important. There's only two ways we can resolve this, Iggok. You either pay the fee equal to the lifetime of contributions the waif you ate would have turned over to the guild..."

"A lifetime!" Iggok exclaimed. "How much is that?"

Kazrallan withdrew a folded piece of parchment from her robe and opened it. "The guild calculations are all here, Zachariah. The tally is based upon the average life expectancy of the deceased and others of his kind, the anticipated success rate based upon his skills, and the wealth potential of the city blocks he would've worked. In the interest of fairness, they subtracted the estimated sick days, the cost of training, the average amount of city fines, the cost of licenses, and the estimated taxes the guild would be expected to pay for their former employee."

"Awfully big of them," Iggok remarked. "How much?"

"Twenty-seven kors, five kronies, and three shecales."

Iggok gulped. "I don't have that kind of money!"

"Then guards will escort you to the capital to Kiss the *Pillar*," Kazrallen replied.

"Yer honor!" Iggok pleaded.

Zachariah shook his head. "That's the law."

"But yer honor..."

Zachariah's communications crystal buzzed in one of his robe pockets. "Iggok, you have forty-eight hours to come up with the fine," he said as he fished the crystal out. "Take him back to his cell, Kazrallan. Then contact his family to see if they'd be willing to pay the fine. I'll follow shortly."

"But yer honor..." Iggok kept repeating as he was dragged away by Kazrallan and several guards.

The Chief Interrogator waited until everyone was well out of hearing range before he answered the insistent buzzing.

"It's been a while, Braz'galar," Zachariah spoke into the crystal.

"I hope I haven't caught you at a bad time, Zachariah, but I'm afraid I need to call in a favor," Braz'galar replied from the other end.

"Actually, old friend, your timing couldn't have been more perfect."

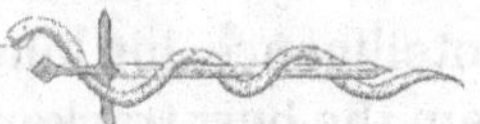

"So a concubine of this Kor demon just shows up on my doorstep..." Lessien looked around the safe-house, "so to speak... claiming to have been sent by the *B'nai Elohim* because you're their spy, for the purpose of seeing the child and I get back to them because 'InnisRos needs her queen,' as you so aptly put it. Just how stupid do you think we mortals are? A back alley ten-year-old waif wouldn't take that story seriously."

There was complete silence as Laylah looked at the queen.

Martin grunted for several seconds and then cooed. Yesper suddenly shook his head as a forewarning to what was coming. Then Laylah crinkled her nose. Martin needed a diaper change.

Lessien, by now well adapted to the situation, ignored the odor and continued to stare at Laylah. She knew from direct experience she had a few minutes before Martin would object, though not by crying. He never cried. But he did squirm, and that made the cleanup much more difficult.

"Can you... can you..." Laylah said as she pointed towards the baby.

Lessien nodded. She lay Martin on her *Mantle of the Sovereign* and changed the cloth diaper. After she had finished, she drew *Ah-HritVakha* and touched its tip to the dirty diaper. The sword glowed, and the diaper disintegrated.

"Impressive!" Yesper said.

Lessien looked at the creature and frowned. *"Am I hearing correctly?"* she wondered to herself.

"We all have our secrets," the beast acknowledged.

"Just because he's on four legs doesn't mean he's like one of your... your..." Laylah stumbled, looking for the correct word.

"I believe they're called dogs on Aster," Yesper remarked. "Or wolves."

Laylah nodded. "Precisely! Yesper's every bit as intelligent as you or I. Besides intelligence, his kind have also developed traits which make them the best trackers in the Abyss."

"Our dogs do that," Lessien observed.

"He's not a dog!" Laylah cried out.

"Laylah, I can speak for myself," Yesper said as he interposed himself between the mortal female and the demon overlord. "Lessien Arntuile, Laylah doesn't lie in this matter. She and I both work for the *B'nai Elohim*. In fact, I suspect we're the only spies used by the guardians who Kor hasn't found and executed... probably because we haven't been in the capital city lately. We've been tracking you on behest of the *B'nai Elohim*."

"Nothing about the games played with and by spies surprises me," Lessien noted, remembering that Argomon, no doubt a creature of Kor's, had betrayed Belladonna. "I suspect Kor had plenty of his own spies to counter the *B'nai Elohim's*."

"I'd wager two or three times as many," Laylah added.

Lessien nodded. She had her own experience with the workings of the spying community and how they're used by their superiors. "Spies being spies, I imagine both the *B'nai Elohim* and Kor are using their spies to spread disinformation to cover the truth... at least, that's how it works on Aster. And every once in a while, each side will kill a few spies and send their heads back on a pike to keep things honest. Unfortunately, as InnisRos's sovereign, I have to play those same games. I don't like it, but my spy master insists lest I upset the delicate balance of spying. It's a complicated process. But if you have the right people decoupling the disinformation from what's real, it's worth playing."

"Not only worth it, but absolutely necessary," Laylah said. "At least if you want to survive."

"Indeed!" Yesper added.

Lessien nodded. "Very well. I accept you for who you say you are… at least for the time being. But from what you've just told me, you're now on the run as much as I. What's your plan for getting us back to the *B'nai Elohim*?"

"First things first, queen," Laylah remarked as she sat in a chair. "I asked for an explanation regarding your other mortal companion and how you came into possession of the child. Also, how have you been able to escape notice and capture by Kor's soldiers? They're all over the city seeking you out."

Lessien grimaced but could see by the look of determination in Laylah's eyes she wouldn't be able to avoid the conversation. She sat across from Laylah while holding Martin and told the story of her and Autumn's abduction and Autumn's rape. She talked of the pregnancy that led to the birth of Martin. Then she talked about taking shelter in a cave and being found by Belladonna, daughter of the demon overlord who had kidnapped them from Aster. With a heavy heart, Lessien described the death of Autumn, Martin's naming ceremony, the escape to the city, and Argomon's betrayal of Belladonna. She didn't mention the close call in the safe-room below when, beyond explanation, both she and Martin hadn't been detected. Lessien believed Martin was the cause. For the time being, that was a hold card she didn't want to play.

Laylah's eyes widened as Lessien told her story. Though she'd never known a mortal, from everything she'd heard from the *B'nai Elohim* and other demons regarding them, they're weak and fragile creatures, though Michael felt there was a strength and nobility of character that argued against present thinking. He believed the only true weakness of the mortals was their tribalism—their inability to act as one—though he saw great promise in the Draugen Pesta giants and the InnisRos elves. Lessien's ability to survive while keeping a newborn child safe, even with the help of Belladonna, spoke strongly to Michael's point of view.

Lessien finished her tale and fell silent. The two beings sat face to face for several long seconds. Laylah's mind worked to absorb everything the InnisRos queen had said while Lessien, already drained of energy and exhausted, held the sleeping Martin while she closed her eyes.

Yesper went over to the closed entrance door and began to sniff. "We've got company," he declared. "I detect the spore scent of a dozen demon underlords and one overlord."

"Do you think they know we're here?" Laylah asked.

Yesper nodded. "They have us surrounded. We're going to have to fight our way out."

Laylah stood and picked up her trident. Lessien, weariness forgotten, took the sleeping Martin to an out-of-the-way corner and covered him with her mantle. When she stood back up, *Ah-HritVakha* was out of its sheath and cleared for action. Both sword and trident glowed with powerful magic. Yesper snarled and retreated just as an explosion blew the entrance door open. When the smoke cleared, the demons at the open door paused when they saw their quarry. The look in the eyes of the two females and the tracker, added to the magical glow of the sword and trident, frightened them.

"Well?" a voice called out. "What're you bastards waiting for?"

Braz'galar inspected Belladonna's wounds again. The burned hand and foot were responding well to the balm he found in the healing kit on the skiff, but she remained unconscious and he was getting worried. She should have come out of it by now.

It'd been two hours since their ship sank. And while the ferocity of the storm had long since abated, it was still raining heavily, and a few of the waves were high enough to break over the sides. During that time, Braz'galar fashioned a protective enclosure at the back end of the skiff using the waterproof cover and moved Belladonna and their supplies under it.

Though he didn't expect any problems, he performed a brief inspection of the skiff's condition to determine its seaworthiness. As he thought, it was in tip-top shape. He even found planks and carpenter tools stowed away to make emergency repairs. But the most important discovery he made was that of a small sail with ropes attached.

"What good is this without a mast?" Braz'galar said aloud as his eyes once again roamed over the skiff's interior.

But now that he knew what he was looking for, he found it easily. What he first thought was a support brace underneath both side railings were actually wooden poles of different sizes attached to the side by leather straps.

"Got you!" Braz'galar exclaimed as he untied each.

He wasn't overly familiar with the framework of a sailing ship but understood enough to recognize the long pole as the mast and the shorter the spar. Setting the mast and spar turned out to be a matter of snapping things into pre-made slots and holes. Getting the sail up took longer to figure out, but it wasn't too long before Braz'galar had the sail catching wind.

Satisfied he wouldn't have to row the skiff to land, he grabbed the two oars, which he knew also doubled as rudders, and retreated under the covered rear half of the boat. He carefully crawled over Belladonna, who was still unconscious, and went to the stern and inserted both oars into metal brackets.

"So… which way to the other side?" Braz'galar wondered as he leaned his back against the rear railing and used the oars to steer the skiff with the wind. He'd lost his bearings after everything that had happened. The overlord shrugged his shoulders. "I'll rely *on the wind and providence,"* he told himself as he drifted off into an exhausted sleep.

The first three demons to rush Lessien, Laylah, and Yesper died a quick death. Lessien, as Landross had instructed her, met the assault with a dodge, whirl, and strike, which brought her blade across the back of the neck as the demon rushed past. His head dropped to the floor as his body took two more steps before falling. Laylah's opponent died just as quickly. The overlord parried the demon's sword thrust with a knife she had pulled from her robes and skewered the demon in the belly with her trident. As the trident entered the body, it flashed and the entire middle section of the startled fiend disintegrated. Yesper, as quick as anything alive in either realm, pounced on the third demon and forced it to the ground. Then he used his forepaws to rend great slashes along the demon's midsection. For good measure, Yesper exhaled a stream of ice-cold vapor into the demon's face.

The rest of the demons at the door only hesitated for a second before they followed the first three. The following free-for-all lasted less than five minutes. In the end, ten demons lay dead on the floor of the room. Two survivors backed out of the room and closed the heavily damaged door, deciding they'd had enough.

Lessien dropped to her knees and whimpered. Besides several shallow cuts, she had a deep gash through the end of her stub, which was bleeding profusely. Laylah, despite being injured herself, moved over to Lessien and used a strip of cloth to apply pressure to the open wound.

Lessien's breath caught as the tension brought incredible pain. "Hurts worse than when I lost it," she gasped.

"If I don't get the bleeding controlled, the pain will end soon enough," Laylah replied. "You'll be dead."

Lessien's thinking was becoming muddled. "Yesper," she whispered.

The tracker already knew what the InnisRos queen wanted of him. "The baby's fine," Yesper said as he looked down on Martin, who was staring back with eyes the likes of which he'd never seen. "Impossibly fine."

Before Lessien could respond, she heard Laylah whisper, "Sorry, but this has to be done the old fashioned way," followed by a few seconds of agony. She screamed. She couldn't help herself. Laylah had used the magic of her trident to cauterize the slash to her stump.

Lessien's sword, *Ah-HritVakha*, glowed as it reacted to its mistress. Though it didn't have the power to take away pain, it could send waves of assurance and calm through the magical link they shared.

The queen responded almost at once... there wasn't time for her to linger through a recovery. She took a few deep breaths and nodded to Laylah. "I'll be alright."

Lessien, with the help of Laylah, crawled over to Martin and Yesper. The child looked back at her with eyes which seemed to ask, "Are you okay?"

"We're not out of danger," Yesper pronounced as he paced around the room. "They're still watching the building and, I suspect, are waiting for more reinforcements. It's only a matter of time before they attack again with overwhelming force. They might even bring in a sorcerer."

"When?" Laylah asked.

Yesper stopped. "For now, I detect no more additional spore scent. But I suspect within the hour."

"We need to make our break before those reinforcements get here," Lessien advised.

Laylah nodded. "But let me hold the child. You've enough problems fighting one-handed."

"I've trained hard to overcome that liability." Lessien

replied as she shook her head. "Besides, Martin's my responsibility."

"Nonsense," Yesper said. "That's not how Laylah and I operate."

"He's right," Laylah agreed. "We protect the innocent. That's why I spy for the *B'nai Elohim* against my kind. That and to prevent the corruption... the depravity... of the overlord rulers from spilling over into your world."

"Sounds strange coming from someone who's an overlord herself," Lessien remarked. "But I believe you. I've seen enough to understand this place is nowhere near what my kind has been taught for generations."

"Not too surprising, though," Laylah remarked. "When it comes to the mortal world, we rarely put our best foot forward."

"We're wasting time," Yesper reminded.

Laylah agreed. "I propose securing the child to Yesper's back. I think we can fit him between the spikes."

Yesper nodded. "Good idea. Grab a weapon harness from one of the bodies. I think something can be jury-rigged easily enough."

It only took a few minutes to get Martin, sill wrapped in Lessien's *Mantle of the Sovereign*, securely positioned on Yesper's back. Yesper took a few steps and moved his shoulders. After a few minor adjustments, he was ready to go. Martin appeared to be just fine with the arrangement.

"Lessien and I will go through the front door and into the city," Laylah instructed. "Yesper... follow after we've drawn them away."

"Wait a minute..." Lessien protested.

"Martin will be fine," Yesper interrupted, reading the concern in Lessie's voice. "My speed and spore scent should be enough to get the child and I through... especially after you've led most of them away."

Lessien reluctantly agreed.

"We'll meet at the usual place," Laylah said.

Yesper nodded.

The demon overlord put her hand on the doorknob and looked at the InnisRos queen. "Here we go!"

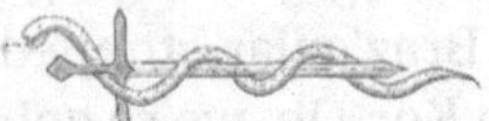

Braz'galar startled awake when a hand touched his arm. Belladonna was sitting next to him, staring.

"What happened?" she asked.

Braz'galar ignored the question and looked out over the water. The rain had stopped, and the surface of the reservoir had calmed considerably. What little wind there was had the skiff slowly plodding forward. But it was still impossible to ascertain the direction.

"What happened?" Belladonna repeated.

"Don't you think it's obvious?" Braz'galar snapped. Then he shook his head to clear his mind. "I'm sorry for yelling at you like that. I'm so damn tired." The overlord took a deep breath. "The ship sank... hit by lightning powerful enough to blow a sizable hole in the deck and practically disintegrated everything topside. It's a miracle it didn't destroy this skiff like everything else. We're the only survivors."

Belladonna softened. "The last thing I remember was talking in our cabin. Thank you for saving me."

Braz'galar closed his eyes and nodded.

"How far away are we from shore?"

Braz'galar grunted. "Which shore? We weren't too far from the center of the reservoir when the storm caught us. I don't know how far the wind took us... or even in what direction."

Belladonna sighed.

"I got us away before the ship sank and set the sail," Braz'galar said. "But remnants of the storm persisted, and

I was tired… or perhaps still feeling the side effects of the lightning strike. I don't know if I slept due to exhaustion or if I passed out. But out I went and we've been at the mercy of the wind ever since."

"Are you still determined to take me to Kor?" Belladonna asked. "Seems the gods might be saying otherwise."

"The gods can…" Braz'galar stopped and shook his head. "I'm not taking you to Kor. Oh, we're going there, but only so I can tell him the resistance is no longer a threat, you're dead, and then claim my city as payment."

"Lessien and the child…"

"I've made certain… arrangements… with an associate of mine who owes me a favor or two," Braz'galar said to calm Belladonna's fears. "He'll get to her before we can… particularly now, since we appear to be hopelessly lost. I keep in touch with him through a communications crystal. Don't worry, he'll find her. After he does, he's got enough clout to keep her and the baby safe until we can get back. I asked him to take her to Zhaarmoth."

"Are you sure you can trust him?"

Braz'galar shrugged. "About as much as I trust anyone. I've known him for a long time, and, for an overlord, he's a pretty decent chap. And he has a soft spot for youngsters."

The two stopped talking as they scanned the horizon for any sign of a passing ship or land. The gentle rocking of the skiff and the sound of the waves as they smacked against its sides mesmerized Belladonna. As the minutes dragged on, she found the lure of sleep impossible to ignore. A slight shake of her shoulder awakened her.

"How long was I asleep?" Belladonna asked Braz'galar as she wiped her eyes. It was now dark. Her companion had conjured a simple light spell to see by, though it was dim enough to stay within the covered area of the skiff.

Braz'galar shushed her. "We've got company."

"What kind?" Belladonna whispered. "A ship?"

"I wish. No… not a ship, though it's as large as one. I'm not sure, but I believe it might be a Behemoth."

Belladonna shook her head. "That's impossible. They're only found in the Kematian Sea. This reservoir isn't large enough to support a Behemoth."

"Not just one, Belle," Braz'galar replied. "And the reservoir, while not large compared to the Kematian Sea, is deep enough and has enough of a food supply to sustain a family of Behemoths. Besides, it doesn't necessarily make its home here."

Belladonna looked at her companion. "What do you mean?"

"You don't know? A series of underwater channels connects this reservoir with the Kematian Sea and all the lakes in the Prefecture. I know the person who mapped them."

"I guess my education is somewhat…" Belladonna stopped and pointed to the starboard side of the skiff. "There!"

A quarter mile away, highlighted by eerie looking lights just underneath the water, was the outline of an immense creature. Its serpentine body was three hundred feet long from snout to the end of the tail. The head and maw of the Behemoth was forty to fifty feet wide. Two large webbed and taloned arms, along with the tail, allowed the creature to swim at a fantastic rate.

"What do we do?" Belladonna asked.

Braz'galar watched the figure as it moved towards the skiff. "They're not known to be aggressive, though if you piss one off, or it's starving, they can be your worst nightmare. I've heard stories of one Behemoth taking down a ship as large as the one we were on."

"Well, we're not pissing it off, are we?"

"No," Braz'galar answered. "At least I don't think we are. But if it's hungry…"

"What a minute," Belladonna interrupted. "I thought

you said this reservoir has enough of a food source to support a whole family of Behemoths."

"True enough. Unless it's gotten a taste for demon blood."

CHAPTER SIX

The Abyss

Kor, Bezrameth, Lilitu, Azazael, and Emprusa sat around a long, garish table and studied a map of the Kor Prefecture. The magic of the map illustrated, in real time, the position of each army being brought to bear against the *B'nai Elohim* fortress. Six armies of twenty thousand demons each were close to being in place and ready to attack the chokepoint. Seven more armies were on the march and only a few days away from their assigned locations, while another seven armies moved to strategic positions around the capital city of Kor and the eastern half of the Prefecture. The latter would serve as a deterrence to any further uprising of the peasant class. Normally Kor and his generals wouldn't have bothered, except the rise of the resistance they had just smashed made the demon lord cautious.

Kor looked at each of the others before locking eyes on Lilitu. "When will the diversion doorway spells be ready?"

"We're working on duplicating them as fast as possible," Lilitu said, though she knew that wasn't going satisfy Kor. "At least ten days."

Kor shook his head. "That's not good enough!" he spat. "You think the *B'nai Elohim* are going to sit by twiddling their thumbs, waiting for you to catch up while thirteen armies take up positions before their fortress? We can't afford to delay the attack. We need to keep them off-balanced and guessing what our actual intentions are. Those doorway spells are necessary to give them a reason to believe the attack on their fortress is only a diversion. We can't afford them the time to figure out the doorway spells are diversions themselves. Bezrameth's spell does us no good if the *B'nai Elohim* are expecting it… or recognize it for what it is."

"My Lord, you can't rush these things," Lilitu responded. "You know that as well as anyone."

Kor stared at his Magic Faction overlord before directing his attention to Azazael. "When will the armies be in place for the attack?"

"The bulk of the armies will be in place three days hence," Azazael replied. "The remaining will take another two days."

"And your war sorcerers?" Emprusa spoke for the first time.

Azazael glanced at Kor who nodded. "I've reassigned most to Lilitu per Lord Kor's orders. But each army still has enough to be effective."

"I don't want the *B'nai Elohim* to think we're holding anything back," Kor said. "If they see halfhearted magical attacks against their fortress, they might figure out the frontal assault is a distraction."

"Perhaps I can be of help," Bezrameth said. "I know of several Order sorcerers who are quite capable of unleashing their spells on the *B'nai Elohim*."

Lilitu shook her head. "Rogue sorcerers, My Lord, who haven't been trained by my Faction. You can't trust them."

"Those 'rogue sorcerers' helped me create the doorway spell that's going to get us to Aster without the *B'nai Elohim's* knowledge," Bezrameth answered Lilitu. "Could you say the same of yours?"

"We were close," Lilitu retorted. "If Lord Kor hadn't..."

"Enough!" Kor said. He waited a few seconds for the anger between the two overlord sorcerers to cool. "Rogue, sanctioned... it doesn't matter to me as long as they can get the job done. Besides, throwing lightning or fire spells against the *B'nai Elohim* should be simple enough. It's all for show, anyway."

Both Lilitu and Bezrameth nodded their acquiescence, though it was clear Lilitu wasn't happy.

Kor nodded. "A most wise decision. Bezrameth, get as many of your Order sorcerers in place with the leading elements of Azazael's armies. I also want you to work with Azazael to put together the assassin team for transport to Aster through your doorway spell. We know where the Talisman is, but not what you'll encounter once over there. So be smart in your selections."

"Maybe we should talk to the Assassin's Guild?" Emprusa remarked.

Kor shook his head. "I don't trust them. The Guilds do nothing but protect their members. And though I've no proof, I suspect they were involved with the resistance. No, we do this with our people. Questions?"

Everyone shook their heads.

"Good! We begin the attack by our armies in six days' time per Azazael's battle plan. An early morning attack, I should think. Lilitu, I want your sorcerers to be ready in five days..."

Lilitu started to protest, but Kor held up a hand to stop her. "With as many of the doorway spells as you have ready. Overwhelm them at first... half should be enough... then use the rest to keep them off-balanced and guessing. A few here and a few there. Keep it constant so they don't have time to let down their guard. Each spell keeps a guardian occupied."

"Only long enough to kill the sorcerer casting the spell," Lilitu remarked.

"I DON'T CARE!" Kor roared.

Lilitu looked down at the floor. If Kor saw the expression on her face at that moment, she'd soon be kissing the *Pillar*... or worse.

"Assign them a few guards if that'll make you feel better," Kor continued. "Bezrameth, have you and your team ready to go on my command shortly thereafter. Once you get to Aster, it'll be up to you to find and destroy the Talisman."

Bezrameth nodded. "Rest assured, its days are numbered.

Then I'll have a world at my fingertips."

"Who's world, Bezrameth?" Kor inquired.

Bezrameth coughed. "Your world, My Lord."

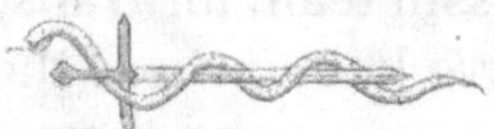

Father Goram, Nightshade, Landross, and Herbie the demon dog, had made their way down the hill overlooking the vast landscape of demon cities, farms, ranches, and crop fields. Of the four, only Herbie looked like he belonged.

Nightshade called a halt after leading the party into a small copse of trees and bushes. "We'll not get far without a disguise," she said. "The common folk will accept us readily enough… but all my contacts are in the cities. Overlords and underlords loyal to Kor control those."

"So how do mere mortals disguise themselves in a world of demons?" Landross asked.

"Skin pigmentation," Nightshade replied without hesitation. "We can get by without horns, body spikes, or talons… but not without different colored skin. And you'll need to cover up your armor. The livery's too obvious and not like anything here."

Landross nodded as he fumbled with his backpack and pulled out a hooded cloak. "It's hot enough without wearing this damned thing."

"Can't be helped," Father Goram said. "Keep it clasped. And get rid of the shield."

Landross nodded but kept mumbling about the unfairness of it as he buried his shield in the soft earth beneath one of the more distinct trees. He then marked the tree trunk with a dagger. "I want to come back for this."

Father Goram ignored the knight as he addressed Nightshade. "What color?"

Nightshade didn't answer. She was staring east. Something

had caught her attention.

"What is it, Nightshade?" the priest asked.

"Huh?" she answered. "Oh, sorry. We should disguise ourselves as members of the Taumaru. They're an obscure clan of demons from highlands on the other side of the Abyss. They have a nasty reputation and most demons, even demons from the Military Faction, give them a wide berth. And since they're a patriarchal society, Landross's insults to me will go unnoticed."

Landross snorted. "Oh, please, Nightshade. My insults are richly deserved."

"That's enough, the both of you!" Father Goram warned.

Nightshade continued. "Though they keep to themselves, they're known to come off their plateau every once in a while. So our presence won't be a huge surprise. Their skin is gray with black accents around the eyes... like a teardrop with the pointed ends going back along the sides of their face to the ears."

Father Goram frowned. "Hmmm... I'm familiar with magic that would work, but it's a sorcerer's enchantment. Eric the Black..."

Father Goram stopped himself before he revealed to Landross that Eric the Black was, besides being a powerful sorcerer, also a master assassin who could disguise himself almost at will. It was an interesting combination of talents. Eric the Black didn't think anyone else knew about his double life, but the priest had figured it out. The confirmation came with the sorcerer's possession and control of the Qénsharma. Only assassins used them. But if Landross were to catch wind of Eric the Black's secret life, there'd be hell to pay. Father Goram had no interest in ending that unusual relationship.

"What about Eric the Black?" Landross asked.

"Just that he explained the enchantment to me once," Father Goram explained. "It's complicated and beyond my training as a cleric."

"Our problems just got bigger," Nightshade said as she pointed.

Father Goram and Landross looked and saw what Nightshade meant. Several demon armies had come into view on the horizon.

"That's a lot of demons," Landross remarked. "The front stretches for as far as the eye can see."

Herbie barked.

"That's why Michael's spies went silent," Father Goram surmised. "They were probably all rounded up before word got out that the demons were going to attack the *B'nai Elohim's* fortress."

Nightshade nodded. "But I bet it's a feint for something much larger. Kor knows he can't take the fortress with a frontal assault… even one as large as this. He's tried before."

"We can't go back, Horatio," Landross said. There was a sudden nervousness in his voice. "We need to rescue Lessien and Autumn."

"No, my boy, we're not turning back," Father Goram replied. "Michael will need to handle this on his own… at least for the time being. It makes our search much more dangerous, however."

The priest turned to his student. "We can't afford to look for Belladonna. Not now. My wife and the queen have always been our first priority."

Nightshade nodded. "I understand. But before we can even begin our search, I need to get inside one of those cities and contact my sources… that is if they haven't been rooted out and killed. Without information, our chances of finding anyone are slim to none."

"We have a little time before those armies arrive and get settled in," Landross said. "Not too much, though. The troops are going to be parched and ready for female companionship after a long day of marching and pitching camp. All three cities are going to be crawling with demon soldiers by tomorrow nightfall… if not sooner."

"Which city?" Father Goram asked Nightshade.

"The southern-most one… Zir Tachoss," Nightshade answered at once. "It's the largest of the three, so we'll have a better chance finding someone to disguise us as Taumaru clansmen. I also have a special friend there who'll help."

"Until then?" Father Goram asked.

Nightshade shrugged. "We hide our faces using the cowls of our cloaks. It's risky, but we don't really have any other options. Having Herbie along will help sell the story."

"Woof!"

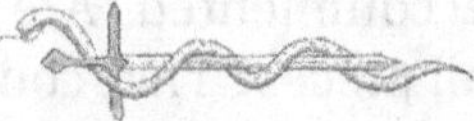

Lilitu stormed into her study and knocked over a small stone statue. "Damn Bezrameth!" she screamed to the empty room. "Damn him! Damn the Order! Damn them all!"

One of Lilitu's junior sorceresses, always on duty, peeked through a slightly opened door from an adjourning room. "Mistress?"

"Get this cleaned up!" Lilitu ordered as she pointed to the broken statue pieces scattered across the floor. "And send someone to tell my Faction underlords that I want them here at once!"

As one assistant cleaned up the broken stone shards, and another ran to collect her underlords, Lilitu sat behind her desk and poured herself a stiff drink of Stenari, her own blend of several different fiery liquors. She took a sip, which caused her to cough as the burning liquid went down her throat. "We're going to do a thousand doorways in five days!" she said. "Or I'm going to tack a few underlord skins to the walls of my bedroom!"

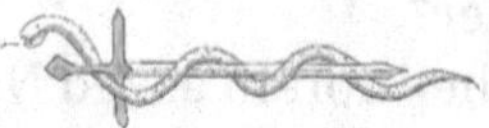

"So, Bezrameth… how many sorcerers do you plan on taking to Aster?" Azazael asked.

Bezrameth glanced sideways at the Military Faction leader. They had left Kor's palace and were walking to the military barracks. "Only two. I can do the binding spells needed to restrain the Talisman myself, but I'll need shielding against her defenses as I cast the enchantment. Once I've done that, your people shouldn't have any problems destroying her."

"It's my understanding that the Talisman could be as large as a small city," Azazael commented. "Are my warriors expected to cut her up into small pieces? That could take weeks!"

Bezrameth cackled from behind the deep cowl of his robe. A boney hand with a few leathery bits of flesh attached came up and rested on Azazael's shoulder. "Relax, my friend. I'll point the way to the Talisman's heart. Then your warriors will only need a few days to hack through." The Order sorcerer laughed. People on the street gave away even more room to the two.

Azazael cringed under the feel of the skeletal touch on his shoulder and physically shuddered at the sound of the sorcerer's laugh. *"Thank the gods I'm not going with this creature,"* he thought.

"Don't worry, overlord," Bezrameth said after a few more seconds of mirth. "Your warriors will be able to get the job done within a tolerable period of time. We're all quite eager to invade the world of the mortals. And I, for one, don't want to keep Kor waiting long."

Azazael nodded but didn't comment. Thirty minutes of silence later, they were inspecting several columns of warriors who would escort the Order sorcerers to Aster.

"Do you really think we'll need fifty warriors?" Bezrameth asked. "I had envisioned a smaller group."

Azazael looked at the underlord who'd be leading the strike force. "Please explain the reality of the situation to our esteemed guest, Vol'goth."

The underlord nodded. "My Lord Bezrameth. The Talisman's an important military target. We've no way of knowing the number of mortals, or other beings, who'll be defending it. Our planners have determined the number fifty allows for rapid deployment while providing enough force to defend you if necessary."

"And if it's an entire army?" Bezrameth asked.

"We only have to give you and your guard enough time to destroy the Talisman," Vol'goth replied. "Our lives mean nothing."

"My guard?" Bezrameth inquired.

"There's one more thing I want to show you," Azazael said as he turned and walked towards a smaller group of ten demons standing in a line one hundred feet away. "You're dismissed," he called over his shoulder to Vol'goth.

As the two approached this new group of demons, Bezrameth could tell right away they were unlike any demon warrior he'd ever seen. Though smaller by a foot than most demons, their bodies had been built for speed, and they were at least twice as strong, if their physique appearance was any indication. Their crimson-colored eyes gleamed with intelligence as they watched Azazael and Bezrameth approach. Instead of talons at the end of their hands, they had fingers like that of the mortal races. This meant they could manipulate tools and other objects that taloned demons have trouble with... a powerful complement to the intellect they possessed. Each of the demons was encased in sleek, emerald-colored armor and had various weapons hanging from the belt wrapped around their midsections—swords, battleaxes, maces, and the like.

Azazael stopped and faced the demons, who, as one cohesive unit, came to attention. Bezrameth thought the sound of the armor coming together in one unified sound was quite remarkable.

"Impressive… but that's not steel they're wearing." The Order sorcerer remarked. "It sounds similar… but more like the carapace of an insect."

Azazael smiled. "Both actually. The insect carapace, besides being strong, is also lightweight. Blended in steel makes it even stronger without sacrificing speed. We have Lilitu's Magic Faction to thank for that."

"That's not all they created, is it?" Bezrameth added, meaning the very existence of the warriors themselves.

"Perceptive," Azazael replied. "But I suggest you reserve that question for Kor. Suffice to say these warriors are special in ability and loyalty. They're yours to command as you see fit in the Talisman's destruction. They'll carry out your orders without exception."

Bezrameth nodded. "I look forward to putting that loyalty to the test."

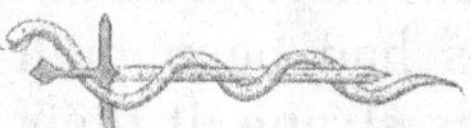

Emprusa was behind Kor, massaging his shoulders. They were both on the massive bed in Kor's equally massive bedroom and had finished a lengthy session of intimacy, though both knew there wasn't any genuine love involved, only familiarity.

"Your shoulders are as tight as a mountain boulder," the concubine said. "I thought we'd be past that… considering."

"There's much riding on this damn operation," Kor replied.

Though he was as tense as Emprusa suggested, her fingers were working out many of the kinks. "If we're able to get past the *B'nai Elohim*, not only the mortal world but the entire connecting universe will be open. Then it'll just be a matter of creating corridors between the worlds to expand our dominance."

Emprusa stopped massaging Kor's shoulders. "You think the other Prefecture leaders connected to our universe are going to permit that?"

"I don't care."

"A very dangerous plan, My Lord."

"How so," Kor asked.

"We're one Prefecture," Emprusa reminded her master. "Despite Bezrameth's confidence, the mortal inhabitants will fight for their world. We're both aware of the success they had against demons during Aikanáro's failed attempt to conquer the elvan island of InnisRos. And even after we seize Aster, what makes you think we'll have the resources available to find and vanquish another world? We'll be blind! Our only experience is Aster… and we don't know if it's one of the more powerful worlds, or a backwater planet in the middle of nowhere. Then there's the other Prefectures to consider. If we find a world to conquer, and it's connected to another Prefecture, we'll be fighting both that world's inhabitants and Abyssian demons."

Kor nodded. "Fair points. But I doubt their validity. I find it hard to believe our Juxtaposition Point would lead to a primitive world. If we can take Aster, it's likely we can take any of the other worlds out there in our universe. As for stepping on the toes of other Prefectures… all I have to do is back away and go for the next world I can find. Don't you see? If we're successful in defeating the *B'nai Elohim* and subjugating Aster, we'll have laid the groundwork for the other Prefectures to do the same to their worlds."

"They're aware of your plans?" Emprusa exclaimed, as she

sat next to Kor on the bed.

"Of course they are," Kor answered. "I told them. The Prefectures don't live in a vacuum." Kor paused before continuing to let what he'd just revealed sink in. "Think of it! Thousands of Prefectures let loose in all the known universes. Demonkind will be unstoppable. And I, Kor, will have made it possible. Everyone will grovel at my feet. As for you, my dear… you'll be my number one consort… and the First Consort over all the consorts in the Abyss."

"Why not queen?"

Kor glanced at Emprusa and scoffed. "Oh, please… let's not get ridiculous."

Emprusa drew back, but not so Kor could see it. "And if you should fail?"

The Prefecture leader laughed… then grew silent. That's why he was so tense. "Then I suppose it'll be time for me to join my predecessors in the *Living Throne*."

Despite Kor's grandiose plans to subjugate numerous worlds and become the Abyss's most favored Prefecture leader… victories that would vastly increase her status… Emprusa decided she might like to see the *Living Throne* claim him after all.

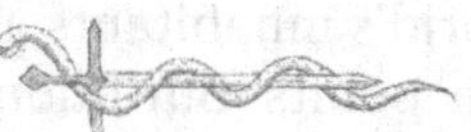

Father Goram, Nightshade, Landross, and Herbie rented a dilapidated hovel in one of the poorer sections of Zir Tachoss to rest. The cities in the Prefecture are much like the cities on Aster in that the neighborhoods of the impoverished are mostly outside the main city walls. Also, like Aster's cities, these places have little organized law enforcement. The people living in these communities keep their heads down, ask few questions, and devote a good part of their existence trying not to become a victim of the rampant crime that's part of their everyday lives. Consequently, the four were able to move around unnoticed.

"I'm surprised we didn't see any soldiers patrolling the streets," Landross remarked as he took a seat on a rickety chair. Herbie dutifully sat next to his new master. "This was much easier than I expected."

"How many cities on the mainland have you ever visited?" Father Goram asked.

"Well, none, actually. But Taranthi..."

Father Goram shook his head. "Elvan cities are the exception. It's a completely different story with the human cities on the mainland. There, soldiers make an even more attractive target for pickpockets and thieves. That's probably true here as well."

Landross paused as he scratched behind Herbie's ears. "I suppose you're right. Though neither Taranthi nor Elwing FeFalas have run-down neighborhoods like this, they certainly have their share of pickpockets. More than once, one of my knights has come to me complaining about a fleecing... though they didn't know when it happened or who did it."

Nightshade, finished with her scan of the streets outside their dirty window to see if anyone had followed them, dusted off a chair and took a seat with the other two—three if she counted Herbie. "The only time troops come from behind the walls into these neighborhoods is to round up people for the *Pillar*. The pickpockets and thieves not protected by the guilds vanish into the background as best they can."

Landross shook his head but didn't comment. Nightshade had explained the *Pillar*, as well as why the guilds had so much influence with the overlords. Surprisingly, at least to Father Goram, Landross understood the guild concept and, given the circumstances as outlined by Nightshade, appreciated why guilds were allowed to exist, though it bothered him they were granted immunity from the law for illegal activities. But as he saw it, this was the Abyss. Different strokes for different folks. Besides, he couldn't let such things interfere with the rescue of Lessien and Autumn. The *Pillar*, on the other hand, was an entirely different story. It personified evil. But even that had a reason for existing.

"Getting into the city is going to be much harder," Nightshade continued. "The gate guards will be even more vigilant, given the circumstances. Then, after we've gotten past that hurdle, we'll find twice as many city guards patrolling the streets. Zir Tachoss's ruling overlord is very fastidious. He can't keep Kor's visiting armies out, but he can do everything in his power to make sure they don't beat too many of the prostitutes or tear up his city in drunken brawls."

"Why don't we just stay here while you contact your sources?" Landross asked Nightshade. But when he looked at her, and then at Father Goram, he understood the two of them had already discussed the matter, and apparently the priest decided against it.

Nightshade looked at her mentor. "Even Landross sees the logic in that, Horatio."

Father Goram shook head. "My decision is final. I'll not let you go into the city alone. You're my responsibility. That's not going to change in the foreseeable future. And I'll not sit here, or anywhere else, wasting time when my wife and our queen languish out there at the mercy of the Abyss!"

"But we'll only be a hindrance," Landross said. His appeal ignited something deep within the priest and caused it to boil forward.

Father Goram whirled on the knight. "Then stay here if you want!" he yelled as he advanced towards his friend. Althaya's high priest's eyes were shining bright blue and blue sparks emanated from his fingers. Neither Nightshade nor Landross had ever seen anything like it. Herbie ducked his head behind

Landross and whimpered.

"In the past year, my wife was kidnapped and brutally raped… twice!" The blue shine in Father Goram's eyes was now tinged with red, and the sparks which came from his fingers turned into blue bolts of lightning which surrounded and spun around, encasing him in magical armor. "And if that wasn't enough, my queen, besides herself being kidnapped, was falsely accused of treason… a charge which damn near brought a bloody civil war to InnisRos! I refuse to lose Nightshade as well in this… this sequence of catastrophes."

Except for the feint crackling sound of magical energies, there was complete silence in the room. Father Goram turned away from Landross. While there was now calm in his demeanor, the magnitude of the forces that surrounded him remained constant.

"Horatio…" Landross began, but a glance from the priest silenced him.

"Don't you understand!" Father Goram barked. "Everything happened under my watch! I failed to save Martin! And now I've failed his daughter, breaking my promise to keep her on the throne! But my greatest failure is with Autumn, the one person I love as much as I love Kristen."

Father Goram closed his eyes and the magical energies that were surrounding him dissipated. When he opened them, they were clear and resolute. He looked at Landross. "No," he said as he shook his head. "I'll not wait behind. Althaya forgive me, I'll use whatever I have at my disposal… including the blackest of magic… to see this through. Only death will stop me!"

Nightshade nodded her acceptance and approval. Landross looked at her and wondered if she'd seen the flicker of red in Father Goram's eyes. Suddenly, he understood that whatever happened from this point on was going to change everything and everyone. Nothing would ever be the same.

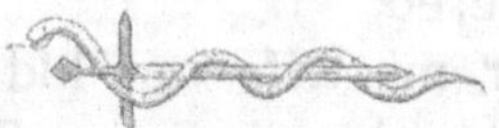

The streets of Zir Tachoss were busy, and the citizens of the city went about their daily business the same as one would see in any city in the mortal realm. As Nightshade had predicted, the city guard patrolled every street, alley, and thoroughfare large enough to accommodate more than two abreast. Also, as expected, there were thousands of demons wearing army identification insignias walking around. This was to their advantage, however. The city guard was so intent upon watching the army and maintaining order, they paid scant attention to three robe-cowled strangers with a dog.

"How much farther?" Father Goram asked Nightshade.

"Several streets over," she answered. "I could get us there quicker by using back streets, but that might be pushing our luck. We need to stay on the main thoroughfares to draw less attention."

"Except from the pickpockets," Landross grumbled.

"An acceptable risk," Father Goram whispered back to his knight companion.

They had just pushed through a group of seven army soldiers when a voice called from behind.

"How much?" the voice asked.

Nightshade stopped, as did Father Goram and Landross. Herbie was a few feet away sniffing the base of a small tree. All three turned to confront the soldiers. Landross went for his sword, but Father Goram stopped him with a firm grip on his sword arm.

"Let Nightshade handle this," the priest whispered.

Nightshade brushed past Father Goram and Landross to face the soldier who had spoken. His companions stood around, waiting to see what would happen.

The soldier leered at Nightshade, though his ugly demon

face made the gesture somewhat comical. "So I have your attention. Good. Again, how much… whore?"

Father Goram looked around them. The scene was drawing attention, which was the last thing they needed. The priest removed his grip on Landross's sword arm and gathered his will. Invisible dark and killing magical energies coalesced around him.

Nightshade sensed the magic building around her master and knew if she didn't settle her score with the soldier quickly, there was going to be trouble. She didn't want to explain to the city guard why a few of Kor's soldiers had been turned to ash.

"You can't afford me, soldier," Nightshade said as she smiled. "Now take your playmates and move along. I've important things to attend."

Even as she said it, Nightshade knew it was a gambit doomed to failure. But she was prepared. Under normal situations such as this, she'd turn into her demon overlord form and dine on the soul of the offending party. But since she now followed the Light, she was determined to handle life, even in the Abyss, from that perspective. What she had in her favor was that demon soldiers are usually dull-witted. They fought and died to serve the purposes of their master overlords. That was their lot in life. All they wanted was food, drink, and an opportunity for regular sexual debauchery. With brains as primitive as that, they were highly susceptible to mental suggestions and imagery, which was something Nightshade could do easily enough with White Magic. An implanted vision of her former demon form should settle the issue.

The demon looked back at his friends and they all laughed. "Guess we'll just take her then… eh, boys?"

But before he had finished, he noticed the look of his friends had changed from amusement to astonishment, then to terror, and finally to abasement as they fell to their knees. From their actions, even the most obtuse of soldiers could figure out fortunes had suddenly taken a turn for the worse. The soldier closed his eyes and slowly turned. When he found his courage, he opened them. A black misty column fifteen feet high towered over him. The inky murkiness of the column swirled and churned before him. The vision mesmerized the soldier as he watched the black column solidify. Out of each side, four arms appeared, each with hundreds of inch long barbed spikes. Two fangs the size of a short sword sprang out of the head as gleaming blue eyes opened and looked down. Every demon in the Abyss was familiar with this particular demon, or at least her family tree.

"Ov... ov... overlord," the demon soldier said as he also dropped to his knees. Regular demon folks walking nearby looked at the scene being played out and shook their heads in confusion.

"So you understand the mistake you've made?" Nightshade inquired.

The unfortunate demon fell face down onto the street. "Yes, overlord," came his muffled reply.

"Stand, all of you," Nightshade ordered. The soldiers scrambled to stand at attention. As they did so, she released the vision she'd formed in their minds. To them, she was once again a hooded female. "I've decided not to kill you. You'll die soon enough for the glory of Kor. But don't think for a second you'll escape unscathed. You've sullied my honor, so I must teach you a lesson."

The demons looked at each other, first with relief, then with fear. Landross, a few paces behind Nightshade, almost laughed out loud when he saw the look on their faces as they realized death might be preferable to the lesson they were about to learn.

Balls of flame materialized in front of Nightshade and moved towards each demon. But unlike the illusion of Nightshade's demon appearance, these were real. Each ball of flame moved towards their intended target slowly, so each soldier had time to consider his fate. Streams of sweat ran down the hideous faces of each. After a few quick moments, a lifetime of anticipation for the soldiers, the moving flames stopped between their legs.

"Not one word," Nightshade cautioned before she turned away and continued down the street, followed by her two snickering companions and Herbie.

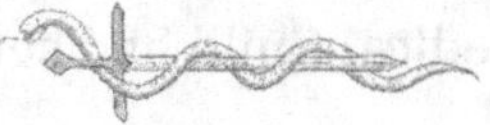

"I heard Nightshade's in the city, My Lord," the underlord, Talvog, reported.

The overlord and ruler of the city of Zir Tachoss, Azzoth, looked up from the papers he was studying. "I send you on a simple inspection tour of the city and this is what you come back with?"

Talvog took a seat on one of the comfortable chairs that ringed the overlord's desk and poured a glass of wine from a decanter that never emptied. Most overlords would have sent Talvog to Kiss the *Pillar* for the familiarity he'd just shown. But it was hard getting good help. As a result, Azzoth was fairly lax with his staff once they gained his trust and as long as they performed at a high level. But if someone ever gave him cause to question either, he could be as merciless as any other overlord. Kissing the *Pillar* wasn't the worst thing that could happen.

"Everything's going quite well in the city," Talvog said as he draped a leg over the chair arm. "The city guard is doing a spectacular job keeping the brawling to a minimum. Money is being spent, which means taxes for the coffers. The brothels have plenty of customers, and the pickpockets and thieves are prospering. For once, all the guilds are happy. It's good to see the army is good for something."

"Careful, Talvog," Azzoth scolded. "Part of that army is mine."

Talvog nodded. "Yes, My Lord."

The overlord smiled. "It's good news to hear the guilds are pleased, is it not?"

Talvog returned his master's smile. "Indeed, it is!"

"So what's this about Nightshade?" Azzoth's complete attention was now directed towards his underling.

Talvog got down to business. "I was inspecting one of those triage stations the Medical Guild had set up… they send their respects, by the way."

Azzoth acknowledged the good wishes with a curt nod of his head, though he wondered why they'd bother. He had about as much control over them as he did over the mating habits of the flamed-wing gnar catcher.

"It was then that I came across several soldiers who were being treated for some rather unusual injuries. Rather amusing, actually. But painful!" Talvog whistled. "Even army buffoons don't deserve that!"

Azzoth waited patiently. He knew Talvog would get to the point… eventually.

"But don't worry, My Lord," the underlord resumed. "They weren't any of our boys. Armor insignia indicated one of the eastern cities… not sure which one. Anyway, each of these soldiers had their crotches burned to a crisp. The clerics say they'll be functional again someday… maybe… but even so, I feel sorry for the poor bastards. I'd rather have…"

"You're getting to the part about Nightshade soon?" Azzoth interrupted.

"Sorry, My Lord. At first, they claimed they only stopped to ask a local female for directions…"

Azzoth laughed. "Of course they did. And with the purist of intentions, I'm sure."

Talvog grinned. "We all know how innocent soldiers

ask for directions, do we not, My Lord? It seems the female objected to the inquiry with fury and… as I've already mentioned… fire between the legs. But before she did, they claim she changed her appearance. Everyone in the Abyss recognizes Nightshade… just like they'd recognize Aikanáro and Belladonna. That family has a reputation!"

"Aikanáro's dead… and no one's heard from Nightshade since his Aster invasion attempt," Azzoth said, "though it's rumored she may have had a hand in her father's demise. Did you try to verify the soldier's story?"

Talvog nodded. "I tried. I went back to where they said it happened and questioned the locals. A lot of them saw or heard about the commotion, but none of them said Nightshade was involved. Just the female and her two companions who only watched the exchange."

"How about a description?" Azzoth asked.

Talvog shook his head. "All three wore cloaks with deep cowls. Oh, there was mention of a dog being with them."

Azzoth took a few moments to consider the situation and its importance. "I suppose we should try to sort this out if we can. With everything that's going on, any complication could be significant. Why Nightshade's here, if she's here, would be something Kor would want to know. Take two of my personal guards and see if you can get me better information. Start with the gorgon. Nightshade spent much of her youth here in Zir Tachoss instead of in Kor with her father. As I understand it, the gorgon became like a second mother to the young Nightshade."

Talvog shivered. "Friends with a gorgon. Imagine that. And here I thought being turned to stone was the only peace you could find with one of her species."

"You know better than that," Azzoth admonished. "Though you're not far off if you make her angry."

Talvog nodded. He stood, saluted, and turned to walk out

of the room.

Azzoth, as he watched his underlord retreat, called out. "Discretion, Talvog! Don't make the gorgon angry with me."

Talvog raised a taloned hand in acknowledgement as he left.

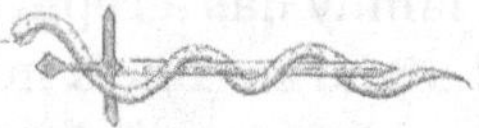

The three entered the front room of a two-story apartment. The bottom floor was a small shop dedicated to the buying, selling, and trading of trinkets, herbs, spices, and hard to find medicinal components such as venom bitterweed, ghost lilac, deathnettle worm hearts, and hammerwort brains. Along one wall was a small shelf of aged tomes and manuscripts. The shop had a peculiar odor about it, which wasn't unusual given the nature of its inventory. Behind a wooden counter sat a nondescript-looking demon reading a tome while puffing away on a large, black cigar, the smoke of which surrounded the demon in a dry, churning haze.

"Any mess that dog makes you clean up," the demon said without looking up from the tome he was reading. "Can I help you?"

Nightshade, with Father Goram, Landross, and Herbie tagging behind, moved to the counter. "I'm looking for a particular root," she said. "And I'm afraid you're my last hope."

That caught the interest of the shopkeeper. He closed the tome and put it down before he removed the cigar from his mouth. "Perhaps we do. What you see around you is but a small part of our inventory. What root do you seek?"

"Root of the assassin vine," Nightshade answered. "But not the rustic brown. It has to be from the stygian black."

The shop keeper put the cigar back into his mouth and studied the deep cowed female standing before him. The other two and the dog were of no consequence at the moment.

"That's a very rare root… one of a kind. In fact, I heard it's no longer found in the Abyss."

Nightshade shrugged. "Perceived truths are not always absolute."

"So it would seem," the shopkeeper admitted. "But who am I to say?"

"Maybe your associate can help me," Nightshade prodded. "I believe her name is Madam Abigail?"

The shop keeper nodded. The cowled female customer had just identified herself as a close friend of his employer. She had kept her true name secret from all but a certain few, and the demon Nightshade was one of them. "Please follow me. I'm Tolves, by the way."

Nightshade hesitated. "A word with my associates before we leave?"

Tolves bowed. "Of course," he said as he moved a respectable distance away.

"The two of you can't follow," Nightshade told Father Goram and Landross.

Landross started to object.

"Abigail is a gorgon."

Landross backed away a step. "Say no more. I'll be perfectly happy to remain flesh and blood, thank you very much."

Father Goram nodded. "We'll be fine here."

Nightshade smiled. "Keep Herbie away from the truffle berries. Animals love how they taste, but it makes them poop purple for a week."

Tolves lead Nightshade into a small, dingy room, which was an obvious workshop. But it wasn't just an ordinary workshop. It was an alchemy laboratory. On the other side of the room was a stairway going up.

Nightshade raised an eyebrow. She knew what the gorgon was attempting to do from the different types of components spread around. "Abigail knows better than this. You can't change lead into gold... at least not without powerful magic. Abigail's a competent enchantress, but she's not *that* good. Besides, Kor's outlawed alchemy altogether. It'd cut his personal wealth in half if gold became as common as lead."

"You know what they say," a voice said from the top of the stairs which lead to the second floor. A veiled and delicately robed figure descended the staircase. Except for her height, which was just under seven feet, her features matched that of an older female elf. Perfectly proportioned, she was beautiful... if one could get past the shimmering eyes hidden behind the veil and the mass of foot long writhing snakes that were intermingled with her waist-long black hair. "Laws are meant to be broken."

Nightshade smiled and approached the gorgon. "And what Kor doesn't know won't hurt him."

The two females hugged.

"I thought you were dead, my dear," Abigail remarked. The relief in her voice was obvious. "At least that's been the rumor spreading around after we learned of your father's debacle on Aster."

Nightshade sighed and took a seat on the stairs. "I was... at least my soul was."

Abigail dismissed Tolves and sat next to Nightshade. "I sensed something was different about you the moment you entered the store."

"A story that needs telling," Nightshade replied. Then she hung her head. "But that's only part of it. You're sensing confliction... and guilt."

The gorgon took Nightshade's hand. "We're all conflicted by one thing or another... at least those of us with a conscious are. The whole business of right and wrong makes it one of life's more unavoidable challenges. We deal with it the best we can and move on, promising ourselves we'll do better next time. I taught you that."

Nightshade nodded. "Therein lies the guilt."

"Child, if you've followed your soul, what's there to be guilty about?" Abigail asked.

Nightshade looked at her lifelong friend and mentor. "You understand what I helped father try to do? We tried to take over Aster. In the process, I did horrible things... things that I did without compunction... things that directly contradicted what you've taught me over the years. Tens of thousands of people are dead because of my father, and I stood right by his side doing my part."

"Your father only cared about one thing... power. I think he had designs on the *Living Throne*."

Nightshade nodded agreement. "That was his eventual goal." The overlord paused. Abigail gave her the time she needed to continue. "But I've been given a second chance... though it's a chance I don't deserve. I should have died like my father as payment. I'm so sorry!" Nightshade suddenly broke down in tears.

Abigail held Nightshade tight and let the younger demon cry her feelings out. She understood how cathartic something as simple as a confession and a good cry can be for the spirit.

After a few minutes, Nightshade ceased weeping and disengaged from Abigail. "Thank you. I needed that. You've been my anchor for so long."

Abigail nodded. "And I'll always continue to be. Now tell me why you're here traveling with two mortals?"

"I need your help."

Abigail smiled. "Take me to meet your companions waiting with Tolves. We'll get acquainted over a hot meal and you can tell me your story. Then we'll see what I can do."

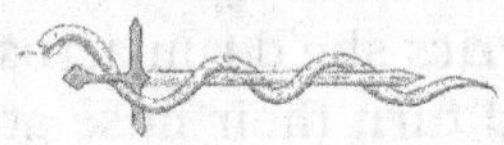

When Nightshade led Abigail into the front shop to meet her companions, Landross averted his eyes. Herbie, however, ran over to the gorgon to make a new friend. Abigail reached down and scratched the Abyssian dog behind the ears, and then on his belly as he rolled over, tongue flopping off to one side of his mouth.

"You need not worry, Landross," Nightshade remarked. "The power of a gorgon only asserts itself when she wishes it. As a further precaution, however, she's hidden her eyes behind a magical veil to make you and everyone else feel more comfortable."

Landross still refused to look at the gorgon. "And the snakes in her hair? Will they be as accommodating?"

"Remember what we discussed?" Father Goram reminded the knight. "Things in the Abyss aren't like the stories we've been traditionally taught. Nightshade explained this. You yourself have seen this since we crossed the barrier with Michael."

"Don't worry," Abigail added as she gave Herbie one last belly pet and stood. "My snakes won't bite... at least as long as you continue to be Nightshade's friend and ally."

Landross looked at the gorgon, then at Nightshade. "That's what worries me."

Father Goram laughed. "My pupil and this knight haven't seen eye to eye on many things. But he's coming around." The priest shoved back the hood of his cloak and extended his hand. "Horatio Goram, madam. It's a pleasure to meet you."

Abigail took the priest's offered hand. She felt the magical energy of a powerful cleric emanating from the touch. His grip was firm but not too firm in deference to the female gorgon. As for the hand itself, it had calluses, which was something she didn't expect. The clerics she'd run across were usually smug little popinjays who'd turn their nose at even the thought of doing manual labor or getting dirty. And also, unlike most other Prefecture clerics, his hand was warm and dry—not cold and wet like a Kematian eel. Then there were the eyes—experienced, intelligent, shrewd, warm, and caring. They were a pleasant combination found only in the peasantry class of the Abyss. If the hands and eyes were any indication of Father Goram's character, Abigail thought she was going to like him very much.

"So you're Nightshade's new mentor," the gorgon remarked. "I'm eager to learn how that happened. She's already accomplished... and powerful. Everyone understands that."

Father Goram's face remained pleasant. "And fears it."

Abigail nodded. "Through necessity."

"Perhaps," Father Goram remarked. "I'm aware of her abilities... but those lie in the Abyss's magic."

"There's another kind?" Abigail asked, genuinely curious.

"Indeed, madam," Father Goram answered. "But it's not only about the magic. It's also about how we use the magic. And most importantly, it's about the spirit behind the magic."

"I could use a hot meal," Nightshade interrupted. "That little shop we always went to... let's see, Tiamat's Horde? Is it still in business, Abigail?"

The gorgon smiled and nodded. "Let's go."

"Should we be out in the open like this?" Landross asked as they walked down the street.

"Woof!" Herbie barked agreement with his master... or was it the strange looking six-legged cat that had just run across their path?

"Look around you," Nightshade said. "What do you see?"

Landross did as his companion asked. "Nothing."

"The people of the Abyss avoid me like the plague," Abigail explained.

"That must be awfully lonely," Landross said. "Wouldn't you be more comfortable around your own kind?"

"You're being rude, Landross," Father Goram admonished.

Abigail smiled. "It's alright, Father..."

"No need for formality, Abigail. Please call me Horatio."

"Horatio it is," Abigail agreed. "Landross, there isn't anyone else of my kind in this Prefecture of the Abyss."

Landross looked confused. "How..."

"It's a story for another day, my new friend," Abigail said. "Let's just say I'm here in this dimension by accident, and I've managed to carve out a pretty decent existence. Besides, I didn't much care for the company of my people. The majority are as cruel as most of the overlords here."

"Woof!"

Herbie caught everyone's attention as he broke away to chase the six-legged cat. He just couldn't control his canine impulses any longer. Landross lunged to grab the dog, but Herbie gave him the slip.

Nightshade laughed. "Relax, Landross. Dogs and cats have been doing this forever. Even in the Abyss. He'll be back. If I remember correctly, that's the café over there."

"Right you are," Abigail concurred.

Since the gorgon frequented the café often, the female demon owner of the café, a dragon-human mix, and Abigail were good friends. She wasn't concerned about the gorgon's effect upon her customers, even as all of them paid their bills and left. They'd be back. Her food was that good.

"It's wonderful to see you again, Abby," the café owner said as she led them to a large table that had just become available.

"Are you well, Eliea?" Abigail asked.

Eliea beamed. "Business is booming!"

Abigail winced. "Sorry I drove your customers away. But my friends are hungry and I've little in my larder suitable for guests. I'll be happy to compensate you for the lost business."

Eliea shook her head. "Don't worry about it. My regulars should be used to you by now. As for the others..." The café owner shrugged. "Their loss. But as I said, business has been great. I've a new cook and his food is the best in the city. First mulled wine and then bowls of steamy hot field strider stew and warm bread, followed by freshly baked pastry slathered with milk-seed frosting. That'll fill up your bellies."

"Milk-seed frosting?" Landross said.

Nightshade smiled. "It tastes like maple on Aster."

Abigail nodded at Eliea. As the café owner walked away, she looked at her guests. "So what's the story?"

"I'm not sure where to begin," Nightshade began.

"Perhaps at your conversion from the Dark to the Light," Father Goram suggested. "I accepted Althaya and Michael's charge to mentor you... but we've never had a chance to sit and talk about it at any great length." Father Goram looked over at Abigail. "We've been busy."

"That's an understatement," Landross added. "Treason against a reigning sovereign, attempted regicide, civil war, invasion, and kidnapping leaves little room for anything else."

For the next three hours, the four, and Herbie, who had returned to beg for stew, sat and talked. The discussion covered everything that had happened on InnisRos, beginning with Nightshade's liaison with Mordecai, including how both she and her father deceived him, and his eventual death by Nightshade's own hand. Much of this Landross didn't know. His cautious acceptance of the former demon overlord became absolute as he listened to her story.

Nightshade talked about how she began to doubt her purpose even before the Dark Elf invasion led by her father. Both Father Goram and Landross were surprised to learn that the shift in Nightshade's point of view began as she was spying on Kristen and Tangus. Their devotion to each other, and to Emmy, had become something Nightshade herself secretly desired. In short, Nightshade wanted to be loved, and to love, regardless of the price she'd have to pay for deserting the dark path. And while the relationship between Kristen, Tangus, and Emmy showed her what was possible, Mariko, a master assassin that Nightshade herself had hired, showed her the way. If a lifelong killer for hire could turn away from such an existence and commit to another way of life, then so could she.

Father Goram took up the narrative and explained how the brief civil war, when Mordecai had sent the queen's army against his fortified monastery, came to be and how it was ended almost as soon as it began… although that ending hadn't come without a significant loss of life on both sides and the complete annihilation of a small town.

Next came the account of Aikanáro's Dark Elf invasion of InnisRos, the battle with, and the subsequent destruction of that army. Father Goram explained how Aikanáro had kidnapped his wife and the InnisRos queen before being slain, which was the reason they had come to the Abyss. Upon arrival, they learned of Belladonna's involvement with an anti-Kor resistance from the *B'nai Elohim* leader, Michael.

"All we know at the moment," Father Goram finished, "is that Aikanáro, before I killed him, released my wife and the queen to the mercies of the Abyss."

"And that Belladonna's resistance was broken," Nightshade added. "We don't know what happened to her. Did she escape? Was she captured or murdered?" Nightshade shrugged. "She's blood. As long as I'm sure she's broken father's influence, I want to give her a chance to live in peace and freedom. Aster offers that opportunity."

"And you don't know where to begin your search?" Abigail asked.

"That's not quite true," Father Goram said. "We're beginning here, hoping to enlist your aid."

Nightshade nodded. "We'd like your help to find an illusionist. We need to interact with the locals without raising suspicions, particularly in consideration of everything that's going on."

"Like finding ourselves in the middle of a bloody great war between the demons and the *B'nai Elohim*," Landross mumbled.

"Woof! Woof!" Herbie sat next to Landross. His tongue dangled out of his mouth and drool dropped to the floor in anticipation of his next handout, which the knight provided without thinking about it.

"A disguise won't fool an overlord," Abigail observed.

Nightshade concurred. "Only if it's more than a cursory glance. We intend to stay out of their way."

"It could work in the current environment," Abigail agreed. "What did you have in mind?"

"Taumaru."

Abigail smiled. "An excellent choice! Yes. I like it. And I know just the illusionist. But let's make things even more interesting. If you and your companions don't mind, I'd like to come with you. No one, even an overlord, is going to approach or challenge three Taumaru and the Prefecture's only gorgon without thinking long and hard about it."

"I was hoping you'd want to tag along," Nightshade remarked with a smile.

"You were correct, My Lord," Talvog said as he walked into Azzoth's office.

The overlord, sitting behind his desk, looked up from the relentless stream of paperwork he was required to complete. The disruption irritated him. Running a major metropolitan complex for Kor wasn't about sitting on a throne, eating, drinking, and gawking at the peasant servants. It required constant attention to such things as city finances, monthly requirements for the *Pillar*, personnel decisions, performance reports, law and order, and everything else the Prefecture leader threw his way. It was the kind of thing he wished he'd known before accepting the position. To make matters worse, his own underlords were incompetent... or lazy. Teaching them to take an active interest in the city's administration had been near impossible, and more than once, the city of Zir Tachoss set a record for the number of underlords sent to Kiss the *Pillar* in a month. "The knocker on my door is there for a reason, Talvog."

"Sorry, My..."

Azzoth cut him off. "I'm busy! Kor's driving me crazy with special orders regarding army support... and I have three generals threatening to sack the city if I don't give them wenches for their beds."

"Uh..."

"They can go to the brothels just like their troops, damn it!" Azzoth snapped. "Now take a seat and shut up! I need to concentrate!"

What Talvog thought was only going to be a few minutes turned into an hour. By the time Azzoth put the paperwork back into its folder, he was even angrier.

"Damn Kor and his war against the *B'nai Elohim*!" Azzoth shouted. "He can't take their fortress with twice what he has!"

"Several other armies are marching this way, My Lord," Talvog mentioned. "I'm sure Kor has thought it out..."

"You mean there's a reason for this madness?" Azzoth interjected. "Oh, I'm sure there is. But as usual, he's not talking and we, the cities, bear the brunt of his... his... his foolhardiness!"

"Careful, My Lord. You're talking treason."

Azzoth glared daggers at his underlord. "I'm not saying something I wouldn't say to Kor's face, Talvog. His army is costing us a fortune. And it's the same in Mar Koozzath and Ith Garrgod. I've spoken to their overlords. Other than our own troops, the army is tearing apart our cities brick by brick. Murder and rape are up, damage costs from marauding drunken soldiers are through the roof, and guild claims for reimbursement have already reached several thousand kronies."

"I'm sure Kor will help with any compensation we need to pay out," Talvog said.

Azzoth let out a quick burst of laughter. "How can you be so naïve? He expects us to do our duty… and this," the overlord said as he picked up the folder he'd just closed and slid it across his desk towards his underling, "is our duty."

Talvog, sitting on the other side of the desk, stopped the folder from dropping to the floor.

Azzoth looked at the underlord, who had wisely decided to keep his mouth shut. "You're here with an update on Nightshade?"

The underlord nodded. "Yes, My Lord. Nightshade is indeed in the city… though her presence is somewhat… un-Nightshade like. That's to say, she never transformed into her demon form. And you were correct. She's with the gorgon… along with two others. They met in the open at a street diner."

"Were you able to get close enough to hear what they were discussing?"

Talvog shook his head. "No one's willing to approach the gorgon that closely. And I have little confidence in our, or anyone's, ability to sneak up on Nightshade… given her reputation."

"I wouldn't want to either," Azzoth agreed as he pulled a communication crystal out of a desk drawer. "Her showing up now is probably just a coincidence, but I best let Kor make that determination… especially since the gorgon is involved. Her special skill set makes her as powerful as most overlords."

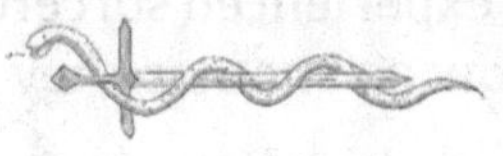

Kor was in a large room he liked to call the "Motivation Affirmation Conference Room." Seated around an enormous table were Emprusa, Azazael, Bezrameth, and Lilitu. Kor only used this room when he was unhappy with the performance of those he trusted to advance his policies. Specifically, when it became clear to him they lacked a certain degree of "enthusiasm" regarding his expectations. He sat at the head of the table made from the skeletons of overlords and underlords who'd displeased him over the years. Decorating the walls were tapestries of overlords being put to death in unimaginable and horrible ways—ways a person wouldn't believe possible until they saw it with their own eyes. The artist had perfectly captured the pain-filled faces of each victim as they endured unspeakable agony. To further the image, each tapestry had been magically enchanted to show the torture live and in real-time. The final touch—the pièce de résistance—was the stuffed bodies of those executed standing against the wall next to their death scene tapestry.

None of these particular underlings had been in the room before, and Kor relished the looks of shock that flashed in the eyes of each before they recovered their composure. Even Emprusa, who'd gotten a little too forward in her perceived position in his court, looked genuinely horrified.

Kor locked eyes with each before he called the gathering to order. "Report! Let's start with you, Lilitu."

The Magic Faction leader cleared her throat. "My Lord, we'll have your thousand doorway spells ready within the next two days."

"Good," Kor purred. "I knew you could do it. What's it going to cost you in personnel loss?"

"All of my seasoned sorcerers," Lilitu answered. "The rest will be new acolytes who'll know that one spell only."

"Any chance your experienced sorcerers will get cold feet?" Kor asked. "They know as soon as they open the doorway, a

B'nai Elohim guardian will close it... after it kills them."

"Death in the service of Kor is much preferable to death on Execution Hill as a traitor."

Kor nodded and shifted his attention to Azazael. "And you?"

"About half the armies are already at the front, though they're currently staying in or around Zir Tachoss, Mar Koozzath, and Ith Garrgod. So far, I've only had one complaint."

Kor steepled his talons. "A complaint? From one of my city overlords?"

Azazael shook his head. "No, My Lord... from a few of my generals. It seems Azzoth of Zir Tachoss denied their request for... ladies... to join them in their bedchambers. I might also mention the Entertainment Guild wasn't too happy about the lost revenue first-rate prostitutes would've charged for the generals pleasures. But they didn't offer up a formal complaint... at least not to me."

The Prefecture leader laughed. "That's as funny as it was when Azzoth told me about it."

"You've communicated with him?" Azazael asked.

Kor nodded. "He works for me, does he not? And he's right. Let the generals go to the same brothels as their soldiers... though I thought they'd have better things to do with their time. Things like planning their assault on the *B'nai Elohim*. Perhaps you should remind them of that?"

"I..." Azazael sputtered.

Kor interrupted him. "Don't bother. I want you to issue orders to all the armies at the front to move out of the cities and begin building their encampments and defensive positions for the assault. That should keep even the generals busy."

"Yes, My Lord!"

Kor wasn't finished. "When will the rest of the armies be on site?"

"A day and a half," Azazael responded as he directed a

smug smile towards Lilitu.

Kor looked at the two and understood exactly what was going on. In a way, he only had himself to blame. He encourages all his Faction leaders to compete against one another for his approval. After all, they can't land the leadership of a more powerful Faction, or keep their own, without it. Underlings perform better when there's something to perform for, and kissing the *Pillar* isn't the motivator it once was.

"When the rest catch up, give them a day to relax before moving them on to join up with the armies already in position," Kor ordered. "I want the troops well-rested, because when we begin the attack, I want nothing held back. I want to hit them like we've never hit them before. I want to hit them hard, often, and without consideration for casualties. They must believe this attack is a serious attempt to breach their fortress. Any hint of duplicity could ruin our chances of getting the assassin team to Aster. If that happens, my wrath will be severe and far ranging. Do you understand, Azazael?"

The Military Faction leader gulped and nodded.

Kor redirected his attention to Bezrameth. The Order sorcerer wasn't one of his Faction leaders, so the hold he had over him was tenuous. And though Kor was the demon's sovereign and held the sorcerer's fate in his hands, both understood the Prefecture leader needed Bezrameth much more than he needed any of his overlords... or anyone. No one else knew the spell that would get the assassin team to Aster under the noses of the *B'nai Elohim*.

"Is your team ready to go?" Kor asked.

Bezrameth nodded. "The underlord assigned to lead them seems to be quite competent. They're ready. My sorcerers are also ready... and eager for the opportunity to please me."

"You mean me," Kor interrupted.

"No, I don't," Bezrameth replied.

"Well played," Kor thought. *"Insult me to my face in front of*

witnesses and there's not a thing I can do about it… for now."

Bezrameth continued as if nothing had happened. "As for those special demons Azazael introduced me too," the sorcerer's jet-black eyes glowed through the blackness of his hood, "they're creepy… even for me. But by all that's evil, they'll get the job done. I could take over all of Aster… or any other world… with just a few thousand of them behind me."

"Was that a threat?" Kor wondered. "Well, you only have ten. Do your part and let me worry about the rest of Aster!"

Bezrameth smiled as he nodded. "Certainly, My Lord. Merely speculation."

Kor understood right then and there that the Order sorcerer and his allies were too dangerous to be left alive after this operation. He looked forward to lighting the bonfires of Execution Hill once again.

"Be ready to go in three days. Dismissed."

CHAPTER SEVEN

Jarsus, Sienna and the Lads – A Backstory

Jarsus and Sienna:

Jarsus Blackmantle, a young dwarf miner and member of the Oakenshield Dwarven Clan living under the Mahtan Mountains, was exploring an undocumented corridor. The exuberance of youth had led him onward into the unknown. Excitement gathered as he followed signs of a potentially large vein of pure silver. If the indications were correct, and he had no reason to believe they weren't, the ten percent finder's fee dwarven law would owe him was going to make him a very wealthy dwarf.

The light on Jarsus's helmet swept across the walls going down the corridor before him. But the silver vein he followed petered out.

"Whit th' hell!" Jarsus exclaimed out loud in frustration. Visions of wealth, females, and a life of luxury vanished as quickly as they had come. "It's juist a normal vein lik' hundreds o' ithers."

Jarsus sighed. He'd been warned about this by a few of the old-timers… veins that appeared to be a sure thing ending in a flash of regret and disappointment. There was only one thing to check before he turned back to rejoin his comrades. Veins of metal will sometimes make right-angle directional changes back into the rock. The young dwarf removed a hammer and chisel from his backpack and approached the place in the wall where the vein sign stopped.

"Nothing," Jarsus said after he opened the rock. "It juist stops. Nae enough silver 'ere tae pay last month's mead tab."

As he scanned his surroundings, hoping beyond hope to spot one more sign of silver before he turned back, he remembered he was in an unchartered tunnel. The discovery of new territories in and of itself was valuable to his clan and worth a finder's fee and well as a small stipend for future royalty considerations. Jarsus thought it was better than nothing, but he had to map it. Then another though struck him. Try as he might, he couldn't remember what passageways he'd taken to get where he was.

"Ah let that vein o' silver distract me 'n' noo I'm lost," Jarsus lamented to the darkness. "I'll be th' laughingstock o' th' entire clan!" The dwarf closed his eyes and took a deep breath. "Bearings! Bearings! Bearings!" he whispered as he concentrated. But no answers were forthcoming.

Jarsus sat down, opened his backpack, and spread everything out to do an inventory of his supplies. Being lost in the labyrinth of corridors beneath the Mahtan Mountains was survivable, but only if he didn't starve or die of thirst before finding his way out. He wasn't deep enough to be concerned about the meat-eating denizens of the lower underground.

"First hings first," Jarsus said as he took stock of his provisions. "Light… magic glow stone in helmet. Check!"

In his mind, the young dwarf continued down the list of survival requirements all dwarves learned from childhood. When finished, he was satisfied he had everything he needed to survive for at least a week.

"Plenty o' time," he thought as he repacked. Only this time he carried his pickaxe for self-defense instead of hammer and chisel.

After five days, Jarsus's confidence had changed to concern. Every corridor he explored either went deeper or turned out to be a dead end. He was exhausted, stiff, sore, and bleeding from wounds he'd received after several encounters with some of the denizens that dwelled underground at this level—such as the huge four-fanged cave spider or the nine-foot long spotted centipede.

Sitting and with his back against a wall, Jarsus had just eaten a half-ration of beef jerky and was considering a quick nap when he heard a faint growl just beyond the illumination of his helmet light.

Jarsus stood, his blood-coated pickaxe at the ready, and calmly awaited this latest challenge to his continued existence. The last five days had taught him many things about himself—amongst them courage, intelligence, and an impeccable ability to stay calm in even the direst of circumstances. He found a source of inner strength that he didn't know he had. Each battle for life he'd endured added to his experience, and it lifted his confidence every time he stood over the dead body of his adversary. Five days is a short time in the lifespan of a dwarf, but an eternity in a fight for existence.

A great hulking figure stopped just outside the light of Jarsus's helmet lamp.

"Why have you intruded upon my domain?" the figure asked. The distinctive female voice had communicated through telepathy.

Startled, Jarsus took a small step closer to the wall at his back. "You talk in mah head!" he exclaimed. "Only th' most powerful sorcerer kin dae this. Urr ye a sorcerer... er... sorceress?"

"Hardly!" a voice thought as an enormous bear-like creature moved into the light. It was multi-colored—blue, white, gray, and brown—with shiny blue eyes and what appeared to be colorful magical runes etched into its back and sides. It stood over ten feet high on its four legs.

"I'm not physically suited for talking with my mouth," the bear said in Jarsus's mind. *"Now answer my question!"*

"A'richt," Jarsus responded aloud. "Ah didn't ken ah wis in yer territory fur ah don't ken whaur a'm at."

"You're lost?"

"Ah prefer tae think o' it as a temporary situation... a moment o' geographical unclarity," the dwarf replied. "Ah will fin' mah wey back tae mah clan soon enough. A'm a dwarf efter all!"

"Harrumph!" the bear remarked. *"I'll lead you back. I'm called Sienna, by the way."*

"Jarsus Blackmantle… 'n' ah kin git back oan mah own!"

"Must I pick you up by your collar and carry you back, Jarsus Blackmantle?" the bear growled.

"Lead th' way," Jarsus replied. Getting lost was bad enough, but to be carried back like a child would be unbearable.

The path they followed filtered through a maze of tunnels and caverns that were unfamiliar to the dwarf. Unfamiliar and less than direct.

"Sienna… surely there's a quicker wey back," Jarsus remarked.

Sienna nodded in the light of Jarsus's helmet light. *"Yes, there is,"* she replied. *"In fact, there's several. But I'm not too keen on you coming back to my home with your clan brothers and sisters… something I'm sure you understand, considering how well you guard your own tunnels and caverns. I doubt even a dwarf can remember all the twists and turns we've taken."*

The protest Sienna expected from Jarsus never materialized, and the light from his helmet behind her dimmed. She turned and saw that Jarsus wasn't following, but instead he was staring at something in the wall.

"You want to get back to your clan?" Sienna asked as she moved closer to inspect what was intriguing the dwarf so.

Jarsus barely acknowledged Sienna. "Do ye ken whit that is?" he asked.

Sienna looked at the crystal embedded in the wall. *"Shiny rocks aren't my specialty. It's pretty, though."*

Jarsus looked at his companion. It suddenly occurred to him she might object if he removed the crystal from the wall and took it. They might still be in her territory.

"My fowk ca' this amethyst rubyhalite crystal. It's extremely rare 'n' valuable… na, mair than that. It's worth a king's ransom… or a dragon's horde. Yin o' th' reason's tis sae rare is that tis ne'er fun in a vein lik' gowd or silver… bit aye by itself. There's na rhyme or reason tae tis discovery… na signs or physical indications whilk leid tae it. Thay say sorcerers kin sense tis presence… bit that's ne'er bin substantiated. Ah ken o' ainlie three that's ever bin found… though this one's aboot a hundred times th' size o' th' others."

Sienna considered this bit of information, but decided it was of no use to her. The dwarves and surface dwellers place value on many things—shiny gems and rocks, wealth, possessions, their position within society—and will kill or be killed defending this accumulation of physical objects or personal power. Her people see things differently. To her, the only thing of value are friends and family, as well as the condition of her soul.

"If you want it, then it's yours. Just be quick about it!"

"I'll split it wi' ye fifty-fifty," Jarsus said as he used his hammer and chisel to chip the crystal out of the stone encasing it.

Five minutes later, he'd loosened the large crystal enough to release it from the wall. He blew on his fingers to dry any sweat before grasping and pulling it out of the surrounding stone. He held the crystal into the light of his helmet and examined it. The amethyst rubyhalite crystal was surprisingly light. But that didn't subtract from its solid composition. Pure amethyst rubyhalite crystal is one of the hardest substances known. Only creation stone, which is rumored to be sentient, is harder.

Jarsus's helmet light unexpectedly sputtered and went out, leaving the dwarf and bear in total darkness.

"That's odd," Jarsus thought. *"Th' magic light o' mah helmet can't be extinguished except be a darkness spell."*

Jarsus knew his vision, like that of all dwarves, would adjust to the darkness enough for him to make out shapes and movements. As he waited for his eyes to adapt, he heard strangling noises.

"Sienna," Jarsus whispered. "Are ye okay?"

There was no response other than the strangulation sounds. With caution the dwarf moved towards the source of the noise, knowing even before he got there, they came from his gigantic companion. The forgotten crystal in his hand abruptly flared in brilliant white light.

The light revealed a fantastic creature even larger that the great bear. It appeared to be ethereal in composition, with pieces of it fading in and out between different otherworldly realms. Jarsus had trouble distinguishing what was and what wasn't real about it. Great tentacles swam in the air around a giant, undulating blob of undetermined origin and composition. Long, stringy hair-like strands with multiple claw-like spikes at the end covered each tentacle. Several of them had attached themselves to Sienna, who, other than making strangling noises, appeared to be in a stupor, unaware of her surroundings or the grip of death the creature had on her.

Sienna suddenly roared in pain and what sounded like despair. Jarsus looked on as he thought about what he could do to help the bear. He relived the last few moments, wondering why the creature appeared when it did. The obvious connection was the amethyst rubyhalite crystal.

"Could it be ah released that thing whin ah took th' crystal oot o' th' wall?" he asked himself.

Following a hunch, Jarsus approached the beast with the crystal held out in front. The interdimensional creature recoiled, released Sienna from its grip, and roared—an ear-piercing, high-pitched sound that was eerily wraithlike. The creature turned on Jarsus but held its distance.

Jarsus, correctly surmising the amethyst rubyhalite crystal was the creature's weakness, slowly moved forward, forcing it to back away from the still stunned Sienna. As he did so, five eyes opened in the central part of the blob-like body. Hatred and fury emanated from those eyes, each directed at the dwarf. With the eyes came the voices in his head.

"Drop the crystal!"

"You will die for your interference!"

"I will strip the skin from your body!"

"You don't comprehend the foolishness of your actions!"

"Your suffering will last a thousand years!"

What was one creature then multiplied into two, then three, until five creatures floated in the air where there once was one. All five approached Jarsus.

"Drop the crystal!"

"You will die for your interference!"

"I will strip the skin from your body!"

"You don't comprehend the foolishness of your actions!"

"Your suffering will last a thousand years!"

The strength of the five appeared to be enough to overcome the effect the amethyst rubyhalite crystal had on the one. Jarsus looked back at Sienna and saw she was still incapacitated.

"Wonderful!" Jarsus thought.

The dwarf rolled the crystal towards the creatures. Though it didn't force them back, its closer proximity was enough to force them to scatter away both from the crystal and each other, which was what Jarsus hoped would happen. With wild abandon, the dwarf raised his pickaxe and attacked the nearest blob. But the blinding speed of his attack wasn't enough to prevent one of the creature's tentacles from reaching out and impaling Jarsus through the thigh. Jarsus screamed in pain as he brought his pickaxe down to sever the tentacle from the embedded claw. The claw vanished in a soundless explosion, which triggered a second scream from the dwarf.

Jarsus nearly slipped on his own blood as he staggered

back a step. But dwarves have a low center of gravity and don't fall easily. He spun to avoid another claw-strike and smashed his pickaxe deep into the eye of the blob, which screamed and flew in all directions, hitting the floor, walls, and ceiling of the corridor as it did so.

Jarsus watched as it went through its death throes. But not for long. He turned to face the other four as he wondered why they hadn't attacked. Another surprise awaited him. The remaining blobs were surrounded by six creatures as unlikely as the blobs. Each of these new creatures was floating in the air, though swimming might be a better term for what they were doing, by beating large wings. The two different creature races hung in the air, staring at each other. Combatants or allies? Jarsus couldn't be sure.

The dwarf backed away while he had the chance and knelt next to Sienna. Several claws had impaled her which, when he removed them, appeared to do more damage coming out than going in. As Jarsus did what he could to control the bleeding, he glanced up at the standoff. Nothing had changed.

"Well, gang ahead, ye blunder-headed twits," Jarsus screamed in frustration, fear, and confusion. "Get oan wi' it!"

Dwarf invectives continued to rain down upon the creatures as Jarsus bandaged Sienna's wounds. Fortunately for the bear, all dwarves going underground packed a kit designed for emergencies and were trained to use it. Within a few seconds, he was so immersed in saving Sienna's life he forgot about the strange creatures altogether. As he tied up the last stitch, he remembered and glanced up. The blobs were gone, as were the six floaters, for want of another name. In their place were six completely different creatures, as beautiful as the others were ugly, calmly staring at him and Sienna.

"Big birds," Jarsus thought. Aloud: "Well, cheers. Noo ye kin gang aboot yer business 'n' ah will gang aboot mine."

"Will your companion survive?" one floater asked. It

sounded like tweets and whistles, but Jarsus's mind translated every word. Familiar with magic in his own world, and how it can be used to make communication between species easier, the dwarf didn't let this new development catch him by surprise. He just accepted it.

Jarsus looked at Sienna. She was no longer making strangling noises and her breathing was steady and unlabored. But the dwarf was still concerned about the amount of blood loss.

"I don't know," Jarsus said in response to the floater's question.

A different floater drifted over to Sienna and hovered in the air above her. "This creature will survive its wounds," it declared. "She only requires a few..." It paused as if searching for the correct word.

"Hours?" Jarsus prodded.

The floater bobbed its head. "Yes... hours of rest. You must guard her from the perils in this realm until she awakens."

Jarsus looked at the beautiful creature. "Laddie, ah git tae git back tae mah clan. Besides, wur in her territory, sae she shuid be safe enough... 'n' she wanted me gaen as quickly as ah kin anyway. I'll juist tak' th' crystal 'n' go."

"This one," the first floater said as it pointed towards Sienna, "needs your help... just as you needed ours against the Apophis."

"So that's whit those things ur called," Jarsus said as he looked at the slumbering Sienna. *"They mak' a valid point,"* he thought. Both he and Sienna would probably be dead without the floater's freely given interference. Besides, in the end, Jarsus knew he wouldn't leave Sienna behind as defenseless as she was, anyway.

"I'll look after her 'til she's fully awake 'n' able tae defend herself," the dwarf conceded. "Or 'til she chases me away."

All six of the floaters nodded, then, one by one, disappeared, presumably going back to wherever they came from.

Jarsus suddenly had a craving to learn more about his benefactors. "Hauld yer horses!" he called out just before the last one left. "Who urr ye? Wull ah ever catch up wi' ye again? Whaur dae ye come from?"

The remaining floater drifted over to Jarsus and settled on the stone floor before him. Even as short-statured as dwarves are, the floater only stood half as tall.

"For reasons you'll never understand, we helped because we're in your debt," the creature said. "We call ourselves the Forseti, and we inhabit another place in time and space. We are what you might call mercenaries... though we seek balance, or equilibrium, instead of financial or personal gain. For many years, we have sought the renegade Apophis... those who you and your friend exposed. And thanks to the both of you, they're once again restrained and in the custody of the Universal Authority."

"Universal Authority?" Jarsus remarked. While it was true he wanted answers, what he'd just heard went far beyond anything he expected. "Uh..."

The floater smiled. "We'll meet again," it said as it faded away.

Jarsus stared at the now empty corridor. All telltale hints of evidence that there was a battle had disappeared as well.

"What happened?" a voice asked in Jarsus's head.

Jarsus looked at Sienna, who was slowly rising. "How dae ye feel?"

"Different..." she answered, *"but well. Something's changed within me. I can't explain it, but I think it's time to end my reclusion and see the light of day once again?"*

Jarsus nodded. "Then we've baith changed... 'n' it's fur th' best, ah suppose. Besides, na self-respecting giant bear wha communicates thro' telepathy shuid remain isolated doon 'ere living aff rock spiders 'n' cave centipedes."

"There's also fish if you know where to find them," Sienna added. *"Big, fat, juicy fish with no eyes. I do missed them cooked, though. So... what happened while I was unconscious? All I remember was a blob... then incredible pain."*

"It's a story ah be telling ye at anither time," Jarsus answered. "Ye ken, I've bin thinking. Mibbie we shuid partner up? I'll split mah commission fur finding th' amethyst rubyhalite crystal wi' ye. That shuid be enough fur us tae stairt oor ain, brave heart mining operation. Wi' yer knowledge o' th' caves 'n' caverns beyond they claimed by mah clan... 'n' mah knowledge o' precious 'n' semi-precious stanes 'n' mining ability, we cuid be extremely successful."

"Well then, pick up your rock... our rock... and let's get out of here," Sienna said.

It took Jarsus a few minutes to empty his backpack of non-essentials to make room for the crystal, after which they began their ascent back to his home. Five days later the two emerged from the caverns and corridors of below to the outskirts of the Oakenshield Clan territory and the safety of dwarven civilization.

As they traveled, the two shared life stories as well as their hopes and dreams for the future. Whereas Jarsus was young and full of excitement for things to come, Sienna, being older and far wiser, was filled with cynicism regarding what life held for the pair... although she came to understand, with Jarsus's encouragement, that whatever lie in front of her was better than the minimalistic existence she was living beneath the surface. Jarsus had also told her about the close relationship the elves of InnisRos had with the giant dire wolves unique to that island. He thought the two of them might share the same connection. Sienna agreed with the dwarf's assessment of their association.

Their arrival into the outskirts of Oakenshield Clan territory didn't go without incident. Because of her enormous size, the guards didn't greet Sienna with enthusiasm, and Jarsus had to convince them she wasn't a threat. Even so, the two were still forbidden to continue until one of the clan elders arrived to give his permission. But any suspicions the dwarves had about Sienna evaporated when Jarsus presented the amethyst rubyhalite crystal to the clan elders. None of the elders had ever seen one as large and as pure. It was priceless... worth at least ten times the platinum, gold, and silver they had in their entire treasury, as well as what they were mining. The elders made Jarsus and Sienna heroes of the clan. The dwarves planned magnificent feasts in their honor and they declared a week of holiday to celebrate Jarsus's return from, and the discovery of, the uncharted regions below. Not only did the crystal he found exponentially increase the monetary worth of the clan, but the new caverns and corridors would at least double the clan's territory and their subsequent mining operation. Images of finding even more amethyst rubyhalite crystal in the newly discovered corridors and caverns danced in the dreams of the clan elders and miners. Dominance over the other dwarf clans of Aster suddenly appeared to be a distinct possibility.

Jarsus and Sienna's celebrity changed when the young dwarf, himself blinded by his new status within the clan and the wealth about to land in his personal coffers, was refused the full ten percent finder's fee commission entitled to him by clan law for discovering the crystal and the new territory. He was told the clan couldn't afford the payment. Instead, they offered him an honorary position as an elder, a small monthly stipend, promotion to mining crew boss, and the hand of a minor noble's daughter. Jarsus didn't believe the compensation offered fully recognized what he'd given his clan. So he stole the crystal, rightfully his by dwarven law, and escaped to the outside world. His clan followed. They wanted the crystal back at all costs, even if it violated their own laws.

They put a bounty on his head. Jarsus Blackmantle would pay for his insubordination and treachery.

Following two months of harrowing escapes from bounty hunters, mercenaries, and Oakenshield Clan hunters, the dwarf and his companion successfully navigated the crossing of the Greater Boreskyre Mountains and into Draugen Pesta—the land of the giants—and presented themselves to the king.

The king of the Draugen Pesta, upon hearing the story of the Jarsus, felt the Oakenshield Clan had broken their own law and granted asylum to the dwarf and the bear. So long as they stayed on the eastern side of the Greater Boreskyre Mountains, Draugen Pesta guaranteed their lives as free citizens, protected from any attempt by the Oakenshield Clan to claim either Jarsus, Sienna, or the crystal. They settled in the nation's capital of Saint Petersburg.

Over years, which turned into decades, Jarsus used the value of the amethyst rubyhalite crystal to build a substantial, and respectable, life in the land of the giants. Sienna, in her own way, also gathered a measure of notoriety because of her size, intelligence, and limited ability to do basic magical spells, such as fire, light, and healing. Her natural affection for children also helped to establish her popularity. Whenever Sienna walked the streets of Saint Petersburg, she'd give rides if asked, provide healing to the poor, and perform simple magic tricks.

The dwarf never forgot the debt he owed the Draugen Pesta people during all that time. Besides securing his position in giant society, he did whatever he could to repay both his adopted country and its citizens. By the time Princess Daphnia came into his life, a meeting of his own design, Jarsus was one of the most learned and powerful persons in all of Draugen Pesta, if not the entire world. Part of that was because of his own perseverance, hard work, and a natural ability to think critically and logically. But another aspect of Jarsus' success—

the true foundation of his knowledge—was his relationship with "the Lads."

The Lads:

The Forseti, or "the Lads" as Jarsus Blackmantle calls them, are a race of eternal beings with the wisdom of immortality. They travel inter-dimensionally between worlds and universes, establishing and reinforcing balance between right and wrong, light and dark, good and evil. They are warriors. They are emotionless harbingers of justice. They are the uncompromisable bringers of retribution. They are the guardians against chaos and entropy.

The old gods created them. But unlike the Sylphs of Aster, they remained true to their calling. And for the first time in their long existence, they owed a debt—a debt to the mortal Jarsus Blackmantle. This caused a period of consternation amongst the Forseti. All debt must be paid. Only this would satisfy the balance ledger. The only question was how that debt should be settled?

Since most of the old gods have long since left in favor of the younger gods, the Forseti had only themselves to rely upon for answers to questions about the nature of their existence. So it was as they considered the debt. With the help of Jarsus Blackmantle, the Apophis were recaptured, which returned the balance they disrupted in the multiverse. These were undeniable facts agreed upon by all. But in the minds of most Forseti, there was no debt for those that hadn't interacted with the mortals to capture the Apophis. But that didn't end the matter. During their discussions about Jarsus Blackmantle and what they owed him, they realized they had undergone a transformation since the abandonment of the old gods. They had evolved from tunnel-visioned creations serving one purpose into beings of independent thought and rationalization. With that came the realization they'd been following a failed mandate.

Chaos and entropy weren't unnatural universal traits that needed to be eliminated to achieve balance. Instead, they were necessary to support the stability of the multiverse. For what value did anything have without its natural opposite to give it worth? Good must have evil to survive. Order must have chaos. There can be no equilibrium without the yin and yang of all forces operating together.

To the logical mind of the Forseti, and in consideration of recent revelations, half of them decided they must represent chaos, while the others supported order. Only through this measure could the Forseti say their true calling, as designed by the old gods, would be fulfilled.

As for the Forseti who banished the Apophis, they opted, because of their own personal convictions, to stay on the side of law and order and to continue their association with Jarsus Blackmantle and Sienna. Their interaction with the mortals in the underground corridors of the Mahtan Mountains during the expulsion of the Apophis had interested them. They found that they genuinely liked the young, brash dwarf and his huge companion. It was just one of many things they were to experience during their relationship with the mortals. In return, the Forseti taught Jarsus and Sienna many new things about the multiverse, its foundation and operation, the need for balance in all matters, as well as many other philosophies and concepts not too dangerous for mortal consumption. To this end, they set boundaries to which of Jarsus's questions they'd answer.

They also determined to do everything they could to protect Jarsus, Sienna, and their friends against any harm that might come their way. Those Forseti believed Jarsus's safety was necessary to maintain balance on the world of Aster. But that wasn't their only motivation. To their great surprise, they also discovered they wished to do so out of loyalty and love… because without him and his bear companion, the Forseti would never have experienced laughter, joy, or hope in a future untainted by the limitations of their immortality. Jarsus taught them how to look towards a never-ending future that can differ from their past. He taught them a way to live life as if it were as fleeting as the seconds that filled the day.

CHAPTER EIGHT

Aster – Draugan Pesta

"Did I just hear you correctly, Michael?" Lord Ternborg asked. "You're asking me to send several thousand warriors to the Abyss to help you fight a demon uprising?"

"We're not short on manpower, Viktor," Sofia pleaded. "You've brought everyone back from the west… we're no longer at war with the Hyrokkin… and Michael helped return Daphnia to us."

Lord Ternborg rubbed his eyes. The herbs he'd taken for the headache he had when he entered the room have done little to curtail the pain. He clapped his hands once. A servant entered the audience chamber.

"Please bring us a tray of cheeses, meat, and bread," the Draugen Pesta king ordered. If herbs and drink wouldn't work on his headache, then maybe food would.

Lord Ternborg then looked sheepishly at Michael. "Sorry. Before coming here, I spent the greater part of the day with my exchequer discussing finances. The size of my headache matches the size of the Greater Boreskyre's."

"He normally comes to me," Sofia mentioned.

Lord Ternborg nodded. "I know. But he flagged me down and cornered me before I had a chance to escape. As he sees it, it's his duty to make sure the king hears about things firsthand… particularly since we now have the added burden of financing the restoration of those lands the Hyrokkin had occupied. He doesn't understand why I won't force the Hyrokkin to pay restitution, by the way."

"Neither do I," Sofia murmured. "Particularly since they're willing."

"The cost of a continued war would be far more expensive," Lord Ternborg answered. "Right now our peace is tenuous at best... and a demand for restitution would, even though the Hyrokkin queen is agreeable, leave a foul taste in everyone's mouth. Well, except for the exchequer."

"Peace will never be as costly as war," Michael added.

Both Lord and Lady Ternborg looked at the *B'nai Elohim* leader.

Michael continued. "You don't measure the price of war in pieces of gold and silver. The true price is the blood, sweat, and tears of those who must wage it. The price of peace is only minor by comparison. A wise leader..."

"A wise leader understands that," Sofia interrupted as she looked at her husband. "And my husband is the wisest person I've ever known."

Lord Terborg cleared his throat. "Let's move on to Michael's request."

"Indeed," Michael agreed. "But I haven't given you as much information as you deserve, considering what I'm about to ask. Like you, Lord Ternborg..."

"Call me Viktor,"

Michael nodded. "With pleasure. As I was saying, I'm used to issuing orders and expecting them to be carried out. And like the other immortals of my kind, I'm somewhat... condescending... towards the mortal races of Aster. I assume I know better than them."

"You mean you're a pompous ass?" Lord Ternborg remarked. "That you're arrogant, contemptuous, and more than just a little self-important towards us country bumpkins here on Aster?"

"Viktor!" Sofia exclaimed.

Michael shook his head. "No, Sofia, he's correct. Consider the conditions I demanded when you used the locket to ask for my help... that I'd help *only* if I approved of the reasoning behind your appeal... never stopping to consider that you might understand what's best for you more than I."

"Listen to him, Sofia," Lord Ternborg said. "It's time to treat each other as allies, and even friends, rather than master and slave… though Sofia and I both realize your immortality makes you wiser by far."

Sofia nodded.

"You were going to give us more background information, Michael?"

Michael nodded. "You already know the *B'nai Elohim* serve as guardians over the Abyss. That we keep demons from crossing the plane between the worlds of demons and mortals."

"Unless a mortal willfully opens a portal from this end and calls forth a demon," Sofia noted. She understood much more about the occult than her husband. "You can't stop that, can you?"

Michael shook his head. "No we can't. Fortunately, most mortals know enough to leave demonkind alone. Only fools think they're powerful enough to keep demons as pets."

"Plenty of those around," Lord Terborg remarked.

Michael nodded. "On both sides. Luckily, or most likely by design, nature has a way of dealing with fools. Many demons have an instinctive desire to control mortals and not the other way around. They'll fight and rebel every second of their captivity, even though it costs them a chance to stay on Aster. Sooner or later the demon will win its freedom, for no mortal can withstand the hatred of an imprisoned demon indefinitely, and exact revenge. This remedies the situation quite effectively… sending the demon back to the Abyss while removing one fool from Aster. But if demons arrive on Aster by way of their own volition…" Michael let the rest of his thought hang out in the open.

Silence reigned between the three as each considered the danger until Sofia broke it. "As my pa-pa was fond of saying, 'Our goose is cooked.'"

Lord Ternborg smiled at Michael. "Sofia's pa-pa always had a way of turning a phrase."

"Most of what I believe the demons are doing is based upon supposition," Michael answered after a brief pause. "But perhaps it's best I start with a brief explanation of the spatial-time relationship between Aster and the Abyss, the *B'nai Elohim's* involvement, and the precautions put in place by the old gods to maintain the balance."

Lord Ternborg rubbed his temples again.

"Your headaches come back, love?" Sofia asked.

Lord Ternborg didn't respond. *"I need a vacation,"* he thought as Michael began his narrative.

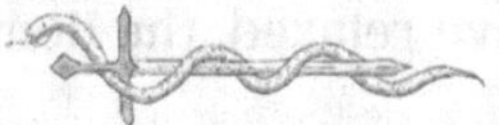

For the next three hours, Michael talked about the political, cultural, and socio-economic history of the Abyss. He explained how the denizens had evolved over the millennia into two distinct and separate classes—ruling and peasant—and how the peasant class, though inferior, had created a safety net from the natural cruelty of their demon overlords by devising a system of guilds which provided the essential services the ruling class required to sustain their coveted and lavish lifestyles.

There was a guild for every kind of convenience delivered to the ruling class—food services, manufacturers, farmers, ranchers, maintenance, sanitation, builders, entertainment, and administration, to name but a few. As the generations passed, the guild format became so successful smaller guild associations, called coalitions, formed within the larger guilds. Such examples of guild associations were "The Coalition of Prostitutes, Escorts, and Streetwalkers" within the Entertainment Guild and "The Coalition of Fieldworkers" within the Farmers Guild. Not only did the guilds and coalitions protect their members from enlistment into the city armies, but they also provided a haven from random selection for the *Pillar*. The formation of the guilds and their coalitions are also credited with the foundational transformation of demonkind itself.

No longer was savagery necessary to survive in the Abyss. Under guild protection, a demon peasant could live a reasonably safe life, raise a family, advance in society through hard and productive work, and be happy. That, in turn, taught demon peasants they no longer needed to be cruel. They learned they could place their trust in the system, and that they didn't need to rely on savagery to continue to exist. With the survival imperative relaxed, the demon peasants learned they could love.

It's uncertain when the demon overlords realized they'd been circumvented. What can be said for sure is that the guild structure, as it stands, works for everyone, and that balance, of a kind, had been achieved. As a result, this particular Abyss Prefecture had developed a civilized society despite the demon overlords.

Next, Michael discussed the physical geography of the Abyss and its space-time relationship with the mortal world. He explained that the Abyss, if viewed from the top down, would appear as if thousands of islands were floating in space. Each of the islands represented the boundary of a distinct and separate Abyss Prefecture... an autonomous Abyssian world. Every single one of the Prefectures was connected to a unique world in the mortal realm... a world that sat in one of many different universes. Michael referred to this intersection between a Prefecture and a mortal world as the "Juxtaposition Point." It was the only link between the demon and mortal domains. If demonkind ever escaped through the Juxtaposition Point and established a foothold on the adjoining mortal world, it was conceivable they could then spread out to other worlds in that universe, or possibly other universes as well.

While there's no physical link between the thousands of Abyss Prefectures, there are communications between each. When one Prefecture leader discovers something significant that could benefit all demonkind, it wasn't long before each of the other Prefecture leaders had that same information. Therefore, if one Prefecture leader figured out how to get through the Juxtaposition Point, soon all the other Prefecture leaders would know about it as well. Then it'd be possible for demonkind to unite and begin a long, bloody campaign to control all the mortal worlds in all the mortal universes.

The old gods created the *B'nai Elohim* to guard against such a possibility. Each Abyss Prefecture has a contingent of one-thousand *B'nai Elohim*, called a *Sayerat*, to guard the Juxtaposition Point and prevent the widespread dispersion of demonkind into the mortal domain. The guardians are impervious to demon magic and physical attacks. The only weakness of the *B'nai Elohim* is the source of their power—the Johari.

There is one Johari for each *Sayerat*. The old gods hid them on those mortal worlds connected to an Abyss Prefecture through the Juxtaposition Point. The Johari takes many different forms. It can be as small as a pebble or as large as a city. It's a sentient being with a gentle disposition. While it doesn't understand its true purpose, it senses its importance to the universal balance between good and evil, and to the survival of mortal kind. To that end, each Johari has natural defenses, such as precognition, to insure its continued existence.

Besides the guardians imperviousness to demon magic and physical attacks, they can also sense when demons open doorway spells... spells that would grant demons access to the mortal worlds... and shut it down. If a Johari were to be destroyed, so would its companion Juxtaposition Point.

Besides losing their imperviousness to demon magic and physical attacks, the *B'nai Elohim* guardians would also lose the power to detect and respond to any attempt to open magical doorways between the Abyss and the mortal world. Without the Juxtaposition Point, entire armies could march from the one realm to the next.

"We'd be powerless to stop the resultant migration," Michael concluded.

Lord Ternborg pulled a cigar from an inside pocket of his vest and chewed on one end as he digested Michael's narrative.

"So you feel the upcoming attack is a ruse to keep your people busy while they open these doorways you spoke of?" Sofia asked.

"It's much more devious than that," Lord Ternborg said as he lit his cigar using a candle.

Michael nodded. "I believe so as well but would like to hear what you're thinking."

"Answer a question for me first," Lord Ternborg asked. "This Johari you spoke of. Is it possible the demons know of its existence and importance to the *B'nai Elohim*?"

Michael shrugged. "I don't see how... but I suppose it's possible."

Lord Ternborg nodded. "Can't ever assume a secret stays a secret for any length of time. How about location?"

"Even I don't know the location... just that it's somewhere on Aster," Michael replied. "Nor do I know its particular form."

A small cloud of cigar smoke wafted around the Draugen Pesta king. "You can bet the demons know... or at least have figured out a way to locate the Johari once they've crossed the Juxtaposition Point. Otherwise, what's the point? The *B'nai Elohim* are the only thing standing in their way, so they need to take you guys out. They can only do that by destroying the Johari... because as long as you maintain your power over them, they lose."

"Stands to reason," Michael said.

"What happens when a doorway spell is used by a demon?" Lord Ternborg inquired.

"We detect it and one of us traces it back to its origination point to locate the demon conjuring the magic and shut it down," Michael responded. "Brutally."

"And if several hundred... or a thousand... sorcerers invoked the doorway spell at the same time?" Lord Ternborg asked.

Michael laughed. "Impossible! For two reasons. One... I doubt very much they have that many trained magic users. And two, the Magic Faction..."

"Magic Faction?" Sofia asked.

"Factions are part of the Prefecture's organizational structure," Michael explained. "Each oversees their own specialty. For example, there's a Faction for magic, military, merchants, and so forth. Similar to your leadership councils."

Sofia nodded.

Michael resumed. "The Magic Faction leader would never allow so many magic users to be killed."

"So that's what you meant when you said 'brutally,'" Sofia observed. There was a slight hint of disapproval in the tone of her voice.

Michael's eyes turned steely hard as he looked over at the Draugen Pesta queen. "Too many innocent lives are at stake to handle things any other way. You yourself withheld mercy when your unlawful possession of the locket I gave your ancestors was discovered."

Sofia returned Michael's stare with a fierce one of her own. "He had it coming," she replied to the accusation. But the guardian made a valid argument.

"Let's calm down," Lord Ternborg remarked. "As for your point, Michael, I don't think the demons will spare anyone if they believe they have a chance to end your dominance over them once and for all... even if it takes their entire army and every single one of their sorcerers to do it. They can replace those at their leisure. Without you or the Johari standing in the way, there's plenty of time to take Aster."

Michael stared at the Draugen Pesta king. "So you're suggesting..."

"I'm suggesting the demons have two feints involved," Lord Ternborg said. "They'll attack your fortress while conjuring the doorway spells, forcing your people to respond to both at the same time. My warriors defending your fortress won't be something the demons will expect, but it won't muck up their plans. In my opinion, the actual attempt to open a doorway to Aster will occur while the first two feints are ongoing. But this spell won't be the same as the others. By that, I mean I believe they've found a way to open a doorway unbeknownst to you... one you can't detect... so they can slip in a team to destroy the Johari."

"Why the ruse?" Sofia asked. "Why not just use the new spell?"

"The answer to that probably lies in their conditioning," Lord Ternborg answered. "Too many millennia of dominance by the *B'nai Elohim* to overcome the doubt all demons are most likely born with. Michael's warriors are their gatekeepers... never defeated... relentless in their guardianship... and all powerful. To most demons, they're probably gods."

"If what you're saying about this new spell is true, how do we guard against it?" Michael queried.

"I'm not sure you can."

There was a sudden knock on the conference room door. The three stared at the door in irritation, though they knew it must be important or else they wouldn't be disturbed.

"Enter," Sofia called out.

Colonel Florentina Antonovich, Lord Ternborg's executive officer, opened the door. "I apologize for the interruption, Your

Grace, but you'll want to hear this."

Lord Ternborg nodded. "I trust your judgment, Florentina."

"We have a runner from the Hyrokkin queen," Colonel Antonovich explained. "It appears she doesn't have as much control over her army as she thought she had. In the name of peace, she wants you to invade."

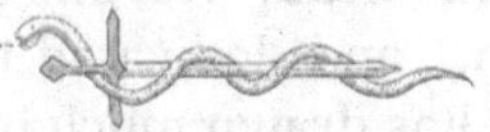

Lord Ternborg adjourned the meeting for a few hours so they could receive the Hyrokkin messenger. He asked Michael to sit in because his impressive size and appearance would intimidate the centaur. It did. The Hyrokkin's superior smirk, one thing peace hadn't put a stop to, dropped from his face when he saw the immortal. Michael flapped his iridescent wings one time for effect.

"Thesonia wants me to invade?" Lord Terborg asked.

Loukocus, the messenger, didn't hear the question. He was too busy staring at Michael.

"I asked you a question," Lord Ternborg said.

"Huh?" Loukocus replied. He took one last look at the *B'nai Elohim* leader before he answered. "Well… not exactly. The queen's been forced to put down several uprisings by the military since this so-called peace between our two races. It's costing the blood of many good Hyrokkin and resources that could be put to better use. She wants you to send a strong contingent of warriors… say two or three thousand… to be her guests. Her Grace believes this show of force, standing side by side with her own personal bodyguard, will be enough to discourage any further rebellions. The queen would also like to see someone who'd be willing to act as your personal representative. It should be someone who won't be afraid to interact with our people… someone whom you think might bridge the gap of distrust between us."

"Sending you foodstuffs and goods isn't enough?" Sofia asked.

"Of which you've been well compensated for," Loukocus snapped back. "We've filled your coffers extensively."

"Filled our coffers? Is that how Thesonia sees it?" Lord Ternborg asked.

Loukocus shook his head. "No. She seems to be sincerely thankful for the help... and dedicated to insuring the peace holds. But that stand has drawn much ire from people within and without the government... people she thought she could count on... people who are now willing to commit treason to end her reign."

"So basically she wants a larger security detail," Sofia observed.

Loukocus nodded. "If you want to put it that way. Keep in mind the peace will hold only as long as she remains in power, or at least until you can win over the people. That's the only thing the fringe elements that want her overthrown fear. Traditionally, the Hyrokkin people have been slow to move. But once they do, they spare no one. If they get behind the queen, her rule will be secure, and your presence will help to guarantee that. It's for your benefit as much as it is for hers."

An idea formed in Lord Ternborg's mind. But it was an idea that was going to require some very deft maneuvering to get it done.

"Alright, Loukocus, I'll give it consideration and have an answer for you tomorrow," Lord Ternborg said. "Florentina!"

"My Lord!"

Lord Ternborg motioned for his executive officer to come closer. "Please show Loukocus to one of the guest rooms. Get him food, drink, and a bath if he wants it."

Colonel Antonovich nodded.

"Then lock him in for the night," Lord Ternborg whispered.

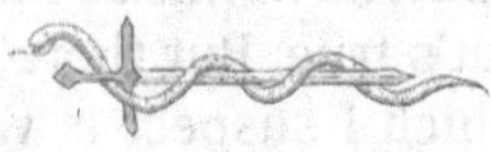

"Make sure..."

"Make sure his room is guarded," Colonel Antonovich added. "I've already anticipated that, Your Grace."

"Are you going to send two or three thousand warriors?" Sofia asked.

Lord Ternborg shook his head. "I don't want the Hyrokkin people to feel they're being occupied. That could actually tip things away from the queen's favor. I believe *who* we send as our representative will carry more weight than the number."

"And who would that be, Viktor?"

"Let's finish our business with Michael first, shall we?" Lord Ternborg turned his attention back to the *B'nai Elohim* commander. "How many of my warriors do you need?"

Michael sighed. "Even behind our fortress walls, the number of demon armies lining up to attack will challenge the strength and courage of the Draugen Pesta."

Lord Ternborg smiled. "Is that your way of saying it's up to me... but as many as I can spare?"

Michael returned the smile. He liked these mortal giants... particularly their king, queen, and their precocious daughter. "I suppose it is. Who better than you to know the strengths and weaknesses of your own people... or what you need to keep your own kingdom safe while you help us? Besides, beggars can't be choosers."

The Draugen Pesta sovereign frowned. "So I get to decide the number of warriors needed to keep Aster from being overrun by demons..."

"If they're not stopped in the Abyss," the *B'nai Elohim* commander added.

"You're not playing fair, Michael."

"Indeed!" Sofia exclaimed. "What about the humans... or

the elves? They have a stake in this as much as we do."

Michael nodded. "That's true. But there's not enough time to negotiate a treaty, which I suspect is what the humans will want to do. As for the elves… they've been through enough already defending InnisRos from the Dark Elf invasion lead by an escaped demon. And let's not forget, they don't have their queen."

"Her sister rules in her stead and from what I've heard, she's very capable," Sofia countered.

Lord Ternborg looked at his wife.

She shrugged. "You were otherwise occupied, so I made my own assessment."

"Even if the elves can be relied upon, there's still a time factor to be considered," Michael replied.

"How many demons are we talking about?" Lord Ternborg inquired.

"Tens of thousands… probably over two hundred thousand, depending on how many armies Kor wants to throw against us," Michael replied. "He's got twenty cities from which to draw, not counting that which he maintains in the capital. Each city has an army of twenty thousand… but he'll hold back at least half."

Lord Ternborg paused as he considered how many troops he'd need. "How big is that fortress of yours?"

"Larger and thicker than the one the humans built in the Olympus Mountains," Michael answered.

"The Hammer," Sofia said. "I've heard of that place, though I only know of it by reputation. We don't trade with the humans much."

"I plan to change that in the future," Lord Ternborg commented offhandedly. "Michael, I can have twenty thousand ready to go by this time tomorrow and another ten thousand in a couple more days."

Michael nodded. "I believe twenty thousand will be

enough... though I think keeping those additional ten thousand ready to go as a reserve would be smart. What about sorcerers?"

Lord Ternborg nodded. "Each our units, regardless of size, have at least one combat sorcerer... and healer clerics... attached."

Michael expressed his thanks and stood. "I need to get back. I'll have a contingent of sorcerers come tomorrow to open a doorway large enough to get your troops through."

Lord Ternborg and Sofia watched as the guardian opened a slit in the floor beneath him and dropped through. As the cracked floor healed itself, Sofia looked at her husband.

"What do you think?"

Lord Ternborg shook his head. "I don't know, dear. We can't control what happens to that Johari creature Michael talked about. And from the way he described the problem, neither can he. The best thing we could do at this moment is prepare for the likelihood that a demon invasion is inevitable. But I couldn't say no to his request for troops. We owe him. Besides, the more demons we kill at the fortress walls, the fewer there'll be to invade if that should come to pass."

Sofia nodded agreement. "Now then, my dear husband. Shall we change the subject and talk about who you plan to send to the Hyrokkin Empire?"

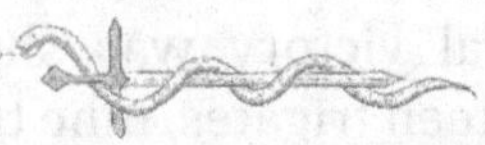

"Jarsus? What do you think the ledger meant about the oblivion... the end of all things?" Daphnia asked. "You think it's the end of the world... like falling off Aster?"

The two were playing their daily game of Belli, a board game of strategy, nation building, war, and peace. Adimar and Sienna, who over the last two weeks had become fast friends, were lying in front of the fireplace. Though the days were warm, Jarsus's gigantic workroom always maintained a chill, so the dwarf kept the fire stoked. Besides the heat it provided, Jarsus and Daphnia both found a measure of comfort in the dancing flames and the alluring sounds of the "crackle" and "pop" of wood as it burned.

"Yer mind's nae oan th' gam, Daphnia," Jarsus responded as he moved his largest army onto one of Daphnia's lightly defended islands. "Now I've control ower yer iron ore deposits 'n' smelting facilities. Na mair iron wirks fer ye, mah bonnie lassie!"

Daphnia smiled. "I just knew you were after that island!" she exclaimed as she sprang her trap. A smaller army—but one large enough to keep Jarsus occupied—sprang out of the mines to confront the invasion. At the same time, a squadron of navy frigates sailed into the harbor to take control of Jarsus's unprotected transport ships and disgorge two divisions of Marines.

"You think ye git me?"

Jarsus countered with seven three-masted warships which sailed around the southern tip of the harbor and into the bay. Daphnia's frigates rushed to intercept the much larger foe. The dwarf smiled as the last of Daphnia's ten frigates was sunk to only one of his warships.

"A'v git mah transports back 'n' noo yer Marines ur threatened. Prepare tae be bombarded!"

But Jarsus's naval victory was short-lived as Daphnia pushed a fleet of thirteen frigates, nine three-masted, and two huge four-masted warships onto the board.

"Where'd they come from?" Jarsus asked. "You can't juist hae fleets 'n' armies poap up oan th' boord oot o' nowhere!"

Daphnia shook her head. "I gambled you'd react to my trap with part of your navy. So I placed mine just beyond the horizon. You won't escape."

"You sacrificed yer frigates tae draw me oot, didn't ye,

lassie?"

Daphnia nodded. "Just like you taught me. Your army, and those ships, are cut off and will soon be destroyed if they don't surrender and join me first. I also have most of your transports. It's just a matter of time before my army on the mainland works its way up your exposed flank to threaten your capital. You gambled and lost."

"Ye think ah, Jarsus Blackmantle, wid be sae careless?"

Daphnia smiled. "Then save yourself, dwarf!"

Jarsus studied the game board. His student was right. She had him back on his heals. Whether he could extricate himself from her trap was questionable. That she'd been his match this time around was not, however.

The dwarf smiled. "Clever," he remarked. "Anything ah dae noo ainlie prolongs yer win. Ah submit tae th' inevitable."

As Jarsus collected the game pieces to put them away, Daphnia's gaze turned towards the fireplace. Adimar, sensing something different in his friend, opened his eyes and looked at the young princess. She was staring into the firelight, seemingly lost in her thoughts, but otherwise okay. The immortal wolf went back to sleep.

"You never answered my question," Daphnia said.

Jarsus looked up. "Yer question?"

"About the oblivion."

The dwarf put the last game piece into its chest and closed the lid. "No, lassie. Tis nae th' end o' Aster... at least nae in ony physical sense. Ye can't pure fall aff a globe floating in space... though ah suppose ye kin fall up, given th' richt circumstances."

Daphnia frowned. "If not that, then what? Darkness?"

"Aye," Jarsus agreed. "The darkness brought oan by evil. Ah believe it's possible there's something wast o' InnisRos... something in th' wilderness o' that vast ocean... that is a serious threat tae us a'. It micht awready be tae late."

"Father's been awfully busy," Daphnia said. "And it's going

to be expensive to pick up the pieces after the Hyrokkin invasion. I can't seem to figure out the best time to ask him about money... or if he'd even be willing after everything that's happened."

"Ah know, lassie," Jarsus replied. "It's nae yer fault. But..."

Both Adimar and Sienna raised their heads and stared at the door to the workroom. Jarsus stopped talking. Soon it became clear what the two animals had heard—knocking from the front doors of the dwarf's apartment.

"Who cuid that be?" Jarsus said as he stood to answer what had become an insistent pounding.

Followed by Daphnia, the immortal wolf, and the gigantic bear, Jarsus went out the workroom, through a small sitting room, and into a long hallway to the front doors.

"Aye, wha ye be," Jarsus asked.

The return answer was muffled and indistinct.

The dwarf rolled his eyes. "Ah keep forgetting ah reinforced th' doors wi' magic weeks ago," he said to Daphnia as he retrieved a ladder to reach a small viewer door nine feet up.

"That ladder seems awfully inconvenient," Daphnia said as she hid a smile behind her hand. "Maybe you should use magic to fly up to the peephole?"

"Ye be making fun of mah stature? Or mibbie her mighty highness believes dwarves be tae wee fur ye giants?"

Daphnia hid another snicker. "Of course not!" she exclaimed, feigning indignation. "As one of only a very few dwarves in Draugen Pesta, you're a national treasure!"

By now, Jarsus had reached the viewer door. "Ye git that richt, bonnie lassie," he said as he opened the panel.

Standing outside were two brawny warriors of the king's personal bodyguard—the First Phalanx. Behind them stood the four guards that always followed Daphnia whenever she went outside the palace.

"Ye be 'ere fur th' Princess?" Jarsus asked.

"And you, dwarf."

Jarsus hid his surprise at being included and nodded. "Well then, juist haud yer horses. We'll be richt oot."

As Jarsus opened the double doors, both of the First Phalanx warriors looked guardedly at the gigantic bear. All of Draugen Pesta knew and trusted Adimar.

"Princess?" one of them inquired, asking for guidance. Or reassurance.

"It's okay," Daphnia replied. "This is Sienna. She's our friend, so you can treat her as you'd treat Adimar."

Both of the First Phalanx warriors nodded. "As you will, Your Grace. We're here to escort you and the dwarf back to the palace. Your father wishes to speak with the both of you."

Jarsus smiled. *"A'm getting mah ship!"*

"Lead the way, gentlemen," Daphnia said in her princess voice. The inflection in her tone brooked no argument or delay. The warriors took it for what it was—a royal command.

"Interesting," Jarsus thought. He'd never seen that side of his student.

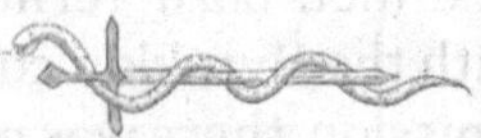

"You want to do what?" Sofia spat at her husband.

Sofia and Lord Ternborg sat at a large conference table in the study of their spacious personal apartment. An enormous fireplace ran along a parallel wall. The jumping and swirling of the flames within reflected brightly in the queen's angry eyes. The Draugen Pesta king had just told his wife about his plans for sending a representative to the Hyrokkin and who that representative was going to be.

"Now Sofia, think before you react," Lord Ternborg pleaded. "Sure, it'll be hard, but it's not near as dangerous as it appears."

Sofia flipped one of her daggers into the air. As the weapon spun back down, she grabbed the hilt and drove the tip into the table to emphasize her point. There were several other deep scars in the polished wood next to the one she'd just created.

"Think?!" Sofia screamed. "You want to send our little girl into that… that… den of four-legged, tail-swishing murderers? There's nothing to think about! It's too dangerous, foolhardy, and… well, husband… someone could also see it as treason to place the next queen into such a perilous position! You're the one who should think about it!"

Lord Ternborg had expected this reaction from his wife. Besides being too soon after Daphnia's abduction, when it came to the welfare of their daughter, she didn't always react rationally. Most mothers don't when their children are threatened. Except this time was different. Daphnia wouldn't be in any real danger. Those with her will be more than capable of seeing to her safety… and the child had a charm about her that made people of all creeds flock to her in adoration. The guards who followed her on her daily forays into the city proper had reported an unabashed affection between her and almost everyone she'd met. Lord Ternborg felt his daughter could do the same with the Hyrokkin common folk. As for her ability to handle the mission, there was no question in his mind Daphnia had the necessary mental capacity and training. She lacked experience, but Jarsus, who'd be going with her, was more than qualified to advise her through any complications. His problem now, as he had foreseen, was convincing Sofia.

"This *is* going to happen, my love," the Draugen Pesta king stated. Though that'd do nothing to win the argument, Lord Ternborg wanted to make sure that part of the discussion was settled.

Sofia put her dagger back into its sheath, laced her hands together, placed them on the table, and stared. Her husband had seen that look before. Anyone who knew Sofia understood that before she was just angry. Now she was dangerous.

"You know how much I love our daughter," Lord Ternborg said. "You also know the last thing I'd do is put her into any serious jeopardy."

Sofia remained quiet but continued to stare.

Lord Ternborg frowned before he continued, as if that'd spare him the daggers being thrown at him from his wife's eyes. "First, she has a special way with ordinary people. You've heard the same reports I have... and you know it's true. Who's better suited to win over an old nemesis than an innocent child who doesn't see them as the enemy? A child whose soul hasn't been tainted by centuries of war?"

Sofia stared.

"As for her safety... she has her own Phalanx of one thousand warriors. Then there's Adimar, her wolf. Let's not forget just who he is... an immortal and the son of the wolf-god Fenrisúlfr. He loves Daphnia as much as she loves him. There's not much harm that could come to her as long as he's around... and that's going to be forever."

Sofia stared, but she was softening.

Lord Ternborg saw that his arguments were hitting home. "Let's also not forget the Hyrokkin queen. I believe she wants this newfound peace between our two peoples to last. I *know* you understand how rare that is for a Hyrokkin leader... and the opportunity we have to find an end to constant war. Give the Hyrokkin people a taste of peace, prosperity through trade, and a better life for their children, and I can guarantee you they'll never look back." Lord Ternborg shook his head. "No, Thesonia won't jeopardize that by letting harm come to our daughter."

Sofia looked at her hands on the table.

"Almost there," Lord Ternborg thought. Aloud, he presented his final argument. "And I'm sending her teacher, the dwarf Jarsus Blackmantle, with her. He wants me to fund an ocean trip west of InnisRos, so he'll be agreeable."

The Draugen Pesta queen looked up at her husband. "He's a dwarf! An academic! What good will he be keeping Daphnia safe?"

Lord Ternborg smiled. "He's much more than a mere dwarf... or academic."

Sofia looked confused.

"What? I'm going to turn the education of my only child over to someone I haven't thoroughly checked out?"

"I checked him out as well," Sofia responded. "He's exactly who he says he is."

"Your spies aren't as good as mine," Lord Ternborg countered. "In his younger days, he was a bit of a ruffian. In fact, the Oakenshield Clan dwarves living under the Mahtan Mountains would love to have him back. Seems they'd like to see him dangling at the end of a rope."

Sofia frowned. "For what!"

Lord Ternborg laughed. "It's kind of funny when you think about it. Seems our dwarf ran off with a rather valuable trinket... a large crystal of amethyst rubyhalite. In fact, it was the largest the Oakenshield Clan had ever seen. Worth a king's ransom... no, a dragon's horde... from what they told my spy."

"So he's a thief as well," Sofia said. "How's that funny?"

"Well, he's the one who found and dug it out of the rock in the first place," the Draugen Pesta king replied. "But the king of the Oakenshield Clan couldn't afford the ten percent finder's fee, which, from what I understand, is standard amongst most of the dwarven clans. In fact, it's the law. Instead, they offered Jarsus the hand of a royal princess, a minor royal title, and a few other things. Essentially, a bribe. Well, most dwarves would rather have the money. Our dwarf was no different. So he stole the crystal back and fled to Draugen Pesta."

"A dwarf fleeing to the land of the giants. If he was trying to hide out, that wasn't going to make him very inconspicuous now, was it?"

Lord Ternborg shrugged. "At the time, we were a bit more cut off from the rest of the mainland. Plus, we scare people. He probably gambled no one would follow."

"As it should be," Sofia remarked. "We've spent hundreds of years purposely developing our reputation. It keeps us from having to worry about interference from the human city states."

Lord Ternborg nodded. "Yes... but I'm trying to change that. Let them fear our strength as a race. Let them fear our military power. But not because they view us as a monster. I think we're well past the point where the humans can threaten us... and we're not a threat to them as long as they don't interfere with our way of life."

"My husband," Sofia said. "I love you. You have a good heart. But that kind of attitude is rather simplistic, don't you think? As long as the humans fear us, we don't have to fear them. But if that were to change..."

"I'd prefer them as friends... or at least partners," Lord Ternborg interjected. "Though my invasion into their lands, regardless of the justification, has undoubtedly ended that... at least for the time being." Lord Ternborg shook his head. "Anyway, back to our discussion about Jarsus. The Oakenshield Clan sent a few emissaries to get him back, but the way my great-grandfather saw it, the crystal was legally Jarsus's since he was the finder and never got his ten percent commission. Great-grandfather sent the dwarves away and he granted Jarsus citizenship so he'd have nothing to fear from his old clan in the future."

"How does that make things different?" Sofia asked. "What more is he that you'd trust the life of our daughter to him?"

"Besides being smart with a talent for self-preservation?" Lord Ternborg remarked. "He used his new wealth to remake himself. He became educated in both the mundane and the spiritual. He worked hard to understand all disciplines...

from mathematics to history... from the physical world to the magical... from the light to the shadow."

Sofia shrugged. "So he's an educated dwarf... an excellent teacher for Daphnia. Does that keep her safe against spears, swords, or arrows?"

Lord Ternborg nodded. "Even the streets of Saint Petersburg aren't completely safe. I asked him the same thing when I interviewed him to be Daphnia's tutor. Aside from his ability to use his mind, which is unlike any I've ever known, he's also an accomplished sorcerer, though he prefers to keep that part of his knowledge secret. But that expertise in the arcane arts, as well as his bravery, has allowed him to garner some... shall we say... unusual allies that are dedicated to him and, by extension, Daphnia. That enormous bear, Sienna, is only but one example. As for others..." Lord Ternborg shivered. "I'm still trying to get over the ones he introduced me to."

Sofia frowned. "You never mentioned this."

"I didn't want to frighten or worry you," her husband replied. "You see, they're not from this world... or even our plane of existence. But I assure you they're safe. Well, at least where Daphnia's concerned. And there's little doubt in my mind they can keep her out of harm's way. Even better than her own Phalanx."

"How do you know?"

The Draugen Pesta king shivered again. "They told me. Actually, they swore an oath... in my mind. It was... unnerving... and irrefutable."

Sofia shook her head. "This is beginning to sound like a fairy tale... too good to be true. And I wouldn't believe a word of it if it weren't you who was telling it."

"Perhaps Jarsus will introduce you to them," Lord Ternborg replied. "But you may wish he hadn't. He calls them 'the Lads.'"

"I'm not a dainty female who..."

Lord Ternborg put a finger to his wife's lips. "I was making no such insinuation, dear. It was simply a warning. The same warning I got from Jarsus."

Sofia thought things over for a few moments before she nodded. "Very well. You've made some very valid points. Provided I'm as comfortable with Jarsus's 'allies' as you are, I don't have any real objection to Daphnia being our representative to the Hyrokkin. It's more than they deserve, but..." Sofia shrugged. "I agree she's probably the best person for the job, considering her way with people. Besides, you can get ten, twenty thousand warriors into Hyrokkin fast enough if things get dangerous."

Lord Ternborg grimaced. "About that..."

"I knew it!" Sofia exclaimed. "You're going with Michael, aren't you?"

"I can't expect anyone else to lead our troops into the Abyss," Lord Ternborg answered back. "I'm the king... and the Abyss is... well, it's not something we've ever experienced before. Who knows what we're going to find... other than demons, that is."

Sofia refuted her husband. "Let Misha take them! He's Field-Marshal of the Army! Isn't that what he's supposed to do?!"

"Sofia, I can't delegate something like this," Lord Ternborg replied. "You know that."

Sofia was almost in tears. "Please, Viktor, make an exception this one time. He's expendable, you aren't!"

"Sofia..."

"I just got my family back!" the Draugen Pesta queen exclaimed. "Now Daphnia... and you..." Sofia sniffed and looked at her husband. "Sorry. I'm afraid I'm not acting much like your queen. Pa-pa would have me over his knee if he saw my tears."

Lord Ternborg covered her folded hands with his own. "Besides my queen, you're also a mother and a wife. There's nothing to apologize for. You're without peer as both... and as my queen. Our kingdom couldn't be in finer hands."

Sofia nodded and straightened. Her transformation from a vulnerable woman to a powerful queen was instantaneous. "Don't worry about your kingdom, Viktor. I'll not let anything happen to it while you're gone."

Lord Ternborg smiled and kissed his wife on the forehead. "The gods help anyone who tries to take advantage of my absence!"

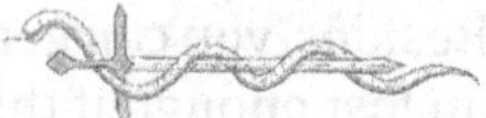

Several hours later, Sofia got her chance to meet Jarsus's interdimensional allies. Through a magical doorway created by Jarsus's mental summons, Sofia saw several multi-colored birds flying effortlessly in the atmosphere of their home plane of existence. Every once in a while, one of them would bridge the distance between the two planes to inspect Sofia. They moved gracefully in both dimensions. They carried about them an elegance that was quite rare… and beautiful.

"Gorgeous!" Sofia exclaimed the first time she saw them.

"Aren't they, mother?" Daphnia said. "And they get along so well with Adimar!"

"Prepare yourself, my love," Lord Ternborg commented. "Looks can deceive."

"Indeed thay kin," Jarsus said. "Tak' me, fur example… braw, wise beyond mah years, genteel… bit ferr ferocious whin necessary. Identical wi' th' lads. Sienna?"

On cue, the bear issued a growl that had an amazing effect upon the flying beings. Instantly, each transformed into savage beasts that had none of the splendor of their earlier manifestation. Their mouths grew saber-like teeth, long, sharp talons materialized out of their feet, and their beautiful colored feathers disappeared to be replaced by black, leathery skin. Three of them rushed up to Sofia while the remaining surrounded Jarsus and Daphnia. As one, the three next to Sofia let out a high-pitched scream while their mouths drooled a thick, black ooze.

Sofia closed her eyes and covered her ears but stood her ground. Once the screaming stopped, she opened her eyes again. The birds were back in their previous forms, flying around in the air as if nothing had happened. The look on Sofia's face when she met the gaze of her husband told him everything he needed to know. She accepted Daphnia would be safe.

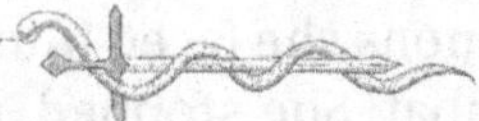

Three days later, Lord Ternborg lead an army of twenty thousand warriors, sorcerers, healers, and clerics into the Abyss. Daphnia and Jarsus Blackmantle, along with Adimar, Sienna, Daphnia's Phalanx of one thousand, and Jarsus's unworldly friends, were in Hyrokkin with Daphnia, Draugen Pesta's new ambassador to the Hyrokkin Empire. Their presence did much to quell the rebellion facing Queen Thesonia. Queen Sofia, once again in charge of the kingdom while her husband was away, put an overwhelming force of fifteen thousand troops on the eastern border just in case there was trouble with the Hyrokkin… or even a hint of danger to her daughter. She was in no mood to coddle anyone, least of all the centaurs. The small opposition party to Lord Ternborg's rule in Draugen Pesta soon learned the queen was far more difficult to contend with than the king and went underground. It was either because of Sofia's stout refusal to allow dissent during this time of emergency, or the knives attached to the belt that encircled her waist.

CHAPTER NINE

The Abyss

Lessien and Laylah dashed through the door of the hut and out into the open. The demons awaiting them, though surprised by the attack, countered with their usual do-or-die response. Lessien released her magical sword, *Ah-HritVakha*, from its restraints and drove into the demons with reckless abandon. The sudden ferocity of her attack, aided by the sword's supernatural enchantments, was enough to kill or drive the demons she faced into full retreat after only a few minutes of combat. She stopped, panting, and watched as the surviving demons melted into the surrounding woods. Laylah waded through her own pile of dead or dying demons to stand by Lessien's side. Both mortal queen and demon overlord had been bloodied and were stiff from several minor cuts and contusions.

"Did Yesper get away?" Lessien asked.

Laylah nodded as she used her trident to spear a wounded demon crawling towards them. "He did." She looked at Lessien. "I've seen good swordplay before... but *damn*... you and that blade of yours are impressive!"

Ah-HritVakha glowed in satisfaction at the compliment.

"Let's just say my concern for Martin motivated me," Lessien replied. "But if you want to see real swordplay, you should watch the knight who taught me. Almost twice my size, wearing armor, using a huge shield, and wielding a great sword one-handed... yet as nimble as I'll ever be."

"That I'd like to see," Laylah acknowledged.

Lessien smiled as she thought about Landross. "You will," she said, knowing in her heart that he was already here, no doubt with Father Goram, combing the Abyss for Autumn and her.

Lessien's eyes went hard as she remembered her dead

friend. "We need to finish off the wounded demons and get moving."

The minute Chief Interrogator Zachariah's carriage entered the city of Uz Urreth, he knew something was amiss. His badge of office always granted him unchallenged access to all parts of any city. Not this time, however. The guards, though respectful, were frightened. But not because the carriage of Kor's chief interrogator had to be stopped and searched. Zachariah, like all interrogators, was an excellent judge of character and knew that wasn't it. As the guards searched his carriage, Zachariah addressed the demon in charge.

"What's going on?" he asked.

"Begging your pardon, but they don't tell me nothing, Your Lordship," the guard replied. An additional complication had entered his life, for he had no doubt the overlord standing before him had the power to send him to the *Pillar*. "But rumor has it something's going on at the amphitheater. It must be serious too if no one's allowed to enter the city without a thorough search... including Kor's chief interrogator."

"I don't hold you responsible," Zachariah said to reassure the guard. "You're only doing your duty."

The guard relaxed, but only slightly. "Thank you, Chief Interrogator."

Two guards ran up and stood at attention. The search of Zachariah's carriage was complete.

"Tell me.. since Trolgroth appears to have his hands full with... whatever... can you recommend an inn close by the palace?" The overlord lied. "I'd like to freshen up before I call upon him."

All three guards stiffened.

"Your Lordship!" the leader exclaimed. "You're not going to

complain about your unfortunate delay here, are you?"

Zachariah frowned. "What? I already said I don't hold you responsible for doing your duty."

"To which we're grateful, Your Lordship. It's just that interrogators usually head straight for the prison to question someone… not to see the city overlord."

Zachariah interrupted with a wave of his hand and a flash of anger, for show only, in his eyes. "By all that's sane! I'm Kor's Chief Interrogator! I go where I want, when I want, how I want! And right now I want to go to an inn! If Trolgroth doesn't care for it, I'll arrange a trip to the *Pillar* for *him*!"

The three guards smiled at the thought of the high and mighty Trolgroth kissing the *Pillar*. "Your Lordship should be most comfortable at Highguarde's Fine Dining and Sleeping Hostel near the palace."

Zachariah nodded his thanks to the guards as he entered his carriage. "Take me towards the amphitheater," he instructed his driver after the carriage started down the street. *"If that's where the trouble's at,"* he thought. *"Then that's where I'll probably find the mortal queen Braz'galar wants rescued."*

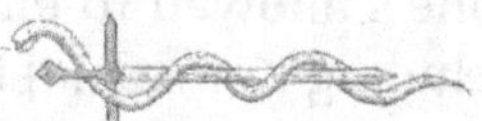

Belladonna and Braz'galar watched as the Behemoth swam closer to their skiff. Then Belladonna noticed another, and then another, until they had identified five Behemoths slowly swimming towards them.

Belladonna shook her head. "They're going to be awfully disappointed if they think the two of us are going to satisfy their hunger."

Braz'galar, who had gone back to the rudder, nodded. "True enough. But that's a family of Behemoths… and I doubt they're looking for food up here on the surface. Usually, it's only the rogues we have to worry about. Families might be inquisitive but will leave us alone after they've satisfied their curiosity. But just in case, hold on to something."

Only one Behemoth swam close enough to be of concern—a juvenile, judging by the size. It bumped the skiff once before it rose its head out of the water to inspect them. The others circled the skiff one hundred feet away. After a nervous minute, the Behemoth slipped back into the water and the family swam away. Both Belladonna and Braz'galar breathed a sigh of relief.

"They're actually quite beautiful... in a way," Belladonna observed.

"As is all nature," Braz'galar said. "From a distance. The trick with these kinds of encounters is living through them so you can tell your grandchildren about it."

They sailed without incident for several hours. Braz'galar did his best to set their course in a northernly direction, but the wind wasn't cooperating, which drastically cut down their speed. By the time night fell, Braz'galar was exhausted, stiff, and sore all over. There was no sign of land.

"You okay?" Belladonna asked.

Braz'galar startled awake and shook his head. "How long was I out?"

"Not long," Belladonna responded. "And it's not like we're going to hit anything."

"We've got to stay on course," Braz'galar said. "And I've got to get a few hours of sleep."

"Hand the tiller over to me. I've had plenty of sleep. I can take over."

Kor's fixer looked at his companion. Right now they were working together, but he knew she hadn't forgotten how he'd betrayed the resistance and kidnapped her. She had every reason to hate him... because regardless of his justification, it was a debt he owed. "So you can slit my throat?"

Belladonna returned his gaze for a few long seconds

before she responded. "If I had wanted to do that, it'd already be done… though I admit the thought had crossed my mind. But maybe… just maybe… you're being sincere. That being the case, you might be our only hope to drive Kor off the *Living Throne*. My personal feelings must be subservient to the cause. Too many lives depend on it."

Braz'galar wanted more from her, but an uneasy peace would have to do for now. "Alright."

He explained the course he'd put them on and how to steer the tiller and work the sail. He also warned her to wake him should she see anything out of the ordinary. Satisfied, he moved under the covered part of the skiff, grabbed a dry piece of discarded sail, and snuggled down for the sleep he could no longer deny.

"I see lights," Belladonna said a few hours later as she shook Braz'galar awake. "There's a ship bearing down on us from the east."

Braz'galar got up, went to the side of the skiff, and splashed water on his face. Dawn was just over the horizon. Though it looked like it was going to be a cloudy day, there was enough light to make them visible from several miles away. He looked towards the east and saw the ship. It was one of Kor's smaller, sleek, and speedy three masted frigates and appeared to be on an intercept course.

"Damn," he cursed. "They've seen us. We can't outrun it, and we can't hide unless we can find a close-by squall."

"I can bring forth a magical fog," Belladonna remarked.

Braz'galar shook his head. "Unless you can cover several miles, it won't do us any good. They'd just follow the fog bank. Besides, those spells don't last long… at least not as long as we'd need it to be. Any other suggestions?"

"Burn them with magic when they get close enough."

"Kor puts at least one sorcerer on each of his ships," Braz'galar countered. "But that's not all. They shield most ships against magic. Not one hundred percent effective… but good enough to withstand several attacks."

Belladonna shook her head. "I didn't know that."

"Kor takes precautions that most would never suspect," Braz'galar responded. "That's one reason your resistance never had a chance. You first need someone who's been on the inside. Someone who understands how Kor operates and knows his tricks and what precautions he takes. Someone who can anticipate his moves."

"*You* were on the inside!" Belladonna exclaimed. "If you're so determined to eliminate Kor, why didn't you use what you know to help us rather than destroying us?"

"I had to," Braz'galar replied. "Kor gave me the job of destroying the resistance. Believe me, I tried hard to think of something else, but came up empty. And if I didn't go through with it, I'd have lost any advantage I have as his fixer. Kor would suspect me of treason… or worse, as a failure, someone who can no longer get the job done. Think about it, Belle. Like all Prefecture sovereigns, Kor doesn't take chances. He's too sly and experienced in self-preservation to leave things to fate. He knows better than anyone how much the overlords beneath him plot every day to end his reign. One incredible advantage he has is the *Living Throne*. Through that he has the combined experience and knowledge of every Prefecture demon lord we've ever had. I'm his fixer… his most trusted advisor and essentially next in line for the *Living Throne*. But even I'm not trusted. No one but Kor knows all the precautions he takes… the plans he's making. Yes, I'm on the inside… as inside as anyone except his number one concubine… and even that's debatable. But that doesn't mean I know everything. Every time he gives me an assignment, he plans for the possibility of my either turning traitor or being found out and tortured for the information in my head. He changes things around, so to speak. He doesn't hide that from me. It's the price of doing what I do for him."

Belladonna shook her head. "First you say any resistance would need someone who's either on the inside or was… that's you. Then you say Kor mixes things up to mislead you in case things go sideways during one of your missions, which negates any advantage you have being on the inside. You're talking in circles. Just tell me this… how do we take him down if we're blind?"

"I've worked around his precautions… at least I believe I have," Braz'galar answered. "What Kor doesn't suspect is that I have my own agents on the inside."

"How can you be sure he doesn't know about your agents?"

"Oh, I'm sure he's aware of the possibility," Braz'galar replied. "Like I said, he doesn't take chances. But my folks are buried deep. Each of them has infiltrated one particular area of Kor's government. They're one part of the whole. Each sends me bits and pieces of information and it's up to me to take what they give and assemble the overall picture. None of them are aware of the others. If one's discovered, it doesn't impact the work of the rest of my spies."

"It must have taken you years to set that up," Belladonna observed.

Braz'galar nodded. "And sacrifice. I had to protect those sources, which was another reason I chose to follow Kor's orders regarding the resistance. Refusal would've raised Kor's suspicions, and when that happens, everything and everyone is at risk." Braz'galar returned to studying the vessel heading towards them. "Let's talk more about it later. Right now, we need to deal with that ship."

Belladonna shrugged her shoulders. "You're Kor's fixer. Let them catch up and then order them to drop us off. It's better than floundering about in this little skiff."

"You're probably right… and I don't see anything else to try," Braz'galar said as he studied the closing frigate. "Wait a minute!"

"What's wrong," Belladonna asked.

Braz'galar ignored the question. "Have you seen a spyglass lying around anywhere?"

Belladonna shook her head.

Braz'galar cursed.

"What's wrong, Braz'galar?" Belladonna repeated. There was a sinking feeling in the pit of her stomach.

"I think that frigate's flying Azazael's flag!" Braz'galar replied as he continued to study the approaching vessel. "No... now I'm sure of it."

"What difference does it make which Faction leader's flag is on it?"

"Azazael's the only Faction leader who doesn't want Kor to join his predecessors in the *Living Throne*," Braz'galar answered. "As Aikanáro's daughter and an overlord yourself, you understand as well as anyone the 'behind the scenes' power struggles that go on... what Kor has to do and who he has to destroy to stay in power. The only difference is you're not after the throne yourself... and neither is Azazael. I don't know how Kor did it, but the Military Faction leader is completely loyal to him. That's only part of the story, however. We have history."

"History?" Belladonna queried.

"Other than Kor, and now you, he's the only other person who knows my true identity," Braz'galar answered. "And he hates me."

Belladonna waited for further explanation.

Braz'galar continued his narrative. "Kor had a somewhat scroungy court hanger-on who was, frankly, an embarrassment. You know Kor... some things he just won't tolerate. And believe me, that's high on his list. He asked me to arrange an 'accident' for the aforementioned embarrassment. But I politely, and with great deference, refused."

"You refused Kor to his face and got away with it?" Belladonna asked incredulously.

Braz'galar nodded. "Doing what I do and being very good at it gives me a little latitude. Anyhow, the next thing I know, Azazael shows up at my doorstep seething with anger and ready to end our relationship… permanently."

"I familiar with Azazael," Belladonna said. "He's ill-kempt, fat, and lazy. You'd have no problem with him in a duel."

Braz'galar laughed. "Azazael's also extremely intelligent. More so than all the Faction leaders save Lilitu. He'd brought twelve warriors to even things out."

"What'd you do?"

"Flash, bang, boom," Braz'galar responded. "I didn't want to take Azazael out… particularly since Kor hadn't given me his permission. Besides, I was curious why he wanted me dead. As far as I knew, I'd done nothing to wrong him. Then there were the warriors to consider. So I created a diversion and teleported to a safe-house on the other side of the city. Then I reached out to my contacts to find out why Azazael was so damned angry."

Again Belladonna waited.

"That court buffoon was Azazael's brother," Braz'galar replied. "Don't get me wrong, there wasn't any love lost between the two… but they were family."

Belladonna frowned. "But you refused to do Kor's bidding."

Braz'galar nodded. "And as a result of my decision, Kor ordered Azazael to do it… which he did with great efficiency, and perhaps some pleasure as well. The point being, Azazael believes it was my responsibility as Kor's fixer to do it, particularly since I was asked. Now he has trouble with his family. No one crosses Azazael's mother. Ergo, the vendetta."

"But…"

Braz'galar shrugged his shoulders. "One of us is going down. As soon as the people on that frigate figure out who we are, they'll probably throw me back into the water and take you to Kor for a date on Execution Hill."

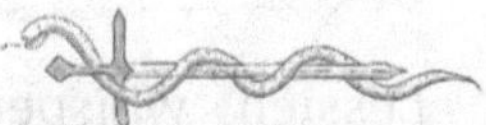

Drorikan rushed to where his underlords and their warriors had the mortal trapped... at least that was the last word he'd received. Belladonna had disappeared, but he'd catch up with her later. One thing at a time. The mortal would please Kor. A messenger hurried to prostrate itself before Drorikan.

"Report!" Drorikan ordered.

"The mortal has allies, My Lord," the messenger said. "We're meeting heavy resistance."

Drorikan looked confused. "Allies? How many allies?"

The messenger still had his face in the dirt. "Many allies, My Lord," he lied as instructed. "The mortal has escaped for now, but we're closing in on it."

The overlord shook his head in disgust. "Who's in charge?"

"Ogis... but they killed him in the first attempt at capture."

One of Drorikan's underlord assistants sniffed. "Ogis... that fool!"

Drorikan ignored the comment. "Who's in charge now?"

"Mazranoch, My Lord."

"Tell Mazranoch I'm on my way," the overlord instructed the messenger. "You three," he said as he pointed to three of his attending underlords. "Take your warriors and go with him. I want the situation contained by the time I arrive."

"I wonder who in the Abyss allies themselves with a mortal," Drorikan pondered as he continued his journey forward. He didn't want to go too fast, lest he be involved in the fight

himself. Good leaders let others do the dying for them.

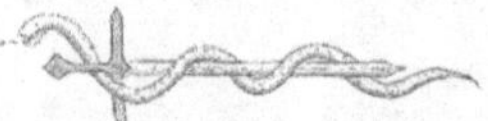

"We're trapped," Lessien whispered to Laylah. The demons had cut the two off in their attempt to get to Yesper and Martin. They'd taken a momentary refuge in an old animal pen, probably field striders, which was abandoned long ago.

Laylah nodded. "They're better organized than they were during the first attack. We're enclosed in their ring and they're doing a patterned search inward, which is surprising. Though it's highly effective, it takes time. Most commanders don't have the patience."

Lessien was feeling helpless again, in the same way as when Autumn and she had first come to the Abyss as caged prisoners. Then, like now, she had no options. "We need to get to Yesper and Martin," she said. There was desperation in her voice.

"Any attempt would lead the city guards right to them," Laylah pointed out. "We need a more direct approach."

"Killing them isn't direct enough?"

"We had the advantage in surprise," Laylah replied. "They now have the numbers to negate that. No, we need something even bolder."

Lessien looked at her companion, curious and waiting for the revelation.

"We surrender."

The InnisRos queen chuckled. "How refreshing… a demoness with a sense of humor."

Laylah shook her head. "I'm being serious, Lessien. I've told you who I am… both to Kor and the *B'nai Elohim*."

Lessien made the connection at once. "But they don't know your relationship to Kor. How will you prove it? And even if you do, how does that help us?"

Laylah removed the scarf that covered her forehead. In the center was a strange-looking tattoo of a serpent that appeared to move rhythmically along its body. It was quite lovely in a strange sort of way.

"Except for his Number One, Kor has his concubines marked," the demoness stated in response to Lessien's shocked look. "It was much uglier when I first got it. But over the decades, it's changed to match my personality. I don't think Kor would invite me into his bedroom now because of it, thank the gods! But the point is, everyone... *everyone*... in the Abyss knows I'm Kor's private property through his mark."

"I'm so sorry," Lessien said. "No one has the right to do that to another person."

"This is the Abyss." Laylah smiled. "Besides, it gives me advantages I can exploit."

"Unless Kor knows your secret identity," Lessien surmised. "And if he does, he can use that against both you and the *B'nai Elohim*."

The demoness shrugged. "It's a risk I take every day of my life. Let's hope that if he figures out who I am, it won't be until tomorrow, after we're safely away."

"Well, they've seen us," Belladonna remarked. "There's no squalls or storms in the area, so we can't hide. And we can't outrun a frigate even with a strong wind at our backs... which we don't have."

Braz'galar remained silent as he continued to watch the frigate. As it sailed closer, he didn't see activity on the deck, which would indicate the crew hadn't been called to arms. "They know the skiff is here, but not that we're on it. That gives us the advantage."

"You intend to fight," Belladonna noted. It wasn't a question.

"Good! How large is her crew?"

"I intend to fight smartly," Braz'galar responded. "As to your question, she'll be of smaller construction..."

"They make them larger?"

"Twice to three times as large," Braz'galar answered back. "But all of those are on the Kematian Sea. Weather conditions... not to mention the underwater inhabitants... are far more brutal there."

Belladonna nodded in agreement. "I've been there once. You're correct... much harsher conditions!"

"Reservoir frigates," Braz'galar continued, "carry a crew of around one hundred officers and crew, at least one overlord, and a sorcerer with a small detachment of ten to twelve personal bodyguards paid for from the sorcerer's private funds so there's never any question of loyalty."

"We can't..." Belladonna paused as she came to understand Braz'galar's meaning that he'd fight smart. "We don't have to fight the entire crew to take over the ship, do we?"

Braz'galar shook his head. "Probably not. It depends upon their loyalty to the ship's captain... or their fear of the sorcerer. If we can neutralize one or both, the crew might be willing to follow another overlord... say you or me? Right now, it's our only chance to get away from this with our lives."

The frigate was now only about half a nautical mile away and closing fast. Individual crew members were taking distinctive forms. Belladonna and Braz'galar, from the moment they saw the frigate, had kept a low profile, and the frigate probably didn't know if the skiff they were about to recover was manned or not.

"You have a plan?" Belladonna asked.

Kor's fixer nodded. "But it's risky as hell," he said as he continued to study the frigate. The crew were acting normal, scrambling to man the wenches that would lift the skiff off the water. Braz'galar didn't see either the captain or the sorcerer on deck, so he was reasonably sure they hadn't spotted the two of them on the skiff. Both would be there if they had.

Belladonna cleared her throat. "Any time, Braz'galar!"

"We need a distraction," Braz'galar answered back. "And I doubt you're going to like it."

Belladonna shrugged. "I'm open for suggestions... short of offering myself to those disgusting demons."

"Cast a fog spell," Braz'galar answered.

"A fog spell?" Belladonna shot back. "But the sorcerer..."

"I know... he'll counter-spell you," Braz'galar responded. "The spell itself isn't important... just that it's a logical reaction to their presence. I don't want the sorcerer to suspect something's up other than the obvious. And I want his attention... and that of the crew... focused on you. In fact, when you cast the spell, make a big deal out of it. Stand in plain view and exaggerate your gyrations as you cast it."

"The sorcerer..." Belladonna repeated.

"The sorcerer won't harm you," Braz'galar assured her. "They'll want to question you first."

Belladonna didn't resist the idea further. As much as she hated to admit it, he was her only lifeline, at least for now, and she was beginning to trust him again despite what he'd done to the resistance movement. Notwithstanding the change of name and the brutal truth that he was a high-ranking member of Kor's dictatorship, she now realized the Argomon she respected and admired was still there inside.

Both waited in silence until the frigate was within range of her fog spell. Belladonna looked at Braz'galar, who nodded. She threw off the slicker she was wearing against the wetness of the weather, stood, and moved to the front of the skiff. No one could deny her station as a powerful overlord sorceress. Throwing caution to the wind, she cast the fog spell... adding several streaks of light which climbed skyward for effect.

"Udara, angin, air, dan cahaya.
Bersatu, menyelaraskan, kembali dan menyalakan."

"Bentukkan siluetmu, tunjukkan venirmu.
Lingkari saya dan semua yang berdekatan." [5]

As she spoke the last word, mist rose from the water and coalesced around Belladonna until the world around her was nothing but a thick, swirling miasma of gray. All sound retreated into the background. The moisture of the summoned fog was so thick it collected on her clothing, soaking the overlord from head to foot.

"Perhaps I overdid it," Belladonna thought.

The sound of water lapping against wood broke the silence. The frigate was rapidly approaching and Belladonna feared it was going to ram her much smaller vessel.

"Braz'galar!" Belladonna cried out softly, but there was no response.

The sound of the approaching ship soon dominated the silence of the fog. As Belladonna readied herself to jump into the water, she heard shouted orders to stop and drop anchor. Sailors yelled and she could hear the footfalls of boots on wood. Two large splashes followed.

"Anchors away!" a voice bellowed.

Then a third voice, shrill and squeaky, called out. "Neat trick with the fog, whoever you are! But such a parlor trick can't save you from discovery... for I am the great Ostrinnauth, and..."

The voice Belladonna heard a few seconds ago giving orders suddenly interrupted the great Ostrinnauth. "Just get on with it!"

"Yes, Captain."

Belladonna closed her eyes. "Where are you, Braz'galar?"

she whispered for a second time as she waited for whatever was coming next.

What came next was a magical incantation that was no doubt meant to counter Belladonna's spell. Despite his shrill and squeaky voice, the great Ostrinnauth hit every intonation perfectly. Belladonna knew without seeing that his hand and arm contortions were as perfect as the lyrics. The magic of the spell created small, three-foot diameter explosions of bright light in the dense fog. As each explosion died out, the light of the day replaced the fog. Within seconds, everyone could see Belladonna standing alone on the skiff.

A figure, the great Ostrinnauth based upon the sorcerer robes he wore, looked down on her from the deck of the frigate and leered. "Well, well, well… what do we have here? A pretty little flower waiting to be picked."

The demon overlord standing next to the sorcerer, the frigate's captain, frowned and shook his head. "Just fer once would ye flay yer shriveled tongue?" he shouted at the sorcerer. "You down there," he said to Belladonna. "Prepare to be boarded."

Belladonna watched helplessly as they dropped ropes from the frigate to the skiff. Several demon sailors prepared to climb down.

"Damnit, Braz'galar," Belladonna whispered. "Do something before I have to. I *will not* let those animals touch me without a fight!"

An underlord appeared at the side of the captain and whispered something in his ear.

"What?" the captain said. "Are ye sure?"

"Aye, Cap'n," the underlord replied. "It's 'er, all right. I've spied 'er meself, I ave. 'Er an' 'er sister. It been a long time ago, but no one forgets seein' Belladonna an' Nightshade! This here one 'ere's Belladonna, she be."

The captain looked at Belladonna. "That puts a different

spin on things. Belay me last order! It seems we've come upon a distinguished… an' dangerous… overlord." He turned to his sorcerer. "Ostrinnauth, bind 'er."

The great Ostrinnauth wasn't expecting that. The last thing he wanted to do was tangle with an overlord, especially one as renowned as Belladonna. "Uh… but Captain… I know you believe that's Belladonna, but shouldn't we verify your information first? Kor…"

The captain made a slashing motion across his throat to silence the sorcerer and turned to the underlord who had identified Belladonna. "You brought me 'er identity," he said. "I'll let ye 'ave the pleasure o' makin' 'er our prisoner."

"But Cap'n…"

"Have ye turned coward like our sorcerer 'ere?" the captain thundered. "Dazarok, that's an order! Either do it or jump o'er the side!"

Dazarok still hesitated.

"Now!" the captain screamed. Spittle flew out of his mouth.

Dazarok called upon several other sailors to join him as he grabbed a rope to climb down to the skiff.

"Do you really think she's Belladonna?" the great Ostrinnauth inquired of his captain. "Sister of Nightshade?"

"Dazarok claims she be," the captain replied. "I'm not particularly convinced, but we'll find out the way o' things once we 'ave 'er in custody." The captain looked at his sorcerer. "Ye look as if ye be goin' to be sick, Ostrinnauth. Perhaps ye should go to yer quarters an' get some rest. Ye be goin' to 'ave a long night interrogatin' 'er."

The great Ostrinnauth complied and returned to his quarters, repeating over and over, "I leered at Belladonna. I leered at Belladonna. Why! Oh, why! Oh, why!"

As this was happening, Belladonna, resigned to the inevitable, studied as much of the frigate as she could from her position on the skiff, which wasn't much. Then she spotted a scarcely perceptible movement in the sail rigging of the foremast. *"Braz'galar!"* her mind screamed.

The almost invisible Braz'galar climbed up to the foremast platform. Belladonna watched as her companion quickly and quietly dispatched the three sailors manning the platform. Any crew in position to have noticed were too busy observing the unfolding scene at the bow of the ship. Braz'galar then arranged each of the dead sailors to appear as if they were still standing watch and used their bodies as temporary cover.

Belladonna smiled as Dazarok and five well-armed sailors dropped into the skiff. She didn't resist as they forced her to climb onto the frigate and then into a small, empty room in the ship's supply cargo bay. There, they bound her hands behind her back, gagged her, and chained her to steel ringed supports embedded in the hull. She even managed to be pleasant when the great Ostrinnauth, accompanied by his own bodyguard, arrived several hours later to begin his interrogation.

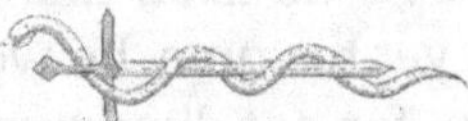

When Belladonna conjured the fog spell, Braz'galar, now in combat mode, slipped over the side of the skiff and waited in the water for the frigate to stop. He submerged and swam the short distance to the bow of the frigate before resurfacing. He pulled himself along the length of the ship until he reached the stern. The frigate's rudder gave him plenty of handholds to climb up to the deck.

Though the crew's attention, including those who manned the frigate's wheel, was directed towards the bow, Braz'galar still knew he'd never get past them without being noticed, and surprise was one of the keys to his plan. Though Braz'galar's success as Kor's fixer was mostly because of his mental and physical acuity, there were plenty of other factors he used to his advantage. Over the years he'd collected a wide variety of magical and mundane devices he used to "grease the wheels," as he liked to say. One of those devices was a *Chameleon Stone*, which he had mounted into a silver ring. It was a magical item which, when triggered, blended his physical form in with his surroundings. Only another overlord could see through its magic.

Camouflaged, Braz'galar made his way forward until he reached the base of the foremast. He climbed the mast rigging until he'd reached the bottom side of the main platform half-way up the mast. He looked at the crow's nest higher up on the mainmast and saw those two sailors were far too busy watching what was happening forward to pay attention to what was happening below them. With practiced efficiency, Braz'galar jumped onto the platform and used a dagger to slit the throats of the three crossbow-armed sailors who had their weapons trained on Belladonna. After restaging the dead to look as if they were still keeping watch, Braz'galar settled in to wait for nightfall. As he used this downtime to rest and prepare for the battle yet to come, he wondered if Belladonna would ever forgive him for not divulging his plan.

"She'll get over it," he told his audience of three corpses.

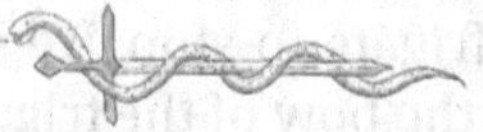

"Well, Mazranoch?" Drorikan asked. "Do you have the mortal in custody?"

"No, My Lord," Mazranoch answered. "But we have it surrounded. I decided to wait until you were on the scene."

Drorikan slapped his subordinate. "Were you not ordered to have the situation contained by the time I got here?!"

"Yes, My Lord," Mazranoch said. "But everyone knows Lord Trolgroth likes his underlings to be involved as much as possible. I thought you'd want to garner his favor by..."

Drorikan slapped Mazranoch again. "You thought wrong!"

he screamed. "You'll soon be kissing the *Pillar* if I have anything to say about it!"

Mazranoch grabbed the hilt of the sword hanging at his side. *"No one will care,"* he thought as he started to pull the blade to kill his superior. A commotion about one hundred feet away stayed his hand.

"We have the mortal!" several demons called out.

"Well, well, well," Drorikan said. "Looks as if someone did your job for you."

Two figures moved through the throng of demons—the mortal so eagerly sought-after and a female demon overlord. The latter had the mortal female bound and was leading her at the end of a chain wrapped around her waist.

"Let me through! Let me through!" the female overlord cried out. "Open a way, you filthy curs!"

Drorikan forced his way through the horde of demon warriors, physically throwing several to the side, to bar the way of the female demon and her captive. "Who are you?" he asked Laylah.

"Who wants to know?!" Laylah shot back.

Drorikan puffed out his chest. "I'm Lord Drorikan, First Overlord to Trolgroth, the ruler of this city state. You're in possession of his prisoner. Give the mortal to me or suffer the consequences."

The surrounding demons growled and showed their teeth, fangs, and tusks to Laylah and Lessien. The one exception was Mazranoch. As he watched, his mind was busy speculating how he could use this situation to his advantage.

Laylah laughed. "Give the mortal to you? My superior, Lord Kor, would have a few choice things to say if I did. Things I don't really want to hear. How about you? Do you want to explain to Lord Kor your reasons for taking his prisoner?"

Drorikan recoiled at the mention of the Prefecture sovereign. But in the long run, he was more concerned about what Trolgroth might think and do if he didn't take the prisoner. "How do I know you're telling the truth?"

"You're not insinuating I'm a liar, are you?" Laylah said. "Blast it all! I'm an overlord!"

"What I'm saying is we let Trolgroth sort it out with Kor," Drorikan rejoined. "I'm saying you either hand the mortal over to me willingly or I'll have to take her from you. I doubt you'll survive if you force my hand."

Mazranoch raised an eyebrow. Drorikan was showing backbone.

It also surprised Laylah to see Drorikan's resistance. Things were spinning out of control, so she played the one advantage she had over most other demons. She removed the scarf covering her forehead to reveal the mark of the serpent.

"You dare to threaten me, Fifth Consort to Lord Kor, the Supreme Potentate of the Kor Prefecture, Warden of the *Living Throne*, Noble and Illustrious Purveyor to the *Pillar* of Captured Souls, Peer of the Realm, and many other titles too lengthy to list?"

Every demon within eyesight of the serpent tattoo recoiled as if the snake had bitten them. Kor had made it clear what happens when someone touches or otherwise bothers one of his consorts. Even overlords weren't immune to his wrath. Anyone who violated this law would willingly run to Kiss the *Pillar*. The alternative was a torture session on Execution Hill and then an even more horrendous death.

Drorikan, now less sure of himself, bowed slightly. "My Lady," he said, though he didn't step out of Laylah's way. "With all due respect, this is Trolgroth's city, which makes the female mortal *his* prisoner. I merely act upon his orders."

Lessien, watching the scene play out in front of her, began to have second thoughts about Laylah's plan. "Michael and the *B'nai Elohim* will come for me," she said, hoping to add fire to the uncertainty of the situation. "Then none of you are safe."

Laylah closed her eyes and sighed. *"Why'd you say that?"* she thought as she whirled on the mortal queen. She slapped her across the cheek hard enough to snap Lessien's head to the side. "You'll only speak when spoken to, mortal!" Laylah ordered. "Michael and his *B'nai Elohim* can't help you now. Your fate will be determined by Lord Kor. Isn't that right, Drorikan?"

"She must first go before Trolgroth," Drorikan persisted.

Laylah stared at the city's second-in-command. "It would seem you leave me no choice. But rest assured that when I leave this city with my prisoner, I'll also be taking your head on a platter."

Drorikan snorted. "Do you think Trolgroth's going to let that happen?"

"Do you think he's going to deny one of Kor's consorts for someone as replaceable as a mere second-in-command?" Laylah countered.

Drorikan was about to answer when his eyes suddenly expanded in pain and confusion. Behind him, Mazranoch was using his sword to cut and slice Drorikan's guts from the rear. As the light of life fled the overlord's eyes, Mazranoch shoved the body off his sword and let it fall to the ground. The surrounding demon warriors began to hoot and holler as they did every time their superiors cold-bloodedly jockeyed for position in the Abyssian hierarchy.

"You're free to go, My Lady," Mazranoch said. "Take your prisoner to Kor... and be sure to mention me, Mazranoch, the new First Overlord to Trolgroth. Drorikan here had gotten fat and lazy. He's the past. Younger underlords like me represent the future."

"Not so fast," an unknown voice called out. Unnoticed until he spoke, an overlord demon, larger than anyone else there, shoved his way through the throng of demon warriors. The few who challenged him were soon spitting out blood and crawling away as fast as they could.

"Who are you?" Mazranoch asked, annoyance clearly written all over his face.

The overlord opened up his cloak to reveal his badge of office. "Zachariah, Kor's Chief Interrogator. And you?"

Mazranoch couldn't believe it. First Kor's consort and now his chief interrogator. All this for a puny mortal? "Mazranoch, Trolgroth's new second-in-command. And you want?"

Zachariah smiled. "Why, the mortal and the consort, of course."

"I'm shocked! Just shocked!" Mazranoch mockingly exclaimed.

The Chief Interrogator smiled at Mazranoch before turning to Laylah. "Kor's most put out with your decision to find the mortal on your own. But I'm sure he'll be happy you succeeded. He might even bump you up to Fourth Consort. Now take the mortal and go to my carriage. It's back behind this throng." Zachariah then turned to several demon warriors. "Make sure they get there unharmed!"

The warriors bobbed their heads up and down in acknowledgement, eager to please.

"How dare you!" Laylah exclaimed. "The mortal is mine and mine alone!"

Zachariah looked at Laylah. "Do not defy me, Fifth Consort. My patience runs thin. You will go with these warriors and wait for me in my carriage."

"Kor will..."

"Kor will do nothing against me and you know it," the chief interrogator said. "Now... do I need to have you chained?"

Laylah shook head.

Zachariah nodded at the demons, who quickly surrounded the two females and led them away. They knew better than to try and take Laylah's trident and sword.

"Now then... what did you say your name was?" Zachariah inquired after Laylah and Lessien had been escorted away.

"As I told Kor's consort, it's Mazranoch, Chief Interrogator."

Zachariah smiled. "Well, Mazranoch, you did yourself a favor here. I overheard you release the mortal to Kor's consort. Though she's out of her league, her intentions were good... and Kor wouldn't have liked her soiled by the likes of Trolgroth, or that creature you disposed of just now. As Kor's chief interrogator, I decide guilt or innocence, and I officially find you innocent of the charge of assassinating your immediate superior."

"I didn't know I needed your approval. He was a coward and didn't serve the citizens of Uz Urreth well."

Zachariah nodded. "Indeed! But let me ask you a question. How close was this creature to *his* immediate superior, the city overlord, Trolgroth?"

"Um..."

"Perhaps... just perhaps, the approval of Kor's Chief Interrogator will carry some weight? Then again, so would my disapproval."

All of a sudden, Mazranoch wasn't so sure of himself. One word from the overlord standing before him could get him sent to the *Pillar*. "Of.. of course, My Lord. I'd be extremely grateful for any help you'd choose to bestow upon me."

Zachariah slapped Mazranoch on the shoulder. "Excellent! I was hoping you'd say that. You see, things are a bit more complicated than one demon taking steps to forward his career."

"They are?"

"Most certainly," the chief interrogator replid. "Normally, what happened here wouldn't matter to me one bit. Nothing wrong with a little career advancement, eh? We expect that from our younger demons. If you survive, you've proven your worthiness. What say you, fellows?" Zachariah asked as he look around at the faces of the demon warriors surrounding them.

Everyone whooped and shouted their endorsement.

Zachariah smiled and smacked the taloned hands of some of the warriors. He had everyone just where he wanted. "See! They all agree you did the right thing!"

"Drorikan was a creep!" one demon yelled.

"Yeah! He stole my poor ol' da's pension!"

"I heard he and Trolgroth played board games together!"

"Eek!" everyone screamed at the same time.

Zachariah held up his hands to quiet everyone down. "One of the many things I'm also allowed to do is make on-the-spot temporary appointments."

"Temporary appointments?" Mazranoch asked.

"It wouldn't be right to leave the peasants leaderless as I take their lord to the capital, now would it?" Zachariah replied. "I grant you temporary control over this city... Uz Urreth... until I can notify Kor and get to you the proper documentation. Of course, you can name whomever you want as your second."

"Me?"

"You'll have my recommendation, naturally, since I'm the one who appointed you. And I'm proud to say I have Kor's ear in matters of this nature."

The bystander demon warriors once again lifted their voices in a cascade of hoots and hollers. Mazranoch was a fairly popular underlord... now overlord... with the troops.

Mazranoch, lost in emotion, grabbed Zachariah's hand and began pumping it up and down. "Thank you! Thank you! Thank... wait! What about Trolgroth? He won't go quietly." Mazranoch dared not ask the obvious question, *"Why was the Chief Interrogator taking Trolgroth in the first place?"* He didn't really care.

Zachariah shrugged. "Does he have any real loyalists in the city?"

The warriors snickered and chuckled. "Only Kor's support keeps his head on his shoulders," one cried out.

Mazranoch shook his head. "No. But even with the entire city behind me, I can't... I can't..."

"Dispose of him?" Zachariah finished the thought. "Blast the legalities, I always say. But you have a point. Kor has a tendency to act... oh, shall we say forcibly if he's been inconvenienced?"

"Forcibly?" Mazranoch stammered. "He'd wipe out the entire city to prove the point no one makes power-grabs without his consent... expressed or otherwise."

"Except for one thing... well, two actually," Zachariah mentioned. "First, Kor's Chief Interrogator, that's me, is the one naming you the temporary leader of this fine city. As I already mentioned, I can do that."

"I still can't believe you'd name me overlord of the city?" Mazranoch interrupted. He shook his head as his mind worked to understand everything that'd just happened... all because of a simple backstab. He came back to his senses when he saw the chief interrogator staring at him. "Apologies, My Lord. And the second reason?"

Zachariah smiled. He didn't let his irritation over the intrusion distract him. "Rounding up the consort is only one reason I'm here. My actual mission is to arrest Trolgroth." The chief interrogator lied. "There's a trivial matter of missing funds... skimming off the top... that sort of thing." This was something that all city overlords were guilty of. Kor expected and allowed it as long as the amount wasn't excessive. Figuring out what Kor considered excessive was something each city leader had to figure out on his own, however. If they figured wrong... "I'm taking him back to the capital for judgment... well, punishment. Judgment's already been passed. You understand."

"Make the retch Kiss the *Pillar*!" someone called out, to which everyone laughed.

"That's the plan," Zachariah said. "Now, if maybe a few of

you might go back to the palace and inform Trolgroth he's leaving with me, I'd appreciate it."

In a flash, all the demon warriors were gone… except for Mazranoch.

"You'd better make sure that crowd doesn't hurt Trolgroth… at least not too much." the chief interrogator said. "He needs to be alive to stand accused before Kor."

"You'll get your prisoner," Mazranoch answered. "I just wanted to say your confidence in me is justified."

"See that it is… overlord," Zachariah replied as he walked towards his carriage. "I don't want to come back to interrogate and pass judgment on you. Now go make sure your warriors have Trolgroth ready to travel. I'll be along shortly."

When he opened the door and climbed into his carriage, he saw two females staring at him. One was sucking on her fingers, red from several light burns.

"You tried to leave, didn't you?" It wasn't a question. "I *did* ask you to wait. But just in case, I put a heat spell on the doorknobs and around the windows. Did you think I'd capture you only to let you escape again?"

Both females continued to stare saying nothing.

Zachariah sighed. "I suppose I need to do some explaining."

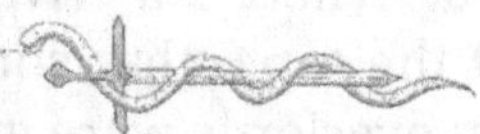

Yesper was concerned. Laylah and the mortal should have arrived by now, if they were going to arrive, which he doubted more and more with each passing minute. The baby was still attached to Yesper's back and had remained silent throughout.

"Where are you?" the creature of everyone's deepest nightmare said aloud.

Martin cooed.

"You can say that again," Yesper said as he walked over to a window to check one more time.

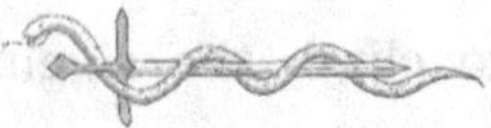

"Grug!" a voice called out from below. "Ye e'er goin' t' come down out o' there?"

Braz'galar looked below to see several sailors looking up at the base of the mast. The approaching night kept them from seeing anything but vague outlines.

"There's a mug o' javah waitin' fer ye in the galley," another called. "And maybe a bit o' rot-gut to go in it."

Braz'galar couldn't afford to have those sailors come up... or draw the attention of the crow's nest on the mainmast above him.

"Give me an' the lads a chance to wake up," he said in his best seaman's jargon.

"Got in a few winks, eh?" the first voice replied. "We'll save ye a seat."

The sailors turned and left. All except one. "That didn't sound like Grug," Braz'galar heard the crewman say as he started to climb the rigging. Braz'galar grabbed a cross-bow from the dead hands of one of the sailors he'd killed, loaded a bolt, and waited. The sailor never appeared.

"Behemoths!" someone in the crow's nest above bellowed.

"Number, location, an' direction!" a voice shouted from the rear of the ship.

"Six, maybe more! I make them four points on the port side, direction due east, range three thousand yards!"

"It's got to be that same family," Braz'galar thought. *"And we're on an intercept course."* He knew one Behemoth wouldn't attack a frigate. That was a battle it'd most likely lose. But the frigate didn't stand a chance against a family of Behemoth's... especially if there was more than one male involved.

"Beat to quarters!" the captain shouted.

"Move it, ye mangy dogs!" This from one of the ship's

officers.

Sailors started to climb the rigging leading up to his position.

"Just what I needed," Braz'galar said aloud as he watched the burst of activity below. His only option was to go straight up and hope he'd remain undetected in his chameleon guise.

"Hard-a-starboard!" the captain ordered. Then he gave several orders in sequence.

"Head to the sky into the wind!"

"Feather an' drift!"

"Back the mainsail!"

As the ship slowed, it made a slow turn to port, away from the direction the Behemoths were swimming. From his new vantage point high above in the upper reaches of the foremast, Braz'galar could just barely make out the Behemoths as they breached the water for air. It didn't appear they'd taken notice of the frigate.

"Good work, captain," he thought.

Unfortunately for Braz'galar, during the emergency, the three sailors he'd dispatched were discovered and another alarm, this one far different, resonated throughout the ship.

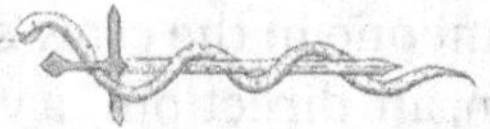

Laylah nodded. "I guess you do, Zachariah."

The chief interrogator smiled. "I should've guessed you'd know who I was, Laylah. I'm not too surprised… though Braz'galar didn't mention you when he asked me to take the mortal queen away from Uz Urreth's overlord."

"Wait?" Laylah said. "Kor's fixer asked you to rescue the mortal?"

"My name's Lessien," the queen protested to deaf ears.

Zachariah nodded. "We've been associates for decades. Between the two of us, nothing much happens that we don't know about. I guess you'd call it a mutually beneficial relationship… though I'd like to think we've actually become friends. Either way, it helps us do our jobs better than any of Kor's other cronies. And that, my dear lady, keeps us in power."

"Then you understand why I've taken the mortal," Laylah responded. "To give her over to Kor and earn a promotion… and power. Except for Emprusa, all his other consorts are morons. I should be at least his number two. This gift," Laylah pointed towards Lessien, "will prove it."

"Nice try," Zachariah said with a grin. "You have no intention of turning the mortal over to Kor. Returning the sword to the mortal says as much. And something both Braz'galar and I have known for some time now is your relationship with the *B'nai Elohim*."

A deathly silence descended inside the coach. Laylah and Lessien tightened their grips on sword and trident, ready to kill at a moment's notice.

"Relax, ladies! I've no intention of turning either of you over to Kor, either."

"Yet you *are* going back to the capital," Laylah said.

Zachariah nodded. "Now I am. Time for Uz Urreth to have a new overlord."

Laylah relaxed, but only a little. "Trolgroth… Mazranoch… what's the difference?"

"Mazranoch will be beholden to me," Zachariah replied. "I saw an opportunity and I took it."

"We're not going anywhere without Martin!" Lessien exclaimed as she unsheathed a part of *Ah-HritVakha's* glowing blade.

"Or Yesper," Laylah added.

Though Zachariah's expression never changed, the mortal queen's remark baffled him. He knew about Yesper. That creature was Laylah's constant companion and a force to be reckoned with in his own right. But who was Martin?

"Of course not," Zachariah said. "If you tell me where they're at, we can pick them up along the way."

Laylah gave Zachariah directions to where they were supposed to meet Yesper. Zachariah's breath caught when his gaze fell upon the child. Martin was a newborn, maybe between one or two weeks old, who had very little in common, appearance wise, with any demon Zachariah had ever seen. But the child's most astonishing feature was his eyes. When they looked at Zachariah, it was as if they were reading his soul... and understanding it.

"A cambian," Zachariah thought. *"This will come to no good."*

Within a few hours, Zachariah's carriage, escorted by a small honor guard provided by Mazranoch, headed towards the capital city of Kor. Trolgroth, battered and bruised, trailed behind the carriage connected to unbreakable chains. At no time during the brief life he had left did he ever figure out how his fall from grace had occurred so suddenly and without warning.

CHAPTER TEN

The Abyss and the Cavern of the Johari

"Arise, My Lord," Emprusa whispered into the ear of Kor. "Your destiny awaits on the morrow."

Kor opened his eyes to see his First Consort staring down at him. "I'm not asleep… and since when do you greet the new day with a simple verse? You're a lot of things, but a poetess isn't one of them."

Emprusa smiled. "Two days hence, and Aster will be yours."

The Prefecture overlord sat up in his gigantic bed and yawned. "Tomorrow the attack begins. But it's going to take longer than one day to destroy the Talisman. And the *B'nai Elohim*, even without the Talisman, won't go down without a long, bloody fight." Kor looked over at Emprusa, lovely as ever, and smiled. "But you're right. Everything will be finalized today, and tomorrow we begin the fulfillment of the destiny you mention. Before that…"

Emprusa allowed herself to be laid back on the bed. "But My Lord," she purred. "We'll be late…"

"I can never be late," Kor whispered into his consort's ear while he kissed the side of her neck.

Somewhere in the back of his mind, his predecessors occupying the *Living Throne* protested the lack of proper discipline during such defining times. As usual, Kor didn't listen.

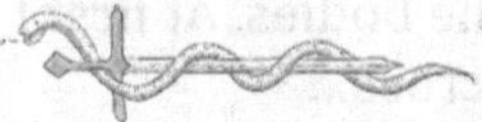

"What the hell's going on?" Max said aloud as he looked down at the dead bat.

"I git one ower here," Azriel yelled out from about one hundred feet away. Azriel and Jörmungander were helping Max canvass the huge cavern the Johari called home for dead bats.

Jörmungander came up alongside Max and studied the corpse. "Just like the others. If I didn't know better, I'd swear they were only sleeping."

"Just get on with it," Max snapped. He was angry. The number of dead bats they'd discovered during the last twenty-four hours rose well past the point of coincidence, or the natural state of life and death. Something was killing them… something even the immortal Johari didn't understand. Max liked the bats, particularly the youngsters. They were like puppies. It hurt him, it hurt all of them, to stand by helplessly while more and more of them mysteriously died. The Johari speculated it was a magical attack. But from where or, perhaps the more important question, who, the Johari couldn't say. It was beyond her experience.

Jörmungander used a small part of his dragon's breath to disintegrate the body. Without another word, he left to do the same to the dead bat Azriel had found.

"Ah be lying, laddie, if ah thought this wis natural," Azriel was saying to his dragon friend as the two rejoined Max a few minutes later. "Tis be evil o' some type tae be sure. Bit a pattern? Can't say ah see one."

Max acknowledged his two friends with a questioning look on his face. "What's this about a pattern?"

"Our young mukker 'ere claims there's a pattern tae th' deaths," Azriel answered.

"What pattern, Jörmungander?" Max asked.

"The location of the bodies. At first I didn't see it, but after the first few we ran across…"

Azriel grumbled under his breath before interrupting. "Just spit it oot, laddie! We dinnae hae time fur yer drawn oot explanations or theories. Lives ur at stake."

"Dying hasn't changed you one bit, I see," Jörmungander said with an affectionate smile. "You're just as crusty as…"

"*That's* what's been bothering me!" Max exclaimed as he held up a hand to silence the two. "Not just the manner of death, but the location as well. They're all in the connecting corridors outside the perimeter of the cavern. But how are they dying? And why here and not in there?"

Azriel turned to Jörmungander. "Laddie, ye hae a close rapport wi' th' bat elders. Explain tae thaim they must warn their fowk tae stay away from th' corridors... at least 'til we git this figured oot."

"Alright, Azriel," Jörmungander replied. "Except the elders don't have much control over the older youngsters. They're liable to enter the corridors just because they were told not to."

Azriel nodded. "Tell thaim tae post guards if thay hae tae. It's a maiter o' life 'n' death."

The black dragon stepped a few paces back to give his wings clearance and flew up towards the cavern ceiling.

"That's a good start, but it may not be enough," Max said as he watched the dragon fly into the darker regions of the cavern heights. "You know the drill, Azriel. What, why, when, where, and how? That method kept us alive for most of our past escapades."

"Aye, laddie," Azriel acknowledged. "But you know as weel as ah that we hardly ever wur able tae answer all th' questions."

"I know," Max answered. Then he frowned.

"What's th' maiter, laddie?" Azriel asked. "Ye look lik' you're aboot tae pass a brick."

"Do you remember that pacifist priest who followed us around for a few weeks?" Max asked. "You know... back in the old days?"

The dwarf laughed. "Oh, aye! Father... Father... ah can't mind his name, bit he didn't dae anythin' right... except fur his rabbit stew."

"What a strange fellow he was," Max mused. "Remember

the evening he resurrected that deer we had killed for dinner? Said his morals wouldn't abide its death. Yet he didn't have any qualms about snapping a rabbit's neck for that stew of his."

"Everyone loved his rabbit stew," Azriel remarked. "Including him."

Max nodded. "But if you think back upon our time with him, more often than not, he managed to help us answer these kinds of questions."

"Aye. He used magic. Whaur ye gaun wi' this?"

"He was a priest, so he used clerical magic," Max said. "Premonition magic that allowed him to see the path ahead or give us words of warning."

"An' we hae a cleric o' oor own," Azriel remarked.

Max nodded. "Perhaps Erika can tell us more about what's going on?"

Two hours later, everyone, including several bat elders, were back at the same corridor entrance where Max had found the dead bat. Jörmungander had warned the elders and made sure they understood the danger. In response, they ordered everyone in the bat clan to stay away from all cavern exits and had guards dispatched to make sure their mandate was obeyed.

Erika stood in front of the others, staring out into the darkness of the corridor. She closed her eyes and concentrated. Nothing about the corridor, or the darkness that reigned within, appeared out of the ordinary.

"I detect no evil to account for the deaths," Erika observed. "Nothing... no, wait! There is something. It's very subtle... as if it's coming from a great distance. I almost missed it."

"Is that the reason behind the deaths?" Solveig asked.

Erika shrugged. "Hard to say."

"What's this 'something' ye mentioned, lass?" Azriel asked.

"That's hard to say as well," Erika answered. "But it's similar to magical stone melding."

Max shivered. "We're familiar with the spell," he said. "But how does that relate to what's happening?"

Erika turned away from the corridor to look at her friends. "Stone melding alters the physical structure of someone or something so they, or it, can move through stone. In effect, the magic changes the recipient's body composition. It's like a ghost's ability to move through solid objects. If I had to guess, I'd say the opposite is happening here. Magic is working to change the air into a denser version of itself. Maybe those who died couldn't get out and suffocated."

"It wis tae thick tae breathe?" Azriel commented.

Erika nodded. "And move. Like a fly getting trapped in honey."

"We've gone in with no problem," Max said. "What makes it different for the bats?"

Erika shook her head. "I don't believe there *is* a difference, except in the capacity of…"

"Our lungs and bodies are much larger and stronger," Jörmungander remarked. Then he looked at Erika. "Sorry."

Erika frowned, then smiled at her mate. "That's alright. Jörmungander's correct. Right now, it's a matter of lung capacity… ours are considerably larger, which adds strength. So we're able to physically process the denser air. Our size also prevents us from getting stuck. The bats… well, with their smaller and more delicate lungs, they never had a chance. There's another thing to consider. If the magic is still working to change the air, who knows how long before we can't breathe or move through it ourselves?"

"Is it safe tae say this is deliberate?" Azriel asked.

Erika nodded. "Without a doubt."

Max sighed. "So what's coming our way?" he wondered aloud. "And why?"

"What makes you say that?" Solveig asked Max.

"What other answer could there possibly be?" Max replied.

"We know it's deliberate. What's happening in the corridors is designed to either keep us from escaping or to isolate the Johari. No one knows we're even alive, so..."

"It haes tae be th' Johari," Azriel finished Max's thought. "Bit how come wid th' Johari be targeted at this particular point in time? Awfy much o' a coincidence. 'N' fur whit purpose?"

"Erika, isn't there a spell you can use to foretell the future?" Jörmungander queried.

"Aye, laddie, ye be oan tae something," Azriel said.

"Divination," Erika answered. "But that requires direct contact with my goddess. I haven't felt Eir's presence since regaining consciousness after the battle with the sylphs. I don't know if she'll answer me."

"Your goddess has already answered you, Erika," Solveig said. "Every spell you've crafted since the sylph battle proves it."

Erika nodded. "I hadn't thought of it in that way." She retreated into a trance-like state. Minutes passed before she came out of it. She'd have toppled over if Solveig and Elbedreth hadn't been on each side to catch her.

Azriel didn't waste a second. "Well, lass?"

Erika took a deep breath. "There are two future timelines possible... and both center on the Johari. Either the Johari lives and our world remains safe from the Abyss. Or the Johari dies and demons rule for the rest of eternity."

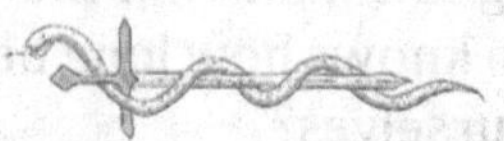

Bezrameth watched as another of his Order of the Talisman sorcerers died, a dried up husk which collapsed into dust under its own weight.

"What kind of magic are your sorcerers doing that causes such a horrible death?" Vol'goth asked. "Are they not aware of the consequences?"

"Powerful magic... the kind of magic that has dire outcomes," Bezrameth responded. "Do they do so without the knowledge they're going to die? No! They understand. They relish the opportunity. They willingly die because of their loyalty to me and the cause we serve. You lead warriors. Are they not as enthusiastic?"

Vol'goth laughed. "Dying in the face of the enemy is something my fifty passionately embrace every waking moment of their lives... which is unique among most of our demon warriors. That's what makes them so valuable. Personally, I believe they're all insane."

"That... and devoted," Bezrameth countered. "Which is what makes them so easy to manipulate."

Vol'goth's fear of the Talisman sect leader intensified. "So, what *are* your sorcerers dying for?"

"Tomorrow I begin the enchantment which will get us to the Talisman. But once there, our success will depend on two things... the strength of the Talisman to resist our attacks, and the possibility of mortal allies it can count on to fight in its defense. To that end, my Order is working... and dying... to send enchantments across the void between the Abyss and the mortal world which will close any attempt to fortify the Talisman once we get there."

"And if its allies aren't mortal?" Vol'goth asked.

"Then your job gets a whole lot more difficult," Bezrameth answered.

Vol'goth frowned. "*I need more than fifty warriors,*" he thought.

Four Taumaru and a dog walked the back alleys of Zir Tachoss, stopping in some of the rougher-looking taverns to drink cheap, nasty tasting ale and listen to drunken gossip from the local citizenry. Though the Taumaru were usually given a wide berth, free drinks opened many mouths. But the only information they gathered centered upon the military and its upcoming war against the *B'nai Elohim*. There was nothing about two mortal females or the overlord, Belladonna.

"This is going nowhere," Nightshade said in exasperation as they sat in yet another rough-looking tavern. "It's been two days and all we've done is make a bunch of rogues drunker than they were when we walked in."

"Not quite true, madam," Landross remarked. "We now know where they're not. I've spent a considerable amount of time in taverns and bars. Don't let the drunkards fool you. If they're anything like the drunken rogues on Aster, they're well aware of everything that goes on in this quarter of the city. Sharing information pays for drinks which keeps their palettes wet. And that's not to mention the thieves, pickpockets, and other ne'er-do-wells who are sanctioned and spying for their guilds. I'd say at least half the demons we've spoken to were sober and probably got as much information from us as we got from them."

"What're you saying?" Nightshade asked. "That our cover's blown?"

"Not at all," Abigail replied. "Our disguises are rock solid… and none of us has said anything to cast suspicion. As far as anyone knows, we're who we appear to be. But the nature of our search won't go unnoticed."

"Look, Nightshade," Father Goram interjected. "Since you've turned from your fiendish heritage, you can't use your demon form to intimidate and scare. Maybe you can throw your name around, but how long do you think that's going to last without the persona to back it up? You've pledged yourself to Althaya. You know what that entails."

"White Magic," Nightshade admitted.

Father Goram nodded. "White Magic which, when used

properly, can be far more effective in the Abyss than black if for no other reason than it has a unique signature that isn't readily identifiable. Look and listen carefully to what's being said... but a tinge of the magic can help decipher between what's true and what's nothing but a story. Information gathering takes times and patience."

"But Lessien and Autumn are on their own," Nightshade replied. "The longer we take to get to them, the chances they don't survive increase dramatically."

"You're forgetting two things, my dear friend," Abigail said. "Two mortal females in the Abyss are just unusual enough to stay any harm that might come to them without having Kor's blessing first. Kor will want to interview them himself. If nothing turns up here, our next step should take us to the capital."

"That sounds real encouraging," Althaya's newest acolyte dryly remarked. "And the second thing, Abigail?"

"The peasants are mostly good people who have no love for the overlords," the gorgon answered. "You could say the same about the guilds... though their primary motivation will be money or leverage. If either has them, they'll be safe enough."

"Besides," Landross added, "the last two days, though fruitless as far as direct information goes, have laid the foundation for an even wider search."

Father Goram caught the look of confusion in Nightshade's eyes. "Think, girl," he said. "Strangers asking questions and willing to pay for answers? Not only will that get out to the common folk but also to the guilds. For the money involved, this entire city... and probably its two neighboring cities... will be searched for the information we seek. All we have to do is wait... and if Autumn, Lessien, and Belladonna have been here, we'll find out about it."

"It won't be cheap, Father Goram," Abigail remarked. "I

know these people… I know the guilds… and they'll demand a top price."

"We can afford it," the priest said. "We only have to make sure the information we pay for is accurate."

"Plenty of guild profits, particularly that of the Thieves Guild, involve information bartering," Abigail said. "Anything we get from them will be verified. You can count on it."

Father Goram nodded. "Then I suggest we get comfortable and wait to see if something comes up."

"But only for a short time," Landross added.

The next day, they received the information they so desperately wanted, though it wasn't what they hoped to hear. Two females, one a mortal, were captured by Kor's chief interrogator, a demon called Zachariah, and were being taken to the capital city of Kor. Belladonna was also heading to Kor… or so it seemed. She'd been last seen boarding a small ship to cross the Grimfail Reservoir south of the capital.

"I guess we know where we go next," Landross remarked.

Abigail noticed Father Goram had suddenly appeared to grow pensive. "Why the long face, Horatio?" she asked. She received no response. "Horatio?"

The priest looked at the gorgon. "Sorry, Abigail. The information only indicates one mortal female. Why not two?"

Abigail had no answer, though she had learned enough concerning the two missing mortal females to understand Father Goram's concern. "Probably just a mis-identification. Don't worry, we'll get them both."

"I hope you're right," the priest said.

Before they could get out of the city to continue their search, the war between Kor and the *B'nai Elohim* began.

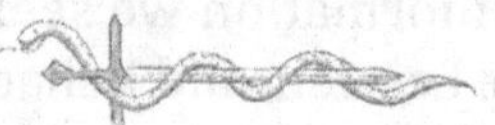

Lord Viktor Ternborg, his executive officer Colonel

Florentina Antonovich, Michael, and Gabrielle stood on the battlements which extended across the entire breadth of the plateau upon which the *B'nai Elohim* fortress stood. Below the plateau and off in the distance, they could just make out three large cities. Between the cities, Kor had deployed several demon armies.

"You expect our twenty thousand to hold this fortress against that… that horde?" Colonel Antonovich observed. "There must be tens of thousands down there."

"The builders magically enhanced this fortress to resist all supernatural and physical attacks," Gabrielle boasted. "We've stood for thousands of years. We could hold it with half our number."

"Yet if we're correct in our assumptions, this is the first time they've ever attacked us under these types of circumstances," Michael countered. "Defending the fortress isn't the primary objective."

The *B'nai Elohim* leader turned to Lord Ternborg. "They'll begin their attack with a series of sorcerer spells, such as magical missiles and explosions of force and fire. These are only designed to get our attention while the armies move to attack. All your warriors have to do is cover up and wait it out. The walls will handle everything else."

"And if they drop their magic behind the walls where my people are exposed?" Lord Ternborg asked.

"The magical resistance of the walls against spells extends both up into the air and down into the ground," Michael replied. "We're virtually impervious to their sorcerer attacks."

"Virtually?"

Michael looked at Gabrielle, who shook her head. "It'll never happen," she said.

"What won't happen?" Lord Ternborg asked.

"We can't have secrets." Michael told his second-in-command. "There's one potential weakness," he admitted to the Draugen Pesta king.

Lord Ternborg waited.

"The builders developed the magic of the walls to absorb the impact of the explosions," Gabrielle said. "But not to deflect it."

"Which means…" Lord Ternborg asked.

This time it was Gabrielle who looked at Michael.

"I don't think anyone here is going to blab it to the other side," Michael replied to Gabrielle's unasked question. "Tell him. He has a right to know."

"When the magic of the explosion or fire hits the magic of the wall, it's absorbed," Gabrielle explained. "If the sum total of the magic is powerful enough, the wall must realign before it can absorb more."

The leader of the giants got right to the point. "How long?" he demanded.

"Just a second or two," Michael answered. "They haven't figured it out yet, though."

"You haven't either, have you?" Lord Ternborg stated.

Michael shook his head. "No. We don't know how to correct this weakness."

Lord Ternborg turned to Colonel Antonovich. "Send runners to all the divisional commanders. Say nothing about the defenses… but when the attack starts, I want our people to take cover from both sides of the wall. Have everyone cover up as well."

"Most will only have their shields."

Lord Ternborg sighed. "I know. But it's better than nothing."

"Really Viktor, none of their magical attacks have ever breached the walls," Michael insisted.

"If this attack is a feint, as you suggest, they're going to try hard to sell it completely," Lord Ternborg replied. "Which means you might never have dealt with the magnitude of the magic that's coming. And if they get a spell through before your shields reset themselves, they may figure out how it happened."

Michael shook his head. "Highly unlikely. The chances are..."

Lord Ternborg gave Michael a withering glare, which caused him to stop talking. "I never leave things to chance," the Draugen Pesta king said. "Not if I'm aware of the possibility... and definitely not when it comes to the safety of my people. I prepare for it."

Off in the distance, they heard bugles, trumpets, and drums. Everyone on the fortress battlements looked towards the demon armies and could see them organizing into three attack formations along a broad front. Behind the armies, dust was kicking up into the atmosphere, signaling even more armies were marching forward.

"That's got to be half of Kor's total strength," Gabrielle noted.

It took the rest of the day for the armies of Kor to get into place. Altogether, eight armies in two rows of four—one hundred and sixty thousand warriors total—occupied the plains outside the three western-most cities of the Kor Prefecture. Though Michael assured his Draugen Pesta allies demons never attacked during nighttime, Lord Ternborg's twenty thousand warriors spent the night on the battlements, nervously watching the demon encampment. Dawn was still three hours away when the attack began.

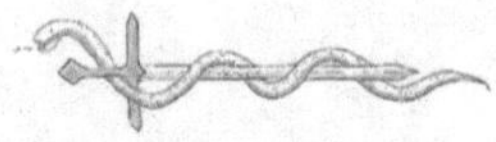

Kor sat on the *Living Throne,* dozing. Javah was no longer enough to keep his eyes opened. The previous day and most of the night had been filled with preparations for the attack on the *B'nai Elohim* fortress. The operation was far too important to leave last-minute decisions to any of his subordinates, regardless of how talented and devoted they were. Before him, advisors, Faction overlords and their assistants, his consorts, and anyone else who felt they could make a mark by being present for what will surely be a historic occasion, filled the audience hall.

"Bezrameth can't be trusted," one of the dead overlords from the *Living Throne* whispered into Kor's mind. *"He'll destroy the Talisman and claim the mortal world as his own."*

"He'll use the mortals to take Kor from you," another suggested.

"Shut up!" Kor thought back.

"Kill him once he opens the doorway!"

"You'll be joining us if you don't!"

"Don't show weakness!"

Kor had enough. He stood and screamed, "Shut up!"

Everyone in the great hall looked at their leader with a mixture of fear and confusion. "Who, My Lord?" Gorzath, the Market Faction leader, asked.

Kor was spared the embarrassment of answering when one of Azazael's underlord assistants burst into the hall and whispered something into the Military Faction leader's ear.

Azazael stood. "The attack has begun!" he called out for all to hear. He then reached down and grabbed his mug of cold javah off the table before him and raised it into the air.

"To victory!" he bellowed. "All hail Lord Kor!"

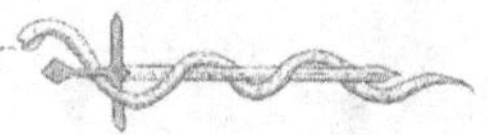

It didn't take long for Zir Tachoss's overlord to shut down the city. To the west, magic lit up the skies in the early morning darkness. The ground shook as explosions over the *B'nai Elohim* fortress rattled window glass and knocked small, light objects off store shelves. Constant patrols of demon warriors marched up and down the streets and back allies of the city. All citizens were ordered to stay indoors, and all guild operations were ordered to cease for the duration. City officials would send any violators to the capital to Kiss the *Pillar*. There was to be no exceptions.

Father Goram, Nightshade, Landross, Abigail, and Herbie took refuge in the gorgon's store and upstairs living areas. Neither Father Goram nor Nightshade had the magical means of escaping Zir Tachoss. They were tired, frustrated, and fearful about Lessien and Autumn's fate in the capital city.

The fortress defenders took cover behind and under anything they could find. As Lord Ternborg had predicted, the magical attacks thrown at the *B'nai Elohim* were unlike any ever experienced, and, as feared, exposed the weakness in the defensive magic. It only took the Draugen Pesta war sorcerers a few seconds to anticipate and prevent the breeches, but that was enough time for some of the demon magic to get through and hammer the stronghold. Parts of the fortress crumbled from direct hits, and some of Lord Ternborg's people, caught without sufficient cover, were wounded by shrapnel, or, sometimes, tragically killed. During the magical attack, the demon armies climbed onto the plateau and positioned themselves for their assault.

After two hours of bombardment, the horde of demon armies began their attack on the fortress. Though damaged, there were no actual breeches in the walls and the defensive magic was still in place, which left the demon armies no choice but to go over the top... warfare Lord Ternborg's warriors were well equipped to handle. All of Michael's guardians had disappeared to prepare for what they believed was stage two of the attack, the attempts to teleport past the Juxtaposition Point and to Aster.

One thousand demon sorcerers, under the command of

their Magic Faction overlord, Lilitu, opened teleportation doorways to Aster. For many, it was the only enchantment they had been trained to do. Each sorcerer, with full knowledge of their probable fate, waited in silence for their doom. The penalty for casting such forbidden magic materialized almost at once. One thousand *B'nai Elohim* warriors pushed through magical teleportation doorways, and one thousand demon sorcerers died a quick and brutal death.

As eight demon armies assaulted the fortress, and one thousand demon sorcerers drew the attention of the *B'nai Elohim*, Bezrameth completed the powerful magical incantation that, unbeknownst to the distracted guardians, opened a doorway beneath the surface of Aster. The dried husks of several Order of the Talisman sorcerers, consumed as the formidable spell developed and coalesced, lay before the iridescent doorway—sacrifices to the desires and goals of Bezrameth and his master, Kor. Bezrameth, unsure about how much time there was before either the doorway collapsed or they'd be discovered, stepped through without hesitation, followed by two Order sorcerers and his personal bodyguard of ten. Vol'goth trailed behind with his fifty warriors.

Deep under Aster, the black dragon Jörmungander felt the unfamiliar presence of an ancient evil. It was a threat even greater than that of the recently destroyed sylph, for the malevolent force he sensed sought to destroy the Johari. He knew the magnificent creature they'd found so far below the surface had to be saved at all costs… that for some unknown reason, the survival of Aster depended upon it. Jörmungander looked at his friends with a great sadness. This was going to be a battle some of them wouldn't survive.

CHAPTER ELEVEN

Aster – Draugan Pesta and the Hyrokkin Empire

"Quiet!" Krasnov Dmitrievich shouted to bring everyone's attention back to the matter at hand. The peace treaty Lord Ternborg had worked out with the Hyrokkin queen had each person in the room outraged and none of them were thinking straight. "I'm as upset as all of you… but our voiced indignation won't solve anything!"

"What does it matter if it's war or peace?" someone shouted. "The Hyrokkin will still want the drugs, and peace will open the border, making it easier to deliver."

"But those beasts won't pay but half as much during peace," another answered. "The risks won't be the same. Any idiot can see that!"

"Hey, now!"

"We're taking the same chances in peace or war," yet a third called out. "Trading in drugs is still illegal… and Ternborg takes a very dim view of it. If the consequences are the same…"

"If we have a problem with our royals, the Hyrrokin would expect us to handle it… permanently," a finely dressed fellow said. "No… we're much better off trading during wartime. The Hyrokkin understand those kinds of risks."

"As long as we control the product, we control the price!"

"We control the drugs but not weapons manufacture!"

"So why do our Hyrokkin contacts want to continue the war if they can force cheaper prices during peacetime?"

"Damn good question!" an overweight, somewhat sloppily dressed shopkeeper exclaimed.

"War is their nature," came the reply from someone in the back of the room. "It's all they know how to do!"

"That and make weapons!" another shouted.

Everyone began talking once again. Dmitrievich sighed. *"This isn't getting us anywhere,"* he thought. He turned to the person on his right and said, "I need to control the room."

Kesha Stanislavovich nodded and drew his rapier. Eight burly warriors standing behind him did the same.

"The next person to utter a word out of order loses his head!" Kesha shouted and waited.

None of those in the room dared challenge Dmitrievich's enforcer. They knew from experience that the former military commander was true to his word.

Kesha nodded. "That's better."

"What do you propose, Counselor Dmitrievich?" someone called out. Dmitrievich thought it might be Vassili Yakopav, Draugen Pesta's Assistant Minister of Weapons. "We stand to lose fortunes if Ternborg puts his peace plan in place and those damned centaurs cut weapons production."

"Even bigger fortunes if we're caught, war or no war!" someone else called out.

Dmitrievich stayed Kesha's hand as he began to draw his sword and make good his threat. "Gentlemen, we have a very limited window of opportunity here. Anything we do must be while Lord Ternborg's away."

"What about the queen?" someone called from the back of the room.

"Yeah," another voice said. "We know she's responsible for the disappearance of Boris Drugov. They won't ever find his body, I'd wager. She's as dangerous as her husband."

"Maybe more so," yet another voice spoke out. "She's from the north. They'd rather let their knives do their talking for them."

Everyone in the room began talking again. Kesha began to draw his rapier once again, but Dmitrievich shook his head.

"Quiet, please!" the Dmitrievich shouted as he held up his arms. "Quiet!"

The noise didn't stop. If anything, it got louder. Dmitrievich looked at Kesha and nodded. The enforcer picked someone close at random, drew his sword, and swung. The unfortunate, a middle-aged, well-dressed banker, ducked at the last minute. Instead of cutting through the neck, the sword connected at the bridge of the nose and sliced, sending half of the banker's head flying a few feet before dropping to the floor. Everyone within five feet was splashed with blood and brains.

The room went silent as everyone looked from Kesha, who was cleaning his sword on the dead man's silk overcoat, to the body of the dead banker.

"I warned you!" Dmitrievich said. "Before leaving, I want each of you to donate five gold coins for his family. You're all responsible for his death. That's not a suggestion, by the way. Do you understand?"

Everyone in the room looked again at Kesha and his warriors, then nodded, though some of them weren't too happy about it.

"That's better," Kesha said to the hushed room.

"Now then… I've been in contact with our associates within the Hyrokkin Empire," Dmitrievich continued. "Having the Princess over there at this moment presents us with a unique opportunity. If our four-legged friends do what they say they're going to do, their queen won't be a problem… and Daphnia will be a hostage. Because of that, I don't think our queen will attack the Hyrokkin… but nor will she hesitate to throw peace out the window."

"And into a very deep hole!" someone called out.

"Just like she did with Drugov," another said.

Antonov Petrova, one of Draugen Pesta's more wealthy merchants, stood. "How are they going to nullify Queen Thesonia or threaten the Princess? I mean, I assume that's what you're talking about. How can they possibly get close enough? The centaur queen has an entire army to help keep her safe. As for the Princess, she's guarded by that wolf of hers as well as her own Phalanx."

"Don't be fooled by the Hyrokkin army's apparent mollification," Dmitrievich replied. "Most consider the Princess being on their land a stain against their honor… and their queen's peace with us the act of a traitor. They'll act when the times right."

"I don't care how the Hyrokkin take care of the matter." another said. "I want to know how long it's going to take. Not all of us have the same unlimited resources as you. Our entire fortunes depend on this 'drugs for weapons' scheme you've arranged with the Hyrokkin. We need that next shipment of weapons to go out soon or we'll not be able to meet payroll, feed our families, or dole out the costs for licenses, fines, and guild dues. We're facing financial ruin!"

"If we don't get the weapons shipped, there'll be hell to pay!" someone else shouted. "Haven't heard from Madeira or Hebron lately, but the black market for Hyrokkin weapons is still going strong in Palisade Crest and Altheros."

There was a general sense of agreement amongst half of those present.

"Then perhaps you shouldn't have gotten involved in the first place," Antonov Petrova remarked.

"Here! Here!" the other half yelled out.

"Your wealth won't stop your head from rolling just as easily as ours if we're ever found out!"

"Is that a threat?"

"If we go down or lose what little we have…"

"That's enough, gentleman!" Dmitrievich bellowed. This time, everyone stopped talking. "No one's going to lose their fortunes because of this. If necessary, the rest of us will cover those of you who need it with no-interest loans. There may even be some funding from the treasury. Isn't that right, Cherganski?"

Kostadin Vasilov Cherganski, Assistant Chief of the Exchequer and an unexpected participant in the treason, nodded. "I think that can be arranged if it becomes necessary." He smiled. "A few minor adjustments to the books is all that's required."

Dmitrievich shrugged. "There you have it. No one suffers because of this minor setback. Now I want you to go back and prepare your product like normal... but sit on it for now. I'll tell you when it's time to ship. Any more questions or complaints?"

"Why can't we make the weapons ourselves... human-sized... and cut the Hyrokkin out altogether?"

The room was quiet.

"We've been through this," Vassili Yakopav responded. "While the Hyrokkin aren't good for much, they *are* sitting on that huge deposit of berlinium ore... the only such deposit known to exist... which makes their weapons twice as strong as any other. The humans aren't going to accept an ordinary steel blade from us when they can get a berlinium blade from the Hyrokkin. Besides, how do we keep the manufacture of human-sized weapons from the king?"

Dmitrievich nodded.

"And we're the only ones who have the Bael trees needed to manufacture the drug the Hyrokkin call Epiphany," Antonov Petrova added.

As the meeting continued, one conspirator slipped out of a door in the back of the room, unnoticed by everyone except Kesha. Taking two of his warriors, Kesha, after a brief conversation with Dmitrievich, left and, despite the head start of the unknown person, was soon following behind at a discrete distance. There was little doubt the one he was following was a spy. But for who?

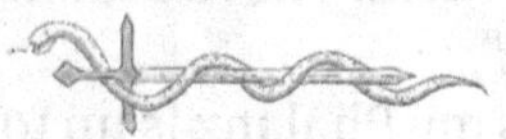

Giorgi had heard enough. His uncle had told him about a wonderful opportunity to invest his recent inheritance into something that would pay big dividends. But what they talked about wasn't only illegal, but also treasonous. Giorgi had no qualms breaking the law now and then. It was how many of the rich merchants in Saint Petersburg amassed their fortunes. But his uncle said nothing about selling drugs to the enemy. And for what? Weapons to sell to the humans for gold? No! Giorgi couldn't stomach that. Without a word to his uncle, he slipped through a back door and left. He wondered if he should tell the authorities, but put that decision away until tomorrow, for it needed close consideration. They'd probably execute his uncle as a result, and loyalty to his family was as important as loyalty to his country.

Deep in thought, Giorgi didn't notice the three barring his way until it was too late to run… not that running would have done him any good. The next three hours didn't go so well for the young giant. Kesha was wrong concerning Giorgi. He wasn't a spy. Unfortunately for the boy, his captors decided he knew too much to be left alive. They never found Giorgi's tortured body.

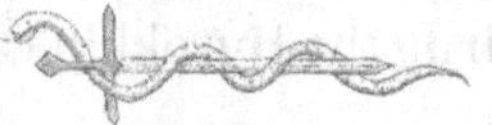

"It's suicide," Jarsus said over a cup of coffee. It was early morning, still dark, and Jarsus was talking to Major Anya Romanova, the commander of Daphnia's Phalanx, over a light breakfast. The princess and her wolf were still sleeping, though it was unlikely Adimar ever truly slept. "This building… oor embassy… is nothing mair than a fancy warehouse. And we're two miles fae th' palace… two miles awa' fae th' queen's guard shuid we need them. That's assuming Thesonia's guards ur even oan oor side."

"You have doubts my Phalanx is up to the job?" Anya asked.

"It's suicide," Jarsus said over a cup of coffee. It was early morning, still dark, and Jarsus was talking to Major Anya Romanova, the commander of Daphnia's Phalanx, over a light breakfast. The princess and her wolf were still sleeping, though it was unlikely Adimar ever truly slept. "This building... oor embassy... is nothing mair than a fancy warehouse. And we're two miles fae th' palace... two miles awa' fae th' queen's guard shuid we need them. That's assuming Thesonia's guards ur even oan oor side."

"You have doubts my Phalanx is up to the job?" Anya asked.

"No... it's nae that," Jarsus answered. "But whit kin a thousand dae against an entire nation?"

"We have Queen Thesonia's word," Anya replied. "Whether or not we can trust that is debatable, I'll grant you that. But we're shoring up the building's weaknesses and adding fortifications. A decent size wall with gates, battlements, and guard towers will go a long way towards keeping away any attack... at least until help arrives. And don't forget the fifteen thousand Queen Sofia has poised on the border."

"Aye, lass, I'm nae forgetting," Jarsus commented as he scratched behind one of Sienna's ears. Though Sienna was as intelligent as both Jarsus and Anya, she still liked the same things most bears liked, including a little attention. "But Thesonia's administration, particularly th' military, doesn't lik' th' peace. Ye kin read it in thair eyes... in th' wey thay react tae oor Princess... in th' furtive gawks thay mak' behind th' Queen's back. Ah believe they're waiting 'til they've convinced enough fowk that peace isn't in thair best interest. Then they'll mak' anither attempt tae overthrow th' Queen 'n' replace her wi' military rule, 'n' oor Princess wull be a hostage."

Anya looked at the dwarf. She only knew him by reputation, but Lord Ternborg's mission briefing made it clear he trusted Jarsus with Princess Daphnia's life as much as he trusted the wolf... and her. She suddenly saw the urgency to the point he was making.

"Excuse me," Anya said as she stood. "I need to inspect the work being done on our defensive perimeter and make a few plans with my staff. Good day, Jarsus."

"That wis a quick turnaround," the dwarf thought as he watched the Phalanx commander leave the room. She had a look of newfound determination in her eye. "Noo she understands," he said to himself as he pushed away his cold coffee. "I think it's time tae go oot 'n' mingle wi' th' centaurs, Sienna. Mibbie ah kin git a feel fur whaur th' common folk staun."

Daybreak had just arrived when Jarsus exited the building. All around the compound, several hundred Phalanx warriors, stripped down to pants and undershirts, sweated in the early morning sun as they built new, and reinforced existing, walls to tighten up the building's defenses. Many of the remaining were digging a spike-filled moat to encircle the embassy. Orderly stacks of weapons, only a few feet away from their owners, were aligned in neat rows and dotted the compound interior. Anya, who was now involved in planning discussions with her commanders, gave him a curt nod as he exited the embassy's perimeter.

Within a few minutes, Jarsus and Sienna had reached one of several marketplaces within the centaur city. Though still too early for most of the merchants, a few shops, particularly those serving food or drink of some type, were already open and doing a brisk business. Jarsus bought a fresh mug of coffee and a purple-colored Danish that turned out to be very tasty.

There were still a few dwarves living in Hyrokkin... distant relatives of the dwarven slaves who tunneled through the Eastern Boreskyre Range... so Jarsus drew little attention. Sienna was another story, however. No bear ever seen in the land of the centaurs could match her size, even the enormous brutes that lived in the mountains. The locals reaction to

Sienna comforted Jarsus, for he doubted he had to worry about pickpockets and thieves. Likewise, as part of Draugan Pesta's diplomatic mission to the Hyrokkin Empire, the badge he wore on a chain around his neck made him off-limits by royal decree.

It wasn't long before Jarsus felt he was being closely watched and followed. Sienna, when asked about it through their telepathic link, wondered what had taken him so long to figure it out. Feigning interest in the merchandise in various shops, Jarsus spent the next hour trying to decide who the watchers were—thieves, suspicious busybodies, spies, or military. Then, on a hunch, he circled the perimeter of the embassy. It was being watched as well, except there were far more, and they were carefully studying the fortifications being added to the embassy.

"They're everywhere," Jarsus remarked to Sienna. *"And ah doubt thare 'ere tae mak' sure Princess Daphnia's kept safe 'n' sound."*

"It could be nothing more than the Hyrokkin playing it safe," Sienna replied. *"Many still consider us invaders, regardless of what the queen has to say about it. You don't forget centuries of hatred overnight. Acceptance takes time."*

"Ah wull tell ye noo," Jarsus countered. *"Th' centaurs wull ne'er accept us as pals, let alone allies. Even oor Princess won't be able tae chaynge that."*

Jarsus noticed a small delegation, each wearing the livery of the queen, making its way through the marketplace and towards the embassy. *"Curious,"* he thought. *"The Princess 'n' th' Queen weren't due tae catch up 'til later in th' week."*

As Daphnia's principle advisor, the dwarf ended his reconnoiter earlier than he wanted and hurried back to the embassy.

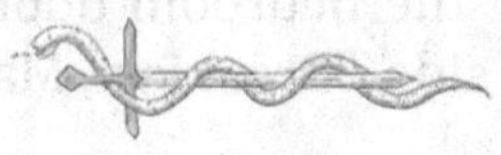

Daphnia awoke and sensed she'd slept way too late. She turned over in her spacious bed and looked directly into the determined eyes of Adimar, her faithful wolf companion. Her first response was to pull the covers over her head and go back to sleep. But that was the reaction of a child. She couldn't afford to be the little girl she was just a few short days ago. Now she had responsibilities to her country and her parents. She was determined to disappoint neither.

In her defense, yesterday had been a busy day. It was the first day of her official duties as Draugan Pesta's ambassador to the Hyrokkin Empire. That evening Queen Thesonia had held court to unofficially introduce Daphnia, and to remind everyone in her administration, as well as the rich and powerful financiers, business owners, and others who held power outside the government, that the brokered peace between the two countries was real and they needed to make the appropriate adjustments for that reality. Daphnia noticed at the time that many of the centaurs in attendance weren't thrilled with the development. Later, there was a modest, hastily prepared dinner for Daphnia, her small retinue, the queen, and a few of the queen's closest advisors. Afterwards, bards entertained everyone with stories of centaur lore, though, by design, none of those stories mentioned the constant war between the two nations represented at the table. Very few of the queen's guests had much to say, and their reaction to her was only just acceptable. It was a bitter affair, and she was glad when it had ended.

Daphnia sat up, yawned, and stretched. Adimar lay at the foot of the bed and closed his eyes. She threw a pillow at him as she got up. He deftly swatted it away with a massive paw and woofed, as if to say, "Is that the best you've got?"

The young princess had just finished dressing when there was a light knock on the bedroom door. An unknown voice called from the other side. "Breakfast, Madam Ambassador!"

With Adimar by her side, Daphnia opened the door and saw a young centaur holding a tray of fruit, steaming hot meat pies, pastry, and a glass of milk. Also included on the tray was a large slab of meat for the wolf.

"Please, put the tray on the table," Daphnia said as she stepped aside. "Would you care to join me?"

"Oh no, Madam Ambassador," the maid responded. "I had my breakfast hours ago."

Daphnia inwardly winced. *"I wonder how long everyone's been up while I slept,"* she wondered. *"That has to change."* Aloud, she said, "Then thank you... ahhh... what's your name?"

"Damaera, Madam Ambassador."

Daphnia nodded. "Thank you, Damaera."

As the princess and her wolf broke their fast, there was another knock on the door. Daphnia didn't have time to swallow her mouthful of food before Jarsus opened the door and walked in, followed by Sienna.

"You hae visitors, lassie," he announced without preamble. "It's th' Queen's foremaist counselor... ah think his name is Thanilus."

Daphnia swallowed the food and wiped her mouth with a napkin. "Lead the way, you old scoundrel," she said before stuffing the rest of the meat pie into her mouth and grabbing a pastry to go. That turned out to be an unfortunate decision as the still hot meat pie burned her mouth. She dropped the pastry and took a drink of milk. "Ow... that hurt!"

"Calm yersel', lassie, 'n' finish yer brunch," Jarsus replied. "He kin hauld his horses. Ah don't lik' him... tae arrogant fur mah taste. We need tae establish boundaries, 'n' ye, mah dear lassie, represent a king... 'n' a powerful nation."

"But..."

The dwarf shook his head. "Finish yer meal. He's nae gaun anywhere."

An hour later, forty-five minutes of which was Jarsus

deliberately procrastinating, Daphnia, Jarsus, and Adimar, entered what served as the receiving room in her compound to find the richly dressed representative of the queen pacing back and forth with a serious and angry scowl on his face. The rest of his retinue stood against a wall and looked worried.

"Do you know who I am, young lady!" Thanilus said with barely contained anger in his voice.

"Jarsus tells me you're the Queen's First Counselor," Daphnia replied.

Thanilus snorted. "And yet I was made to wait for an hour before you received me!"

Adimar sensed a change in Daphnia's attitude and issued a low, barely perceptible growl as the hackles on his back rose. The young princess brushed Adimar's side to calm him as she remembered her training.

"First Counselor Thanilus, it was you who showed up on my doorstep seeking an audience," Daphnia responded. "I've no obligation to drop everything I'm doing to attend to you."

"Good fur you, lass!" Jarsus thought to himself.

"Now we can continue to banter or you can tell me why you're here unannounced," Daphnia continued.

Thanilus stared for a few seconds before nodding. "The Queen is having a banquet tonight in your honor. Last night was more for the benefit of the Queen's court. Tonight is her formal introduction of you as Draugen Pesta's ambassador to the Hyrokkin Empire. The dwarf, your Phalanx commander, and a small token guard of four may also come. But there will be no animals."

Jarsus bristled at the thought of Sienna being considered a simple animal and began a terse remark when Daphnia held up her hand to still him. "The only animals we brought are our warhorses."

"You know who I mean," the First Counselor replied.

"My friend, Adimar, is the son of the immortal Fenrisúlfr,

father of all wolves, and the grandson of the old god Loki," Daphnia said. "Surely such a heritage makes him more than just an animal."

"Well..."

"As fur mah bear companion, Sienna... huv a go tae keep her awa'," Jarsus added.

The Hyrokkin's eye's narrowed. *"We can adjust,"* he thought. Aloud: "I'll inform the Queen. We'll expect you at the palace in six hours."

Thanilus clapped his hands once and led his entourage out of the room.

"Something's nae right," Jarsus said, confirming Daphnia's own feeling of disquiet.

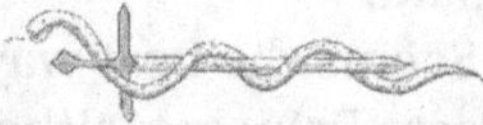

Thanilus was sitting around a large wooden table with other members of the queen's counsel—Perrius, Hyrokkin's master armorer, Tritocus, the Army's new Chief of Staff, Casillos, high priest to Skerrit, god of Centaurs, Kadotus, owner of Hyrokkin's largest bank and Hyrokkin's chief financial officer, Cretandrou, Minister of Mines and Precious Stones, and Antephone, the female crime boss of the seven cities. Together, these seven centaurs represented the most formidable block of notables in the Hyrokkin Empire's power structure. And together they were making a fortune by procuring and selling Epiphany, a hallucinogenic drug made from the bark of the Bael fruit tree only found in Draugen Pesta, in exchange for berlinium made weapons which Draugen Pesta in-turn sold on the black market to the humans for a handsome profit. They were also the main powerbrokers behind the latest assassination attempt on the queen. Only the threat of a Draugen Pesta invasion forced them to back off for a time and drop the blame on a few of their lackey generals.

"You said the wolf wouldn't be a problem!" Casillos exclaimed.

Thanilus shook his head. "I told you it wasn't a sure thing. Now that I've seen it close up, there's no doubt in my mind the wolf's lineage does indeed go back to Loki. I'll not be the one to tell it where it can and cannot go!"

Casillos sighed. "Skerrit doesn't want a confrontation with Loki. Nor do I want a confrontation with Skerrit. Only through him does my magic flow."

"You mean the ley lines," Antephone remarked.

"Which are..."

"Enough!" Thanilus said.

"So we need to neutralize the wolf... but cause it no harm in doing so," Tritocus said.

Casillos nodded. "Seems the best way. And we can't afford to hurt the Draugen Pesta Princess, either."

"We have to act this evening," Thanilus remarked, "or drop the effort for now... and I don't see when we'll get a better opportunity. But I warn you, if we don't take care of this soon, we can't send our weapons to our friends on the other side of the mountains."

"And if we don't do that," Perrius said, "we'll not get our next shipment of drugs."

"Not to mention a truce between our two countries may actually go into effect if it isn't stopped," Kadotus added. "Once formalized, it'll be harder to break."

Tritocus nodded. "Without war with the Draugan Pesta, the queen will order a decrease in weapons manufacture. That means less to send across the mountains and less of the drug coming back. No war also means fewer troops, one of our principal users of Epiphany."

"Once hooked, always hooked," Kadotus remarked. "They'll never be off the stuff, so we lose no profit."

"But they buy twice as much," Tritocus countered. "And

we're able to hook the new recruits, which, I might add, drops dramatically during times of peace."

Cretandrou, a big burly brute who seldom spook, shook his head. "I, for one, am not ready to sacrifice my lifestyle for the sake of peace."

There was a nod of heads around the table. "Here! Here!"

"So we take the queen out of the picture and blame Draugan Pesta... but we're agreed the Princess and her wolf are off limits," Antephone said as she cleaned her fingernails with a sharp dagger. The crime boss wasn't beautiful by any standard, too much hard living, but she was fastidious when it came to personal cleanliness.

"That leaves the dwarf," Tritocus remarked, "or one of their garrison warriors."

Antephone shook her head. "Not a garrison warrior, particularly the commander."

Thanilus nodded. "Antephone's right. Phalanx warriors are a special breed. No one would believe one of them would go rogue. But the dwarf actually works to our advantage. According to the information I've received from Dmitrievich, the Draugen Pesta queen has no love for him. She'd be more likely to believe the dwarf was responsible than anyone else. She might also be willing to sacrifice the dwarf to keep the peace in effect."

"So you're thinking we kidnap the queen and blame it on the dwarf?" Antephone asked.

Casillos shook his head. "Not kidnap... assassinate. Just like we tried to do earlier... only not as clumsy."

"Clumsy?" Tritocus bristled with indignation.

"Yes, clumsy," Casillos repeated. "All you army types know is brute force. Sometimes that works. But regicide requires sophistication... a deft hand, so to speak... to be successful. And by successful, I mean it should not only result in the queen's death, but there must also be a logical scapegoat that the people will be accept, particularly since our queen is so popular. We don't want suspicion to fall on us. Considering our experience with dwarves, it should be easy to make Jarsus Blackmantle the fall guy. All we'll need is a basic cover story. It doesn't have to be anything elaborate because it won't matter to the people, for they'll be out for blood. My priests will see to that. As for the Draugen Pesta princess... we keep her as a hostage. That should stay their queen's hand for a time."

"If she believes our story and allows us to punish the dwarf, how does that prevent the peace?" Tritocus asked.

Thanilus smiled. "If she doesn't, she'll have to go to war to get her daughter back," he said. "If she does, there'll still be enough justification for us to re-declare war on Draugen Pesta. And that, my friends, puts us back to where we started... only we'll have eliminated our weakest link."

Thanilus looked around the room. "Any more questions or concerns?"

"Just one," Cretandrou asked. "How do we assassinate the queen and blame it on the dwarf?"

"Leave that to me," Antephone cackled.

The banquet was low key by Draugen Pesta standards, but a grand affair for the Hyrokkin. All the rich and the powerful were in attendance and dressed in their finest apparel. As each guest was announced to the hall by a herald, they joined the reception line for Queen Thesonia and Daphnia. But other than formal introductions, little communication passed between Draugen Pesta's first ambassador to the Hyrokkin Empire and the Hyrokkin people. Not unexpectedly, they viewed her as an outsider, an interloper who didn't belong regardless of her official standing, and treated her as such. Adimar, whose wolf's senses picked up on the tension, stood. His hackles were up and a deep, low, almost imperceptible growl issued from his throat.

Jarsus grimaced. *"Oh, boy,"* he thought. "Keep th' wolf under control," he whispered to Daphnia. "We don't need an international incident."

Daphnia nodded and placed a calming hand on Adimar's side. He ceased growling and his hackles lowered, but he remained alert and standing. The Hyrokkin still in the receiving line gave the wolf even more leeway.

The guests wasted no time breaking up into different factions based upon position within the government and individual wealth. Queen Thesonia and Daphnia sat on a dais at one end of the room with a few of the queen's closest friends, along with Jarsus and Anya. Daphnia's four guards, as well as several of the queen's, stood against a wall behind them. Except for an occasional furtive glance in their direction, the guests ignored Daphnia and her party.

"Nice crowd," Jarsus remarked. "Ye don't seem tae be well-liked, Queenie."

"Jarsus!" Daphnia snapped as she looked sternly at the dwarf. "It's not your place to say! And address our host by her proper title!"

"It's just an observation, lassie," Jarsus retorted. "Don't git yer backside up."

"It's alright," Queen Thesonia responded. "The proposed peace treaty between our two countries isn't popular with those not accustomed to wondering where their next meal's coming from. But the people... the ordinary person on the street and in the fields... like food on the table for themselves and their families. They'll appreciate your help whenever we have drought... which happens more than we'd like."

"Aye, Queenie... er, Yer Grace," Jarsus replied. "Bit yer problem isn't wi' th' fowk, bit instead wi' yer upper class... yer generals, merchants, 'n' bankers. War mak's those folks rich.

Enough that thay hate tae gie it up regardless o' th' cost yer common fowk hae tae pay."

Queen Thesonia nodded. "I understand... but I have most of the army behind me."

"Dae ye noo," Jarsus answered.

The Hyrokkin queen remained silent. In the absence of conversation, Daphnia took the opportunity and tried to steer the conversation in another direction, like to the drought and what Hyrokkin needed to keep its people fed. But the queen wouldn't allow it. It was clear she had something else on her mind.

Queen Thesonia looked at Daphnia. "What would your mother do if your father was away and she feared an overthrow attempt?"

Daphnia shook her head. "That'd never happen."

"Hypothetically," the queen said.

Daphnia knew exactly how to answer. "My mother's from the north... as are her attendants and personal guards. Their knives would be out in open display for all to see. Everyone knows what that means... don't tempt fate or you die. There's not a person in Draugen Pesta who doesn't know how dangerous northern men and women are with their knives. If I were you, I'd start by surrounding myself with only those whom I knew were absolutely trustworthy... preferably kinfolk. Then I'd make sure they're trained appropriately and arm them to the teeth."

"You're so young to be so wise," Queen Thesonia mused.

"That she be," Jarsus observed. "But she's had a lifetime o' training... training that's aye ongoing."

Daphnia blushed. "I have excellent teachers."

"Dae ye hae spies in yer employ, Yer Grace?" Jarsus changed the subject.

"Of course!" Queen Thesonia responded. "Doesn't everyone?"

"Do they work directly for you?" Daphnia queried. Jarsus had asked a legitimate question, and the queen didn't seem to fit the typical Hyrokkin mold—ruthless, bloodthirsty, and calculating.

Queen Thesonia shook her head. "The army handles that for me and gives me weekly reports. Most of the spies are in Draugen Pesta. But don't worry. I'll have them withdrawn as soon as your father has formally signed the peace treaty."

Daphnia sighed and looked at Jarsus, who shook his head.

"Do ye think th' army's aff tae report oan th' spies thay hae peepin' you?" Jarsus asked.

"Peeping... oh, watching me? Why would they want to do... oh! I'm such a fool!"

Daphnia shook her head. "No, Your Highness. Maybe a bit too trusting, but not a fool. Even the most beloved rulers need to keep a constant eye out for treachery. But considering the recent assassination attempt, I'd say you need to be extra careful."

"Och, aye," Jarsus added. "You need tae hunker doon. Tell me, dae ye hae none o' yer own? Spies wha report tae ye alone? Spies that watch yer people?"

"I probably should, shouldn't I," the queen stated after a few moments' thought.

"Aye!" Jarsus explained. "Or else how kin ye expect tae keep from losing yer heid?"

"Jarsus is right, Your Grace," Daphnia added. "If history is any indication, sovereigns are far more likely to be overthrown by their own followers than another country."

"It be fact, plain 'n' simple," the dwarf acknowledged. "Considering th' opposition tae th' peace treaty, I'm surprised yer aye alive."

"I may be a little naïve where spies are concerned, but I guarantee you I've safeguards that will keep my head on my shoulders," the queen snapped. "I can be just as merciless as any enemy, Hyrokkin or Draugen Pesta."

Daphnia looked down. "Forgive us, Your Grace," she said apologetically. "The peace treaty represents hope for your people. We in Draugen Pesta very much want to see that hope fulfilled. We also know how important you are to realizing that goal. Naturally, we're concerned for your safety."

Queen Thesonia smiled and shook her head. "Think nothing of it. Let's speak of more pleasant things, shall we?"

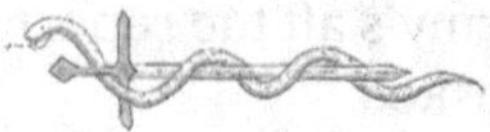

Several days after the banquet, in the deep of night, an assassination team composed of five humans breached the Hyrokkin queen's palace. They moved over, under, and around barriers no centaur could ever hope to negotiate. Along the way, they left several palace guards dead, victims of poisoned bolts from small handheld crossbows. The rest, identified by red armbands and part of the larger army faction that favored war with Draugen Pesta, had been warned of the incursion and looked the other way as the assassins went about their clandestine mission.

The queen's inner chambers offered tougher opposition. Her personal guards were there because of their unwavering loyalty. And like Daphnia's Phalanx warriors, they had specialized training which went far and above that of the ordinary guard or soldier. The hand-to-hand combat that ensued played out in only a few seconds and left all the centaur guards dead along with one of the five assassins. Though victorious, none of the remaining assassins escaped injury.

The assassins wasted little time entering the queen's chamber. Six female attendants, armed and ready for battle, stood guard around the queen's bed. The assassination team had been warned of this. Poisoned tipped throwing darts dropped all six. The exposed queen cowered in her bed. The nearest assassin walked over and cut her throat. The assassins watched indifferently as the queen thrashed about, choking and gagging on her own blood.

As soon as the queen stilled, her murderer examined the cooling body. He looked up at the team leader. "She's the decoy," he said.

The leader nodded, unsurprised. "We were told that might be the case," he responded. Using hand signals, he directed the rest of his team to search the room for concealed doors that might lead to secret rooms or passageways. They had the room searched within a few minutes and found what they were looking for... a long corridor leading to an iron reinforced door.

"Hachiro," the leader said.

One assassin approached the opened entrance to the secret corridor and shrugged off a backpack. He opened it and stepped back. A black mass slithered out and moved down the corridor. Qénsharma!

"You stay here with me, Hachiro," the leader ordered. "You two... get Kiyoko's body and bring it back."

Unconcerned about time since the only guards left in the palace were allies, of a sort, they carefully wrapped the body of the dead assassin in sheets and placed it on the bed. They waited an hour before entering the corridor. The Qénsharma needed time to work.

The assassins picked the locked door and entered. Three female attendants and one guard stood transfixed by the sight of the true queen's remains and didn't notice the assassins approach. They died quickly.

The assassins collected the slumbering Qénsharma and the head of the Hyrokkin queen. Hachiro raced back to the bedroom and carried back the body of his fellow assassin and a small spark from flint and steel left the room in a blazing inferno.

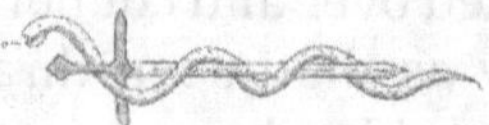

"We're surrounded," Major Anya Romanova said. She was sitting at a circular wooden table in a small chamber that was temporarily serving as a conference room. Also seated were Princess Daphnia, Jarsus, and Major Romanova's executive officer, Captain Dominika Yerzova. Adimar and Sienna were lying on the floor next to the door.

"I'm nae surprised," Jarsus said as he nodded. "That tracks wi' whit yer mither said lest nicht oan th' crystal. Yer folks kept thair self-restraint, Anya?"

Major Romanova nodded. "As difficult as it was. But I don't like the tactics, dwarf."

"We can't mak' th' foremaist move," Jarsus replied. "At least nae 'til we know how come th' Hyrokkin decided tae reverse coorse 'n' break th' peace."

"If they attack, how long can we hold them off, Anya?" Daphnia queried.

"Our defenses leave a lot to be desired," Major Romanova answered. "I won't be happy with anything short of twenty-foot stone walls and a moat."

"I'd lik' a fortified keep tae," Jarsus remarked. "Bit times run oot. Give yer best guess."

Major Romanova took a few seconds to consider the question.

"Spit it oot, lass!" Jarsus exclaimed, his impatience clear to see.

"Jarsus!" Daphnia warned.

"It's okay, Your Grace," Major Romanova said. "There's not a straightforward answer, Jarsus. I can think of at least two unknowns that impact the answer. First, the obvious unknown is how many they'll send against us. We can be reasonably certain they won't bring everyone, not with your mother keeping fifteen thousand of our warriors on their western border. The only thing keeping her from invading is you, Your Grace, and they know it."

"Father's inadvertently made me a hostage," Daphnia remarked. "I thought the queen was being sincere. Instead, she was playing us all along."

Jarsus shook his head. "We don't know this is th' queen's daein', noo dae we. We've heard nothing from her sin th' banquet, which leads me tae think she's a hostage herself... or worse."

"Whether it's the queen's doing or not is irrelevant," Major Romanova said. "The second question mark is how are *they* going to play it? They can't afford to let any harm come to you, Your Grace. So what's their approach going to be?"

There was a sharp knock on the closed doors to the room. Captain Yerzova answered and had a brief conversation with the guard on the other side. Rejoining the meeting, she whispered into Major Romanova's ear.

"We're about to get a few answers," the Phalanx commander announced. "There's a Hyrokkin delegation waiting at the front gate requesting to talk with you, Your Grace."

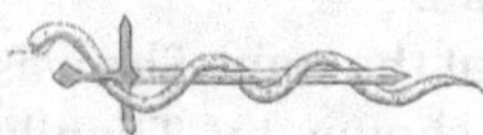

First Counselor Thanilus, the same centaur who invited Daphnia to the banquet, led the group of Hyrokkins waiting at the front gate. Only this time, instead of being accompanied by a civilian retinue, following him were several army officers and a dozen well-armed warriors.

"We meet again, eh, Princess," Thanilus ignored the normal pleasantries reserved for diplomats.

"And once again you've come unannounced," Daphnia replied. "As do your soldiers surrounding my embassy. We had assurances from the queen..."

Thanilus interrupted. "The queen is dead," he said without preamble. "Assassinated, we believe, by your dwarf. I'm here to arrest him."

"Preposterous!" Jarsus and Daphnia both yelled. The news rocked Daphnia back on her heels, but she knew for a fact Jarsus wouldn't have done such a thing. Her concern for the dwarf overcame her sorrow that someone had killed the Hyrokkin queen.

"Don't worry, dwarf, you'll get a fair trial. If you're innocent, you'll be released."

Jarsus drew a dagger. Sienna and Adimar growled. "I'll go nowhere wi' ye, ye dirty, stinkin' centaur!"

"Nor will I allow it," Daphnia added.

Major Romanova held up her hand, calling for calm. "How do we know you're telling us the truth?" she asked. "And if true, what evidence do you have it was Jarsus?"

Thanilus reached behind him as an officer handed him a heavy wool bag. The bottom of the bag was stained a dirty red. The first counselor reached inside the bag and withdraw the queen's head by the hair. He raised it up to show everyone before throwing it in the dirt at Jarsus's feet. "There's your proof the queen is dead."

Daphnia recoiled at the sight. She was even more disgusted with the disrespect shown by Thanilus to his sovereign's remains.

"Actually, I suppose I should thank you, dwarf," Thanilus said as he looked at Jarsus. "I never liked the queen. You could even say I hated her." The first counselor shrugged. "Still, she was Hyrokkin. And an outsider murdered her. It's now a matter of justice... and national pride."

The Hyrokkin turned to Daphnia. "Will you surrender the

dwarf to me, Princess?"

"Tell me of your evidence," Daphnia asked.

"You'll hear it at the trial," Thanilus responded. "Not before."

Daphnia shook her head. "You're lying. You've no evidence because there's no way Jarsus murdered your queen. He had neither the motive nor the opportunity. You'll have to take him if you want him… and I'm ready to fight should you try."

"Unfortunate, though not unexpected," Thanilus retorted. "I suggest you use one of those crystals you and the west are so fond of and communicate with your mother. Let's see if she values the dwarf as much as she does her daughter."

"We have diplomatic privilege," Major Romanova reminded the first counselor.

Thanilus laughed. "Granted by the queen," he replied as he pointed at the queen's head still lying in the dirt. "As far as I'm concerned, that privilege ended with her life."

Jarsus could stay silent no longer. Nor could he ignore his race's legacy of impulsiveness and colorful usage of language. "Ye foul-smelling, four-legged, troll-kissing, chamber pot! Ye 'n' me, one-on-one, richt 'ere 'n' noo!"

The first counselor smiled. "Charming. Princess, you have twenty-four hours to turn the dwarf over for trial."

"As I said, that's not going to happen," Daphnia said.

"Then I suggest you sharpen your swords," Thanilus barked. "As of right now, we're at war. Again!"

The Hyrokkin delegation turned and walked away.

Daphnia watched their backs for a couple of minutes. "Anya, please put together a detail and bury the queen's head with honor," she ordered. "I'll say a few words when you're ready. Then prepare my Phalanx for battle. Jarsus…"

"Ah know whit tae dae, lassie," the dwarf said. "And ye?"

"I'm going to talk to my mother."

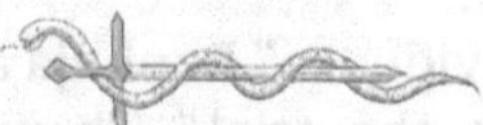

Sofia was reading crop production reports while eating a light breakfast of bread slathered with butter and jam with coffee to wash it down. "How long before the eastern fields and fruit trees fouled by the Hyrokkin are back into full production?" she asked.

"Next growing season at the soonest," Anna Merkulova, Draugen Pesta's Minister of Agriculture, replied. "But I wouldn't worry too much. It's been a good season. I doubt we'll have to tap into our reserves."

The Draugan Pesta queen shrugged her shoulders. "That's what it's there for. Anything else?"

"Nothing more, Your Grace," Anna said.

Sofia breathed a sigh of relief. Dealing with the mundanity of running a government can be so damn tedious. "Thanks for your report. You're dismissed."

As Anna Merkulova left, Major Raisa Stanislav walked through the double door entrance to Sofia's large office. The queen could see from the major's bearing and the look on her face that something was wrong.

"So what brings one of our scout commanders in from the eastern frontier?" the queen asked, not sure she wanted the answer. "The Hyrokkin not behaving themselves?"

"How'd you guess?" Major Stanislav answered.

Sofia sighed. "They're the Hyrokkin. What's going on?" In her voice was both dread and anger.

"The Hyrokkin have closed the border," Raisa said as she sat and poured herself a mug of coffee. "Their war banners are flying over their side of the pass."

"Damnit!" the queen exclaimed as she stood. "I knew they couldn't be trusted!"

Raisa stood as well.

Sofia placed her hands behind her back and paced back and forth before stopping in front of a map of both nations hanging on a wall. She already had the troops in place to invade and defeat the Hyrokkin. One thing stayed her hand, however. Her daughter was now a hostage. Undoubtedly, the Hyrokkin knew she'd understand the implications and would hold any kind of military response.

"Daphnia's got a complete Phalanx protecting her," Sofia said to herself. "Plus that wolf. She should be safe enough. Right?"

"I beg your pardon?" Raisa said.

Sofia shook her head. "Just thinking out loud," she answered the scout commander. "Get back to your command. I want every inch of our eastern border under watch at all times."

"Yes, Your Grace."

"And on your way out, get me General Valeryevich," Sofia ordered.

CHAPTER TWELVE

The Abyss

Zachariah preferred crossing the Okoris Run instead of the Grimfail Reservoir whenever he went south from Kor… or returned north. It added three days to his travel time, but the chief interrogator was never comfortable with the reservoir crossing because of the uncertainties of the weather and the beasts that swam in the waters… not to mention the extra cost for his oversized carriage.

Zachariah used the additional travel time to get to know his guests. He had heard of Laylah by reputation, of course, though the more he engaged her in conversation, the more he came to believe there was more to her than any of Kor's other consorts. She was smart, a skilled conversationalist, and had a great sense of humor. But mixed in with that was a hardness that only came from profound personal sacrifice. Unmatched in reading people, the chief interrogator determined that there was something Laylah was hiding, something potentially threatening to the Kor regime. Whatever this secret was, she had surprisingly shared it with the mortal queen. *"Things are getting interesting,"* he thought with delight. *"I wonder if Braz'galar knows as well?"*

As for the mortal queen, there was no question she was unusually intelligent, though she was as closed mouth as Laylah was talkative. She was clever, suspicious of most things, thoughtful, and her responses to his questions, though generally truthful, always seemed to turn the conversation back onto him as if she was the interrogator. That is to say, she was a natural-born queen familiar with word-play and used to getting to the crux of the matter. The more Zachariah got to know her, the more he enjoyed the back and forth of their conversations. He came to respect the mortal queen as much as he respected Laylah, or any other citizen of the Abyss.

The baby Martin, much-loved by the queen, was like no other child Zachariah had ever known or observed. Never once did he cry. The cambion child seemed to look upon the world with eyes that understood much more than his age allowed. That he had a special relationship with Lessien, and vice versa, was clear. How this relationship would end, not so much. One thing was certain, however. The child must remain in the Abyss for the sake of two worlds—demon and mortal.

Finally, there was the beast Yesper. He fell into the category of demon dog, though there were aspects of Yesper's behavior that reminded Zachariah of a dragon. Whatever he was, it was far from typical. He was as ugly as any demon Zachariah had ever seen, but extremely intelligent and protective of the people in his life. As for his ability to safeguard those he cared about, there was little doubt on that score. He was as strong as a goliath and as quick-witted and sprightly as a vampire cat. And his ability to spore-scent gave him advantages no other demon or creature of the Abyss had.

"How much longer?" Lessien asked. Though the carriage was luxurious, after a few days of traveling with two other adults, a baby, and an oversized dog-monster, she was feeling the restriction of captivity multiplied by her mind's imagination as she anticipated their arrival at the capital city of Kor. Can she trust Zachariah? Laylah? Could Kor discover her despite attempts to keep her hidden? And what would happen to Martin if they were to be discovered?

"We'll should arrive dusk tomorrow," Zachariah answered. "Once there, we'll wait for a couple of hours before entering the city."

Lessien raised a questioning eyebrow.

Zachariah expected the questioning look. "Shift change," he said. "I want to go in just before, so we're dealing with guards that are tired, hungry, and ready for a visit to the Entertainment Guild."

"The guild headquarters are located there," Laylah remarked. "As are the finest prostitutes. Nothing but the best for our troops."

Lessien rolled her eyes. "Some things remain the same regardless of where you are." The mortal queen changed the subject. "You think your prisoner has it left in him to make it? He's looking pretty ragged."

"It doesn't matter," Zachariah answered back. "He's collateral damage."

The response came out cold and matter-of-factly. The chief interrogator realized how he must have sounded almost immediately. "Forgive me if I sounded cruel, Lessien. I guarantee Trolgroth isn't someone to feel compassion for. He's guilty of terrible things and has earned his fate many times over. Being dragged to death or kissing the *Pillar* is mercy compared to what he deserves. You know what the *Pillar* is, don't you?"

Lessien nodded. "I know what it is and why it exists," she said. "Demons being demons, I first thought the more fed to it the better."

"And now?" Zachariah asked.

The mortal queen shrugged. "Let's just say I don't feel the same. Oh, don't mistake that as sympathy for the overlords, underlords, warriors, and all the other demons in the ruling power class. You're cruel, unconscionable brutes who use your fellow citizens ruthlessly. Only the guilds save them. But only as long as they serve the guilds. The common folk I've been associated with since my forced arrival, those you take for granted, would be welcomed in my kingdom. I've seen their hard work, how much they care for their families and loved ones, and their overall decency. They've helped me, a complete stranger, even if it would mean their lives."

"That's quite an indictment," Zachariah remarked with resentment. "Yet here we are… a demon overlord and one of

Kor's consorts… your boogeymen… trying to get you back to your own world."

"She's right and you know it," Laylah refuted.

The chief interrogator looked at Kor's consort. "I know," he admitted. "It's just hard hearing such a truth from a stranger."

Laylah agreed. "Of course it is. But ofttimes it's the stranger who sees things for what they truly are."

Lessien put a hand on Zachariah's arm. "I don't mean to be so damning. If it helps, from what I've observed, there appear to be more exceptions than I would ever had believed. Laylah, Nightshade, Belladonna, you, even Yesper, for all his apparent ferocity, have a goodness about you that's to be admired, considering the societal norms of the Abyss and how you were raised."

"Maybe that will change one day," Zachariah said.

Laylah and Lessien looked at each other. Did he know about the resistance? "What do you mean?" Laylah asked.

Zachariah chuckled. "I am what I am," he replied. "Kor's chief interrogator. And the existence of the resistance… any resistance… is high on the list of information I gather whenever I open the mind of a detainee. No one can resist… no one is immune to my ability. I can even strip Kor of his secrets. What I know…" Zachariah paused briefly as he gathered his thoughts. "Well… suffice to say, the Abyss is at a critical point, and Kor's ability to stave off an overthrow rests on a razor-thin probability. The smallest thing could tip his rule one way or the other."

"Why does he let you live?" Laylah asked.

"He once expounded on that very thing," Zachariah replied. "Other than my ability to interrogate as I do, I'm afraid I can do little else in the way of magic. But my ability to read people… to gather information and the truth… is valuable and the reason I'm so… esteemed, if you want to call it that. While there's very little I can do to Kor, physically or magically, under the correct set of circumstances I can open him up like a book. I can expose all his secrets. But he doesn't fear me for that, else he'd have murdered me long ago. No, instead, he uses me. And I let him. That needs to change as well." Zachariah took a deep breath, then sighed. "The truth be known, most of who you see is bluster... well, that plus Kor's support and my friendship with his fixer, Braz'galar."

"That traitor!" Lessien hissed.

"There's more to it than you know," Zachariah said. "One thing you should never forget while you're here, my mortal friend. You're a stranger in a strange land. Assumptions can, and will, get you killed."

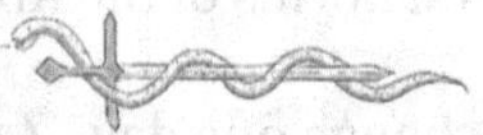

Ostrinnauth stared at Belladonna. They were deep within the ship in a room that had been hastily set up for interrogation. At the moment, the overlord sorceress didn't represent a threat. Her hands were manacled together, and they had shackled her to a sturdy bulkhead. But Ostrinnauth wasn't prepared to take chances. As a final safeguard, he gagged her.

Satisfied that Belladonna couldn't cast spells or counter spell any magic he himself attempted, Ostrinnauth smirked. "The great Belladonna. Who would've ever thought the daughter of Aikanáro and sister of the assassin Nightshade would one day be the prisoner of the great Ostrinnauth?"

Belladonna wanted to shrink the private parts of the idiot sorcerer standing in front of her, but she could only scowl at him instead. Ostrinnauth flinched slightly, barely enough to be noticed. But Belladonna saw it and her eyes reflected her satisfaction.

The door to the room opened and the ship's captain strode in, followed by a couple of hulking sailors.

"Report, Ostrinnauth," the captain ordered.

"Captain, I've only just started," the sorcerer protested.

"What's taking so long?" the captain roared.

The sorcerer winced and ducked like a child afraid to get cuffed by an adult. "She's going to be a tough nut to crack, Captain, so I had to take certain precautions."

The captain waved a hand in dismissal and went to stand in front of Belladonna. He removed the gag. "Where's Braz'galar?"

"What makes you think I know who this Braz'galar person is?"

The captain slapped Belladonna across the face. "Try again," he said. There was no emotion in his voice. "Or perhaps ye know 'im as Argomon, eh?"

Belladonna spit blood from her mouth but remained silent.

"No matter," the ship's master remarked after a few moments of silence. "I've 'eard from reliable sources ye two was together in Uz Urreth. I've also been told Braz'galar 'ired a ship to get the both o' ye across this here reservoir. What 'appened? Did the ship sink? Perhaps from that there freak storm? Or maybe ye stole the skiff because they discovered you're a traitor an' wanted by Kor... or that there Azazael wants Braz'galar dead an' will pay 'andsomely fer 'im."

Belladonna wrinkled her nose. The captain's breath smelled of rotten meat and decaying teeth. "I'm alone," she said.

"Sure," the captain snorted. "Ye launched the skiff on yer own."

"Who's to say I didn't," Belladonna retorted.

The captain shook his head. "I've 'eard a lot o' things about ye, Belladonna, but none o' them mention any seafarin' experience. No... ye 'ad 'elp. An' I'm bettin' that there 'elp came from Braz'galar. That there fog magic ye conjured been only a distraction. 'E's 'ere on this here ship somewhere, I'm sure o' it. We'll find 'im, don't ye worry."

Belladonna looked away.

The captain re-gagged his prisoner and turned to Ostrinnauth. "Keep 'er 'ere just as ye 'ave 'er. If ye can get any more information out o' 'er, fine... but it's unnecessary." The captain turned and grabbed Belladonna by the chin and jerked her head up. "Braz'galar will come for 'er soon enough. I know I would," he leered as he looked her over.

"What am I supposed to do when Braz'galar comes to rescue her?" the sorcerer asked.

The captain shook his head. "I'll post the sailors I brought with me outside the door. If 'e gets past them, you'll 'ave to 'andle the situation yerself."

"But..."

"Ye be the great Ostrinnauth, be ye not?"

"But..."

"Or die trying," the captain replied to the unasked question. "Kor an' Azazael get what Kor an' Azazael want. As we speak they want Belladonna an' Braz'galar. We'll make that there possible. Do ye understand?"

Ostrinnauth gulped.

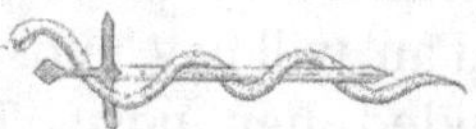

Braz'galar had his own problems to worry about. The crew knew he was on the vessel, and they had instigated a ship-wide, patterned search that was leaving very few places to hide. For the moment, Belladonna would have to fend for herself.

Braz'galar, camouflaged by his *Chameleon Stone* ring, stealthily climbed down the foremast to the main deck. He had to arm himself, so his goal was the ship's armory, which would be located belowdecks, probably in a closet-sized room. To get below he had to either open one of the crew access hatches in the deck, risky even with his camouflage, or make his way to the door located underneath the quarterdeck, which meant crossing the length of the ship and beat the ongoing search while doing so.

"No problem," he thought sarcastically as he looked around the base of the foremast.

He got on his abdomen and crawled to the ship's railing, knowing the magic of his ring would hide him from detection... at least as long as no one tripped over him. Once against the railing, he got up on his hands and knees and paused for the ring to adjust. Several long minutes later, he was in front of the door leading below. Above on the quarterdeck, orders were being shouted by the ship's officers. All around sailors were either busy running the ship or involved in the search for him.

Braz'galar nimbly sidestepped as the door unexpectedly opened. Out walked the ship's captain, who turned to his left to climb the stairs going up to the quarterdeck. But on the first step, he paused and looked directly at Braz'galar. The fixer stilled. He didn't even breathe.

"Oh, great! The damn ring needs to be recharged."

The captain, after a few tense seconds, decided he'd been imagining things. He shook his head to clear it and mounted the stairs. Within a few moments Braz'galar could hear the captain shouting his own orders in his own colorful language. The captain spared no crewman or officer his verbal abuse.

Braz'galar used the distraction to open the door, slip through, and close it behind him. But any thought he had about a reprieve, regardless of how brief, was dispelled when he saw two huge sailors standing guard in front of a door a few feet away. Neither looked in his direction, so it appeared they didn't notice the door open and close. Braz'galar sighed in relief. Then he saw lamplight shining from under the door they were protecting.

"Not the armory," he knew without a doubt. *"But I'd bet my*

life it's where they're keeping Belladonna."

Belladonna—still bound, chained, and gagged—watched Ostrinnauth as he stared at the closed door. The captain scared the life out of the sorcerer, but from what she'd just observed, the possibility of meeting Braz'galar frightened him even more.

The sorcerer turned and looked at Belladonna. "Why couldn't you have jumped into the damn water and drowned?" he snapped. Remembering who he was talking to, he walked over and removed the gag. "Sorry, madam," he apologized. "As you can imagine, your presence, as well as Braz'galar's, has everyone on edge... especially the captain. And now me. Imagine Azazael's disappointment if he ever discovers the captain had Braz'galar on the ship and lost him."

Belladonna shook her head. "You've no evidence Braz'galar is on the ship."

"Please spare me your lies," Ostrinnauth countered. "Azazael has spies everywhere. He's followed your movements... at least until you started the crossing. Where else *could* he be?"

"And if I admitted we were together, but he drowned when our ship sank," Belladonna said. "Would that be so hard to believe?"

"Kor's fixer... drowned?" Ostrinnauth remarked. "I don't think so. Considering his reputation, he'd probably hitch a ride on one of the denizens that swim below us. Why are you protecting him?"

"I'm wondering that myself," Belladonna thought.

The sorcerer didn't wait for an answer as he turned and went to the door. He fashioned several protection wards on it as well as on himself. The efficacy in which he created and shaped the magical spells surprised Belladonna. Until now, she believed the sorcerer lived a shallow, cowardly existence buoyed only by a high opinion of himself... an opinion not shared by the captain or the ship's crew. But from what Belladonna had just witnessed, both her and the captain's opinion of his ship's sorcerer was woefully deficient, for, despite his cowardly demeanor, Ostrinnauth was not only capable but also strong enough to be dangerous.

"So what now?" Belladonna inquired. "We wait?"

Ostrinnauth nodded. "I've my orders. If Braz'galar does figure out you're here, and if he gets past the two guards out front, the wards I placed on the door will kill him."

"Just for the sake of argument, let's say Braz'galar is here on the ship and shows up," Belladonna said. "If your wards don't kill him, then what?"

"I suspect the captain and the rest of the crew will be down here by then," the sorcerer answered. "If not, I'll have you as a bargaining chip."

The capital city of Kor was three times the size of Taranthi, Lessien's own capital of InnisRos. Kor's palace was a city in its own right, as large as Taranthi, though not as beautiful. Inside the hundred foot walls surrounding the palace were buildings upon buildings—private residences, multi-level apartments, shops, markets, mansions, government buildings, headquarter buildings of the various guilds, and all the other buildings housing the things needed for the efficient management of a world. Hundreds of demon guards roamed the perimeter of the palace, and Azazael, acting on Kor's behalf, had stationed several thousand within the walls at various locations throughout the palace grounds.

"I got to give it to you demons," Lessien said as she held Martin from inside Zachariah's carriage. "You build intimidating cities. But there's a special grandeur to this one."

"It's because of the guilds," Laylah remarked. "Kor doesn't concern himself with the city's appearance. Neither do any of his subordinates. They only care that it works efficiently. But the peasant folks who work for the guilds, and the guilds themselves, care about structure, form, and beauty… very much so despite Kor's indifference."

Lessien shook her head. "There's much Kor could learn from his subjects. A wise leader understands this."

"Like most overlords and underlords, his arrogance prevents him from appreciating other points of view," Laylah said. "It's a common occurrence here in the Abyss."

"As well as other places," Lessien added. "Aster also has its share of arrogant leaders. I've concluded it's a result of too much power… and not enough self-deprecation."

"Having the former means you don't need the latter," Zachariah noted.

From outside the carriage, someone barked, "Hold and prepare for inspection!" The carriage stopped as ordered.

"That's my cue," Zachariah said as he slipped the chained pendant that identified him as Kor's chief interrogator over his neck. "Don't, under any circumstances, leave this carriage," he ordered. "You're protected as long as you stay here. Not by me personally… but by the office of the Chief Interrogator." Without another word, Zachariah opened the door and exited the carriage. There was a slight "bump" from the rear of the coach when Trolgroth was unchained and taken away.

Several hours later, Zachariah opened the door to his coach and tossed in a large sack of food and wine. "Give me a minute to speak to my driver," he said before re-closing the door.

"What was that all about?" Lessien asked.

Laylah shrugged as she opened the sack. "Whatever it is, we'll be well-fed… field strider steak, bread, cheese, sweet cakes, and fine wine. There are even several bottles of milk for

Martin."

Zachariah climbed back into the carriage, which renewed its slow passage through the crowded streets of the capital city. "We need to make one stop before leaving," he said as he looked out a window at the passing city scenery.

It was obvious to Laylah and Lessien that Zachariah was preoccupied with whatever had happened between himself and Kor, though it appeared the chief interrogator had been true to his word and hadn't turned them in to the authorities. Neither wanted to disturb their benefactor and kept their mouths shut.

The carriage rolled to a stop. From through the open window, Zachariah pointed to a figure picking the pockets of an unsuspecting citizen.

"Iggok!" Zachariah called out. "I thought you kissed the *Pillar*."

Iggok looked around until he found the source of the voice calling his name. "Yer honor?" he replied when he saw the chief interrogator.

By now the subject of Iggok's attention, a demon of questionable intent himself based upon his rough façade and hatred-filled eyes, realized his pocket was being picked. "Why you..."

"Take them both and tie them to the back of the carriage," Zachariah ordered.

"But yer honor," both demons said as they were bound by several demon warriors who had been trailing behind the carriage.

"You got a second chance, Iggok, which you squandered," Zachariah said. "As for you..."

"I'm the victim here, yer honor!" the second demon exclaimed.

"Really?" Zachariah retorted. "I don't think you've ever been a victim. To the *Pillar* of Captured Souls!" he ordered the driver.

Both prisoners protested.

"And gag them," Zachariah charged before closing the shutter to his window.

Lessien looked at the chief interrogator, horrified. "You're going to execute them without at least a trial? Even us lowly mortals have higher standards than that. You alone can't be their judge and jury!"

"Yes, I can!" the chief interrogator snapped. "As I'm sure you've done as a queen. So don't give me your sanctimonious indignation."

Laylah laid a hand on Lessien's arm. "He's right. Now hush… it's how things work in the Abyss," she said, not willing to upset Zachariah any further. He was a wild card that she still wasn't sure about. "It could've been us just as well as them."

"But…" Lessien began.

"Did you even look at them?" Zachariah asked. "The way they've lived their entire lives is an indictment. We're demons, remember?"

The edge in Zachariah's voice convinced Lessien to follow Laylah's advice and calm things down. She took a bottle of milk from the sack and fed Martin. "I didn't mean that as it sounded," she apologized.

Yesper, quiet since they had entered the capital, looked at Zachariah. "This is not like you, Chief Interrogator. This is all new to Lessien. You should give her a measure of leeway."

Zachariah sighed and nodded. "You're correct, Yesper. Lessien, I apologize as well. As an outsider, I can't expect you to understand everything that's going on. What I do is necessary for appearance's sake. The chief interrogator is expected to… well, to act like the chief interrogator. Particularly here. Any deviance from that sends up red flags which will sooner or later get back to Kor. We can't afford that. I need to make sure Kor forgets about the both you… not that he needed much of a push. Something much bigger than the two of you, something I don't know about, is going on. That, ladies, is very disconcerting. And it makes him even more dangerous."

Zachariah was quiet for the rest of the trip to the *Pillar*. Lessien dared not challenge him further.

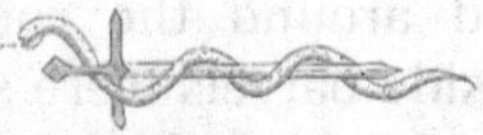

Braz'galar put a vertical support beam between him and the two hulking sailors. He only had a few minutes before the power of the magical ring which kept him camouflaged would run out. He looked around and spied a door marked "Armory."

"You've got to be kidding me," he thought. *"I didn't think sailors could read."*

Braz'galar suddenly knew what he was going to do. From their position, the two sailors had a direct line of sight to the armory door. They may not be able to see him yet, but the door was another matter. But if things went as he expected, he'll only have to deal with one crewman at a time.

The experienced fixer moved silently towards the armory, using the cover provided by barrels and crates of supplies as much as possible. Before the door, he checked to see if it was locked.

"Still living right," he silently thought as he heard the doorknob click open. Braz'galar took a deep breath before opening the door and slipping through.

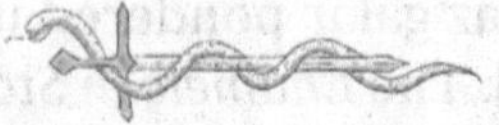

"Ye see that there, Luca?" one of the two sailors asked.

"What now, Guido?"

The one called Guido drew a club from his belt. "I thought I saw the armory door close."

"Didn't see a thing," Luca answered.

"I'm fixin' to check it out," Guido answered.

Luca drew his own club. "Ye be careful," he whispered.

Braz'galar looked around the room. Hanging against walls and stacked inside barrels were swords, spears, clubs, halberds, crossbow bolts, and plenty of crossbows to shoot them with. Standing in a corner was a barrel that contained different types of swords—two-handed swords, long swords, and several epees.

"What the hell are they doing with epees?" Braz'galar wondered. *"Though I suppose a few fencing lessons wouldn't hurt anyone."*

Then his eyes lighted upon three strangely hilted blades. *"Those are made by the four-legged mortals on Aster. They're supposed to be twice as hard as regular steel. Let's see, I believe they're called... uh..."* He smiled. *"Katanas! Who needs a saber or cutlass when you have those!"*

Braz'galar had just finished arming himself with two of the three katanas when the door opened. With grim determination, he turned to confront one or both of the sailors. At least that's what he thought he'd have to deal with. Instead, he watched as the blood drained from the sailor's face and his eyes grow to twice their size.

"Ghost!" the sailor screamed as he ran out of the room.

"What the...?" Braz'galar pondered until he realized what must have happened. The *Chameleon Stone* hadn't discharged all of its magic. He looked at himself and sure enough, his left arm holding a katana and his right leg were plainly visible, while the rest of him was still blended into the background.

Braz'galar snickered. "I guess he doesn't like ghosts," he mumbled.

"Ain't no ghosts on this 'ere ship, Guido," Luca said as the two guards walked towards the armory door. "You know as well as I that there ghosts be banished from servin' as ship crewmen 'undreds o' years ago. Too much bad mojo."

"But, Luca… there's a black market fer ghosts," Guido protested.

"No cap'n worth 'is salt would allow it," Luca replied. "Particularly our cap'n."

"But Luca…" Guido persisted.

Luca stepped in front of Guido just before they entered the armory. "You're wrong! Now flay yer shriveled tongue, why don't ye!"

When Luca turned to enter the armory, what he saw wasn't a ghost waiting for him, but a demon overlord, holding a katana in each hand while swaying back and forth, spoiling for a fight. He immediately realized he was facing Braz'galar, Kor's fixer and the second most powerful demon in the Prefecture.

"I hear you're looking for me," Braz'galar announced.

Luca and Guido charged, clubs raised above their heads, screeching war cries at the top of their lungs.

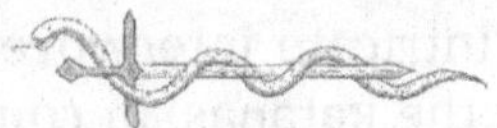

Belladonna heard the battle cries coming from outside the room. "Braz'galar's here," she told Ostrinnauth, though from the look on his face she could see he knew very well what was happening. "Your options are quickly running out."

The sorcerer laughed, albeit nervously. "Luca and Guido are more than enough to keep your precious Braz'galar busy long enough for the captain to get here with reinforcements," Ostrinnauth boasted.

"Now it's my turn to laugh," Belladonna responded. "Two ship's sailors against an overload. And not just any overlord… but Kor's fixer. Someone who makes his living surviving impossible odds. I've seen him work, Ostrinnauth. I've seen him kill. You're betting on the wrong horse."

Ostrinnauth shook his head. "I have you," he answered. "After we've satisfied Azazael's vendetta by delivering Braz'galar's head, we'll all be handsomely rewarded… and you'll be handed over to Kor."

"You think Azazael's vendetta matters to Kor where Braz'galar's concerned?" Belladonna replied. "You think Kor's going to reward you for killing his fixer without permission?"

Ostrinnauth looked from Belladonna to the door.

"You're going to have to decide soon, Ostrinnauth," Belladonna pressed. "Your wards won't hold Braz'galar back for long. But they *will* make him angry."

The sorcerer didn't appear moved. He approached Belladonna and re-gagged her.

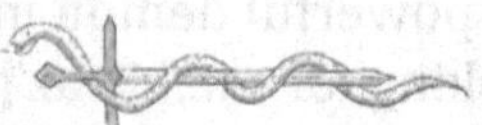

The katanas felt as light as a feather. Braz'galar swept them back and forth as he weaved an impenetrable shield of steel in front of him. The intricate interwoven pattern of defense and offense made by the katanas, in concert with each other as they flicked through the air in front of their user, defied belief. It was as if an unworldly force directed them through their delicate dance of death. But while the skill belonged to the overlord, only the katanas made it possible. They became extensions of Braz'galar's arms—and his mind.

Luca and Guido never stood a chance. Both were laying on the deck within seconds, each cradling a stump which was once a functioning arm. The shock of what had just happened left them speechless and too stunned to feel pain. Without hesitation Braz'galar sprinted over the two sailors and out the door, only to be confronted by the captain, his first officer, and a room full of sailors.

Zachariah felt Lessien should witness at least one execution by the *Pillar*. The InnisRos queen wasn't very enthusiastic and voiced her resistance as the chief interrogator led her from the carriage to a viewing area. But Zachariah's request was tantamount to an order that she, and she alone, was required to obey. She didn't know if it was as benign as him believing she needed the education... or if it was because he wanted a small measure of revenge for her earlier condescension.

The *Pillar of Captured Souls* is a huge, swirling column of dark energy which gets its power from the consumption of physical and spiritual bodies fed into it. Similar in looks to a tree, the *Pillar* "trunk" is roughly three hundred feet across and goes up several thousand feet until it branches off at the top, where tentacles of dark energy expand upward in all directions from the *Pillar* to penetrate the grayness of the *Veil of the Infinitus Atrophia*.

There was no shortage of victims being forced to Kiss the *Pillar*. Each condemned demon, arms tied behind their back with sturdy hemp rope and supported by a guard on either side, was dragged forward and forced to kneel before the *Pillar*. The guards tethered both legs to the ground, placed a simple metal circlet on the head, and moved away to another prisoner further down the line. The guards repeated this procedure until prisoners encircled the entire base of the *Pillar*.

Several minutes after preparing the last prisoner, multi-colored lights flashed thousands of feet up in the *Veil of the Infinitus Atrophia*. One by one, tentacles of colored energy descended down the trunk, launched itself from the *Pillar*, and struck each prisoner. Possessed by powers they couldn't control, each prisoner jerked back and forth in different directions. Bones, unable to cope with the forces now streaming through them, snapped and broke. The eyes of the condemned rolled back until only the whites showed and smoke streamed upward as blood boiled and organs burned from the inside out. After a few seconds, a black tentacle of light replaced the colored lights going into each prisoner and returned to the *Pillar*, disintegrating the prisoner in the process. The *Pillar* had completely annihilated every single physical aspect of each. The only thing left behind at the end of the execution was the circlet.

Lessien watched in horror as Iggok, his pickpocket victim, and all the other demons were made to Kiss the *Pillar*. "What a terrible way to die," she observed.

Zachariah shook his head. "Terrible… yes, mortal queen. But not the worst. Kor reserves those deaths for Execution Hill."

Lessien looked at the overlord. "I can only imagine." There was a hint of contempt in her voice.

Zachariah redirected his attention from the *Pillar* to Lessien. "Once I was interrogating an underlord who'd been called to the mortal world by a middling sorcerer. Generally speaking, when that happens, the demon has only two choices… obey, which we all find appalling, or kill the summoner the first chance we get. But when we do that, we're immediately returned to the Abyss… something not all of my kind really want."

"I've heard about that," Lessien replied. "On InnisRos, demon summoning can only come to no good, so we vigorously discourage it. It's punishable by death."

Zachariah resumed his narration. "It took several months before this underlord killed his captor. During that time, he had an opportunity to witness several executions."

The more Lessien got to know Zachariah, the more she understood the techniques and patterns he used to tell a story... or to interrogate. He'll be driving home a point soon. All she could do was wait for the other shoe to drop.

"You use the death sentence as punishment by your own admittance," Zachariah said. "In fact, you yourself have used that magical sword to carry out executions on individuals who have committed certain offenses. I believe it's a requirement for one of your stature."

Lessien nodded. A quick glance at the *Pillar* showed a new set of prisoners being prepared to kiss it, or, more accurately, to be kissed by it. "You're well informed. But that's not your point, is it?"

Zachariah laughed. "You're a quick study. The more I learn about you, the more I'm convinced it's worth the risk getting you back to Aster. You're much too dangerous to be let loose here in the Abyss."

Lessien waited.

"You mortals developed the one method of execution Kor favors above all others," Zachariah said. "You call it 'drawn and quartered,' I believe. In it..."

"I know what it means to draw and quarter someone," Lessien snapped. "Only the humans do it. Elves would never consider such a thing! It's barbaric!"

"Are there any non-barbaric ways of taking a life, mortal queen?" Zachariah challenged.

Lessien looked away from the overlord and to the *Pillar*. The latest round of executions was about to begin.

"The method of these killings, as well as their purpose, serve the greater good," Zachariah said as he too looked at the next round of executions about to begin. "Whether or not you choose to believe it, most of the prisoners executed really are criminals. Then there's the value of the *Pillar* itself. There wouldn't be an Abyss without it."

Lessien couldn't argue with the logic. She winced as the latest group of detainees was evaporated by the *Pillar*. This time she could make out the grunts as air was forced out of their lungs. She heard the snap and pop as bones broke and dislocated. Then she heard a faint noise, a slight crackle, as the life force of each joined the *Pillar*. Lessien thought she was going to be sick and began to sway.

"Careful, mortal queen," Zachariah said as he put an arm around her shoulders to prevent her from falling.

"I'm fine!" Lessien remarked, though she didn't try to shrug off his support. "As you say, I'm a queen! I've seen worse!"

"Laylah!" he called as he led Lessien to the carriage. "It's nothing to be ashamed of," he told Lessien. "Death is never clean and you haven't eaten or rested much over the last few days."

Lessien knew it was more than that. She had a hole in her heart left by the death of Autumn. She needed to get back to InnisRos, to the lands and people she loved, to grieve and to heal. What she'd just witnessed emphasized that longing.

Together, Zachariah and Laylah helped Lessien back into the carriage.

"Time to leave the city," Zachariah told his driver. "We go east to Zhaarmoth."

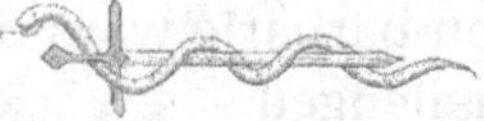

"So, we finally meet," the captain proclaimed. "Lord Kor's fixer... the great Braz'galar."

Braz'galar kept his katanas at the ready. "Captain," he said as he nodded. "I was hoping to avoid the pleasure, but suspect it was inevitable."

"Oh, I assure ye, there'll be no pleasure once Azazael 'as 'is 'ands on ye," the captain replied.

There was a moan from inside the armory. The captain nodded at a couple of sailors. "Get them to the sawbones. As for ye, Braz'galar, drop the swords. Yer time as me prisoner doesn't need to be... uncivilized."

Braz'galar smiled. "It's a bit too late for that, don't you think?"

The two sailors Braz'galar had disabled were taken out of the armory and through a passageway which Braz'galar presumed led to the sickbay. Both sailors, holding their bleeding stumps tightly, looked at the overlord as they passed and nodded their respect and gratitude for their lives. That didn't go unnoticed by the captain.

Braz'galar noted it as well. "I can protect you from Azazael, if it comes to that," he said. "Kor won't interfere."

"Me loyalty doesn't come an' go like the tide," the captain replied. "Me word is me bond."

"And your crew?" Braz'galar inquired.

"Azazael pays all o' us well," the captain countered. "That's the only loyalty they need to understand."

Braz'galar saw what the captain couldn't. The crew behind him, to a man, frowned when they heard their captain dismiss them so easily. "Sure about that, Captain?" he asked.

The captain laughed. "I know what ye be tryin' to do. It won't work. I 'old all the cards. Now drop the swords an' surrender. If ye do, I guarantee decent treatment fer both ye an' Belladonna as long as you're on me ship."

Braz'galar whirled his katanas through the air in an intricate pattern of thrusts, lunges, and parries. The swords disappeared into flashes of light as he performed each maneuver. "I propose single combat, Captain," he said. "You and me. Winner take all."

"And why would I want to do that there?" the captain retorted. "As I said, I 'old all the cards. Take 'im!" he ordered the crew standing behind him.

No one moved.

"You're not afraid, are you, Captain?" the captain's underlord second-in-command asked.

The captain lashed out at the underlord with a closed fist, which knocked the demon to the deck. Several of the sailors muttered their disapproval while a couple others helped the first officer back to his feet.

"I gave ye an order!" the captain shouted as he turned away from his armed prisoner to focus on the crew. "Now take 'im, Gar'os, or I'll 'ave you..."

The sharp end of a katana suddenly burst through the captain's chest. He looked down in stunned silence as he dropped to his knees, then his eyes glazed over as he fell to the deck, helped off the katana by the heel of Braz'galar's boot.

Braz'galar had earned and kept his position as Kor's fixer not because Kor owed him a favor or felt obligated, but because he was very good at his job. Part of the reason he was so successful was that he never hesitated to act when an opportunity presented itself.

"Not very sporting of you, Braz'galar," Gar'os commented. The ship's second-in-command spoke without a seafaring accent.

Braz'galar shrugged his shoulders. "Sometimes fair play's overrated. Who's next?"

While none of the crew stepped forward to accept Braz'galar's challenge, neither did they show any fear or reluctance to do so.

"As good as you appear to be, we still outnumber you an entire ship's crew to one," Gar'os remarked.

"Two."

Gar'os frowned. "Oh! You mean Belladonna!" he exclaimed. "Our sorcerer has her safely locked away."

"Well... I won't let you turn me over to Azazael," Braz'galar declared. "And I'm not leaving Belladonna. So let's get on with it!"

Gar'os held up a hand. "Then again, I have you to thank for my captaincy... unless anyone wishes to challenge me for it." He addressed the last to the sailors standing behind him.

After a few moments of silence, one of the crew in the back yelled, "Hail, Cap'n Gar'os!" Soon all were cheering their new ship's master.

Gar'os held up a hand to settle everyone. "I suppose we can give you the skiff back and sail on," he told Braz'galar. "I doubt Azazael will know the difference. As for our former captain... I guess he just wasn't strong enough to hold the position."

Braz'galar nodded. "The natural order of things. Who wouldn't understand that? Congratulations, Captain Gar'os."

Gar'os smiled. "Captain Gar'os. It does have a decent ring to it, doesn't it?"

It didn't take long to convince Ostrinnauth to release Belladonna from her bonds. He wasn't particularly fond of Gar'os, but trusted the new captain much more than the now deceased former captain. The ship's crew overhauled the skiff to repair all damage and loaded it with fresh supplies. They would sail until the northern shore of the Grimfail Reservoir was just beyond the horizon before launching the skiff with Braz'galar and Belladonna onboard back into the water.

The morning they parted ways, Braz'galar gave Captain Gar'os a small bag of semi-precious gems for his troubles and a bit of friendly advice. "Never let your emotions control your response to any situation," Braz'galar warned. "Your captain did just that and, as a result, turned his back on an armed opponent."

Gar'os bowed. "Thank you, Braz'galar... but I'm not the same as he. I trust no one and suspect everyone, particularly those under my command. They have the most to gain should any misfortune befall me."

Braz'galar nodded. "Good. There's one last thing. Below in

the armory is a third katana, like the two I carry. Retrieve it and use it."

"I prefer the longsword," Gar'os replied.

"Perhaps now," Braz'galar said. "But give the katana a the armory is a third katana, like the two I carry. Retrieve it and use it."

"I prefer the longsword," Gar'os replied.

"Perhaps now," Braz'galar said. "But give the katana a chance. I guarantee you won't regret it."

The ship's log omitted its encounter with Kor's fixer and the sorceress Belladonna but went into fine detail about the former captain and his attempt to smuggle contraband across the reservoir. It described how the captain was caught, court-martialed, and, along with the contraband, sent to the bottom of the reservoir as punishment.

Gar'os wisely distributed the gems Braz'galar contributed amongst the sailors in equal percentages, a gesture that helped seal the loyalty between Gar'os and his new crew. Wisely, the new captain also made it clear the payment wouldn't be recorded in the ship's log. This meant there'd be no taxes and union fees collected, the failure of which is a death penalty offense. By doing this, Gar'os guaranteed there'd be no open mouths to give away their involvement with Braz'galar and Belladonna once back on shore.

chance. I guarantee you won't regret it."

The ship's log omitted its encounter with Kor's fixer and the sorceress Belladonna but went into fine detail about the former captain and his attempt to smuggle contraband across the reservoir. It described how the captain was caught, court-martialed, and, along with the contraband, sent to the bottom of the reservoir as punishment.

Gar'os wisely distributed the gems Braz'galar contributed amongst the sailors in equal percentages, a gesture that helped seal the loyalty between Gar'os and his new crew. Wisely, the new captain also made it clear the payment wouldn't be recorded in the ship's log. This meant there'd be no taxes and union fees collected, the failure of which is a death penalty offense. By doing this, Gar'os guaranteed there'd be no open mouths to give away their involvement with Braz'galar and Belladonna once back on shore.

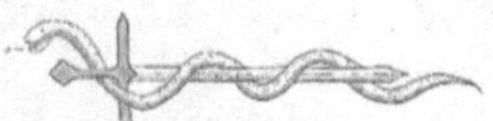

Zachariah's carriage made it out of the capital city of Kor without incident. They followed a main road through a deep forest that was heavily patrolled by warriors from Kor's army. The only thing needed for them to pass through unmolested was the seal of the Chief Interrogator. Four long and boring days later, the forest opened up to a great plain. Off in the distance lay two cities and beyond them a large plateau. Accentuating the plateau was a thousand foot waterfall.

Everyone had exited the carriage and were enjoying a few moments to exercise their legs. Lessien, holding Martin, couldn't help but stare at the distant waterfall. Zachariah, munching on a piece of salted kaika, a four-legged game bird similar to a pheasant on Aster, noticed and walked over to her.

"Beautiful, isn't it?" he said. "We call it the Duhová Kaskáda, or the Rainbow Cascade in your native tongue. If you look closely enough, you can see how three rainbows at the top of the falls combine to make a much larger rainbow at the bottom."

Lessien nodded. "I see it. And yes, it's beautiful. We've nothing like this on Aster."

"Does it surprise you?" Zachariah asked. "That splendor can exist in such a place as the Abyss?"

Lessien looked down at the miracle that was Martin. Then she thought of the people who had helped her since being exiled to the Abyss, help that was given freely and required no recompense, and found that it didn't surprise her.

She looked at Zachariah and then at Laylah and Yesper, who had walked up and stood by her side. "No... not anymore," she conceded.

CHAPTER THIRTEEN

The Abyss and the Cavern of the Johari

Temperance looked at the beaten and battered body. "He's just a child," she whispered.

Like most of her brethren, the *B'nai Elohim* warrior had just prevented the young sorcerer from invoking a doorway spell which would have opened a channel between the mortal world of Aster and the Abyss. It started out like all other such conjurations when a slight, spell specific change in the magical ley lines surrounding the Abyss exposed the attempt. While these kinds of changes are very subtle, and demon sorcerers did what they could to disguise them, the *B'nai Elohim* had the power to recognize and shut the magic down along with the sorcerer who attempted the spell casting. Never before was the sorcerer been so young, however.

"Why would they use someone so immature?" Temperance wondered. She knew the answer to her thought even before she had finished it. "They needed a thousand sorcerers to attempt what they did," she said aloud. "At least, that's what Michael told us. But this... this... butchery leaves a foul taste in my mouth!"

Her job finished, she teleported back to the fortress. There was still the demon army to defeat.

Throughout the stronghold, *B'nai Elohim* warriors were coming back from their completed missions of dealing death. A good many of them felt the same as Temperance... disgusted with the circumstances that forced them to kill children and angry it had to come to that. When it came time to fight the demon army, they took out their frustrations with a savagery that's rarely indicative of the normal, business-like manner they're accustomed to when dealing with demons.

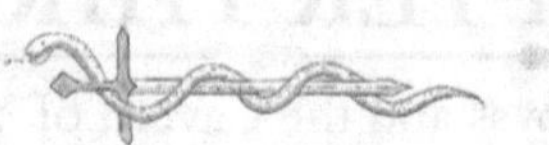

Lord Ternborg looked out from the battlements of the *B'nai Elohim* fortress and studied the demon army's advance. Flanking Lord Ternborg on the walls were his First Phalanx commander, General Angelica Gargarin, and his executive officer Colonel Florentina Antonovich. The initial bombardment by the demon sorcerers reached its apex several hours ago and had ceased altogether shortly thereafter. Sorcerers on both sides were now doing everything they could to recover their strength and rejoin the fray. An army captain rushed up and saluted the Draugen Pesta king.

"As you were, Captain," Lord Ternborg said. "You have the casualty reports?"

"Yes, Your Grace," the captain replied. "Inconsequential."

General Gargarin shook her head. "We'll be the judge of that, Captain."

"Yes, ma'am," the captain answered. "Twenty-five dead and fifty-seven wounded… though of those, only three are serious. Everyone else is combat ready."

"Light indeed," Lord Ternborg remarked. "And the *B'nai Elohim*."

"Most of them are still off on their missions," the captain replied. "The ones that have returned are in an ugly mood."

"Ugly? How?" General Gargarin asked.

"Ugly like Michael forced them to do something they didn't want to do," the captain answered. "Like when you mercy kill an old and dying horse. That kind of ugly."

"Unsurprising, all things considered," Lord Ternborg said. "Return to your unit, Captain. And thank you for the report."

"It could've been much worse," Colonel Antonovich remarked after the captain had left.

Lord Ternborg didn't respond and remained quiet for a

a few minutes as he watched the charging demons. Even though this was only a ruse, at least according to Michael, the battle to take place during the next few hours, or days, was going to be monumental, nevertheless.

"Prepare to repel invaders," Lord Ternborg screamed.

Unit commanders repeated this order up and down the fortress battlements. No one had time to think after that as they let their battle instincts take over their actions.

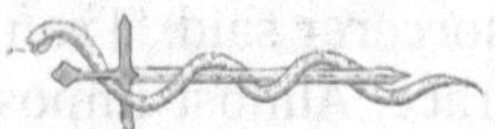

Michael sat and waited patiently as the sorcerer finished his conjurations. The sorcerer was tapping into the nearest magical ley line, searching for any unusual power reductions which would indicate the manipulation of magic.

"Well?" Michael asked, impatient for information. He was sure Kor staged the demon attack to hide something much larger. He was also reasonably sure that the "something larger" wasn't the deluge of doorway spells being simultaneously conjured by demon sorcerers... spells that were taking his entire force away to deal with them. "Anything else?"

Anakim, the sorcerer, shook his head. "Nothing, Michael. While I can't be sure, the power drains I'm detecting don't conflict with what the demons are attempting to do."

"That can't be all," Michael said. "We've been playing this game with the demons for several millennia. They know they can't overwhelm us, that they need to sneak past. Keep looking at the ley lines. There has to be something there you're missing... some sign more power is being used for incantations other than simple doorway spells."

Anakim nodded. "Again, it'd help if you told me what it is you believe they're attempting to do."

Michael frowned. "Perhaps you're right," he responded

after a few seconds. "I suspect... no, I believe they've learned the location of the Johari and are attempting to cross the Juxtaposition Point to destroy her."

"*We* don't even know where the Johari is," Anakim said.

"You think I don't know that?!" Michael snapped. "Otherwise, I'd just pop over to Aster and see for myself!"

Michael quickly calmed down and started to apologize for his outburst. But when he began to speak, Anakim raised a hand to stop him.

"There it is," the sorcerer said. "I can see it now. So faint... so delicate... just a trace. Almost impossible to detect. Oh... damn! Whoever did this is good!"

Michael waited. He'd get no answers until Anakim was ready.

Anakim shook his head to clear it. "We're too late," he said. "They've already gotten past us."

"You can track them, right?" Michael asked. "You know where on Aster they went?"

"No," Anakim answered. "At least I can't trace the magic that was used bypass us. Barring a miracle, I'm afraid the Johari is on her own."

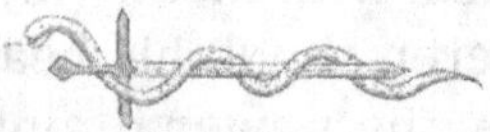

"Report!" Kor ordered the army general. He was sitting on the *Living Throne* and waiting for a report on the status of his latest gambit to rid himself of the *B'nai Elohim* and gain control over the mortals of Aster. Emprusa was standing behind the throne and massaging Kor's neck and shoulders. Never far from her lover, lately she'd been keeping herself extra close. She had a good feeling about the campaign and wanted to be "up front" when they finally destroyed their ancient enemy. Kor was a harsh master, but he rewarded handsomely when things went his way. Who's to say he wouldn't make her his queen, even after his earlier scoffing of the idea? Never has a queen sat upon a throne next to a Prefecture ruler. But Kor could change that if he was in the correct frame of mind and properly motivated. Emprusa was an expert in the latter.

The army general, more of a high-ranked messenger, cleared his throat. "Hail, My Lord!" the general shouted. "General Sol'gonath sends his respects and..."

Kor nodded. "Yes, yes..." he interrupted. "Now, unless you want to Kiss the *Pillar*..."

Emprusa squeezed Kor's shoulders extra tight to calm him down.

Kor put his hands over hers to convey that he had received her message. "General," he said. "Forget the official salutations and get on with your report."

The general gulped, knowing the terrible news he was about to disclose wouldn't be well received by the Prefecture demon lord. *"Curse Sol'gonath for sending me,"* he thought. Aloud: "Our attacks at the fortress aren't going as anticipated."

"Explain, General," Kor commanded, not that the statement surprised or disappointed him. Though he was hoping for better, the attack on the *B'nai Elohim* ramparts meant nothing.

"Our ancient enemy has enlisted help from mortals," the general said. "General Sol'gonath says to inform you the mortal race called the Draugen Pesta is there in significant numbers."

"Do you understand what that means?" Emprusa whispered in Kor's ear.

Kor nodded. "The B'nai Elohim knew about our plan," he whispered back. "At least enough of it to realize the attack is a feint and to have allies available while they take care of other things... such as killing every sorcerer trying to open doorways to the mortal world."

"But it doesn't mean they know about Bezrameth," Emprusa said. "Nor does it mean he didn't make it across."

"No, it doesn't. But it does mean I have a spy close by." Kor looked around the room at the silent sycophants, wondering who it might be.

"Kill them all!" the souls in the *Living Throne* screamed. *"Trust no one!"*

The Prefecture leader ignored the voices in his head.

Emprusa squeezed Kor's shoulders again. "Not necessarily. Michael's smart. He could've figured it out on his own. Then there are the mortals. Who knows what kind of advice Michael's getting from them?"

Kor nodded his understanding. "Anything else to convey, General?" he asked the waiting officer.

"Thousands of our warriors lie dead at the base of the fortress walls, My Lord," the general replied. "Nothing we've done so far has succeeded, and the fortress shows no signs of weakening. Those mortal devils fight like male field striders during breeding season! General Sol'gonath says that we can't take the *B'nai Elohim* citadel and wishes to withdraw."

Kor stood. This time, Emprusa wouldn't calm his anger. "Withdraw?! You're fighting against wretched mortals and you want to withdraw? After less than a day of combat? Sol'gonath's probably spending more time entertaining his consort than he's spending on the battlefield!"

The general, eyes wide with fear, looked at his feet. He sensed rather than saw the Prefecture leader come down off the dais to stand in front of him. Without hesitation, the general prostrated himself. "My Lord! Please! I'm but the messenger," he pleaded.

"And expendable, which is no doubt why General Sol'gonath sent you," Kor reminded the general who, by now, trembled all over. "Has Azazael been told about this?"

"I don't know, My Lord. I haven't personally seen the Faction leader involved… and General Sol'gonath said nothing about him. But I find it hard to believe Lord Azazael wouldn't have concurred with the withdrawal request."

Kor sighed. "Get up!" he ordered. He then looked around the room at his advisors. "Anyone want to tell me how this happened? Why is General Sol'gonath so eager to withdraw? Why has our army suddenly become so impotent? Anyone?"

There was a deep-seated silence in the room. And with good reason. Kor, in his current mood, was just a look away from sending people to the *Pillar* or, even worse, Execution Hill.

"I didn't think so," Kor remarked after a few seconds of silence. "General, I don't care if the attack on the *B'nai Elohim* fortress has left a stack of dead warriors a mile high before its walls. Tell General Sol'gonath he's to continue the assault until I say different. You can also tell General Sol'gonath that his continued service... and by that I mean his life... depends upon how well he performs this task. I never expected him to win. But damnit, I wanted something better than so quick a withdrawal! It's humiliating!" Kor studied the general for a few long seconds before dismissing him.

The general bowed and made a hasty retreat. As he was leaving, Lilitu walked into the room. She looked terrible. All traces of the fastidiousness she was known for had vanished. Her hair was disheveled, clothes wrinkled, and her face was haggard looking, as if she hadn't slept in a week, which Kor knew wasn't true.

Lilitu ambled forward to stand before the dais. She never attempted to bow or acknowledge Kor. Instead, she kept her head down and stared at the floor. There was a barely perceptible groan from the others in the throne room.

Kor, more confused than angry at her lack of respect, waited for her to speak, though it soon became obvious no words were forthcoming from the Magical Faction overlord.

"Look at me," Kor demanded.

Lilitu slowly raised her head. "My Faction... all of my sorcerers... are dead," she said. "Beaten to bloody pulps by the

B'nai Elohim! They spared no one! Not even the children!"

Kor shrugged. "We discussed this. You knew it was going to happen."

"All gone," Lilitu whispered. She once again lowered her eyes to stare at the floor.

"Stop this nonsense," Kor admonished. "Your sorcerers died in my service. That's a good death, by any account."

To Lilitu's credit, she had the presence of mind to keep her mouth shut.

"You'll train new sorcerers," the Prefecture leader continued. "And soon you'll have an entire world of mortals to choose from for your magical experiments."

"You don't understand," Lilitu said. "It was more than a slaughter. My sorcerers, from the youngest to the oldest, were connected to a ley line when they died. I had connected to the same ley line... connected to make sure all did as they were supposed to do. I heard their screams! I felt their fear and their pain! I experienced their deaths!"

There was a sudden commotion at the back of the audience chamber. Azazael, with several of his top generals, marched into the room and straight toward the *Living Throne*. Everyone, including Kor, directed their attention away from Lilitu and towards the Military Faction overlord.

"We'll discuss this later," Kor said to the sorceress. "You're dismissed."

Because of Azazael's grand entrance, no one noticed Lilitu as she raised her head to gaze at her lord. Anyone who did would have seen the madness in her eyes.

"Dismiss me, will you," she whispered as her mind reached out and grabbed the only ley line over the palace, an extraordinarily powerful ley line known only to Kor and herself as his Magical Faction leader. Her hands moved in slow, rhythmic motions as she mouthed words of magic.

"Dismiss me, will you!" she repeated in her mind as she

gathered the magic to do her bidding.

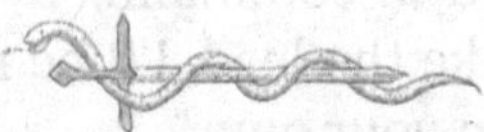

"What's taking them so long?" Vol'goth asked for what seemed like the hundredth time.

Bezrameth was tired of the demon commander's constant whining over the relative inconvenience of their location. To wit, they didn't know where the doorway Talisman sorcerers had opened to Aster led, just that it was underground in a series of caves and corridors. Vol'goth decided early on to send a small scouting team to figure it out. Bezrameth, realizing the possibility of those warriors becoming hopelessly lost was high, had advised against it. But the commander was determined to follow proper military protocol.

"I told you not to spare ten of your warriors for so precarious a mission," Bezrameth remarked contemptuously. "It's not just the chance of them getting lost… but who knows what manner of creatures they might come across?"

"Trained demon warriors against mortal creatures?" Vol'goth snapped back. "I don't see the danger."

"Or they could run into the Talisman herself," Bezrameth continued, "since we don't know where to find her. She's *not* mortal, I assure you. And if not her, perhaps her guardians… if she has any. If either of those two scenarios turn out to be the case, then she knows we're down here."

"It's not like you gave me any other options," Vol'goth replied.

Bezrameth sighed. "I told you to keep everyone together!" he pointed out. "At least until we're more comfortable with our position. But you assured me you knew best." The sorcerer shook his head. "Regardless… the decision's been made and your orders carried out. So quit complaining. We're wasting time waiting for them to come back."

Vol'goth nodded. "*That* we can agree upon," he said as he turned to his second-in-command, a slimy snake demon named Gazginius. "Take the lead. I'll be right behind, so don't make any decisions on your own."

Gazginius nodded, motioned towards six warriors to join him, and began the march down the blackened corridor.

Vol'goth and Bezrameth walked side by side as they followed. "You'll give me a heads-up if you detect anything, right?"

Bezrameth nodded, not caring if Vol'goth could see him or not in the darkness. His mind was far too busy thinking about what lie ahead. Soon he'd realize his life's work. Soon he'd achieve the destruction of the Talisman and a free entrance into the mortal world. The sorcerer smiled.

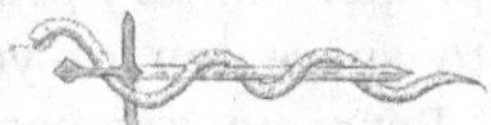

As night fell, Father Goram, Nightshade, Landross, and Herbie waited for Abigail to return from scouting the safest route out of the locked down city of Zir Tachoss. They'd make their attempt to escape under the cover of darkness. If possible, they wanted to get away without forcing the issue. But fleeing the city was a prime objective, so they were prepared to fight their way out if necessary. They had wasted too much time already.

Father Goram looked at the big knight as he sat and repeatedly oiled his massive sword. Landross hadn't taken the delay very well, and now he was distant and uncommunicative. He was even ignoring Herbie. Concerned about where the knight's mind was, Father Goram reached down and grabbed Landross's shoulder. "Landross," he said.

The knight stopped what he was doing and looked up at the priest, though he said nothing.

"I'm worried too," Father Goram remarked. "But we'll get

them back. We just have to be smart about it."

Landross returned to oiling his sword.

Father Goram sighed and looked at Nightshade, who'd been watching. She shook her head as if to say, *"It is what it is."*

Herbie barked as Abigail came up the stairs from her ground floor shop. "Nothing's changed," she reported. "I don't think even me or your disguises as Taumaru will stop the guards from questioning us."

"Any word on the battle?" Landross asked as he stood and sheathed his sword.

Abigail shook her head. "Not specifically... but none of the guards I spoke too cared to talk about it, so I assume the *B'nai Elohim* fortress still holds. Otherwise, they'd be bragging and drinking... or already drunk."

"We're ready to go, then," Nightshade commented.

Both Father Goram and Landross shouted, "No!"

Nightshade looked bewildered. "I thought we couldn't wait any longer?"

"Our best bet is to wait until it's towards the end of the late afternoon shift," Landross said. "Say around midnight. That way, those on duty will be tired and looking forward to being relieved. They won't be as attentive as they normally are... and certainly not willing to investigate anything that might extend their time on duty."

"Such as movement in shadows," Abigail added.

"Precisely," Father Goram answered.

Nightshade nodded as she sat back down. "For the record, I'm as tired of waiting as you are, Landross."

At midnight, two mortals, a demon, a gorgon, and a six-legged dog entered the gloomy and dirty corridors of Zir Tachoss's deserted alleyways and back streets. They carefully negotiated what protection they could find in shadows, behind walls, and alongside buildings. Landross had been right concerning the guards. Few showed interest in slight or unusual noises or movements. They preferred to pretend it was either their imagination, the wind, or some other natural phenomenon that didn't need their immediate attention. It wasn't until they'd reached the eastern main gate of the city, the last barrier to leaving, that they realized they had a serious problem. Not only were the guards very much alert and active, but the massive wooden and steel reinforced doors were closed and barred.

Jörmungander, in his dragon form, landed near his friends on one of the "streets" that ran next to the Johari. He'd just returned from the ledge they used to enter the huge cavern several days before.

"Weel, laddie?" Azriel asked.

Jörmungander changed to his human form. "Same as down here," he answered. "The air on the ledge is barely breathable even using my dragon lungs and as thick as tree sap. No escape from that quarter."

"How about near the ceiling?" Erika asked. "Any problem with the air up there?"

Jörmungander shook his head. "It's fine up there. The bats should be safe enough. I've already talked to the elders regarding that."

"So we wait," Solveig said. "We wait for whatever's coming to attack the Johari."

Max nodded. "That and plan."

"Aye, laddie," Azriel responded. "Ah just wish we knew whit it's wur planning fur."

"Demons would be my guess," Max answered. "Do we have any idea what kind of defenses the Johari has?"

Elbedreth spoke for the first time. "According to what

I've been able to decipher in my conversations with her, she doesn't have anything in particular… at least nothing like magical spells she can use to defend herself on this plane."

"Great!" Max exclaimed as he shook his head.

"However," Elbedreth continued, "her strength lies in her invulnerability to most, if not all, forms of physical and magical attacks."

"It'd tak' a lang time tae hack apairt a bein' o' her size," Azriel stated.

"Unless one knows just where to strike," Elbedreth said.

"So there *is* a weakness," Jörmungander commented. "But she's so big! As big as many of the cities on the surface. You could attack for a hundred years and not find the weakness."

"Aye, laddie, ye'r nae wrong," Azriel remarked. "But here's th' one thing ye'r forgetting. If th' demons ken th' Johari's location 'n' howfur tae git 'ere, it stauns tae reason thay ken whit it'll tak' tae murdurr her. 'N' if thay dae that, we'll lose Aster tae th' demons forever if Erika's premonition is correct. That's a risk we can't afford tae tak'!"

Jörmungander laughed. Everyone stared at him as if he were crazy.

"Have ye gaen insane, laddie!" Azriel exclaimed.

"Can't you see it, Azriel?" Jörmungander asked. "Elbedreth? Max?"

No one answered.

"We saved the world from the sylphs," Jörmungander said. "Now we're going to save the world from the demons of the Abyss. And just like with the sylphs, not a single person up there will know about it!"

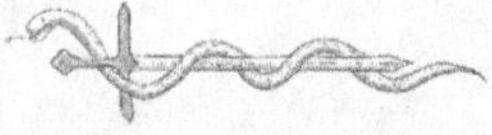

"How much longer can they keep coming?" Colonel Antonovich asked her commander, Lord Ternborg. The two of them, along with General Gargarin, were on the battlements of the *B'nai Elohim* fortress and looking out over the field of battle. "Their dead are stacked halfway up the walls."

Lord Ternborg shook his head. "I don't know. Even behind these walls, we've suffered more causalities than I like. At least they've stopped for now. I understand it's a feint... at least according to Michael... but..."

"It is," Michael interrupted as he walked along the battlements towards them, with Gabrielle following close behind. "And the secondary feint, if we've guessed correctly, has also been negated. Most of their sorcerers, if not all, are very much dead right now. As for the reason behind both gambits, there's nothing we can do to alter that. The demons going after the Johari are already on Aster."

"You're absolutely sure about that?" General Gargarin asked. "Perhaps our sorcerers can locate her through magic, so we can send help?"

Lord Ternborg shook his head. "Aster's a big place... the Johari's located underground... and we don't know what to look for."

"How about the sorcerers at Havendale?" General Gargarin continued, undeterred.

"No time," Michael said. "I'm afraid we can only hope the Johari can take care of herself."

"Here they come again!" someone shouted.

"If they've gotten someone over to Aster, why are the demons still attacking?" Colonel Antonovich asked. "If it's a ruse, they've already accomplished their objective."

"That's a good question," Michael replied.

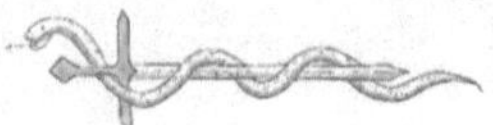

Muffled screams suddenly filled the darkness ahead.

"Now what?" Vol'goth pondered aloud to no one in particular.

"I suspect we've reached the outskirts of the Talisman's cavern," Bezrameth said as he walked past the demon overlord and to the source of the screams. His two subordinate sorcerers and bodyguards shoved their way past Vol'goth as they hurried to catch up with their master.

Like insects caught in amber, a trio of the demon scout team were stuck in a thick and sticky substance which enveloped the passageway. The faces of those ensnared were turning different colors as they struggled to breathe.

Bezrameth wasted little time conjuring the magic necessary to clear the corridor. A searing hot beam of plasma issued forth from his hands and melted the thick amber-like substance. With their mouths covered, the three demons weren't able to scream as their flesh and bones disintegrated into ash.

"What did you do!" Vol'goth demanded. He'd arrived just in time to witness the corridor being cleaned and the death of his warriors.

Bezrameth shook the incident off with a shrug. "They were dead the moment they walked into the enchanted part of the corridor."

"You could have warned us!" Vol'goth shouted.

"We'd get nowhere if your scouts kept testing the air," Bezrameth reasoned. "And the longer we're searching for the Talisman, the greater the risk of discovery. You want surprise on our side, do you not?"

Vol'goth couldn't argue with the logic. Besides, Bezrameth's personal bodyguard was looking irritated, which might escalate into deadly violence… something he didn't want to be on the receiving end of. Still, he hesitated to order the rest of his scouts forward.

"It's safe now," Bezrameth remarked, understanding the

other's reluctance.

"Go!" Vol'goth ordered his scouts who obeyed, if somewhat reluctantly.

"But not into the cavern," Bezrameth called out. "I want to see it before we carry out our attack."

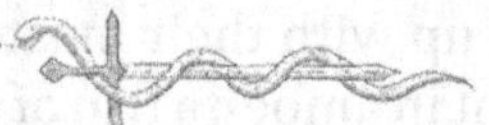

A bolt of electricity hit Kor and dropped him like a rock face down on the floor. All overlords and underlords have natural defenses against certain types of offensive magic. In Kor's case, he was partially immune to electricity, which prevented instant death. Emprusa, who was standing near her lord, was knocked across the floor, unconscious.

With Kor down, Lilitu directed her attention to the Military Faction leader, who had just entered the room. While everyone was staring and trying to make sense out of what had just happened, the sorceress guided two beams of cold energy at Azazael, knowing his immunity didn't include that kind of magic. But Azazael, a trained warrior, recovered from his surprise in time to dodge the beams. Two of his generals weren't so lucky. The force of the magic knocked them over, but by the time they hit the floor, their bodies had already frozen. Brittle body parts scattered in all directions, kicked around by scrambling demons trying to escape Lilitu's insanity.

Lilitu laughed at the spectacle before her. Azazael lie on the floor face down and covering his head with his arms while his generals, those still alive, sought their own escape. Demons with tails held them between their legs as they ran. Kor's personal bodyguards, trained to respond to emergencies without hesitation, looked as surprised and confused as everyone else. Lilitu whirled around in a tight circle. As she did so, she flung spheres of pure magical energy around the entire room. At least three spheres hit each of the guards who dropped to the floor like sacks of wet grain, alive but unconscious. All of the others still left in the room suffered the same fate as the guards.

The room had suddenly become ghostly quiet. The only one left standing was Lilitu. She moved to stand over Kor, who was too stunned to think clearly. She knelt and turned him over so she could look into his face.

"Before I kill you, I wanted you to know why I betrayed you, Mighty Lord," Lilitu said.

She was still quite insane, but in a devious and malicious way. Her objective, and how she'd carry it out, remained clear in her mind. But the psychosis from which she suffered had distorted that goal to the point that nothing short of her death would ever take priority in what remained of her life.

Kor stared, desperately trying to focus on Lilitu's words, the look on her face, her body language, and anything else that might help him understand why she had turned traitor.

"You murdered every member of my Faction!" Lilitu screamed. Drool flew from her mouth as she shrieked. "Every sorcerer... every potential sorcerer... butchered by the *B'nai Elohim*, those devils, so you can expand your realm!"

Kor sat up and covered his eyes with his hands. The electrical attack by the sorceress had given him a severe headache. "You agreed it was necessary," he forced himself to say. "Necessary for a chance to dominate the mortals."

"That's what has me so angry... and sad," Lilitu said. Her attitude had calmed somewhat. "That I agreed with you to do it. That I destroyed my own Faction. The children... the trusting and innocent children. Bodies beaten and mangled."

"There are no innocent and trusting demon children," Kor countered. "At least not real demon children."

Lilitu remained silent.

Kor looked at his Magic Faction leader. "Lilitu, this isn't like you."

"Stop talking!" the sorceress yelled, furious once again. "You're going to pay! We both are!"

Lilitu closed her eyes and started another enchantment. Power pulled from the ley line coalesced around her. Kor, himself a sorcerer of means, recognized the spell she was calling forth and started to crawl away, though he knew he'd never get far enough to save himself. In just a few seconds, the room, indeed, the entire palace, along with everyone in it, would be nothing but a crater in the ground. In all the Prefecture, only Kor and the Magic Faction leader had that kind of power.

Suddenly, Lilitu's chanting stopped and her eyes opened wide in shock and pain. The magical upsurge she was building fizzled around her. The sorceress looked down to find the hilt of a dagger sticking out from between her breasts, piercing her heart. It was only then she realized that in her madness she'd neglected to weave protective spells around her. As Lilitu dropped to her knees, she looked out over the room and saw Azazael, with a smirk on his face, walking towards her.

"Stupid witch," Azazael said as he came up to stand over her. "Did you think I'd stand by and let you ruin everything for Lord Kor?" He bent down and roughly removed the dagger.

Blood spurted from the now opened wound and Lilitu's eyes closed as the darkness rushed in. The last thing she saw was Azazael helping Kor to stand.

"I owe you my life," Kor told his Military Faction leader. "She was going to destroy the entire palace and everyone in it."

"Only my duty, My Lord," the ever faithful Azazael responded.

Kor nodded. "Yes, but even so, you have a huge favor coming. Just name it."

Azazael didn't even have to think about it. "I want the fixer," he replied. "I want to see him drawn and quartered on

Execution Hill."

"You're still holding that old grudge against Braz'galar, I see," Kor said.

Azazael nodded. "It's a matter of family honor."

"Still... my fixer?" Kor questioned. "Isn't there anything else? Perhaps one of my consorts?"

Azazael didn't reply. He'd made his request.

Kor stared at the other for a few seconds, knowing Azazael wouldn't change his mind, but wishing he would. "Very well. As soon as Braz'galar shows his face in the capital, I'll have him arrested and executed."

"Don't execute him too fast," Azazael remarked. "I want him to know who's responsible for bringing him down. I want to look into his eyes as his entrails are slowly pulled out of his gut."

Emprusa, battered and bruised, sat up and watched the exchange between Kor and Azazael. There was no concern, or interest, in her well-being whatsoever. The First Consort narrowed her eyes. *"I'll destroy you!"* she thought.

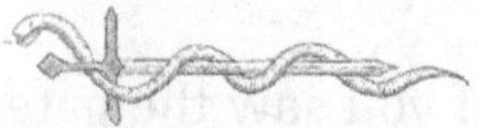

Abigail, followed by Father Goram, Nightshade, Landross, and Herbie, walked up to the gate. "Open the gates," she ordered. The Taumaru, besides being openly hostile and imperious, considered all other demon races inferior. It wasn't in their nature to "ask" for anything.

Facing off against four Taumaru was enough to make the guards hesitate, but not enough to neglect their duty. Of the five guards, two crossed their halberds to block the way further, two fanned out to either side and the last one, the captain of the guards, approached to stand in front of Abigail. He bowed slightly as a show of respect, unwilling to risk any more confrontation than what was already coming.

"I'm sorry, madam, but I'm afraid I can't do that," the captain replied. "The city's on lockdown until further notice."

"I don't care about the petty squabbles you have with the *B'nai Elohim*," Abigail said.

By now, Father Goram, Nightshade, and Landross had come up to stand alongside the disguised gorgon. Landross added a snarl for affect. Herbie was off to the side, sniffing at the base of a small bush before relieving himself.

"I wish I could," the captain responded. His hands tightened on his sword. "But I have my orders."

Abigail sighed and looked over at Father Goram. "He thinks I care about his orders."

Father Goram let out a guttural laugh, and Landross snarled again.

Several other guards had, by now, appeared to reinforce the original contingent. Though this propped up the captain's courage, he still didn't relish a fight. Rumors about the tenaciousness and sheer brutality of the Taumaru were legendary. If true, the *Pillar* might be an easier death. He decided to defer.

"Madam, maybe if you saw the gate commander, he'd see fit to let you through," the captain said.

"We don't have time for your bureaucracy," Abigail answered with contempt.

"Perhaps we should talk to him," Father Goram said. "It'd probably take less time to convince him to let us through than kill the guards. And I just had my robes cleaned."

Abigail paused as she pretended to consider. "Oh, I don't know," she said before redirecting her attention to the captain. "Very well. Bring your commander to me."

The captain breathed a sigh of relief before motioning for one guard to retrieve the gate commander. The guard disappeared into an unusually large door next to the gate and reappeared flying in the air through the opened door to land on his back a few feet away. He was still alive but stunned into unconsciousness. The captain and his guards cringed when the unfortunate landed.

Into the torchlight strode a truly impressive demon overlord. He stood over nine feet tall and had six arms and four legs. He wore armor made of steel plates that covered every inch of his body. Holes had been designed in the armor to prevent interference with his natural defenses—boney ridges and horns that stuck out all over. In one hand, he held a fifteen-foot long steel spear. Attached to a belt around his body were several swords and battleaxes. The gate commander went over to the hapless guard laying on the ground and kicked him in the side.

"Put yourself on report," he said before striding towards the captain. "So why did you feel the need to interrupt my sleep, Captain?"

"Well… um…" the captain stammered.

"You're here at my insistence," Abigail said. "We wish to leave the city."

The gate commander snorted. "Permission denied." Then he turned and slapped the captain in the face. "Taumaru or not, no one leaves the city!" he ordered as he walked away.

"Not good enough!" Abigail called out.

That stopped the gate commander in his tracks. He turned back around and looked at the insolent Taumaru. "You dare?" the overlord said as he walked back while tightly gripping his spear.

Abigail crossed her arms and stood her ground as he approached. "My kind dislike being denied simple requests, Commander," she said. "Now open the gates!"

With unnatural speed, the gate commander thrust his spear at Abigail's midsection. Landross was faster. He drew his great sword and blocked the spear onslaught away from his ally. Just as quick, Abigail's eyes caught the overlord's attention. They flared with supernatural light and the gate commander turned to stone. Landross, never one to miss an opportunity, sheathed his sword and drew out a heavy mace. He brought it down on the statue and smashed it into hundreds of pieces.

Abigail, power spent, leaned heavily against Father Goram as she closed her eyes. He put his arm around her to keep her from falling.

"She'll be weak for the next twenty-four hours," Nightshade whispered.

Though disabled and supported by Father Goram, Abigail behaved as if she was still in the fight. Nightshade and Landross moved to the front and prepared to battle the captain and his guards with sword and spells of White Magic. Herbie, who sensed the change of attitude in his master, growled and showed his teeth. The playful Abyssian dog had changed into a very intimidating opponent.

"Your move, Captain," Father Goram said. "And make it soon. As my lady here explained, we don't have time for delays."

The captain looked from the pile of rubble that once was the gate commander to Abigail. "You're not Taumaru, you're the gorgon Abigail."

Abigail took a weary breath and leaned even more heavily against Father Goram. "You've caught me, Captain… but I guarantee you my friends *are* Taumaru. You don't want to doubt me in this."

The spikey frill that ran down the captain's back lay flat and he held up his empty hands. "Whether they are or aren't, I'm not going to challenge. I think we can accommodate your request. Open the gates!"

"A wise decision, Captain," Father Goram said as the guards rushed to follow the captain's orders.

The captain smiled. It was a smile that made him look even

uglier. "What choice do I have?"

This time, it was Father Goram's turn to smile. "We all have a choice. The key is knowing and understanding the consequences of those choices."

"Like the *Pillar*?" the captain replied.

"Maybe," the priest agreed. "But even so, you get to live another day. As long as you have that, you have a future. And who among us can really know what the future holds... except for hope?"

"I'm no damn philosopher," the captain replied. "And my superiors aren't the forgiving type. But I take your point."

The gate creaked slowly until it was open enough to allow someone to pass through. The gate guards stood around looking in all directions to see if anyone was watching. They were anxiously waiting to close it as soon as possible. They each knew discovery could be lethal.

"Now hurry and go," bid the captain. "And don't come back!" he called out as the gate doors closed behind the four travelers and their dog.

"Think we're in the clear?" one guard wondered aloud.

The captain wiped the sweat off his brow with a dirty rag. "Only if I can explain this pile of rubble."

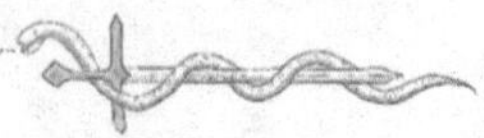

Vol'goth and Bezrameth entered the great cavern of the Talisman. The sorcerer immediately recognized the warding spell placed close to the entrance and abolished it with a flick of his hand. Before them was an enormous field of giant mushrooms. Above, darkness shrouded the ceiling. The faint echo of water and screeches of some type of unknown creature resonated throughout the immense cavern. Luminescent moss covered the stone floor and provided enough light to see, though not enough to prevent shadows from obscuring anything that might wait in ambush. That possibility didn't go unnoticed. Vol'goth's warriors, who'd just seen three of their comrades die unexpectedly, nervously stared off into the murky darkness. A few were even shaking in fear.

"Settle them down," Bezrameth told Vol'goth. "You're experiencing clerical magic. It's making you and your fighters anxious."

Vol'goth couldn't help himself. "Maybe if you magicked a little light?" he asked hopefully.

Bezrameth shook his head. "Think, idiot! That'd only make the shadows deeper as well as give our position away." Bezrameth then looked closer at Vol'goth and realized he was as frightened as his troops. "Do your duty!" he admonished. "Or face the *Pillar* when we get back!"

"If we get back," Vol'goth thought.

High above, Sqreecco, the bat who guarded this section of the cavern, felt the intrusion of the demons through his echolocation ability. He screeched his findings to the next bat down the line of pickets, who, in turn, repeated the warning. Within minutes, the entire bat community knew about the interlopers. Not long after, so did the Talisman and her mortal protectors.

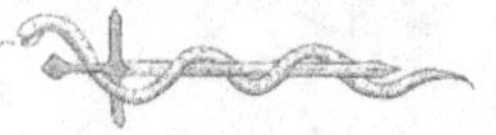

"They're here," Jörmungander, in human form, announced needlessly. Everyone had already figured it out based upon the excited chattering of the bats on the cavern ceiling.

"How mony 'n' fae whilk direction, laddie," Azriel asked.

Jörmungander shook his head. "They don't count exact numbers, Azriel."

"Not enough toes," Max commented. His joke fell flat,

although it did convey his nervousness.

"But from what they're saying, I'd guess between fifty and one-hundred," the young black dragon continued. "As for direction, the other side of the cavern."

"You mean fae th' ledge?" Azriel asked. "But that means thay wur comin' up… lik' th' sylph. Elbedreth?"

Elbedreth shook her head. "This is uncharted territory for me. I never expected to find the Johari this deep… and who knows what we'd find if we went deeper."

"They're demons from the Abyss," Solveig said. "They teleported here from there."

"Right yer are, lass," Azriel admitted. "Glad thay didn't teleport doon oan tap o' us."

"Erika?" Jörmungander asked.

The black dragon priestess shook her head. "Not now, Jörmungander!" she snapped. "All the wards I'm maintaining have me stretched pretty thin!"

Jörmungander drew back. Though surprised at the chastisement, he understood the pressure she, all of them, were under. He reached out and touched her arm. "I'm sorry."

Erika sighed and covered his hand with hers. "I'm the one who should apologize," she said before turning to the others. "The number is closer to fifty… warriors mostly, but three sorcerers are with them." She suddenly winced. "Something has just revoked one of my wards… with a simple spark of its own magic. Whatever's coming is powerful… better than me."

"We git whit we wanted, lass," Azriel said. "Drop th' rest o' yer ward spells 'n' prepare tae uise yer clerical magic. It'll be pure tough enough, ah reckon."

Jörmungander backed away and turned into his dragon form. Erika did the same. Not only did she still have possession of her clerical spells, but now she could use her dragon breath and would be much more resistant to physical and magical attacks.

“You two understand what needs to be done?” Max asked.

Both nodded. The two had discussed with Azriel and Max their part in the defense of the Johari and, now that they knew the direction of the threat, were ready to proceed.

“And don’t tak’ ony unnecessary chances,” Azriel told them. “Hit ‘n’ run! Hit ‘n’ run! We’ll git thare as soon as we kin. ‘N’ keep yourselves ready tae defend th’ Johari if ony o’ thaim git through.”

The remaining four watched as the two dragons disappeared up into the inky black heights of the great cavern. The natural coloration of their dragon scales blended in with the darkness to obscure them even further.

“The gods be with them,” Solveig prayed.

Max clutched her hand. He wasn’t sure if his intention was to comfort her or him.

“Well, mah friends,” Azriel declared. “Now that we know they’re ‘ere ‘n’ whaur they’re at, it’s time tae gie thaim a bit o’ a reception, don’t ye think?”

CHAPTER FOURTEEN

Aster – Draugan Pesta and the Hyrokkin Empire

"What's the situation, Misha?" Sofia Ternborg asked her General of the Army, Field Marshal Mikhail Grigorievich. She had called together her war council to discuss the Hyrokkin's claim that Jarsus Blackmantle, her daughter's close friend and advisor, had assassinated their queen, Thesonia. They were meeting in her husband's large conference room, which adjoined his office.

"Though the Hyrokkin fly their war flags over the pass, there's been no further sign they're on a war footing," Field Marshal Grigorievich responded.

"You're keeping the eastern frontier guarded?" Sofia questioned.

Field Marshal Grigorievich nodded. "As per your orders, Your Grace. All along the entire border. They won't surprise us again."

"They shouldn't have the first time," Sofia pointed out.

"Why don't you just order the Princess to turn the dwarf over to the Hyrokkin," Krasnov Dmitrievich asked.

Sofia looked at the questioner. She didn't like him. He harbored secrets, and she knew from her sources he was involved in his fair share of shady dealings, though no one could bring her proof of his corruption, which was unfortunate. She'd love to have any excuse to remove him from the council. Too bad her husband wouldn't allow her to handle him like her pa-pa would have... like she did with Boris Drugov.

"I've communicated with the Princess," Sofia said. "She won't hear of it. She says he's being framed... that there's no way he'd do such a thing. He didn't have the motive, means, opportunity, or a desire to see the Hyrokkin queen dead. In fact, he very much wanted her alive. Even I can attest to that." Sofia looked around the table to glance at each of those present. "As much as I questioned my daughter's choice of Blackmantle as her advisor, he's one of ours and I believe he's been wrongly accused. So I support her decision."

"Then it's war," Dmitrievich declared. *Things were falling into place very well.*

"You don't believe in negotiation, Dmitrievich?" Sofia asked.

"Their queen's dead," Dmitrievich continued. *Maybe things weren't going so well after all.* "Just who are you going to negotiate with? Not the army. We know where they stand."

Sofia eyed the counselor. *"What's his game?"* she wondered.

Dmitrievich shook his head. "No, Your Grace," he pressed. "We'll need to go in and get her. Granted, with Lord Ternborg gone, along with a substantial part of the army... again... that might be easier said than done. And the Hyrokkin will fight hard for their lands, and our strength and position will be less than ideal." *As long as there's war, there's a need for Hyrokkin soldiers and the weapons which the humans pay so dearly for. And as long as there's a need for soldiers, there's a need for our drugs to exchange for those weapons.* "But go in, we must! For the Princess!"

"Then they'll attack the Princess for sure," Field Marshal Grigorievich curtly responded. He didn't like Dmitrievich either.

"The Princess has that wolf and her Phalanx to protect her until our own forces arrive," Dmitrievich countered.

"We try diplomacy first," Sofia said with finality.

"Perhaps we should wait for the king to return from the Abyss, Your Grace," someone suggested.

Sofia shook her head with indignation. "I'm the queen and quite capable of handling this situation. Gentlemen, I'll not leave my daughter dangling in the wind. We'll try a diplomatic solution first. If it comes to war, however, I'll lead the army myself!"

"And there it is!" Dmitrievich thought. *"If the Hyrokkin can assassinate the Princess as they did their queen, there'll never be peace!"*

"The army awaits your orders, Your Grace," Field Marshal Grigorievich declared. "Peace or war, we're yours to command."

"Mother wants to try to negotiate with the Hyrokkin first," Daphnia announced as she walked into the large storage room turned conference room. With priority given to the exterior defenses, they'd done little to improve the interior of the compound and its main building. The storage room was the only downstairs room with four walls.

"Negotiate wi' they heathens!" Jarsus shouted. "Tae say a'm skeptical wid be an understatement! Only mah heid oan a platter wull satisfy them!"

"Calm down, Jarsus," Daphnia said. "They'll have to go through my Phalanx and me to get to you."

Jarsus shook his head. "Ah can't let that happen. But ah will nae gang doon wi'oot a fight!"

"As young as I am, and as much as I need your counsel, I'm in charge here and I give the orders. You're to stand down!" Daphnia ordered.

"Stand doon fae what?" Jarsus asked.

"Whatever you're planning!" Daphnia replied. "Is that understood?"

"Oh, aye, lassie," the dwarf answered, though everyone knew very little would stop him from doing what he thought was necessary to protect his young charge.

The Draugen Pesta princess turned her attention to Major

Romanova. "Anya?"

"Our battlements are as good as they're going to get, considering we're out of building materials," the Phalanx commander answered. "We've fortified the entire compound... but not to my satisfaction. There're too many weaknesses for my taste."

"How long can we hold if mother's mediation doesn't work out?" Daphnia asked.

"Perhaps a few days... a week at the most, Your Grace," Captain Dominika Yerzova, the Phalanx's executive officer, responded. "Or..."

Jarsus whispered under his breath. "A'm a deid dwarf fur sure."

"Or what?" Daphnia queried.

"We take the fight to them," Anya answered. "When your mother attacks, we do as well, forcing the Hyrokkin to fight on two fronts."

Jarsus spit on his hands and rubbed them together. "Now wur talking!"

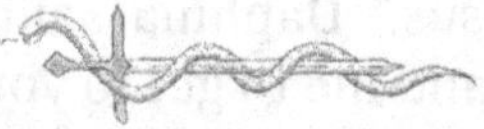

"You're dismissed for the rest of the day," Thanilus told the crew of army soldiers who were moving furniture from his private quarters. He was relocating his belongings into the palace since his position as first counselor put him temporarily on the throne when the queen expired. The inconvenience of her estranged son, the exiled rightful heir to the Hyrokkin Empire, would be dealt with soon.

"You're taking an enormous risk, Thanilus," Antephone remarked. The two were meeting without the others in the first counselor's current living quarters. Thanilus paid Hyrokkin's crime lord handsomely to use her resources to spy on everyone and everything, including his fellow conspirators.

"We want war," Thanilus argued. "That's the whole point."

"Yes," Antephone agreed. "But we don't want the Draugen Pesta to invade, do we?"

Thanilus shook his head. "They won't… at least not as long as we hold their Princess hostage."

"You're not giving them much choice," the crime boss countered. "And why the dwarf? I saw the Princess and him at the banquet and they appeared close."

"That's exactly why I picked the dwarf," Thanilus remarked. "My sources tell me he's her mentor and friend. She'll not give him up… and I don't really want him. The last thing I need is a speedy resolution."

"Agreed," Antephone replied. "But *my* sources tell me the Draugen Pesta queen's not too enamored with him. She might order he be turned over if for no other reason than to save her daughter from his ilk."

The first counselor shook his head. "I don't think so. She may not like him, but he's still a citizen of Draugen Pesta, and, as I've already mentioned, the Princess would never consent. Her mother will try to save him."

"You sure that's not your own addiction to Epiphany talking?" Antephone asked.

Thanilus frowned.

"No one I work with has secrets I don't know about," Antephone said by way of explanation.

Thanilus shrugged his shoulders. "I'm not surprised you know. Information gathering is what I pay you for. But don't think I allow my addiction to influence my thinking. To the point, I know they'll not turn him over because the Draugen Pesta have principles. You don't know what principles are… and I don't have them. But their king and queen do. She'll work to save the dwarf. Probably through diplomacy first… which I'll ignore, of course."

"I know what principles are," Antephone said in rebuttal. "Though I dislike them. I ask you... is war worth all the suffering that comes with it? Now that we've dispatched the queen, what's keeping you, as the first counselor, from keeping troop strengths up and weapons production going, peace or no peace?"

"We're agreed, remember?" Thanilus replied. "It's the best way to prevent the discovery of our trafficking in black market drugs for weapons with the Draugen Pesta. If their royals find out..." Thanilus shrugged. "It goes two ways. No, despite my new-found authority, peace is still bad for business."

Though Antephone had reservations, she nodded agreement. "But only if Draugen Pesta stays on their side of the mountains," she added.

Thanilus nodded. "They will."

"I hope so," the Hyrokkin female answered. "Our lives depend upon it."

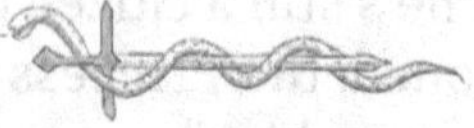

Adimar was laying comfortably next to the massive fireplace in the conference room. To an ordinary observer, he looked as if he was dozing, drifting in and out of sleep-induced unconsciousness. But like Sienna, who was only a few feet away, he was listening intently and heard as well as understood every word being uttered by Daphnia, her military advisors, and Jarsus. Being born a son of the father of all wolves came with advantages that mortal wolves don't have, such as enormous strength, massive size, high intelligence, and immortality. As for Sienna, Adimar wasn't sure how she had developed the ability to understand language, unless it was a by-product of her capacity for mind-to-mind communication. While Daphnia knew he could understand her language, he was reasonably certain she, and Jarsus, didn't suspect the mind link he shared with Sienna, though both knew the bear could communicate with anyone she choose.

"Anyone coming for Jarsus will have the surprise of their life," Sienna declared. *"And not just from me. I suspect the Lads will get involved as well."*

"The ones you call 'wildcards,'" Adimar said as a matter of fact. He and Sienna had many discussions about the Lads. He had even met them in their attack mode persona, though he'd never seen them in an actual fight. Sienna assured him he'd be quite impressed. They were a vicious, take no prisoners type of creature.

Sienna smiled in her bearish way. *"Those are the ones."*

Adimar growled a low chuckle. *"Maybe Daphnia should let them have him?"* he thought at Sienna. *"It'd be the last dwarf the centaurs would ever want to take again... if they survived."*

"Of that, there's no doubt," Sienna agreed.

"Even so, it might not be a bad idea if I were to go on the prowl tonight," Adimar added. *"Perhaps I can convince those four-legged jokers to let us go. I can be very persuasive when pressed. Want to come?"*

"I think I'll pass," Sienna responded. *"If you haven't noticed, I'm slow with little acumen when it comes to moving stealthily. I don't want to give you away. Nor do I want to become a pincushion for their spears."*

Adimar nodded. *"I thought so but I wanted to ask. Courtesy to a fellow comrade and all that. Guess I'll take a nap... could be a busy night. Let me know if anything important comes up."*

The last thing Sienna heard from her wolf friend was a distinct thought pondering the taste of centaurs. She smiled. *"Probably chicken."*

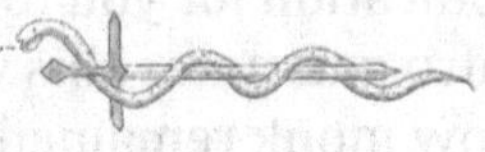

Dardandros heard a soft knocking on the door to his small, spartan room. At first, it irritated him. He didn't like being disturbed when he was in daily prayer to Kihara, the Goddess of Life. But the young warrior-monk realized it could be something important.

"Come," Dardandros called out as he stood.

Brother Theodasius entered. "I'm sorry to disturb you during evening prayers, Brother Dardandros, but I have news from Grimsturm."

"What's my mother done this time?" Dardandros asked.

For the first time since the two met all those years ago, Brother Theodasius looked uncomfortable. "Forgive me, but my tidings are of a different nature. I'm sorry to inform you that your mother's dead… assassinated by a foreigner if the messengers are to be believed."

"There's nothing to forgive, Theodasius," Dardandros responded. Not unexpectedly, he didn't really feel any emotion—no sorrow, no anger, no regret, no guilt. His mother had sent him away when he was a very young child, ostensibly to keep him safe. Since then, however, she hadn't bothered to send him a note or even check on his well-being. "I *am* surprised it was a foreigner, though. She had plenty of enemies in her own council and amongst our ruling elite."

Theodasius shrugged. "The messengers sent from the capital can explain what happened in more depth. They've asked to see you."

Dardandros frowned.

"They insist. There's a question of succession since you're her only heir."

"I don't want to be king," Dardandros insisted.

Theodasius nodded. "As the abbot explained it to me, they have documents of abdication for you to sign."

"Does the abbot also guarantee this will be the end of it?"

Dardandros's fellow monk remained silent.

The soon to be ex-prince sighed. "Very well."

Four messengers waited for Dardandros in the monastery common room. The moment he saw them, he suspected something other than a simple message delivery and document signing were in the offing. The "so-called" messengers looked more like seasoned warriors than low-ranking members of the bureaucracy typically used for such purposes.

Dardandros stopped walking towards the four couriers. When Theodasius turned to leave, Dardandros grabbed his arm and shook his head.

"You're here with news concerning my mother?" Dardandros asked.

One of the four stepped forward. "We bring sour news, Prince," he said.

"Don't call me that," Dardandros answered. "Mother made sure I wasn't a couple decades ago."

"As you wish," the other replied. "Your mother's been murdered. A foreign guest of our nation killed her most foully."

Dardandros nodded. "So I've been told."

"Then you know you're the legal heir. To officially abdicate, there are documents that requires your signature before we can install a new monarch upon the throne." The speaker held out his hand and snapped his fingers. Another of the messengers pulled a roll of scrolls from a cylindrical leather case hanging from his belt. Then he produced ink and quill.

Poison recognition is part of every warrior-monk's training, and both Dardandros and Theodasius smelled the poison coming from the quill. It was a quick acting and deadly toxin called tiger lily.

"Poison," Dardandros warned.

Both monks took defensive stances while three of the four messengers spread out. The speaker cursed as he threw the poisoned quill at Dardandros, who deftly stepped aside.

"They told me you might be more than a spoiled royal,"

the speaker remarked. "It'll do you no good... even with your friend to help."

"I've no interest in anyone's politics," Dardandros said. "Leave now while you still have your lives."

The speaker shook his head. "I can't do that."

Neither Dardandros nor Theodasius needed any more prompting. Though carrying their usual weapon compliment while in the monastery was prohibited, they could keep daggers upon their person. Dagger hilts blossomed out of the eye and throat of the speaker. He dropped without making a sound. The three remaining messengers drew swords and attacked the warrior-monks. Dardandros ducked to evade the sword thrust of the nearest and hit the assassin in the chest with his leg, causing his opponent to lose balance and step back a few paces. Dardandros was on him in an instant and drove the heel of his hand into the nose, pushing it up into the brain, killing the assassin. Meanwhile, Theodasius used his weight and positioning to knock his opponent off his feet. He then moved to the head and broke the neck. By now, several other monks, including the abbot, had entered the room and were watching.

The last assassin stopped and held up his hands. "I didn't sign up for this," he said as he backed away towards the door.

"Then go in peace," the abbot announced.

After the assassin had left, the abbot looked at Dardandros. "Perhaps you need to look into this," he remarked.

Dardandros nodded. "It would appear so. Would you allow Theodasius to accompany me?"

"It's his choice," the abbot smiled as he responded to the query. He already knew what the answer would be.

"Give me a few minutes to put together my travel pack," Theodasius replied with his own grin.

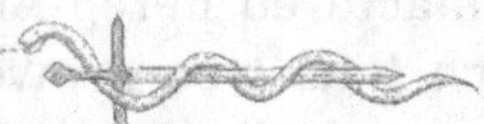

Sofia was finishing up her latest council meeting when she noticed Aleksei Smirnov, her most experienced and trusted spy, enter the back of the room unnoticed. She kept giving instructions and orders as he skulked into the nearest shadowed corner.

"Everyone understand what I want done?" Sofia asked.

"Yes, Your Grace," all those around the table agreed.

Sofia nodded. "Then let's get to work, ladies and gentlemen. The safe return of my daughter is to be your only concern... and that might very well depend upon how well you do your jobs."

As everyone filed out of the room, Sofia looked around the room. Only after the last person had exited and closed the door did a shadow step into the light.

"I appreciate you keeping your arrival secret," Sofia remarked.

Aleksei nodded.

"Successful?" the queen queried.

"Not entirely," the spy responded. "I understand what's going on. I just haven't identified the ringleaders yet. And the only reason I know what I do is because we're watching the eastern border so closely."

Sofia frowned. "Not exactly what I wanted to hear, but as my husband would say, 'One step at a time.' Continue."

"Yes, Your Grace," Aleksei answered. "There's a drugs for arms scheme being played out between a few of our people and the Hyrokkin. Apparently, our people are smuggling a drug made from the Bael tree... the Hyrokkin call it Epiphany... for weapons of berlinium ore, which are then turned around and sold by us to the humans."

"Who's actually making the drug?"

"It's being manufactured here," Aleksei replied. "We're checking to see which Bael tree growers are involved and where the drug's being made. But I don't have that information just yet."

"When you do, let me know," Sofia instructed. "But do nothing to stop it."

"Yes, Your Grace."

"Thank you," Sofia said as she nodded. "Now, as far as I can determine, the Hyrokkin have the only deposit of berlinium ore on Aster. Tough stuff… twice as strong as steel and worth a fortune on the black market. Very difficult to work, but our centaur neighbors have obviously figured it out. If they'd learn to tolerate other races and sell their weapons themselves, they'd be quite wealthy… though they wouldn't have the drugs, which I suspect is the real crux of the matter. Interestingly enough, our generals once put together a war game that tested our ability to capture and hold that mine."

"How'd that turn out?" the spy inquired.

Sofia shrugged. "Touch and go. Taking the mine wasn't the problem. Holding it was." The queen leaned back in her chair and looked at a framed map of both nations hanging on the wall next to her. "Do you have any clue how far up in the government this goes?"

"No… but there's at least one on the council," Aleksei replied.

Sofia had expected that, and she even believed she knew who it was. She rose from her chair and began pacing, both hands behind her back.

Aleksei remained silent.

"Where did you get your information and how dependable is it?" Sofia asked.

"Most of it came from a driver," Aleksei answered. "Someone who's been making deliveries of drugs to the Hyrokkin on a weekly basis."

"And the weapons coming back?" the queen inquired.

"They used different drivers for that part of the operation," the spy answered.

Sofia nodded. "Smart. About the driver?"

"He's just a boy who wanted extra money for the usual things... drinking and partying with members of the opposite sex."

"So he looked to do that by illegally smuggling drugs to our hereditary enemy," Sofia commented.

"The boy claims he didn't know he was doing anything illegal," Aleksei answered back. "He saw what he said were official-looking documents and a bill of sale. He also swears he thought he was delivering medicine."

"Yet he wasn't caught going through Eagle Pass where all *legal* shipments go to the Hyrokkin," Sofia wondered aloud. "He should have known better! What the hell are we teaching our children these days?"

Aleksei sighed. Education wasn't the problem... gullibility was. "He used a different pass... really only a trail... they showed him to get across the Boreskyre's. As I said, he thought it was legitimate."

Sofia shook her head. "A trail off the beaten path and he thought it was legitimate. Unbelievable!"

"It's partly my fault, Your Grace. I should've known the pass was there and had it guarded."

"I'll hear of no such thing," Sofia said. "You're not to blame. Did the driver know whose signature was on the bill of lading?"

"Some minor functionary working for the Office of the Chief Exchequer," Aleksei replied. "Probably another pawn, like the driver. That person is under observation. We should be able to work ourselves up from there."

Sofia nodded. "Just what I was thinking. What did you do with the driver and his cargo of 'drugs?'"

"After our questioning, we told him everything was in

order and let him go," the spy said.

"Very well," Sofia agreed. "Good job. Keep that trail open and work your way up the food chain. I'd love to give my husband a fist full of traitors when he gets back."

"Any word from Lord Ternborg?" Aleksei asked.

Sofia shook her head. "Nothing."

"He'll be back, Your Grace."

"Oh, he'll be back," Sofia said. "I just hope and pray to the gods it'll be in one piece."

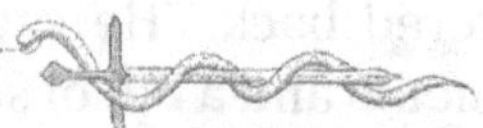

"What!" Dmitrievich exclaimed. "You're telling me they stopped one of our drivers, questioned him, and then sent him on his way?"

Kesha Stanislavovich nodded. "At least that's what Cherganski said. Now he's worried it'll lead back up to him, since the signature on the bill of sale is someone who works underneath him."

"Cherganski's an idiot. The larger question is why did they let the wagon through? Either they're being sloppy, which I don't believe, or someone's caught a whiff of what we're doing and didn't want us to know."

Kesha shrugged. "Right now Cherganski's the only one with his neck out."

"If they bring him in for questioning, he'll expose us all," Dmitrievich said. "Ternborg may have scruples about torture, but his wife doesn't. They do things different in the north. She'll not hesitate if it'll get her the evidence she desires."

"He'll faint before the first drop of blood."

Dmitrievich nodded. "Or spill his guts. Torture up north... at least torture for information... is more psychological than physical. Do we have anyone else in the Chief Exchequer's office?"

"We've been grooming someone… an ambitious young female who doesn't see the law as an absolute," Kesha replied. "I think she's ready."

"Then sign her up," Dmitrievich ordered. "Make that your number one priority. Once she's totally committed, arrange for Cherganski to have an accident."

Kesha agreed. "Already working on it."

Dmitrievich smiled. "Thought you might be. Obviously the pass we were using is being watched. We need to use the northern route."

"That way's much more dangerous," Kesha commented. "The terrain's far steeper and there're more predators roaming around… particularly Royal Mountain Saber Cats. Big brutes… and intelligent…"

Dmitrievich held up a hand to cut Kesha off. "Then provide a stronger escort."

"Very good," Kesha replied.

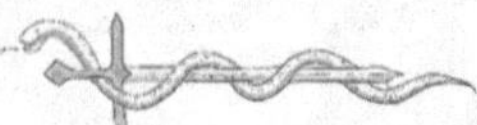

Thanilus looked up from the letters he was studying. "Damn paperwork!" he said as Antephone entered the room. "What's on *your* mind?"

"My assassins failed to dispose of Dardandros," Antephone commented without preamble.

"Finding and eliminating him is your responsibility, remember?" Thanilus replied. "Try again."

Antephone nodded. "Don't worry on that score. Did you know he was traveling from that monastery of his to Grimsturm?"

Thanilus looked at the crime boss. He'd already been informed. But he wasn't surprised she knew. Her spies and contacts were probably better than his. "Of course I know! Just like I knew you failed to take care of him the first time. Is that why you're wasting my time?"

Antephone shook her head. "If he links up with the queen's loyalists… or if he contacts the queen's former bodyguard, who'll be just as devoted to him as they were to his mother… we could have a real problem on our hands. Nothing I can't handle… but you should be prepared to open the coffers."

Thanilus waved a hand. "Then maybe you should intercept him *before* he reaches the city?"

"He's already here."

Thanilus winced. He *didn't* know that. "Whatever it takes," he said as he went back to his paperwork. "We'll negotiate the price later. Now, have we concluded our business? I've got a mountain of correspondence that requires my attention."

Thanilus looked up at the silence. Antephone had already left.

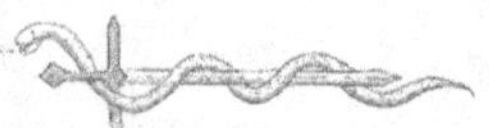

Wolves and equines have been natural enemies since the dawn of time. This is also true of the centaurs of Hyrokkin. The Hyrokkin hate wolves even more than they hate the Draugen Pesta and the humans. Any wolf who found itself wandering across the mountains and into the lands of the Hyrokkin could expect to be hunted down and killed. No expense, monetary or otherwise, is spared in this butchery. Therefore, the reaction to Adimar since his arrival couldn't have been clearer to both the wolf, his friends, or his allies. Even so, the Hyrokkin were forced to make an exception since the immortal wolf was part of Daphnia's retinue.

When the threat to Daphnia, Jarsus, and their entire party materialized through the queen's assassination and subsequent accusation that Jarsus was the assassin, Adimar decided to make things interesting for the Hyrokkin by giving them something else to worry about. Sienna, who knew what the wolf was about to do, advised him to do it without the foreknowledge of Daphnia or anyone else. She told him it gave them "plausible deniability" should they need it.

The first night the Draugen Pesta compound came under blockade, Adimar, using his natural wolf ability augmented by his supernatural capabilities, snuck through both lines of defense, evading both the Phalanx and Hyrokkin guards, until he was free of the city walls. That first night, his only goal was to announce his presence, which he did by catching and consuming two cows, leaving only skin and bone behind.

Adimar didn't hide the two carcasses but hid all signs of his having been there. Let the Hyrokkin figure it out on their own. Tomorrow night, however, he'd have a much different story to tell.

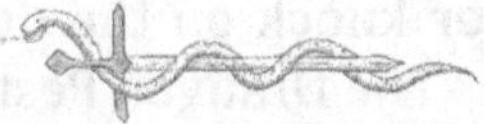

"Damn that wolf!" Thanilus said aloud as he looked at the latest reports of widespread howling the previous night. He'd even heard it himself, and it was enough to send shivers down his spine. Thanilus knew who was doing it and why. And it was succeeding! The populace was operating in panic mode and his guards were chasing phantom reports of wolves all over the city, which was, among other things, weakening the blockade around the Draugen Pesta compound. If it kept up, he'd need to bring in reinforcements... troops he couldn't afford to take away from the western border. There was a sharp rap on the door just before someone entered.

Thanilus looked up from his desk. "Ahhh... Casillos," he said when he saw the high priest enter his office. "What brings you here? Special instructions from your god?"

"Skerrit is your god as well," Casillos answered. "You need to make your peace with him."

"Ha!" Thanilus laughed. "All he's good for is overseeing the constant suffering of our people. Maybe if he actually helped every so often… like bringing rain during droughts… or giving us a cure for colic or encephalomyelitis!"

"Or stopping you from poisoning our people with drugs," Casillos countered.

"Touché," Thanilus replied. "Though you've never turned down your part of the profit from the sale of those drugs."

The priest shrugged. "Most go into church coffers."

"Why are you here?" Thanilus asked.

"The Draugen Pesta delegation has arrived," Casillos announced.

The Hyrokkin leader frowned. "I wasn't expecting them until tomorrow."

"Which is why they're here today," Casillos remarked.

There was another knock on the door. "My Lord," a low, gruff voice called out. "The Draugen Pesta are here."

Thanilus looked at the high priest, who had already made himself comfortable on a pillow-seat, and raised an eyebrow.

"I wouldn't miss this for the world," Casillos said in answer to Thanilus's unasked question. He poured himself a glass of wine from a bottle on Thanilus's desk.

Thanilus sighed. He knew better than to force the priest to leave. "Let them in!"

Seven Draugen Pesta marched into the room. One was an obvious diplomat from the expensive clothes he wore and the deference the others showed him. His escort comprised six fierce, no-nonsense warriors who seemed much more comfortable on a horse and in a field of battle than being on protection detail. Even though the Hyrokkin had confiscated their weapons, Thanilus suspected they could do almost as much harm with their fists alone. Tagging along behind the Draugen Pesta were a dozen Hyrokkin guards.

"Care for a cup of wine?" Thanilus offered.

The finely dressed diplomat nodded and sat cross-legged on the pillow-seat in front of Thanilus's desk. "That would be delightful."

As Thanilus handed over a wine-filled cup, he asked for a name.

"Terribly sorry," the diplomat replied. "Pavel Shubin at your service, First Counselor Thanilus... or should I say King Thanilus."

"Thanilus will be fine for now," the new Hyrokkin leader responded. "There are still certain formalities that have to be observed."

"Ahh... but of course," Shubin said. "We must always observe the proper rituals. It makes the civilized world go round."

Thanilus wondered what the Draugen Pesta meant by that. "Yes, of course. Anyway, I have to admit, considering the current standing between our two nations, I had deeply concerning reservations about allowing you past the border."

"Yet you did," Shubin returned. "Surely that's evidence of your belief that peace between us is paramount."

"You dare talk peace after one of your own assassinated our queen!" Thanilus shouted. "How arrogant can you people be?"

There was a sudden sense of unease in the room. Everyone tensed. The Draugen Pesta warriors turned and faced the Hyrokkin guards. Thanilus and Casillos stood. But Shubin remained seated and stayed calm. He didn't even blink at Thanilus's outburst and remained in complete control of his emotions.

"Cease and desist!" Shubin ordered his escort in a low voice, though there was no mistaking the authority in his command.

The Draugen Pesta warriors stood down. They never relaxed, but they were no longer on the verge of violence. The Hyrokkin guards followed suit after receiving a curt nod from Thanilus.

"Perhaps you should hear the terms Queen Sofia has laid out before rejecting any sort of compromise between the two of us out of hand," Shubin said, unbothered by what had almost just happened.

Thanilus and Casillos sat back on their pillow-seats. "At this point, what's there to lose?" Thanilus said. "So... how will your queen smooth over regicide?"

Shubin met Thanilus stare for stare and didn't flinch. "We know about the drugs for weapons smuggling going on between certain elements of our two countries."

Casillos choked on his wine while Thanilus couldn't stop a brief look of horror from crossing his face.

"Caught you!" Shubin thought. He also deduced from the panic that flashed in Thanilus's eyes that he had become addicted to the drug. *"Not only have I caught you, but I have you!"*

"Preposterous!" Thanilus lied.

Shubin continued unabated. "Furthermore, she's prepared to let the exchange continue." The Draugen Pesta diplomat paused to let his last statement sink in. "But only as long as you end your blockade of the Princess, giving her the freedom to come and go as she pleases. That and keep the drug for weapons arrangement... oh, shall we say... somewhat less than common knowledge."

Thanilus looked at Casillos. "Otherwise?" he asked.

Shubin shrugged. "Otherwise we shut you down. That and we'll come over here with enough force to destroy your entire army... hell, your entire empire."

Thanilus looked at Shubin. He didn't appear so soft, so

pompous any longer. "So, if we allow your Princess..."

Shubin shook his head. "Not so fast. There are other conditions."

"What else could your queen possibly want?" Casillos queried. "We have little else to offer."

"You don't give yourself enough credit," Shubin answered. "You know the names of my countrymen providing the drugs. We want them. We also want you to drop the pretense of Jarsus Blackmantle being an assassin. You know as well as I that's not true. Finally, we want peace between our two peoples... a peace that your dear, departed queen wanted as well."

Thanilus cleared his throat. "Just for the sake of argument, let's say that there *is* a drug trade..."

"Drug smuggling, my dear sir," Shubin interjected. "Let's call it what it is."

Thanilus nodded. "Very well... drug smuggling. Let's say I know the names of your people helping us. And let's suppose I give you those names, drop the charges against the dwarf, and pursue peace. How will your queen keep the drugs flowing, considering how your king feels about it?"

"Fair question," Shubin concluded. "For the time being, the king doesn't have to be brought into our little secret. Oh, he'll eventually find out. But the queen can be quite persuasive. He'll accept it as the price for peace... and getting his daughter back."

"Why not just let everything continue without change?" Casillos asked.

Shubin turned his attention to the high priest. His steely gaze made Casillos wonder if he'd crossed some kind of line with the Draugen Pesta emissary.

"Because, priest, they're traitors who need to be punished," Shubin snapped. Then his gaze softened. "I'm sure you understand."

Thanilus and Casillos both gulped before nodding. For the

second time, the giant sitting across from them exposed just a brief hint of his capacity to command a room with authority. There was also a hardness to him neither centaur wished to challenge.

"Then we have a deal?" Shubin purred.

"I don't know everyone involved…" Thanilus began.

Shubin frowned.

"But I do have a couple of names you might be interested in," Thanilus hastily added. "One of them is the leader."

The Draugen Pesta envoy smiled. "Cut off the head and the body dies. That'll be sufficient. Then we're agreed?"

Thanilus sighed, thinking he had much to learn about negotiation. "We do."

"Excellent!" Shubin said as he reached into his robes and produced a leather messenger tube containing documents of agreement. "These will seal our treaty. Oh, I understand they're just pieces of parchment… but I wouldn't recommend breaking any of the articles of covenant contained therein. My queen can be very disagreeable if pushed."

"I bet," Thanilus whispered under his breath as he prepared to sign. More loudly, "We have a wolf problem that you might be able to help us with."

At first, Shubin looked slightly confused. Then he made the connection in his mind and laughed out loud.

Upon entering the Hyrokkin capital city of Grimsturm, both Dardandros and Theodasius knew at once they were being watched. They were in one of the poorer neighborhoods, believing they'd have a better chance of remaining anonymous. They had figured wrong.

"Are you seeing what I'm seeing?" Theodasius asked Dardandros.

Dardandros nodded. "Palace guards. At least half a dozen following and watching every move we make."

"Where to, then," Theodasius asked. "Not the palace... especially after what happened at the monastery."

Dardandros considered. "No... not there. We need to get the lay of the land first. As much as I deny any desire to be king, they won't believe me."

"Eight," Theodasius said.

"Huh?" his companion questioned.

Theodasius tilted his head to the right. "Two more just latched on to us."

Dardandros nodded. "I see them. Let's go visit that tavern over there."

Three hours and several mugs of ale later, Dardandros and Theodasius had, through the extensive rumor mill running throughout the poor side of the city, a complete picture of the queen's assassination. They learned of the dwarven foreigner accused of the crime and the compound blockade of the newly minted ambassador from Draugen Pesta, who was harboring the alleged assassin.

"To sue for peace with our traditional enemy," Dardandros commented. "I didn't think mother had something like that in her."

"Pretty amazing," Theodasius agreed. "I don't know about you, but I approve. Our people could use a friend."

The other centaur monk shook his head. "The military would never accept that. In fact, I'd be willing to bet they'd rather see her dead than have peace."

"So perhaps..." Theodasius said.

Dardandros nodded. "Yes. This whole thing about accusing the Draugen Pesta of her assassination is a sham to cover up their own culpability and treachery in my mother's death."

Theodasius whistled. "What're you going to do about it?"

Dardandros finished his cup of ale. "Two things to consider.

One, I can't turn my back and walk away from mother's death. I must try to bring her true murderer to justice, and our estrangement shouldn't interfere with that."

"I'm glad to hear you say that," Theodasius said. "I'd be wondering what happened to my friend if you hadn't. And the other?"

"You said it yourself," Dardandros replied. "Our people need the peace she gave her life for."

As Dardandros and Theodasius left the tavern, two female centaurs, dressed in attire common to ordinary folks, watched from across the street at an open-street market. They made note of the guards from the palace and the direction the two monks headed. Though they couldn't be absolutely sure, they believed one of those monks was the queen's long absent son. One female followed while the other disappeared into the crowd of shoppers.

The palace guards, just augmented to ten, continued to follow the two monks. Two of them broke off and ran in the palace's direction after it became clear their quarry was heading towards the Draugen Pesta compound.

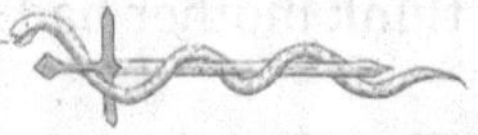

Adimar was running through golden fields of wheat, chasing one of his many brothers and sisters. He was content and carefree, living life as one of Fenrisúlfr's immortal offspring. But somewhere in the back of Adimar's mind rested the knowledge that something was wrong... as if a piece of his heart was being held elsewhere. The young wolf stopped and cocked his head.

"What's wrong?" he wondered. "Why do I feel so alone even though I'm with my family?"

His father, the immortal giant sire of all wolves, suddenly stood by his side.

"You no longer belong in this world, my son," Fenrisúlfr said. "Someone else needs your companionship. That person holds the missing piece of your heart... and your spirit."

"How did this come to be?" Adimar asked. "How could you turn your own flesh and blood over to someone else?"

"I am your father," Fenrisúlfr answered. "It is the way."

Adimar sighed. That was the only answer he could expect from the great wolf demi-god. Then he heard another voice, a familiar and heartwarming voice, call his name from far, far away. "Adimar! Adimar! Adimar!"

"Wake up, sleepyhead," Daphnia said.

Adimar open his eyes. They felt like sandpaper. But the smell that assaulted his senses forced him to come wide awake. Fresh meat! Fresh blood-soaked meat! Saliva worked overtime in his mouth. But before he had a chance to savor his meal, he perceived another, someone who was a stranger, sitting next to the princess. Adimar uncoiled from his sleeping position, stood, and faced the stranger.

"I figured you needed a hardy meal considering what you've been doing the last few nights," Daphnia said, ignoring the sudden attention the wolf was giving the stranger.

"I've seen him from afar," Pavel Shubin remarked. "But never up this close. Impressive! No, more than impressive! He's magnificent! And his size..."

Daphnia petted Adimar's side. "He's a very special wolf," she said with pride. "The son of Fenrisúlfr, god of the wolves. The demon Nightshade brought him to me for company after she'd kidnapped me to force father to invade the land of the humans. We've been best of friends ever since."

Shubin laughed. "Indeed! His nightly forays have been driving the Hyrokkin to the point of insanity! Absolutely delightful!"

Daphnia kissed the wolf on the head and whispered, "Eat."

Adimar didn't need more persuading and attacked the bloody meat like he hadn't eaten in days, even though it was just yesterday. As he downed the succulent slab, he realized just how ravenous he was.

Shubin continued his discussion with the princess. "We've reached an agreement..."

"So mother said," Daphnia commented as she pointed to the communications crystal on the table between them. "Do you think they'll keep the peace?"

"As I mentioned, their new leader... I won't say king just yet... is probably the drug for weapons smuggling ringleader on this side," Shubin said. "And I strongly suspect he's addicted to the drug. He'll keep the peace as long as the drugs keep coming."

Daphnia shook her head. "He's killing his own people. And mother's going to allow it to continue?"

"It's peace or war, Your Grace," Shubin explained. "The latter will kill many more... including our own. Besides, it was the price for your safety."

"We weren't in any real danger," Daphnia said. "We have... certain supernatural resources at our disposal."

Shubin nodded at the wolf. "Adimar?"

The wolf, at the mention of his name, looked up. Blood dripped from his snout.

Daphnia nodded. "Among others."

The queen's diplomat frowned. But before he could ask for clarification, there was a knock on the door and Jarsus, with Sienna trailing behind, walked into the room. The dwarf took a seat while the bear shared in Adimar's flavorful windfall.

"Sorry tae disturb yer meetin, lassie," Jarsus said. "But twa o' they de'il centaurs ur asking fur entry intae th' compound."

"Hyrokkin officials?" Shubin asked.

Jarsus shook his head. "Not th' wey they're dressed. No

fancy-dandy duds. I'd say monks. Aye, definitely monks... 'n' they're running fae a hail bunch o' Hyrokkin soldiers."

"Are they fighting?" Daphnia inquired.

"No, lassie," Jarsus answered. "There's a standoff atween th' monks 'n' th' soldiers... though Anya is making sure that's as far o' it goes. At least 'til we hae yer orders."

Daphnia stood. "Let's go take a look."

The scene before them when they reached the main gate of the compound was as Jarsus had described, except the number of soldiers had doubled over the last few minutes. Anya had archers posted along the battlements facing the standoff. There were several Draugen Pesta black-feathered arrows buried in the ground before the Hyrokkin soldiers.

"Situation, Anya?" Daphnia asked her Phalanx commander.

"So far, they've respected our warning arrows," Anya replied. "But the number of soldiers keeps escalating... and I can't pull more troops away from the rest of the battlements in case this is a prelude to an attack."

Daphnia leaned over the battlements. "You two," she called. "What's your names and why are you here?"

Jarsus pulled his princess back behind the wall. "Are ye doolally! You're making a perfect target!"

Daphnia shrugged off Jarsus's hand and his concern. "Oh, posh. They'll not shoot me." She leaned back over the battlements. "Well?" she hollered.

"My name's Dardandros and my friend here is called Theodasius," the bigger of the two answered. "I'm afraid we need sanctuary from our own people."

"Dardandros?" Daphnia wondered. "Where have I heard that name before?"

"At the Queen's introduction dinner," Anya replied. "That's the name of her son."

"Aye," Jarsus added. "Her alienated son 'n' th' heir tae Hyrokkin. Na doubt auld what's-his-face haes some no nice 'n' unpleasant hings planned fur him."

"You shouldn't get involved in Hyrokkin politics, Your Grace," Shubin warned.

Daphnia shook her head. "I don't *care* about the politics, Shubin. Hyrokkin or not, I won't stand by while they're butchered. At least not when I can do something about it. Open the gates."

"Belay that order," Jarsus shouted before turning to the princess. "Lassie, ye *hae* tae care aboot politics. It's th' reason how come you're 'ere. You're th' ambassador."

Daphnia turned to Shubin, who nodded in support of the dwarf. "He's mostly correct, though I've always found politics, combined with a touch of civility, works under the right circumstances. But the risks must be considered. That's particularly true in this case. We can't trust Thanilus… yet."

The princess thought about it for just a moment before shaking her head. "No. Nothing I've learned about politics says it must be devoid of common decency. Father would make this same decision. Open the gates!" she ordered.

But before they could get the gates opened, twelve Hyrokkin females shoved their way through the throng of army soldiers. They quickly disarmed and disabled any soldier who attempted to stop them. The twelve centaur females broke through the army perimeter and stopped before the two monks. Together, they bowed.

"They lasses kin fight!" Jarsus observed.

"Those are Thesonia's personal bodyguard," Shubin said. "See the medallions around their neck? They'll be loyal to the Hyrokkin prince."

Jarsus shook his head. "This is anither situation altogether. You can't let that four-legged airmie in here, lassie!"

"They'll augment our defenses if there's a fight for the prince," Shubin countered. "If we're going to let the prince in, they should be allowed as well. In fact, they'll probably insist on it."

"They didn't seem tae be gey effective stopping th' Queen's assassination," Jarsus remarked.

"For whatever reason, they weren't there," Daphnia said. "If they had been, either Queen Thesonia would still be alive or they'd be dead. Get the gates opened!"

Shortly thereafter, the two Hyrokkin monks and their new bodyguard were safely behind the walls of the compound.

"There's aff tae be repercussions," Jarsus mentioned.

Shubin nodded. "Perhaps. But the Princess is in a much stronger position than twenty-four hours ago."

"Howfur's that?" Jarsus asked.

"Thanilus has become addicted to a drug made from our Bael tree," Daphnia said. "And we know it. I'll explain the details later. For now, let's go see what our guests have to say for themselves."

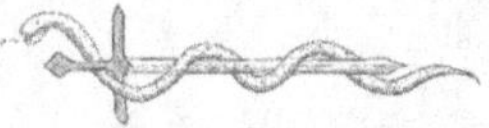

The knock on Krasnov Dmitrievich's door irritated him. He had little free time and didn't appreciate the interruption. The knock became more insistent and a gruff voice called out, "Open in the name of the Queen!"

When he answered, three army warriors stood in the entranceway. "The Queen wishes a word."

Irritation turned to concern. "What does she want?" Dmitrievich asked.

"The Queen doesn't confide in us. She just expects us to carry out our orders... which are to deliver you to her. Her preference is alive."

Dmitrievich didn't like the sound of that.

As he and his escort marched into the street, another group of guards were approaching. Kostadin Chenganski was in their midst. He was sweating and looked as if he was going to cry.

"They know about the drug smuggling," Dmitrievich concluded. *"And if they don't, Chenganski will sing soon enough."*

Back at Dmitrievich's apartment, Kesha Stanislavovich decided it was time to leave Saint Petersburg for good. He slipped out of a back exit and disappeared into the streets.

CHAPTER FIFTEEN

The Battle for the Johari

"We go that way," Bezrameth said.

Vol'goth shook his head. "We shouldn't split out forces. We've no idea what we're facing."

"No, we don't," Bezrameth answered. "Which is exactly why we shouldn't concentrate everything together. You, my ten, and I will circle around while my sorcerers and the rest make a frontal assault."

Vol'goth protested. "I should stay with my command."

"You want to survive?" Bezrameth asked. "You want Kor's thanks and accolades? Perhaps a promotion to overlord? Or even your own city?"

Vol'goth considered. Just a hint of rewards and riches will entice the rudimentary instincts of most demons, and Vol'goth was no different. Then a thought came to him.

"You don't expect my command to survive, do you?" he said. "But we..."

Bezrameth held up a hand to stop Vol'goth mid-sentence. "I don't know, but there will be resistance. Something as important as the Talisman will have strong defenses. In fact, I worry our current numbers won't be enough. I'd have brought an entire army through the doorway if I could've."

"So my warriors are nothing but bait?" Vol'goth concluded.

"Not necessarily... but what if they are?" Bezrameth asked. "If it gets the job done, do you have a problem with it?"

Vol'goth smiled as he thought about the good things that could come into his life if this mission is successful. "No... not at all," he answered before giving the orders.

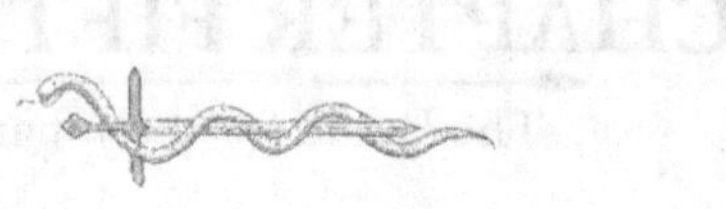

Jörmungander and Erika flew high enough that the darkness clinging to the ceiling above covered their approach. They had left the others well behind. The strategy involved an attack from above by the two dragons which, if everything went according to plan, would allow Azriel, Elbedreth, Max, and Solveig to surprise the intruders. Once everyone was engaged in the fight, Erika would fly back to the Johari and circle the supernatural being on the off chance another attack materialized from another direction.

"Remember," Jörmungander said. "The mushrooms are the bat's only source of food. Don't breathe on the enemy or use a spell that might spark a fire."

"I'll remember," Erika replied. "Look! Down there!"

Jörmungander nodded. "I see them. As Azriel is so fond of saying, 'Arrrggghhh! Let's murdurr th' bastards!'"

The two dragons dove out of the darkness from the upper reaches of the cavern. The demons, their attention directed forward into the forest of mushrooms, were taken by complete surprise. But the dragons, restrained from using their devastating breath weapons or fire spells, weren't able to take full advantage of their superior tactical position. Jörmungander, as soon as he was within range, used a lightning bolt spell to vaporize half a dozen of the demons, along with a few mushrooms. Erika used clerical magic to banish several others back to the Abyss.

The demons, unhindered by concern for the mushrooms, overcame their initial surprise within seconds of the dragon's aerial assault. The two sorcerers hit the dragons with heat rays as they flew over. A rain of magic-tipped arrows followed. Neither the spells nor the arrows did much to hurt the dragons, but it was enough to cause concern. Both realized the battle wasn't going to be a "walk in the park," as Max might say when something was going to be easy. The dragons stopped once they were out of spell and arrow range and hovered.

"They've sorcerers!" Erika exclaimed. "Powerful sorcerers who don't need to worry about the mushrooms while we're fighting without our best weapon... and no surprise this time. We should wait for the others."

Jörmungander shook his head. "Not part of the plan. Azriel and Max would have my tail spikes if I ignored the script."

"You're too subservient to those two," Erika said. "It's a weakness."

"No!" Jörmungander disagreed. "It's common sense. They've had much more battle experience! You wouldn't be saying this if you'd seen Azriel and Elbedreth take out the sylph."

Erika didn't relent. "You're a dragon!" she rebuked her mate.

"A very *young* dragon," Jörmungander reminded Erika. "Let's make another run at them."

Erika reluctantly followed Jörmungander's lead. As it turned out, her fears about attacking alone without the element of surprise were well-founded.

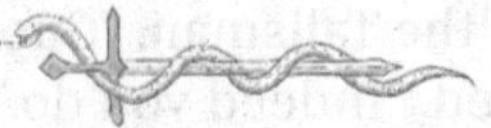

"That must've hurt," Max commented. "I counted at least two magical attacks."

They'd just witnessed the attack on their two dragon allies from afar. They expected a response to Jörmungander and Erika's attack, though they weren't sure about the nature.

"Aye," Azriel responded. "But noo we know. Let's step it up, a' body, afore they twa git intae ony mair trouble!"

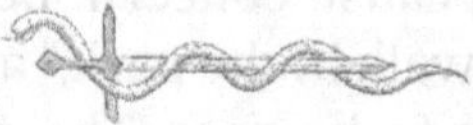

"Did you see that?" Vol'goth asked. "Two dragons are defending the Talisman!"

"Among others," Bezrameth replied. "I suspect the dragons are only part of the Talisman's defenses."

Bezrameth, Vol'goth, and Bezrameth's ten guards traveled through the mushroom field for an hour before the Talisman came into view.

"That's a city!" Vol'goth exclaimed.

Bezrameth rolled his eyes. "Quit getting so excited," he admonished. "You think I'd be here if I didn't know how to destroy it? We go after the heart."

"If it has one," the underlord remarked.

"Of course it does," Bezrameth answered.

"Do you know where to find it?" Vol'goth persisted.

The Order of the Talisman leader nodded as he stared at the Talisman. "I've worked out the magic that will allow me to locate the heart… the center of its soul… the essence of its being. All one in the same." Then Bezrameth looked sideways at Vol'goth. *"And you'll be playing a key role, my emotional friend."*

Vol'goth nodded as he started forward through the mushrooms towards the Talisman. "Guess I have to trust you."

Bezrameth nodded. "Indeed you do."

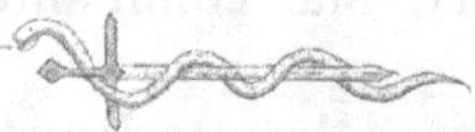

After a quick strategy discussion, the two dragons decided Jörmungander would concentrate his attack on the sorcerers while Erika dealt with the invading warriors that accompanied them. The two also decided their breath weapons would now be necessary in their defense of the Johari. In the end, they agreed any destruction to the mushrooms caused by their attack was necessary collateral damage if they were going to save her.

With Jörmungander leading the way, the two dragons made their second strike. Once again, magic-tipped arrows rose through the mushroom canopy and into the sky to meet the dragon's attack. But like earlier, they had no effect.

Jörmungander, unable to locate the sorcerers, joined Erika's assault on the demon warriors. Their breath weapons cleared a broad swath through the field of giant fungi. Dozens of demons died along with the mushrooms, their flesh corroded down to the bone. As Jörmungander made the turn for a second onslaught, he felt a strong disturbance in the magical ley lines running through the cavern. He stopped Erika, and they both hovered.

"I felt it too," the female dragon commented before Jörmungander could say anything. "The Johari?"

Jörmungander nodded. "I believe so. This is only a ruse to distract us from her."

"We must..." Erika began.

Jörmungander shook his head. "No... you must go as planned. I need to keep fighting until Azriel arrives. I need to expose the sorcerers."

"You don't know when they'll even show up!" Erika exclaimed. "Alone, you're too inexperienced to stand much of a chance against the demons and the sorcerers. They'll be the death of you! And the threat to the Johari is more immediate. Who knows how formidable those attackers are? We both need to go."

The younger dragon realized his companion was making a great deal of sense, and that Azriel and Max's plan was faulty... that this wasn't the main threat. He decided his friends would need to deal with the sorcerers and warriors themselves. The

Johari took precedence. He nodded and turned away to fly back to the Johari. It was at this moment the sorcerers stepped out from behind their magically enhanced concealment and made their attack. Two beams of black energy, directed at Jörmungander, flashed through the cavern atmosphere from the sorcerer's hands. Jörmungander's natural magic resistance intercepted one of the beams and drained it before it could do any damage. The second beam, however, sliced past his defenses and struck him at the base of his left wing and burned its way halfway through the flesh and bone. Jörmungander roared in pain and, unable to use his maimed wing, crashed down to the cavern floor, sliding fifty feet and knocking over several mushrooms as he did so before coming to a stop. Erika followed him down.

"Don't worry about me," the injured dragon screamed through his pain. "Get to the Johari!"

"Let me help you," Erika pleaded.

Jörmungander shook his head. "No time," he said. "Now go!"

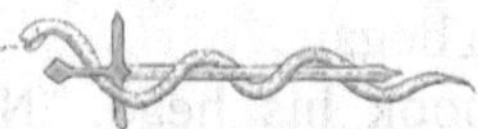

The demon warriors and sorcerers moved towards the injured dragon with caution. They realized wounded animals, especially when cornered, are even more dangerous and difficult to kill. The warriors, now numbering sixty-three from their original one hundred, stopped and waited behind thick mushroom stalks while they awaited orders from the two sorcerers. The dragon was in a clearing of knocked over mushrooms several hundred feet away.

The sorcerers stopped as soon as they came into view of the injured creature and prepared the invocations that would finish the beast. In a harsh tone, one sorcerer ordered the warriors to fire arrows, even though he knew it was a futile effort since none had magic arrows strong enough to penetrate dragon scales. As the projectiles flew outward, the dragon stood and towered over them. The sorcerers saw, for the first time, how seriously their original attacks had damaged the dragon's wing. Smug, as all sorcerers are, the two smiled as they readied their deadly magic. That smugness turned to fear when it became clear the dragon was preparing to use its dragon breath. Spells forgotten, they dropped to the ground as caustic acid sprayed the mushrooms all around.

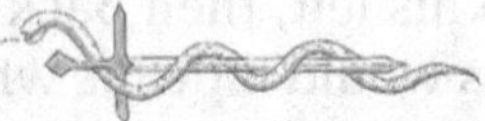

Jörmungander grimaced in pain as he steadied himself for the demon onslaught. Already he could hear their approach. *"Where's Azriel,"* he wondered.

Several arrows breached the mushroom stems, but didn't pierce Jörmungander's tough hide. He stood and roared his annoyance and sprayed the trunks of the mushrooms before him with caustic acid before dropping back down. Several demons screamed in agony. His antagonizers, though fewer in numbers, wasted little time continuing their assault and resuming arrow fire as they inched closer, moving from mushroom stem to mushroom stem.

Jörmungander ignored the ineffective arrows and listened. The demons were aligning themselves in a broad arc before him. As inexperienced as the young black dragon was, he had enough presence of mind to understand he was being surrounded. He roared as he stood again. It was a roar of both defiance and agony as the movement involved the reposition of his injured wing.

Jörmungander took a few precious moments to prepare himself for battle. He induced an enchanted cloud of darkness to surround and cloak his location and movements. Then he enhanced his resistance to the inescapable magical attack spells that will come from the sorcerers. He didn't think he could defeat all the enemies arrayed before him, but hoped he could buy enough time for his friends to join the battle. That is, if they arrived within the next few minutes. If not... well, he knew he'd not survive.

The arrow fire became sporadic as soon as he encircled himself with the cloud of darkness. But Jörmungander knew the cloak of anonymity he now wore was only a temporary advantage. The sorcerers would solve it soon enough. He moved several feet to his left, then back into the mushrooms, hoping the huge stalks would hide his whereabouts, if only for the briefest of moments. The relocation brought another wave of anguish from his wing.

Black magical rays of destruction searched the blackness around Jörmungander, weaving back and forth like a spider forming a web to catch its prey. As the beams of black energy crisscrossed their way through the cloud, they shattered it and exposed everything that hid within.

Jörmungander attempted to move silently further back into the mushrooms, but the pain of his wing made the attempt all but impossible. Discovered, he knew he was living on borrowed time. He saw demons come out of their hiding places from behind the mushrooms and race forward with weapons raised. The magic of the blades on the swords and battleaxes gleamed in the cavern light. But that wasn't what terrified Jörmungander the most. He saw the sorcerers, both of them, move forward whilst gesturing with their hands and whispering chants. He saw the look in each of their cold, dark eyes. They looked amused as they prepared to kill their quarry.

Jörmungander wasn't about to be like a rabbit slaughtered for their supper. No! He was a dragon. The last male black dragon. He'd die with honor. He'd die making a good accounting of himself. He'd die in a way that would make Azriel and Erika proud. The pain in his wing forgotten, Jörmungander stood taller and bid his deadly breath come to him one last time. He left nothing behind as he released it. Every demon within one hundred feet dropped to the ground, writhing as the acid dissolved them to the bone. But the intensity of Jörmungander's breath didn't stop there. Though it was incapable of hitting the sorcerers who had kept themselves out of range, it intercepted their lethal shafts of black energy.

The two beams released from the sorcerer's enchantments sliced through the dragon's breath. Jörmungander felt the magic enter his body. Though his own breath had reduced the severity, the beams still had enough power to engulf him in a fresh torment that was too much to endure. He toppled over. He welcomed the pain-free oblivion that was quickly overcoming him. Just as he surrendered, he heard a vaguely familiar voice scream: "Ye wull regret th' day ye left yer maws womb!"

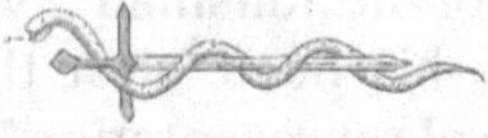

Bezrameth, Vol'goth, and Bezrameth's guards stopped just short of the open field that surrounded the Talisman.

"The Talisman's even larger than I thought," Vol'goth remarked.

Bezrameth sat on the moss-covered ground. "Sit next to me, Vol'goth, and learn… for what I'm about to show you will amaze and astound you!"

Vol'goth sat next to the sorcerer. The guards took defensive positions around both demons. Bezrameth began chanting while making impossible looking contortions with his arms, hands, and fingers. As his taloned-tipped skeletal hands moved, sparks flowed outward and left traces in the air before him. Circles, triangles, squares, and rectangles formed the foundation of the pattern being weaved by Bezrameth. Then came more complex shapes—cubes, polygons, ellipses—all interconnected with each other and with the base. Over that, Bezrameth sketched out a pentagram which hovered above the original design. In each arm of the pentagram, he drew magical symbols that emitted enormous power. Vol'goth shielded his eyes against the intense radiant light of the symbols. But his curiosity was too great to withstand. He peaked through his fingers to see what would happen next.

The symbols twisted and turned in the air. The points of the pentagram arms reached down and bonded with the foundation. Strands of power from the symbols within each arm, like the appendages of a solar flare reaching into space, snaked up, down, and around to meet in the absolute center of the pentagram. There was an instantaneous, soundless explosion of energy and light. When the light faded away, floating in the middle of the pentagram was a heart.

Thump! Thump!

"Is that the heart of the Talisman?" Vol-goth asked.

Bezrameth shook his head. "Not the actual heart… but close enough. A magical representation."

Thump! Thump!

"It's the guide to finding the heart," Bezrameth continued.

Thump! Thump!

Vol'goth cocked his head. "It seems to be fading away," he commented. "Is it dying?"

Thump! Thump!

"No, Vol'goth," Bezrameth answered. "It'll come back. The spell just lacks one more component."

Thump!

Vol'goth looked on in fascination. "What's next?" he asked.

"This is where you come in," Bezrameth said. "Come around and face me."

"I have a part to play?" Vol'goth asked as he scooted over

to face Bezrameth.

"The most important part!" Bezrameth replied.

Vol'goth smiled.

The heart-centered design, still hanging in the air, was now between them. Bezrameth didn't hesitate. His taloned-tipped hand flashed forward through the center of the pentagram, through the floating heart, and into the chest of Vol'goth. Bezrameth withdrew Vol'goth's still beating heart as the demon fell backwards, astonishment still written on his dead face. The sorcerer pulled back his blood-soaked hand until he had the flesh and blood heart positioned in the center of the pentagram, where it hung, still beating.

Thump! Thump!

The Order of the Talisman sorcerer wove a series of new incantations. One by one, the symbol strands interconnected at the center point of the pentagram withdrew until the beating heart hovered alone. Bezrameth then snatched the heart and dismissed the pentagram. He stood, approached the guard nearest to him, and offered the organ. The guard nodded, took the heart, and ate a small portion. Bezrameth repeated this with his remaining guards and finished what was left over.

Thump! Thump!

Though no heart remained, the continued beating Bezrameth and his guards heard in their minds was undeniable. It was the true sound of the Talisman, and it would lead them to the most vulnerable part of its soul. To a place between reality and illusion. To the place where the struggle for Aster will be won or lost.

Bezrameth smiled as he opened a doorway to the Talisman's spirit. It felt light and airy. Bright illumination—cascading colors of reds, blues, greens, and purples—emanated through the doorway. Each demon covered its eyes against the brilliant hues. Since they were used to the semi-darkness of the Abyss, the vibrant light made it difficult for them to see. Or was it because the strength of the Talisman's soul was enveloping the blackness of their own? Either way, Bezrameth didn't care for this unforeseen development, yet he didn't hesitate. Followed by his guards, he stepped to the other side.

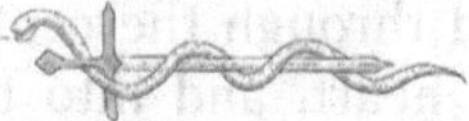

Erika flew over the gigantic bulk of the Johari several times but found no evidence of anything amiss.

"This is a waste of time," she thought. *"And Jörmungander needs my help."*

"Damnit!" she exclaimed aloud. "What do I do!"

In the end she decided there was no direct danger to the Johari. In the end, she decided that she and Jörmungander were the last of their kind, the last of the black dragon race. She turned and bolted back, terrified that it was too late.

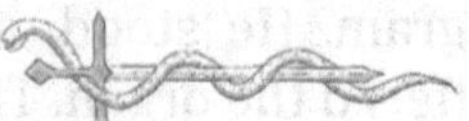

The brutal assault by Azriel and his companions stunned the demons attacking Jörmungander. Azriel, brandishing his deadly battleaxe, hit the front line of the demon warriors like a boulder rolling over a nest of insects. Azriel banished three demons back to the Abyss within seconds of his attack. The demons surrounded Azriel and attacked from all sides to bring the fighter down. But he only grinned and laughed as he cut down even more demons, now within ready reach of his weapon. Though not unscathed, Azriel shrugged off the wounds he did suffer in an adrenaline-induced fury.

While Azriel fought the warriors within their midst, *Elbedreth* attacked them from the periphery. She formed appendages of razor-sharp blades and sliced her way through the warriors from all around. The two sylphs worked in concert and after a few minutes, the battle shifted in their favor. Of the original one hundred demons who had crossed over from the Abyss, only thirty-one were now left… and that number was diminishing by the second.

As the two sylphs fought the warriors, Max and Solveig attacked the two sorcerers. Even though the two ghosts had yet to work together as a team in any combat engagement, Max, a veteran of many battles throughout his mortal career, instinctively understood how to make the most of their ghostly abilities and outlined a quick stratagem. They masked their movements by using their ability to enter and exit the ethereal plane at will. This kept the sorcerers off balanced. The spells they used fell on empty spaces in the material plane while the ghosts would appear here and there to attack or harass. After a few minutes of failed responses to the withering attacks by the ghosts, the two sorcerers, their spells mostly depleted, retreated back into the mushrooms. Instead of pursuing, Max and Solveig hurried to Jörmungander's side. He was still alive, but Solveig, after a brief examination, knew that might change if she delayed healing.

By the time Erika arrived, the battle with the demons was winding down. Both Azriel and Elbedreth looked as though they had things under control. But both also looked hurt and exhausted. Seeing that Jörmungander was still alive, and that Solveig was looking after his wounds, she attacked the demons still engaged with the two sylphs. Together, the three quickly banished the remaining demons back to the Abyss. Azriel wasted little time confronting the dragon.

"Aren't ye suppose tae back wi' th' Johari!" he exclaimed.

Erika nodded. "Yes, Azriel… and I was. But there wasn't anything or anyone there. It was all quiet. And I needed to get back to Jörmungander… to make sure he was alright."

"We cannae afford tae think this wis th' ainlie threat!" Azriel shouted. "Ye shuid hae stayed! Noo th' Johari is unprotected!

Whit if this wis juist a ruse, lass!"

"Calm down, Azriel," Elbedreth advised. "What's done is done."

Azriel looked at his mate but withheld further comment.

Max approached. "The sorcerers got away," he remarked. "They retreated back into the mushrooms."

Azriel looked at his friend. "Ah don't think they're th' main threat tae th' Johari… bit we cannae afford tae let thaim run free doon 'ere. They'll need tae be hunted doon 'n' dealt with."

Max nodded agreement. "And sooner than later. They'll have their spells back this time tomorrow."

"Ah ken that," Azriel said as he looked over at Jörmungander and Solveig. The dragon was now standing and flexing his newly healed wing. The sylph-dwarf saw other wounds, but they looked superficial. After Solveig's healing, the dragon was probably in better condition than he was.

"Laddie," Azriel called.

Jörmungander and Solveig walked over to join the rest of the group. "A'm glad tae see yer nae dead!"

"Thanks, Azriel," Jörmungander said. "I thought I was… going to die, that is."

"Ur ye pure tough enough tae fly?" Azriel asked.

The black dragon flapped his wings. "Yes, sir."

"Than a'm waantin' ye 'n' Erika tae hunt doon 'n' destroy th' sorcerers," Azriel instructed.

Jörmungander's visage turned unusually harsh. "It'll be my pleasure. Let's go, Erika," he said without need for further inducement.

As the two dragons flew off in the direction the sorcerers had taken, Max shook his head. "I've never seen Jörmungander look like that."

"It was the look of our ancestors," Solveig remarked. "Before the *Maelstrom*. Pray that the evilness hidden in his heritage doesn't come back."

"Jörmungander's a pussycat," Max said. "I don't see him..."

"You know nothing about us, my dear," Solveig retorted. "The *Maelstrom* no longer exists to guide our behavior. But I agree. I don't see Jörmungander or Erika returning to our old ways."

"We'll worry aboot that later," Azriel said. "Noo we need tae git back tae th' Johari."

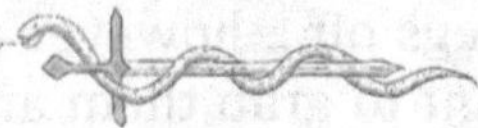

The two sorcerers, their magic depleted, ran for their lives. They didn't believe, even with all their magic spells available to them, they were strong enough to defeat the Johari's defenders... particularly since at least two black dragons were involved. Their only chance for survival was with their master, Bezrameth. But first they needed to get to him, which meant getting to the Johari. The only problem was those same defenders stood in the way.

The sorcerers used the stalks and canopy of the mushrooms to cover their retreat. After thirty minutes of fleeing, they changed direction to a course that would take them back to the Johari on a circular route. As they made their way through the mushroom field, they noticed flying animals observing their movements. They looked like small black dragons.

"I don't like that," one sorcerer noted.

The other sorcerer shook his head. "Just some type of indigenous animal. Probably the source of the screeching we heard when we first arrived. I'm not too concerned."

High above, partially obscured by the darkness of the cavern roof, two dragons flew in the middle of a colony of bats. Every now and then, a bat would fly up from the cavern floor and report the whereabouts of the demon sorcerers. Though the dragons knew where the demons were, they didn't try to attack, preferring to shadow them instead.

"What are you waiting for?" Erika asked.

Jörmungander looked over at his mate. "Now that the *Maelstrom* prophecy is a thing of the past, do you think you and I will return to the ways of our ancestors?"

"You're asking that now?" Erika replied.

"I've been thinking about it for a time," Jörmungander said. "What those sorcerers did to me hasn't set too well. I want to pull their arms and legs off... however many they have... the more the better. I want to grab them and squeeze until their eyes pop out of their eye sockets. I want to..."

"You understand you can't kill them, right?" Erika stated. "All you can do is banish them back to the Abyss. They can only be truly slain in the land of their origin."

Jörmungander sighed. "I know that. Read all about it in Tielron's *'Demons, The Inside Story.'* But a little pain and suffering before they go back would do my heart a lot of good. Is that backsliding?"

Erika laughed. "You call that going back to the ways of our ancestors? Honey, you want revenge. It's natural and doesn't mean you and I... or our children... are going anywhere. The prophecy may be finished, but the change it triggered in us is permanent."

Jörmungander was blushing. "Yes... well... uh... our children... I mean..."

"Of course we're going to have children together," Erika said. "As far as I know, we're the last of our kind... so we're stuck with each other. So buck up, lover. Now, are we going to do this or what?"

Jörmungander breathed a sigh of relief over the change of subject. Without further delay he dove on the sorcerers who, with few spells left in their repertoire, offered little resistance and were quickly banished back to the Abyss as acid from breath weapons washed over them. After all was said and done, Jörmungander found he didn't need hate, or even revenge, as a motive to do what was necessary.

As the two dragons flew to the Johari, Jörmungander's thoughts returned to what Erika said about children. He hadn't considered that. But she was right… they needed to produce offspring if the black dragon race was going to survive. By the time they reached the Johari, the young Jörmungander was determined to "buck up."

By the time Azriel and the others made it back to the Johari, Jörmungander and Erika were circling above. The two dragons landed shortly thereafter.

"We banished the two sorcerers to the Abyss," Jörmungander reported.

"And we saw nothing out of the ordinary from above," Erika added. "We overflew the area several times to make sure."

"Well, something's wrong," Solveig said. "I've been trying to contact the Johari, but she's not answering."

"I guess we can assume the worst," Max remarked.

Azriel nodded. "Aye, laddie. 'N' we need tae figure oot what's gaun oan bonny damn quick. Solveig, is thare anythin' ye kin dae tae fin' her? Magically, ah mean."

Solveig shook her head. "I can't read her presence at all. It's as if she's not there."

"You mean she's dead?" Elbedreth asked.

Solveig shook her head. "No… I don't think that's the case, though I can't be sure. For what it's worth, I can't feel any signs of corruption… no sign that her body's decaying. I'd say she gone but not dead."

"You're saying her spirit is juist flapping aroond somewhere unknown?" Azriel remarked. "like in another…"

"Dimension, realm, domain, and so on," Solveig interrupted. "Yes, I am. And I doubt she's alone."

"We did think there was a possibility the attack from the west could be a feint," Max observed.

"We wur wrong tae think it wasn't!" Azriel exclaimed. "Oh, mah aching heid. Howfur cuid ah be sae stupid! 'N' how come didn't th' Johari call oot if she wis in trouble?"

"Don't blame yourself," Max said. "If anyone let us down, it was our bat friends for not warning us about the danger."

"Besides, we don't know yet if there truly is a problem," Elbedreth pointed out.

"There's a kinch, a' right," Azriel said. "Solveig, we need tae fin' whit damn dimension… or whatever… th' Johari's gaen tae! Then we need tae git thare! 'N' we need tae be fleet aboot it!"

"Solveig, honey…" Max pleaded.

Solveig shook her head. "I don't know. I'm not a sorcerer. My magic isn't the same."

"Yer a ghost," Azriel said. "Ghosts kin shift thro' dimensions. That shuid gie ye some idea aboot it."

"We can only go through one plane, Azriel," Max responded. "The ethereal plane."

"And she's not there," Solveig added. "I would've known when I tried to contact her."

"You know, it occurs to me we don't understand that much about the Johari," Elbedreth remarked.

Everyone turned to look at the female sylph.

"Well, how do we know she isn't taking care of her own business?" Elbedreth replied. "No law of nature says females need males to protect them."

Azriel chuckled. "True enough, mah dearest."

"So what are we supposed to do?" Max asked. "Just sit around and wait?"

Everyone looked at each other and shrugged.

Solveig spoke for each of them after a few seconds. "I guess we do."

Azriel spat on the ground. "That grinds me tae na end!"

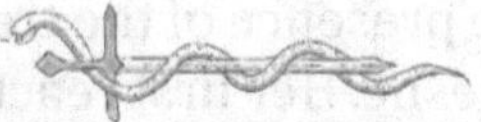

The deeper Bezrameth and his warriors moved into the Talisman's soul, the more uncomfortable he felt. It was the opposite of the Abyss. Even the smell of the place was disgusting. But if the Talisman's here, then here is where he and his associates would end it.

The first demon to die didn't have time to either call out a warning or scream. One moment it was fine, the next its head and body lay in two separate pieces on the ground. There was no banishment back to the Abyss. The demon was dead. Permanently. Two more demons died as the first. Bezrameth, resolved to finding the Talisman, didn't take notice of the deaths until after the third. Now alerted to the danger, he had his bodyguards close ranks while he conjured several spells of warding around all of them.

The fierce demon warriors looked around them, uncertainty and fear on their hideous faces, as they followed Bezrameth's instructions to stay within the warding perimeter. In the sorcerer's brief relationship with his demon guards, he'd never seen fear in their eyes. That fear forced upon him second thoughts... enough so that he looked for a potential escape route. There wasn't one.

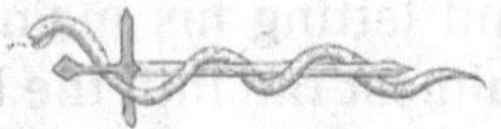

The Johari was alone. At first she'd considered asking her two sylph friends for help... Azriel was a fierce and battle-hardened warrior while Elbedreth, of all the original sylphs, was the only one who remained true to her calling. But despite their role in stopping the sylph invasion, she still had trust issues with what remained of the sylph race and decided against it. Besides, this was her battle to fight.

The Johari felt the presence of the trespassers the moment they entered her demesne. Her first reaction was to investigate the intrusion and determine friend or foe, though the chances of the interlopers being friendly was remote. Friends wouldn't enter uninvited.

As the Johari approached the interlopers, she detected the evil long before she identified the demon sorcerer and his ten demon allies. Their presence could only mean one thing. They were here to destroy her. The Johari understood if she were to survive the encounter, she first needed to isolate the sorcerer. To do that, she had to kill off his escort. The first three demons died before the sorcerer realized what was happening.

Bezrameth, surrounded by a circle of protectors and magical wards, moved forward. It was the only direction he figured made any sense. They hadn't moved very far before the wards he had constructed warned him of trouble. He stopped and concentrated, hoping to discover the nature of the threat. Nothing imminent materialized. But like everything else in this land, he knew that when it did, it would be ethereal.

Undeterred, Bezrameth continued to move onward. Regardless of the potential for danger, he rejected any notion of turning around and letting his main objective slip away. Deep in thought, he almost ran into the back of the demon in front of him. He looked around and saw that everyone else had also stopped.

"What's the matter?" Bezrameth asked the warrior, but didn't receive a response.

He looked into the demon's eyes, but only emptiness stared

back at him. The next demon was in the same condition, while the remaining five moved closer to Bezrameth. It seemed to the sorcerer that they were now seeking his protection rather than the other way around.

Bezrameth looked out into the colorful expanse of the Talisman's domain and sighed. "Did any of you see anything?" he asked.

"A ghost, My Lord," one of them replied.

Bezrameth slapped the demon across the face. "You're afraid of ghosts?" he asked. Then he looked at the others. "Are all of you afraid of ghosts?"

"You see what she did to those," another said as it pointed to the two who weren't moving. "This wasn't just any ghost."

"She?" the sorcerer asked.

The five remaining warriors nodded their heads vigorously.

"The Talisman," Bezrameth said, more to himself than for the benefit of the warriors. "I never expected a female." He then redirected his attention to his guards. "Let's keep moving forward. Only this time I'll lead."

The remaining warriors thought that was a fine idea.

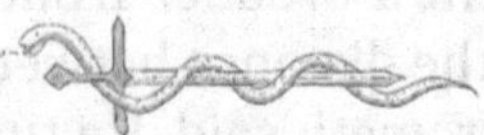

The Johari watched from a distance as the sorcerer and what remained of his guards continued to push forward. Though she had hoped her phantom attack would affect more of the guardian demons, she was at least grateful for the success she had. Now for the next phase of her plan.

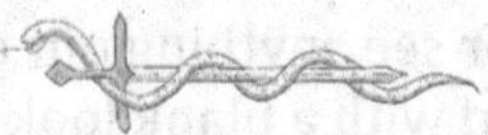

"Arrrggghhh!" Azriel cried as he walked back and forth. "Ah can't tak' this anymair. Thare haes tae be some wey tae figure oot what's gaun oan... or at least gab tae th' Johari."

"If we could communicate, we'd know what's going on," Max remarked somewhat flippantly.

Azriel sent daggers towards Max with his eyes. He knew Max had a way of making light of things when he was worried, but the dwarf-sylph wasn't in any mood to appreciate the rogue's attempt to lighten the mood.

"Smartass," Azriel whispered as he sat down next to Elbedreth.

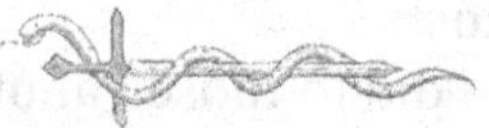

The fog appeared in front of the demons without warning. Sensing danger, Bezrameth stopped everyone before they entered. He detected the magic being used, but it was strange and unfamiliar, neither sorcerer nor clerical. Without knowledge of the magical foundation of the spell, he couldn't dismiss it. When he attempted to lead his party around, it repositioned itself back before them. When he spread his demons out to present a broader front, the fog stretched to match, regardless of the distance between each.

"Interesting," Bezrameth said. He turned and grabbed the shoulder of the demon nearest to him. "Go in five steps, then turn and come back. Call out with each step."

"But My Lord..." the demon began.

The withering look Bezrameth gave the demon was enough to end further discussion.

"Call out on every step you take," Bezrameth repeated. "Tell me if you hear or see anything out of the ordinary."

The demon stared with a blank look on his face.

Bezrameth sighed. "Something different, moron. And if you do, don't take another step until I tell you to."

The demon took a step forward into the fog. The misty

vapor enveloped him almost at once. "One," it said.

"Can you hear me?" Bezrameth asked.

"Hello, My Lord?" the demon called out. "Can you hear me?"

"I hear you," the sorcerer replied.

"My Lord?" the demon said. "I'm lost. I can't see anything."

"Damnit!" Bezrameth swore. "Come back!"

"Help me, My Lord!" the demon's voice sounded different, as if it was coming from far away and through a filter. "I don't..."

As the voice withered away, the fog lifted. There was no sign of the demon who had entered... and no sign that something was amiss. Another one gone. That Bezrameth was being purposely stripped of his guardian warriors wasn't lost upon him.

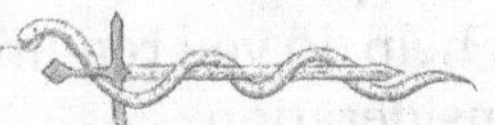

The Johari was whittling down the number of demons, but she was also expending valuable energy in the process. It concerned her that when it came time to confront the sorcerer, she'd be helpless in front of him. She could delay the encounter to rest, but the sorcerer was getting close to her innermost chamber, the place where she'd be most vulnerable. It was protected, but, unrestrained, the demons would ultimately break through.

The Johari moved behind the group of demons and turned herself invisible. Despite the threat to her existence, she needed time to contemplate her next move without fear of discovery. Alone with her thoughts, she soon realized there wasn't much she could do to stop the encroachment. Any energy expenditure to further isolate the sorcerer would further drain her spell-casting ability, making her survival in a direct confrontation with the sorcerer less and less a probability. She knew physical attacks would be pointless since the sorcerer had them safeguarded with a magical shield… and any attempt to dispel the shields would not only weaken her but also signal her location to the sorcerer. She was in a no-win situation. The Johari dropped to her knees, clasped her hands together, and chanted a prayer to the Elder gods for guidance and aid. Within moments, there was a response. The Johari fell on her side as the voice of Ghidia, Goddess of Battle, filled her head.

"What is it you desire, daughter?" the goddess asked.

The Johari rose to her feet. "Your help, My Lady," she responded. "The fate of my world is in great jeopardy."

"The world of which you speak has stopped believing. It has rejected me."

"But I have not, My Lady," the Johari said. "The Elder gods created me to keep my world safe from the Abyssian demon hordes. I honor that calling."

"What manner of help do you require?" Ghidia asked after a few moments of consideration.

"Send me a representative of your divine retribution, My Lady," the Johari petitioned. "To defeat the interlopers."

There was a pause before the Elder goddess replied. "Very well," she said. "But there will be recompense."

"What payment will you demand, My Lady?" the Johari asked.

"You shall face the sorcerer alone," Ghidia replied. "Your world lives or dies by your own actions. That's how it is with all Johari. That's how it will be with you."

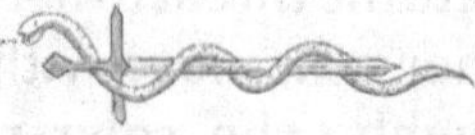

Bezrameth continued to move forward. He hoped he'd find the center of the Talisman's heart before he lost all of his guards. He was tired and getting more so by the minute. The adrenaline rush from opening the gate, exposing himself to possible repercussions from the *B'nai Elohim*, and finding the

Talisman, was long gone. Now he faced dwindling power with which to destroy the Talisman. Things were no longer going as he had hoped, and he wondered what else could go wrong. When the beast appeared within his circle of protections, Bezrameth knew, and wasn't a bit surprised.

The Johari watched as the help the goddess Ghidia promised appeared as Mahfuz, the Void Guard. It materialized within the circle of the sorcerer's protection wards. The creature was thirty feet tall, had four arms with five taloned-tipped fingers, multiple tentacles in place of legs, a triangle shaped face with no eyes, two long antler horns coming out of its head, and three foot long hair-like appendages covering its body which moved back and forth similar to writhing snakes. The Void Guard used a beam-like ray to disintegrate the remaining demons and then disappeared. True to Ghidia's word, Mahfuz left the sorcerer unscathed. The sorcerer looked around and spied the Johari, who no longer hid behind her shield of invisibility and a cascade of colors.

Bezrameth imagined many different scenarios when he faced the Talisman, but he never considered appearance. The body was tall, slender, and covered in long, dark-colored purple flowing hair. She had two sets of wings, which were covered by long hair as well. Her arms were like the wings, but there were no hands and fingers. Hair flowed down her body and curled upward from the floor. If she had legs, they were well concealed. Hair partially covered both sides of her face. Other than large, expressive eyes, there were no other features—no mouth, nose, or ears. "You have powerful allies," Bezrameth said. "The old gods? I thought they had moved on."

"The old gods created me," the Johari replied. *"I asked one*

of them for help."

Bezrameth heard the voice in his head. The creature was indeed feminine.

"Why didn't you have me killed as well?" Bezrameth asked.

"Unlike the younger gods, the old gods required compensation for favors bestowed. I must face you alone."

Bezrameth smiled. "Levelling the playing field. I understand that. You don't look as I had expected."

"Does it matter?" the Johari replied.

He shook his head. "No. You'll die regardless. And with your death, the *B'nai Elohim* will fall and the mortal world will belong to the demons of the Abyss."

The Johari didn't respond or wait for the demon sorcerer to attack. She directed an electrical bolt towards Bezrameth, hoping to surprise him. It hit him in the chest. But a magical shield surrounding the sorcerer absorbed the power of the spell.

"As I said," Bezrameth laughed. "You're going to die."

His counterattack followed a split-second later, the force of which knocked the Johari back and to the ground.

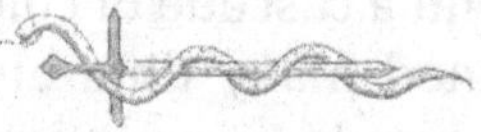

Above the Johari city-structure, a multitude of different colored lights suddenly lit the black cavern ceiling. Bats who were using the blackness to mask their presence scattered in different directions. Max pointed to the display to bring it to everyone's attention, though it was unnecessary, since the entire cavern had lit up.

"That's where the Johari is," Jörmungander observed.

"How do we get into her world?" Elbedreth asked.

"We gang up 'n' walk richt in," Azriel said. "Fortunately we hae tae dragons tae fly us there."

Max chucked. "Just like the old days, eh, Azriel?"

"Aye!" Azriel responded with a hardy laugh. "We wing it wi' hawp 'n' a prayer."

The two sylph rode on the backs of the dragons while Max and Solveig drifted up under their own ghostly power. But once in the lights, they couldn't distinguish one area from another. It all looked the same.

"I don't see a doorway," Elbedreth called out over the sound of the rushing wind.

"Ye didnae think it'd be that easy, did ye noo, mah bonnie lass?" Azriel shouted back. "Jörmungander, ye ken magic! Cast an enchantment! Fin' th' doorway in!"

Jörmungander stopped and hovered. He whispered a strange-sounding incantation and the magic he called flashed into existence. It turned his eyes into glowing golden embers, a dazzling contrast against the pitch-black coloration of his dragon scales.

"There," Jörmungander said as he pointed.

"Ah kin barely see it," Azriel remarked.

"That's because it's far away," Jörmungander replied. "And not exactly in our world. Max! Solveig! Hold on to me! Erika... follow!"

At break-neck speed, Jörmungander flew towards the doorway with Erika close behind. As they got closer, the physical appearance of the doorway became clearer... a multicolored opening surrounded by an ominous looking dark ring that kept expanding.

"What's that circle?" Azriel asked.

"The passage," Jörmungander replied. "To leave our world, we must travel through the passage that connects the two. If the Johari were dead, it wouldn't be there."

"So if she dies while we're on the other side, we're trapped?" Max asked.

No one said a word.

Max sighed. "Just great!" he exclaimed as they passed through the opened doorway into the Johari's realm. "Just freaking great!"

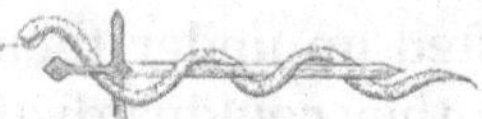

Bezrameth didn't give the Johari a chance to respond to his first attack. He'd planned this confrontation for years and knew each spell he was going to use as well as the order he was going to cast them. But since the Johari was a creature of legend, he couldn't be sure how her spell defenses or magical immunities would alter or impact the effects. His strategy was to strike her with a wide variety of different spell types to see what would stick. If things went according to plan, one of those spells, or a combination of, would either destroy her or make her powerless to defend herself.

The Johari was still shaking from the remnants of the last spell when a lightning bolt hit her. This time, though, she was not only invulnerable to the spell, but it rebounded back to Bezrameth, who was forced to deflect it off to one side.

But while Bezrameth was quick to respond to the lightning, it took valuable time and allowed his opponent to take the initiative. All of a sudden, it felt as if his internal organs were being turned inside out. Pain from the spell drove him to his knees and forced him to scream out. The pain eased after a few moments, though he was still weak. The Johari's next attack was an attempt to force Bezrameth to leave her realm through a banishment incantation, but his wards blocked it.

The Johari didn't wait to see if her banishment spell worked before she chanted her next. A streak of frozen lightning flew at Bezrameth and hit him in the chest. The force of the impact knocked him backwards and to the ground. He was still alive, but all the defensive wards he had surrounded himself with were gone.

Bezrameth slowly stood. His opponent was casting another spell… disintegration from the sounds and looks of it. The demon's counter-spell was simpler and, therefore, quicker. A four foot long curved blade appeared above the Johari, sliced down, and cut deeply into her shoulder. She screamed in agony. The pain from the injury forced an interruption in her spell summoning. The blade came down again and cut further. This time, the pain caused her to lose consciousness. Bezrameth then used an enchantment to raise the Johari's stunned and gravely wounded body, shifted it to horizontal, and caused it to spin at an incredible speed while he opened a doorway to the plane of Hell.

"Let the Talisman be Hela's problem," he said aloud. Just as he sent the Johari to Hell, he heard a voice behind him praying.

When Solveig saw the spinning creature, which she assumed was the Johari, and the opened doorway to an alternate reality, she understood the demon sorcerer's intent and did the only thing she could, though she believed it was already too late. She spoke an incantation to dismiss the doorway. Her counter-spell caused the doorway to wobble and become slightly insubstantial, but the demon sorcerer's magic proved too strong and it quickly returned to normal. The demon sorcerer, Bezrameth, wasted little time sending the Johari through the doorway and closing it.

"Ye son-of-a-bitch!" Azriel screamed as he raised his battleaxe over his head.

Bezrameth turned, pointed a finger at the dwarf-sylph and sent him flying backwards. Next, he snapped a finger and disappeared. Everyone looked around, hoping to locate the sorcerer.

"He's teleported!" Max shouted. "He could be anywhere!"

Azriel had just returned to the group. "Whaur's th' Johari?" he asked. "Did th' demon mak' the lass disappear?"

Elbedreth nodded. "He sent her to another dimension."

"Another dimension?" Azriel repeated. "Howfur dae we git the lass back? Solveig?"

"I'm working on it," the ghost replied.

An explosive globe of fire engulfed Azriel and left him rolling on the ground to put out the flames. Still smoking, he rose and looked at the source of the attack. The demon sorcerer was standing only a few feet away.

"I've won," Bezrameth said. "The Talisman, your protector, is gone forever. Kor and his hordes will soon be on your world, and there isn't a thing you can do about it." Then the sorcerer laughed. "But take solace. With the Talisman gone, you're stuck here in this... this..." Bezrameth looked around. "This psychotic world of her creation."

Everyone stared, stunned.

"Fortunately, I have no such..."

Suddenly a dark form flashed forward, and all that was left of the demon wizard Bezrameth was his legs and lower torso. The upper part of his body was being gobbled down by Jörmungander.

"What urr ye doing?" Azriel demanded.

"I'm saving you, Azriel," Jörmungander responded between chews and chomps. "Stopping evil... killing the bad guy... pulling your bacon out of the fire. Yuck! This is dreadful! I need a toothpick."

"Ye muckle, blithering idiot!" Azriel yelled. "We don't ken whaur he sent th' Johari!"

"He wasn't going to help us anyway," Jörmungander remarked.

"Peace, my love," Elbedreth said. "Jörmungander did what

he thought was right."

Azriel sighed. "Ah ken he did. Bit now… howfur dae we… whaur th' hell…"

Jörmungander and Erika both nodded. "Exactly!" Erika said.

Azriel shook his head. "Whit urr ye talking aboot?"

"He sent her to the plane of Hell," Erika replied.

"Ye ken that howfur?" Azriel snapped.

"Remember when we first met?" Jörmungander asked. "I told you dragons had extraordinary hearing? Erika and I both overheard the demon brag about where he'd sent her. It was the dimension of Hell. And I can open up a doorway to there just like he did."

Azriel didn't even have to think about it. "Then dae it! Ah've bin thare afore. Ah will juist sneak in, grab her, 'n' come richt back."

"You've been to Hell?" Elbedreth remarked, stunned. "That's a story I want to hear!"

"Max 'n' ah baith hae, haven't we, Max," Azriel said. "It's a story fur annur day. Now git it dane, laddie."

"Nope!" the young dragon answered. "I gotta go along to open a doorway back."

Azriel stared at the dragon with sylph arms crossed but saw the logic behind the dragon's remark. And if Jörmungander was going, they probably all were. And he couldn't do anything about it. "Then chaynge intae yer two-legged form 'n' git oan wi' it, boyo!"

"I'm right behind you, Azriel," Max said as the magical doorway opened.

"We're all going," Solveig stated.

Azriel shook his head as he led the way into Hell.

CHAPTER SIXTEEN

The Abyss

Braz'galar and Belladonna approached the capital city from the south through dense woodlands. Braz'galar had paid a kronie to passing peasants for two worn-out hooded robes to disguise their identities as much as possible. Kor's fixer hoped to obtain as much information as possible before he presented himself to Kor. He'd been away from the capital for a while and politics, those still in favor with the Prefecture leader and those not, had a tendency to change often. He also wanted to hide Belladonna away so Kor couldn't get his hands on her. He'd sworn on his life he'd not let her go to Execution Hill, and the only way to prevent that was to get her to Zhaarmoth.

The scene at the main gate was relaxed. The normal discipline usually displayed by the gate guards appeared to be replaced by a sense of great excitement. Braz'galar and Belladonna were passed through after only a brief inspection.

"I wonder what's going on?" Belladonna asked.

Braz'galar shook his head. "Not sure… but whatever it is helps us. Let me get you stashed away before I go see Kor."

"Is it safe?" Belladonna wondered.

"My hiding place? I'm the only one who knows about it. Not luxurious… and it may be a little dusty… but it's comfortable enough. It has travel packs, a stash of money, and a secret way out of the city for when a quick escape…"

"Not that," Belladonna interrupted. "Is it safe to see Kor? You've been gone for quite a while… and I don't like the mood we're seeing in the city. It's almost too… too…"

"Too relaxed for the capital?" Braz'galar suggested.

Belladonna nodded. "Like they've won a glorious victory of some kind."

"No better time to approach Kor," the fixer replied.

Belladonna looked at Braz'galar. "Except what have they won?"

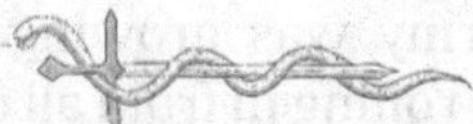

"Lilitu going mad like that was the last thing I expected," Kor remarked.

"Who can ever understand the minds of sorcerers?" Azazael responded. "I mean, they have to be half-way insane to become sorcerers in the first place."

"Perhaps," Kor answered. "But Lilitu wasn't like any other sorcereress I've ever known. She was very much in control of her art. Very logical… probably the finest mind I've ever witnessed."

Azazael glanced sideways at his leader.

"At least until the end,' Kor continued. "I guess losing all her sorcerers was too much to bear. But she knew that was going to happen. I just don't understand it."

"My Lord!" a door guard called. "Message from General Sol'gonath."

Kor motioned for the guard to come forward. Once he had the parchment, he dismissed the guard, opened it, and read.

"It appears we're finally making progress," Kor remarked. "The general says they've killed one of the *B'nai Elohim*."

Azazael looked confused. "How can that be? Unless…"

"Bezrameth got rid of the Talisman," Kor finished for his Military Faction commander.

"We won?" Azazael whispered.

Kor nodded. "Order a full frontal attack on their fortress," he ordered. "Then mobilize my special strike force. We're going to Aster!"

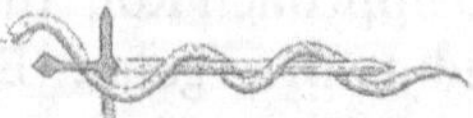

Michael was staring out over the field before his fortress walls. The demon army was growing in front of his eyes. Reinforcements were rolling in from all over the Abyss. Worse, he'd personally witnessed several of his precious *B'nai Elohim* warriors, warriors he couldn't replace, killed by demons. In his long lifetime, he'd never seen a demon kill a *B'nai Elohim*.

"Michael?" Lord Ternborg asked. "You still with us?"

Michael shook his head. "Uh? Oh, sorry."

"We've just entered uncharted territory," Gabriella, who'd come up to the battlements with Michael, explained. "It's going to take some getting used to."

"Gabriella, it's worse than that," Michael said. "It means something's happened to the Johari and as a result the Juxtaposition Point is collapsing."

Gabriella nodded. "And once the Juxtaposition Point comes down..."

"Aster's in grave danger," Michael finished.

Lord Ternborg sighed. "Is there anything we can do?"

Michael shook his head. "You're already doing so much... and now we'll need you more than ever. I'm asking for your troops to fight longer. We need to stop the demon armies here... for once they get to Aster, it may very well be too late."

Braz'galar made his way to the palace using the citizens that inhabited the capital city as cover. By eavesdropping on guards roaming the streets and getting drunk in taverns, he was able to determine a "glorious victory" had been won against the *B'nai Elohim*. That demonkind had, for the first time in history, killed several of the winged guardians. It irritated him that such a significant occurrence had happened while he was out of circulation, even if it couldn't be helped. After four hours of mingling, taking side streets, alleys, and sometimes rooftops, Braz'galar stopped two hundred feet from the front entrance of the palace to observe. Everything appeared to be normal. Kor's fixer decided it was now or never, so he took one last look around for anything out of the ordinary before walking towards the gate.

Belladonna, who decided not to remain behind at Braz'galar's hideaway despite her promise, followed her friend and wasn't far behind when he walked up to the front gates of the palace. She saw the guards tense as soon as Braz'galar pulled down his hood to reveal his identity. She watched as twenty-five more guards joined the twelve who manned the gate to confront the demon overlord. Apparently, these guards had different orders than those at the city's front gate, for they were in no mood to blithefully pass Kor's fixer through the palace gates unchallenged. And Braz'galar wasn't the kind of demon who accepted confrontation and confinement gracefully. A furious battle ensued which left ten guards dead and Braz'galar unconscious. It took every ounce of her discipline to keep from running to Braz'galar's aid, but she knew it was hopeless and she needed to remain free to rescue him. But to do that, she needed allies… allies she didn't know where or how to find. She retreated.

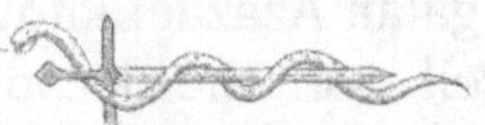

Eleven demons sat around a table in a small dingy room. Though each demon was comfortable in the darkness, they had placed fire-lit torches in all four corners to dissuade wraith spiders, the most venomous arachnid in the Abyss, from dropping down and creating a scene. Water beads from the high humidity in the room ran down the walls and settled in small puddles on the stone floor.

"Lord Braz'galar's been taken by Kor," Trozzan announced.

"Stating the obvious, chief," Talrak said. "We all know what happened at the palace gates. The boss made a damn fine showing of himself. So what're we going to do about it?"

"Here! Here!" the rest added.

Trozzan smiled. "We're going to walk in and pluck him right out of the hands of Kor."

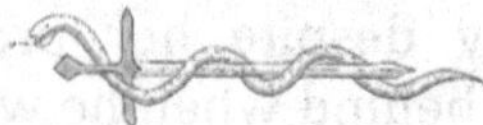

"What kind of swords are these?" Azazael asked as he clumsily handled the two katanas taken from Braz'galar. "They're like no blades I've ever seen. From whose dead hands did you take them?"

Braz'galar, beaten and battered, stood before Kor and Azazael in the throne room. He looked at the Military Faction leader. "They're called katanas. And how they ended up in my hands isn't your concern. Now give them back!"

Azazael laughed. "You think you still have standing in the court of the great Kor? You killed ten of his guards who were simply fulfilling their orders to detain you. By doing so, you committed high treason."

Braz'galar looked at Kor, but there was no hope from that end. The Prefecture lord shook his head before speaking. "My hands are tied, Braz'galar. Azazael knows the law, as do you. You've served me well over the decades, but you of all my subjects understand I can't tolerate open defiance."

"They attacked me first, Lord Kor," Braz'galar pleaded. "I've a right to defend myself… even against *your* guards. They should have known I'm your fixer and treated me accordingly!"

Kor looked at Azazel.

"Not true, My Lord," Azazael replied as he held the katanas

out before him. "He attacked the guards with these... these... katanas." He threw the swords down as if they were cursed. They clattered on the floor but appeared undamaged. "If not for the additional troops I ordered at every gate to the palace, he'd have gotten past and disappeared. Who knows why he's here? Perhaps even to assassinate and replace you, Lord Kor?"

"I'm only here to claim what you promised me, Kor... the city of Zhaarmoth," Braz'galar responded.

"And what of the resistance leader, Belladonna?" Kor asked. "Are you going to bring her to me per our agreement? I know she's still alive. You were seen entering the city with her."

"I've quashed the bulk of the resistance and brought her to the capital by your orders," Braz'galar answered.

"Then why isn't she here with you?" Kor asked. "Why don't I see her standing before me in shackles and chains?

"You intend to execute Belladonna," Braz'galar replied. "Don't deny it. I wanted to talk to you before bringing her in. I think putting her to death would be a mistake."

"You do, huh," Kor said.

"I believe you should give Belladonna a reprieve," the fixer answered. "She can be a valuable asset against any remaining resistance forces still aligned against you."

"There are no resistance forces left," Azazael countered.

Braz'galar shook his head. "Belladonna says there're still many individual cells remaining, particularly in the outlying areas of the Prefecture. Unfortunately, she doesn't know their locations."

"She doesn't..." Kor began.

Braz'galar held up his hands. "Not her fault. They set the organization up so that no individual person knew the location of all the cells. It's how you or I would've set it up if we were resistance leaders."

Azazael started to say something, but Kor stopped him with a look. "Not good enough, Braz'galar. Assuming what you're saying about the resistance is true, I still don't see how leaving Belladonna alive benefits me."

"Belladonna knows their tactics... their strategies," Braz'galar replied.

"So do you," Kor remarked. "Besides, if they suspect Belladonna's working for me, wouldn't they take steps to change that?"

Braz'galar nodded. "No doubt. But who better to recognize those changes for what they are than Belladonna? Who better to hunt these cells than Belladonna and me? Besides, who says anyone has to know she's alive and working for you?"

"There are warrants out all over the Prefecture for her arrest," Azazael mentioned. "And by now it's widely known she's here in the capital. Lord Kor would show weakness if she's not detained and executed."

"I can fix that," Braz'galar answered.

Kor nodded. "Yes, I imagine you can. That's what you do best, isn't it? Go on."

"You're not seriously considering keeping him alive," Azazael said, outraged. "I saved your life! You promised him to me!"

"Watch your tone!" Kor snapped.

Azazael looked at the floor.

"And don't you dare question me again!" Kor continued. "No one's too good for the Pillar... or Execution Hill!"

Braz'galar looked between the two. "What the hell's going on," he thought. "Azazael saved Kor's life? How? From whom?"

Kor brought his fixer out of his musings. "How are you going to fix it?" he asked Braz'galar.

"She has to die," Braz'galar answered.

"But I thought you said..." Azazael started.

Kor whirled on his military leader. "Not physically, you idiot," he said before turning his attention back to Braz'galar. "Explain!"

"We'll fake her death," Braz'galar replied. "I've done that kind of thing hundreds of times."

"You've what!" Kor exclaimed.

Braz'galar looked at the Prefecture leader. He was treading on thin ice. "When you say to make someone disappear, I make them disappear. That doesn't necessarily mean they have to be killed. A technicality, I grant you, but people have more intelligence value alive than dead. Not to mention people who receive death reprieves have a tendency to feel obligated. I use that obligation to get them working for me... which benefits you. So I ship them out to other cities and trouble areas with new identities and they keep tabs on things. No one has ever resurfaced to embarrass you. No one has ever been the wiser. And I've received good information from most... so it works. Really, Lord Kor, I couldn't do my job if I didn't use informants."

Kor stared at Braz'galar. "Okay... though you're pushing it," he said after a pause to consider Braz'galar's words. "But fine... go on."

"You already know I have Belladonna," Braz'galar stated. "And don't get any ideas about finding her on your own. I've got her in one of my many safe-houses scattered around the capital."

"My spies..." Kor began.

"Your spies are now my spies," Braz'galar announced. "All dead and replaced."

Kor's face changed colors. He was about to explode in rage.

"I value my life, Lord Kor," Braz'galar said. "No one knows how you operate better than I. Any good fixer would do the same. It's protection against sudden betrayal. If it helps, my spies serve you better than yours ever did."

"If it helps?" Kor shouted. "You've just confessed to being a traitor!"

"I confessed to doing my job!" Braz'galar fired back. "Which you expect from all your subjects... My Lord."

Azazael smiled. No one speaks to Kor like that and lives.

Kor paused as his anger drained away. "You just reminded me why I've kept you on for so long as my fixer. Courage… courage to remind me from time to time that I should fear you. But it's a very dangerous game you play."

Braz'galar nodded. "Worth it. I'm looking forward to someday retiring to Zhaarmoth… with my head still upon my shoulders."

"Perhaps one day I'll grant you that retirement," Kor said.

Braz'galar nodded while Azazael held back an inaudible groan. His enemy was going to get a reprieve, despite Kor's earlier promises.

"May I continue?"

"By all means, Braz'galar," Kor replied. Azazael shook his head and sat down on the dais steps.

"By your own admission, Belladonna's been seen with me in the city, so word of that has probably already made its way back to the resistance… what's left of them. Right now, she's undoubtedly their prime suspect in the treachery. Hell, I wouldn't be surprised if they already have a price on her head. But if they see her publicly executed, it might be enough to convince the remaining resistance cells that they no longer have a problem… or that she wasn't involved in their betrayal."

"She *should* have betrayed them," Kor remarked.

"Yes, My Lord," Braz'galar said. "May I continue?"

Kor wave a hand.

"Right now, those cells still left are closed up tighter than a strider bull's butt. And they'll continue to lie low until they feel safe again… which a live Belladonna may prevent. But if they believe she's dead, and their secrets are secure, they'll eventually loosen up. When that happens, and with Belladonna's help, we'll pounce, and you'll be able to destroy the resistance once and for all. What you do with Belladonna after that is your own affair."

"Hmmm," Kor said as he nodded. "I see the logic of your plan. But why can't I just torture any information I need out of her? Surely the resistance would wonder the same thing?"

"Torture information out of an overlord?" Braz'galar replied. "Particularly one as powerful as Belladonna? No... I believe seeing her on Execution Hill will be enough to convince most people she preferred death to revealing information. Besides, she doesn't know everything. I've already explained that. But she does know how they operate, and she can identify trademarks. Imagine being able to predict when, where, and how a cell will strike."

"Why do you need Braz'galar for that, My Lord," Azazael asked. "Have Belladonna bow to you and let her run the operation."

"Fool!" Kor shouted. "For this to be successful, we'll need a network between all the cities in the Prefecture. Braz'galar already has that. Besides, even after she gives her oath, how can I ever trust her again? She's broken it before. I need someone loyal to me to be her handler. Who better than my own fixer? Besides, you and I are going to be busy enough eradicating the armies of Aster."

"So that's why everyone's in such a lighthearted mood," Braz'galar thought. *"They found a way around the B'nai Elohim."*

"What do you need, Braz'galar?" Kor asked.

"We need a show, My Lord," Braz'galar answered. "Ergo, Execution Hill. We can't just announce her death. That satisfies no one... particularly the remaining resistance cells. We need to give the people irrefutable evidence of her death."

"Alright," Kor agreed. "I'll make the necessary arrangements. I so love that part... almost as much as the execution itself!"

"It's fake," Braz'galar reminded Kor. "A grand illusion only."

Kor laughed. "It'll be grand all right! You can count on it!"

Braz'galar nodded. But he knew from the sound of Kor's voice and from his body language that Kor would never release Belladonna once he had her, and the trip to Execution Hill probably wouldn't be an illusion. The Prefecture demon lord was playing him. It was time to change strategies. It was time to run. "I'll bring Belladonna in," he lied.

"Good! Good!" Kor acknowledged and called out for the guards on the other side of the throne room doors. "Pick up your swords, Braz'galar. You're dismissed. Go and bring me Belladonna. My guards will accompany you. And Azazael, you're dismissed as well. Prepare to invade Aster."

Four guards marched into the room. "Don't let Braz'galar out of your sight!" Kor ordered.

The four guards saluted in unison and surrounded Braz'galar. As Braz'galar turned to leave, one guard caught his attention and winked.

Braz'galar recognized the guard. *"Trozzan!"*

As the two overlords, walking side by side, left the room, Kor called out. "And the feud between the two of you ends now!"

"Fat chance," Azazael whispered under his breath, but loud enough for Braz'galar to hear.

"Something I've been wondering for a time now," Braz'galar said just as low.

"What!" Azazael barked as he turned into another corridor.

"Why pick a fight with me," Braz'galar answered back. "It makes no sense. One word and I can have your intestines pulled out through your damn arse and used to strangle you."

Azazael stopped walking and turned to answer his antagonist. But by then, Braz'galar and the guards had disappeared down the other hallway.

As the party continued to march through the palace, seven more guards, Braz'galar's men, one and all, joined the procession and were still escorting the overlord when he went through the front gates of the palace grounds.

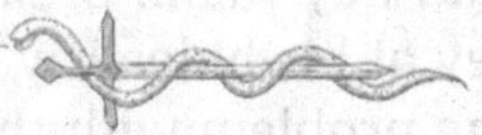

Kor smiled as he sat on the *Living Throne*. The spirits of his predecessors were noisy as usual, but he didn't care. Defeat of the *B'nai Elohim* was within reach and the mortal world of Aster soon thereafter. Added to that, Braz'galar was bringing in Belladonna. Even on the cusp of a glorious victory, he decided he needed to set an example. Neither mercy nor magnanimity was part of his personality. And what a thorn in his side she'd been. There's no way he'd accept her oath. She'd already exposed herself as an oath-breaker once and she'd not get a second chance. The fake execution of the titular head of the resistance would be anything but fake, and Braz'galar would follow soon thereafter. He could no longer be trusted, either.

"You've done well," one soul in the *Living Throne* remarked in Kor's head.

"Yes, Kor," another remarked. *"Perhaps good enough to join us!"*

But several other souls... souls whose voices were distant and barely perceptible, disagreed. *"Leave Belladonna alone!"*

Most of the souls contained within the throne laughed... and laughed... and laughed.

Instead of being annoyed, Kor felt euphoric. Soon he was laughing just as hard.

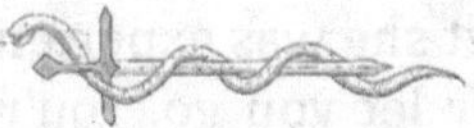

Belladonna carefully made her way back to Braz'galar's safe-house. But while she traveled the back-alleys and byways of the city to keep out of sight, her mind stayed focused on her latest problem... how was she going to rescue Braz'galar? Since she couldn't do it herself, she'd need to find trustworthy allies. Maybe she could buy them. Braz'galar had told her of a large stash of money at his hideaway, so hired mercenaries were a possibility. The problem with that, however, was that no one in their right mind would accept any amount of money to challenge Kor in his own palace. Besides, Kor could pay anyone she hired twice as much for her.

Perhaps a resistance cell would help, but again, there were several problems. First and foremost, there wasn't any sign of the resistance in Kor. If nothing else, Braz'galar was thorough. Any cells who had avoided his hunt would be in the outlying areas and cities and not the capital. Second, even if she found a cell, they'd probably be more inclined to kill her than help. She couldn't get rid of the feeling she was now persona non grata to the resistance. And if *she* were persona non grata, she could only imagine how they felt about Braz'galar.

By the time Belladonna returned to Braz'galar's safe-house, she didn't have any idea what her next move was going to be. She poured herself a stiff drink and sat in a large, cushioned chair to think. But it wasn't long before the drink and her own exhaustion claimed her, for the next thing she remembered was Braz'galar walking through the front door.

"What are you doing here?" Belladonna asked as she stood. "I mean, I saw you captured at the palace gates."

"Followed me, eh," Braz'galar answered. "Even after I asked you not to?"

Belladonna shrugged. "How'd you escape?" she asked while peeping through a window. Several well-hidden guards were lolling about, but she was experienced and spotted them with little effort. "Kor let you go. You're here to turn me in, aren't you?"

"You don't really believe that, do you?" Braz'galar asked.

Belladonna was silent.

"Relax," Braz'galar said as he opened a small compartment underneath the mantle over the fireplace and removed a bag of coins. "They're *my* people."

"Dressed in Kor's livery and so soon after being captured by Kor's guards?" Belladonna shook her head. "I'm just surprised to see you. I mean, after the reception you received, I'm surprised your head isn't sitting on a pole somewhere. So I just figured..."

"You figured I made a deal to turn you in," Braz'galar finished for her. "I did... kinda."

The female overlord stared at her companion. "But you just... I knew it!" Her voice was just above a whisper, but her fury was still clear for anyone to read. "I knew I couldn't trust you! All that crap about re-establishing the resistance... about seeing the light... about loving me. And I believed you! You vile, despicable..." Belladonna stopped talking and slapped Braz'galar across the face.

The force of the blow rocked Braz'galar. He reached up and wiped away a small amount of blood that had escaped from his lower lip. "I guess I had that coming. But it's not what you think."

"How 'bout you explain it to me," Belladonna said as she reseated herself into the cushioned chair. She was shaking with rage.

"Later," Braz'galar replied. "Right now, we need to get out of the capital. I got a message to my people who are making arrangements to..."

"I'm not going anywhere until I get an explanation!" Belladonna shouted.

"Then you're going to die!" Braz'galar retorted just as loudly.

Braz'galar waited for Belladonna to calm down and then poured his own drink and sat in another chair. He rubbed his temples and took a deep breath before he began. "I need you to trust me."

Belladonna looked at Braz'galar. "Trust you!" she

exclaimed. "Our entire relationship was a lie. A lie to get close to the resistance, which you then destroyed along with many of my friends. Then you convinced me it was the only way to save the cause."

"It *was* the only way!" Braz'galar exclaimed. "Once the resistance acquired Kor's attention, and he put me to the task, there's no way it was going to survive."

"Because there's no way Kor's fixer can fail," Belladonna wryly observed.

"That's correct," Braz'galar responded. To him, that fact was irrefutable. "But my relationship with you, though not planned, changed my opinion of Kor... my entire core beliefs, actually. The feelings I developed for you are not a lie. Getting to know you... to understand you... was an epiphany. Yet I still needed Zhaarmoth. So I made it my mission to figure out how to keep myself on Kor's good side and keep you and the cause alive."

"And now you're going to turn me in to do that," Belladonna said. "For a city?"

"Yes... well no," Braz'galar answered. "I fed Kor a story to convince him we're valuable assets... that there were still resistance cells in the remote areas of the Prefecture and we'd be the perfect individuals to help root them out and destroy them. You because of your intimate knowledge of the resistance and me because I'm his fixer and have the resources to do so. I told Kor you were willing to re-swear a loyalty oath to him. He doesn't believe me and plans to betray us both. But it bought us time. Time we shouldn't squander."

"Why Zhaarmoth?" Belladonna asked.

Braz'galar sighed. *"She'll not be denied,"* he thought as he got up and poured himself another drink. He took a sip to let the whiskey-burn warm his insides and started pacing back and forth in front of the small fireplace.

"Zhaarmoth is isolated and backs up to the *Veil*. And the

dominant race of beings on the plateau where it sits is the Taumaru. You understand what that means."

Belladonna nodded. "Pretty nasty dispositions. Tough, independent, honor driven, and not too keen on having relationships with other demons. No one messes with them and..."

"No one messes with Zhaarmoth," Braz'galar finished. "They're not so bad once you get to know them, by the way. All things considered, Zhaarmoth is *the* ideal place to base my operations. And it's under my control."

"Does the current city overlord realize that?" Belladonna asked.

Braz'galar smiled. "That arrogant bastard and all his hangers-on have been dead for a while now."

Belladonna appeared confused.

"I've been planning and working towards this for several years," Braz'galar said. "To that end, I've replaced the entire administration there with my own people. I've also worked out a treaty with the Taumaru. We're allies. If someone goes to war against either of us, the other joins in. It's a damn good safety barrier against my enemies. And I have quite a few of those. I wanted Kor's blessing... but that's pretty much out the window. He's going to kill the both of us the first chance he gets."

"You were going to tell Kor I was dead, remember," reminded Belladonna. "That was the original plan."

"Someone saw through our disguises after entering the capital," Braz'galar said. "They identified you with me... and that information got back to Kor and Azazael. So the 'you being dead' story wasn't going to work. And that's not all. Apparently, someone tried to assassinate Kor, and Azazael saved him from joining his predecessors in the *Living Throne*."

"Who'd do that?" Belladonna asked.

"Only a Faction leader would have the power... and the

backbone… to try it," Braz'galar answered. "But I don't know who, and my palace spies haven't caught up with me. Anyway, Azazael now has Kor's ear... and gratitude. I've told you about Azazael's hatred for me." Braz'galar paused his pacing for a moment before continuing. "Whether we lived or died depended on how I handled that meeting. I only had a few seconds to come up with a plan to get me out of the palace and us out of the city." Braz'galar took a sip of whiskey. "It was a close thing. Kor doesn't trust me… that much I know. He let me go… under guard… only because he needs me to bring you in. He's gambling I don't see his plans for us."

Belladonna looked up at Braz'galar. "Sit down. Your pacing's making me nauseous."

Braz'galar drained the last of his drink and sat.

"Answer a question?" Belladonna asked.

Braz'galar nodded. "Just one."

"Since you won't have Kor's blessing, how are we going to rebuild the resistance?" Belladonna inquired. "You won't be his fixer anymore. And what stops Kor from retaking Zhaarmoth?"

"I've built a large organization since becoming Kor's fixer," Braz'galar replied. "Built it for just this occasion… the day when I fall out of Kor's favor. I made sure I'd still be able to operate throughout the Prefecture and have a defensible base of operations. And I doubt he cares about Zhaarmoth... particularly now."

Belladonna raised an eyebrow.

"Apparently Kor's found a way around the *B'nai Elohim,*" Braz'galar explained. "That means he's going to invade the mortal world."

Braz'galar ignored Belladonna's look of surprise as he fished a couple of palace guard uniforms out of a trunk and threw one to Belladonna.

An hour later Braz'galar, Belladonna, and eleven of Braz'galar's people, dressed as Kor's guards, marched out of the city and disappeared into the surrounding forests.

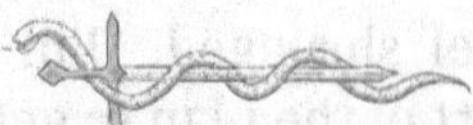

Kor looked out from the battlements surrounding the westernmost city of Ith Garrgod as his armies gathered on the nearby plains. Though there was a lull in the combat at present, he saw Azazael was getting ready to pull out all the stops, leaving very little in reserve. The Prefecture demon lord was uncomfortable with the tactic but understood the importance of the battle to come… not only to his plans but to history. It was going to take a mammoth effort, and Azazael knew that. They needed every single soldier for what was shaping up to be the confrontation of a lifetime. Even considering the vulnerabilities of the *B'nai Elohim* caused by the presumed destruction of the Talisman, a full third of his entire force already lay dead and stacked up at the base fortress wall from the first few attacks. The Draugen Pesta warriors from Aster that were reinforcing his eternal nemesis caused a good portion of those losses. If all of Aster's defenders were so brutal, conquering the world might not be so easy after all. But it was better to know that now and not later when he was on Aster. So far, the only positive was that *B'nai Elohim* were also dying, though not in great numbers.

"We'll be ready to attack with all our armies in a couple of days," Azazael said as he approached his lord.

"Why did you pull everyone back and why are you waiting so long?" Kor inquired. "Everything's in place right now."

"I want to give the warriors who's already been engaged with the enemy a couple days to rest and get healed," Azazael replied. "We should be at full strength when we attack."

"One big push, eh?" Kor asked.

Azazael nodded. "Even those Aster bastards won't be able to stop us."

The attack wasn't the only thing on Kor's mind. "How many war sorcerers are attached to your armies?"

"In total?" Azazael shrugged. "I'm not sure. Lilitu took quite a few for her part of the plan to get Bezrameth to Aster."

"Find out for me," Kor ordered. "I want all of them here by tomorrow morning. Then I want one… no, make that two of your armies."

"But, My Lord," Azazael protested. "I need…"

"Think, Azazael!" Kor demanded. "While you're keeping the *B'nai Elohim* occupied, I'll lead an army through the back door… a sorcerer created back door… and attack Aster. It could be over even before you defeat the *B'nai Elohim* and their allies. But to be on the safe side, I want an army held back in reserve. I'll let you know when to send them over."

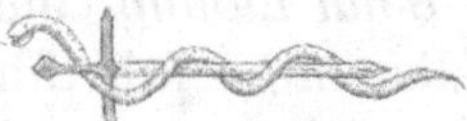

"Why are we going west?" Belladonna asked. "Zhaarmoth's to the east."

"I mentioned Kor was attacking the *B'nai Elohim* fortress," Braz'galar replied. "I want to see what's going on. Besides, there's someone out there I want to retrieve. Someone who's important to me. I want her back at Zhaarmoth with us."

"A lover?" Belladonna asked.

Braz'galar shook his head. "More like a daughter."

Belladonna looked at her companion. She didn't detect any duplicity in his voice. "If she's like a daughter, then she's probably even more competent than most of your people and could get back to Zhaarmoth on her own. No… I suspect it's more than that. We just barely pulled ourselves out of Kor's fire. Now you're putting us back in. What's the real reason?"

"Do you believe we should invade Aster?" Braz'galar asked.

Belladonna shrugged. "I've never really given it much

thought. It didn't work so well when father and Nightshade did it with the dark elves of Svartalfheim. I've never been there myself... but from what I've heard, it's a demon paradise. We're clearly superior to the mortals and the land is supposedly rich and abundant... teeming with life but without the dangers we face here. I can understand why Kor wants it. I'd be inclined to live there myself if given the choice."

Braz'galar shook his head. "No! Don't you understand how wrong that would be? If Kor gains a foothold on Aster... or worse, conquers it... he'll enslave the mortal populace. Surely you can see the parallel between what Kor's done here with what he'll do over there?"

Belladonna didn't expect the passion in his voice. "What are you? An advocate? Their champion? They're just mortals."

"Just mortals?" Braz'galar exclaimed. "Did you get that from your father? Nightshade? You're wrong, Belle. In the things that count, we're no different from the mortals of Aster. I've been there. I've seen it for myself."

"You've been there?" Belladonna remarked. While it's true a demon can get caught in a summoning spell, she'd never heard of it happening to an overlord who has the power to resist it.

Braz'galar nodded. "Some fool of a sorcerer over there captured me in a summoning spell while I was sleeping. It was before I became Kor's fixer. I'd just had a strenuous day and was exhausted. I didn't put out my customary protections before collapsing into bed. It only took me a few minutes to free myself of his bewitchment once done. But since I was already there and had nothing pressing over here, I thought, why not? I spent three of their years traveling around the primary landmass... well, the known landmass. There's an even larger landmass far to the west they know little about. Anyway, during those travels I met a lot of people across all spectrums of the economic landscape. In fact, I came to know a few of them rather well. I observed their cultures, their morals, their strengths and weaknesses. I saw how they loved their families and the sacrifices they were willing to make to keep them safe. Not so much unlike our own people… those outside the ruling class, that is. And like us, they have the same problems on Aster with despots and dictators, though they have many compared to our one. But even so, they were free… for the most part. Besides you, my time spent over there reshaped my thinking regarding Kor and the resistance."

Belladonna was silent for a few seconds before saying anything. "You mean that, don't you?"

"With all my heart," Braz'galar replied. "But it's not just one world. Once Kor conquers the mortals, he's free to jump to any inhabited world in that universe. I know it's possible because the Elves of Light on Aster have been doing it for centuries to and from their home world of Alfheim. So we're not talking about just one world. And even worse, if he succeeds, you can bet he'll relay that information to the other Prefectures. He's too full of himself to resist taking a bow."

Belladonna made the connection at once. "If what you're saying is true, we're talking thousands of worlds in potentially hundreds of universes!"

"It could be tens of thousands of worlds in thousands of universes," Braz'galar said. "Bella dear, I want to see the people of all worlds free of Kor and his ilk. Our kind should stay in the Abyss, where we belong."

"Can the mortals stop him once he's over there?"

Braz'galar shook his head. "Unlikely, but possible if they can unite and the elves don't retreat back to their home world. But if he manages to gain control over them, he'll have a plethora of new resources, both in manpower and natural materials, from which to draw. Any future resistance would stand little chance on both sides. I imagine that would stand true for any world and any Prefecture… though who really knows? But we can't take that chance."

"How are you going to stop him?" Belladonna asked.

Braz'galar shook his head. "I don't know yet," he replied. But in truth, he did. The only way to stop Kor was to kill him, an objective now even more challenging since Kor wanted him dead as well. "We need strong, fast horses."

"I have a herder friend nearby," Belladonna said. "But it'll cost you."

"Maybe your lovely face will get us a discount," Braz'galar said with a smile.

Belladonna laughed. "This one's got good, fast horses. But nothing will change his opinion of their value. Be prepared to pay through the nose."

CHAPTER SEVENTEEN

The Abyss and Hell

Father Goram, Nightshade, Landross, Abigail, and Herbie entered the capital city of Kor just a few days after leaving Zir Tachoss. They had commandeered four of the Abyss's six-legged horses for the overland trip and soon discovered this version of horse was twice as fast and much more robust as those on Aster. Landross commented on more than one occasion how much he'd like to take several hundred back to Aster for his knights. Throughout the journey, their disguises as Taumaru held fast. Most of the people they met in route gave them a wide berth, and those with whom they did business refused to look at them directly.

The capital city of Kor was much like the other cities they had observed during their trip, except twice as large. Even the elvan city of Taranthi on InnisRos or the human city of Palisade Crest on the mainland of Aster couldn't match it in size, though both cities were much more beautiful, particularly Taranthi.

Abigail and Nightshade explained the capital was the headquarters of the different Factions and guilds that comprised the political makeup of the Kor Prefecture. It was also the location of Kor's palace. Because of this, its layout and purpose differed from that of the other cities. There was a much stronger military presence stationed within the city's boundaries. But unlike the other cities, the guards at the gates and patrolling the streets had no qualms about stopping and questioning Taumaru. The ordinary citizens of Kor, however, were the same as those of the other cities, except more guarded concerning the information they were willing to disclose.

"Our best sources are still going to be in the taverns," Abigail said shortly after they had passed inspection at the main gates.

Nightshade agreed. "And those are going to be in the Merchants and Market Factions. Mostly the Merchants."

Landross frowned. "Can't go into a tavern without drinking… and Abyssian ale is terrible!"

"You just can't handle it," Nightshade teased.

"Mock me not, witch," Landross countered. Though the words sounded serious, there was a lightness in his voice and a grin on his face which said his response was from one familiar traveling companion to another. This banter had become common between the two over the last few days. The knight had finally accepted Nightshade as an ally and a friend. It was a friendship that was long in coming. Nightshade had worked hard to get there and accepted it with gratitude.

"Try the spiced wine," Nightshade continued. "It goes down much easier… hardly any burn at all."

Landross rolled his eyes.

To spite Nightshade, in the next tavern they visited, and on the advice of one of its patrons, Landross ordered the strongest, most noxious drink the tavern served. And true to the patron's word, it had a burn that felt like Hell's blazing brimstone and lasted an eternity plus a day. At least that's how long it felt to the knight. Landross's choice of drink for the next few days was strider milk, if available, or just plain water.

The taverns of Kor were a goldmine of information. They learned something big was happening at the fortress of the *B'nai Elohim*. There was a rumor floating around that guardians were dying in the face of the demon attack, something that had been impossible before now. At first, Father Goram had a hard time believing the stories, but they remained so consistent from tavern to tavern that the priest had to concede it was at least possible.

There were also stories, and eyewitness accounts, of Belladonna, disguised as one of Kor's guards, leaving the city with several other guards. They'd been seen heading to the west. As for Queen Lessien and Autumn, very little information was forthcoming. One old geezer, a demon with tuffs of gray hair scattered over his twisted and crippled body, swore on his mother's rotted tusks that he'd seen a mortal female in the carriage of Kor's chief interrogator, Zachariah. The carriage was last seen leaving the city and heading towards the east.

"We have a decision to make," Abigail said as they sat around a table in the small inn room they'd rented to be their base of operations.

"Not much of a decision for me," Landross said. "I'm going east."

Herbie barked an acknowledgement.

"Landross, I understand your need to follow any lead that might lead to finding Lessien," Nightshade said. "But if what's happening to the *B'nai Elohim* is true and they're destroyed, I've little doubt a demon invasion will threaten Aster soon thereafter. The stakes are higher than a single queen."

"Not for me," Landross retorted. "Nothing's more important!"

Nightshade shook her head. "You're thinking with your heart."

"And you're not?" Landross responded heatedly. "Your sister's going west, which is where you want to go, I'd wager."

"Stop it, the both of you!" Father Goram exclaimed.

"Surely you want to go east with me," Landross said. "Autumn's..."

The priest shook his head. "No, my friend," he whispered sadly. "You heard the same story that described the mortal as did I. She has one hand. Lessien's with this Zachariah demon, not Autumn. And Lessien wouldn't leave Autumn's side, unless... I don't think Autumn's alive."

There was silence around the table.

Abigail placed a hand over Father Goram's to give him what little comfort she could. "I'm sorry."

Father Goram appreciated Abigail's comfort. "After what happened to her in that cave, I don't think she had the will to live any longer." Tears rolled down his cheeks.

"We can't know for sure," Nightshade said.

"Nightshade's right, Horatio," Landross added. "I'm sure she just got separated from Lessien. We'll find her. Don't you worry none."

Father Goram wiped the tears from his eyes. "Sorry. Can't afford weakness in this place."

"It's alright," Abigail responded as she squeezed his hand. "Love, regret, sorrow, and all the other emotions mortals have exist here in the Abyss. No one except the ruling class would consider what you're feeling as a weakness. And they're fools."

Father Goram nodded. "Nightshade, you go east with Landross and find our wayward queen. Abigail and I will go west and see what we can do to help Michael fend off the demon attack."

"Shouldn't I go with you, Horatio?" Nightshade asked. "Two clerics are better than one... particularly in a war zone. You need me. I'd also like to know my sister's safe."

The priest shook his head. "While you're correct, I'll be just fine with Abigail. I imagine just the appearance of a gorgon will have entire platoons of demon warriors running for their lives. Landross will need your knowledge of the Abyss and your magic to keep him out of trouble as he searches for the queen. It's still important to get her back. As for your sister, I'll find her if I can."

Nightshade acquiesced. "As you wish, Horatio. What about the Qénsharma?" she said as she pointed to her backpack.

"I'd like to leave the Qénsharma here in the capital," Father Goram answered. "Maybe as close to the palace as possible?"

"That'd give Kor something to worry about," Abigail said. "Very little he or his cronies fear more."

Father Goram nodded. "They've proven to be quite

valuable to us, but it's time to give them their freedom."

"Alright," Nightshade answered.

"Good," Father Goram said. "Now, once you have the queen, make your way back west to the *B'nai Elohim* fortress as fast as you can. We'll wait for you there. If you can't find us, find Michael. He'll get you safely back to Aster. Questions?"

Everyone shook their heads.

"Very well," Father Goram said. "No point wasting any more time. You two be careful."

Nightshade reached over and gave Father Goram a quick kiss on the cheek. Landross and the priest shook hands while Nightshade and Abigail hugged. The four left the inn and parted ways, each determined to complete their mission and meet once again.

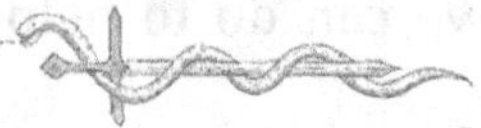

"We've bin 'ere afore, Max," Azriel commented as he looked over the river before him. It was dark and foreboding. "The water Styx."

"The one and only," Max said. "Now we only have to wait for Charon to carry us across."

"For a price," Azriel added. "There's aye a cost. By th' gods, ah hate tae gie up mah gold!"

"Why don't Erika and I just fly you across?" Jörmungander asked.

"Ah wish ye cuid, laddie," Azriel said. "But that micht bring a hail lot o' grief doon upon oor heids. Max 'n' ah hae bin 'ere wance before. Thare ur rules doon 'ere that need tae be followed. One o' they is th' Ferryman mist boat us ower."

"Or there'd be hell to pay," Max snorted. "Get it? Hell to pay? We're in Hell?"

"Oh, laddie," Azriel said as he shook his head. "It might've bin funny th' first dozen times ye tellt it. Bit really?"

Max looked at Solveig for support. "Different audience," he said sheepishly. "But what isn't an attempt at humor is what's on the other side."

"Max?" Jörmungander said.

Max shook the dragon off. "Not now, big guy. What waits on the other side are three heads of the biggest, meanest, scariest dog..."

"Max!" insisted Jörmungander.

The rogue turned on his winged companion. Jörmungander backed up a step. "Please let me finish! You think that just because you're this huge flying monstrosity you can trample all over another person's freedom of speech? Let me tell you something, boyo! I'm not just some ordinary bug you can stomp on! I'm Maximillian Darkshadow, the world's foremost..."

"I think Jörmungander's trying to tell you something's coming across the river towards us, love," Solveig said.

Jörmungander nodded. "Charon's coming," he declared.

"Aye, it's him a' right," Azriel confirmed.

Max silently worded "Sorry!" to Jörmungander before he turned to meet their transportation across the River Styx.

As the boat of Charon approached, both Jörmungander and Erika took human forms, though Azriel assured both the boat would magically adjust its size to accommodate dragons. The boat moved forward until it was three feet from the shore of the River Styx. A plank covered the remaining distance, and the black-robed Charon crossed it until he was standing on the water's edge. He brought his arm up and a skeletal hand opened, palm up. He didn't say a word.

"Yeah, ah git yer ransom," Azriel said as he dug into a belt pouch and brought out six pieces of gold. "Ye better nae lea 'til ye pay me back, Max!"

"Ghosts don't carry gold, Azriel," Max replied.

"Cheapskate," Azriel mumbled under his breath.

Azriel, Elbedreth, Max, and Solveig crossed the plank and settled into the boat. When Jörmungander and Erica tried to cross, however, Charon blocked their way and held out his hand.

"I guess dragons cost more," Elbedreth said when she saw what was holding up the two dragons.

"But we're not in our dragon shapes," Jörmungander said.

"Aye, 'n' ah awready paid a gowd fur th' baith o' ye," Azriel said as he stormed across the plank.

Azriel closed in with the Ferryman and was about to put a hand on its shoulder when the creature turned. Inside the deep hood of Charon, two bright red orbs stared at the dwarf. Azriel froze and dropped his arm back to his side. The world stopped for him as he stared into those eyes. To Azriel, only Charon and he existed. In those eyes, he understood Charon had recognized him from his last visit. A memory floated to the forefront of his mind. It was that of an earlier companion, one of the many mercenaries hired during his adventuring days, who had fallen into the water of the Styx. He remembered the man's death as if it had happened only yesterday. At first there was only shock on the man's face. Then his eyes registered the pain. It must have been agonizing. The memory of the dying man's scream brought tears to his eyes.

Charon pointed to his boat.

Before Azriel turned to go back, he looked at Jörmungander. He knew the dragon, his friend, carried a pouch of jewels he'd taken before he'd left his people's lair. "Pay Charon, laddie," he said. "There is na ither wey across."

Jörmungander nodded as he dug into his pouch of jewels and brought out the most beautiful sapphire Azriel had ever seen. "If you say so," Jörmungander said as he held it out for Charon.

But Hell's chauffeur didn't accept the offer. Jörmungander replaced the sapphire with a diamond and still Charon ignored the recompense. Confused, the dragon grabbed a handful of jewels and gems from the pouch and held them out in his open palm. Charon looked at the precious stones, choose a small pearl, and stepped aside. Jörmungander and Erika, followed by Charon, crossed the plank and settled into the boat.

"Apparently I was offering too much," Jörmungander commented as the boat lurched off the shore and started its journey to the other side… to Hell itself.

The second the bow of the boat left the shore, darkness closed in from all around. The only light came from a lantern on the boat's bow and the river itself as bubbles rose to the surface and exploded in gas and steam. The water churned in response and shook the boat. The sounds of the small eruptions were muted, as was any attempt at conversation between the companions. Here and there, deformed skeletons of various kinds of creatures covered in yellowish-colored moss floated to the surface. Several minutes later, they entered calm waters, and the boat stopped lurching back and forth. As the companion's eyes readjusted, new images became visible in the blackout. Eyes, hundreds of thousands of eyes, peered up from the surface of the water. Each pair of eyes reflected back at the travelers the anguish and misery of the doomed souls behind them. Each pair of eyes pleaded to be released from the Hell they found themselves in… from the Hell of their own making. Azriel and Max were prepared for the sight and did what they could to calm the fears of their fellow travelers. They assured them that every soul they saw staring up at them deserved to be there, and that the best thing they could do was to close their eyes. Then the two provided small strips of cloth to each with instructions to plug their ears. Everyone in the boat was even less prepared for the sounds of despair that followed. The cloth could only muffle the sounds.

"Why, Azriel and Max, did you not prepare us for this sooner?" Elbedreth asked. Azriel could hear the melancholy in her voice.

Azriel sighed. "Lass, ye git tae understand. Max 'n' ah hae bin thro' sae much th'gither, we... we..."

Max jumped in to cover Azriel's stutter. "What your lover is trying to say, Elbedreth, is we weren't expecting the eyes either? The wailings, yes. But not the eyes."

"But you've been here before!" Solveig exclaimed. "You've made two crossings... there and back. How could you not have seen that? Did you forget?"

"They weren't there the last time we crossed," Max said.

Solveig wanted more answers. "But you did see something terrible, right?"

"Aye, we did," Azriel said. "We've seen mony things in th' years o' oor adventuring. Mony horrible 'n' disturbing things. Sae much sae that we've developed... ah..."

"An immunity," Max suggested.

Azriel nodded. "Aye, an immunity tae whit we've seen, heard, fought, 'n' bolted fae. We juist weren't thinking, fur whilk ah apologize."

"We both do," Max added.

"'N' in hell there'll be muckle mair disturbing hings awaiting us," Azriel went on. "Hings Max 'n' ah wull be seeing fur th' foremaist time as weel. Sae be prepared, a' o' ye."

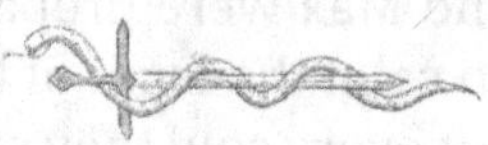

Father Goram and Abigail left the city of Kor and followed the Kor Canal to the Kematian Sea. Both decided the fastest way to the *B'nai Elohim* fortress was across the inland sea instead of overland. The trip to the seaport occurred without incident, though every interaction they had with the local populace convinced Father Goram more and more that the people, while looking vastly different, were not unlike the normal farmer, herder, or merchant on Aster. They worked hard to build a life for themselves and their families. They loved, they played, and they had a unique sense of humor, all extraordinary qualities for a people ruled by demon overlords. He also found there was an unexpected amount of freedom. Abigail told him it was because of the various guilds that existed to give the people not only a voice in how they lived their lives but also a decent amount of protection from excessive persecution. Michael had told him about the guild system and how it worked, but Father Goram now saw it in operation. All things considered, he felt it was a remarkable arrangement, though he wondered about its continued success.

"It's a system that's worked for thousands of years," Abigail had said after he'd expressed his doubts. "As long as the guilds produce the things the overlords refuse to live without, their existence is assured."

Two days after they'd arrived at the seaport, a ship came in that looked large enough to accept horses in its hold. As it turned out, the horses weren't the problem. When they talked to a representative of the ship about passage and costs, they discovered the captain had no intention of allowing a female, Taumaru or not, to take even one step onboard.

"Would it be possible to speak directly to the captain?" Father Goram asked.

The crewman shook both of his two heads. "Not possible," the heads said in unison. "We're unloadin' an' will set sail soon fer the trip outbound. We 'ave a schedule to meet."

"Perhaps it'd be wise if you let your captain decide," the priest insisted.

"'E'll not change 'is mind," the crewman replied.

"He doesn't know what I offer," Father Goram said as he directed the crewman's attention to Abigail who, though she kept her head well hidden within the cowl of her cloak, revealed just enough of herself to make the priest's meaning clear. "The captain will reward you handsomely for bringing this beauty to his attention."

Both heads of the crewman nodded enthusiastically. "I take yer meaning," he responded. "You wait 'ere while I get 'im."

"Try to keep your head hidden until we've set sail," Father Goram said to Abigail.

The gorgon smiled within her concealment. "This is going to be fun."

The captain was a huge, ugly brute of a demon. He looked like a cross between an earth elemental and a small dragon. Yellow pus excreted through openings all over his body and mucus ran down his checks from copper-reddish colored eyes. His mouth was a hole in the middle of his face, with foot-long fangs going up and down over each cracked lip. Three legs as thick as tree trunks jutted out from beneath the torso and ended in talon-tipped toes, three to each foot. Behind the creature extended a long tail that had a vaguely human-like hand on the end. Inch-long flies hovered around the captain's armpits and at the base of his two small wings, and the smell that assaulted the priest and gorgon was almost enough to drive them to their knees.

Behind the captain was a small, petite female demon that looked, except for her dainty wings, more like an elf from Aster than a demon. Her beauty easily circumvented the captain's ugliness. Both Father Goram and Abigail recognized the intelligence in her eyes and knew she was the actual brains of the ship, while the captain was obviously the muscle. Together, they represented a formidable duo.

"Who call captum?" the creature asked.

Father Goram and Abigail looked at each other, knowing that the ploy they were going to attempt was a non-starter. Abigail straightened her robe.

The priest cleared his throat. "I did, captain. I wish to buy passage on your ship for myself, my companion, and our two horses."

"No female except Laurette allowed," the captain said as he turned. "She ship's number one officer."

"I have gold," Father Goram said as he opened a pouch from off his belt and let the sparkling coins run through his fingers and to the wooden dock below his feet. "Lots of gold. You understand as well as I how rare it is."

The captain stopped and looked at the coins laying on the dock. "Bah! Kor take all gold. Against law to have. Kiss *Pillar*."

The captain began to walk away when his assistant stopped him. "Perhaps there's a way, Oknog," she said.

The captain stopped and looked at Laurette. "You think maybe get round Kor?"

Laurette nodded. "Let me discuss this with these strangers and see what we can work out."

Oknog nodded and walked away, stopping only to knock a resting crewman into the water.

"That's a lot of gold, stranger," Laurette said. "Especially for one of the Taumaru, which I doubt either of you are."

"What makes you say that?" Abigail asked.

"Oh, I don't know," Laurette responded. "Maybe it's the way you carry yourselves?"

"What's wrong with the way we walk?" Father Goram asked.

Laurette shook her head. "It's not you," she told the priest. "It's you, madam. You're far too graceful to be a Taumaru female... and way too tall. It's a good disguise and one that'll fool most. But you're not Taumaru. Neither of you are."

Father Goram and Abigail looked at each other. "Let's say we're not," Father Goram said. "Does that influence how much gold you'll charge?"

"It affects whether or not we accept you as passengers,"

Laurette replied. "I'll not allow anyone on board that's potentially dangerous to my ship and its crew. If I'm not satisfied, no amount of gold will get you a berth."

"I can assure you we mean no harm to you or your crew," Abigail said. "Unless, of course, you seek to harm us. We only wish to reach the other side of the Kematian."

"Uncover yourselves or walk away," Laurette said. "It's as simple as that."

"Do you know what a gorgon is?" Abigail said as she removed the hood of her cloak.

Laurette's eyes went wide, and she took a step back. "There's only one in the entire Abyss. Depending upon whom you're speaking to, she's either royalty or evil incarnate. Even Kor's afraid to challenge her."

Abigail revealed her head just enough for Father Goram and Laurette to see, but no one else. A thin veil which hid her brightly glowing eyes covered the gorgon's face. Snakes, intermixed with her black glossy hair, stared back at Laurette, who immediately closed her eyes.

"Don't worry," Abigail said. "Much of my reputation rests upon rumor and innuendo, which I encourage. My power to turn flesh to stone is completely under my control. Only my enemies need to fear for their lives."

Laurette opened her eyes, reached up, and slowly pushed aside the veil. Abigail didn't try to stop her.

"Your face is quite lovely," Laurette said. "Even your deadly eyes."

Abigail nodded as she readjusted her hood. "Thank you."

Laurette turned and addressed the priest. "Now your turn."

Father Goram did as requested.

"A mortal elf," Laurette commented. "What an unusual pairing!"

"Now that you know…" Father Goram began.

Laurette nodded. "You're both acceptable," she said. "And

you can keep your gold. Oknog's right, it's more of a problem than it's worth."

"But payment?" Abigail inquired.

"Conversation," Laurette answered. "Crossings are boring... and I imagine the two of you have a few interesting stories to tell."

Father Goram nodded with a smile. "Indeed we do, madam. Indeed we do."

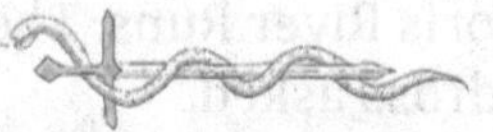

It only took Landross and Nightshade a few hours to get reliable information concerning Queen Lessien. Several sightings, each corroborated by separate sources, indicated the queen was in fact being transported in the carriage of Kor's chief interrogator, Zachariah, and was heading eastward. By all accounts, Lessien was traveling with Zachariah, a baby, and another demon female with her pet. There were no reports of the queen being mistreated, or of a second mortal female.

"That didn't take long," Landross remarked. "This Zachariah person's not trying to hide her, that's for sure."

"Why should he?" Nightshade asked. "No one's going to challenge him. After Kor and Kor's fixer, he's the most powerful overlord in the Abyss."

"If he's hurt the queen, he'll be the third most powerful *dead* overlord in the Abyss," Landross said as he smashed one gauntleted hand into the other. "What's to the east?"

Nightshade considered for a moment. "To the southeast is the city of Drog'dronnan. It's a rare city in that the guilds control a weak overlord. That he's a relative of Kor's is the only reason he remains in power. We should be able to resupply there without too many questions being asked. Further southeast and on the other side of the Okoris River Run is another city called Zor'gothan. It's larger than Drog'dronnan and the ruling overlord isn't one of Kor's favorites. He suspects all strangers, so I think we should steer clear by staying on this side of the Okoris. Due east is a plateau. That's where the Taumaru call home. There's only one city up there, Zhaarmoth, with a few surrounding towns. The souls that inhabit Zhaarmoth and the towns are a hardy bunch... much like the Taumaru. A great lake covers about a third of the landmass. Close to the base of the plateau is the confluence of the Arlinggamau and Okoris River Runs. The Duhová Kaskáda..."

"The what?" Landross asked.

Nightshade smiled. "That's its demon name. It translates to Rainbow Cascade. It's one of the most beautiful places in the Abyss... a three thousand foot waterfall that drops from the top of the plateau." The warrior didn't react. "Which you're probably not interested in," she added.

"After the plateau?" Landross asked, confirming her suspicion.

"The end of the Abyss," Nightshade responded. "We call it the *Veil of the Infinitus Atrophia*. The end of all things. It marks the border of the Prefecture."

"What happens if someone accidentally enters the *Veil*?" Landross wondered.

Nightshade shook her head. "No one's ever returned after entering the *Veil*. It's postulated that when someone enters, they're either destroyed, magically transported elsewhere, or eternally lost."

"Sounds like the perfect place to get rid of unwelcome problems," Landross said.

Nightshade knew to what her companion was referring. "It is," she answered. "But we have strict laws about using the *Veil* as in such a way... with serious consequences. Besides, other ways exist to get rid of 'unwanted problems,' as you call them."

Landross nodded. "That thing you call the *Pillar*."

"And Execution Hill," Nightshade added. "Which is worse."

"So if the queen's not on the plateau, then where do we go from there?"

"She'll be there," Nightshade said. "That's the only thing that makes sense. You've given up on Autumn?"

Landross nodded. "Father Goram may hold out hope, but no one's seen her. And we've almost crossed the entire length of the Abyss. You know as well as I how close Lessien and Autumn were. Lessien wouldn't let Autumn out of her sight."

"There could be many reasons the two aren't together," Nightshade said. "Autumn's death is only one possibility."

"Maybe so," Landross replied. "But mortals here in the Abyss are rare enough that we'd have heard something if Autumn were still alive, even if someone... or something... forced the two to separate. But we're only hearing about Lessien." The knight shook his head. "Autumn didn't make it. That's what my gut tells me."

Nightshade agreed. "And Horatio?"

Landross shrugged. "I believe deep down he knows as well. Lessien will tell us for sure."

"What do you think about Abigail?" Nightshade changed the subject.

"She seems a decent sort," Landross replied. "Cool in a fight, and, well, she's a gorgon. I'd much rather have her as an ally than an adversary."

"I've known her for most of my life," Nightshade said. "I know how she thinks... how she feels. She's developed a soft spot for Horatio."

Landross laughed. "Saw that, did you?"

Nightshade glanced over at her companion. "Yes, I... oh. You saw it as well, didn't you?"

"You don't have to know someone your entire life to understand when that person's in love," Landross replied. "She should be a great comfort when Horatio decides to deal with the emotions of Autumn's death."

"Pretty perceptive for such a huge, lumbering knight of questionable intelligence," Nightshade added.

"Bigger head, bigger brain."

Six hours later, Landross decided it was time to stop for the night, or what passes as night in the Abyss. They got off the well-traveled road and set up camp roughly one hundred yards into the forest. They didn't need a fire for warmth or to cook food since they had plenty of trail rations. After removing the saddles and brushing the horses, the two laid out their bedrolls and pulled out strips of strider jerky before settling down for much needed sleep.

"You're not eating," Landross said as he munched on his jerky. "You should eat to keep up your strength."

Nightshade shook her head. "Too tired to eat. Give Herbie my share."

Landross studied his companion for a few moments. She'd already stretched out on her bedroll. He felt concern for the sorceress, something he didn't think possible a year ago. "You sleep," the burly knight said. "I'll take first watch."

"I warded us with magic," Nightshade sleepily replied. "We don't need a watch."

Landross thought about that for a few moments before answering. She was right, her wards are strong. But he had a sinking feeling things in the surrounding forest weren't as they appeared. "I think we'll do things my way for a change," he said to no one as he threw a piece of jerky to his dog.

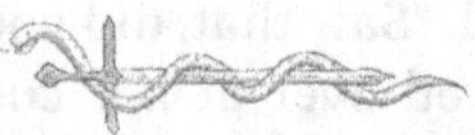

The other side of the River Styx wasn't as Azriel or Max had remembered. Instead of a cave which housed Hell's guardian, Cerberus, and a road for them to travel, all they saw was a great blight. Lava rock covered the ground with occasional scrubs or trees of various sizes, the tallest of which measured several hundred feet. Small explosions of fire and magma, accompanied by a release of noxious gases, dotted the landscape. Off in the distance, there appeared a gigantic cloud which was gaining in size as it rushed towards them.

"This isn't the Hell I recall," Max observed. "And that cloud looks as if it's heading our way."

Azriel drove the business end of his magical battleaxe into the lava rock, spit on both hands, and rubbed them together. Satisfied, he raised the battleaxe for combat. "Now we git tae see howfur mony ither ways Hell haes changed," the dwarf-sylph said.

In response to the upcoming threat, multiple razor-sharp blades materialized from Elbedreth's body. Max and Solveig flanked their friends so they'd be ready to attack from the sides. And the dragons changed into their natural forms and flapped their wings a couple of times to ready them for flight.

"Haud that," Azriel called out to the dragons. "Ah think ah know what's comin' 'n' yer flying wull ainlie antagonize it."

"You think it's Cerberus?" Max shouted. By now, both of the ghosts were at least fifty feet to each side.

Azriel nodded. "Aye, laddie. And if wur nae goin awa from Hell, he'll lea us alone... at least ah think."

"You're gambling our lives on that?" Elbedreth asked.

"It's one o' th' few constant hings aboot Hell, at least according tae legend 'n' mah afore experience," Azriel responded. "That 'n' th' souls."

"Poor things," Elbedreth said.

"They're getting whit thay deserve," Azriel answered back.

The cloud stopped moving fifty feet away. It was huge, at least as large as ten Jörmungander's. No one moved as they watched the cloud, unsure what to expect. It didn't take long before the cloud dissipated, revealing the creature that was inside.

"By the gods," Max whispered, too far away for anyone to hear. "That can't be!"

The creature inside the dispersing cloud was monstrous, easily the size of a small castle. It had the body of a dog, but fifty heads instead of three… and all fifty of those heads were staring at Hell's interlopers.

"That's not three heads," Erika said.

"Och, brilliant!" Azriel exclaimed. "The lass kin count."

"Hey! Leave her alone," Jörmungander protested.

Azriel ignored the dragon. "That's Cerberus, a' right. Everyone, haud yer positions… 'n' don't threaten him. We'll be okay if we keep oor heids aboot us."

The massive creature moved forward. As it walked, an enormous explosion of fire, magma, and gas erupted in front of it. Cerberus walked through unharmed, impervious to the dangers of its home. Hell's guardian stopped a few feet away and several heads sniffed each of the companions. Satisfied, the heads drew back, and the creature sat on its haunches.

"Some of you are not dead," each of the fifty heads said at once. The sound of all those deep and eerie voices forced the travelers to cover their ears.

Azriel took a step forward. His ears were still ringing. "We come fur one wha does nae belong in yer domain."

"Once in Hell, forever in Hell," the creature replied. "Turn back now or prepare for your eternity."

"We brought someone out once before," Max called out. "Including ourselves."

The fifty heads turned to inspect Max. "Yes," Cerberus said. "I recognize your smell… and yours," the heads said as they shifted their attention to Azriel. "But you're different. One of you is dead yet still walks in the land of the living and the other died, but one of the young gods revived your essence."

"We're 'ere tae again claim th' soul o' one wha does nae

belong," Azriel said. "We hae na issue wi' ye or th' rules o' th' deid. Wur 'ere ainlie tae correct an injustice."

Cerberus raised up. "An injustice! There are no injustices in Hell! The souls that cross into its domain do so to *serve* justice. Hell delivers punishment. Hell delivers balance to the natural order of things. Hell puts the souls of the innocent at peace by torturing their abusers."

"But the blameless..." Elbedreth began before being interrupted.

"No one crossing the Styx is blameless!" Cerberus exclaimed. "Charon refuses all innocents seeking passage into Hell."

"Souls pay Charon to cross the Styx, knowing the other side leads to eternal torment?" Elbedreth said. "That makes little sense."

"It's either that or swim!" Hell's guardian replied. "The depths of the River Styx can be even more cruel." Cerberus then shifted its entire focus to the female sylph and studied her for a few moments. "I know of you. You're a creation of the old gods... almost as ancient as the mortal realm itself. You should not be here. For you, Hell is exempt and cannot hold you."

"We come for another such as me," Elbedreth said. "Ancient and..."

"Made from the souls of the old gods," Cerberus finished for the sylph. "Another such as you has recently passed this way, only it didn't cross the Styx to get here."

"If she's like me and doesn't belong in Hell, why didn't you stop her?" Elbedreth asked.

All fifty heads of Cerberus shook back and forth in unison. "I don't interfere in the affairs of the old gods. Since she is of them, her fate is theirs to determine. As is yours."

"I am as free-willed as any other," Elbedreth remarked heatedly. "The old gods don't exercise their will upon me!"

Cerberus smiled. "So says you, Elbedreth, last of the true sylphs."

"How do..."

"How do I know your name?" Cerberus replied. "I'm of the old gods myself."

"Enough o' this," Azriel said. "Where'd she go?"

A small road, its boundaries marked by a faint shimmering, materialized in the lava rock and led away from the River Styx and deep into Hell itself.

"The other went that way," Cerberus told them. "If you stay on the road I've outlined, you will find it. Be forewarned! Remain on the path!"

"Thank you," Elbedreth said.

All fifty heads of the dog of Hell laughed. "Do not thank me. The task ahead of you will be dangerous, and not all of you will survive. The one you seek is quite mad... and guarded by Hell Hounds."

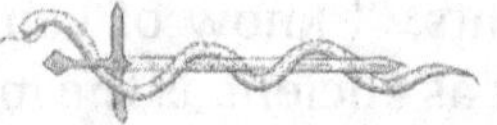

The crossing of the Kematian Sea took three days. Captain Oknog wasn't as slow mentally as he appeared. He ran the ship with the kind of competence one gained only through long years of experience. And despite his occasional harshness towards the crew, they seemed to like him well enough. Also during that time, Abigail and Laurette became steady companions, trading stories of lives spent as the unique individuals they both were. Although Father Goram occasionally spent time on deck trading a few of his own stories with the two, he preferred to spend most of his time alone, either below deck in the hold with the horses or in his cabin.

It was during the afternoon watch and Abigail and Laurette were on the main deck, leaning against the ship's railing and staring out over the water. Behind them, Oknog was calling out orders, and the crew were dutifully carrying them out.

"Your friend seems to prefer staying to himself," Laurette mentioned to Abigail. "He keeps much of who he is hidden. Have you known him long?"

Abigail didn't answer right away. "How does one ever truly get to know someone else?" she finally said. "Have we had a relationship over a long period of time? No. I only met him a few days ago. A beloved friend of mine introduced us. I've spoken of her before..."

"You're talking about Nightshade," Laurette said.

Abigail nodded. "He's her mentor, her friend, and I suspect in many ways her protector, even though she's an overlord. I guess you could say I know him because I know Nightshade so well. Her regard for him gives me all the information I need to understand him. But there's another way to know someone... a way that's even more intimate, more certain, than time or association alone. It's an immediate connection of souls. For that to happen, though, one or both must be willing to let the other in. I... I feel that bond. I have from the very beginning of our relationship. But I don't think Father Goram is one to expose himself so. There have been a few fleeting moments when I'm allowed to see what might be, but then he covers it up so well I'm not even sure I saw it in the first place. He's very good at hiding his feelings."

"He's married and looking for his kidnapped wife," Laurette stated. "You said so yourself. It's rare for a mortal to find themselves in the Abyss. And mortals who don't have some kind of demon patron don't live long. From everything you've told me about Father Goram's wife and her situation, it's reasonable to assume she's no longer alive. He probably already understands that. But still, he'll need time to mourn. And even then, there're no guarantees."

Abigail sighed. "Of course you're right."

Laurette continued. "You don't really want to get yourself involved with a mortal, do you? They have such brief lives compared to demons and are infinitely weaker."

"That's only what Kor would have us believe," Abigail countered. "In many aspects, mortals are stronger than we've been told. Father Goram is from race of elves who are much longer lived than humans... on par with my own race. And he's a powerful cleric. Nightshade told me he was more than a match for her father. You know who her father was, right?"

Laurette nodded. "Aikanáro."

"One of the stronger overlords in the Abyss and a close ally of Kor's," Abigail said. "Then there's Nightshade herself. She's a powerful overlord in her own right. Nightshade told me he was stronger than she was. In the end, he, along with his goddess, converted her from the assassin overlord she was to a follower of White Magic... though she admitted she was having thoughts about converting beforehand."

"White Magic?" Laurette asked.

"According to Horatio... I mean Father Goram... and Nightshade, the magic we practice here in the Abyss is called Black Magic, though we don't follow evil gods," the gorgon said in response to her companion's query.

Laurette frowned.

"If someone follows what the mortals consider good-aligned gods, they are practitioners of White Magic, and vice versa," Abigail clarified.

Laurette shook her head. "We don't follow the gods... good or evil. Nor do we count on them for our magic. We use ley lines."

"So I've been told," Abigail replied. "But their beliefs make a strange kind of sense. According to Nightshade, there are distinct differences between the two kinds of magic, just as there are differences between the gods. Even so, both kinds of magic still depend more upon the strength of nearby ley lines rather than the gods, though Nightshade did mentioned an exception… a young child named Emmy and her mother, Kristen, Father Goram's adoptive daughter. Both can practice certain kinds of magic without ley lines. They can pull the magic they need from their very essence."

"How amazing!" Laurette exclaimed.

The conversation between the two trailed off, replaced by the silent familiarity of two close friends.

"Laurette," Oknog called out from the quarterdeck. "Need you at wheel."

The ship's first officer frowned. "The only time he wants me up there is when there's a problem. Please find your priest and go back to your cabin."

Abigail nodded. "He's usually with the horses at this time of the day. See you at dinner?"

"We'll see," Laurette responded.

Abigail found Father Goram where she expected… below decks with the horses. By then, the ship was rocking and rolling in agitated waters. Abigail explained to Father Goram what she knew as the two further secured the horses against the unexpected movement. But Father Goram decided against going back to his cabin. He wanted to know exactly what was going on and if he could help.

As they headed back up to the main deck, something big hit the side of the ship and sent Father Goram and Abigail scrambling for handholds. The cracking of wood caused by the impact reverberated throughout the ship like the death rattle of a gigantic creature.

The priest grabbed Abigail's hand as they climbed out of the hold, onto the main deck, then up the ladder to the quarterdeck. There was a look of fear and desperation in the eyes of the crew as they scrambled to save their watery home. But one look at the churning water surrounding the ship spoke to the futility of their efforts. Oknog and two other sailors, secured to the deck by strips of rope, were at the ship's wheel, struggling to keep it steady. Each impact upon the ship made control of the wheel even less likely. Laurette was at the front railing, shouting orders to the crew. She looked at Father Goram and Abigail as they reached the quarterdeck and shook her head.

Oknog noticed Abigail and pointed. "You should be thrown overboard!" he screamed. "Female bad luck!"

"Don't mind him," Laurette said. "He's embarrassed he's gotten us caught in a Behemoth spawning which he should have seen and steered around."

"They're huge," Abigail commented as she observed one swimming next to the ship. "I've never seen one before, but I've read about them. Isn't it awful early in the season for them to be mating?"

Laurette nodded. "Yes. And their spawning grounds are much farther north. This has happened before, but it's very rare. Some say it's a portent of things to come. Good or bad, I don't know nor do I care."

"Nature isn't always consistent," Father Goram said. "And reading good or bad in natural events more often than not gets you in trouble."

Another violent impact rocked the ship and threatened to knock anyone who wasn't holding on to something off their feet. One of the crew members on the mainmast lost his grip and fell to his death on the deck below. Calls of "hull breech" echoed throughout the ship. Oknog's struggle with the wheel intensified as he used all his strength to hold the ship parallel to the swimming Behemoths. Laurette's orders to the crew intensified. Father Goram grabbed one of several strips of rope secured to the deck and tied it around Abigail.

"You need one too," the gorgon called out above the sounds of wood breaking, Behemoth's breaching, and Laurette yelling orders.

"We'll not survive if I don't do something," the priest said as he moved closer to the railing. "I can't afford a rope! It's too restricting!"

"What are you going to do?" Abigail asked.

"I'm going to move the ship," the priest responded.

Another blow to its hull rocked the ship. Father Goram stumbled but didn't fall. Abigail watched as Father Goram's arms, hands, and fingers wove complex patterns into the air while he prayed for his goddess to hear and heed his call. Shimmering strands of power extended from the ley lines overhead, entered the priest, and were then released through his fingers and into the air before him. A large rift in the air appeared about one hundred yards before the ship. It wasn't large enough to accept the entire ship... but it was enough to make a difference.

"Steer into the magic," Father Goram called out to Oknog.

As unlikely and dangerous as it seemed, Oknog didn't need further encouragement. He didn't see any other way to save his ship. The captain followed the priest's request and set his course for the middle of the rift. As the ship closed to within fifty yards of the atmospheric rupture, those looking forward watched as Behemoths, perhaps sensing the magic, skirted to either side of the rift instead of swimming into it.

Twenty yards from the rift, the Behemoths disappeared, which calmed the water and gave the captain greater control over the ship. Since it was now obvious the ship was too large for the rift, Laurette ordered the crew members manning the sails to climb down to the main deck.

Ten yards from the rift, Father Goram stumbled as the power needed to keep the rift open drained from him. Though he still had strict control over the energy being used to keep the rift open, he could feel what the consequences of casting such a powerful spell was having on his body. He was lightheaded and felt like he was going to vomit. The world was spinning.

Arms appeared out of nowhere and wrapped themselves around his waist. If they had come a second later, he'd have fallen over from sheer exhaustion. Someone whispered words of encouragement into his ear. They sounded so familiar. Autumn? No. They belonged to Abigail.

Oknog steered the ship dead center into the rift. The hull fit through without incident, but the top halves of the masts sliced off and fell into the water. The instant the bowsprit entered the rift, the entire ship, minus the cut parts of the masts, disappeared and reappeared five miles behind the Behemoth spawning. Crewmen took a few minutes to look around at the now still water. Even the echo of Oknog and Laurette's orders was silenced, if only for a few seconds. The ship came to a dead stop and began to list to the starboard side.

"Get your asses moving," Oknog screamed.

Laurette's orders weren't far behind. "Man the pumps!" she commanded. "And get me a full damage report!"

While everyone was busy trying to keep the ship afloat, Abigail was administering to an unconscious Father Goram. His pulse was weak and intermittent and he was struggling to take a breath.

"Father Goram… Horatio," Abigail whispered into the priest's ear. "You did it! You saved the ship!"

Father Goram opened his eyes and smiled before falling back into a deep sleep.

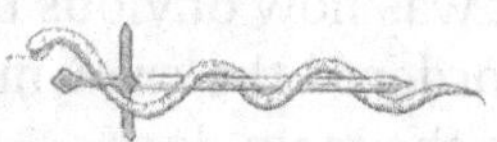

The attack came at dusk, when Landross and Nightshade were both exhausted after another full day of travel. They were still in the forest, but only just barely. The trees were thinning out and the curves in the road gave them occasional glimpses of the open field and city lying beyond.

Landross saw a slight glimmer of metal ahead and called out a warning just before a flight of nine arrows flew towards them. The knight's warning gave Nightshade just enough time to ward herself against harm. Landross ducked down on his horse and the three arrows aimed at him deflected harmlessly off his armor. Both dismounted their horses and took shelter behind trees. Landross looked for Herbie from behind his cover and what he saw caused him to close his eyes and shake his head. The dog was lying on the road with an arrow sticking out of his side. A terrible feeling in the pit of his stomach rushed over him.

"Damn it!" he whispered. Then, so his antagonists could hear, he shouted, "You shot my dog, you whoresons! You're going to pay handsomely!"

Laughter came from the trees and bushes ahead. "You're outnumbered five to one," a female voice called out. "And we don't fear the Taumaru... even one who's lost his dog." More laughter. "Give us your coins and perhaps we'll let you live."

This time it was Landross who laughed. "What do you want written on your tombstones?" he yelled as he bolted to a tree that was only a few feet away from Herbie. The bandits fired several more arrows at him, but each missed. Landross looked at Herbie and saw he was still breathing.

"I'm here, boy," the knight said.

Herbie whimpered.

An arrow dug itself into the dirt next to the dog's head. "The next one goes into his eye," the same female voice called out. "Throw your coin pouches on the road."

Several fiery explosions occurred near the sound of the voice, and smoke covered the area. Most of the thieves coughed. Landross took advantage of the diversion and darted to Herbie. He dragged the wounded animal back to the cover of the tree. The wound was serious, but very little blood streamed out of it. Landross's training and experience told him the injury wasn't deadly as long as it was treated within the hour. He pulled a metal flask off his belt and had Herbie drink it. The medicine would begin the healing process and stabilize the dog until he could cut the arrow out.

Nightshade had also taken advantage of her distraction and moved to Landross and Herbie using the cover of several trees. "How is he?" she asked.

"He'll be fine once we get the arrow out," the knight responded. "How much damage did you do?"

"Not much, I'm afraid," Nightshade replied. "It was mostly for cover so you could retrieve Herbie."

"Maybe it scared them away," Landross said. But the "twang" of a bowstring and the "thunk" of an arrow into a nearby tree said differently.

"Calm yourself, Landross," Nightshade advised.

"Calm myself like hell!" Landross fired back as he drew his sword. "I've had enough of this. Watch Herbie for me."

Nightshade shook her head. "You're not doing this on your own."

Landross swiped his magically gleaming sword through a couple of bushes and quickly built a small shelter to hide Herbie. "I'll draw their attention while you go around and attack from the rear. Do you have magic prepared to do the job?"

"I don't want to use killing magic," Nightshade replied.

Landross stood. "I don't care what you do," he said crossly before leaving.

Nightshade watched as the knight moved forward from tree to tree. A thought suddenly occurred to her. Maybe Landross would be more effective in his normal appearance. When the knight made his charge, she dropped his magical Taumaru disguise. By the time the demon bandits caught sight of him, they saw an angry, armored, sword-swinging maniac rushing towards them. They fired several arrows at him but missed. Landross charged into the bandits and killed three in the blink of an eye. Three more bandits turned and ran away. But the remaining four kept their composure and took a few steps back while reloading their longbows. Landross turned to face them and two arrows hit him—one in his sword arm and another in his leg. He dropped his sword and toppled over.

Nightshade, who had circled around and behind, watched in horror as thieves moved up to Landross and aimed arrows at him. At such a close range, arrows would penetrate his chest plate. The knight used his sword as a crutch and stood, though it was quite clear he couldn't maneuver without falling over again.

Landross spied Nightshade in the background and sought to buy time. Grunting, he raised his sword up in his opposite hand and leveled it at the thieves. "Are you ready to give up?" he asked.

The thieves laughed. "To a dead man?" one thief said as he released his arrow into Landross' uninjured leg. "That armor won't protect you now."

The knight hit the ground hard and mumbled in pain. Nightshade saw Landross slowly stand again. His courage, sense of resolve, and refusal to surrender any show of vulnerability to the thieves fascinated her. Her delay came with a price as another arrow pierced the other arm of her comrade. He dropped his sword but with a Herculean effort stayed on his feet. The faint sound of the arrow penetrating first his armor and then his flesh stirred something in Nightshade that she had thought to be lost forever. It was something that she no longer had control over... something that she had feared ever since her conversion. It wasn't possible on Aster, but she was in the Abyss.

"No!" Nightshade screamed. "Please! No more!"

All four of the thieves turned to stare at the figure that had materialized unnoticed behind them.

"Nightshade!" Landross shouted to the priestess. Even

filled with pain, he understood what was going to happen. He saw Nightshade's eyes and recognized the Black Magic that was filling her soul. "Your vow to your goddess, Althaya, and Horatio! Run away! Don't let me be the cause of your damnation!"

But Nightshade didn't listen... couldn't listen. It was too late. Beauty turned to hideousness... white turned to black. Nightshade became a black, misty column fifteen feet high. Out of each side, four arms appeared, each with hundreds of inch long barbed spikes. Two fangs the size of short swords sprang out of the head as gleaming blue eyes opened and looked down. The thieves found they couldn't move, couldn't scream, couldn't take their attention away from Nightshade's blue eyes. Their bowels released as eight arms engulfed them together in a group-like hug, forcing barbed spikes into their bodies. The spikes weren't long enough to kill, only to immobilize. And though their voices wouldn't work, their eyes shrieked with the pain.

Nightshade let the thieves' fear and torment wash over her. The emotions revitalized her. Once again, she felt the seductive allure of Black Magic. Their fear and pain were like a soothing balm to her eternally ravenous soul. It satisfied her... almost. There was still one thing left to do. As each thief watched, Nightshade's fangs descended and entered their chest one by one. For just a few moments, they each felt their insides liquefy before dying. But death wasn't the end of their terror. She ate their souls. Only then did the terror stop. One doesn't sense oblivion. Nightshade let the dried husks drop to the ground.

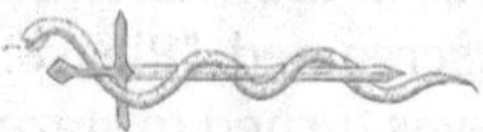

"It's hot," Jörmungander said for the third time.

"What'd you expect?" Erika asked. "A nice, cool cavern?

We're in Hell."

The two dragons, in human form, were bringing up the rear as the group followed the road which Cerberus said would lead to the Johari.

"Quit yer bellyaching," Azriel called from the head of the line.

They'd been walking for what seemed like hours—time doesn't exist in Hell—with no sign of the Johari. The road itself was evenly paved with smooth lava rock, which had a slight spring to it. It made walking easier. But the true horror of Hell lined the road. Like tall stalks of corn, souls stood along both sides of the road and pleaded for their release in a brutal cascade of sight and sound. Each of the companions, even Azriel and Max, couldn't help but feel a sense of sadness for those spirits fated to eternal suffering. It didn't help that they understood each of the condemned had earned every second of their damnation.

"I don't know how much longer I can take this," Solveig said as she covered her ears with her hands. "No wonder the Johari went mad."

Max put an arm around her. "It'll be alright. We'll get through this."

Solveig leaned against her beloved. "We're dead. Maybe this place is where we're going after we've finished whatever destiny requires of us?"

The rogue ghost shook his head and squeezed Solveig even harder. "If that were the case, we'd already be here. Hell waits for no soul."

The ghost dragon remained unconvinced. "Maybe Cerberus won't let us leave," she speculated.

"Then he'll hae tae deal wi' baith edges o' mah battleaxe, he will!" Azriel exclaimed. "And you'll tak' yer dragon form alang wi' Jörmungander 'n' Erika."

"Don't forget about me," Elbedreth said as sharp blades

formed on appendages up and down her body.

"Or me," Max added with a sly smile, thinking of all the things an experienced rogue could do to Hell's guardian.

Azriel laughed. "Aye! A' o' us stoatin warriors 'n' mukkers!"

Solveig smiled. "I expect even the dog of Hell would think twice before taking on this bunch."

Azriel laughed. "I expect he wid at that, lass."

Not long after, they could hear the baying of creature or creatures unknown. The keening sapped the souls of all who heard it. A look of terror came over the dead who lined the road. They turned into a mist that cleared away after a few moments, revealing the desolate landscape of Hell. It was a landscape they were all too familiar with. Off in the distance and all around were large, four-legged black figures with glowing red eyes and fiery breath coming out of their mouths. At first they only watched, but then something seemed to click in their minds and they began running at once. They moved along the surface of Hell in gigantic, fluid motions. Their paws created flames each time they struck the ground. As they drew closer, the size of the beasts became more clear-cut. Each was at least as big as a large warhorse.

"Hell Hounds," Azriel remarked.

"We'll never outrun them," Max said.

"Aye," Azriel returned. "We'll hae tae staun 'n' fight."

Jörmungander morphed into his dragon form and stepped forward. Erika followed his example.

"Get back oan th' road, ye twa beastie nitwits!" Azriel shouted.

Jörmungander used a wing to scoot Erika back. "Sorry, Azriel," he said as he followed suit.

"Get ready!" Max called out.

The Hell Hounds were within ten yards when they unexpectedly held up their charge. They snarled and stomped the ground but refused to go any closer. Max played a hunch and walked a few feet down the road. As he expected, several of the Hell Hounds on both sides of the road broke from the pack and followed him on a parallel path ten yards from the road.

"Just as I suspected," Max said after he'd returned. "Cerberus was right when he warned us to stay on the road."

"Then we should be fine," Solveig remarked.

"Aye," Azriel agreed. "Let's git going."

No one knew how much time had passed when they found the Johari—a day, a week, months, or even years. There was never a night, they never felt tired or needed to rest, and they never had any need for food or water. The only thing they felt was the constant, overbearing heat.

Max was several hundred feet ahead of the rest of the party doing the thing he did so well when alive, scouting, when he saw a figure ahead lying twenty yards off the road. He stopped, as did the Hell Hounds, and signaled for the others to come forward.

As soon as everyone had joined him, Max pointed. "Look over there."

"I see it, Max," Azriel said. "It looks lik' a lump o' purple hair."

"Is it the Johari?" Elbedreth asked.

Max shrugged. "Hardly looks like something that's alive. But in all of this gods-forsaken place, that's the only thing we've seen that looks like it doesn't belong."

"Aye, me boyo," Azriel said. "Which means wur aff tae hae a fight oan oor hands. Jörmungander, Erika, Solveig… turn intae dragons. Solveig, ye git that lump 'n' bring it back tae t' road while th' rest o' us hae a go at they de'il dogs."

Jörmungander and Erika flapped their huge wings to gain altitude while Azriel, Elbedreth, and Max charged off the road and directly towards the Hell Hounds nearest the recumbent figure. Azriel and Max screamed war chants from the old days while the Hell Hounds barked and snarled. The two dragons appeared over the Hell Hounds first and let loose with their deadly dragon breath, which killed two of the creatures and sent seven more scrambling away, yelping in pain. More Hell Hounds appeared to take their place. When the dragons turned to make another attack, their companions and the Hell Hounds were already engaged in close combat. Further use of their acid breath would be too dangerous.

Azriel, brandishing his magical battleaxe, Elbedreth with her multiple blades, and Max hit the charging Hell Hounds with a distinct crash of grunts, groans, snarls, and barks. Azriel and Elbedreth hacked and slashed while Max attacked with his fists, relying upon his devastating touch to deal out necrotic damage. The dragons landed next to the melee and were immediately confronted by their own contingents of Hell Hounds. It wasn't long before the Hell Hounds had scratched, gashed, and burned Azriel, Elbedreth, and the two dragons. Smoke rose into the surrounding atmosphere. Max, though similarly wounded, wasn't in as bad a shape as the others because of his ghostly immunities and limited resistance to certain kinds of their attacks.

The Hell Hounds had fared little better. Several lay dead in bloody lava rock, while most of the others had wounds. Their only advantage was in the numbers. As soon as one Hell Hound died, another appeared to take its place.

While the battle was ongoing, Solveig took to the air. As she gained altitude, she felt the hot winds in the atmosphere of Hell—its updrafts, downdrafts, and currents. She had spent her entire life beneath the ground. There were a few caverns large enough to accommodate flying, but she'd experienced nothing like this. It was her and the sky. Nothing else mattered. She felt free as she sailed through the air. She closed her eyes and drifted, unfettered by the restraints of life and death. It was liberating.

"Hell has released me," she whispered. "I never have to touch the ground again!"

Then she remembered the fighting below and the duty that called to her. With a jealous sigh, Solveig turned to retrieve the figure. She spotted it lying on the ground below and dived. She used her enormous wings to break her descent just before she hit the ground, gently picked up the figure with her claws, and returned to the air while trumpeting her success. After landing back on the road, she shifted from her dragon form so she could tend to her patient.

The eyes of the limp figure opened and she—Solveig knew it was female—attempted to stand. Solveig, worried the creature might further damage herself, tried to stop her. But the creature was surprisingly strong and broke her grasp. For a brief moment, the two stared at each other. The creature Solveig looked at was tall, slender, and covered in long, dark colored purple flowing hair. She had two sets of wings which were also covered by long hair. Her arms were like the wings—covered by long purple hair. They remained down by her side. She had no hands or fingers. Hair flowed down her body and curled upward from the ground. If she had legs, they were well concealed. Hair partially covered her face on both sides. Other than large, expressive eyes, there were no other features—no mouth, nose, ears.

"Johari?" Solveig asked.

The being said nothing, but Solveig could tell the mythical being was terrified. "I'm Solveig. I'm here with Max, Azriel, Elbedreth, Jörmungander, and Erika. Remember us? We're your friends from the cavern."

The Johari said nothing, but her eyes appeared to calm.

"We're here to take you back home," Solveig continued.

"Home?" The Johari said in Solveig's mind. She shook her head. *"I don't remember."* She backed up and stepped off the road.

Four Hell Hounds appeared out of nowhere and charged. Solveig didn't have time to turn back into her dragon form. She rushed over and knocked the Johari back onto the road. The Hell Hounds, deprived of their target, attacked Solveig instead. Being a phantom did nothing to stop her ghostly flesh from being torn and ripped apart by Hell's minions. The Johari, frozen in place by her fear, watched as Solveig died under a mountain of teeth and claws.

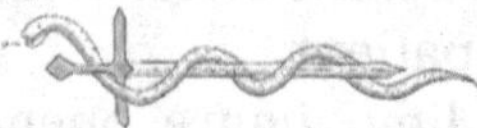

The ship finished the crossing of the Kematian Sea five days after the run in with the Behemoth spawning and docked at a port city called Dral'gaman. Except for Oknog, both Father Goram and Abigail were treated like royalty by the crew for the rest of the trip. The captain still believed Abigail's presence onboard was the reason for the trouble in the first place. He thanked Father Goram for saving his ship and wished them goodbye, but with orders to never set foot on the ship again. Laurette, standing behind the captain, rolled her eyes and mouthed they'd be welcomed any time.

The taverns and inns of the port city are unlike cities that are landlocked... for their main clientele are sailors from docked ships who's travels are far more extensive than the ordinary citizen of the Abyss. As a result, they had much more information to trade for money or mugs of ale.

At first, the Taumaru disguises both wore discouraged sailors and made information sharing difficult. But Father Goram had the ability to make anyone feel comfortable. Though it was part of all clergy training, Father Goram's talent far exceeded that of most individuals, trained or not. It never took long for the priest to put most at ease, even in his masquerade as a fierce Taumaru warrior.

Two days after arriving in Dral'gaman, Father Goram and

Abigail rode horses southwest towards the battlefront opened up against the *B'nai Elohim* fortress. Based upon information they received from their drinking buddies, the demon armies were having a good bit of success, even managing to kill a few of the guardians. It was something that had never transpired in the long adversarial history between the two.

"Something's happened to the Johari," Father Goram said. "That's the only plausible explanation for the *B'nai Elohim* deaths. And if the Johari is dead or otherwise compromised, that means the Juxtaposition Point is shutting down."

"Or already gone," Abigail added.

Father Goram nodded. "Which means a demon invasion on Aster is imminent."

"So if that's the case, the *B'nai Elohim* fortress is the last line of defense for your world," Abigail concluded.

Father Goram shook his head. "No... well, yes. But that's only a ruse. Don't get me wrong... now that the Johari's gone, they'll kill as many *B'nai Elohim* as they can. But the true endgame is to get a demon army on Aster... something they couldn't do until they eliminated the Johari's control of the Juxtaposition Point."

"That's news to me," Abigail said. "I thought it was the *B'nai Elohim* who stopped the demons from getting access to your world."

"That's only partially correct," Father Goram responded. "The Juxtaposition Point separates the Abyss and Aster. Specifically, it keeps the two dimensions apart. Imagine two opposing walls in a room closing in on each other, crushing everything in between. Now place a steel rod horizontally between the two walls. If strong enough, it stops the walls from closing. The rod is the Juxtaposition Point. But if the rod's not strong enough, the walls will snap it and come together. Without the Johari's magic controlling and keeping the Juxtaposition Point strong, both dimensions would come into alignment… meaning they'd phase into one singular reality. The *B'nai Elohim* control the demon's entry to the mortal dimension because they control the Juxtaposition Point. If they lose that, the demons will overrun them, and Aster, in no time."

"So stopping the war won't stop the demons from invading Aster," the gorgon stated.

Father Goram nodded. "Correct. I need to figure another way to stop the invasion from getting that far."

"You'll not be alone," Abigail said. "I'm as committed to this as you are. What can I do to help?"

The priest paused while he considered. "Even with the Juxtaposition Point weakened or gone, it'll still take a lot of magic to transfer an entire army to Aster. Any draw on that much magic will be easily detectable on the ley lines."

"So you'll know when they do it?" Abigail asked.

"Knowing and stopping it are two different things," Father Goram responded.

Abigail sighed. "I'm sorry."

"For what, my dear?" Father Goram asked. "For being a kind and gentle soul?"

Abigail laughed. "I don't think, in the history of creation, anyone's ever called a gorgon a kind and gentle soul. It's…"

"It's not who you are?" the priest said before Abigail finished. "What would Nightshade say about that?"

"Well…" Abigail stuttered.

"People can be so ignorant," Father Goram stated. "Both here and on Aster. Everything I know about your race is what I've read. But from what I've observed, everything I've read is about gorgons is all claptrap. Hell, everything I thought I knew about the Abyss is claptrap. Except for most overlords, the Abyss is populated by the same kind of folks that inhabit Aster. I believe the Abyss has a population of citizens who have all the characteristics necessary to create and maintain a moral society... a society that has no use for the brutality of the overlords. You're no different."

Abigail blushed.

Father Goram smiled and took her hand. "Are you shocked I could say such a thing?" he asked. "I'm not one to let my preconceptions blind me from the truth. I see the goodness in you... the value. Being a gorgon is part of who you are... just like being an elf is part of who I am. But it doesn't completely define you." Father Goram placed an open hand over Abigail's heart. "The rest of you is defined by who you are in here."

The gorgon placed her hand over that of the priest. "Thank you. No one understands that."

Father Goram shook his head. "Nightshade does. As does everyone who's taken the time to get to know you. I'm sure of it. So stop selling yourself so short."

Abigail nodded.

"Now we need to figure out how to stop the demon invasion of Aster," the priest said.

"That's easy... we prop up the Juxtaposition Point you spoke of," Abigail concluded.

Father Goram nodded. "Seems simple enough... but how? Obviously it's a magical item that gets its power from the Johari. But I can't prop it up without a basic understanding of how it works, what type of magic is being used by the Johari, or if and how the ley lines are involved. In other words, except for what's been explained to me, I know nothing about either the Johari or the Juxtaposition Point."

"Then we need to go to the Juxtaposition Point," Abigail decided.

Father Goram sighed. "That appears to be the only answer. Unfortunately, there are several demon armies standing in our way. And we don't have much time."

Abigail smiled. "I bet a couple of gorgons can get through."

The priest hesitated. "A couple..."

"We'll veil your face," Abigail said. "I'll lead and do all the talking. As long as you keep your face buried in that great hooded cloak you wear, they'll never know the difference. And if a demonstration is needed… well, I can provide that."

"That just might work," Father Goram agreed. "Except for one thing. Most everyone believes there's only one gorgon in the Abyss. How do we explain two?"

Abigail smiled and her eyes glowed slightly. "You think anyone's going to ask?"

CHAPTER EIGHTEEN

Aster – Draugan Pesta and the Hyrokkin Empire

"Are you sure you can do it?" Kesha Stanislavovich asked the Madeiran sorceress for the third time.

The former bodyguard for Krasnov Dmitrievich sat at a table in a hastily repaired tavern in the city of Madeira. Throughout the city, carpenters, fine woodworkers, plumbers, and other skilled laborers were rebuilding the city which had been flooded a few months earlier. The current warlord was pulling out all the stops and costs didn't seem to be a factor. While this was taking place, a restored Madeiran army kept themselves busy by patrolling the muddy streets, insuring Madeira's remaining citizens were taking part in the reconstruction. The soldiers that were off duty frequented the many taverns that had already been rebuilt and opened for business—getting drunk, bothering serving wenches, and offering opinions to the civilian builders regarding everything from how to drive a nail into a plank of wood to finishing a fine stairway banister. In short, they were being a general nuisance to everyone around them.

The sorceress nodded for the third time. "You paid your gold..."

"A lot of it," Kesha reminded the sorcerer.

"Yes, you met my price. And I'll honor the agreement. Except..."

Kesha jumped on the sorcerer's last comment. "Except what?!"

The sorceress sighed before she haughtily replied. "Clearly, you don't understand how magic works. Or the conditions under which we're paid."

Kesha pulled his rapier from its scabbard and slammed it down on the table. Several soldiers looked over at the two, but one glance from Kesha drove them back into their mugs of ale. None were prepared to challenge the giant, especially for a witch.

"Perhaps it's you who doesn't understand," Kesha said.

The rapier didn't bother the sorceress as much as the look on the face of the giant Draugen Pesta sitting across from her did. When she continued, her tone was much more conciliatory. "Forgive me. I believe I get your meaning. A full refund it is if I don't follow through."

Kesha left the rapier sitting on the table. "Much better. So, what are the problems?"

"Only a few, actually. The ley lines over Hyrokkin aren't very strong. Strong ley lines are key to long distance magic such as this."

"So you may not be able to do it?"

The sorceress shook her head. "Oh, I can do it. It's only... how do I explain this? I'll have to draw upon two or more ley lines if one isn't strong enough. That takes more effort and energy from my life force."

Kesha took out ten more gold pieces and added them to the bag of gold already sitting on the table. "Will that take care of it?"

The sorceress looked up at the giant and nodded.

"Now explain to me what you're going to do for all this gold," Kesha said.

"I'll put a spell on her communications crystal..."

Kesha stopped her. "There'll be more than one crystal in the compound. How are you going to know which one?"

"Each communications crystal has its own unique magical signature," the sorceress answered. "I'll tap the ley lines over your Princess's location and listen in."

"You'll be able to hear their conversations?" Kesha asked. If so, it was news to him.

"No," the sorceress replied. "Nothing that specific. But I'll be able to zero in and identify any crystal powered up around the coordinates of the compound."

"I'd wager the Princess isn't the only one operating communication crystals over there," Kesha observed.

The sorceress shrugged. "It's the best I can do. Take it or leave it."

"Then what happens?"

"That's another question mark," the sorceress replied. "I'm working off the assumption the Princess will have a backup crystal linked to the original."

Kesha nodded. "I'd expect a royal to have one."

"Then no problem," the sorceress said. "Providing the ley lines allows me to overload the first one. The second will be ready to explode upon activation after a day."

"Why will it take that long? Why not at once?"

The Madeiran sorceress was about to make an ill-tempered remark involving civilians who'd never understand magic and the sacrifices sorcerers go through to conduct it when Kesha touched the hilt of his rapier. Instead, the sorceress took a sip of wine. "The magic needs that long to establish itself on the second crystal. That, of course, presumes that both crystals have the same activation sequence."

The giant picked up his rapier and slammed it back into its scabbard. "Damnit! That's a lot of 'ifs.' Are you sure you can do this?"

"Of course I'm sure! Just being honest with the customer. Why do you want to main or kill this Princess of yours, anyway?"

Kesha looked at the human female sitting across the table. "That's none of your concern."

The sorceress shrugged. "No, it's not. Just curious."

Kesha considered. "Revenge. Pure, simple, soul-searing revenge. Though I'll take it, I don't really want the Princess killed. I'd much prefer the explosion to maim her. Then I'll know, for as long as the Princess lives, her mother…"

"Your queen," the sorceress stated.

Kesha shook his head. "She's no queen of mine. She forced me into exile and threatens my life. I want retribution! Maiming her child will insure she never forgets the price that I, Kesha Stanislavovich, forced her to pay!"

"How will the queen ever know it was you?"

Kesha smiled. "One day I'll tell her."

The sorceress suddenly noticed something she hadn't seen before. It was a tinge of madness in the eyes of the Draugen Pesta giant.

"Do we have all the traitors rounded up?" Sofia asked as she and Aleksei Smirnov, her chief spy, walked along a deserted hallway in the palace.

Aleksei nodded. "For the most part, Your Grace," he replied. "Krasnov Dmitrievich's the ringleader. Along with him there's Vassili Yakopav, the Minister of Weapons, Antonov Petrova…"

"One of our wealthier merchants?" Sofia asked.

"Correct," Aleksei agreed. "And there's Kostadin Vasilov Cherganski, the Assistant Chief of the Exchequer, and Kesha Stanislavovich…"

Sofia frowned. "He's one of yours, isn't he?"

"Correct again, Your Grace," Aleksei said. "And on the run. We'll get him, eventually."

The queen nodded. "I know you will. And when you do, deal with him in your own way."

"No trial?" the spy asked.

I already have plenty of traitors for my trial," Sofia replied. "He doesn't need to be handled like the others. Anybody else?"

Aleksei shook his head. "No one of note… some low-level

level government types and a few of the more insignificant merchants hoping to profit through the weapons for drugs trade."

"That's everyone?" Sofia asked.

Aleksei looked at this queen. "We used a few persuasive techniques to get the information we wanted. Except for Stanislavovich, we have them all. I can guarantee it."

The two traveled in silence for a few minutes.

"Gotta admire their ingenuity," Sofia remarked after a time. "Even if they are traitors."

"Not everyone believes that," Aleksei said. "There are those who feel they were only taking advantage of an opportunity."

Sofia let loose a harsh laugh. "Trading with the enemy to profit one's purse is acceptable? Who are these people?"

"Mostly merchants, bankers, and the like," the spy answered. "But a few of them hold prominent positions within your government."

"Have you identified them?" Sofia asked.

Aleksei nodded. "I believe so. It's skewed reasoning, that's for sure. But it's also the kind of thinking that could free the traitors... or be the basis for even more underhanded negotiations with the Hyrokkin."

"They're no longer the enemy... at least according to my husband," Sofia countered.

Aleksei sighed. "Your Grace, they fly their war banners!"

"A mistake which I intend to rectify," Sofia answered. "Just as soon as I can get Daphnia out of harm's way."

"Very well," the spy said. "They're not the enemy... just misguided children."

"Please, Aleksei," Sofia said. "We're both from the north and share a kinship, but I'm still your queen. I don't have time for your quick tongue."

Aleksei averted his glance. "My apologies." Aleksei took a deep breath before continuing. "I know you're tired of hearing this, but I beg you… again! Put the traitors before a military tribunal with you at the head. It's the only way you can be assured of a conviction."

The Draugen Pesta queen shook her head. "You know I can't do that, Aleksei. Military authorities shouldn't judge civilian officials of the government. It's a matter of law. I want them to get a civilian trail before a judge and their peers. This has to be completely above-board and open for all to see. It should be out there in the domain of public opinion. When my husband hears of it for the first time, I want it to be a fait accompli. The only thing I'll leave for my husband is the execution orders to be signed."

"Can you get an execution recommendation in a civil court, Your Grace?" Aleksei asked. "You can guarantee it in a military tribunal."

Sofia shrugged. "Nothing is guaranteed… but yes, I believe so."

"The information about the drug trade will come out," Aleksei mentioned.

Sofia shrugged. "So? That *is* why they're being put on trial."

"It's a dangerous business, Your Grace," the spy observed. "If it gets out that we're continuing the drug trade, the king will find out about it soon enough… perhaps before you're ready for him to know."

The queen sighed. "Relax, Aleksei," she said in reassurance. "I can trust the few people who do know about it to keep their mouths shut. As for the centaurs, half of them are already addicted and won't talk for fear I'll shut it down. The other half know nothing and it'll stay that way. I'll inform my husband as soon as he returns from the Abyss. We'll decide together how best to move forward." Sofia looked over at the spy. "It's the best way I know to keep Daphnia safe."

"If there's a better way, I don't know what it might be," Aleksei agreed. "And stronger minds than mine have been looking into the matter."

"I know, my friend," Sofia said. "That's true about the both of us. What's that all about?"

They had just rounded a corner and spied two guards standing on either side of a large set of double doors… doors leading to one of several conference rooms throughout the palace. This wasn't unusual. Guards are always posted at strategic locations in the palace. But guards posted next to conference room doors usually meant an important meeting was occurring inside. Both guards came to attention as soon as they saw their queen. Sofia stopped before the doors.

"I wasn't aware of any meetings being conducted," Sofia said to Aleksei.

"Neither was I," Aleksei responded as he nodded to the guards, who immediately opened the double doors.

Inside, several heads that were bent over a large oaken table examining a map glanced up. "Your Grace!" one of them exclaimed. They looked as if they'd gotten caught with their hands in the proverbial cookie jar.

Sofia recognized all of them. "Why is my general staff hunched over a table studying a map without my knowledge, Misha?"

The General of the Army, Field Marshal Mikhail Grigorievich, cleared his throat. "Please, Your Grace," he said as he offered his chair to the queen.

Sofia sat in the proffered chair. When Aleksei took the chair next to her, several eyebrows raised, but they made no comments. "Well?" Sofia asked again.

Field Marshal Grigorievich looked at General Anatoli Valeryevich and nodded.

"Your Grace," General Valeryevich said. "Obviously we're aware of the latest communique received from the Princess…"

"I've made no secret of her predicament," Sofia inserted.

"Yes, Your Grace," General Valeryevich responded.

Sofia's eyes bored into Field Marshal Grigorievich. "And I also made it clear that we'll manage this diplomatically. That would be my husband's wishes if he were here... which is why I sent a delegation led by Pavel Shubin to the Hyrokkin to negotiate. We want peace with the Hyrokkin and Shubin's brokered one. Daphnia's safe for now."

General Valeryevich nodded. "We understand that, Your Grace. But still their war banners fly and elements of their military still surround the Princess's compound. She is, for all intents and purposes, still a prisoner of the Hyrokkin. Then there's the fact that Her Grace the Princess provided sanctuary to their dead queen's son. He's the rightful heir. The current military junta that now controls the Hyrokkin Empire no doubt wants him dead. If the Princess doesn't surrender him, the diplomatic solution Shubin crafted could go out the window. We need an extraction plan ready if it becomes necessary."

"You don't think a full Phalanx is enough to keep her safe?" Sofia asked. "Or that immortal wolf of hers? Or the dwarf sorcerer Blackmantle and his gigantic bear?" She didn't mention the Lads. Very few people knew of them.

"Do you think it's enough, Your Grace?" General Valeryevich asked. "If so, why do you have most of our remaining army sitting on the eastern border? Why are you prepared to strike Hyrokkin with overwhelming force on a moment's notice?"

The general's comments struck home. Sofia looked around the table. None of the generals flinched in the wake of her steely gaze. It was proof, at least to her, that they each had the courage of their own convictions. Not a coward in the bunch.

"Then why behind my back?" Sofia finally said. "Why not involve me in your planning?"

"May I be blunt, Your Grace?" General Magdalena Petrovna, overall commander of the royal family's three Phalanx's, asked.

Sofia looked at General Petrovna. She had personally

appointed her and trusted her judgment implicitly. "Of course, Maggie."

"None of us at this table believe that peace, at least a lasting peace, is possible with the Hyrokkin," General Petrovna stated. "We believe it to be… folly, Your Grace."

"It's absolute madness," Field Marshal Grigorievich chimed in. "Begging your pardon, Your Grace."

Sofia looked to her top military advisor and then back to General Petrovna. "Go on, Maggie."

General Petrovna nodded. "We also believe the Princess was the last person the king should have sent as ambassador. She's too young and inexperienced. We have many diplomats who could have done the job… and none of them are as valuable to the kingdom as Princess Daphnia. Why put her in harm's way?"

While her husband accepted such criticism with grace and might even act if he saw it had merit, she was from the north and saw things differently. She had little to no tolerance for his generals questioning her husband's decision-making after the fact and behind his back.

"My husband's reasoning for sending her, though none of your business, was well thought out and perfectly reasonable," the queen replied angrily. "Daphnia's far more capable than many people give her credit for. Anything else?"

"Everyone around this table loves the Princess," Field Marshal Grigorievich said, clearly trying to tone down the queen's annoyance. "Each of us knows her personally. Her smile and her caring nature has graced us all. We'd give our lives for her. Not because it's our duty, though there is that. But because of who she is and what she means to our kingdom. We didn't want to sit around and wait for something to happen to her before we took action."

"I understand and appreciate the motivation," Sofia said. "But none of this answers my original question. Why are you being so secretive? What are you hiding?"

"We're not hiding anything, Your Grace," General Petrovna replied. "We didn't want to involve you until it was necessary for fear it might cause friction between you and the king. That and we fear the king is far too enamored with the idea of peace with the Hyrokkin."

"That sounds awfully close to treason," Sofia said. She didn't bother to tell them she felt much the same. But she'd never raise her doubts or objections behind her husband's back. And though Viktor valued the opinion of his commanders, once he made a decision, it was their duty to carry it out. Just as it was hers.

"Never, Your Grace!" Field Marshal Grigorievich exclaimed.

"Typically a king's generals do what the king tells them to do," Sofia continued. "Is that not so, Misha?"

"Of course, Your Grace," Field Marshal Grigorievich answered. "But we're not plotting to overturn the king's decision, regardless of how ill-informed we believe it to be. We just want to save his daughter… peace or no peace."

"Again, it's not the planning I object to," Sofia retorted. "It's the secrecy."

There was silence once again.

"Listen to yourselves," Sofia said to the quiet room. "You sound just like the Hyrokkin generals." She took time to look around the table. "You're convinced you know better than your liege. I'm very disappointed with the lot of you. While I understand your desire to see Daphnia home and safe… we all want that… I'm disheartened you feel the need to covertly plan a rescue… or that you would even dare!"

"Your Grace…" Field Marshal Grigorievich began.

"Stop!" Sofia barked. "Each one of you knows you're free to come to me with anything. With anything! I've made that clear time and time again. Yet here I find you making plans that involve my daughter without my knowledge. Only happenstance has brought your actions to my attention. Do your oaths to my husband and me matter so little?" Sofia stopped and sighed.

"Your Grace, if I may?" General Petrovna asked.

The queen closed her eyes and shook her head. "Not now, Maggie. I need to think."

Silence permeated the room. Despite the displeasure of their queen, the generals still felt the course of action they'd chosen was appropriate for the situation... a situation that neither the king nor his queen, in their judgment, fully understood. Diplomacy won't work with the Hyrokkin.

"Very well," the queen said after a time. "No one gets fired or strung up. This time. So... what's your plan?"

There was an uncomfortable stillness in the room.

"You've got nothing, do you?" Aleksei broke the silence. He couldn't help himself. "After all this, you got nothing!"

Sofia let out an abrasive laugh. "Unbelievable!"

"Those devils have the Princess in a tough spot," Field Marshal Grigorievich said. "If we attack from the border, they'll overrun her compound before we can get to her. If we try to get her out through subterfuge... well, how do you sneak someone around with a giant wolf and an even larger bear following along?"

"He's got a point," Aleksei mentioned. "Besides, knowing the Princess as I do, she'd not leave without every single member of her Phalanx, their horses, and probably a few Hyrokkin as well."

"Did you consider magic?" Sofia asked.

Field Marshal Grigorievich nodded. "We've discussed it with several of our war sorcerers."

"And?"

Field Marshal Grigorievich shook his head. "They'd need to cast a doorway spell which, for several reasons, isn't practical."

"Explain," the queen requested.

"I'll need to defer to General Valeryevich, Your Grace," Field Marshal Grigorievich replied. "He understands sorcerer business far better than I."

Sofia looked at General Valeryevich and nodded. "The floor is yours, Tolly."

"Well, Your Grace, first and foremost, to open a doorway to the Princess's compound, a sorcerer has to have been there so he or she can visualize where the doorway will open. None of our sorcerers have ever been in Hyrokkin territory."

"I really need to educate myself on magic use," Sofia remarked to herself.

"Your Grace?" Field Marshal Grigorievich asked.

Sofia shook her head. "Just thinking out loud. Tolly, please excuse my ignorance if this is a stupid question, but can't sorcerers use magic to read the thoughts of others? Perhaps we can find someone who's been there and get the information we need from their mind."

General Valeryevich shook his head. "Not a stupid question at all, Your Grace. Unfortunately, the sorcerer or sorceress has to have intimate knowledge of the other end beforehand. That means, as I said, he or she must have been there. There's really no exception to this hard fast rule. But suppose we had that worked out. The next problem is the amount of power needed to keep the doorway open. As Master Smirnov insinuated earlier, the Princess's proclivities towards people would suggest she'd not be willing to come alone. They'd need to keep the doorway open long enough for our people over there to come through. That necessitates an exorbitant amount of power... power that we don't have. That's also why the Princess's Phalanx sorcerers can't open a doorway from there to here. What would be the point if she won't leave unless everyone else can leave as well?"

"They did it on the elvish island of InnisRos to get an entire army there from an entirely different dimension," the queen said.

"But only with the help of relic-powered magic," General Valeryevich countered. "We don't have that luxury."

Sofia frowned. "Alright... point taken. Is there anything else, Tolly?"

"Regarding the magic, just one more thing, Your Grace," the general answered. "We've learned from the Princess's own Phalanx sorcerers that the ley lines over there aren't very strong... certainly not strong enough to support the magic required to pull everyone back, even if we solved the first two drawbacks. Worse, the attempt could cause the ley lines over there to overload, which could lead to a catastrophic explosion. And not just in Hyrokkin. The blowback through the opened doorway, as demonstrated on InnisRos, would be even more disastrous over here."

Sofia leaned over to Aleksei. "I thought the blowback on InnisRos was unconfirmed?" she whispered to her chief spy.

"As did I, Your Grace," Aleksei whispered back.

"Viktor's always bragging about how much better his spies are compared to mine," the queen muttered. "Is he right?"

Aleksei shrugged. "Vasiliy Sergeyevich and I don't consider ourselves vying against each other. We're both loyal to the crown and we trade information all the time."

Sofia took a deep breath. "Well then?"

"You know as well as I how secretive the elves can be, particularly when their relics are involved," Aleksei murmured. "Besides, I don't have people over there. It's not cost effective to have people on InnisRos doing the same thing for both the king and you. Too much of an overlap. In all likelihood, the information regarding the blowback has just been verified and Vasiliy hasn't gotten the data to me yet. Not unsurprising since I've been out of pocket locating traitors for you."

"You're forgiven," she whispered with a smile.

"Your Grace?" General Valeryevich inquired.

Sofia looked from Aleksei then back to the general. "Sorry, Tolly... please continue."

General Valeryevich shook his head. "Not much else to add. In short, magic isn't the answer."

Sofia looked around the table. "Anything else before I leave?"

Everyone shook their heads. "That covers everything, Your Grace."

Sofia nodded. "Keep pursuing your planning. Let me know when you have something that's truly actionable."

The queen stood. Everyone around the table stood as well. "There's peace between our two nations... but that doesn't mean the Hyrokkin are going to make things easy for my daughter. I doubt she'll get the supplies she needs from them. Put together a month's worth and send them over on wagons. We need to make this a monthly occurrence, so please see to it."

"Don't forget the Hyrokkin military is in control, Your Grace," the Field Marshal Grigorievich remarked. "If they don't get the legitimate heir from the Princess, there's no telling what they might do.... or when."

"I'm aware," the queen replied as she walked out of the room, followed by Aleksei.

"I wish Daphnia hadn't let the Hyrokkin into her compound," Sofia said as soon as they had exited the room. "She put herself right in the middle of something she has no business being involved in. Let the Hyrokkin handle their own damn politics!"

"You'd have done the same thing," Aleksei remarked. "Heir or no heir."

Sofia stopped.

Aleksei had taken several steps down the hall before he realized she wasn't at his side. He stopped and turned.

"That one little act, done in kindness, jeopardizes the

peace my husband so craves," Sofia said. "It got her compound surrounded by the Hyrokkin army with demands she hand over the prince… which she'll never do. At least not against his will. It was a terrible decision… a decision that could cost her, and maybe thousands of others, their lives. No, Aleksei, I wouldn't have done the same thing!"

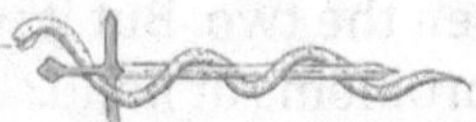

Daphnia, Jarsus Blackmantle, Major Anya Romanova, Shubin, the two Hyrokkin monks, Dardandros and Theodasius, and the leader of the dead queen's personal guard, Galissa, were in the compound's make-shift conference room. The giant wolf, Adimar, and the even larger bear, Sienna, were both lying near the only doorway out of the room. Both of these very special animals were awake and alert. Unlike all the other Hyrokkin, neither Dardandros, Theodasius, or Galissa appeared to have any problem with the wolf, though they still kept their distance as much as possible.

Dardandros looked around the room with disdain. "The only diplomatic mission between our two nations in history and this warehouse is the best they could give you?" The Hyrokkin prince shook his head. "You're right, Lady Daphnia. I know from personal experience those that rule my people since mother died have no intention of making peace with you. In fact, I'm surprised they haven't already attacked."

"Your information appears to be outdated," Shubin remarked. "We've signed peace accords with your people, Dardandros. But your arrival, and the Princess granting you sanctuary, has put a bit of a kink in everyone's plans."

"A kink, he says," Jarsus said. "Tell me, Shubin, dae a' diplomats hae th' knack fur saying hings wi' sic aplomb? Th' Hyrokkin hae thair panties sae far up thair arses, thay can't think straecht, I'd wager. Nae a peep oot o' thaim sin they twa 'n' Galissa's wee pairtie git 'ere."

"I think what our dwarf friend means is that, if nothing else, your arrival has confused them just a bit," Shubin said.

Daphnia was smiling. Ever since Shubin's arrival, he and Jarsus have been jabbering at each other relentlessly. It looked like a game between them, and she was having fun watching the interaction between the two. But it was only a momentary distraction from the problems at hand.

"We believe the peace would've been assured if not for your arrival, Prince Dardandros," Daphnia said. "But now who knows? Shubin's correct, however. Your sudden appearance has no doubt thrown them off balance. At least enough to force them to rethink the situation. Even so, I expect I'll soon be getting an ultimatum demanding we surrender you to them."

"Maist likely wi' yer heids oan a spike," Jarsus remarked under his breath.

"Anyone who lays a hand on the prince answers to my maidens and I," Galissa said.

"Galissa, stop," Dardandros snapped. Then he sighed. "Sorry. That was uncalled for. Princess Daphnia, please don't consider me the prince. I've renounced my claim to the throne."

"Yet as you've explained it, they're trying to assassinate you," Daphnia commented. "Why do you think that is?"

The Hyrokkin prince shook his head. "I don't know."

"For the same reason they assassinated the queen," Galissa remarked.

Shubin nodded. "Galissa's right. One seldom denies the lawful heir to a throne. It's a birthright. It doesn't matter how many official papers of abjuration you sign. Anyone can easily explain those away as forgeries. The only real exceptions to the laws governing the rules of inheritance are mental or physical disability or incapacity. Unpopular monarchs are generally overthrown and executed or, in rare cases, banished for life upon pain of death. Heads of state replaced by another ruling body, the military in this case, are usually killed as a matter of course… as are their heirs."

"So my options are to die or run away from the land of my birth?" Dardandros asked. "I can't just live my life as a monk?" The centaur prince looked at Theodasius and shook his head. "I don't know what to do, brother."

"You have a third choice," Daphnia said. "You can accept your heritage and fight for that which is rightfully yours."

"Fight?" Dardandros inquired. "With what army?"

"The queen's Shield Maidens, for one," Galissa said. "And the people of Hyrokkin, for another."

Dardandros shook his head. "Even if you're right, Galissa, what a slaughter that would be."

"If you decide to fight, Draugen Pesta will ally itself with you," Daphnia added.

"Your Grace!" Shubin exclaimed. "You can't speak for your father about such things… particularly when the lives of Draugen Pesta citizens are at risk!"

"The lassie kin speak fur baith th' king 'n' th' queen o' Draugen Pesta," Jarsus said. "At least whin th' Hyrokkin ur concerned. Need ah remind ye she's nae ainlie th' Princess bit th' ambassador as well."

Shubin looked at the dwarf and nodded. "Technically you're correct, Blackmantle. But *should* she speak for them? At least in this instance?"

"That's enough, the both of you," Daphnia ordered. Then she looked at Dardandros and shrugged. "Just a discussion between advisors. You don't have to worry. My father will honor all promises I make to you as ambassador to the Hyrokkin Empire."

"I won't run," Dardandros explained as he shook his head. "I'm not craven. But I still deny the throne. I've no wish to sit upon it either now or in the future. As for your offer of military aid… that means war. I don't want that on my conscience."

"My Prince!" Galissa exclaimed.

"That's just the way of it," Dardandros said.

"You're pentin yersel' intae a corner, laddie," Jarsus commented.

"For once I agree with Blackmantle," Shubin said. "You don't have many options, and your rejecting the ones you do. Which brings me to a question. If you don't want our help to put you upon the throne or to leave Hyrokkin, why are you here?"

"We came to discover why Thanilus sent an assassination team to my monastery to take my life," Dardandros explained. "But you've explained things quite satisfactorily in that regard."

"May I say something?" Theodasius asked.

Dardandros smiled. "Of course, brother."

"Let's disappear into the Northern Boreskyre Mountains," Theodasius suggested. "I doubt they'll send anyone to search… at least not there. The mountains have plenty of game to hunt and streams to fish. And there are several small tribes there for companionship."

"Those small tribes don't take too kindly to strangers," Dardandros snorted.

"They always welcome monks," Theodasius refuted. "They'll keep us hidden."

Dardandros nodded. "Perhaps you're right."

"You'd be doing your people an injustice if you took that course of action," Daphnia advised.

"Listen to her, My Prince," Galissa added.

Dardandros looked at the Shield Maiden and then the Draugen Pesta princess. "As I've already stated, I've no desire to rule Hyrokkin. I don't know how much clearer I can make it. I just want to be left alone!"

"As a monk, you're familiar with duty and responsibility?" Daphnia asked.

"Of course I am," the centaur replied. "But we're also taught the importance of personal freedom. We're trained to wander and survive alone... to offer our help to as many people as we can throughout the land."

"And 'ere ah thought ye stayed cloistered behind they monastery walls o' yours," Jarsus said. "Tell me, boyo. Howfur mony o' yer brother monks ur heirs tae a nation? Howfur mony fowk kin a lone monk hulp compared tae th' king o' an entire fowk?"

Shubin began to object to Jarsus's hard questioning, but a motion of Daphnia's hand silenced him.

Dardandros looked at Jarsus. Daphnia couldn't tell if there was anger or shame in his expression. Whichever it was, the princess didn't think it was enough to change Dardandros's mind. But from the look on Jarsus's face, she didn't believe he was finished with the young centaur. She was right.

"Princess Daphnia mentioned duty 'n' responsibility," Jarsus continued. "When ye'r th' member o' a ryle fowk, ye don't git tae forgoat aboot yer duty or responsibility oan a whim, fur it's pernicketie, or fur ye don't lik' it. Ye don't git tae pat yer tail atween yer legs 'n' mak' a run fur it lik' a spineless feartie-cat. Some hings tae decide aren't yers tae mak', laddie."

The young centaur slammed his fist on the table in anger. "I said it once and I'll say it again! I'm no coward!"

Jarsus slammed his own fist on the table just as hard as the centaur did. "Then quit acting lik' one, ye damned four-legged, beardless, pig-headed, rust bucket!"

Dardandros, Theodasius, and Galissa stood, backed away from the table, and drew quarterstaffs and sword. "We were wrong to believe that the Draugen Pesta had truly changed," Dardandros said. "We were wrong to have come here."

Jarsus didn't move. "Ye idiots! If ye hadn't come 'ere, you'd be deid by noo. We saved 'yer mangy hides. 'N' if ye haven't seen it by noo, wur also trying tae save th' hides o' yer fowk! If ye ken what's guid fur ye, ye'll pat they tree limbs 'n' sticker awa', sit yer bottoms doon, 'n' listen tae th' Princess... fur she's someone wha understands 'n' bides by her duty 'n' responsibility."

The centaurs looked at each other, at Jarsus, then at Daphnia. They nodded and put their weapons away before lowering themselves back down. "You did save our lives," Dardandros remarked. "We can't deny it and owe you a debt as a consequence."

Daphnia shook her head. "You owe us no debt, Dardandros. We provided you sanctuary because it was the right thing to do, even though your presence here complicates things for us."

"Remember that," Jarsus said.

"That's enough, my friend," the princess ordered. "We expect nothing in return and will respect your wishes, regardless. But your people... and mine... won't be well served with the military in charge of your empire. I'm sure my mother and father would agree with that assessment and be willing to help return your country back to its lawful ruler. But only if you're willing."

Dardandros took a deep breath. "It's just that..."

There was a sharp rap on the conference room door and one of Major Romanova's Phalanx officers marched in. He saluted the princess and his commander.

"Captain Aslanov, Your Grace," he said without preamble. "There's a Hyrokkin delegation at the front gates requesting an audience. He calls himself Thanilus."

"The heich 'n' mighty Thanilus 'ere again tae mak' his demands known," Jarsus said. "Just say th' word, Daphnia, 'n' I'll hae th' Lads remove his private bits 'n' feed thaim tae Adimar 'n' Sienna."

Both of the animals growled their displeasure.

"We've got to hear him out, Your Grace," Shubin remarked. "Preferably before removing his private parts."

Daphnia nodded. "At least they're still willing to talk. You three stay here and consider our discussion. And Galissa... no coming after Thanilus with your Shield Maidens while he's in the compound."

"He killed Queen Thesonia!" Galissa snarled.

"In this compound my word is law," Daphnia said. "And I have a thousand warriors of my Phalanx to back it up."

Jarsus held back a smile. He couldn't be prouder.

The centaur female nodded acquiescence.

Daphnia nodded. "Very well. The rest of you with me. Lead the way, captain."

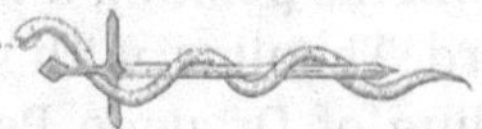

Thanilus waited in the blistering sun of mid-day outside the walls of the Draugen Pesta compound underneath a temporary canopy set up by his attendants. From what he saw of the breastworks hastily built around the complex, his warriors would have little trouble breeching them. But any aggression at this point would be political suicide. The cost in blood to his army would be so high both here and on the border even his hand-picked generals would object. And it hadn't been that long since they had invaded Draugen Pesta, only to be driven back in disgrace. Then there were the insidious effects of his addiction. He'd do anything to keep the drugs flowing from Draugen Pesta. He'd even given up Dmitrievich's name for the promise. Dmitrievich, along with his cronies, had been rounded up by their secret service and are now being held pending trial. It turned into a very public display orchestrated by that queen of theirs.

"She's a smart one," the centaur thought. *"What's taking so long?"*

Thanilus's attention returned to the present as the doors of the main gate opened. Two guards marched through and posted themselves on each side. Through the gates, Thanilus could see the Draugen Pesta had erected their own pavilion. A double line of warriors led from the gate to the pavilion. Underneath the pavilion, the child ambassador was sitting at the head of a small table. Behind her stood that damned dwarf, Jarsus, the envoy, Shubin, and the military commander of the force guarding the compound. Then there were the two animals, the wolf and the bear, lying on each side of the table between the princess and the other end where pillows had been placed for him to sit on.

The presumptive king of the centaurs saw no reason to bring his attendants, but his position did demand he take with him his personal guard. Thanilus, with six warriors, marched through the double line of Draugen Pesta warriors with as much dignity as he could muster. He knew one word from the child and her warriors would slaughter him. At least that would be an honorable death, not that honor was important to him. But even as he considered his predicament, it was the wolf that unnerved him the most. It was so big! The fear was so great he thought he might urinate all over himself. By the time he sat on the pillows at the table, his whole body was shaking. The wolf suddenly rose on all four legs, stretched, walked to the child, and laid back down. Thanilus knew that was by design. And it worked. He thought he was going to pass out. The wolf was bigger than big. It was enormous! Then the bear did the same thing. It was even larger!

"I hope this is acceptable, Thanilus," Daphnia said. "A bit hot in the mid-day sun, but it's so much stuffier inside. At least out here we have a delightful breeze to cool us. And to satisfy our hunger and thirst, chilled wine with fruits and cheeses will be brought out shortly."

Thanilus nodded. "This works well enough, Princess. And wine with a mid-day meal will be most welcomed. We can discuss our business and fill our bellies at the same time."

"And what business is that?" Daphnia asked. She didn't bother with pleasentries, preferring to get directly to the point.

"You invited several of my countrymen inside your compound," Thanilus stated. "One of them is a Prince of the Empire, the son of our late queen. And while I appreciate the hospitality shown to them, there's talk amongst my advisors you now hold them as possible bargaining chips should the peace between our two countries fail. I must now ask you to turn them over to me."

Daphnis smiled. "I can assure you they're not prisoners, Thanilus. And unlike you, I believe the peace will hold."

"Yes, Princess, but..." the Hyrokkin began.

"Nor have I put limits on their stay," Daphnia continued unabated. "I've made it clear they can leave whenever they want. Right now, they choose to remain."

Thanilus stared at the Draugen Pesta princess. He'd entirely forgotten about the wolf as he wondered how the young child opposite him could be so refined. Most her age, royal or not, would still be playing with dolls and stuffed animals.

"Ah, the wine," Daphnia said as two of her Phalanx warriors, each armed to the teeth, carried from the main house trays filled with fruits, cheese, and bread, along with a decanter of wine and several goblets. "It's a meager offering, I know... but we haven't been resupplied since our arrival. The good news is several wagons of supplies should cross the border soon. You'll hasten matters, I trust?"

Thanilus poured himself a goblet of wine and nibbled on apples and cheese. He noticed the princess was drinking water. "You'll get your supplies," he said between mouthfuls. "The wine is excellent!"

Daphnia smiled. "So I've been told," she said with a nod towards Jarsus. "My parents have forbidden me from drinking alcohol."

"Aye, lassie," Jarsus remarked. "Not 'til yer sixteen. Yer

parents hae bin ferr insistent aboot that. It muddles th' mynd."

"So it does, Blackmantle," Thanilus responded. "If you can't handle it."

Jarsus smiled. "Richt ye ur, Thanilus… though A'd need tae be oot 'ere swallyin vino fur a week afore I'd hae tae worry aboot a muddled mynd."

"That must be the dwarf humor I've heard so much about," Thanilus replied.

Jarsus laughed and raised his goblet up to Thanilus. "Mibbie someday I'll prove it tae ye."

"Don't doubt that he will, Thanilus," Daphnia said. "Now, if I may, I'd like to get back to our business at hand."

Thanilus nodded. "As you wish, Princess. I repeat my request that Prince Dardandros come with me. As for the queen's Shield Maidens…" Thanilus shrugged. "Well, I have no actual interest in them. They failed in their duty to protect the queen from assassination. As far as I'm concerned, they should each fall on their swords."

"As I understand it, the queen ordered them outside my compound to protect me from any… wrongdoing," Daphnia remarked. "Not that I needed protecting by them. As you can see, I'm quite secure."

"Aye, she is, Thanilus," Jarsus said. "You hae na idea juist howfur protected. Bit ah hae tae wonder… juist wha wis it that advised th' queen tae send her Shield Maidens 'ere in th' foremaist steid?"

"Insinuating what, dwarf?" Thanilus angrily replied.

"You very weel ken whit I'm insinuating!" Jarsus answered just as angrily.

Shubin held up his hands. "Gentlemen! Calm yourselves!"

If the dwarf and the centaur had anything else to say, they kept it to themselves.

"Thank you, Shubin," Daphnia said. "As I said, Thanilus, your prince is more than welcome to return with you. I'm not holding him against his will. But he's chosen not to. He's been very specific regarding that. We in Draugen Pesta don't like to force someone to do something against their will. Well, except for paying taxes… or if the person is a prisoner… or in the military…"

"There are exceptions to every rule, Your Grace," Shubin said to the princess. Then he turned his attention to the Hyrokkin leader. "This is not one of those exceptions, Lord Thanilus."

"I'm afraid I must insist," Thanilus countered. "He's a Hyrokkin, and you have no jurisdiction over him. Nor does my request go against the peace accords."

"If I may, Your Grace," Shubin inquired.

Daphnia nodded. While she'd received training in diplomacy, Shubin was a master. It was a good time to watch and learn.

"Is Prince Dardandros a criminal?" Shubin asked Thanilus.

"No… at least not at the moment, though he and his companion ran from my guards," Thanilus answered.

"It's our understanding that someone tried to kill him," Shubin responded. "At least that's what he told us."

"And you think it was me?" Thanilus shouted.

"Of course not," Shubin returned while thinking the angry response was a bit over-played. He suspected the Hyrokkin before him was at least partially responsible, which didn't surprise him in the least. "But given the circumstances of his mother's death along with the attempt upon his own life at the monastery, you can understand his reluctance to turn himself in to your guards."

Thanilus seethed with false anger. "That was the dwarf who killed the queen," he insisted. "Who sits here at this very table as free as you or me because of political convenience. It's a damned insult to the entire Hyrokkin Empire, though I've chosen to ignore it for the sake of the peace."

Jarsus shook his head but refused to get riled up. "Everyone aroond th' table kens th' truth, Thanilus. And that's nae it!"

"Indeed," Shubin remarked in support of the dwarf. "Just as everyone around this table knows why you excepted the peace accords… and what happens if you decide to break it." Shubin paused to let his words sink in. "Let's be frank about things, shall we? You don't get Prince Dardandros… unless he decides of his own free will to go with you. Any attempt to take him by force will break the peace and be met with force here, as well as overwhelming force at the border."

"You'd invade over this… this internal matter that doesn't even concern you?" Thanilus asked. "You'd give up the peace?"

"And you'd lose your daily fix of Epiphany over this?" Shubin countered.

Thanilus pulled back as if Shubin had slapped him across the face. "How dare you!"

Shubin remained unfazed. "If we're going to have this discussion, we're going to put everything out on the table. We know you're addicted to the drug. We also know that you're making a substantial profit selling the drug to your people. Tell me, is that profit why peace with Draugen Pesta is acceptable to your military? Or are your generals addicted as well?"

Thanilus didn't say a word. But if looks could kill, Shubin would be dead.

"And I suspect that's the real reason behind your invasion several months ago," the Draugen Pesta diplomat continued. "To gain control of the Bael trees, though your dead queen probably didn't recognize that part of the plan when she gave her authorization."

"She certainly did not," Daphnia agreed. "Queen Thesonia told me as much during the state dinner she hosted for us. She wanted access to food for her starving people. Too bad she got faulty advice on how to go about getting it."

"Still, we almost succeeded!" Thanilus insisted.

"You were never going to be successful," Shubin stated. "If our king hadn't had half our armies west on the other side of the Boreskyre's, you wouldn't have gotten past Dragon Pass."

The centaur leader took a drink of wine as he gathered his thoughts. "May we return to the matter at hand? At least let me hear from Dardandros's own mouth. Grant me that."

"You're nae believing th' Princess, laddie?" Jarsus asked. "She said Dardandros doesn't wantae gang wi' ye. Anyway, dae ye think we'd be gowk enough tae let him shaw his-sel oot in th' open sae ye kin shoot him wi' an arrow or bolt? Ur ye dunderheided?"

"Jarsus is correct... he doesn't want to see you, much less go with you," Daphnia reiterated. "That you heard this from me is the only proof you need."

Thanilus shook his head. "Not really satisfactory... but I'm forced to accept it for the sake of the peace."

"Ye mean th' drugs, don't ye, laddie?" Jarsus corrected.

Thanilus ignored the dwarf. "Have it your way, Princess. We'll do this officially. Please inform Dardandros and his companion they're both exiled from Hyrokkin. They have two days to leave our borders. The penalty if they're captured after two days is death. That's the law here, and that means it's my right within the parameters of the peace."

"Is that true?" Daphnia asked Shubin. "Is it within the peace accords?"

The diplomat nodded. "There's nothing in the peace to indicate we can interfere with their jurisdictional processes. After two days, if they take as much as one step outside our walls, they're fair game for bounty hunters, law enforcement officers, or even common citizens."

"The arrest warrants will be dead or alive," Thanilus added. "They'll also offer a significant bounty."

"Ah don't lik' ye, centaur," Jarsus remarked.

"I don't care what you like, dwarf," Thanilus replied before turning his attention back to the princess and Shubin. "You should probably know that if he decides to leave within the two day deadline, I can't ensure his safety outside this compound."

"And why not!" Daphnia demanded.

The centaur smiled. "Grimsturm's a big city with more than its share of hooligans and rogues. We do the best we can to maintain the law..." Thanilus shrugged. "But you know how it goes. You just can't control one hundred percent of the population at all times. Someone with a grievance against the queen might find her son a reasonable substitute for violence. Or maybe someone not quite in their right mind takes a pot shot. It's a shame, but you never know. Of course, if something were to happen to him... say an arrow in the gut... we'd vigorously pursue and punish the offender to the fullest extent of the law. That much I *can* guarantee."

Daphnia and her entourage watched as the centaur stood, turned away from the table without another word, and strode out of the embassy.

"What do you think?" the Draugan Pesta princess asked.

"The eejit admitted he's aff tae huv a go 'n' hae Dardandros murdurred at th' foremaist opportunity," Jarsus said as sipped from his wine. "And he set it up sae that th' peace won't be goosed 'n' th' drugs wull keep flowing."

Shubin nodded. "Blackmantle's right, Your Grace. One way or the other, Thanilus is determined to see Dardandros in his grave."

"Perhaps we can sneak Dardandros and Theodasius out on the return trip of our incoming supply wagons?" Daphnia speculated.

"They're probably expecting that," Major Romanova commented.

"Ye be richt, Anya," Jarsus said.

"What about a magical solution?" Shubin asked. "Maybe we can have one of Anya's Phalanx sorcerers open a doorway back to Draugen Pesta for the two Hyrokkin to go through?"

Daphnia shook her head. "Anya and I have already discussed that. According to Anya's sorcerers, it won't work for two reasons. The ley lines above us are too weak and the Hyrokkin have placed some type of magical restrictions on us. Mother has confirmed the information concerning the ley lines. She also said that even if we were free of the Hyrokkin's magical meddling, any attempt to use the ley lines would have dire consequences."

"A've clocked that as well," Jarsus commented.

"You noticed it?" Shubin remarked skeptically.

"Jarsus is a full-fledged sorcerer in his own right," Daphnia said.

Jarsus nodded. "Aye, lassie. Th' Hyrokkin hae us locked doon tight... at least in th' magic department."

"Can't you break it?" Shubin asked.

Jarsus shook his head. "Under normal conditions, sure... except th' conditions aren't normal. Hyrokkin's ley lines ur aboot as puny as A've ever seen. Bit they've learned ower time howfur tae mak' th' maist o' it. One o' th' hings they're pure guid at is manipulating they ley lines. They've fun a wey tae boost power or reduce it... clever wee buggers... 'n' ah kin tell ye th' ley lines gaun ower th' compound aren't pure tough enough. At least fur that level o' magic. Think o' a water slowing doon 'n' then speedin' back up again. It's th' slowing doon that's ower us. There's wee ah kin dae aboot that."

"How about the combined strength of all our sorcerers?" Shubin suggested.

"Good thought bit aye nae powerful enough tae break th' stranglehold th' Hyrokkin hae ower th' ley lines," Jarsus replied. "A've looked at this up, doon, 'n' fae side tae side. It can't be done. Even if it cuid, as th' Queenie said, it'd be tae dangerous."

A shroud of silence dropped over the group as each

thought about the dilemma of the two Hyrokkin.

"Let me send th' Lads," Jarsus suggested. "They'll set hings richt. Or better aye, send that stoatin wolf o' yours. Adimar wouldn't even hae tae dae anythin' bit let th' centaur git a guid glimpse o' him. He'd fall ower deid in fright."

"We can't do either, my friend, even if we wanted to," Daphnia said. "Let's take this inside. We need to talk with our centaur guests before we come to any conclusions or develop plans. They might have a few ideas. Can't do much without their approval, anyway."

Jarsus shrugged. "We cuid aye juist kick thaim oot, lassie."

The Draugen Pasta princess didn't bother to respond.

That evening when Daphnia retired to her room to call her mother, she found her communications crystal had exploded. Someone had overloaded it. Without delay, she sent Adimar to retrieve Jarsus. He'd figure out what was going on.

"All richt, wolf, A'm hurrying as fleet as mah legs kin carry me!" Daphnia heard Jarsus yelling long before her door guards opened the door to allow him entry. Sienna followed him into the room a few moments later. "Daphnia, what's sae god's awfy important ah hae tae be pushed by that wolf o' yours!"

Daphnia said nothing. She pointed at the wreck of a table with a large black smudge on it. A burned out communications crystal was lying next to it.

The dwarf went over to the overturned table and picked up the blackened husk from the floor. "Overloaded," he declared as he turned it over and over to inspect it. "Did ye lea it activated, lassie?"

Daphnia shook her head. "I'd never be so careless."

"Thae hings aren't known tae activate themselves," the dwarf said. "Does a'body else ken th' activation sequence fur this crystal?"

Again, Daphnia shook her head. "Not here. Mother and father do."

"Weel, someone turned it oan! It mist hae bin thro' magic. By th' gods, if ye wur close by whin it exploded, it cuid hae blown yer heid aff! Ye cuid hae bin murdurred!" Jarsus again looked at the burned out crystal. "Do ye hae a spare?"

The princess went over to her bed, grabbed a leather travel sack from underneath, and rummaged around until she brought out a small box, which she handed to Jarsus. Inside was another communications crystal, which at first glance looked intact.

"Staun back 'n' activate it," Jarsus said. The crystal worked as it should.

The Draugen Pesta queen answered almost at once. *"Daphnia?"*

"No, Queenie, it's me, Jarsus Blackmantle," the dwarf replied. "Don't be worried. Yer wee lassie is braw 'n' sittin' neist tae me."

"Hi, mother," Daphnia called.

"Why is the dwarf calling me?" Sofia asked.

Daphnia looked at Jarsus and frowned.

"We were testing my backup crystal," Daphnia said. "We didn't think you'd be so quick to answer."

"What's wrong with the other?" the queen demanded.

The princess looked at Jarsus and nodded. "The foremaist crystal overloaded," the dwarf said. "Efter talking tae Daphnia aboot it, I think it kin hae bin a result o' sabotage."

There was silence on the other end.

"Are you there, mother?" Daphnia asked.

"I'm here," Sofia said. *"Sabotage, Blackmantle? You think someone's trying to kill my daughter?"* There was a pause. *"An overloaded crystal explosion can be serious if you're close enough, and Daphnia knows that. She wouldn't have forgotten to turn it off."*

"Now don't ye fret..."

"Don't I fret!" the queen screamed. *"Don't I fret! I'm holding*

you personally responsible for the safety of my daughter, you mangy dwarf. If it was sabotage, find out the particulars and then act upon it. Do not... I repeat... do not spare the rod! Take whatever action is required short of breaking the peace. I want to know if that's necessary first. Is that understood?"

"Ye don't hae tae worry oan that accoont, Queenie," Jarsus replied. "Daphnia's lik' mah ain daughter. A'd die afore ah let anythin' happen tae her."

"Yes you will!"

"Don't coddle me, mother," Daphnia warned.

"Or what?" the queen asked. *"You'll throw a temper tantrum? You'll hold your breath?"*

"Mother!" Daphnia cried out.

Both Daphnia and Jarsus heard a sigh on the other end. *"I'm sorry, sweetheart. I know you're not just any child, that you've been educated and trained like no other, and that you're more capable than most adults. But that's not the point. It never has been. You're the very future of Draugen Pesta. Your father and I are willing to risk everything to keep you safe. And right now, it appears someone close to you in that Hyrokkin snake pit we've sent you to is trying to strike. Now, tell me everything that's happened since our last conversation."*

Jarsus sat in a chair in one corner of Daphnia's room while the princess briefed her mother on the events of the last twenty-four hours. Sienna and Adimar hadn't moved from their position and still blocked the door into the room. The conversation between mother and daughter dragged on for what seemed like hours, and Jarsus soon lost interest. He was there. He knew everything that had happened. Instead, he let his mind wander to the question of the overloaded communications crystal... specifically, who or what caused it to overload?

"If Daphnia hadn't unintentionally left it oan," he thought, *"then someone deliberately overloaded it. Bit howfur? Besides*

th' Princess, ainlie her mither or faither cuid activate it. Th' logical conclusion wis Daphnia hud left th' crystal activated instead o' shutting it aff efter her lest blether wi' th' Queenie. Bit that wid be oot o' character fur th' Princess. Her mither wis right... Daphnia wasn't lik' ordinar bairns. She wis gey diligent aboot sic matters... almost tae th' point o' obsession. She understaun howfur neglected wee hings cuid add up tae muckle larger 'n' dangerous hings. Fur th' sake o' argument, let's rule oot an accidental overload. Sae 'twas intentional. Either someone did it thro' magic or discovered whit th' activation sequence wis, snuck bygane twa brawny guards 'n' intae th' room, 'n' turned it on."

"My foremaist assumption wis wrong... thought o' in th' heat o' th' moment. No one could've known whin th' wee lassie wid be in th' room fur it tae be an assassination attempt. It mist be either a warning or a message. But how come? 'N' who would've dane it? Who could've dane it? Who'd wantae warn her aff or send her a message? Shubin or one o' his aides? Major Romanova? One o' th' Phalanx warriors?"

Jarsus shook his head. While they couldn't be one hundred percent eliminated, he doubted any of those had anything to do with it. Everyone in Daphnia's Phalanx was devoted to her. And Jarsus knew for a fact that Lord Ternborg ensured his sorcerers performed magical invocations to test each one's loyalty. They'd not be in the Phalanx if they hadn't passed. As for Shubin... Jarsus had known him for quite some time. They teased each other brutally on occasion, but behind that façade was a long-lasting friendship. Shubin's dedication to the royal family was beyond question. And Shubin would've made sure those working for him were as well.

"That leaves Dardandros, Theodasius, 'n' Galissa or yin o' her warriors. Dardandros doesn't seem tae fit th' profile o' assassin or saboteur. Everything we ken aboot him matches up wi' whit th' Hyrokkin deid queen hud said at th' banquet... 'n' there's na

quaistion Thanilus wants him deid, sae how come wid he waant his yin benefactor harmed? As fur Theodasius, a' we ken is that Dardandros haes vouched fur him. Galissa?" Jarsus shook his head. *"Possible, ah suppose. Bit ah ken her type. Th' identical as th' Phalanx. Devotion 'n' honor ur foremost tae them."*

"Then again, mibbie none ur wha thay claim tae be 'n' planted in th' compound by Thanilus. Mibbie th' 'heir seeking refuge' narrative is juist a story tae git in? Ur th' Hyrokkin stupid enough tae huv a go at assassinating th' Princess? Or whit wid thay be trying tae warn th' Princess aboot? Either wey, thay likelie shuid go."

Jarsus sighed. "Ah don't ken whit tae think," he said aloud. "Mibbie we let centaur assassins wi'in oor midst. It'd be juist lik' they four-legged, dung-sniffing, goblin kissers tae advertise thair intentions lik' this!"

"Blackmantle," Sofia said to no response. *"Blackmantle!"* The queen was more insistent the second time.

The dwarf heard his name being called by the queen through the crystal. He shook his head to clear his thoughts. "I'm richt 'ere, Queenie."

"As I said earlier, I'm holding you personally responsible for the safety of my daughter."

"Ah tak' yer point," Jarsus replied. "But don't ye worry yer bonny wee heid, Queenie. Forby me, there's a stoatin muckle wolf 'n' a hail Phalanx guarding her. 'N' don't ye forgoat th' Lads. We'll keep her safe."

Sofia shivered as she remembered her encounter with the Lads. *"She might be even safer than I,"* the queen thought. Aloud: *"Even so, should harm befall Daphnia, don't bother to come back. Tell that to everyone else! And keep me informed!"* The queen broke contact.

Jarsus shook his head. "Yer mither has a richt tae be worried."

Daphnia looked at her friend. "You're scaring me."

"Don't worry, bairn," Jarsus replied. "Ye'll be safe enough. Let's fin' Anya 'n' Shubin sae ah kin explain mah suspicions."

A knife, one of several always carried by the Draugen Pesta queen, buried itself into the wooden mantle above the fireplace in her private chamber.

"Damnit!" Sofia swore. "I don't know who to string up first… the Hyrokkin for being the Hyrokkin, or my husband for putting my daughter there in the first place."

CHAPTER NINETEEN

The Abyss

Belladonna wasn't wrong about being thrust from the frying pan and into Kor's fire. The road west was full of Kor's warriors, all heading in the same direction. It was impossible to avoid them. But it wasn't until the third day that Braz'galar saw the first signs they were being followed.

"There are those whom I suspect know our identity trailing behind us," Braz'galar announced to Belladonna and Trozzan.

"What're we going to do?" Belladonna asked.

Trozzan smiled. "We're going to get lost in the hustle and bustle. Watch and learn."

Braz'galar's small party mixed itself in with a much larger group of soldiers, easily done since there were so many on the way to the western front. Now and then they'd leave the road and blend in with whatever background provided cover—trees, small towns and villages, tall grass, and the like. After a day of playing cat and mouse, both Braz'galar and Trozzan agreed they'd lost their pursuers. But while the common warrior had no particular interest in them beyond basic camaraderie around a campfire, Braz'galar knew they still couldn't let their guard down. After several more days of traveling with no other signs of being followed, they reached the western-most city of Mar Koozzath, where they made their way to one of Braz'galar's safe-houses.

Belladonna plopped herself down on the first available hide-covered chair in the main room. "Water, please," she said to the house servant who had appeared by her side. "Then a bath, if that can be arranged."

"Yes, ma'am," the female demon said before scurrying away.

Braz'galar went into another part of the house with Trozzan and three other demons who had been waiting for him in the safe-house.

"I assume you'd like a look-see from the ramparts, Braz'galar?" one demon asked.

Braz'galar nodded. "Yes, Ral'gorith... but later. I could use a quick nap after our meeting. Have you been out and about? Any rumors regarding Belladonna and myself?"

"None that we've heard," another demon named Troramal answered. "Meg'thannes and I spent most of the morning speaking with soldiers in taverns and inns. Nothing concerning either of you."

"Most of the chatter's about how the *B'nai Elohim* are dying..." Meg'thannes, a female demon, was saying when Braz'galar stopped her.

"We heard rumors on the road, but most of them were just scuttlebutt between the troops," Braz'galar said. "Has it been verified, Meg?"

Meg'thannes nodded. "Verified it myself. Actually saw one hit the ground on this side of their fortress. It was mostly dead by then, but still killed a dozen soldiers before falling for the last time. Still hard to believe something that fierce could be brought down in the first place."

"A sign of the times," Braz'galar remarked as he looked at the diminutive female. She was without doubt the best rogue he'd ever known, and he'd known quite a few over his lifetime. Her lithe body was built for speed and stealth, and she was smart—very smart. So when she said she'd done something, regardless of how impossible it seemed, she was telling the truth. And that was another thing about her. She never lied. Braz'galar had become fond of her over the years. He'd ask her to go back with him to Zhaarmoth when his business here was concluded. For as valuable as she was to him traveling the Abyss and gathering intelligence, her safety was even more important.

A few hours later Braz'galar, Belladonna, Trozzan, Ral'gorith, Troramal, and Meg'thannes had found a perch in one of the taller belltowers of Mar Koozzath. The belltower gave them a three hundred and sixty degree view of the land surrounding the city. To the west, steep hills led to the *B'nai Elohim* fortress. As they watched, demon warriors climbed those hills. Every few minutes there'd be a bright light on the horizon followed by the rumble of an explosion accompanied by dead demon body parts which flew through the air and landed at the base of the hill. Many of those body parts were jagged and sharp enough to impale any demon unlucky enough to be caught in the downward trajectory. To the north, south, and east were open fields with row upon row of demon warriors standing in formation, waiting for their turn to assault the fortress.

"It almost looks as if Kor's using every demon warrior he's got for this," Belladonna remarked.

"The *B'nai Elohim* are dying," Trozzan said. "This could be an opportunity of a lifetime for him. I'd be doing the same."

"Too bad the resistance is gone," Meg'thannes remarked. "They'd probably have no problem taking over a few cities right now."

"Not sure the guilds would allow it," Ral'gorith commented.

"I'll be damned!" Braz'galar suddenly exclaimed. He was using a spyglass and looking to the northeast. "That's Kor! He's here. And it looks like he has his own army."

"What's he doing?" Belladonna asked.

Braz'galar handed the spyglass over to her. "See for yourself. But I suspect getting ready to invade Aster. There's no other answer. My guess is they're only waiting for the Juxtaposition Point to fall for good."

"What do you want to do, boss?" Trozzan asked.

Braz'galar looked out over the demon armies as he thought

about Trozzan's question. He could see several sorcerers circled around Kor, using a strong ley line to weave protective magic over him. There was no way he'd ever get close to the Prefecture leader, even with long ranged magic. If he was going to kill Kor, he'd need the help of the *B'nai Elohim*. "I, for one, don't believe our invasion of Aster will be a good thing in the long run. I intend to find my way to the *B'nai Elohim* and offer my services."

"As will I," Belladonna said unexpectedly.

Braz'galar grabbed her hand and squeezed. Belladonna squeezed his in return. He then turned to Trozzan. "But this isn't something I'm comfortable asking you to do as well. Follow me if you will... or not. It must be your decision. I'll think none the less of you."

"Oh, I think me and the boys will go with you, boss," Trozzan announced. "We've gotten pretty attached to you over the years."

"I'm going too, Braz'galar," Meg'thannes declared.

"Ral'gorith?" Trozzan asked. "Troramal?"

"Huh? Oh, sure, we're going," Ral'gorith answered for both. "Just thinking about someone who I know that might be of some use. He's as big as a small mountain and no one... I mean no one... dares bother him. Not even army jerks."

"I know of him," Meg said. "If it comes to hand-to-hand fighting, he'll be invaluable."

"Sounds like a good match," Braz'galar said.

Ral'gorith nodded. "Oh, yeah, he is. Except he doesn't work for you, Braz'galar, and I'm not too sure how you feel about that. Plus... well, he's a little on the stupid side. He may be smarter than a rock, but only if you give him the benefit of the doubt."

"I don't need brains over brawn," Braz'galar said. "We've got enough of that." The fixer pulled a kronie out of his money pouch and handed it to Ral'gorith. "Put your small mountain on the payroll. We leave for the fortress in four hours."

"How are we going to get in without getting killed?" Belladonna asked.

Braz'galar shook his head. "I'm not sure. Guess we'll just knock on the front door and hope for the best."

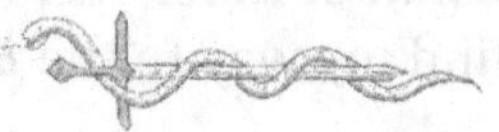

Ashryn, like most of the other demon warriors in Kor's army, waited for her chance to assault the fortress of the dreaded *B'nai Elohim*. As she waited, she and her fellow demons could talk of one thing only. The guardians of the mortal world were dropping out of the sky. In all of history, no demon had ever killed one of the winged fiends. But now they were falling under the claws, bites, swords, and magic of demonkind, and she'd be part of it. It promised to be a grand adventure!

Ashryn was young by demon standards—only two hundred and seven Abyssian years old. And like every other demon in her lineage, which goes back several generations, she was a warrior through and through. Her father and his father before him had trained her for years and years. The training was both physical and mental. She dedicated her whole life to fighting threats to the Prefecture leader, Lord Kor.

But despite Ashryn's training, her consummate skill with different weapons, her ability to understand tactics and apply them on the battlefield, her knack for operating independently, and her ability to improvise when necessary to carry out orders… one thing held her back. She was small. Too small by far to be on the front lines of battle. Measuring just under six feet tall, her fellow demon soldiers, on average, stood closer to nine feet. No measure of skill or bravery would make up for her diminutive stature in the eyes of her peers or her superiors. They'd never consider her for more than messenger duty.

But an irresistible call to glory pulled at Ashryn. She was determined to prove herself once and for all. She decided she'd abandon her messenger duties the first chance she got and face off against a guardian. Maybe if she brought back the head of one, she'd get the credit she felt she deserved. More importantly, she'd make her family, and the families of her ancestors, proud.

But once she found herself in battle, the haze of combat overcame Ashryn's self-determination to battle the enemy. After her unit had ascended the hill and reached the top, things quickly got out of hand. The *B'nai Elohim* were behind the huge walls of their fortress, along with another race of warriors she'd never seen before. The battlements on top of those walls provided the enemy exceptional cover from demon arrows, spears, and sorcerer magic. Any attempt to flank the fortification was impossible because of the *Veil*. The bodies of thousands of her brethren lay at the base of the wall.

The small plain between the top of the hill and the wall was full of craters caused by the explosions of *B'nai Elohim* magic. Attacking demons had to run over a field of blood, entrails, and the body parts of those who had gone before. The sight and smell of the slaughter that took place, was still taking place, made Ashryn retch.

But the worst sights Ashryn witnessed occurred when the explosions ceased. For that's when waves of *B'nai Elohim* flew out from the fortress and over the field. Some of the *B'nai Elohim* would conjure magic that exploded in the demon's midst, leaving behind more dead demons and dense smoke. Others selected demon commanders and messengers, drop under the cover of the smoke, grab them, and fly straight up until they were only specks in the sky. The bodies of falling demons became another hazard on the battlefield. But coming so close to the ground to snatch up commanders and messengers made the *B'nai Elohim* vulnerable to attack, though Ashryn knew why they took the risk. They sought to destroy her army's command and control, forcing individual demons to act on their own initiative, which was something few were intelligent enough to do. Fortunately, there were far more commanders and messengers than there were *B'nai Elohim*. Though doomed to failure—they'd need to destroy Kor himself to end the attack—it was an effective short-term strategy.

Ashryn didn't have to wait long for her first mission. Amid loud explosions and the sound of dying demons, her division commander shouted for her to make her way to their left flank and order the battalion commander to move in from the perimeter for a more frontal assault.

"Tell him to get his arse closer to the center!" the division commander ordered. "We attack within the hour!"

As Ashryn ran over the battlefield, she caught a closer look at the death and destruction wrought by the *B'nai Elohim*. She heard the wretched crying of the injured and saw demons scooping up their entrails to put them back into their bodies as their faces contorted in agony. She saw looks of fear as demons tried to stave off the bleeding that came from missing limbs or large rips in their bodies. She saw demons torn to pieces by explosions.

It was too much for the young messenger. She stopped running and looked around her while crying uncontrollably. What she saw, what she smelled, and what she heard were incomprehensible. Suddenly she understood the true consequences of war and wondered when, or if, it was ever worth all the pain and suffering.

Ashryn then remembered she still had a role in whatever grand design was being played out. There was a message to be delivered. She fought through her melancholy and tears as she ran again. She didn't see the bloody intestines on the ground until it was too late. Ashryn slipped and fell hard on top of a corpse. When she raised her head, she was looking directly into the open eyes of one of the dead. Flying bone had sheared off half of its skull just above the eyebrows. Gray brain matter ran down its nose and into its open mouth and over its ears. Other than that, there wasn't a mark on the body. The tumble, however, saved her life.

There was an explosion off to her side. Ashryn's instincts drove her to take cover on the opposite side of the body as shrapnel-like bones whizzed all around. She felt her shield of flesh and blood shudder under the weight of each fragment impact. The sound of the explosion was still ringing in her ears when she tried to stand to continue her mission. But the sudden movement brought on a dizziness which threatened to overwhelm her. The last thing she wanted to do was lose consciousness on a battlefield. She closed her eyes tight and lowered her head in a futile attempt to keep the darkness at bay. The next thing she remembered seeing was the face of a female overlord before she passed out again.

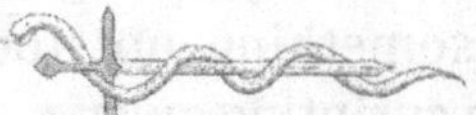

Getting to the top of the hill was easy enough for Braz'galar, Belladonna, and the rest. The demon army commanders were too busy trying to win a war, and the demon warriors were too busy trying to stay alive to worry about a group of fugitives running from Kor's justice. They made the climb up the hill without challenge. Once there, however, both Braz'galar and Belladonna knew a straight approach toward the fortress would be much like kissing the *Pillar*. Either was a death sentence.

"What do you think?" Braz'galar asked Belladonna.

There was a sudden explosion and everyone dropped to the ground.

Belladonna looked around the battlefield as they regained

their feet. The surrounding warriors were beating their chests and shouting war cries.

"Looks as if they're gearing up for another charge right up the center," Belladonna observed. "And that's where the *B'nai Elohim* will concentrate their firepower. I think we need to go to the left and hug the *Veil* to the fortress."

Braz'galar looked to the left and then the right. "I like it. Let's go back down the hill, at least enough for cover from more explosions, and move left."

When they came back over the apex of the hill, the attack on the center was ongoing. *B'nai Elohim* warriors were flying over the attacking army in groups of twenty or more. Some were casting destructive magic which blew entire swathes of demons into scraps of flesh and bone, while others dropped and went back up with struggling demons clutched in their talons... demons who were later dropped back onto the battlefield like bombs. But very little attention was being given to the extreme flanks of the battlefield.

As they made their way along the edge of the *Veil*, Belladonna noticed something not too far away. "Be right back," she said before sprinting away.

Braz'galar told Trozzan to keep moving and ran after Belladonna. By the time he reached her, she was kneeling over the body of a young female demon, a messenger from the looks of her uniform. Both of the youngster's feet were gone at the ankle from an apparent explosion, and what it left of her legs lie in a pool of blood.

"We don't have time for the dead," Braz'galar said as he put a hand on Belladonna's shoulder.

"She's not dead," Belladonna replied. "She breathes still and opened her eyes."

"She's just a wisp of a child," Braz'galar said as he knelt next to his companion and felt the injured demon's pulse. It was barely there. "She'll be dead soon enough."

"I can save her," Belladonna answered as she began a healing spell to stop the bleeding.

"Why would you?" Braz'galar asked. "She's one of thousands littering the ground. She choose her profession and paid the price. Let it go."

"You said it yourself... she's just a child," Belladonna protested. "She's not the same as the others."

Braz'galar studied his companion's desperate attempt to save the army messenger. "What's the real reason? Do you know her? Does she remind you of someone you once knew? Perhaps *you* at her age? Let her die in peace. It's an honorable end for a warrior. We've got to move."

Though Belladonna had stopped the bleeding, she knew her help may have come too late. An impossibly large amount of blood had already soaked the ground. The child needed a soft bed, a trained healer, and, most importantly, a second chance.

Belladonna looked up at Braz'galar. "Do you even see the horror in what's happening here?" she asked. "Open your eyes and take a good look around, Braz'galar. She's like a flower in a field of dung... a speck of beauty surrounded by ugliness."

"You're making a rather large assumption," Braz'galar commented. "I doubt she's any different from all the other soldiers on this field... seeking glory and a chance to kill one of the *B'nai Elohim*."

"What choice did she have?" Belladonna countered. "Her entire life they've trained her to kill Kor's enemies."

"And no doubt cruelty was part of that training," Braz'galar responded. "This 'flower' could be no more different from Kor's other killing machines. Leave her to the death beetles and carrion eaters like the rest of her companions."

Belladonna shook her head. "I understand what you're saying, Braz'galar, really I do. But I have a feeling about this one. I think she's redeemable. I think she deserves an opportunity to live a life of peace… a life minus the brutality she probably experiences every day. You say you love me. Give me this one."

Braz'galar sighed and looked over at the rest of his group. Trozzan was waving frantically for them to return. He looked back at Belladonna, who was applying makeshift bandages to both of the child's stumps. "Yes, I love you, but…"

At that moment, the child opened her eyes. She had the most beautiful emerald-green colored eyes Braz'galar had ever seen, despite being filled with pain and fear.

"What's your name," Braz'galar asked.

"Ashryn," the child answered as she raised her head slightly and watched for a few moments as Belladonna covered what remained of her legs. "A messenger with no feet," Ashryn said as she laid her head back down. "That's going to go over well with the brigade commanders."

Braz'galar looked at Ashryn as he chuckled at her remark. Suddenly, he thought Belladonna might be right. "You have to make it off this battlefield alive before you need to worry about that."

Ashryn looked up. Fear glinted in her pain-filled eyes. "I don't want to die."

"Kor wants you too," Braz'galar said. "Or should I say, he doesn't care one way or the other?"

The messenger winced as Belladonna tightened the strips of cloth covering her injuries. "You're both overlords," she said. "You could…" Ashryn closed her eyes as tears ran down her cheeks. "Why do you help? I'm just a lowly messenger."

Belladonna moved from the child's legs to look into her the eyes. "You have magnificent looking eyes. Has anyone ever told you that?"

Ashryn shook her head.

"Someone should have," Belladonna continued. "How's your pain?"

"I can manage," Ashryn remarked.

Belladonna looked at Braz'galar, who nodded and scooped the young demon up into his arms.

"You're going with us," Belladonna said. But Ashryn didn't hear the overlord. She was unconscious once again.

Michael, Gabrielle, Lord Ternborg, his First Phalanx commander, General Angelica Gargarin, and his executive officer Colonel Florentina Antonovich were meeting in Michael's study on the status of the demon war. Gabrielle had the floor and her news wasn't good.

"There's been no real threat to the walls yet," Michael's second-in-command said. "But while we've killed thousands, tens of thousands are waiting below the hill for their turn to attack. More worrisome is the enemy is organizing all their winged demons into a singular attack force."

"Strength?" Michael interrupted.

"At least a battalion," Gabriella answered.

Lord Ternborg shook his head. "That's going to be a problem. Especially if they use their magic to bombard us from the sky."

Michael nodded. "To put it mildly. But we'll be able to provide enough cover. At least I believe so."

"You're going to be outnumbered… by a lot," the Draugen Pesta king remarked.

"Even in our current state, one of my warriors is worth ten of theirs," Michael responded.

"But you can't replace your losses," Colonel Antonovich mentioned. "They can with ease."

Michael nodded. "No one's more painfully aware of that than I. Please continue, Gabriella."

"Kor himself is out there and not within the walls of his city," Gabriella said. "From what our intelligence is telling us, he's putting together an entire army of his more experienced and vicious warriors. We're not sure of his intentions but believe it's to attack Aster now that they've compromised the Juxtaposition Point."

"He'll need more than an army to take Aster," General Gargarin observed. "Please consider... to be victorious, we don't have to actually win here."

"Meaning?" Lord Ternborg asked.

"I know the destruction of the Juxtaposition Point puts us at a tremendous disadvantage," General Gargarin said. "But as long as we fight, we're draining Kor's resources and making it less likely he can reinforce the Aster invasion with significant numbers. And without those numbers, he can't win... at least not with only one army. My people, the Hyrokkin, the humans, the dwarves, and even the elves, will come together to stop him."

"So you see it as a numbers game, General?" Gabriella said.

"Angelica's right," Lord Ternborg answered for his general. "If you look at it that way, it *is* a numbers game. And it makes perfect sense. I think it's time to consider doing more than just defending the fortress. We need to get emissaries to the humans, dwarves, and the elves, so they're prepared to defend Aster. Even the Hyrokkin if they'd be willing... though things are tentative with them right now. As for here, our only job should be to kill demon warriors. As many as we can. All of them if necessary. No quarter given. You also mentioned demons willing to overthrow Kor? We can definitely use that to our advantage. Maybe we should look into inciting a few riots in the cities. No leader wants trouble at home while he's making trouble somewhere else."

Michael shook his head. "No riots. The guilds won't go for that. But they might be willing to go on strike if convinced. You'd be surprised how much influence they have over their overlord masters. But it won't be an easy sell... and they can't know we're behind it."

"The *B'nai Elohim* do not play roles in domestic politics," Gabriella reminded her leader. "It's unheard of."

"So is the loss of the Johari and from that, the Juxtaposition Point," Michael said in rebuttal to his second-in-command. "We just need to find the right person to negotiate for us. No small feat, there. We know there was an underground resistance amongst the people, but we never discovered who their leaders were."

"There's Belladonna," Gabriella mentioned. "From all reports, she was most prominent leader of the resistance."

Michael nodded. "Ah yes, Belladonna... Nightshade's sister. But we don't know where Belladonna is or if she's even still alive. Probably not. The resistance has been crushed by Kor, with most of its leaders either killed outright or sent to the *Pillar*. There's not much of a chance Belladonna escaped that fate. We have Kor's fixer to thank for that."

"Nightshade," Lord Ternborg remarked. "I've dealt with her. She's a strange one to figure out. First, she kidnapped my daughter to force me to attack the humans. Then she started a war between the elves on InnisRos while her father brought the Dark Elves from the Svartalfheim to invade Aster. But that's not the end of it. For good measure, she helped to end the whole affair by changing sides. Even though she's now apparently working for the good, I'd still like to ring her neck. She should answer for her crimes. But who's this fixer you mentioned?"

"An overlord who does Kor's dirty work," Michael answered. "No one knows his identity, part of the reason he's so successful. He wields a tremendous amount of power... smart, wealthy, and very personable, with connections all over the Prefecture. If Kor were to have a successor, this demon would be it. Now, back to the matter at hand. I'll have our emissaries contact the guilds to gage their interest in a general strike. But don't count on it. Without a clear cut victory, I can't give them any of the assurances they'd want to go against Kor. They may even see the conquest of Aster as a good thing... something that would allow them to expand. I'll pass along any information regarding this matter as I get it. Anything else, Gabriella?"

"Casualties, Michael," Gabriella replied.

"Ah, yes," Michael sighed. "My favorite part of the briefing."

"Another twenty-seven dead, I'm afraid," Gabriella said. "On a more pleasant note, the number of our wounded has gone down... less than one hundred, and none of those serious."

"That makes almost two hundred total dead, by my count," Lord Ternborg remarked. "That's twenty percent of your total force. Two hundred *B'nai Elohim* that can never be replaced. If the Juxtaposition Point isn't restored soon, you may not have enough left to keep the peace."

"I'm well aware," Michael responded. "I want to talk to you about that after this meeting."

Lord Ternborg nodded. "Sure... we'll talk. Whatever I can do to help. But first, promise me you'll stay behind the walls, Michael. Stop sending your people out there."

"I'm having a lot of success taking out their command and control, which is making it easier for you to kill them when they reach the fortress walls," Michael countered.

The Draugen Pesta king shook his head. "The tactic is sound, except they outnumber you twenty, thirty, forty to one. They can replace the dead faster than we can kill them. Besides, we need your folks to fend off any flying attacks."

Michael looked into his wine cup and nodded. "Perhaps you're right. Gabriella, please scrub all missions outside the walls." The *B'nai Elohim* leader shook his head. "I don't enjoy playing defense. It just delays the outcome."

"That's how it might feel," General Gargarin said. "But when you consider our options, it's the smart move. And it doesn't mean we'll lose the war as a consequence. The walls of this fortress are virtually impregnable. Let the demons bash their heads against them. My warriors can hold out even if the odds *are* twenty, thirty, or forty to one."

Michael looked at General Gargarin and nodded. "Possibly," he conceded. "Though I wish we could at least sortie to stop that army Kor's taking to your world. Keeping the two separated is the purpose of our existence."

The Draugen Pesta king shrugged. "Don't beat yourself up over that. Things spiraled out of control through no fault of your own. What's done is done."

Michael looked at Lord Ternborg. "I'll provide the means for you to send your emissaries back to Aster. Coordinate with Gabriella." Michael then looked at his second and nodded before announcing the meeting was over.

Gabriella, General Gargarin, and Colonel Antonovich walked out of the room. Lord Ternborg and Michael stayed behind.

"What did you want to speak to me about that couldn't be said in the meeting?" Lord Ternborg asked.

Michael poured himself another goblet of wine. "It concerns our future together."

Lord Ternborg leaned back and crossed his arms. "Our races are forever linked. We have been ever since that incident in Dragon Pass several centuries ago. You were there, so you know better than I."

Michael nodded. "Yes... and it was I who gave the locket to Irinushka Abramovich. And we've answered your call for help many times since."

"I don't deny that," Lord Ternborg answered. "And we're grateful."

"But considering our current situation, I think we need more than gratitude," Michael said.

The Draugen Pesta king unfolded his arms and took a sip if javah. "We're here, aren't we? But I don't know if I can spare more troops... particularly in light of the upcoming demon invasion of my home world."

"That's not what I'm thinking," Michael replied in answer to Lord Ternborg's assumption.

But Lord Ternborg knew what Michael was thinking. "You want to keep some of my people over here?"

Michael nodded. "I've lost two hundred already. Who knows what the final tally will be?"

"What will it matter if the Johari, and then the Juxtaposition Point, never returns," Lord Ternborg asked. "That chokehold was the only thing that allowed you to stop demons from getting to my world. Without it, you're trying to dam up an ocean." The lord of the giants shook his head. "Perhaps your time has come. And perhaps it's time we, the people of Aster, started taking care of ourselves."

Michael was silent.

Lord Ternborg sighed. He knew he didn't have a choice. Honor demanded it. "Neither one of us knows how this is going to turn out. "But if there's still a need for our help, you have it."

Michael smiled, though it pained him to do so for many different reasons. *"The gods never had this in mind when they created the B'nai Elohim,"* he thought. To the Draugen Pesta king, he nodded. "Thank you."

"You should stay behind, My Lord," Azazael said. He, Kor, and Kor's First Consort, Emprusa, were at the head of an army of the Abyss's most feared warriors. They were sitting atop pure white Abyssian stallions, in stark contrast to the state of their blackest of black souls. "It could be dangerous. And besides, you still need to select a new Magic Faction leader..."

Kor laughed. "I don't have enough sorcerers to make a new Faction leader necessary," he said. He patted his horse's neck as it stomped the ground, displaying its anxiousness to run with the wind. "Lilitu may have betrayed me, but she showed true courage... showed some real bollocks. Still, it was stupid to challenge me."

"I believe she went mad after losing all her fellow sorcerers," Azazael remarked.

"You're probably correct," the Prefecture leader said. "No one in their right mind would've done such a thing." Kor took a deep breath. "It's a wonderful day, don't you think?"

"Yes, My Lord," Azazael responded.

"Here we are, on the precipice of a glorious victory," Kor said. "It'll be the greatest victory in our history, and I'm the one who achieved it. Defeated the *B'nai Elohim* and soon the mortal world. Me... Kor... the one hundred and... oh, I don't know... one hundred and something Prefecture ruler of the Abyss. None of my predecessors in *The Living Throne* has even come close to what I've been able to accomplish. I'll go down in history as the greatest ever. I *am* the greatest ever!"

Kor stopped talking and looked at his military leader. "Dangerous? Look out over the field. Do you see any mortal getting to me? And if one does, so what? It'll be the last thing it ever did. I'm not afraid of a little danger, Azazael. It would be quite stimulating, actually."

Azazael sighed. "Yes, My Lord."

"You stay here and complete the destruction of the *B'nai Elohim* and their mortal pawns while I win us a world. We'll have a great victory celebration... the greatest of all time. I'll grace the table with succulent mortal children roasted in nuts and herbs and slathered with the fat of strider calves. And you'll be right there by my side. How's that sound?"

Azazael knew he needed to let it go. "Yes, My Lord."

Kor smiled. "Now run along. Army sorcerers are getting

ready to open up a doorway to the mortals and I have to leave." The Prefecture leader suddenly laughed. "It's going to be grand!"

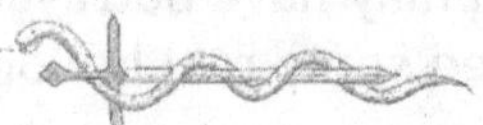

Emprusa listened to Kor boast about his victories over the *B'nai Elohim*, the mortal giants from the land of Draugen Pesta, and soon the mortal world itself. She watched and listened to the interaction between Kor and Azazel and saw anger, or was it despair, in the latter's eyes as they discussed Lilitu? And no wonder. Kor had completely changed the narrative. Though Azazael had saved him from Lilitu's betrayal, Kor didn't declare the Military Faction the hero as expected. This should've came as no surprise to anyone who knew the Prefecture leader for the creature he was.

The First Consort had taken Azazael's advice and decided not go with the army, despite Kor's wishes otherwise. And her lover, consumed as he was with the intoxicating allure of success, didn't insist, for which Emprusa was grateful. She didn't believe things on the mortal world were going to go as smooth as Kor thought. She was extremely apprehensive about the entire campaign to eliminate the *B'nai Elohim* and conquer the mortals. Did Kor think the people of Aster would just roll over and play dead? Did he think the mortals were going to be pushovers? Sure, he was taking his strongest army, but he was facing an entire world full of warriors and sorcerers who'd be fighting for their lives as well as the lives of their loved ones. Emprusa had a feeling Kor's cavalier approach to the invasion was going to lead him straight into a trap. And secretly, she hoped it led to the end of him.

"Sure you won't go with me?" Kor asked. He'd dismissed Azazael, who was riding away.

Emprusa smiled. "Though I know you'll lead our armies

to a magnificent victory, My Lord, there's no place for a weak female like myself. Besides, I must prepare your household for a great victory celebration. All the overlords will be attending..."

Kor interrupted with a laugh. "No doubt."

Emprusa smiled. "And, My Lord, as much as it pains me to say, your other consorts sometimes neglect the simple things running the household of the great Kor requires."

"I have servants for that," Kor said. "What I need from you is to run the bedroom to my satisfaction." Kor grabbed one of Emprusa's breasts. "Which you do spectacularly."

Inwardly, Emprusa winced. She wanted to knock him off his horse and have hers trample him to death. Outwardly, she fawned over his touch as expected. "I have something special planned for your triumphant return, My Lord."

Kor leered. "Hope it includes captured mortal females," he said as he kicked his horse into a trot to get closer to his army.

Emprusa watched Kor's back with hate-filled eyes as he rode away. *"I hope my sense of dread turns out to be true,"* she thought. *"I don't want him ever touching me again."*

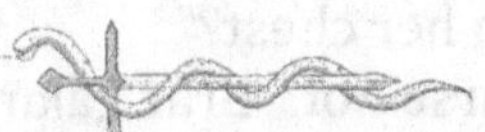

Braz'galar held the young messenger close to his chest as he raced to the fortress wall. He held her tight enough to feel her heart beating. It was racing, which concerned him. Braz'galar stopped and knelt.

"Are you okay, child?" Braz'galar asked. Ahead of him, he heard someone calling for him to "get up off your arse and hurry up!"

"Don't call me child," Ashryn insisted. "I know who you are! I know you're Kor's fixer!"

The comment surprised Braz'galar. "Who told you that?"

"I heard her call you Braz'galar," Ashryn replied. "Your name's been common knowledge since Kor put a warrant out for your arrest."

Braz'galar shook his head. "I'm not surprised," he said as he stood, still cradling the messenger in his arms. "Now try to remain calm. I'm not sure how much more your heart can take."

"Where are we going?" Ashryn asked.

"Child... Ashryn... we're going to the last place you expected when you opened your eyes this morning," Braz'galar answered.

"I expected to be dead," Ashryn said.

Braz'galar laughed. "This is going to be worse!"

Belladonna wasn't too happy with Braz'galar when he finally caught up. "That was stupidly dangerous," she commented in a low voice.

"Don't blame me," Braz'galar whispered. "Ashryn's heart was beating so fast I believed she was having a heart attack. I thought I'd better check it out."

"And what would you have done if she had been?" Belladonna said more loudly this time. "Rip open her uniform and put a bandage on her chest?"

"Well... no, of course not," Braz'galar sheepishly replied. "I would've brought her to you."

"Knock it off," Trozzan yelled. "See that?" he asked as he pointed to the battlefield before them. "Those are real explosions. We're only a hairsbreadth away from being blown to bits or knocked into the *Veil*!"

"We don't really need a reminder," Braz'galar said.

Trozzan just shook his head.

The group continued their journey along the *Veil* towards the fortress. Trozzan's earlier remark turned out to be prophetic when an explosion occurred close enough to knock four of Braz'galar's group into the *Veil* and slightly injured two others, including Meg'thannes. They made it to the base of the wall without further incident.

"Damnit!" Braz'galar yelled. "I hate losing people!"

"Now what?" Trozzan asked unemotionally. To him, death was simply the cost of doing the business they were in.

Braz'galar shook his head. "I don't know. To tell the truth, I never thought we'd make it this far. Let me think."

Braz'galar didn't have to think for too long. A door opened where there wasn't one before and twenty black-clad, black-robed giants quickly surrounded the entire group. Braz'galar and his party were disarmed, restrained, and led into the open door. The tunnel, for that's what it was, through the wall leading into the fortress interior was surprisingly long and made of rock and stone which was magically sealed.

Once inside the fortress, the passage through the wall they'd just traveled closed and looked as if it never existed. The buildings on this side of the wall were imposingly large to accommodate the size of the *B'nai Elohim*. Braz'galar, when he looked around, could only see the mortal giants. These impressive warriors surrounded them, manned the walls, and went about the business of defending the fortress as if it was theirs. They acted professionally in all respects, including their treatment of the prisoners. Their language was much the same as the demons except with heavy accents, so there was little chance of miscommunication. Healers took Ashryn from Braz'galar and at once began the work of healing her bloody stumps while others inspected the minor injuries of those affected by explosions. As that was being done, the guards encouraged the rest to sit and rest. After a few minutes, food, and water were brought out. Braz'galar didn't get his first look at one of the *B'nai Elohim* until thirty minutes later.

Except for demon sorcerers trying to open doorways to the mortal world from the Abyss, most demons have never seen a *B'nai Elohim* up close. Braz'galar had caught glimpses of them as they flew over the battlefield, but they were far away and obscured by smoke from explosions. When the ring of giants surrounding Braz'galar and his group finally opened up, it revealed two of the *B'nai Elohim* trailed by three giants who looked to be leaders by the difference in their dress. Braz'galar, along with everyone except Ashryn, stood.

The sheer size of the *B'nai Elohim* surprised and impressed Braz'galar. One was at least twenty-seven feet tall while the other, a female, was a foot shorter. Atop their dragon torsos were large dog-like heads, but instead of two eyes, there were six, three to each side. The gold-colored eyes sparkled with intelligence and wisdom. The scales on their bodies shimmered with a shiny black coloration, which reflected light back at the observer. Four powerful arms protruded out of the torso, each ending in a three-talon hand. Four clawed legs, as thick as the trunk of a large tree, and ten feet high, secured these great beasts to the ground. Their tails extended another fifteen feet and ended in a three-talon tip. But the most significant part of these creatures were the wings. Each wing was twenty feet wide, with huge claws protruding outward from the point where the delicate wing skeletal structure began. The membrane on each wing was flexible and nimble, but also appeared to be very tough. The wings shimmered a deep purple, which faded half-way down and turned crimson. Gold flakes covered the wings and sparkled even in the dim light of the dreary day.

"Who speaks for this group?" the *B'nai Elohim* male spoke.

"That would be me," Braz'galar said before hearing Belladonna clearing her throat. "Well, the two of us, actually. We share leadership."

"I'm Michael, commander of the *B'nai Elohim*. This is Gabriella, my second, Lord Ternborg, king of the Draugen Pesta from Aster, and his assistants, General Gargarin and Colonel Antonovich."

Braz'galar identified himself and each member of his party. Then he asked the one question that had been gnawing at his gut ever since being brought inside. "Why did you give us sanctuary?"

"Wasn't that your intention when you made your mad dash across a battlefield to the base of my stronghold?" Michael asked.

Braz'galar nodded. "Yes, of course. But..."

"Besides, I'd hardly call it sanctuary," Michael said. "You're prisoners until I say otherwise. But to your point, when I received a report you helped an injured demon on the field of battle, I was... intrigued."

Gabriella picked up where Michael had left off. "It may surprise you to know we understand the politics of the Abyss. We know the extent of the peasant folk's desire for peace and that it's Kor's blind ambition that prevents this from becoming reality. The overlord and warrior class are more than happy to follow Kor's lead because it assures them positions of power. But power in the hands of the greedy and the evil leads to unrelenting brutality... a viciousness that isn't easily controlled. This cruelty is normally turned towards those less powerful... specifically the peasant class. But in your society, guilds exist to keep the peasant folks moderately safe... at least those that don't turn to a life of crime or operate outside guild jurisdiction. From what we understand, the guilds do an excellent job protecting its members. Denied the peasants, the warrior class turns inward to satisfy their proclivity towards violence. Promotions are earned by the blade of a sword or battleaxe... not by merit. A simple derogatory comment... or a wrong look... can quickly turn deadly. Life becomes cheap. Even more so on the battlefield."

Michael cut off his second-in-command. "Thank you, Gabriella." The *B'nai Elohim* leader looked at Braz'galar and Belladonna. "So you see, we've never seen a warrior stop to help one of his own kind upon the field of battle. It's just not in the nature of a warrior… particularly an overlord… to help a common soldier. Or anyone else, for that matter."

Michael paused as he looked at the two overlords. He began to say something else, but instead nodded towards Gabriella and, along with the three giant leaders, turned and walked away.

Gabriella stepped forward and pointed at Braz'galar and Belladonna. "You two, follow me." Then she addressed the Draugen Pesta warriors guarding the demons. "Take the rest and make sure they're comfortable. But keep them under close watch."

Gabriella turned and walked away. Braz'galar and Belladonna looked at each other and shrugged before following. "Don't get into any trouble," Braz'galar yelled over his shoulder to his people.

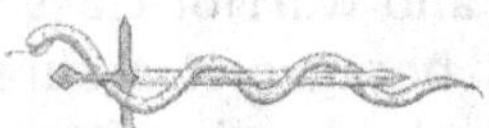

Michael, Lord Ternborg, General Gargarin, and Colonel Antonovich were sitting on one side of a huge, shiny, lacquered wooden table in a small cavern-sized room when Gabriella arrived with Braz'galar and Belladonna. Each had drinks before them—Michael a wine goblet while the others had mugs of steaming javah. Gabriella directed Braz'galar and Belladonna to sit on the opposite side of the table.

"Wine or javah," Gabriella asked.

"I think javah might be best," Braz'galar replied.

Belladonna nodded. "Same, please."

"You're the spitting image of Nightshade," Michael said to Belladonna.

"You've seen my sister?"

The *B'nai Elohim* leader nodded. "She's out there on the other side of the wall. She came back to look for you… among other things. Nightshade's not the same as she was when she went to the mortal world with your father to stir up trouble."

Belladonna sighed. "I cut off contact with her years ago... afraid she'd find out I was one of the resistance leaders and turn me in to Kor."

"She expressed an abundance of surprise when given that tidbit of information," Michael said before taking a sip of wine. "It appears the both of you have taken unexpected directions in your life's journey."

Belladonna shook her head. "Hard to believe."

Gabriella, after pouring her own goblet of wine, took a seat next to Michael. "She follows one of Aster's newer gods. She's here with a mortal priest who acts as her mentor. Powerful magic radiates from him. He has a strong character and is well-versed in the arcane arts. I assure you, from what I've seen, he has her under his complete control. She'll not turn from her new path."

"I hope you're right," Belladonna remarked.

"Then there's the knight," Michael added.

Gabriella chuckled. "Ah yes, the knight." She swirled the wine in her goblet and smiled. "A stern fellow who's everything a paladin should be... and then some. Between him and the priest, she walks the straight and narrow or suffers the consequences. It's a somewhat unusual relationship with a rigid system of checks and balances between them. Believe me when I tell you she's got her hands full with those two. But I think she's sincere."

Michael cleared his throat. "Time to get to the reason we're here. It surprised me to hear from my sources that the leader of the resistance..."

"One leader," Belladonna interrupted as she shook her head. "Not *the* leader. I don't know who that is." The overlord looked at the quiet faces around the table. "It's better that way... that I don't know."

Michael nodded. "Forgive me. As I was saying, how is it a resistance leader and Kor's fixer are here together, especially considering that it was you, Braz'galar, who broke the resistance? Were the two of you in on it together?"

"We were never in it together!" Belladonna protested.

Braz'galar shook his head. "Belle's correct. At the time, she didn't know who I really was and the nature of my mission."

Michael nodded. "I stand corrected. Please continue."

"It's a long story..." Braz'galar began. When he saw Michael begin to say something, he held up his hand. "Which I'll summarize for brevity's sake."

Michael nodded and leaned back, ready to listen.

Braz'galar looked over at Belladonna before starting. She wasn't going to like hearing what he had to say. "As Kor's fixer, I go where Kor wants, when Kor wants, and I do what Kor wants. I'm his assassin, foreman, gopher, and many other things all rolled into one. In other words, I do just as the job title says... I fix things. I decided to do it because, like the other fixers before me, the position meant power... power second only to Kor." Braz'galar took a break to take a sip of javah. "In the beginning and after some early success, Kor gave me a little latitude, which expanded with each completed mission. I used that latitude for my own purposes. For example, when I received orders from Kor that someone had to be eliminated, my first goal was to gather as much information as possible. Specifically, who was the target, what did he or she do to earn Kor's attention, was a family involved, were there future beneficial considerations to be had if the person remained alive, how serious was Kor's motivation, and so on. I only had two rules. I'd never hurt or ruin someone who was innocent, and I never messed with the peasants."

"Excuse me," Gabriella said. "Why not the peasants?"

Braz'galar let out a short laugh. "The first is rather obvious. You mess with the peasants, you mess with the guilds. Just between you and me, Kor fears the guilds… or I should say, he fears the luxuries the guilds can withhold if they're so inclined. Then there's the paperwork. You get caught harming a guild protected…"

"And the second reason?" Gabriella interrupted.

"Peasants, though not perfect by any means, are usually far too busy eking a life out for themselves and their families to get involved in illegalities or politics… except for the resistance, of course." Braz'galar replied. "Kor only rarely had any reason to go after them."

"Thank you," Gabriella remarked. "I apologize for the interruption."

Braz'galar nodded. "Where was I… oh… if I found through my information gathering that a targeted person was innocent or did something I felt was justified, instead of seeking a more permanent solution, I'd relocate them and their families as far away as possible. Usually to Zhaarmoth. The city sets on the plateau the Taumaru call home. Even Kor would hesitate to tangle with that tribe. Over the years, as Kor's fixer, I've accumulated more wealth than I could spend in several lifetimes. I used this wealth to set up an organization, based in the aforementioned Zhaarmoth, that's filled with people who are either grateful or owe me. It's an organization that expands across the entire Abyss." Braz'galar looked at Michael. "About the only thing I couldn't do was penetrate your circle of spies… though I believe Kor has managed to do so."

Michael nodded. "Yes… yes, he did. And apparently he had them dealt with. Right now, I've no eyes beyond the wall."

"Don't beat yourself up over it," Braz'galar said. "There's a lot of things Kor does very well. Getting rid of spies is one of them." The overlord didn't mention he'd replaced Kor's spies with his own and had little trouble doing so. It was a matter of finesse. Michael probably didn't have access to the right people.

Braz'galar emptied his javah mug. "Eventually, the time came when Kor ordered me to destroy the resistance. Their acts of aggression and defiance were, up to that point, insignificant and beneath Kor's attention..."

"We were only testing the waters early on," Belladonna remarked.

Braz'galar ignored the interruption. "But instead of keeping their operations confined to the outlying cities, they turned to the capital. Bands of resistance fighters started ambushing members of the Military Faction... and they became good at it. But they got cocky. Those early victories culminated in the attempted destruction of a barracks full of sleeping soldiers."

Belladonna shook her head. "I had nothing to do with that attack."

"Of course you didn't," Braz'galar responded as he covered Belladonna's hand with his own. "You're not that stupid. Anyway, five minutes after the news got to Kor, he summoned me. It was in the middle of the night. I'd been aware of the attacks occurring across the Abyss, as well as the ones in the capital. But this final one took me by surprise because of its audacity... and foolhardiness. When I arrived at the palace, guards escorted me to Kor's bedchamber. He had three words for me: 'Destroy the resistance!' Then he returned to his sleep."

"Were any of the resistance in the capital captured?" Michael asked.

Braz'galar nodded. "Yes. Very quickly. By nightfall of the next day, the Military Faction had them all rounded up."

"And you didn't take part in that?" Michael asked.

Braz'galar shook his head. "No. I left almost immediately after receiving Kor's orders and had already left the capital when it happened. My job was to break the resistance. To do that, I knew I had to start outside the capital. That's where the true leaders were... at least according to the reports I had. What occurred in the capital involved one cell only... albeit the largest cell the resistance had at the time. As for the capture of the responsible participants within the capital, I was neither requested nor was I needed. The military had everything under control."

Michael looked confused. "You weren't even there for the questioning?" he asked. "I'd have thought the information they had would be invaluable to your mission."

"If there were any interrogations, perhaps," Braz'galar replied. "But there wasn't. They immediately sent the leaders to Execution Hill while the ordinary foot soldiers went to the *Pillar*. Kor takes great delight in planning unusual deaths for those going to Execution Hill. Though I wasn't in the city at the time, I understand he was particularly brutal."

Belladonna lowered her head as she spoke. "He had them flayed of their skin and then boiling oil poured over them." There were tears in her eyes as she recounted the deaths. "I was there. I knew several of them and their families. The screams still haunt me!"

Braz'galar gathered the weeping Belladonna in his arms to comfort her.

Michael and Gabriella looked at each other. The emotions generated by the two overlords surprised them. Even more so the tenderness shown by Braz'galar. Lord Ternborg sadly shook his head.

After Braz'galar gave Belladonna a few minutes to compose herself, he continued his commentary. "As I mentioned before, whenever I'm given orders to fix a problem, regardless of the situation, the first thing I do is gather information. If it's a person, I want to know everything about them. How do they live their lives? Do they have families? What do they do for a living? What motivates them? What are their dreams and hopes for the future? Things of that nature. Information is the backbone of my methodology. I don't act until I'm sure I understand everything there is to know about the subject, because that's what I used to decide how to solve the problem. Sometimes brutal actions are necessary… but only rarely. We all know Kor's penchant for overaction. My sources inside the resistance…"

Michael cut off Braz'galar. "Wait a minute! You had spies within the resistance?!"

"I'm Kor's fixer. And I'm very good at it. Of course I had spies in the resistance."

Michael shook his head in disbelief. "By the gods, if you could place them, why haven't you been able to put spies within the *B'nai Elohim*?"

"I thought long and hard about how to do that," Braz'galar replied. "Never could figure it out. You don't use demon servants… well, behind this wall, anyway. So I couldn't sneak someone inside. That meant turning one of your people, which was never going to happen. I was aware of your employment of spies on the other side and thought I might recruit some of those, believing I could gain access to you that way. But I could only identify a few. Those I approached chose to remain dedicated to you. Unfortunately, Kor was much better turning them than I."

"Yes, he was," Michael said.

"That's probably because I don't use coercion or torture to recruit a potential spy. But unlike Kor's, my spies stay faithful, which makes them both dependable and trustworthy." Braz'galar held out his mug to Gabriella, who sighed and signaled one of the Draugen Pesta guards to refill it with javah. After taking a sip, the fixer continued. "If you lost contact with your spies, it means they choose death over Kor."

"Even more deaths on my conscious," Michael remarked to no one in particular.

Gabriella put a hand on Michael's shoulder, which he briefly covered with his own. "Continue," he told Braz'galar.

The overlord nodded. "The job of destroying the resistance

was going to be a large undertaking. I understood that from the onset. But at the time, I hadn't actually decided if I was going to destroy it or just send it underground until Kor found something else to interest him. That would be a profitability decision based upon what information I was able gather."

Belladonna jerked her hand away from Braz'galar's.

Braz'galar didn't try to take it back. "I'm sorry," he said to Belladonna. "It's just the way I thought about things back then. Information, power, and wealth all help to immunize a person against Kor's whims. It's just life in the Abyss. You know that to be true."

"Being true doesn't make it easier to hear," Belladonna snapped back.

Braz'galar sighed and turned his attention back to the other side of the table. "Even though I had sources within the resistance, it was important enough that I felt I needed to personally gather the information I'd need to get the job done. That meant I had to infiltrate it."

Braz'galar turned to Belladonna. "It wasn't difficult to do. That's the first flaw I found in the organization."

"Of course we failed that test!" Belladonna exclaimed. "The identity of Kor's fixer has always been a state secret! How could we had known it was you?!"

"Someday I'll show you how," Braz'galar said. "I warned you this was going to be difficult to hear."

Belladonna looked at her hands folded in her lap and nodded.

Braz'galar worriedly glanced at Belladonna before he continued. "Once I was on the inside, it wasn't too hard to find out who the leaders of the local resistance cell were. That's when I learned of Belladonna. She's a powerful overlord and the daughter of a rather significant, though now dead, overlord in Kor's sphere of advisors. To think someone of her background would be a resistance leader intrigued me. So I arranged to meet her. What happened in that meeting was something… unexpected. And wonderful. My life… my entire perspective on everything… changed from that point on." Braz'galar looked at Lord Ternborg. "You may not realize it, mortal king, but demons fall in love. That became true for me from the moment I laid eyes on her."

"Your actions tell a different story. It's common knowledge you're the one responsible for destroying the resistance in the city of Uz Urreth," Lord Ternborg pointed out.

Braz'galar nodded. "Yes, I was," he replied. There was sadness in his voice. "And a lot of good people died as a consequence. That's something I have to live with."

"As do their families," Michael added.

The fixer looked at his mug. "You're right, of course," he replied after a few moments of silence. "I know money can never take the place of a loved one, but I've made sure the families of those who died are taken care of for the rest of their lives."

"I didn't know you did that," Belladonna said.

Braz'galar didn't look up. "I had reasons for what I did… but I'm not proud of it. And I felt if I told you about the payments to the families of the dead, you'd think I was trying to buy them off to assuage my guilt over the slaughter… or improve my standing with you."

"And just what were those reasons?" Michael prompted.

Any regret or guilt Braz'galar was feeling evaporated. He looked up at Michael. "The resistance… its basic structure… had serious flaws. Essentially, anyone with a guild card could get in."

Michael turned to Lord Ternborg. "I explained the guilds and their impact on Prefecture society."

The Draugen Pesta king nodded. "I'm following him."

Michael nodded at Braz'galar to proceed.

"Once someone joined, it took little digging to find

names, including those of cell leaders, cell locations, planned operations, strengths and weaknesses, finances, and even the date and time each cell was going to meet. The list goes on." Braz'galar took a sip of javah. "You have to understand. By this time, the thought of a resistance to Kor's rule had my complete support. But the one that was in place had no chance of surviving, let alone bringing down Kor. With apologies, Belle, a first year fixer could have done what I did. The only reason the resistance survived as long as it did was because Kor was ignorant of its existence… until the barracks debacle in the capital."

"So I decided the best course of action was to bring the resistance down and then start over. New organization, new leaders, new base of operations, new attack strategies, and so forth. That meant I had to get rid of the current leadership to make way for people I'd hand-pick. People who I trusted to get the job done. People who I knew would keep their mouths shut."

"In other words, it'll be your resistance and not of the people," Belladonna said.

"What do the people understand about freeing themselves from Kor's domination!" Braz'galar retorted. "Nothing… except how to get themselves killed. And what does it matter how freedom is won as long as it is?"

"Freedom?" Michael asked. "Is that what you offer? Sounds as if the people might be trading Kor for Braz'galar. Is there a difference?"

Braz'galar held his tongue. He fought back the rage that suddenly threatened to overcome him. Now more than ever, he knew he needed to keep his emotions in check. He looked at Belladonna. "Still don't trust me, do you?"

Belladonna's silence was all the answer he needed. Braz'galar looked at Michael. "Kor's overthrow isn't going to come from any type of homespun resistance."

"Which you conveniently had butchered," Michael mentioned.

Braz'galar sighed. "Yes. I've already admitted to it. Sacrifices had to be made. I... we... can build a new and stronger resistance. But we need a more professional organization. One that'll have a decent chance of defeating Kor."

Michael looked at the two overlords for a good long minute before saying anything else. "I choose to believe you, Braz'galar. I'll leave the question of how your resistance to Kor's rule should proceed up to the two of you... though success may be difficult if you can't resolve your obvious differences. I even wish you success. Now, moving forward, you're aware of what Kor's attempting to do right now?"

Both Braz'galar and Belladonna nodded. "We learned about it a few days ago," Braz'galar remarked. "I've been out of the capital or else I'd have learned of it sooner. But from what we've seen and heard, it's clear the Talisman is gone and the Juxtaposition Point has collapsed. That *B'nai Elohim* are dying confirms it."

"The Juxtaposition Point hasn't completely collapsed," Michael pointed out. "But otherwise, you're correct. What do you know of the Talisman?"

This time it was Belladonna who spoke. "That its existence made your kind immune to demon attacks and kept the Juxtaposition Point from failing. Since both things have happened... or are currently happening... it appears Kor's figured out a way to destroy the Talisman. This leaves him free to move between worlds without your interference, which gives him the opportunity to conquer the world of the mortals."

"He'll need to get by us first," Lord Ternborg pointed out. "I can only speak for my people, but we'll give him the fight of his life once he gets his army over there. Hell, we're doing it on these walls as we speak! And the elves, dwarves, and humans won't be pushovers."

"Nor will his army," Braz'galar countered. "And don't assume he won't be able to recruit from those living on your world. Demons don't have exclusive rights to greed and power. I've spent time there, so I know."

Lord Ternborg reluctantly agreed. "You're right. Even amongst my own people, there are those who favor riches over love of country."

Gabriella jabbed Michael in the side with her elbow. "All this talk about the demon resistance and the Talisman. We're wasting time."

"Your correct," Michael said to Gabriella. "What do you want from us?" he asked Braz'galar and Belladonna. "That's why you're really here, isn't it? You want our help."

Braz'galar looked Michael in the eye. "Yes... we want your help."

Gabriella snorted. "What a surprise! Why else would you be here... to offer us *your* help?"

Michael gently chided his second-in-command. "Gabriella, stop."

"No, Michael, she has a right to be cynical," Braz'galar said. "But these are different times. Wouldn't you agree, Gabriella?"

Gabriella quieted. "Perhaps."

"Tell us," Michael said.

"I want your help to kill Kor," Braz'galar answered. "Short of a miracle, it's the only way to keep him on this side. And with Kor out of the picture, we all benefit."

No one appeared surprised.

"So you can take over?" Lord Ternborg asked.

"I'd be a damned sight better at it than Kor," Braz'galar responded. "But I've no interest in sitting on the *Living Throne*."

"If you were to kill Kor without an alternative in place, the power vacuum would tear the Abyss apart," Michael commented. "With the Faction leaders and other overlords vying for the throne, there'd be civil war."

"Would that bother you so much, Michael?" Braz'galar asked.

Michael nodded. "Yes! Innocents will die! None of us want to see that!"

"I'll sit upon the *Living Throne*," Belladonna suddenly declared.

Everyone on the opposite side of the table stared at the female overlord. Braz'galar smiled. He didn't know she was going to volunteer, but now that she had, he fully supported the idea.

Belladonna returned their stare for a few moments before she made her case. "I have the bloodline. I possess wealth and power... as much as my father. I have many relationships with the peasant class, including most of the guild masters. I'm allied with the second most powerful demon overlord in the Abyss who'll back me up against any other suitors for the throne."

"I certainly will," Braz'galar confirmed.

Belladonna took her companion's hand. "And lastly, I'll have the support of the ancestors. I mentioned my bloodline? It goes back to several distant rulers of the Abyss... all of whom will enjoin the others in the *Living Throne* to back my claim. As for the Faction leaders... they'll fall into place once they understand I've secured the patronage of the ancestors. So you see, there'd be no power vacuum if Kor were to die. Michael, my way means peace... peace between demonkind, the mortals, and the *B'nai Elohim*."

"How long have you been planning this?" Gabriella asked.

Belladonna frowned and shook her head. "There's no plan... at least not one I've actively pursued. It just... feels right."

"I've never considered her in that position, but from everything I know about her capabilities, she's as well qualified as anyone," Braz'galar said. "I'd say more than well qualified.

She's got my vote. Different times, eh, Michael?"

"Indeed!" Michael remarked. "And if you don't kill Kor?"

Braz'galar shrugged. "Then I'll probably be dead and Belle will carry on with the resistance... only she'll have my resources to work with. I never realized it until this moment, but I believe Belle represents a bright future for the Abyss... if she's given the chance. Think you'll need to get involved, Michael. No more business as usual."

Michael looked first at Gabriella and then at his allies. Lord Ternborg shrugged. "Can you trust a demon, Michael?"

"I believe it's worth taking the risk," Michael replied to Lord Ternborg before turning to Braz'galar. "So how do you propose killing Kor?"

Belladonna suddenly jerked, her eyes rolled back into her head, exposing only white, and she fell back in her chair and to the floor before Braz'galar could stop it. The fixer knelt next to the stricken Belladonna and held her in his arms while everyone else gathered around.

"She's having a fit!" Braz'galar yelled. "Call your healers!"

By this time, the female overlord's whole body was convulsing as the seizure took control. White foam escaped her mouth while thin strands of blood streamed from her nose, ears, and eyes. But as quickly as the seizure began, it quieted. Belladonna's breathing returned to normal and her eyes closed.

When the healers entered the room, the female overlord was resting comfortably in Braz'galar's arms. The healers could only do a cursory assessment of Belladonna's condition, since Braz'galar refused to yield her to them.

"The seizure's over and she's in a deep sleep," one of the healers said. "But she should be fine when she wakes up. She needs more attention than what I can give her here to determine the underlying cause."

Michael nodded and dismissed the healers. "I can have her

carried to a bed," he suggested.

Braz'galar nodded as he gently laid her on the flat stone floor. He used a pillow-seat for her head and then wiped the blood off her. "But I must go as well. I'll not leave her."

"Of course..." Michael began, but then stopped.

Belladonna's eyes fluttered open. At first she had a hard time focusing, but when she found Braz'galar's face, she smiled. He helped her to sit up.

Belladonna apologized. "I'm sorry for the commotion."

"Think nothing of it," Michael responded. "There's a warm bed waiting for you, if you choose. You must be exhausted."

Belladonna wiped her brow. "That can wait. What just happened was a visitation from my ancestors residing in the *Living Throne*. It would seem they've been keeping tabs on me. My becoming the next Prefecture ruler has plenty of support. As for Kor, his destiny may have already been written," she cryptically remarked.

A sharp rap on the entrance door to the room drew everyone's attention.

CHAPTER TWENTY

The Abyss and Hell

"No!" Max cried out when he saw the shredded body of Solveig lying off the road. Four Hell Hounds were standing over it and snarling. To Max, it appeared they were laughing.

"She's gaen, laddie," Azriel said. "There's nothing ye kin dae noo. Sae git ahold o' yourself!"

Max turned on his friend. In his eyes there was rage tinged with madness. "By the gods, I'll have my revenge! Nothing will stop me!"

"We have the Johari," Elbedreth remarked. "Solveig died to keep her safe. Don't make her sacrifice the cause of your own."

Azriel looked at Max's ghostly form. "It's time tae lea, Max."

Max turned to his friend. "You go without me. I'll not leave Solveig!"

"No, Max!" Jörmungander pleaded. "They'll kill you just like they killed Solveig! Don't leave us!"

Max took a deep breath. As he did so, the madness in his eyes vanished. "This isn't the end. Solveig's waiting on the other side and I'm going to find her. Fate be damned."

"Laddie, please!" Azriel make one last appeal. Max ignored him and charged the Hell Hounds. Azriel began to follow, but Elbedreth and Jörmungander held him back.

"Please, my love, don't leave me alone again," Elbedreth implored her mate.

Azriel didn't fight the two. But he didn't turn away, either. Instead, compelled by loyalty and love, he silently gave witness to his friend's death.

The ensuing battle was intense. Max fought well, killing six Hell Hounds. But as each Hell Hound died, two others appeared to take their place. Max cleared a small circle around him and, for the briefest of moments, he and the Hell Hounds took a respite from combat. Max, standing over the body of his beloved, saluted Azriel as a dozen Hell Hounds descended upon him. After it was over, the shredded bodies of both Max and Solveig slowly faded away.

"Hell's bells," Azriel said as he turned away with tears in his eyes. "It wis a guid 'n' heroic death, mah mukker. A campfire stoory fur th' generations, that's fur sure! Bless ye and yer lass oan yer further travels."

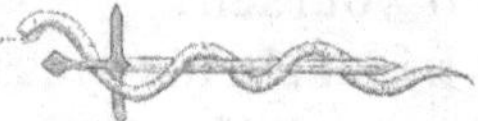

"What have you done?" Landross shouted as Nightshade moved towards him. Her black misty-like body moved over and through the forest landscape as she approached the injured knight. "You've broken your solemn vows to turn from the Black Magic!"

Nightshade said nothing as she inched closer to Landross. She was looking through the fog of Black Magic. All she saw was another soul to devour.

"Coming for me too?" Landross asked.

Now only a few feet away, arms reappeared out of Nightshade's body.

"When you're done with me, at least spare the dog," Landross said. "He's a good boy who deserves a long and happy life."

Nightshade towered over the fallen knight. A mouth, and fangs the size of small swords, appeared in the inky column. Acid saliva dripped from each fang and sizzled on the forest floor. Her blue eyes swirled as she looked down at her next victim. Though she eagerly looked forward to the sound of his scream as she devoured his soul, something about the knight lying on the ground gave her pause. She found she didn't want to eat the spirit of this prey. He was special to her. He was her... companion. Her father had warned her about emotional hazards such as fear, happiness, loss, contentment, and love. Evil cannot prevail once they've been allowed to fester inside. "You don't have to do this," Landross said as he scooted away as best as he could, considering his injuries. "You killed evil demons. So what if you used Black Magic to do it. Father Goram believes that evil is to be destroyed by whatever means necessary. But that doesn't mean it controls you. Resist the urge!"

The mention of Father Goram stopped Nightshade for good. Even through her evilness, she could see him. He was her mentor, the bright white light that ever shines through the blackness that always surrounds her, her anchor in a world full of uncertainty, the only mortal she genuinely loved... not as couples love each other, but as a drowning person loves the hand of the one reaching down to save them. The restrictive blackness of her soul suddenly dispersed to be replaced by the freedom of the white. Self-determination replaced subjugation. Nightshade returned to her normal self.

"You're not looking in too good a shape, knight," Nightshade said as she dropped onto her knees to inspect Landross's wounds. "Getting those arrows out is going to hurt like hell."

Landross breathed a sigh of relief. "Never mind that. You're back. Praise the gods."

"It was Horatio's doing," Nightshade commented as she gratefully looked into the knight's eyes. "But thank you for reminding me how much I stood to lose."

Landross shook his head. "Shucks... nothing to it, my lady. Would you go get Herbie?"

Nightshade smiled. "Sure you won't run when I do?"

The knight chuckled.

"Be right back," Nightshade said as she left to fulfill Landross's request.

Herbie wasn't too far away and was able to limp back to

Landross with Nightshade's help. Once reunited with his master, Herbie laid his head on Landross's chest and patiently waited for his turn to be healed.

Nightshade rolled up her sleeves and went to work.

Father Goram and Abigail had little trouble with Kor's armies during their journey west, though there was one instance when Abigail had to prove the legitimacy of their claim to the gorgon race… and the encounter nearly took her life. They were traveling through a field with Abigail about ten feet in front when a squad of nine soldiers hidden in the tall grass attacked. Father Goram heard the "twang" of bowstrings and created a magical force field in front of Abigail to deflect five arrows released by the attackers just before they stood and charged. Abigail tore off her veil and used her power to turn the first three into stone. But the enormous drain of energy caused her to drop to the ground, unconscious. Two soldiers stopped where she lay while the other four continued their advance towards Father Goram. The priest, terrified over the prospect of losing Abigail, drew as much power from the overhead ley lines as they would give. The soldiers standing over the gorgon vanished into a warm, wet mist. Then two twenty foot tall earth elementals, made of rock, stone, and sinew, grew out of the earth before Father Goram. The priest ran to Abigail as the elementals beat three of the four remaining soldiers to a bloody pulp. One lone survivor ran away.

While the elementals stood guard, Father Goram knelt over the downed gorgon. Her skin was pale, her breathing shallow, and her heart was barely beating. The priest cupped Abigail's head between his two rough and callused hands. As he did so, one snake caressed him before dropping limp. Father Goram used all the healing magic he could muster to save the gorgon's life. Even considering his mastery in the healing arts, it was touch and go for a few minutes.

One by one, the snakes intermingled with Abigail's hair regained consciousness until finally she opened her eyes. Father Goram, engrossed as he was in keeping the gorgon alive, had his eyes closed as he worked his magic. Only after Abigail covered his hands with her own did the priest know he'd been successful. Father Goram dropped over on the ground next to the gorgon and took several deep breaths.

"Don't ever do that again," Father Goram remarked before falling into an exhausted sleep.

Abigail smiled and took his hand before she went to sleep as well. With two gigantic elementals standing watch, six uninterrupted hours passed before the two began their travels once again.

After the confrontation, word quickly spread about a couple of gorgons traveling west on a pilgrimage and that one disturbs them at the risk of certain death. By the time the two reached the westernmost city of Mar Koozzath, they were celebrities of a sort. The ordinary peasant folks had always treated the two travelers with respect and kindness. But now even Kor's soldiers were willing to buy drinks, meals, or anything else to keep from being turned to stone or into a warm mist.

Abigail, after days on the trail, wanted a warm bath and a soft bed to sleep in. Father Goram agreed that they both deserved at least that much. Although all of Kor's regular soldiers stayed in their military camps, the officers preferred to stay in the city. So finding a decent inn that also had a vacancy turned out to be a problem, but only temporarily. Officers were dying in front of the *B'nai Elohim* fortress walls with almost as much regularity as the foot-soldiers. They found a recently unoccupied second story room in one of the better inns. Their reputations didn't save them from paying a premium price… though unlike Captain Oknog, the inn owner had no trouble accepting gold.

"What's our next move?" Abigail asked as she removed her cloak.

There was a discrete knock on the door, and Father Goram opened it to find several servers lined up in the hallway outside their room with food and buckets of hot water for Abigail's bath. The priest didn't answer the gorgon's question until after everyone had left.

"Get to the Juxtaposition Point," Father Goram replied after swallowing a bite of bread slathered in butter and jam. "Though I don't know if it's a physical location or somewhere in a different dimension or universe. I need to speak with Michael."

By this time, Abigail had removed her veil. The snakes intertwined within her long hair were limp and appeared to be sleeping. Father Goram asked Abigail to sit on the bed so he could inspect them.

"Are these separate entities?" the priest asked.

Abigail took a few moments to think about her answer. "Yes… separate entities. They're somewhat like pets, though very intelligent and completely loyal."

"What happens if one dies?"

"Another grows back… well, it's born, actually… to take its place," the gorgon replied. "But the new snake has its own distinct personality… as they all do."

"Can they act independent of you?"

Abigail nodded. "Yes… with limitations. If I go unconscious, as I did in that field, so do they. If I die, so do they. But if someone hurting or attacking me gets too close, they'll bite on their own. And one other thing, Horatio. None of them would ever hurt you."

"Good to know," Father Goram said as he gently lifted one with his hand. It looked at him and went back to sleep.

Abigail, unconcerned with modesty in front of the priest, stripped away the rest of her clothes until she was down to her undergarments. She sniffed, wrinkled her nose, and threw everything into an empty corner of the room. "I could use some new clothes. These are ruined."

"We can do that first thing tomorrow," Father Goram said as he turned his back on the gorgon to give her privacy... but not before he got a glimpse of her partially nude body. Except for the eyes and snakes in the hair, gorgons are human-like in appearance. The few scars she had didn't mar her natural beauty. He heard splashing as she stepped into the bath.

"Ahh," Abigail said as she settled into the hot water. "Horatio, why is your back turned? Come join me."

"I'll use it after you're done."

"But, Horatio..."

Father Goram sighed. A great melancholy suddenly came over him as the hole in his heart caused by the loss of Autumn threatened to swallow him up once again. "I'm still married," he said. "Autumn..." The priest stopped talking for fear he'd have a complete breakdown.

The room became silent. Abigail closed her eyes and shook her head. "How damned insensitive of me. Horatio, I'm so sorry. I... there's no excuse." The gorgon sighed. "I just got caught up in the moment."

Father Goram turned to face the gorgon. "You've nothing to apologize for, Abigail."

"Even so..."

Father Goram shook his head. "Don't you go there. I know Autumn endured terrible things here in the Abyss... things that... well, things she'd not have survived, given her gentle nature. And she's not been seen while Lessien has. Only death would separate the two. Autumn's..." The priest closed his eyes and took several deep breaths. Abigail patiently waited. "Autumn's gone. I feel it in my heart. But with everything else going on, I made the choice to set aside my grief."

"How can I help?" Abigail asked.

The priest smiled. "You already have. You and I... we're somehow connected. To me, and I think to you as well, there's little doubt about that. But until..." The priest shrugged.

Abigail remained silent as she finished her bath. Father Goram left the room and was gone for two hours. When he returned, he had packages of clothes for both of them, including long night-shirts. He stripped, threw his dirty clothes onto the same pile Abigail had made with hers, and stepped into the tub of freshly heated water to wash off the dirty trail. After eating a light meal, they went to sleep together in the only bed the room provided. During the night, Abigail held the priest close as he spilled silent tears.

The small group of survivors approached Hell's guardian, Cerberus, who was lolling about on the banks of the River Styx. Jörmungander and Erika were in the lead, followed by Elbedreth supporting the Johari. Azriel brought up the rear. The Hell Hounds had stopped trailing them thirty minutes ago. The skeletal Charon was waiting in his boat at the shoreline.

"You're not the same number as when you came," the fifty heads of Cerberus bellowed. "Less gold to pay Charon, eh?" For some reason, Cerberus found his remark amusing and laughed. It sounded like a cross between the howl of fifty dire wolves and the screech of fifty harpies.

"Keep yer remarks tae yersel', ye over-sized, rabid, clump o' compost!" Azriel yelled. "I'll hae none o' it!"

"Calm down, my love," Elbedreth said over her shoulder. "Let's just get out of here and take the Johari home. Max and Solveig died so that we could."

But it was too late. Cerberus stopped laughing and all fifty

heads turned their attention directly to Azriel. "You wish to join the souls here in Hell?"
Elbedreth sighed. Neither she nor anyone else could deter Azriel's anger or the battle that was probably coming. She gently set the Johari down before calling forth her many bladed appendages. Jörmungander and Erika prepared themselves as well.

The dwarf-sylph slapped the snout of one head with the flat side of his battleaxe. "Ah wish fur ye tae shut up!"

Cerberus reared up and growled. Azriel raised his battleaxe and prepared for the onslaught. But Cerberus stopped in mid-strike, turned, and walked away. When he was about one hundred feet away, an enormous cloud formed around him and moved away. When it dissipated on the horizon, Cerberus was no longer visible.

Azriel looked confused. "Ah don't understand," he said to Elbedreth. "Why did th' stoatin beast run?"

"It wasn't anything you said or did," Elbedreth replied as she helped the Johari back up.

"Which is fortunate for us," Jörmungander angrily added. "You could have gotten us killed!"

The dwarf-sylph looked down. "Ah know. 'N' a'm sorry. It's juist that huvin tae come 'ere tae save th' Johari... 'n' then losing Max 'n' Solveig... well... it a' juist seemed tae boil tae th' front o' mah thinking. Bit how come did Cerberus nae swallow me lik' a doggie bone?"

Jörmungander pointed to the shoreline where Charon's boat waited. "I think the 'stoatin beast' stopping might have had something to do with that."

Charon was standing at the front of his boat with his hand out, awaiting payment for the crossing back to the mortal world. Waves on the river rose and fell, but the boat remained perfectly calm.

"Ah still don't understand," Azriel said while shaking his

head.

"We were watching," Erika said. "The moment Charon's hand went up and opened, Cerberus broke off his attack."

Azriel sighed. "Hell's rules, ah suppose. Let's git tae th' ither side."

Cerberus was right… the price to cross the River Styx was cheaper by one passage.

Landross, Nightshade, and Herbie ended up spending four days and nights not far from the ambush site. A couple of Landross's wounds had become infected, which led to two days of feverish delirium and two days of recovery before he was strong enough to travel again… and even then he had a hard time staying on his horse for the next day. Everyone was more than ready for a roof over their heads, a hot meal, and a soft bed when they entered the city of Drog'dronnan. Once in the city, they settled into the nearest inn that didn't look too flea-bitten. Before entering the common room of the inn, Landross stabled their horses and paid to have them well brushed and fed.

The clientele within, though not wealthy by any means, appeared to be just normal folks enjoying a mug before heading home to their families. It was the same thing you'd find at most inns and taverns in Taranthi on the elvan island of InnisRos. Two burly looking demons, nursing a mug, sat at small tables on either side of the front entrance. Neither seemed particularly concerned as Landross and Nightshade, still disguised as two fearsome-looking Taumaru, walked in with Herbie trailing behind… though they gripped the handles of the clubs hanging off their belts.

"No dogs allowed," one of the door guards said.

Nightshade fished out a hand full of coins from her belt pouch and put a remadie on the table. The guard looked up with a blank expression on his face. Nightshade added another remadie and the guard nodded.

A waitress appeared soon after they took a seat around an empty table. "What's your pleasure?" she asked.

"Whatever you have that's hot," Nightshade answered.

"For three," Landross added. "One for the dog."

"And to drink?"

Landross thought about it for a second. "Whatever's on tap. Water for the dog."

"I'll have javah," Nightshade said. "And do you have any rooms available?"

"Plenty," the waitress answered. "Most of our regulars headed west with the rest of the army. One bed or two?"

"One room but two beds," Nightshade replied.

"It'll cost you a remadie for the meal and a kronie for the room."

Nightshade laid a kronie and three remadies on the table. "Keep the change."

The waitress smiled. "Thank you. Your meals and drinks will be out in a minute or two, and I'll make sure the room is extra clean."

As the waitress walked away, Landross turned to Nightshade. "Do you think a Taumaru would be so free with their money? I mean, considering their disposition."

"On the contrary, the Taumaru are quite generous as long as they receive excellent service," Nightshade responded. "It's a shame most people don't understand that about them."

"How long before we reach the base of the plateau?" Landross asked.

Nightshade shrugged her shoulders. "I'd say another two days of travel across open grassland. I've only been there once, but that seems about right."

The waitress arrived with a tray of food and drink. The bowls were filled with strider stew, there was a large loaf of bread, Landross's mug contained a dark, rich, and tasty ale, and the javah was steaming hot. Several days of jerky had taken its toll. The three had little time for conversation as they dug into the food.

"I just had a thought," Landross said as he cut off his third slice of bread. "The closer we get to the plateau, the greater our chances of running into real Taumaru."

Nightshade nodded. She'd eaten her fill and was sipping her javah. "You're right. They don't take kindly to impersonators. We should drop our disguises once we're outside the city."

Landross leaned back in his chair, belched, and farted. "Guess it's time to show folks who we really are."

Herbie barked a couple of times.

Nightshade couldn't stop laughing.

Father Goram and Abigail grabbed a quick breakfast of a hardy and good-tasting mash of different grains, along with fruits, nuts, and plenty of javah. Neither mentioned what happened the previous night, though it was on both their minds.

"How are we going to get to Michael when there's a war being fought in front of his fortress?" Abigail asked. "We can't just walk in."

"I've been there," the priest said as he downed the last of his breakfast mash. "Recognizing where you want to go is one prerequisite for casting a dimensional doorway spell. I should be able to get us there from our room. When we're done here, I'll go provide for the horses and settle accounts while you go back to the room and get our things together."

An hour later, they were ready. Father Goram drew a circular pattern on the floor with chalk he always carried and stepped inside. Then he reached out towards the gorgon.

"Take my hand, Abigail," he said.

She stepped inside the circle, took his hand with both of hers, and stood close by his side. "I should tell you I've never done this sort of thing before."

"I'll keep you safe." Father Goram gripped her hand tightly. "Now... no matter what happens, don't let go until I say it's okay."

"Never," Abigail replied.

With one hand, the priest constructed different shapes in the air before him while articulating words of magic. The ley lines that ran through the sky above dipped down in answer to his call and provided him with all the power he'd need. The pattern on the floor shimmered and a small, black spot appeared in front of the priest. As Father Goram's incantations became louder, the spot doubled, then tripled in size until it was large enough for both the priest and the gorgon. Through the doorway was the courtyard inside the *B'nai Elohim* fortress.

Abigail took a step towards the doorway, but Father Goram stopped her with a shake of his head and more pressure on her hand. "Unnecessary," he whispered.

As Abigail stared at the courtyard on the other side of the doorway created by Father Goram, her vision blurred and turned gray. She closed her eyes. When she opened them, they were both standing in the courtyard of the *B'nai Elohim* fortress and the magical doorway was gone. Suddenly she felt faint and darkness seemed but a moment away. A strong arm wrapped itself around her waist and held her up.

"Steady, Abigail," Father Goram said. "The first time through a dimensional doorway can be taxing on the body."

Several Draugen Pesta warriors ran over to them. "Father Goram?" one of them asked.

"Heard of me, eh, my boy?" the priest said as he smiled. "Please take us to Michael."

"Right away, Father!"

As the warriors escorted them inside the fortress, Abigail leaned over and whispered, "They're not afraid of me."

Father Goram shook his head. "One, you're with me and apparently they know me well enough to understand I'm one of the good guys. Two, I've never heard of a gorgon on the other side except in ancient manuscripts which may not be familiar to them. So they probably don't know about your special abilities. And three, Draugen Pesta warriors aren't afraid of anything. I'm surprised to see them over here, though. But if Michael was going to ally himself with mortals, the giants are an excellent choice. No other race can match them on the battlefield. Besides being over twice the height of humans or elves, they're all extremely intelligent, ferocious in combat, and very well led."

Father Goram, Abigail, and their guides entered a large room. Michael, Gabriella, and several Draugen Pesta sat on one side of the table while two demons occupied the other.

"Father Goram!" Michael exclaimed. "I'm surprised to see you. Have you found your wife and the queen?"

The priest shook his head. "Unfortunately, we haven't. But Landross and Nightshade have an idea where the queen might be. They are, at this moment, still searching... but I'm sure they'll find her soon enough. As for my wife... there's been no word on her for some time now." There was a small catch in Father Goram's voice. Abigail squeezed his hand, which she had held ever since their transition through the dimensional doorway. "I've accepted the fact that she's most likely dead."

"I'm so sorry," Michael said. There was genuine sorrow in his voice. "I see you've brought with you the only gorgon living in the Abyss."

"You know of me?" Abigail asked.

"The whole Abyss knows of you, Abigail," Michael replied. "Be welcome in the fortress of the *B'nai Elohim*."

Abigail nodded. "Thank you for your kindness."

Michael introduced the priest and the gorgon to everyone else sitting around the table.

Abigail couldn't help but to stare at Belladonna. "You're the splitting image of Nightshade," she said. "I knew from her you were twins, but I never imagined how close."

Belladonna smiled.

"If I may," Michael interrupted. "Now then, Father Goram, have you come to be sent back home?"

Father Goram shook his head. "I've decided to stay in the Abyss," he replied. His willingness... his desire... to remain and live in the Abyss surprised everyone, including Abigail. "It's time for me to settle down... to live a simpler life, free from the responsibilities of my priesthood. Here I can live away from all the intrigue and catastrophes I faced day after day on InnisRos. I haven't abandoned Althaya. Nor will I give up the calling completely. But my days as a high priest are over."

"Don't be so sure," Belladonna blurted out. "Good leaders can be hard to come by. Rest assured, someone here will find a need for your talents."

Michael shook his head. "Never mind that. If not to go back to Aster, why are you here?"

Father Goram smiled. "Blunt as always. I want to repair the Juxtaposition Point, if possible."

There was silence around the table until finally Braz'galar spoke. "You think you can do that?"

But Michael was shaking his head. "No, not without the Johari. We appreciate the gesture, Father Goram, but it's just not possible."

"Michael, how do we know until he at least tries," Braz'galar countered.

Father Goram looked at the demon who'd just spoken.

"Braz'galar's your name, right?"

Kor's fixer nodded.

"Braz'galar's correct, Michael," the priest said. "At least take me to the Juxtaposition Point and let me see what I can do."

"You can't fix the Juxtaposition Point," Michael said again.

"But what if I can brace it up to buy you some time?" Father Goram argued. "It's not just the future of the Abyss that lies in the balance. There's also a real and imminent danger to Aster. Besides, what have you to lose?"

"But my sorcerers have already..."

Father Goram interrupted the *B'nai Elohim* leader. "Your sorcerers don't practice the same type of magic I do."

"What's the harm?" Lord Ternborg asked.

Michael looked at the Draugen Pesta king. "Plenty to the priest."

"Isn't that his choice?" Gabriella interjected.

Michael looked at his second, at Lord Ternborg, and then stood. He was convinced. "Do you need time to rest or prepare?"

Father Goram stood as well. "There's no time for that."

As the priest and the gorgon followed Michael and the others out of the room, Abigail, still holding Father Goram's hand, leaned in and whispered, "Are you sure you understand what you're doing?"

"Not really," Father Goram whispered back. "But we both know I have to try. It's why we came."

Abigail tightened her grip on the priest's arm and hand. "You're right. But I'm worried. What if... I don't want to lose you! I remember our discussion from last night, but that doesn't change how I feel about you."

"We've been taking risks ever since we came together. This is just another."

Abigail shook her head. "No, Horatio. This is different. I

can sense it."

"So can I," Father Goram admitted.

The Juxtaposition Point was housed in what amounted to a small castle complete with moat, drawbridge, thirty foot high walls that were ten feet thick, battlements, and magic-infused stone gargoyles that acted as guardians. Inside the walls there sat one massive building. The stone doors, the only entrance or exit in the building, opened by an unseen force as Michael approached. A dim, dirty looking blue light and a loud shriek escaped the opened doors.

"The light used to be a brilliant white!" Michael shouted as he entered the building containing the Juxtaposition Point. "When it's working properly, you need special magical eye coverings to see it."

The Juxtaposition Point, a large, bluish colored orb, floated in the center of the fifty foot high room. All around the orb, streams of light left the surface, only to be recaptured by the orb, bent into an arc, and drawn back in. The orb itself turned on its own axis, but the spin was off balanced. Each wobble of the orb produced a high-pitched whine. Occasionally, a stream of light would escape recapture, only to fizzle out before it could travel very far.

"When did this happen?" Father Goram bellowed over the sound of the orb.

"A few days ago," Michael answered. "Most of our sorcerers can't concentrate long enough to cast any kind of diagnostics spells. The few who did found the Juxtaposition Point orb absorbed their magic and the whine only got louder. Our sorcerers have thousands of years of experience and don't fail often."

Father Goram shook his head. "Your sorcerers don't have a

goddess helping them. Give me some time alone with the orb."

Michael nodded.

"I'm not leaving!" Abigail shouted.

Michael took the gorgon's arm and began to drag her away. Abigail tried to shrug his grasp off, but couldn't. Snakes suddenly animated around Abigail's head and hissed. Her eyes took on their deadly shimmer.

"I'm warning you!" Abigail shouted at the *B'nai Elohim*.

Father Goram didn't know if Michael had a natural immunity to Abigail's particular ability, but he wasn't willing to take the chance. "Leave her be, Michael. Abigail and I decided we're in this together. I find strength in her presence."

Michael consented and let go of Abigail's arm. With a curt nod at the priest, he and the others left the building.

As soon as they were gone, Father Goram turned on Abagail. "Have you taken leave of your senses? This is going to be dangerous… as in it might kill me! I don't want you to be collateral damage! I don't want you to die!"

"But you said…"

Father Goram cut her off. "I didn't want you to turn Michael into stone, if that's even possible."

Abigail crossed her arms while the snakes on her head weaved back and forth in response to their mistress's irritation. "I don't care what you or anyone else says, I'm not leaving! Not while you're risking your life in here!"

The priest's eyes softened. He cupped the gorgon's face in his hands and kissed her on the forehead. "Just don't die."

"As long as you don't."

Father Goram nodded and turned to study the orb. He checked the ley lines overhead to make sure they were powerful enough to support the magic he felt he'd have to conjure. Then he sent an identification spell followed by a truth seeking spell into the orb. When he did so, he found that negative energy surrounded the orb by means of a very old and powerful enchantment.

"I wonder who put that there," the priest wondered. *"The older gods?"*

Father Goram ramped up the magic he was drawing from the ley lines and punched a hole through the destructive force encasing the orb. In response, the orb turned from blue to a vibrant green. The priest could sense relief, though it was short-lived. The wobble soon became more severe and the noise louder. Father Goram didn't expect it would be easy.

The identification spell, besides revealing the negative energy, gave Father Goram a potential solution, albeit only a temporary one. First, he'd have to remove the negative energy. Then somehow he'd have to stabilize the wobble. If he was lucky, that would allow the orb's light to fully escape, which was, as he came to discover, the crux of the entire matter. But what he thought he needed to do was going to be dangerous.

Father Goram grabbed Abigail by the shoulders. "Are you sure I can't convince you to leave?" he yelled above the din of the orb screech.

Abigail didn't try to answer. She shook her head and unexpectedly hugged the priest for a few moments before letting go. She mouthed the words, "You and me," before motioning him to get back to the business of saving two worlds.

Father Goram nodded and turned to the floating orb. First, he cast several protective spells over the gorgon. She'd never know they were there, and they'd last for at least twenty-four hours... plenty of time to bring this to a conclusion. Then he cast the same warding spells on himself. Regardless of what some people believed, he didn't have a death wish.

The priest next turned his attention to the negative energy covering the orb. He understood putting a hole in it was one thing... but removing it altogether would be a completely different challenge. Father Goram didn't believe he could remove or strip away the negative energy surrounding the orb.

But he could cancel it out using a surge of positive energy such as a burst of sunlight. Except one wasn't enough. He'd need the power of several, set to go off simultaneously, to do the job. He crafted the spell he thought might destroy the negative energy and placed it off the surface of the orb by a few feet. He repeated the same spell construction three more times, one for each primary direction of the compass.

Father Goram turned to Abigail. "Do you have a piece of cloth? About two feet long by two or three inches?"

The gorgon reached into a belt pouch and withdrew a small knife. She pulled up her skirt, cut a piece off at the hem, and handed it to the priest.

"That'll do," Father Goram said. He tied the strip around Abigail's eyes and turned her so that her back faced the orb. Then he took her hands and placed them over her eyes. "It's about to become extremely bright in here... bright enough to blind. I'd hate for you to lose those beautiful, shimmering eyes. Don't move from this position until I tell you."

Abigail nodded.

Father Goram, largely immune to the effects of the spell since he was the conjurer, closed his own eyes anyway and concentrated. An eruption of intense light fill every nook and cranny of the room, followed by an explosion around the entire orb. Even before the priest opened his eyes, he could sense the absence of the negative energy field. His magic did nothing to affect the wobble or the screeching, but that wasn't an intended consequence.

Father Goram untied Abigail's blindfold. "It's safe."

"Did it work?"

The priest nodded. "Yes. Now I have to figure out how to stop the wobble. I'm going to make an attempt to communicate with the orb."

"It's not a living thing, is it?"

"I don't know," the priest answered. "Certainly not as we

know life."

"Will it be dangerous?"

"Perhaps," the priest responded. "Anytime you venture into the unknown, there're risks involved. But at this point, attempting to connect with the orb is the only thing I know to do." Father Goram kissed Abigail's cheek. "Now step back."

Again, the priest closed his eyes. But just before he lost himself in the spell he was going to cast, he heard a voice.

"Horatio," Abigail said. "Make sure you come back to me. I love you."

Inwardly, Father Goram smiled before he returned to his spell creation. He directed energy at the orb and opened his mind. It was as if the orb had been waiting. In an instant, blackness surrounded Father Goram's mind. He sensed movement, his movement, as he rushed towards some unknown destination. Then he was floating. He didn't feel the transition. A streak of red light passed close by. Father Goram watched as it moved away from him until he saw a small detonation far off in the distance. Through trial and error, the priest figured out how to move through the blackness and towards the point where he saw the explosion. Another red streak of light passed by. Then another. And another. All heading in the same direction and exploding at the same point ahead.

Father Goram redoubled his efforts to reach the explosion point. After what seemed like an eternity, a small pinprick of blue light came into view. From all around, red streaks of light crashed into the blue speck. He continued to move towards it until he could clearly see what was taking place. The priest realized he was witnessing the destruction of the Juxtaposition Point in real time. The explosions he was now observing caused the orb wobble in the physical world. Worse, with each explosion, a tiny part of the Juxtaposition Point flew off into the nothingness that surrounded both it and him.

As he watched, he tried to figure out how the Johari

shielded the Juxtaposition Point. Did the Johari prevent the red streaks from attacking? Or did she protect the Juxtaposition Point so the red streaks couldn't affect it? Perhaps it was the combination of both? And just what were the red streaks? Where did they come from? And why do they act as they do? In the end, the priest decided to let Michael's scholars work that out, if they hadn't already. All he needed to do was stop the explosions, which would end the wobble and prevent the Juxtaposition Point's essence from being chipped away.

Trapped as he was in nothingness, Father Goram wasn't sure if magic was going to work, for there weren't ley lines to draw power from. But upon closer observation, he didn't believe he needed them. There was magic everywhere. He could sense it. Whether it was enough to get the job done, however, was something the priest couldn't know for sure.

Father Goram began with a simple warding incantation around the orb. He felt the magic build and release. The blue hue of the orb became deeper, but only for a brief moment before the red streaks overcame it once again. The priest anticipated this. It was a simple spell after all. What he didn't expect was the momentary sensation of weakness that followed. While it made sense that without ley lines the magical energy had to come from somewhere, Father Goram didn't expect part of it would come from his own life force. If the amount of drain corresponded with the power-level of the magic he conjured, it probably meant more potent magic would drain enough of his life force to kill him.

As Father Goram floated in the void, he considered his options. There was no question he should make the attempt. Too many people on two worlds depended upon him. The only decision was selecting the spell he'd use in an effort to stop the wobble. He had to choose carefully because, given the circumstances of his life force drain and the magnitude of the spell, there'd be no second chance.

The orb wobble worsened. Father Goram sensed there wasn't much time left before the orb would stop functioning altogether. The magical spell he chose wouldn't stop the assault, but he hoped it might heal the orb enough to delay its eventual destruction. Maybe that might buy enough time for Michael and his Draugen Pesta allies to defeat the demons and stop the invasion of Aster. That was, after all, his intended purpose.

Father Goram shaped the spell with words and hand gestures, but hesitated before speaking the final verse to trigger it. He felt the magic building from within, ready for release. He stopped it for just a moment as he reviewed his life and all the people he loved who had filled it. Then he thought of Abigail and the future that might have been. Tears rolled down his cheek as he whispered the final stanza of his incantation. A cascade of White Magic left his fingers and rushed forward. A brilliant flash of light consumed the orb.

CHAPTER TWENTY-ONE

Aster - Draugan Pesta and the Hyrokkin Empire

Princess Daphnia, Jarsus, Shubin, and Major Romanova were meeting over goblets of wine—water for the princess—not long after Daphnia had discovered the ruined communications crystal in her room.

"Yin or a' th' centaurs cuid hae bin involved," Jarsus said. "Let me sink th' Lads oan thaim, lassie. Thay wull be telling th' truth o' it soon enough."

"Not the best plan I've ever heard," Major Romanova remarked. "But I reckon it'd be effective."

"Hells bells, Anya, effective isn't th' word fur it," Jarsus countered. "The Lads..."

"We all know the abilities of the Lads, Jarsus," Shubin interrupted. "But we don't want to make an enemy of a prince of the Hyrokkin. Particularly since he seems to view us in a favorable light right now."

"Prince o' th' Hyrokkin," Jarsus mocked Shubin's description of the centaur. "Shubin, if he is whit he claims, he doesn't wantae sit oan th' throne, anyway! Howfur does that hulp th' peace... or oor position 'ere? Lassie, if th' Lads can't hae th' centaurs, turn thaim ower tae Thanilus. Let's keep peace wi' him even though he's a lying, thieving, drug-sniffing dry boak. As lang as th' drugs keep comin', at least we hae some semblance o' control ower him. We hae none wi' Dardandros."

Major Romanova nodded. "Again, I agree with Jarsus. The bottom line here is your life could very well be on the line, Your Grace, and we don't know from who. The centaurs are the most likely culprits... the *only* culprits in my estimation... and I'd prefer they were on the other side of our walls. Keeping you safe from all threats is my sacred duty as your Phalanx commander. That comes from the king himself... and it's in the oath I swore to him. Please don't force me to choose between your orders and his."

"Yes. Yes." Shubin said as he bobbed his head up and down. "I agree with the both of you. I only ask that we be smart about it… that we consider the long-term consequences."

"Peace or th' lassie's safety?" Jarsus asked Shubin.

Shubin sighed. "Obviously, your safety comes above every other consideration, Your Grace."

"Now yer talking!" the dwarf exclaimed. "Throw thaim oot! Let Thanilus deal wi' th' critters!"

Daphnia had heard enough. "Stop talking, everyone. I appreciate your counsel… all of you. But we're not throwing them out. Nor are we going to let the Lads have a go at them. You want to give them heart attacks? It's bad enough we force them to deal with Adimar, given their racial fear of wolves."

The son of Fenrisúlfr, laying at the room entrance next to the great bear Sienna, raised his head at the mention of his name. Once he saw everything was well, he went back into a light slumber.

"Anya, did we not have eyes on the centaurs while we met with Thanilus?" Daphnia asked.

The Phalanx commander shook her head. "Not directly… but I had guards posted at the door to the room where we're holding them."

"Could they have gotten past the guards?"

"I don't believe so, Your Grace," Anya replied. "I questioned all of them before coming here. None of the centaurs left the room. And there's no other way in or out."

"That we ken o'," Jarsus remarked.

"I'm sure there's a simpler explanation," Shubin said. "One that doesn't involve all this skullduggery. Maybe they didn't do it."

"Then who?" Daphnia asked.

"Does there even need to be a who?" Shubin questioned.

"Insinuating th' lassie left th' crystal oan even though she swears she didn't?" Jarsus asked.

Daphnia shook her head. "I know in your eyes I'm still a child, Shubin. But few children have had the training or the life experiences I've had. My mother and father both feel I'm ready to start acting as a princess should... and they also believe I can handle being our ambassador to the Hyrokkin Empire. I believe it as well. I'm smart enough to turn a communications crystal off when I'm done using it."

"Of course, Your Grace," Shubin replied. "Then either someone had the activation sequence or it was turned on with magic."

"Mah thinking exactly," Jarsus said. "But ah don't see howfur it cuid be a'body wi' th' knowledge tae activate it. Nae ainlie wid thay hae tae git th' sequence, they'd hae tae git by th' guards tae git intae th' room." Jarsus frowned. "Why didn't ah ask this quaistion afore? Lassie, did yer muckle wolf sniff anythin' unusual whin ye foremaist entirt th' room... lik' a body or anythin' else oot o' th' ordinar?"

Daphnia shook her head. "Not really. Oh, he sniffed at the table, but that's understandable considering what happened."

"Then it hud tae be magic," the dwarf concluded.

Both Shubin and Anya nodded.

"I think Jarsus is probably correct, Your Grace," Anya said. "I didn't think it was possible, though I can't envision any other explanation."

"It's possible," Shubin offered. "But only at the highest level. The Hyrokkin sorcerers... well, I'm not so sure they have the finesse to pull off something like that."

"Anybody in Draugen Pesta?" Anya asked.

Shubin nodded. "Oh, sure. Several, in fact. But why? What would be their motivation?"

"You cuid stairt wi' money," Jarsus remarked. "That's aye a guid motivator."

Daphnia considered. "Perhaps. But if that were the case, what motivates the person paying to have it done? Could it possibly have been a warning, message, or blackmail? Maybe they only intended to scare me."

Jarsus snorted. "Mayhap 'twas yer mither. She'd lik' tae see ye come back hame."

"You're way off base, Jarsus," Shubin responded. "The Queen knows how dangerous that would be."

"You're right, Jarsus… mother would like to see me come home," the princess answered. "But not before I've accomplished my mission here. She knows how important this is to father."

"Your Grace?"

"Yes, Anya."

"If your crystal was vulnerable to a magical attack, then it's likely all of them are," the Phalanx commander said. "Perhaps we should keep them in steel containers until we need to use them."

"Separate steel containers," Jarsus added. "We don't waant thaim exploding together."

Daphnia nodded. "See to it, Jarsus."

"Lassie…"

"Aren't dwarves supposed to be noted for their metal work?" Shubin said.

"But lassie, ah don't hae ony smithy tools or even a steid tae light a gid fire," Jarsus protested. "Besides, ah haven't dane ony real metal wirk in decades."

Daphnia rolled her eyes. "By my Uncle Philmore's armpit hair," she said. "Anya, don't the troops carry satchels containing emergency healing supplies?"

"Why, yes, they do," Anya replied.

Daphnia continued. "And don't those satchels contain metal containers which have glass vials of different kinds of salve?"

"Again correct, Your Grace," Anya said. "We use glass vials because any other kind dilutes the efficacy of the medicine."

"Are the metal containers sturdy?" the princess asked.

By now, Anya was enjoying the princess's little show. "It only stands to reason, Your Grace. They do have to protect glass from breaking in battle, after all."

Daphnia turned to Jarsus, who had a scowl on his face. "There you go, Jarsus. Problem solved."

The dwarf stood and bowed to the princess. "Sae it wid appear, lassie." He turned to go, stopped, and turned back around. "If ye'r aff tae cuss lik' a dwarf, at least git it richt. Ye don't hae an Uncle Philmore."

"There you are!" Queen Sofia called out. Down the hall, she recognized the back of her chief spy, Aleksei Smirnov. "Hold up!"

Aleksei turned and waited for Sofia to catch up with him. "Yes, Your Grace?"

"I've been looking all over for you," the queen said. "I knew you were in the palace and wanted to get to you before you left on spy business."

"The spy business is good, but it doesn't take me out of the palace today," Aleksei replied. "Why not send a messenger to track me down?"

Sofia looked around the hallway. "Over here," she said as she led the spy into a small alcove. "I didn't want to wait."

"Is this the best place to have a conversation, Your Grace? State secrets being what they are and all."

"Perhaps not." The queen looked at the two guards who always accompanied her, when she allowed it, and directed them to stand watch on both ends of the hallway. "That better?"

Aleksei nodded. "What's so important, Your Grace?"

"Let's knock off the 'Your Graces' for the sake of brevity... at least for this conversation."

"As you wish... Sofia," Aleksei agreed.

"There's been an attempt on my daughter's life," Sofia said. "Though neither she nor the dwarf know if it really was an assassination attempt. And both claim she's safe... which I've a tendency to believe considering everyone... and everything... over there acting as her personal bodyguards. Still..." The queen sighed. "I sent separate messages to Shubin and Major Romanova... neither knows anything for sure. One wants to interrogate the Hyrokkin's Daphnia's given sanctuary, to the point of death if necessary, while the other wants a more reasoned response. That would be Shubin, of course." The queen shook her head. "I don't think it's the centaurs. But I have to tell you, Aleksei, I'm worried. If..."

Aleksei grabbed the queen by her shoulders. "Slow down, Sofia."

Sofia stopped talking long enough to consider how she must have sounded. "Sorry."

"What happened to make you suspect someone's made an attempt on the Princess's life?"

"Her communications crystal overloaded," Sofia responded.

Aleksei grimaced. "That could kill someone if they're too close. And it's not as if the Princess would forget something like turning hers off."

"That's the general consensus," Sofia said. "In fact, Daphnia's been considerably adamant that she'd never be so careless."

"I assume her room's guarded around the clock by her Phalanx warriors."

The queen nodded.

"So there's no possibility someone with the activation sequence snuck in and turned the thing on," Aleksei concluded.

"We probably should assume it was through magic... though I wouldn't want to rule anything else out entirely." The spy paused as he considered the ramifications of the act. That there was something happening beneath the surface was unmistakable. The only questions were who and how. They would discover the why when they revealed the who. "What do you want me to do?"

"I want you to find out if anyone here in Draugen Pesta is responsible," Sofia said. "And I don't want your spies limiting the search to this side of the Eastern Boreskyre Range. Go west to the other side if necessary... particularly to the human cities of HeBron and Madeira. Enough gold will buy much in either of those two whorehouses. How my husband could have ever allied us with them is beyond me."

"There were other considerations at the time... such as the Princess," Aleksei mentioned as a reminder. "I'm sure the king regrets it even as you do. Anything else?"

"When you find who's responsible..."

Aleksei nodded. "I know what to do."

Sofia held up a hand. "On second thought, maybe we should give the traitor over to my pa-pa?"

The spy smiled. "Northern justice! I like it! Your father would know the exact punishment for someone who tried to harm his granddaughter."

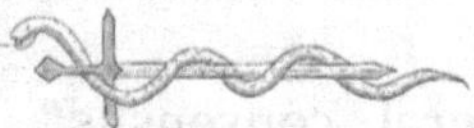

"Is it done?" Kesha Stanislavovich asked the Madeiran sorceress.

The magic user nodded. "Once I was able to coax those damned Hyrokkin ley lines to cooperate, it was surprisingly easy. The first crystal overloaded a day ago, give or take a couple of hours. So the next time she powers up the second... boom!"

"How do you know the first one has already overloaded?"

"A girl can't give away all her secrets," the sorceress replied.

Kesha wasn't buying it. "I need proof!"

The sorcerer sighed. "Alright… as long as you keep that rapier in its scabbard."

"That's to be determined," Kesha said.

The sorceress grabbed her goblet of wine. "This is me." Then she put two copper pieces beside each other a few inches apart. "The two crystals." Reaching down to the floor, she picked up a handful of straw and laid several of them in a horizontal pattern at arm's length. "As I mentioned, the ley lines over Hyrokkin aren't strong. First, I had to pull several together…" she combined the horizontal lengths of straw into one, "… so I'd have enough power. Once done, I put together the spell and cast it." She placed a piece of straw from the ley lines to one of the copper pieces, which she connected with the other copper piece using another length of straw. "Next I tagged it with my own unique signature using a faint strand of power, which I can sense until it's broken." The sorceress laid several pieces of straw length to length from one of the copper pieces to the goblet of wine. "When this one overloads and explodes…" she removed the copper piece connected to the ley lines, "… it sends a ripple through the strand of power from the tagged crystal to me. I've already felt that ripple. If there's a second crystal slaved to the first, the magic is activated…" she brushed away the straw which connected the two copper pieces, "… and it'll overload when she uses it."

Kesha watched and learned. "You don't have a strand tagged to the second crystal. Why is that? And without it, how do you know when the second crystal explodes?"

"I guess we'll hear about it someday," the sorceress answered somewhat flippantly.

Kesha slammed his fist on the table. His giant strength, unchecked for that brief moment, sent the table crashing to the floor and everything on it flying. "This isn't a game!" he shouted.

"You're paying for that table," the tavern owner yelled.

Several soldiers who'd been drinking stumbled to their feet and drew their swords.

The sorceress stood as she hastily prepared a fire spell and got ready to run for her life.

Kesha held up both his hands. "Just a misunderstanding," he called out. He dipped into his money pouch and withdrew a gold piece, which he flipped to the tavern owner. "I'll not harm you," he said to the sorceress. "Will you answer just one more question?"

The sorceress reluctantly nodded and sat back down.

"Are you sure there's no way you can tell me when the second crystal explodes?"

The sorcerer shook her head. "I'm sorry. It's just not possible."

Kesha sighed. "Very well," he said as he stood and walked out of the tavern. *"Guess I need to go back to Draugen Pesta and wait,"* he thought to himself.

"We've got a problem," Daphnia began the meeting. "Well, several, actually."

Dardandros, Theodasius, and Galissa nodded. "We understand Thanilus has given us forty-eight hours to leave the city," Dardandros said.

"And we're under the opinion that's non-negotiable," Shubin added. "Thanilus has been quite adamant about it."

"But the moment you walk out those gates, you're going to be killed," Daphnia said. "Thanilus made that clear as well, though not in so many words. Since I've given you sanctuary, I can't allow that. It's Draugen Pesta law, and technically, this compound now rests on Draugen Pesta soil."

"So you're not going to throw us out, then?" Theodasius asked.

"Don't ye be sae sure," Jarsus commented.

"But the Princess just..."

"Someone tried tae murdurr th' lassie," Jarsus hissed. "If we fin' oot 'twas ye, th' law be damned. In fact, I'll murdurr ye myself."

There was silence around the table.

"Do you really believe we'd do something like that?" Galissa asked. "Do you think we're so barbaric we'd try to kill the only benefactor we have in this city?"

"Ye wid if ye wur spies sent by Thanilus," Jarsus said. "Efter a', we ainlie hae yer word ye'r wha ye say ye ur. Lies 'n' deception come easy wi' yer people."

The Hyrokkin looked at the princess for support but found none.

Dardandros shook his head. "This can't be happening. We didn't do it, Princess!"

Daphnia remained silent. She didn't like what was going to happen next. But everyone, including her, though only after some deep soul searching, agreed it was necessary.

"Ye mist prove it," Jarsus stated.

Theodasius looked scared. "How the hell are we going to do that?" he asked. "Isn't it enough that we've been under constant guard ever since we arrived at your compound? Ask your own guards!"

Jarsus shook his head. "Means nothing. Fur a' we ken this compound's stowed oot o' secret passages 'n' doorways."

"So what are you going to do with us?" Galissa asked.

Jarsus laughed. "A four-legged wha gets richt doon tae business! Ah lik' it!"

"Jarsus, please," Daphnia said. "This is distasteful enough without you making light of the situation."

"Aye, lassie." The dwarf looked at the centaurs. "All ye hae tae dae is sit thare. Th' Lads wull dae th' rest."

"The Lads?" Dardandros questioned.

Jarsus ignored him. "If ye huv a go tae resist, it won't gang easy oan ye. Bit ah think ye'll ken th' necessity o' bein' forthcoming wi' th' Lads. Ready?"

The Lads suddenly appeared in front of the Hyrokkin. They appeared to study the three for a few seconds before flying around the room a few times, as if they were stretching their wings.

"They're beautiful!" Dardandros exclaimed.

The Lads flew back and hovered in front of the centaurs for a few seconds. Daphnia knew what was coming next and closed her eyes. Two terrified, pathetic screams fill the room, followed by the sounds of crying. Both male centaurs had broken down. Galissa, however, didn't appear the worst for wear. After a few seconds of silence, Daphnia opened her eyes. The Lads were gone and Dardandros and Theodasius, their eyes wide open and still wet with tears, sat staring off into nothing.

Jarsus looked at Galissa. "How urr ye nae affected?"

"My Shield Maidens and I have seen worse," Galissa replied. "We've seen large-scale death. We've seen whole families… youngsters… slaughtered and killed for no good reason other than sport. Entire villages…" Galissa shook her head. "Our dreams are already so haunted that nothing ever really surprises us."

"How terrible!" Daphnia exclaimed. "That your people would do such things!"

Galissa nodded. "Queen Thesonia was beginning to change our culture, which I suspect is why she was assassinated."

Shubin shook his head and changed the subject back to the Lads. "I've seen them before… but it's still horrifying! I can only wonder what it feels like to have one of them in my head."

"Will the Prince and his friend be okay?" Galissa asked.

"Well, Jarsus?" Daphnia asked.

"Each body reacts differently," Jarsus answered. "They teuk it ower badly... bit ah think they'll recover. Maist importantly, we noo ken thay didn't sabotage th' communications crystal. 'N' Dardandros pure is th' Prince."

"Wish we didn't have to do that to them," Daphnia said as she shook her head.

The dwarf, sitting next to the princess, covered her hand with his. "It wis th' richt decision, lassie. We hud tae ken if thay wur responsible. Noo we kin shift oan tae ither possibilities."

The centaurs came out of their momentary stupor and shook their heads. They looked angry. "Believe us now!" Dardandros exclaimed.

"Don't tak' that tone..."

"It's fine, Jarsus," Daphnia said. "Yes we do. And I'm sorry."

"What's next, Your Grace?" Shubin asked. "The centaurs are still under time restrictions?"

"You three try to come up with a plan," Daphnia answered, meaning Jarsus, Shubin, and Anya, before she shifted her attention to the three centaurs. "We'd be grateful for any help you can give us."

Dardandros nodded. "Of course," he said. Daphnia could tell by the stiffness in his voice he hadn't forgiven her for their exposure to the Lads.

The princess sighed as she stood. "I need to talk to my mother."

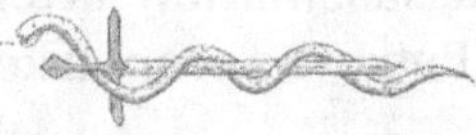

The entire general staff of the Draugen Pesta military, minus those campaigning in the Abyss with the king, sat around a large table in one of the larger conference rooms in the palace. Though the meeting started in mid-morning, it was now late afternoon with no signs of it wrapping up anytime soon. The remnants of food and drink, what was left of lunch, lay scattered on one end of the table as generals and their staff officers huddled around a large map of the Hyrokkin Empire on the other.

"Is that map giving you any answers?" Queen Sofia said as she walked into the room.

Everyone stood at attention.

"As you were," Sofia said as she waved her hand at them.

She walked to their side of the table and took the empty chair at the end. They gave her a few minutes of silence to study the map. The detail was outstanding. She'd have to remember to congratulate Aleksei when she saw him next. Acquiring that much information out of a land so hostile couldn't have been easy.

"Of course, it could have been Viktor's spies who managed it," she said under her breath. More loudly: "So… where are we?"

"Much the same place as when we last discussed the matter, Your Grace," Field Marshal Mikhail Grigorievich answered his queen. "Getting to Princess Daphnia before they do appears to be impossible… with one exception."

"Which is?" the queen asked.

"Recall the Princess and name Shubin the new ambassador, Your Grace," Field Marshal Grigorievich answered.

Sofia shook her head. "No… for two reasons," she replied. "My husband and my daughter."

"But surely the assassination attempt changes things," General Magdalena Petrovna remarked. "The king would understand."

"The king knows as well as I… as well as all of us… the protections my daughter surrounds herself with," Sofia said. "How can I expect her to believe she's in danger when she's probably safer there than I am here in my own palace? Besides, assigning someone else as ambassador is one argument I used before she went. You can see how that turned out. The assassination attempt, if that's what it was, won't change the minds of either, I'm afraid. But it's a good thought. Anything else?"

"I'm afraid we're stymied, Your Grace," the Field Marshal replied.

Sofia put one leg up on the chair, bit her lip, and twirled her long hair as she thought about matters. "Alright then, I know what I have to do," she said to no one in particular. "Generals, thank you for your time and considerations. You're all dismissed. Oh, and Mikhail..."

"Yes, Your Grace?"

"I want to dictate a message for the Hyrokkin leader, Thanilus," Sofia said. "Send me your clerk and a messenger... preferably one who'll not crap his pants at the sight of the Hyrokkin up close."

"Yes, Your Grace."

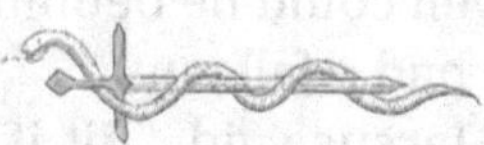

Jarsus looked at the three centaurs. The princess had left for her bedchamber only a few minutes before to confer with her mother. "So whit ur we aff tae dae wi' ye?"

"We passed your damned test, dwarf," Theodasius said. "What more do you want?"

"Jarsus isn't talking about the overloaded crystal," Shubin replied. "We still have the time limit imposed by Thanilus to consider. Add to that the obvious threat to your lives if you try to leave before the forty-eight hours are up and you can see the dilemma."

"Do you really think Thanilus would attack if we stayed here?" Dardandros asked.

"No," Jarsus replied. "He's got awfy much at stake tae risk

anither war wi' Draugen Pesta. Bit ye can't spend th' rest o' yer days 'ere. 'N' th' Princess haes tae much a hert by far tae force ye out… afore or efter th' forty-eight hour limit… knowing it wull leid tae yer deaths."

"He's right," Shubin said. "They won't attack directly. It's what they'll try to do indirectly that concerns us."

"Lik' overloading a communications crystal," Jarsus interjected.

Shubin nodded. "This isn't going away as long as you're in the compound. That's how bad Thanilus wants you. As long as you're here, the Princess is in danger. Personally, if not for her, I'd throw you to the wolves myself if it served to keep her safe. And don't think for a second Jarsus, Anya, or anyone else here wouldn't do the same."

Jarsus echoed Shubin's remarks. "Absolutely!"

"Thanilus isn't an idiot," Shubin continued. "I believe he understands that by removing the Princess he's removing the only reason you're here and not outside the walls getting your throats cut. He very well could be behind the crystal overload, but only as long as he had a fall guy."

"That wid be ye," Jarsus said. "Bit if he is responsible, ah doubt he'd ken aboot th' Lads 'n' howfur thay kin git tae th' truth o' th' matter."

"We're not incapable of saving ourselves," Dardandros said. "We're both highly trained monks. Besides, Galissa and her Shield Maidens would scare most of them away. All we need is a head start."

"If ye believed that, why'd ye come 'ere in th' foremaist place?" Jarsus asked.

Before any of the centaurs could answer, there was the sound of a small explosion which shook everyone and rattled everything on the table.

"The Princess!" Anya cried out as she stood and ran towards the door of the room. By this time, her training had taken over and all her responses became automatic. As she raced through the doors and towards the stairs, she ordered one of the door guards to retrieve as many healers as he could find. The other she told to find her second-in-command, Captain Valeria Konstantinovna, and have her place the entire Phalanx on high alert.

Shubin and Jarsus were just coming out of the conference room as Anya climbed the stairs two at a time. Jarsus was warning the centaurs to stay where they were. When Anya entered Daphnia's room, she saw signs of an explosion—tables overturned, personal items scattered on the floor, and a second set of scorch marks on the main table. Adimar was standing over a recumbent Daphnia, growling and snapping at the guards as they used swords in an attempt to prod him away so they could help the princess. If Adimar attacked, the guards didn't stand a chance.

"Stand down!" Anya ordered. "Keep your eyes on him and back away slowly!"

The guards complied immediately.

Once they were out of harm's way, Anya crossed the few feet from the doorway to the princess and knelt with her hands up while maintaining eye contact with Adimar. There was a sheen in the wolf's eyes that Anya had never seen before. The massive wolf stopped growling, but didn't give ground.

"Adimar, it's me, Anya," the Phalanx commander said. "We've been friends for a long time. Remember?"

The wolf's eyes cleared in response to a voice he knew well.

"Your father would be very proud of you," Anya continued. "You've protected Daphnia so well! But now she needs protection of a different sort. You need to let her friends... people who love her just as you... protect her from the wounds caused by the explosion. Can you do that for me?"

Adimar briefly studied Anya's face before reaching over

and sniffing her.

Anya took a chance and scratched the wolf behind his ear. He accepted her attention for just a second before moving a short distance away from Daphnia. It was far enough to stay out of the way, but close enough to watch everything that was going on. Anya inspected the princess's injuries more closely. Not only was blood flowing from her neck but also from her right eye... or what was left of it after a wooden splinter had done its work.

"By the gods," Anya whispered. "Give me one of your aid kits," she said to the guards.

The Phalanx commander pulled bandages from the aid kit. She looked at the neck wound as she gently placed a dressing on it. The blood flow was already beginning to stop and the injury appeared to be mostly superficial. The eye wound, however, was another matter altogether. A three-inch piece of wood shrapnel was sticking out of it. There was no doubt in Anya's mind the splinter had ruined her eye. Only the healers could determine if any of the wood had penetrated the brain.

Daphnia moaned.

Adimar softly whined.

"Shhh," Anya said as she did what she could to immobilize the splinter. "Try not to move your head, Your Grace."

Daphnia lapsed back into unconsciousness.

"By mah father's forge!" Jarsus exclaimed as he and Shubin came running up. "Oh, wee lassie, howfur cuid this hae happened!"

"Where are those healers?!" Anya said to no one even though she knew the answer as she heard the sound of many boots sprinting up the stairs. Anya glanced at the dwarf. "The other crystal overloaded."

"By Thor's hammer, ah will murdurr th' loathsome, dung-sniffing, whelping that did this!" Jarsus vowed.

"Stand in line," one of the guards said.

Jarsus caressed Daphnia's brow and then bent over and kissed her on the forehead. "Ah shuid hae figured it oot. Ah shuid hae bin 'ere fur her."

Shubin broke his silence. "Save your self-recriminations, Jarsus. It does neither you nor the Princess any good."

The healers arrived and didn't waste time taking over Daphnia's care. The guards continued to watch over the princess as the healers worked. Adimar was only a few feet away. Everyone in Daphnia's Phalanx was familiar with the wolf, so the healers were able to work unintimidated by his presence. Anya, Jarsus, and Shubin retreated into a corner of the room.

Anya shook her head. "I've never seen Adimar that close to attacking before," she said. "Scared the crap out of me. Thought I was going to lose a couple of guards."

Jarsus nodded. "That wolfie o' hers, lik mah Sienna, don't appreciate thair friends bein' attacked. Neither dae ah. Bit if he thought th' guards wur th' enemy, they'd hae bin jibbed tae shreds afore ye arrived."

Anya nodded agreement.

"None of us could have known or prevented this," Shubin remarked.

"Aye, Shubin," Jarsus replied. "Ye hae th' richt o' it. Thare wis na wey tae know... it worked juist braw th' lest time she used it. Whoever did this is yin dead hard scoundrel."

"The last time she used it," Anya said. "That might be when the magic caught the crystal and made it overload."

"I wonder if our own sorcerers can trace the magic back to its source," Shubin suggested. "And if so..."

Suddenly Jarsus's own communications crystal, which was wrapped in a small steel container and carried in a belt pouch, went off. The dwarf frowned. "Fae th' soonds o it, it's th' Queenie."

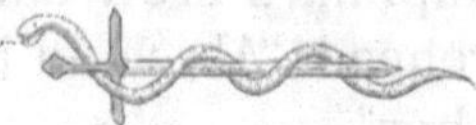

Sofia was in her private chambers eating a quick dinner. Though the roasted meat and potatoes were as tasty as always, all she really had an appetite for was wine. She pushed her half-eaten plate away, scooted her chair back from the table, and draped one long leg over the chair's armrest. Then she took one of her knives from its belt pouch sleeve and began balancing the tip of the blade on her fingertip. She flipped the knife into the air and it came down point first onto the table. The hole it made matched many others already there. Sofia pulled the knife out of the table and repeated the process. It was automatic. It was what she normally did when she was deep in thought.

"I've got to get Daphnia out of that snake-pit," she thought to herself. *"But I can't just order her home. It has to be in a way that will satisfy my husband, the Hyrokkin, and Daphnia herself. Invasion is out. That'd generate a dangerous reaction from the Hyrokkin that even their thirst for the drugs we provide won't stop. Think I'll save that option for later. Magic isn't the answer either, for reasons the general staff had made clear. I can't order Aleksei to spirit her away. She'd refuse, and that wolf and dwarf would back her up. I guess I could have him drug her so there'd be no objection... but she'd never forgive me for that. Neither would Viktor. I don't want to lose my husband and daughter. The letter I sent? Maybe I can scare the Hyrokkin into letting her go? We'll have to wait and see."* Sofia sighed. *"Wish I could confer with Viktor... but there's no way to communicate with him in the Abyss, short of calling Michael with the amulet. Considering what's going on over there, Michael probably wouldn't answer. And if he did, he'd be angry... very angry... and tell me I'm a queen, so handle it myself. And he'd be right."*

A buzz from Sofia's communications crystal broke her

concentration. It was Daphnia.

"Yes, dear," Sofia answered.

"Mother, I need..." Then there was silence.

"What's going on?" Sofia said aloud.

Sofia tried to reconnect with Daphnia but failed each time. She checked to see if her crystal had been powered out, but it still had half a charge in it. Sofia next wondered if Daphnia's crystal powered out instead, but knew almost before the thought came to her that her daughter wouldn't let that happen. Sofia then forced herself to think about the unthinkable, another crystal overload. That's when the panic set in.

"Who do I call?" she wondered. "Shubin, Major Romanova, or, the gods help me, the dwarf?"

In the end, she decided to contact the dwarf. If something was wrong, she didn't want Major Romanova's military training to interfere, nor did she want Shubin's diplomatic wordplay. She needed direct answers. Not only would the dwarf be more forthcoming, but of the three, he was also the one closest to Daphnia. She'd be able to tell just from his tone how serious the situation really was.

"The dwarf it is," Sofia said.

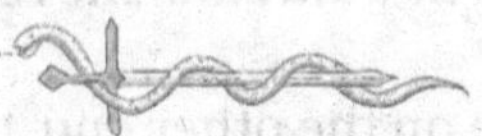

Jarsus rubbed his eyes and took a deep breath.

"You want me to talk to her?" Shubin volunteered.

"Thank ye... bit ah kin dae it," Jarsus replied. "Awright, Queenie. Jarsus speaking."

"I was talking to Daphnia when contact was abruptly cut," the queen said without preamble. *"I haven't been able to contact her since. Is she there with you?"*

"The wee lassie's 'ere, Queenie," Jarsus grimaced as he responded. "But she can't blether richt now."

"You don't hide emotions well, dwarf," Sofia said. *"I can hear your anger... and your fear. Tell me what's wrong and don't spare the details."*

"Ye waant it straecht 'n' true, Queenie," Jarsus said through clenched teeth. "I'll gie it tae ye straecht 'n' true. Some cowardly, dirt-licking curd overloaded th' Princess's crystal while she wis talking wi ye. It exploded. That's th' truth o' it."

"How badly was she hurt?"

"The healers ur aye workin' oan her," Jarsus replied. "She haes a neck wound which bled a lot bit turned oot tae be ainlie superficial."

"And?"

Jarsus sighed. Shubin motioned for the crystal, but the dwarf shook his head. He'd be the one to tell her. "Queenie, prepare yersel'."

"Spit it out, dwarf, before I strangle you and have your body cut into pieces, taken to every point on the compass until the stench of decay no longer bothers me, and left for the carrion eaters to consume!"

Jarsus could feel a headache suddenly coming on. "A wooden splinter lodged itself in th' Princess's richt eye, Queenie. Th' healers don't ken yit if ony o' it's in th' brain. Bit her eye is goosed. Oan th' guid side, she regained consciousness fur a few moments."

There was silence on the other end, though Jarsus, Shubin, and Anya could hear heavy breathing coming from Jarsus's crystal. Then there was a "thump" which sounded very much like something sharp digging itself into wood.

"I told you I was holding you personally responsible, dwarf!"

Jarsus nodded. "Aye, Queenie, that ye did."

"There wasn't anything Jarsus could have done about it, Your Grace," Shubin said.

"Is that you, Shubin?" the queen asked. *"I thought you'd at least keep a handle on things. It was one of the reasons I sent*

you."

"Yes, Your Grace," Shubin replied. The queen's reprimand didn't bother him in the slightest. "Right now, everyone's questioning their whole reason for existence. Major Romanova's ready to fall on her sword. Blackmantle's threatening to take the Lads and fight the entire Hyrokkin Empire. And the Princess's wolf is acting like he wants to eat everyone, including us. But I repeat, there was *nothing* anyone could have done to prevent this from happening, short of getting rid of all our communication crystals… which we considered. What was used to hurt the Princess was magic… extremely powerful magic."

"Why would the Hyrokkin do that?"

"We don't think…" Jarsus began.

The queen interrupted. *"Let me stop you right there, Blackmantle. Things are bad enough without me trying to interpret your dwarvish accent. Let Shubin speak."*

"Ye hurt me grievously, Queenie," Jarsus replied.

"Get over it! Shubin?"

"We don't believe the Hyrokkin sorcerers are sophisticated enough to do this, Your Grace," Shubin answered. "Major Romanova has already ordered her Phalanx sorcerers to see if they can trace the magic back to a source inside Hyrokkin. But as I've already mentioned, this is too much for Hyrokkin sorcerers, so I don't think ours will have any luck. That's about all we can do on this end… at least from a magic perspective."

"I've had someone working on this end since the first crystal overloaded," the queen said. *"If it came from over here, he'll figure it out."* There was a pause. *"Is there any word about my daughter?"*

Anya looked over at the healers. They had moved Daphnia to her bed and had healed the wound that was in her neck. At the moment, they were discussing the best way to remove the splinter. One healer, an older gentleman, noticed Anya looking at them and walked over.

"Is that the Queen you're speaking to?" he asked.

Anya nodded.

"Give me the crystal," he said.

Anya, Shubin, and Jarsus looked at him.

"C'mon, girl! Let me speak to the Queen."

"Is that Boris Nikitovich I hear?" the queen asked.

The healer took the communication crystal out of Shubin's hand. "The one and only, Your Grace."

"Oh, thank the gods! I didn't know you were part of Daphnia's Phalanx!"

"Switched with one of the Princess's Phalanx healers when I found out where the Princess was going," Boris said. "Didn't think you'd mind, Your Grace."

"Didn't we agree you were going to call me Sofia?"

Boris smiled. "Not in front of my commander, Your Grace."

"Never mind that," the queen said. *"Boris... how's my daughter? And don't pull any punches!"*

"Have I ever?" the healer answered. "Other than a few superficial burn marks, the Princess only had two other wounds of note. One was a neck gash, which fortunately missed the carotid artery. Though it caused a moderately heavy amount of blood loss, there wasn't enough to be a serious threat to her life. I healed it personally. The other injury is much more complicated."

"The splinter in her eye."

"Yes, Your Grace. One positive is the splinter didn't enter the brain. That I'm sure of. But I'm sorry to say I can't save the Princess's eye. There's nothing we can do about that."

"Are you sure?" the queen asked.

Boris shook his head. "Like arms and legs, once they're gone, no magic will bring them back. Again I'm sorry, Your Grace."

"You're sorry?" the queen suddenly exploded. *"Tell that to*

Daphnia... or her father!"

Boris had experience dealing with victims and their families, knowing full well emotions always ran high during times like this. The outburst didn't bother him at all. "The problem we face now is removing the splinter without causing more damage or causing a major bleed. At the moment, she's in no condition to survive either."

Anya, Shubin, and Jarsus exchanged worried glances. The healer had just verified their worst fears.

"What do you recommend, Boris?" The queen's tone had returned to normal.

"We keep her comfortable for a day to give her body a chance to replace lost blood and to stabilize," Boris replied. "Then we remove the splinter."

"I trust your judgment. Let me know as soon as it's done. Now give the crystal to Shubin and get back to work."

"Shubin here, Your Grace."

"Tell Anya I suspect the two overloads are related, so she should have her sorcerers take that into consideration. We're chasing ghosts... I understand that. But I don't want any stone left unturned."

"Anya hears and understands, Your Grace. We're as determined to sort this out as anyone."

"I doubt that," Sofia snapped. *"I'm sorry, Shubin,"* she said after a slight pause. *"Not knowing if the king is alive or dead while he fights a war against demons in the Abyss... and now this... well, as you can imagine, my patience is running thin. I know you and everyone else are doing everything you can and that Daphnia's in the best of hands. One last thing. I want you to notify me the second anything changes with Daphnia. If not, then at least every four hours. Is that understood?"*

"Perfectly."

"Now give me Blackmantle."

"A'm richt 'ere, Queenie," Jarsus said as he took the

communications crystal from Shubin's hands.

"About those two centaurs Daphnia gave sanctuary to..."

"It wasn't thaim wha did this, Queenie," Jarsus interrupted. "We a' 'greed 'twas best tae sink th' Lads oan them."

"Daphnia allowed that?"

"In th' end she wis convinced 'twas necessary," Jarsus replied. "Ah saw tae it."

"Well, dwarf... I never thought I'd ever say this, but I'm glad you're with Daphnia right now."

"A've tellt ye ower 'n' ower... it's as if she wis mah ain daughter. 'N' don't forgoat Sienna 'n' th' Lads. Thay hae a particular fondness fur th' wee lassie as weel."

"No, I'd never forget about them." There was a pause at Sofia's end of the crystal. *"I need to talk to you alone?"*

Jarsus looked at Anya and Shubin who both nodded and went over to confer with healer Boris. "Speak yer peace, Queenie."

"I sent a personal letter to Thanilus via messenger. I'm afraid I wasn't very nice..."

"Good!"

"... but I didn't want to mince words. I wanted to make sure he understood my meaning in the letter."

"Ye hae a natural proclivity regarding that," Jarsus commented.

Sofia laughed. *"I'd guess you'd know. Anyway, Shubin doesn't believe Hyrokkin sorcerers had anything to do with the attack on Daphnia..."*

"None o' us dae, Queenie."

"Well, I'm inclined to believe you. But I want to make sure."

"Ye waant me 'n' th' Lads tae pay a visit tae auld Thanilus 'n' ask him directly," Jarsus said.

"You've read my mind."

Jarsus laughed. "It wid be mah pleasure, Queenie! Dae ye waant him tae be kicking whin th' Lads ur dane?"

There was a momentary pause. *"It's tempting to say no... but keep him alive and kicking. As long as he's addicted to the drugs we provide, he's the devil we know."*

"As ye wish. Anythin' else, Queenie?"

"Let me speak to Anya."

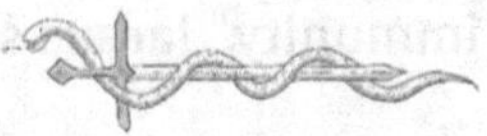

Jarsus figured he'd just walk out of the compound telling no one and demand to speak to Thanilus. It was the dwarven way... direct and above-board... a "you show me your cards and I'll show you mine" sort of thing. The dwarf waited until after midnight. He made one last check on Daphnia and saw that she was sleeping soundly while being looked over by Boris, several other healers, as well as Adimar and Sienna. He scratched Adimar's belly, patted Sienna on the head while telling her to stay, and left the room. The guards at the front gates challenged him, but quickly gave way after Jarsus reminded them who he was and his relationship with the princess in a way that would have made his daddy proud. Two Lads flittering in the surrounding air helped as well. Once outside the front gates, Jarsus didn't have to walk far before being stopped by Hyrokkin guards. They towered over him almost as much as the Draugen Pesta people did, but Jarsus was used to that and didn't allow it to intimidate him.

"What's your business, dwarf?" one guard asked. Several of the others snickered when another called out "short tail," which Jarsus guessed was a centaur insult.

"Squash you like a bug, short tail!"

"Hey, Plateon! You see anything?"

"Can't say that I do, Linackos! Oh, wait! There it is. But you gotta look real close!"

"I didn't know the gods made things that small!"

Jarsus smiled. "If yer finished huvin yer fin, a'd lik' tae be taken tae Thanilus."

"Oh, you would, would you?"

"How about I run you through with my sword instead so we can have a hot meal for a change?"

"Only be enough for two of us!"

"I hae diplomatic immunity," Jarsus said. "Ye ken whit that means nitwit?"

The centaur laughed. "Do I 'ken whit that means' he says."

"It means that, by order o' yer ain leader, ah can't be harmed, molested, or held back in ony way," Jarsus told them, hoping that Shubin was right about the meaning of diplomatic immunity… or that the centaurs would honor it. "But don't tak' mah word fur it. Ask yer superiors. Ah will hauld yer horses."

"Hey!" one centaur exclaimed. "That's not funny!"

"We'll take you to our superiors, all right," the one who appeared to be in charge said.

Four of the centaurs surrounded the dwarf and marched him down a street until they came to an old, dilapidated barracks-type building.

"You three wait here while I get the captain," the one in charge said. "And keep a close watch. Don't want the bug to disappear into a dung heap."

There was general laughter all around. But when Jarsus looked up into their eyes and at the blades of the swords pointed at him, he knew they meant business.

"What's this I hear of someone wanting to visit with the king?" an exceptionally burly centaur said as he came out of the building. "Don't you know how late it is?"

"So Thanilus is th' king now," Jarsus thought.

"This one 'ere, cap. Can't miss him… oh, wait! I guess you can."

Jarsus had to suffer through another series of guffaws. This time, even the captain took part.

"Well, short tail," the captain said. "I'm wondering why my equines didn't run you through on the spot?"

"He's from the Draugen Pesta compound, sir. Says he has... ahhh... ahhh..."

"Diplo mune, you idiot."

"That's right, sir. Says he's got diplo mune."

The captain butt slammed the speaker. "You moron! It's called diplomatic immunity! And if he's from the compound, which he probably is, since there're no other dwarves in the city, he's got it!"

"But, sir! He says we can't skewer him because of it!"

"He's right!" the captain answered.

"A'm glad ye ken th' situation, captain," Jarsus said.

"All too well, short tail," the captain replied. "I want three of you to come with me to keep a close watch on our guest as we head to the palace. The remaining one is to report back to your post. Figure out who's doing what."

The march to the palace through the city streets took an hour, which garnered plenty of attention from those city residents still awake. The longer Jarsus studied the Hyrokkin people, the more he felt sorry for them. They lived in what basically amounted to shacks. The people themselves showed the early signs of starvation, while more than a few also looked to be hooked on the drugs being sent over by his own adopted country.

"Oh, Queenie! If ainlie ye cuid see th' devastation yer allowing," Jarsus thought.

On the other hand, the soldiers guarding him looked healthy and well fed. And they treated the common folk... peasants, Jarsus concluded... with contempt. A slow, simmering anger burned within the dwarf. His anger only got worse as they neared the palace. The homes there were actual buildings, and the few Hyrokkin he saw looked far more healthy and much better fed. Obviously, the crown favored these people. But they paid a price for their good fortune. Most of the ones he saw showed signs of drug addiction. It wasn't as apparent as it was on the faces and bodies of the peasant class, but it was still there to see if one was paying attention. Jarsus wondered if one dwarf could be the catalyst for regime change.

"Ah think a'd lik' tae gie it a try," he thought.

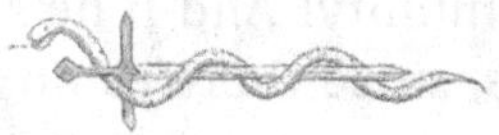

"Where's Jarsus," Shubin asked. He and Major Romanova were in Daphnia's room. Boris and his healer assistants were preparing to remove the splinter from the princess's eye.

Anya shrugged her shoulders. "I've been asking that same question for the last few minutes. I had his room checked. It's empty. But Sienna's still here, so he's around somewhere."

"Major!?" one of Anya's officers called from across the room.

Anya and Shubin waited for the officer to join them.

"Yes, lieutenant?" Anya said after she returned his salute.

"It's about the dwarf."

"You have information regarding Blackmantle?" Shubin asked.

The lieutenant nodded. "He went through the front gates a little after midnight. It was Jarsus, so the guards figured he had his reasons. And they sure weren't going to keep him from leaving."

"And why was that?" Anya inquired.

"Jarsus became quite… shall we say, animated… when they stopped him for questioning," the lieutenant replied. "Something about lice-ridden, clumps of compost…"

Anya held up a hand. "We get it, lieutenant."

"Then there were the Lads who were accompanying him, ma'am."

Anya and Shubin looked at each other. "That can't be good," Shubin said to Anya. "I need to get to Thanilus and you better get the troops ready for whatever's coming."

"But the Princess..." Anya began.

"The Princess is going to be fine," Boris, holding a bloody splinter of wood in a pair of forceps, said from across the room to the puzzled diplomat and Phalanx commander. "It's not like I can't hear you. Now go do what you need to do. She'll sleep for a few more hours yet and I'd better contact the queen."

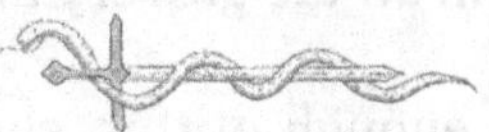

They'd kept Jarsus waiting long enough. He got up from the pillow he'd been sitting on... there weren't chairs, tables, or any of the other amenities one might expect in a normal room, particularly one in a palace... and walked over to the four guards who were playing a of game with dice.

"A'm tired o' waiting in this damned stall lik' ah wis a brain-rotted, troll-kisser! Ah demand tae see Thanilus!"

"Oh, do you now, short tail," one guard said as he rolled the dice.

There was loud laughter from the other guards as the three dice came to rest. "A triple hoof!" one of them exclaimed as he racked in a few copper coins.

"Now look what you made me do," the dice thrower said. "Go back to your pillow before I stomp you into a bloody smudge on the floor."

Jarsus watched as the guards went back to their dice game. "Take me tae Thanilus noo or suffer th' consequences!"

The four centaurs rose from their pillows and drew their

swords. "To the gods with your diplo mune, short tail! If you don't get back to your pillow and quietly wait, we're going to send you off to the king without an arm. Two if you persist."

"Are ye th' leader o' this motley crew?" Jarsus asked.

"Hey now! Don't you be calling us a crew!"

The centaur Jarsus originally addressed smacked the other centaur across the mouth. "Shut up, Horace!" he said. Then he looked down at the dwarf. "I'm in charge. Sergeant Ed. But you can call me Mister. And Horace has a point. We don't like being called names, particularly from a short tail."

Jarsus sighed. *"How hae thae idiots survived culling fae th' herd?!"* he thought. Aloud: "A'm giein' ye one lest warning. Tak' me tae Thanilus or a'm aff tae git very angry. Dinnae ye doubt me!"

"Alright, I've had enough of this, short tail," the sergeant said. "Grab an arm, one of you!"

Jarsus walked out of the room ten minutes later. The screams had finally quieted down. Two of the Lads followed him and flew on either side. Back in the room, the four drooling, bug-eyed, and babbling centaurs had collapsed into heaps on the floor.

Jarsus questioned the first centaur guard he met in the hallways for directions to Thanilus, wherever he may be. The Lads played nice and remained in their unthreatening manifestation. But as soon as the centaur began to show its obnoxious contempt for Jarsus, they changed. The centaur suddenly had somewhere else to go, but gave Jarsus an approximate location for Thanilus after a little prompting.

"Ye micht as weel keep looking lik' ye dae now," Jarsus said to the Lads. "It'll save time."

Jarsus met little opposition as he made his way through the palace. The centaur guards and staff he met as he walked the halls of the palace avoided him and the Lads at all costs. Thanilus wasn't in his personal quarters, so the dwarf headed off to the throne room, the other place he was told the new king of the centaurs might be.

As expected, there were four guards outside the throne room doors. But unlike the others he'd met in the hallways, these were seasoned troops. The minute they spied Jarsus and the Lads, they pulled swords and, except for one who slipped inside the room, attacked Jarsus and his two allies. The dwarf, only a little surprised, raised the sword he'd taken from one of his previous guards and, screaming a dwarvish battle cry, charged to meet the Hyrokkin onslaught.

"Gnarr!"

When the opposing sides met, there was no clash of bodies, nor were there sounds of steel upon steel. Jarsus, at the last moment, slide underneath the leading guard, opened the belly with his sword, and quickly crawled out from under so fifteen hundred pounds of collapsing centaur wouldn't crush him.

The Lads were much too quick to be hit by their opponents. As centaur swords passed through empty air in futile efforts to strike them, the Lads darted in and out, leaving devastating slashes in flesh not protected by armor. In a matter of moments, the remaining two were lying dead in their own blood.

Jarsus wasted little time. He rushed to the doors of the throne room and opened one a crack to peek in. A crossbow bolt slammed into the door at about the height of a dwarf's head. Jarsus closed the door and leaned his back against it.

"Ah don't ken howfur thay did it, bit thay hae a wee airmie in thare hiding behind overturned tables," he said to the Lads. "Hells bells... ah doubt Thanilus is even in thare still. This didn't wirk oot lik' ah wanted it to."

"Surrender and we'll give you a quick, clean death!" someone called from inside the room.

Jarsus knew he couldn't delay much longer. More centaur warriors would soon fill the hallways of the palace... centaur guards who wouldn't run away at the sight of the Lads.

A voice came into Jarsus's head. *"Where are you, Jarsus?"*

"Not noo, Sienna," Jarsus replied aloud. "A'm in a ticht spot."

"You're in the Hyrokkin palace, aren't you?" Sienna said. *"I'm coming. And so are Adimar and Shubin, who has asked that you not kill Thanilus."*

"Ah think Thanilus is aff tae end up killing me afore then. How's th' Princess?"

"The healers have removed that piece of wood from her eye," Sienna replied. *"She's going to be fine, or else Adimar wouldn't be coming."*

"Sienna, if ah git th' chance, a'm aff tae murdurr Thanilus. He's nae worth th' air he breathes 'n' it needs tae end." There was a sudden pause. "Here thay come!" Jarsus exclaimed as guards charged from both ends of the hallway.

CHAPTER TWENTY-TWO

The Abyss

The light from inside the building that housed the Juxtaposition Point turned from dirty blue to a cleaner white. The squealing which came from the orb had changed as well… from almost mind deafening to where it was only a nuisance.

"Whatever the priest did worked," Braz'galar said. "If not completely, at least it bought us a little time."

"So it would appear," Michael said. "Hopefully, there's still a live priest inside." Michael began to walk into the building, but stopped and turned instead. "Gabriella, better get a healer down here."

When everyone entered the building, they saw that Father Goram had stabilized the orb, as suspected. The wobble had been drastically reduced and the orb's coloring was much closer to its natural hue. It hadn't been repaired completely, but as Braz'galar said, they now had more time before a complete breakdown. It was time that came at a price, however.

Over in a corner of the room, Abigail held a recumbent Father Goram. The gorgon's head leaned over his face and tears flowed down her cheeks and dropped into that of the priest. The snakes in her hair were agitated. Their eyes swirled bright green, and they moved around her head in a rhythmic pattern, looking for an excuse to strike at something.

Abigail looked up at Michael, Lord Ternborg, and the others. "He hasn't come back to me," she said through her tears. "I know he's trying… but…"

Michael approached Abigail. The snakes in her head calmed since their mistress didn't see the *B'nai Elohim* leader as a threat. "Are you sure he's gone?"

Abigail didn't look up. "He's not gone. He won't wake. But

he's not gone... just trying to get back."

Gabriella and a healer hurried into the orb fortress and went to Father Goram's side at once. As the healer knelt to examine the priest, Gabriella pulled Michael back to the others.

"The elf may have bought us some time before the Juxtaposition Point completely collapses, but the demons aren't letting up. It looks as if a full-blown attack is about to begin," Gabriella reported.

Lord Ternborg looked at General Gargarin and Colonel Antonovich. "We better get up there."

As the three Draugen Pesta leaders left, Belladonna looked at Braz'galar. "If we could take out Kor, I could stop this."

"You mean by taking over the throne?" Michael asked.

Belladonna nodded.

"He's with his demons getting ready to invade the mortal world," Michael said. "It'd be impossible to get to him."

"Especially since they know the two of us are outlaws," Braz'galar added. "We can't talk our way close to him. That won't fool anyone."

"So what do we do with the extra time the mortal priest bought us?" Belladonna asked.

Michael shrugged. "Same as we discussed. Kill as many demon warriors as we can and hope the world of Aster can withstand Kor's invasion. Perhaps, Belladonna, if you can take Kor's place on the *Living Throne*, the Abyss will be changed as a result. And it could be that, if you do represent a new age for the Abyss, we won't need a Juxtaposition Point."

One of the Draugen Pesta warriors left behind by Lord Ternborg had picked up Father Goram and, followed by Abigail and the healer, exited the building. As the healer passed by Michael, he shook his head.

Michael sighed. "Let's go."

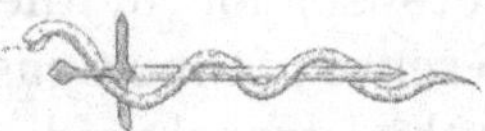

A sorcerer rode up to Kor. "My Lord!"

"Tell me you and your colleagues are ready to open the doorway to the mortal world?" Kor asked in anticipation.

"We are, Lord Kor," the sorcerer replied. "But there's been a slight complication."

Kor shook his head. "I should've known. What is it?"

The sorcerer looked at his master with apprehension. "The Juxtaposition Point hasn't collapsed as soon as we had anticipated. It was about to when magic, completely foreign to us, somehow strengthened it. We can still open the doorway, but with the Juxtaposition Point active, it becomes far more dangerous to travel through."

Kor turned and looked towards the demon warriors at his back. They were primed and ready to go. "We'll take our chances. Open the doorway," he ordered. But to be safe, he decided he'd make the interdimensional journey to the mortal world from the rear of his army instead of the front. "Then report to the *Pillar*."

The sorcerer gulped and began to turn away when he remembered protocol. He saluted the Prefecture leader, who had already forgotten he ever existed. After the sorcerer relayed Kor's order to his superiors, he stashed his badge of office in a nearby latrine and disappeared into the hustle and bustle of the military activity all around. The *Pillar* would have to get along without him.

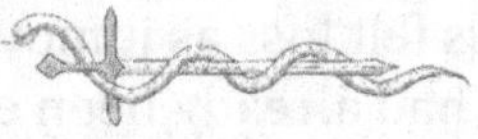

The disembodied consciousness drifted in an ethereal sea of perpetual oblivion. None of the consciousness's physical senses functioned because, for it, the physical no longer existed. There was no sense of time's passing or of placement. Reality, if it existed in this eternal void, was defined only by a sense of being—the feelings and memories the consciousness had of a different place that blew somewhere in the winds of time, unattainable. This was the cruelest of all fates.

The faces of people and animals the disembodied consciousness didn't recognize lined up and marched across it's memory. Then came remembrances of places and landscapes, again unrecognizable. It saw, yet it didn't. Who did these reminiscences represent? What did they mean? Were they phantoms of a mind gone mad? Or did they really exist? And if so, where?

Whatever the faces, places, and landscapes meant, the consciousness concluded it could use them as anchor points against the endless abyss which encircled and threatened to consume him. The consciousness mentally locked on to the first face it saw—a female with beautiful red hair. She smiled.

"Follow, my love," she said.

The consciousness didn't remember her, nor did it understand how it could hear her speak. It experienced a sense of longing, but that feeling flickered away almost as soon as it had appeared. The consciousness heeded her request. But before its guide relinquished it to the next anchor point, she spoke again before fading away.

"I'm very proud of everything you've done since my departure... as I am of the daughter we raised. Find your way back to where you belong, my love. There are many who need you."

The consciousness felt loss as it moved away, but it was an old pain... a pain that had already been endured and accepted.

And so it went. The disembodied consciousness followed each anchor point one by one. Most faces smiled encouragement. But there were several, perhaps too many, who spat invectives and tried to lead the consciousness astray. But each time the spiteful sought to send the consciousness into the emptiness, others would appear to keep it on the straight and narrow.

Four huge, purple-colored statues in the form of dragons and made of pure crystal appeared along the line of anchor points. The consciousness sensed a strange familiarity with the crystal dragons. It struggled with the intimacy it felt for creatures it didn't recognize. The consciousness sensed each had a name, but couldn't find them in the miasma of its reality. It searched and searched, but only found the nothingness that enveloped its sense of being. Then an astonishing thing happened. The first crystal dragon opened its eyes and the names of all four rushed in—Horvath, Duffy, Brand, and Klaus.

"How do I know you?" the consciousness asked.

"To answer that question, you must first come to re-know yourself," the crystal dragon named Brand responded. *"We're here to help you find your way... to find the truth of who you are."*

"Why would you do that?"

"Because we died for you," Brand replied.

The consciousness grew frustrated. *"I don't remember! Why did you die for me?"*

Brand smiled. *"Because you loved us. Because we loved you."*

The consciousness considered. Then more names came from the furthest reaches of his mind—Golanth, Renart, Talamanth, Hoth, Tremorlyne, Jyoranth, Pytor, and Eddrych.

"Our brothers," Brand commented.

"You can read my mind?" the consciousness, now suspicious, asked.

"We're in your mind... and will be there always. Follow us to find your way, beloved master."

The consciousness didn't believe the crystal dragon would lie. Somewhere in the recesses of its mind, the love it felt for them and their brothers, untouched by anything other than simplicity and truth, cried out, begging for release. But the shield that blocked those emotions remained in place.

"I don't doubt your words... but I still don't remember," the consciousness said.

"For now, that's not important," Brand responded. *"What's important is that you trust us to help you find the true path back to yourself."*

"I do," the consciousness answered with sincerity.

"Then follow."

Each crystal dragon led the consciousness to the next. The final crystal dragon, Horvath, steered the consciousness deep into the darkness... further than the others combined. If not for the crystal dragon's guidance, the consciousness understood it'd never have found its way to the next anchor point.

"Go," Horvath said.

"I hope I never forget this," the consciousness replied.

Horvath smiled. *"Now that you have found us, we'll not be that easy to lose again,"* the crystal dragon's voice remained strong even as it faded.

As the consciousness approached the latest anchor point, feelings of despair, grief, guilt, regret, and loss overcame it. Though there were no memories associated with the feelings, the pain that sprang from them was almost beyond its ability to endure.

"Why am I experiencing this?" the consciousness asked the last anchor point, a feminine face framed in long hair and displaying a heart-stopping smile. *"What are you doing to me?"*

"Nothing, my love."

"Don't call me that!" the consciousness railed. *"I don't know you!"*

"And yet you do," the female stranger replied. *"Once you were all that I needed... all that I wanted. And the same was true for you."* A look of sadness came over the female stranger's

face. *"But that hope has escaped us both. Your future lies with her now."*

"I'm sorry," the consciousness said. Despite the blankness that was as dark as the blackness of the surrounding void, it sensed she had at one time been the most important person in a prior reality. She wouldn't lead him astray.

"The memories are here, my love," the female stranger replied. *"There're all around. But you must retrain yourself to see them... to feel them... once again. That begins by breaking the barrier."*

The consciousness looked and saw they had come to an invisible barrier. It didn't remember how it got there.

"Your last hurdle," the female stranger said.

"How do I break through?" the consciousness asked.

"That's for you to discover, my love."

The consciousness accepted the term of endearment. Now it seemed appropriate.

"Remember," the female stranger said as she faded away.

"I'll remember," the consciousness promised. *"I'll remember you, the crystal dragons, and all the others who helped to make this journey possible."* But as the consciousness faced the barrier, it wasn't sure it would.

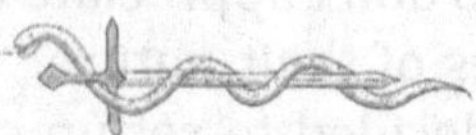

Lessien, carrying the baby Martin, Laylah, Yesper, and Zachariah reached the apex of the plateau after a long and arduous climb. The path they used, located along the side of the plateau, was a rough and tiring ascent. While it was wide enough to safely accommodate Zachariah's carriage, it was too steep for the horses to pull as long as the occupants remained inside. Zachariah refused to leave it or the horses behind, and no one blamed him. In many respects, the carriage had become a home to them, and the horses were steady and sturdy friends. Lessien, following a mortal tradition, had named each of the four—Brandy, Fancy, Scout, and Sunshine.

Once on top, they stopped to catch their breath and eat a light mid-day meal. They were near a wide river that flowed over the side and dropped a thousand feet. The noise of the water from the river as it dropped over the edge drowned out the sound of the water crashing upon the rocks below.

"What feeds this river?" Lessien asked. Martin had finished a skin of strider milk and, unbothered by the tumult caused by the rushing water of the river, was fast asleep in Lessien's *Mantle of the Sovereign* and safely tucked away in the carriage.

"There's a small, freshwater sea further inland that feeds it," Zachariah replied. "A large river feeds the sea… that and the unusually large thunderstorms that occur over the plateau. The river runs deep underground and is itself always reinvigorated by the water dropping off the side of the plateau… water that doesn't go into the Okoris and Arlinggamau Runs. It's a gigantic, circular self-sustaining system."

"And the city we're going to is at the other end of the plateau?" Laylah inquired.

Zachariah nodded. "Indeed. But first we have to get past the Taumaru. Though not complete savages, they're a rough bunch of demons who don't appreciate trespassers."

"I've heard stories of their nature," Laylah said. "And this is where Braz'galar decided to set up camp? Zhaarmoth and the Taumaru have never seen eye to eye. For a long time, the city did everything it could to wipe out the Taumaru, who tried the same with Zhaarmoth several times themselves. That they hate each other is an understatement. Seems like an awful lot of trouble for Kor's fixer. Why would he want this city?"

"Things have changed considerably over the years," Zachariah explained. "Kor owes much to his fixer and rewarded him with the lordship of any city in the Abyss. Braz'galar deliberately choose Zhaarmoth for strategic reasons, which

I'm sure he'd be willing to discuss once he shows up. As for Kor, he was more than happy to give it to him. One less thorn threatening him. All Braz'galar has to do is go to the capital and officially claim it."

Lessien shook her head. "So all we have left is to get by the Taumaru, who are as likely to kill us as look as us, and then negotiate our way into a city run by one of Kor's own overlords since this Braz'galar fella isn't there to let us in. Sounds easy enough... if you like death traps."

Zachariah laughed. "Oh, how I love this mortal!" he exclaimed. "Is the blade of that sword you carry as sharp as your tongue?"

Lessien stared, unamused. "Perhaps you'd like to find out?" she asked as she gripped the hilt of *Ah-HritVakha*.

The InnisRos queen's remark sent Zachariah into a fresh set of chuckles. "No, my dear, I've no intent on discovering what your magical sword can do." The Chief Interrogator turned serious. "It'll be much easier than that. For years now Braz'galar has secretly been replacing anyone of any importance within the city with his own people. That includes administration, law enforcement, and the upper echelons of the city militia. He even disposed of the city overlord... an oaf of a demon named Mangrod... without Kor's knowledge. The city, for all intents and purposes, has belonged to Braz'galar for quite some time now. We'll have no problems on that front. As for the Taumaru, Zhaarmoth, or should I say Braz'galar, has a treaty with them. It's a 'you scratch my back and I'll scratch yours' kind of agreement. The Taumaru knows who I am and that we're coming... at least that's what Braz'galar told me. Does that satisfy your fears, mortal queen?"

Lessien nodded. "Thank you, Zachariah," she said as she climbed back into the carriage.

"You must give Lessien her due," Yesper said after the mortal queen had closed the door. "She's been in a difficult situation for a long time. An overlord forcibly sent her to a foreign land. She had to stand by helplessly as a demon brutally raped her best friend, which resulted in her friend's death during childbirth. Now she cares for an orphaned infant, the consequence of that rape, and I suspect a constant reminder of her own perceived failure to defend her friend. She's a queen in her own world, but is completely reliant upon strangers to survive in ours. Yet she remains strong. Think how hard that must be."

"And I've seen her use that sword of hers," Laylah added. "Even one handed she's a deadly adversary."

"I know all that!" Zachariah snapped, then shook his head. "I'm sorry, Laylah. It's just that she frustrates me. One minute she's good-natured and pleasant and the next she's a viper, ready to strike. When I'm around her, I feel like I'm constantly walking on eggshells… not knowing which Lessien I'm dealing with. One thing's for sure, though. She'd make a worthy opponent during an interrogation."

A day and a half of travel put them on the shores of the inland sea Zachariah had mentioned when they had first reached the top of the plateau. During that time, there were signs they were being watched by the Taumaru… signs that were left behind deliberately according to Yesper. But the Taumaru never challenged them.

"There're no docks… no ships for a crossing," Laylah mentioned. "You'd think at least the Taumaru would have a settlement here."

"The Taumaru are all around us," Zachariah said. "But they live much closer to Zhaarmoth. I said the other day that Braz'galar had strategic reasons for selecting Zhaarmoth. Obviously, the Taumaru are one. But this sea is another. If Kor or another overlord were to send an invading army, first they must ascend up the only path to the top of the plateau. You experienced yourself how difficult that is. Then, upon reaching the sea, they'd have to march around it. During the march around, they'd be constantly harassed... whittled down is more like it... by the Taumaru and Braz'galar's own special forces. Any invading army would be at half strength or less and exhausted by the time they got to the other side to face the main strength of Braz'galar's own army and the Tamarau."

"And if they brought their own ships?" Laylah asked. "They could build them in the forest-rich lands below. I know the climb is prohibitive, but they can do anything if Kor has given them the proper motivation. Or they could build them once on top."

Lessien shook her head. "There's no way they could get sea-ready ships up to the top," she said. "If they were to build ships once they got up here, they'd have to bring their own materials. I haven't seen large enough trees or anything else in the last day and a half they could use. And even if they managed to bring enough material, building ocean or sea-going ships takes time and a lot of experienced shipwrights. Other than moving stuff around, the labor an army provides isn't good enough. That's a lot of additional personnel, which leads to the problem of feeding everyone. It's not as if they can plant crops, and the wild game around here isn't even close to being enough. Without bringing a mile-long supply train, they'd be starving inside of two weeks. It's a logistical nightmare. Finally, I doubt the Tamarau and this Braz'galar you speak of would just sit on their haunches swapping tales of glory days gone by while this was happening. An army bivouacked in one place for as long as they'd have to be to build ships would be inviting disaster, something I'm sure the Tamarau and Braz'galar wouldn't take long to arrange. It's an impossible situation and one I doubt any general worth his salt would consider."

Zachariah nodded. "Impressive."

Lessien looked down at a grinning Martin as she tickled him on the belly. At the moment, she looked like nothing more than a mother and her child. But when she looked back up at Zachariah, there was a glint in her eye that betrayed that entire image.

"I rule an island nation," she said in a voice that left no room for dispute before going back to tickling Martin.

Zachariah looked at Laylah, who smiled. Yester chuckled.

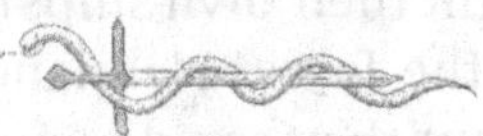

"There it is," Nightshade said as she and Landross looked out over the grassy landscape at the plateau still several miles away. "I doubt we'll get there by nightfall."

Landross squinted his eyes as he looked at the plateau off in the distance. "Is that a waterfall?" he asked.

Nightshade nodded. "Yes. It's quite lovely... but mostly I remember how loud it is. You can't hardly think it's so loud."

Herbie barked.

"I think he already hears it," Nightshade remarked.

"No... it's not that," Landross replied as he got off his horse and knelt down by his dog.

Herbie barked again. Then his hackles rose and he growled as he stared in front of them. It was a low, deep snarl that came from the lower reaches of his chest.

Landross rose and unsheathed his great two-handed sword.

"What is it?" Nightshade asked.

"I'm not sure," Landross answered. "But there's something out there. Even I can sense it now. You stay here with the horses. And keep a tight hold on the reins so they don't bolt. Herbie and I are going to check it out."

Herbie stayed close to Landross's side as they moved forward. The trail they'd been following turned from the east to a more southeasterly direction. But Herbie kept going due east and soon they were in chest-high grass.

"I don't like this," Landross said aloud.

"Neither do I," Nightshade said from a few feet behind. She held the reins of both horses who followed.

Landross jumped. He and Herbie had been so intent on the perceived threat ahead of them, they never heard her come up from their rear. "Really, Herbie?" he said to the dog before he turned his attention to his other companion. "I thought I told you to stay on the trail!"

"You thought I was going to listen?" Nightshade countered. "How chivalrous of you. Landross, until now, you've refrained from treating me as a damsel who needs protection... and I appreciate that."

"But..."

"No 'buts' about it," Nightshade scolded. "We're in this as equal partners. That means you don't get to boss me around. You know better than most that I can take care of myself... and you might need my help. Besides, who's to say whatever's out there wouldn't come around and..."

Herbie growled again, but this time it had more urgency to it. Landross and Nightshade looked, but saw nothing.

"See the line of trees over there?" Landross pointed to the north.

Nightshade looked. "I see them. They run along the banks of the Arlinggamau Run." She shrugged. "A run is basically like most rivers but larger. To the south is the Okoris Run... also lined on both banks with trees. They meet a few miles ahead."

"What kind of critters live near or in the water?"

"Oh, I don't know," Nightshade replied. "The normal kind, I guess."

"For you, maybe," Landross said. "You're from the Abyss. But for me... what I'm really after is whether or not there's something that might crawl out of the water looking for a meal?"

Nightshade froze. Suddenly she had a pretty good idea

what might be out there. "Get on your horse!" she yelled as she mounted hers.

Landross wasted little time heeding her warning.

"Now let's get back to the trail," Nightshade said as she used the reins to turn her horse before kicking it in the side.

Again, Landross wasted no time following but held his horse up after a few steps. Herbie hadn't moved and was barking wildly. Landross dismounted, pulled out his sword, and slapped his horse's rear-end to make it gallop away. Despite the gathering darkness, Herbie's barking allowed the knight to locate the dog in the tall grass. As both looked out over the grassy field, they could just barely make out movement. Stalks of grass flattened along a broad front before them and headed in their direction. Herbie showed his teeth as he growled a challenge to whatever approached.

"Get back here!" Nightshade screamed. "You can't defeat what's coming! The trail's protected!"

"What's coming?" Landross yelled back.

"The spiny h**ummeri** are spawning!"

"The spiny what..." Landross began before he stopped. He'd just caught a glimpse of one. It ran three feet off the ground on twelve legs. Its body was six to seven feet long. Two foot-long claws on arms twice that length protruded from its sides, like a crab or lobster, and a double tail ending with a stinger on each curled up and over its body. Down the back of the creature ran a triple row of spikes, which appeared to be dripping a slimy substance of some sort. They were incredibly fast and there were a lot of them.

"Never mind," Landross yelled to Nightshade. "No time."

A bolt of white lightning suddenly struck several feet in front of Landross and Herbie. Bits and pieces of spiny hummeri flew into the air, dropping tissue, blood, and guts over both.

"Get back here!" Nightshade repeated.

Landross didn't have to be told again. "C'mon, boy," he said as he turned to run. Herbie followed this time.

But it was too late. Another bolt of lightning from Nightshade eliminated a few more, but there were just too many. And Landross knew it. Although they were only twenty yards from the safety of the trail, the knight realized they'd never outrun the creatures. Herbie was running a few feet ahead, so Landross turned to fight, hoping Herbie wouldn't stop and continue onward.

"You'd die for a dog!" Nightshade screamed.

Landross had never faced creatures with the spiny hummeri's speed and agility. For every one he sliced, two grabbed him with their claws. Each claw strike dented his armor. Above the din of chitin on metal and Landross's own grunts came another sound... the "ping" that the tail stingers made when they hit the knight's metallic shell. Each stinger that hit lacked enough force to penetrate the armor completely, though they left small holes.

A minute, or was it an eternity, passed before Nightshade and Herbie arrived to help. The priestess created a wide arc of fire in front of them to keep as many of the spiny hummeri away as possible. A countless number burned before they learned to go around. Herbie, though the same size as the spiny hummeri but heavier, moved almost as quick, which allowed him to dodge the claw and stinger attacks. He struck back at the river creatures with a ferocity that surprised both Landross and Nightshade.

The priestess felt the drain of the power she used to help keep the spiny hummeri at bay. Soon she'd no longer be physically able to use the magical force from the ley lines that fed her. If she didn't do something soon, the three of them would be dead within minutes. Nightshade withdrew into herself, whispered an entreaty to Althaya, and reached up once again to contact the ley lines that passed overhead. A shimmering dome appeared over the three which evaporated any spiny hummeri within its confines. Nightshade dropped unconscious to the ground.

Landross, panting, his armor now useless, looked around for more of the spiny hummeri to kill. Hundreds stared at him from outside the shimmering walls of the dome while others tried to claw their way through. The dome remained intact—for now. The knight looked at Herbie, who was sitting close by. His faithful friend appeared to be unharmed. Nightshade, however, lay unmoving a few feet away. Landross dropped his sword and took a step towards the priestess, but suddenly his vision failed. An incredible pain from an unnoticed puncture wound in his hand shot up through his arm and into his chest. His heart beat wildly and then fluttered. Breathing became difficult, then stopped altogether. The knight dropped to the ground just a few feet from the priestess. His armor clattered and broke away in many places. Herbie lay next to Landross and placed his head on his master's chest.

The clamoring of Landross's armor when he fell startled Nightshade into consciousness. She looked over at the knight with weary eyes and saw one of his hands had ballooned up to three times its normal size.

"No!" Nightshade whispered in a hoarse voice as she crawled to Landross. "You will not die! Do you hear me, you elvan bastard! You will not die!"

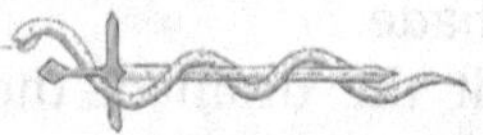

Zachariah had his coachman move the horses pulling his carriage at a leisurely pace. Now that they'd made it to the plateau that housed both the Tamarau and Braz'galar's city of Zhaarmoth, the Chief Interrogator didn't feel threatened. Any highwaymen trying to set up camp on this plateau would soon find themselves either flying without wings or roasting in a Tamarau bonfire. The locals were known to enjoy a little "sport" with their captives every once in a while. It was a narrative that, though they didn't nurture, they didn't bother to discourage either.

It was a lazy afternoon and Martin was asleep, though he was little trouble when awake, and everyone else in the carriage was doing their best to imitate him as the motion of the carriage rocked them back and forth. Only the occasional drone of a gnar—a small, six-winged flying insect—kept them from falling asleep themselves.

"Whoa there, beasties!" the coachman shouted. "Master Zachariah... you better get out here!"

Zachariah frowned. "I wonder what's going on?" he said as he pulled aside the curtains covering a window. "Uh oh. You two ladies stay inside. Yesper, I think you should come with me."

"What's happening?" Laylah asked.

"The Tamarau have decided to make an appearance," Zachariah replied.

"But Braz'galar said..."

"I know what Braz'galar said, Laylah," Zachariah answered. "But you can't take anything for granted with this tribe."

The Chief Interrogator and Yesper stepped out of the carriage. Standing in front of it were three Tamarau, but that wasn't all of them. Interspaced in the grasslands that made up this part of the plateau were another fifty Taumaru. Zachariah had known his carriage was being watched, but the number surprised him.

"Which one of you is the leader?" Zachariah asked as he and Yesper approached the three in front of the carriage.

"You have a Highland Taupe Dragon with you," the middle of the three said. Then he addressed Yesper. "My tribe is honored to make your acquaintance."

Yesper bowed his head. "Thank you. I'm Yesper Duskborn

of the Shadow Peaks Highlands."

"I wanted you to act real mean and bloodthirsty... not recall your family lineage," Zachariah whispered.

Yesper ignored the overlord.

"You may call me Uraxas," the Taumaru replied as he returned Yesper's bow. Then he turned to Zachariah. "You are Braz'galar's friend?"

"I am. My name is..."

"We know who you are, Chief Interrogator," Uraxas said. "We haven't received word from Braz'galar in quite a while. But the last time we spoke he asked us to let you pass onward to Zhaarmoth. All except for the child you have with you."

"You mean Martin?" Yesper asked.

"If that is the name of the child, Yesper Duskborn of the Shadow Peaks Highlands, then yes."

Zachariah shook his head. "Nothing will get Martin away from Lessien. Nothing!"

"It's a condition of your passage, Chief Interrogator Zachariah," Uraxas explained. "The child is a cambion... the child of a mortal and one of us..."

"I know what a cambion is," Zachariah responded with agitation.

"Calm yourself," Yesper whispered.

"Then you understand why we must take him," Uraxas said. "He must not be allowed access to the mortal world! If he were, every superstitious monster-hunter there would hunt him. They'll force him to defend himself. They'll force him to unleash his power. Many will die... including him."

"You think we in the Abyss will be any more accepting?" Zachariah demanded. "Here, he'll be an outcast! At least over there, he'll have a queen to guard and provide for him."

"Even a queen cannot prevent his eventual awakening," Uraxas replied. "And yes, it's true that here in the Abyss, he'll be a pariah... a half-breed with fewer rights than most peasants.

But not with us. We're already outcasts."

"Are you sure about this?" Zachariah asked.

Uraxas nodded. "As sure as one can be. You either hand the child over willingly or we'll take him by force."

"You'd kidnap Martin?" the Chief Interrogator remarked. "Do you know what you're dealing with? You think we'll just lie down and let you do whatever you want? You'd lose many of your warriors! Perhaps even your own life!"

The Taumaru chieftain shrugged. "Death is part of life, and there are many more to take our place."

Zachariah sighed and looked at Yesper. "At least growl or something!"

"Don't fight this," Yesper said to the Chief Interrogator. "It's what's best for everyone, especially Martin."

Zachariah looked at Yesper and then at the faces of the Taumaru and sighed. "Lessien's going to be crushed."

"Bring the child to me," Uraxas requested. "We've already placed him in a family. Don't fear. He'll be loved. You must explain this to his mortal caregiver."

"Oh, sure. She'll understand all right," Zachariah said to himself as he turned back towards his carriage.

"Both will get over it," Yesper remarked. "In time."

"Of course they will," Zachariah answered. "I'm just worried about what Lessien will do to me with that big, long, demon-sticker until she does."

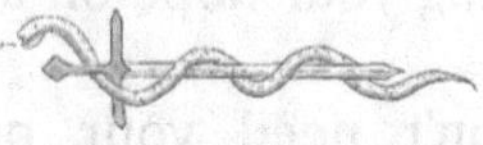

The child Martin wasn't asleep, as everyone had assumed. He had sensed the Taumaru long before they stopped the carriage. With his keen hearing, he heard and understood everything the Tamarau, Zachariah, and Yesper discussed. The Tamarau request didn't shock him. In fact, to him, it made perfect sense. He understood the reasons he couldn't stay with his second mother in the mortal world, and he understood the problems he'd have growing up off the Tamarau plateau in the Abyss. A decision—a life-altering decision—was necessary.

"I love both my mortal mothers," Martin thought. *"One I'll never know and the other will never know me."*

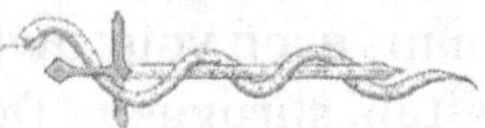

"No!" Abigail demanded once again. "I'm not letting you take him!"

"Listen to reason," Michael said. "He's not coming back. All our healers agree that his condition is irreversible. His people… his friends… should be allowed to bury him at his monastery, don't you think?"

"This isn't his native land, Abigail," Lord Ternborg added. "It's what he'd want."

Abigail shook her head. "Don't you see! He's not dead! I'll not allow him to be buried alive!"

"His mind's gone," Gabriella added. "Every one of our healers who examined him has said the same thing."

"No!" Abigail screamed. "Don't you tell me that. I don't care what your healers say. Or yours, Lord Ternborg. He'll come back. I know it."

Michael sighed. "Abigail, you're only thinking of yourself."

"And you're putting your hope on an impossibility," Lord Ternborg added.

"Besides, we don't need your permission," Gabriella remarked. "We've included you as a courtesy since you were his traveling companion. But you've no real claim over him… at least not as much as the island of InnisRos on Aster does. That's his home. That's where the people who love him the most live."

Both Michael and Lord Ternborg winced. As usual, Gabriella's directness spared no feelings and came across as being overly harsh, given the circumstances. The last thing anybody wanted was a grieving and angry gorgon. As it stood, even the *B'nai Elohim* weren't immune from her special kind of ability.

"Rein Gabriella in," Lord Ternborg whispered to Michael. "I don't want to be a statue decorating the foyer in my palace."

But the explosion of fury they expected from the gorgon never materialized. That Gabriella's remarks took Abigail aback was plain to see. But instead of becoming angry, the gorgon closed her eyes and took a deep breath.

"The person Horatio loves the most, other than his daughter Kristen, is his wife, Autumn," Abigail said. Her voice was steady and measured. "But she's likely dead. He admitted as much to me. It's not so much that there's direct evidence to support that assumption. But rather, it's the lack of evidence of her presence here that's convinced him. Everywhere we've heard rumors of the queen... a one-handed mortal who wields a magical sword. But no one has ever tied the queen to another of her kind. And Horatio doesn't believe the queen would leave his wife unless she *was* dead."

Michael nodded agreement. "I see the logic. And even though he believed his wife dead, he'd still stay to look for the queen, along with Nightshade and Landross. But what does that have to do with Father Goram being... comatose... or your relationship with him?" Michael had almost said "dead," but caught himself. He didn't want to disturb the delicate hold the gorgon had on her emotions.

"I'm getting to that," Abigail responded. "Nightshade's like a daughter to me. I served as the mother she never had as a child. And though I didn't care for the person she was under her father's talon, she always came back to me as the person I grew to love. I'm not surprised Horatio and his goddess could turn her from the dark… for the light was always within her, just waiting to escape. When she showed up the last time, the time when I met Horatio and Landross, she enlisted my help in the pursuit of the mortal queen, Lessien. During our travels, Horatio and I became… close. When he heard of the difficulties you were having here and the threat it presented to his native world, he decided to come here instead. I stayed with Horatio while Nightshade and Landross continued east in search of the queen."

"For which we're eternally grateful," Michael said.

Abigail looked at the *B'nai Elohim* leader. "I only hope it's not in vain." Tears flowed down the gorgon's cheeks. "I don't believe he's gone. Not Horatio. None of you know him as I do. We're connected, as impossible as that might sound. He's still fighting to get back. I can sense it." The gorgon paused. Her tears had stopped flowing. "I love him, Michael," Abigail said with conviction. "I love him like I've loved no other in my life. With his wife gone… well, I think I can say no one here, or on Aster, loves him more. And… and though he'd never abase the memory of Autumn, I know he loves me too. Let me take him back to my shop in Zir Tachoss. I'll care for him. I'll do whatever's necessary. And I'll wait however long it takes for him to find his way back to me."

"You're putting us in a difficult position, Abigail," Michael said. "I'm sure the people in his monastery will want him back as well."

"As will the entire island of InnisRos," Lord Ternborg added. "Perhaps you could go to Aster with him instead?"

Abigail shook her head. "That'd only put him in more danger. Here I'm accepted… or feared… and have built a life. They'd never accept me on the mortal world. Because of who I am, they'd hunt me relentlessly. Horatio would seek to protect me, but it'd never end. That'd be putting Horatio and every person around us in danger. I can't live with that."

"Let's say Father Goram wakes up and wants to go back to Aster," Gabriella asked.

Abigail looked at the *B'nai Elohim*. "Did you not hear me when I said I loved him? Any sacrifice isn't too great. If he wanted to go back, I'd not stand in his way."

Gabriella shook her head. "Short of a miraculous recovery, there's only one way to resolve this. He's a subject of the InnisRos queen, isn't he?"

Michael, Lord Ternborg, and Abigail looked at Gabriella.

"Let her decide... if she ever shows up."

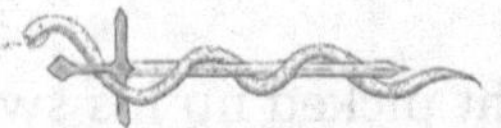

Landross startled awake. It was morning. He'd been having a bad dream... a dream in which Nightshade had died. That bothered him more than he expected. He looked over and saw her sleeping on her stomach with one arm outstretched and resting on his chest. Then he heard a familiar lapping sound. He looked over at Herbie. The dog was only a few inches away and licking his front paws. When Herbie realized Landross was awake, he reached over and began to lick the knight's face while he wagged his tail furiously.

"Oh, yuck!" Landross exclaimed as he used the back of his sleeve to wipe away the dog's slobber.

"Woof!"

Landross gently placed Nightshade's arm to the side so he could sit. He put his great cloak, which looked to have survived unscathed, over the recumbent priestess.

"Come here, boy," Landross said to Herbie. The knight scratched behind the dog's ear. "How you doing?"

Herbie rolled over to one side as he accepted the attention.

The knight looked around. Dead spiny hummeri were all around the perimeter of the barrier Nightshade had placed to protect them. As for the rest, there was no sign. Landross stood and stripped away the bits and pieces of his broken armor that still clung to him. Then, on impulse, he also took off the chain mail he wore underneath. When the ringed metal shirt hit the ground at his feet, it felt as if he'd been released from a great burden. A great awakening rose from deep within. He felt liberated… liberated from duty to an ideal… from the demands of principals… from the tenets of knighthood. It felt good to be rid of everything. It was a freedom he hadn't experienced in a long time.

"I'm ready for a new life," Landross thought. *"Ready to be who* I *am."*

The former knight picked up his sword from where he'd dropped it and sheathed it. He saw the trail they'd been traveling the night before about one hundred feet to the southwest. Their horses were still there. Nightshade had the presence of mind to stake them before coming to fight with him the previous night. Then he wrinkled his nose. He noticed the stench of the dead spiny hummeri for the first time. They smelled like rotten fish.

"What say we wake up Nightshade and get back to the trail, Herbie boy," Landross said as he knelt next to the priestess.

But she didn't respond. Landross looked more closely at her face. It was pale and clammy. He placed his ear over her chest. Her heartbeat was slow and irregular, and she was barely breathing. He briefly inspected her body for signs of poisoning from a stinger strike and found none, which meant she must have overextended herself when she healed him.

The former knight straightened up and cursed. "Damnit! Why didn't she stay on the trail?"

Landross knew he had to get Nightshade to a healer, or she'd be dead within a few hours. The plateau was too far away. He scooped up Nightshade and, with Herbie sticking to his side, ran to the horses.

"Back to Drog'dronnan, Herbie boy!"

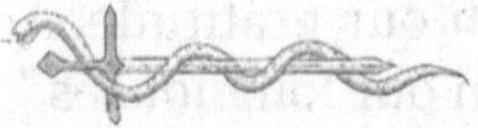

When Zachariah and Yesper opened the carriage door, both Lessien and Laylah were asleep.

"That's strange," Zachariah said.

"Indeed," replied Yesper. "Though perhaps it's for the best."

"Regardless of how we do this, the mortal queen's going to want me dead… or severely incapacitated!"

Yesper smiled. "You mean she'll try to cut off your…"

"Precisely," the chief interrogator responded. "Especially if we're caught in the process."

But extricating Martin from Lessien's *Mantle of the Sovereign* went smoother than expected. Neither Lessien nor Laylah woke from their nap, and Martin, though awake, stayed silent. Zachariah and Yesper took the child to the Taumaru.

"His name is Martin," Zachariah said as he handed the child over. "Martin… Martin…"

"Goram," Yesper said. "Martin Goram. Queen Lessien explained to me that it's common on the mortal world to name people with a first and last name. The last name identifies the family. And so it was given in the naming ceremony."

"His mortal and Abyssian name, yes," Uraxas replied. "But his Taumaru name, the name we shall call him, is Xerxes."

"Meaning?" Yesper asked.

Uraxas looked at the Highland Taupe dragon. "It means 'lord' in the language of the Taumaru, Yesper Duskborn of the Shadow Peaks Highlands."

"I didn't realize the Taumaru had a word for that, Uraxas," Yesper said.

"An outsider wouldn't," Uraxas replied with finality.

"Understand this, Yesper Duskborn of the Shadow Peaks

Highlands. Our days of being outcast are coming to an end… and Xerxes will play a major role. It has been foretold. You may now go in peace with our gratitude. And know that you will always have a place in our longhouses."

Yesper bowed. "I'm honored and hope to see our paths cross again."

"That was curious," Zachariah commented as the two returned to the carriage. "I wonder what he meant by 'Our days of being outcast are coming to an end?'"

Yesper laughed. "Whatever it means, I suspect your friend Braz'galar… and Zhaarmoth… are going to be involved."

As the two drew closer to the carriage, they noticed the driver had fallen asleep. "That's curious as well," the chief interrogator remarked. "Thozzin! Wake up!"

"Huh? Oh, begging your pardon, My Lord. I can't for the life of me understand why that happened."

Zachariah smiled. "It's been a long trip, my friend," he said as he opened the door of the carriage. "We can go now."

Inside the carriage, Lessien and Laylah were awake and talking as if nothing had happened. The empty *Mantle of the Sovereign* lay across the queen's lap. Both glanced up at Zachariah in acknowledgement before returning to their discussion. Zachariah shook his head. The scene inside the carriage, though like many others he'd witnessed since beginning this journey with the two females, seemed strange. It was as if he'd expected something else… that something was missing. But he couldn't quite place a finger on it. He took one last look out over the grasslands before entering the carriage. Empty. He shook his head again before going inside, wondering why he had gone outside in the first place.

Yesper followed Zachariah into the carriage. Unlike the others, he remembered everything. *"Clever lad,"* he thought. *"Always knew there was more to him than meets the eye."*

"I just heard from my people in Zhaarmoth," Braz'galar said to Michael. He'd walked in on a strategy meeting between the *B'nai Elohim* and the Draugen Pesta leaders. Belladonna was at his side.

"And?" Michael impatiently replied.

"The mortal queen has arrived safe and sound," Braz'galar said.

"Any sign of Landross and Nightshade?" Michael asked.

Braz'galar shook his head. "None as yet. But they're heading that way. I'm sure they'll turn up."

Michael raised an eyebrow.

"My sister knows her way around," Belladonna said in response to Michael's silent uncertainty. "Don't worry. She'll get there with the knight."

"Now that we know Queen Lessien's in Zhaarmoth, do you think one of your sorcerers can open a doorway from there to here?" Lord Ternborg inquired of Braz'galar. "I want to get her returned as soon as possible. She's important to the elves of Aster... and if Kor attacks, she'll be instrumental in leading the effort to counter his invasion."

"So Kor's still here?" Belladonna asked.

Michael nodded. "As far as we know. According to my sorcerers there's been no large usage of magic. So his army's still here."

"As to your question, Lord Ternborg... no," Braz'galar said. "It'd have to go across the entire expanse of the Abyss. None "What if I were to fly there?" Gabriella interrupted.

Michael shook his head. "Too dangerous. You couldn't make the trip without needing to stop and rest. Any landing would expose you to an attack even more so than when you're in the air."

"And from what I've seen, there's plenty of demons with wings," Lord Terborg remarked. "Without all of your immunities, you'd be a sitting duck either way."

Everyone looked at the Draugen Pesta king with frowns of confusion on their faces.

"Sorry. It's an Aster expression," Lord Terborg explained. "Easy target."

Michael nodded. "It's out of the question, Gabriella."

"Maybe one of your sorcerers could teach Braz'galar the spell which will allow him to open a doorway to Zhaarmoth from here," Belladonna offered. "He's a powerful sorcerer in his own right... plus he's been there enough to know it by heart, so familiarity wouldn't be a problem."

This time it was Braz'galar who put down the suggestion. "I already know the spell, Belle. But if it were that simple, I wouldn't be wasting my time on horseback whenever I traveled. Nor would anyone else. Unfortunately, besides distance, there's another problem when using a dimensional doorway spell. You all know about ley lines, right?"

Everyone nodded.

Kor's former fixer continued. "Here in the Abyss, we're so busy going about our daily business we tend to forget the reasons why some magic... magic that would ease our lives considerably... isn't used regularly. The simple answer is the *Veil*. As a learned old demon once explained, the ley lines and the *Veil* are in constant conflict with one another. No one in the Abyss completely understands the problem... or the relationship between magic and the *Veil*. It's why magic isn't as common in the Abyss as you might think... and when it *is* used, it's only after complicated safeguards have been put into place. For reasons no one understands, the *Veil* affects the ley lines in unpredictable ways. One moment, they're strong and the next, they're weak. Something seemingly as easy as magically lighting a campfire becomes a risky proposition when you don't know if it's going to fizzle out, flare up and burn everything within a few hundred yards, or light up as intended."

"Any competent sorcerer could tell what's coming before activating the spell," Gabriella said. "And as you said, there are safeguards put into place."

"Safeguards that may or may not work," Braz'galar responded. "Gabriella's correct. A competent sorcerer should be able to tell what he's dealing with when he derives his power from the ley line. But there's no sorcerer alive that can foresee what the end result will be when the nature of the ley line changes after they've tapped it but before it activates. Sorcery in the Abyss is a dangerous business. That being said, there are ley lines that are more stable than others. Knowing which is which is almost as important as knowing how to cast the spell. For example, the ley lines going over Kor's palace are about as stable as there is in the Abyss, though an inexperienced sorcerer will still have problems."

"But we respond to tapped ley lines when we prevent doorways from being opened to the mortal world," Gabriella said.

"The Johari makes that possible," Michael replied. "But without her, we're as susceptible to the problems with the ley lines as any other Prefecture sorcerer."

"So flying over to get the mortal queen is still our best and quickest option," Gabriella concluded. "With the additional time the elvan priest gave us before the Juxtaposition Point completely collapses, I should be able to get her back here."

"Again, Gabriella, it's too dangerous," Michael said.

"Then send several of us," the *B'nai Elohim* second-in-command offered. "Surely one of us will get there."

"That makes you an even larger target," Michael replied. "And if you should lose the queen?"

Gabriella didn't have an answer for that possibility.

"Maybe I have information that can help," a familiar-sounding voice said.

Everyone stopped and turned towards the voice. Abigail was standing in the open doorway. "The guards let me in," she said.

"They should have announced you," Lord Ternborg commented. It was his guards at the entrance. The *B'nai Elohim* were far fewer and had other responsibilities.

"I asked them not to," Abigail remarked.

Lord Ternborg frowned. "That's not how it works."

"Don't blame them, mortal king," Abigail replied. "I'm afraid I bullied myself in. Though I don't enjoy doing such things, I'm awfully damned effective at it."

"I guess you are," Braz'galar commented. "Showed them a little of those two shiny pearls, I bet."

"Why are you here?" Michael asked. "Has there been a change in Father Goram's condition?"

Abigail shook her head. "I'm afraid not. But there's been a change in my position. That's why I sought you out and was told you were here. Speaking of which, do you mind if I make an observation? You seem to be conducting the entire defense of the Juxtaposition Point from behind a table. Is that wise?"

Gabriella started to say something, but Michael grabbed one of her arms to shush her.

"Since you said you have knowledge that might be of help, I assume you stood at the doorway long enough to hear what we were talking about," Lord Ternborg said.

Abigail nodded.

"What information do you have?" Michael asked.

"First, I want a few things from you," Abigail replied.

"This isn't a time to be making demands!" Gabriella exclaimed. "Or to withhold vital information that we might need in this battle!"

"Settle down," Michael ordered his second. "What do you

want, Abigail?"

"Nothing much... a covered wagon, a month's worth of supplies, and two horses. I'm not waiting for Queen Lessien to decide Horatio's fate. I'm taking him out of here at dawn tomorrow."

Michael looked at the gorgon. "If this information you offer..."

Abigail interrupted Michael. "I don't care if what I offer helps or not! At dawn tomorrow, I'm leaving with Horatio one way or the other. Now... you can always forcibly stop me... or even kill me. You'll probably even succeed. But if you do, I'll unleash my power. And you'll have to explain to the loved ones of those trying to stop me why their bodies are being returned as stone statues."

"Fortunes of war, gorgon," Gabriella said. "That's all any family needs to be told." Her leader was being manipulated, and she didn't care for it.

"And is that what Horatio is to you, Gabriella?" Abigail countered.

Michael waved his hands for silence. The tension in the room was too high for his liking. "Please stop!"

"Michael, from what I know of the elvan queen, she won't appreciate you letting the body of her priest... the husband of her friend... go," Lord Ternborg said. "Besides being her friend and close ally, he was the one most responsible for her victory over the Dark Elves. If it were me, my Sofia would move heaven and earth to get my body back. She'll be the same, mark my words."

"Then the elvan queen will have to live with it... or deal with her objections on her own," Michael said. "There are too many important things that need doing to get caught up in a disagreement over a body... excuse me, Abigail... over Father Goram." Michael looked around the table. This wouldn't be a popular decision. "You can have your wagon, supplies, and horses. And for both your sakes, I hope you know what you're doing!"

Abigail nodded while everyone else held their tongues.

"So, how do you think you can help?" Michael asked.

"During our time together, Horatio talked a lot about his queen," Abigail answered. "From what he said, in many respects, she's like Kor… short-tempered, impatient, controlling, manipulative, and so on. But she differs from Kor in that she's regal. She deeply cares for the lands she rules as well as her subjects… enough so to risk her life, or even give it, to prevent harm to them. Horatio says she's a good person, if a bit strong-willed, and an even better queen. As part of her station, she was given two items when she became queen. One's a sword, named *Ah-HritVakha*, and the other's a cloak called the *Mantle of the Sovereign*. Not only do both items have strong magical properties, but there also appears to be a link between them and the queen. Horatio suspects that both sword and cloak are sentient. He says they're relics." Abigail stopped. "Can I have wine, please?"

Michael nodded and directed a servant to pour the gorgon a glass goblet. The liquid was gold-colored instead of red. Abigail paused before drinking.

"It's quite good," Lord Ternborg said. "Better than wine."

"Ambrosia?" Abigail asked.

"Yes," Michael said.

"I've heard of it." The gorgon took a sip and coughed. She wasn't expecting the burn as it went down, though she enjoyed it. As it settled into her belly, she felt refreshed, as if she'd taken an eight hour nap. She took another sip before continuing.

"We all know how powerful relics are. I'm no sorcerer, but with magic that potent it occurs to me you could use the relics not only instead of the ley lines but also as a homing beacon."

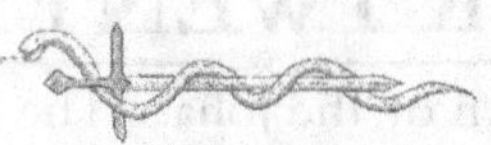

The next morning, a lone wagon left the *B'nai Elohim* fortress through a side gate. As usual, the main gate was being assaulted by Kor's demon minions. Warriors made several attempts to accost the wagon, but each time the offending demons slowly backed away with their hands held up. Word quickly spread throughout the demon armies to leave the lone wagon alone.

CHAPTER TWENTY-THREE

Aster - The Cavern of the Johari, The Hyrokkin Empire, and Draugan Pesta

The crossing of the River Styx out of Hell was much the same as the crossing going in the opposite direction. As Charon's ferry neared the opposite shore, a dense cloud formed around the boat. The boat hit a solid mass and stopped. The wet fog didn't dissipate, so they didn't know exactly where on Aster they were.

"That's oor cue tae leave," Azriel said.

"Exit stage left, eh, Azriel?" Jörmungander exclaimed.

"Oh, laddie," Azriel said as he shook his head.

The ferry, once everyone had exited, silently slipped away and disappeared into the fog.

"We're officially oot o' Hell," Azriel said. "Though we left two dear mukkers behind… 'n' a piece o' mah hert. Ah ne'er thought Max 'n' Solvieg wid hae tae die twa times tae fin' peace. Bit enough o' that slobbering, tear-jerking sentimentality fur noo. Ah will grieve fur Max 'n' Solveig efter. We git tae git th' Johari home."

The fog lifted and they looked around to get their bearings. They were standing in a dark, underground tunnel. All but the Johari, who didn't appear to be aware of anything, felt comfortable in the blackness.

"I think I've been here before," Erika said as she placed a hand on the stone wall. "There's a small ledge on the other side of this wall that overlooks the Johari's cavern. I was with Max and Solveig at the time. It was during the sylph invasion, and we needed a quick place to hide. So I did the only thing I knew to do. I took both of their hands… they were in their corporeal forms… and I magically melded through the stone. I didn't stop to think both could have done so themselves if they turned incorporeal. Max was… well, the whole notion of being pulled through a stone wall didn't really agree with him. He was quite pissed off, actually."

Azriel chuckled. "Ah bet he wis, lass. Ye aff tae dae th' identical fur us?"

Erika nodded. "If that's what it takes. The only problem is I don't know how the Johari's body might react… and she's unable to tell us at the moment."

"Who knows if she ever will," Jörmungander observed. "Maybe I can knock a hole through it with a spell?"

Erika shook her head. "It's too thick. It'd take days to bust through, even with magic."

"Ye'r forgetting a'm still a dwarf, lass," Azriel said. "Let me see whit th' stane tells me afore we git oor knickers in a bunch."

Azriel used his dwarf brain with sylph hands to feel the stone. After fifteen minutes of inspection, he produced a hammer and chisel from his body. For the next ten minutes, he chiseled gashes out of the wall in a circular pattern with one in the exact center.

"Ye'r richt, Erika, it's thick," the dwarf-sylph said. "'N' hollow oan th' ither side. But it haes weaknesses as weel. Watch 'n' learn."

Azriel retrieved his magical battleaxe and placed the blade on the ground with the handle between his legs. As he always does before using his battleaxe, he spit on his hands and rubbed them together. After taking a couple of practice cuts at the marked center, he swung with all his might.

The part of the wall outlined by the chisel marks crumbled into pieces. Erika was right. There was a small ledge on the other side of the wall, and it overlooked the cavern of the Johari. The forgotten smell of the cavern battered their senses—mushrooms, bats, and air freshened by the city-like structure off in the distance.

The Johari opened her eyes and breathed deeply. "Home!" she exclaimed as she flew through the hole and into the cavern, trailed by a streak of purple. Bats joined her flight and soon all of them were performing intricate maneuvers in the air. Outlines of purple stripes crisscrossed the air before fading. Bat youngsters squealed in laughter as they playfully surrounded the Johari, darting in and out. The Johari was laughing just as hard.

"She seems tae be back tae normal," Azriel remarked.

"We don't belong here, my love," Elbedreth said. "Not anymore."

Azriel looked over at his sylph companion and took her hand. "Ye'r richt, lass. 'N' it seems lik' we bonny muckle pure good enough tae deserve a lee o' peace 'n' quiet ourselves."

"Peace and quiet?" Jörmungander remarked. "That doesn't sound like you, Azriel."

"It is noo, laddie," Azriel replied. "Though ah juist micht meander up closer tae th' surface juist in case thay need me... or if life gets tae boring."

"Can Erika and I tag along?" Jörmungander asked. "You know... just for a little while."

Azriel laughed. "We'd be happy fur th' company, laddie. Fur as lang as ye baith waant. Bit foremaist, gang ahead 'n' use yer magic tae fix that nook in th' dyke ah made. Wouldn't waant th' Johari tae git oot again, wid we."

"Right away, Azriel!"

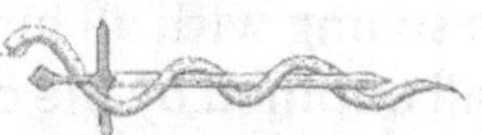

Adimar, with Shubin riding on his back, and Sienna sprinted from the embassy and through the city. Neither guards nor citizens dared to get in their way. The sight of an immortal, gigantic wolf and an even larger bear thundering down upon them was enough to make even the bravest of the centaurs reconsider any heroic notions they might have. The sound of Shubin screaming from the top of his lungs for them to move was the final straw for any stragglers. They moved.

But the guards at the palace were a different story altogether. There were six of them, and they stood in front of the gates and refused to get out of the way. Shubin had expected this and stopped the frantic charge before either side could attack one another. If he couldn't reason with the guards, then Adimar and Sienna would have free rein. But not until then. Shubin was very careful about not inviting unnecessary bloodshed.

"I'm here on behalf of the Daphnia, Princess and heir to the throne of Draugan Pesta, Duchess of the Northern Boreskyre Mountains, Commander-in-chief of the Third Phalanx, Ambassador to the Hyrokkin Empire, and daughter of Their Majesties King Viktor Ternborg and Queen Sofia Germanovna Ternborg." Shubin was laying it on as thick as possible. He didn't want to give the guards a chance to think, even though that wasn't usually their strong suit. "I'm here to see King Thanilus to inform him about a grave transgression carried out upon said Princess. It's a dire matter of life and death."

"Huh?"

"Maybe that was too thick," Shubin thought.

The centaur standing next to the one who'd expressed confusion shook his head. "Lazolio, you're a moron. He means he has a message for the King from that female muckety-muck over at the compound. And that it's important."

"Oh! Thanks, Bastorus."

"How do I know any of what you just said is true?" Bastorus asked.

Adimar growled and pawed the ground in front of him, leaving deep marks in the stone with his claws.

Except for Bastorus, the rest of the contingent of centaur guards backed away a few feet. A few of them looked as if they were getting ready to bolt.

"Steady, boys," Bastorus said before redirecting his attention back to Shubin. "You can go in... under escort. But that damned wolf and the bear have to stay out here."

Adimar growled again. Shubin held on for dear life as the wolf grew to twice his size. But that wasn't the only change. If the wolf looked menacing to the centaurs before, he was ten times more so now. His eyes became blood-red and turned feral. He showed his fangs, which dripped saliva, and growled. Each exhalation surrounded the centaurs in a steaming hot zephyr which smelled of freshly devoured meat. All the centaurs except Bastorus and Lazolio took off at full speed through the gates and back inside the palace walls.

Inwardly, Shubin smiled. *"I didn't know he was capable of that."*

"Eek!" Lazolio exclaimed.

Bastorus took a couple of steps back and raised his sword. "Perhaps I can make an arrangement. After all, you do represent the... the..."

"Ambassador?" Shubin prompted the centaur guard.

"Yes! Yes! Of course. But first, maybe your wolf friend could return to his normal size? Just as a show of good faith, you understand."

Shubin smiled. "What do you think, Adimar?" he said as he patted the side of the wolf's neck.

The wolf reverted to normal form, which was still massive and intimidating.

"Can he understand talking?" Lazolio asked.

"Every word," Shubin replied as he dismounted. "So can the bear."

Both Bastorus and Lazolio had forgotten about Sienna. They leaned to the side so they could look around the wolf and at the bear. She was multi-colored—blue, white, gray, and brown—with magical runes etched into her back and sides. She stood over ten feet on all four legs. Neither had seen anything like her. Sienna looked back at the two centaurs with shiny blue eyes.

"This is Sienna," Shubin said. "She understands what's being said just like the wolf."

"Hi ya, boys," Sienna said into the minds of Bastorus and Lazolio. *"A pleasure to meet you."*

Lazolio feinted dead away. Bastorus stared at the bear.

"But unlike the wolf, Sienna also enjoys talking to people," Shubin added.

Bells rang within the palace complex. Bastorus looked back through the gates and saw centaur guards running from barracks towards the palace. He kicked the recumbent Lazolio awake.

"Get off your arse and guard this gate," Bastorus said to Lazolio. Then he looked back at Shubin. "You three, follow me!"

As Sienna, the last in line, passed Lazolio, she stopped and looked at him. The centaur stood in place like a statue, almost too afraid to breathe. Sienna gave Lazolio a bear smile.

"Have a nice day."

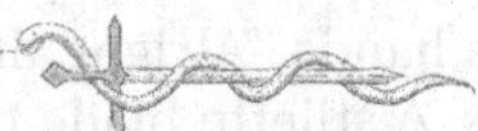

Two of the Lads appeared from their dimension, but that only stopped the centaur guards for a moment. Even Jarsus wasn't foolish enough to believe the Lads and he could defeat that many centaurs without starting a war... and perhaps being killed in the process. The centaurs surrounded him on three sides while his back was against the throne room doors.

"My mukkers, a'm thinking ye shuid skedaddle afore ye git yourselves murdurred," Jarsus told the Lads. "A'm nae feart tae die if that's mah fate 'ere, bit ah don't waant ye tae follow. Gang hame 'n' be wi' yer wee lassies 'n' laddies."

Both of the Lads appeared in the air before Jarsus. *"We*

could call others," one of them said. *"We haven't paid our debt to you."*

"Then wash th' ledger, buckos," Jarsus replied. "Ye'v dane mair than enough fur me. Forby, ah cam tae murdurr Thanilus, nae tak' pairt in a bloodbath."

"We shall meet again," both called out in Jarsus's mind before disappearing.

"Not if ah don't hae mah head," Jarsus said as he threw the sword he was using onto the stone floor.

Behind him, the doors to the throne room opened. Centaur guards stood all around, pointing swords and spears at him. "Drop the rest of your weapons," one of them called out.

Jarsus sighed as he did as ordered. A steel quarterstaff, pickaxe, hammer, chisel, and several knives clattered across the floor.

Not satisfied, the one who'd given the order thrust his sword at Jarsus a few times. "We want all of it."

"Ye damn, bloody, four-legged, spider winchin' jackass!" Jarsus cried. "I don't hae anythin' else!"

"Search him!"

Jarsus held up his hands. "Alright already!" he shouted as he removed his shoes. A stiletto blade thrust out the front of each when Jarsus triggered it. "That's all. Ah swear."

Several of the centaurs wrinkled their noses. "By the gods, short tail! Your feet!" one of them cried out.

"Ye don't hae tae git sae personal aboot it," Jarsus commented. "It's ainlie bin twa weeks sin ah teuk a bath."

"Only two weeks, he says," another said. "I'd wager more like two years!"

"Ye'r na cup o' rose water either, ye muckle lug," Jarsus replied.

"How do you want to die, short tail?"

"Just put his head on a spike!"

"Boil the 'muckle lug' alive!"

"To the rack with him! Then he might be closer to normal size!"

"Give him to my mother-in-law!"

Everyone stopped and looked at the centaur who made the comment. Then they all laughed.

"Have you seen his mother-in-law? What a horse's face!"

Another round of laughter ensued.

"She's... she's... the only centaur uglier than a dwarf!"

Several of the centaur guards were laughing so hard they had to lean against walls for support or fall down.

"None of you are going to do anything to him!" a voice called from down the hallway. Thanilus and Shubin, surrounded by members of Thanilus's personal bodyguard, walked towards the pack of guards who held Jarsus. Any of the guards who could get away unnoticed escaped back into the throne room or down the opposite end of the hallway. The rest came to attention.

"So, dwarf, what did you hope to gain with this little escapade of yours?" Thanilus asked.

"Ah cam 'ere tae murdurr ye, Thanilus, fur whit ye did tae th' Princess," Jarsus responded. "Ye think ah wis aff tae staun aroond 'n' let ye aff th' hook?"

"Blackmantle," Shubin said.

"The wee lassie means mair tae me than lee itself!"

"Blackmantle."

"To think some dirt-licking, lice-ridden troll kisser wid dare tae tak' her..."

"Blackmantle!" Shubin screamed.

"Damnit, Shubin, ah wis juist getting warmed up!" Jarsus yelled back.

"He's shown me proof," Shubin said. "He nor anyone in Hyrokkin were responsible for the attack on the Princess."

Jarsus shook his head. "Ye believe this proof o' his?"

Shubin nodded. "Hyrokkin sorcerers aren't really that

good... at least not compared to ours. Begging your pardon, Thanilus."

"Quite all right, Shubin," Thanilus replied. "It's all true, unfortunately. But dwarf, one of the few things our sorcerers actually do well is reading ley lines. It's necessary since ley lines are so weak and inconsistent over here. And after centuries, it's become second nature. As soon as Shubin explained what had happened to the Princess, I had my sorcerers check. They found remnants of a large spike of power along the ley lines around the time the first crystal overloaded. We figure the magic that triggered the spike set the second crystal to explode the moment someone activated it. When we followed the spike backwards, we found it came from Draugen Pesta, though we don't know for sure if that's where it actually originated from."

"From Draugen Pesta, huh," Jarsus said. "Boy oh boy, th' Queenie isn't aff tae wantae hear that."

"I've already told her," Shubin remarked. "Both Thanilus and I felt it best she not believe any Hyrokkin was responsible."

"Ah bet ye did," Jarsus commented. "Aah... aboot a' this..."

"You and those monsters of yours killed four of my guards," Thanilus said.

"To which Queen Sofia has offered a very generous recompense," Shubin reminded the Hyrokkin king.

"Say it," Sienna said in Jarsus's mind.

"Where are you?"

"Adimar and I are making sure everything is good outside the palace," Sienna replied. *"Now say it!"*

"Whit dae yi'll waant me tae say?"

"Apologize!"

Jarsus sighed. Though it went against his nature, he admitted to himself an apology might help sooth things over. "Thanilus, ye hae mah heart-felt condolences. A'm sorry th' Lads 'n' ah hud tae murdurr they flea-infested... ah mean they brave warriors. A'm sure thay hae a seat o' honor at th' table o' yer gods, 'n' that they're families kin pride themselves in sic fabulous deaths. It'd be..."

"That'll be just fine, Blackmantle," Shubin said.

"By Odin's anvil, ah hope so," Jarsus whispered to himself. "Ah wis laying it oan slicker than a water o' snot running ower ice."

"Yes, it was a somewhat articulate apology," Thanilus said. "Though I'd still like to have him voice it in public... say, a marketplace square?"

"Ah will kick yer four-legged..."

"We already discussed this," Shubin remarked, interrupting the string of invectives that were about to come out of the dwarf's mouth.

Thanilus smiled. "You're too easy, short tail." The Hyrokkin leader turned to Shubin. "While you're here, perhaps we should discuss our other little problem."

"Yes, perhaps we should," Shubin replied as he and Thanilus turned and walked down the hallway side by side. "The Princess will never let you kill them, you know."

"How unfortunate," Thanilus said. "Over lunch?"

"You still got that red you imported from us?" Shubin asked.

"Of course!" Thanilus replied.

Jarsus shook his head. "Diplomacy!" he whispered to himself before calling out. "Shubin!"

Both Shubin and Thanilus stopped and turned.

"Am ah juist suppose tae hauld yer horses 'ere twiddling mah thumbs while ye hae dinner wi' that four-legged... wi' Thanilus?" Jarsus inquired.

"Go back to the embassy, Blackmantle," Shubin said.

"And take those animals with you," Thanilus added.

Jarsus watched as the two continued their journey down the hallway, talking as if they were old friends.

"Diplomacy!" Jarsus repeated to himself.

"C'mon, short tail," one guard prompted. "Back to the compound and your Princess."

This time Jarsus didn't argue.

It was midday and the Madeiran sorceress sat at the same table in the same tavern she frequented every day for her lunch. She was dipping a fresh slice of buttered bread into a bowl of rabbit stew when a stranger joined her. He had blond hair, blue eyes, bulging muscles under his simple workman's tunic, and a ready smile she immediately fell in love with.

"The stew's pretty good," she said as she sat back to enjoy the view, thinking a noon tryst might do her a lot of good.

"Forgive me, madam sorceress, but I'm not here to eat lunch with you. I've something much more pressing to ask."

The sorceress suddenly became suspicious. "Then see me at my shop during normal business hours."

The man shook his head. "I'm afraid this can't wait."

The sorceress dropped her bread and spoon to spin warding spells around her. The stranger didn't try to stop her. None of her protection magic activated. "What the..."

The stranger held up a hand and exposed a simple-looking ring on one of his fingers. "Anti-magic. And there's no point calling for help. Most everyone around us works for me and I paid the tavern owner to look the other way. You've no allies here."

"What do you want?" the sorceress asked.

"You recently performed a service for a giant from Draugen Pesta," the stranger said. "I wish to know his name and where I can find him."

The sorceress shook her head. "He never told me his name," she answered truthfully. "Nor did he tell me where he was going afterwards... though I assume back to Draugen

Pesta,"

"Please describe him to me."

The sorceress shrugged and gave the blonde stranger a thorough description of the giant.

"And the nature of your service?"

The sorceress had little scruples regarding client privacy. If it would get this suddenly very scary person away from her, she was willing to sing like a bird. "He wanted me to magically rig a couple of communication crystals to overload."

"Did he say against whom?"

"Some princess or other," the sorceress replied. "She was across the mountains east of here. The gold was real and there was a lot of it."

The stranger stared at the sorceress for a few moments. "You did what he asked, knowing it was going to hurt or even kill someone?"

"Like I said... it was a lot of gold."

"Do you know if your magic spell was successful?"

The sorceress shrugged. "No, I don't. But the giant never came back for a refund, so I assume it was."

The stranger nodded to his men in the tavern and they all stood. He threw a silver piece on the table, which the sorceress greedily pocketed before going back to her stew.

"By the way," the sorceress called out to the stranger who had started to walk away. "Can you tell me if my spell was successful?"

The blonde-headed human paused. "It was," he finally said.

The sorceress smiled as she tore off a piece of bread. "Good."

The stranger whirled about, grabbed the sorceress's head on both sides with open hands, and violently twisted. Everyone in the room heard the snap of her neck. The body fell over on the table, face in the stew, and lay there for a few seconds before it slithered off onto the floor.

Later that evening, the stranger pulled out his own communications crystal and contacted his Draugen Pesta handler. “It’s Kesha Stanislavovich.”

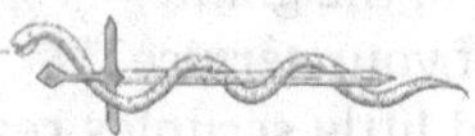

“Are you sure it’s him?” Sofia asked.

“Not much doubt about it,” Aleksei Smirnov replied. “The Madeiran sorceress’s description of him was quite accurate. We know he had motive, and now we’ve placed him with the sorceress, who actually crafted the spell to hurt the Princess.”

“And do you know where he is?”

“We think he came back to Draugen Pesta, though we haven’t been able to verify that,” Aleksei replied. “We’re leaving no stone unturned. If he’s here, he’ll show up eventually.”

“Take him alive if you can, Aleksei,” Sofia ordered.

Aleksei raised an eyebrow.

“Northern justice,” was all the queen said.

Being from the north himself, he understood exactly what the queen was referring to. He smiled. “I’ll see to it, Your Grace. Do you want to see him before?”

Sofia shoot her head. “I never wish to set eyes upon that cur.”

“Yes, Your Grace.” Aleksei rose from his chair to leave. “I’ll keep you informed. Should I notify the northern chieftains in advance?”

“I’ve already done that. Oh, and Aleksei… what happened to that sorceress?”

“As it was relayed to me, she was rather proud of her accomplishment, even after being reminded her spell hurt someone.” Aleksei shook his head. “You know how magic users are… full of hubris. My operative thought the world would be better off with one less sorceress. He snapped her neck.”

"Too bad she didn't suffer."

"It was a spur-of-the-moment decision, Your Grace."

"Ahhh… I see."

Aleksei bowed and left the queen's study.

"Svetlana!" Sofia called out to one of her handmaidens waiting in the next room after Aleksei had left. "Draw my bath and then notify the kitchen that I'll want dinner brought up in about an hour."

"Yes, Your Grace."

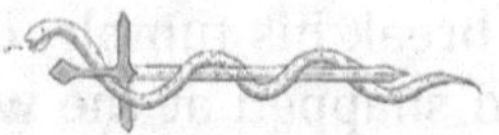

Kesha Stanislavovich ducked behind a small cottage on the outskirts of Saint Petersburg. A dense fog had settled down upon the city, which was most likely the reason he still had his freedom. But the fog wouldn't last much past daybreak, roughly two hours away. So it was important to find somewhere to hide by then.

It seemed as if the whole of Saint Petersburg was looking for him. It wasn't what he'd expected when he returned from Madeira. He found that the authorities had tacked up copies of the warrant for his arrest with an amazingly accurate illustration of his face on every wooden beam, pole, and wall in the city… or so it appeared. With his former boss, Krasnov Dmitrievich, and the other conspirators rounded up and in dungeons so deep they'd never see the light of day, if they were still alive, there were few allies to lean upon. Those who might help had either gone underground or slammed the door in his face when he came calling. And considering how well loved Princess Daphnia was, every person on the street was a potential accuser.

Kesha peeked around the building. Several city guards were standing underneath a street lamppost. The effect of the flames from the lamp combined with the fog gave them an eerie look... like ghosts who were undecided about their incorporeality. One second they were fully visible, the next obscured by shadow and fog.

Cut off as he was in that direction, Kesha, his back flattened against the outside wall of the cottage, moved along its length to peer on the other side. Nothing but dense fog. In his case, the unknown was better than the known. He took off in that direction hoping he'd find sufficient cover. He'd taken only a few steps when he tripped on the uneven ground and fell. As he used his arms to break his tumble, one hand landed in a small depression and snapped at the wrist. He did what he could to stifle a moan, but the surprise and severity of the pain from his broken arm forced one out anyway.

Kesha paused and listened. No other sound broke the stillness of the foggy night. He used his belt and wrapped it tight around the break. It'd have to do until he could fashion a splint. On his feet once again, he continued to move in the same direction. But the pain in his arm soon became all-encompassing, so Kesha decided he'd stop for the rest of the night. He'd try again to escape Saint Petersburg the next evening.

The next cottage he came upon had a lit candle in one of its windows, so he continued on. By the time he made his way to the next cottage, the night was lifting, taking the fog with it. Kesha picked the lock on the front door and slipped inside, peering one last time into the lifting fog to see if he'd been spotted. Seeing nothing, he breathed a sigh of relief and turned. A family of four stood by the dying fireplace staring at him. A well-used sword hung above the mantle. Kesha's pain-addled mind could barely keep up as the father grabbed the sword from its resting place and had the tip pressed against his throat.

Later that same day, Aleksei Smirnov entered Kesha's cell.

"I was wondering if you'd show up," Kesha said. The two of them had been brief acquaintances a long time ago. "I assume you know of my involvement with Krasnov Dmitrievich?"

"That and so much more," Aleksei replied. "How's your arm?"

"Good as new," Kesha responded as he wiggled his fingers. "Though I wonder why you bothered, since the queen will no doubt take my head."

"The queen doesn't want anything to do with you."

"I don't understand," Kesha said.

"We know about the human sorceress you hired to assassinate the Princess."

Kesha smiled. "I didn't really want the Princess killed... just maimed. Was I successful?"

Aleksei shook his head. "Injured, but very much alive."

"Then why am I not going to face the queen's justice?" Kesha asked. "Waiting for the king to return from the Abyss?"

This time it was Aleksei's turn to smile. He wasn't a cruel person by nature, but he had no sympathy for anyone who deliberately set out to hurt a child. "You're to be turned over to the northern tribes. You leave tomorrow."

Kesha frowned. "I don't understand," he repeated.

"The northern tribes are the queen's people," Aleksei explained. "And they have an even greater fondness for the Princess... particularly her grandfather. But they have different ideas concerning crime and punishment than we do here in the capital. I believe the penalty for deliberating hurting a child of royal descent is the Blood Eagle. Or is it flaying? I could never get them straight."

Daphnia startled awake from the latest of several nightmares she'd been having. The setting for each was different, but all involved the same communications crystal exploding in her face. She looked around her bedchamber once again to orient herself… and once again she had to re-remember why there was nothing but black from where her right eye should be working.

A grizzled, smallish hand covered hers. "Calm yersel', mah bonny lassie," Jarsus said. He'd been sitting next to her bed, unbothered, for a long time. There didn't seem to be anything anyone wanted him to do, which frustrated him. But when he considered what he tried to do at the Hyrokkin palace with the Lads, he didn't really blame them, or Shubin, who was running the show now. That was the queen's decision.

"You and the Lads were like a bull in a glass shop!" Sienna said in Jarsus's mind.

"They'd hae gotten me guidd, Sienna," Jarsus thought back. *"Ah wis a deid dwarf if Shubin hadn't shown up."*

"You'd have killed every Hyrokkin in the palace," Sienna countered. *"The Lads told me they were coming back with reinforcements. You know what two can do. Imagine twenty."*

"That'd hae bin a stoatin nightmare!" Jarsus agreed.

There was mild laughter in Jarsus's mind. *"Like I'm going to believe you would have minded."*

Jarsus had sounded concerned, but secretly he enjoyed the idea. He hated the centaurs even more than he did before coming over, and Sienna knew it. *"A've git ither talents."*

"Really! Since when?"

"Jarsus?" Daphnia said. "You still with me?"

"Huh?" the dwarf said as he looked at the princess. "Oh! Sorry, lassie. Juist talking tae Sienna."

Daphnia smiled. "She talked to me while I was asleep. She told me many interesting things about you."

"Now ye'r juist trying tae friten me," Jarsus replied with a warm chuckle.

Daphnia suddenly became serious. "What's happening?

You know... out there," she said as she moved her head towards the window in her bedchamber. "Are Dardandros and Theodasius still here? Galissa and her Shield Maidens? Do you reckon Thanilus really wants to kill them even if they leave within their time limit? How mad is mother?"

"Sienna hasn't filled ye in?" Jarsus asked the princess.

"I left a few things for you," a sleepy voice said in Jarsus's mind.

Daphnia shook her head. "No, silly. And I can't get a thing out of Adimar. He just doesn't care as long as I'm alright."

"Give th' wolf credit," Jarsus commented. Then he sighed. "Princess... mah wee lassie... there's aff tae be some changes... 'n' ah think they're fur th' best."

"It's mother, isn't it?"

"Aye," Jarsus answered. "And wi' guid reason!"

"Oh, Jarsus," Daphnia said as she shook her head. "Spill the beans. How bad is it?"

"Ye'r bein' replaced, darlin'," Jarsus answered. "Shubin's taking ower. 'N' th' wey he gets alang wi' Thanilus, can't say ah don't understand it."

"Diplomacy," Daphnia said.

"Ah see ye understand as weel."

The princess shrugged. "What's not to understand? Shubin's a career diplomat and mother's been looking for any excuse to get me back home that father wouldn't object too. Didn't do much, did I? Except, of course, to cause a bunch of problems for mother, you, and everyone else."

"Ah will nae hae ye talking that way," Jarsus scolded. "Ah don't care howfur muckle training ye'v hud in a' that heich 'n' mighty stuff. Ye'r aye a bawherr lassie wi'oot a lot o' lee experiences. Wance we git back, we'll pick up mah instruction whaur we left off... if ye mither allows it."

"She won't dare stop that," Daphnis vowed. "What else?"

"Shubin git Thanilus tae gree tae allowing Dardandros

'n' Theodasius… they're aye safe, by th' way… tae migrate tae Draugen Pesta. Yer mither says thay kin dae thair monkish hings in th' Northern Boreskyre's."

"My mother's from up there," the princess said.

Jarsus nodded. "Aye. Whilk is how come ah suspect she insisted upon that. Can't hae na damned centaurs running aboot unsupervised. 'Ere lately th' Queenie 'n' ah hae bin seeing eye tae eye oan mony mair things."

"Oh, no! The end of civilization as we know it!"

"Watch yer mouth, lassie."

Daphnia smiled.

"Oh, 'n' anither thing. Galissa 'n' her Shield Maidens ur tae be added intae yer Phalanx. Anya hud thaim swear oaths tae ye 'n' said she wis glad tae hae thaim. 'N' thay wur glad tae hae someplace tae gang ourside o' Hyrokkin."

"Interesting. I'd have thought they'd go north with the Prince?"

Jarsus shook his head. "The Prince didn't waant them. They'll dae weel in yer Phalanx. They're mighty warriors yin 'n' a'."

There was a sudden pause in the conversation as both ran out of things to say. Indeed, no words were necessary between the two friends. Both realized how close the world had come to ending for Daphnia. Even as changed as it was now going to be, what could have been would have been far worse.

Jarsus sniffed. "Daphnia?"

"Yes?"

"When wis th' lest time ah tellt ye howfur important yer tae me? Lik' mah ain daughter."

"Go easy on the old coot," Sienna said into Daphnia's mind. *"He has trouble expressing emotions beyond anger, frustration, righteous indignation, and the like."*

Daphnia didn't need Sienna, or anyone else, for that matter, to tell her about Jarsus's feelings for her. She felt much the same. It was as if he were a second father. "I know, Jarsus."

The dwarf was looking at his hands, which were clasped together in his lap. "Guid. It's guid that ye ken. Noo ah shuid let ye git some sleep."

The princess suddenly had an urge to yawn. "Perhaps you're right."

"And a'm needin' tae see howfur muckle trouble ah kin git in. Shubin's bin free o' mah charm far tae long."

As Jarsus was on his way out of her bedchamber, Daphnia had a thought. "Jarsus!"

The dwarf stopped and turned.

"Which do you think I should wear... a glass eye or a patch?"

Jarsus smiled. "Arrrggghhh!"

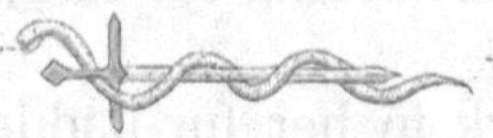

"Do you know about crops, Aleksei?" Sofia asked her chief spy.

They were in her study. It was late, the fireplace was beginning to die down, and the queen had pushed the empty wine decanter over to the side of her desk in favor of a coffee pot.

Aleksei shrugged. "Ten years ago I'd have not only said no, but hell no."

Sofia nodded. "Pretty much how all us northerners see it."

"But now I recognize entire economies can run off of crop production. I know that drought, particularly persistent drought as they have in Hyrokkin, can crush an entire people. No one really thinks of anything else when their belly is empty... except to find food and, instead of that, throw out the leaders, who they'll almost always blame for their predicament. Those leaders, in response, will protect themselves with a powerful military, and before you know it, you have a two class system... the military and everyone else. Cause and effect. That's an oversimplification, of course."

"But pretty astute," Sofia commented. She picked up several pieces of parchment she'd been reading and tossed them across her desk in front of Aleksei. "Crop reports for wheat, barley, soybeans, and maize. Production is down by roughly a third for each."

"Results of the Hyrokkin invasion?" Aleksei asked.

Sofia nodded. "So I've been told. Oh… we're okay, providing we don't have any drought conditions of our own to deal with. But it just gnaws at my gut to make peace with the Hyrokkin, knowing they're responsible for harm… or the potential for harm… to our people. The world would be a much better place without them."

"You and the dwarf seeing eye to eye," Aleksei remarked. "Amazing!"

Sofia leaned back in her fur-padded chair, crossed her arms, and closed her eyes. "Blackmantle. My daughter admires him. No. If I were being truthful, she cares deeply for him as a friend and a mentor. I believe he feels she's the daughter he wishes he had."

A young servant knocked on the door to the queen's study before entering. She carried a tray of fresh coffee and another mug. There were also several small, steaming hot meat pies.

"Right there, dear," Sofia said as she pointed to an empty spot on her desk.

The servant poured fresh mugs of coffee for both Sofia and Aleksei. "Will there be anything else, Your Grace?"

Sofia, her eyes still closed, shook her head. "No, Alisa, that's it. Sleep well."

"You should too, Your Grace," Alisa replied. "We all worry about you."

Sofia smiled. "I will. I promise."

"You shouldn't make promises you won't keep," Aleksei said after the servant girl had left. He was gingerly holding one of the meat pies and blowing on it. “Spicy!” he exclaimed after swallowing his first bite.

Sofia opened her eyes and sat up straight. “I’ll sleep when Viktor returns. Where’d we leave off?”

“We were talking about the dwarf,” the spy said. “An observation, if you please.”

The queen nodded. “Speak your mind.”

“I know you have your problems with Jarsus, but he’s an excellent influence on the Princess. Despite his gruff appearance and nature, he’s very learned. He’s also experienced in things none of our people could ever hope to be. Things he’s passing along to the Princess. And as you yourself have already mentioned, he loves her like a daughter. With that bear and the Lads, not to mention Adimar, she couldn’t have better security. They can do things even her Phalanx can’t do.”

“Yet Daphnia was damned near killed… lost an eye… on his watch,” Sofia countered.

“Even you couldn’t have prevented that.”

Sofia sighed. “I know.”

There was an uncomfortable lapse in conversation. Sofia had closed her eyes again and her breathing became slow and steady. Aleksei thought for a second she’d fallen asleep. He was just about to quietly leave when she abruptly opened her eyes and took a sip of coffee.

“I apologize for the lateness of the hour,” Sofia said. “But there was a reason I called for you.”

Aleksei shook his head. “No apologies necessary, Your Grace. Like all your subjects, I’m at your beck and call.”

“How’d the matter with Stanislavovich go?”

Aleksei smiled. Under normal circumstances, he’d never celebrate another’s misfortune. But Stanislavovich deserved everything he got. “The northern chieftains were more than happy to delve out justice for their Queen and in the name of the Princess. I’ve never seen flaying and the Blood Eagle done in that combination before. He survived the flaying, but his heart gave out just before they spread out his lungs. He was quite mad long before then, however."

Sofia took no pleasure in the traitor's death, but she was relieved it was over. "I don't want any of this to get back to Daphnia."

"Of course, Your Grace... though I'd like to tell Jarsus. I think he'd take great comfort in the nature of Stanislavovich's execution."

Sofia nodded her approval. "Daphnia comes back home in a few days... and that means her Phalanx will come as well. I want you to embed a few of your spies with the army contingent going over to replace them. I want to keep a keen eye on the Hyrokkin. As much as I trust Shubin, he can't see everything."

"As you command, Your Grace."

"Also, get word to your father in the north about the two centaur visitors we have coming," Sofia continued. "I'd appreciate it if he'd watch out for them. They're monks, so survival shouldn't be an issue. But there are orders of monks who allow fraternization between males and females, so if that were to happen, I don't want any of our northern brothers and sisters to get all sanctimonious and hang the two by their gonads."

"Really, Your Grace," Aleksei huffed. "A relationship between one of our females and a centaur?"

"You're as aware of the stories as I am," Sofia replied.

"Stories are all they are. Show me a cross between one of our people and a centaur, and I might well believe. But there's no such thing."

"No issue between the two races is viable according to those same stories," Sofia retorted. "But the heart wants what the heart wants. If something were to happen, just ask your father to use a little common sense when dealing with it."

"Shouldn't be a problem as long as one of my sisters isn't involved. Then I can't guarantee anything."

Sofia smiled. "Oh, my dear Aleksei, but you can."

"I don't understand, Your Grace."

"I've decided to make you a duke and give you the Varencastle Slopes," Sofia replied. "You've more than earned it. Viktor will approve. I'll see to that."

"I don't know what to say, Your Grace. Father might be angry some of his lands are…"

"I've already communicated with your father," the queen interjected. "He's very proud."

Aleksei stood and bowed. "Thank you, Your Grace."

"Don't thank me just yet. You'll find being a duke carries much more responsibility than being my master spy. Speaking of which, I need you to send me your replacement."

Aleksei smiled. "I know just the person. You're going to love her."

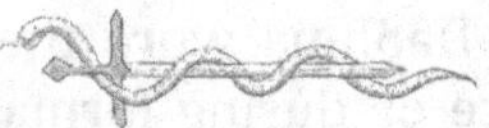

Daphnia, Adimar, Jarsus, Sienna, and Daphnia's Phalanx returned home a week later. The two centaur monks, Dardandros and Theodasius, as well as Galissa and her Shield Maidens, made it safely out of Hyrokkin as well. Thanilus was true to his word. There were no attempts on the former prince's life. At the border, one hundred of the queen's own Phalanx took control of the two centaurs and escorted them to their new lives in the Northern Boreskyre Mountains. The queen's Phalanx commander tested the Shield Maidens and deemed them more than suitable to join Daphnia's Phalanx.

Thanilus offered Shubin, Draugen Pesta's newest ambassador to the Hyrokkin Empire, an entire wing of the palace. But Shubin decided to remain at the newly refortified compound for security reasons. Thanilus later admitted that was best for all concerned. The secret to Shubin and Thanilus's relationship wasn't the drugs that the latter was addicted to, but instead it was Shubin's ability to drink Thanilus under the table. It turned out a wine sopped Thanilus had a free tongue. Shubin soon knew most of the centaur king's most intimate secrets... secrets the Draugen Pesta diplomat used to his advantage when he felt the need. Such gifts, and the games he could play with them, made Shubin's life worth living.

Princess Daphnia and Jarsus returned to their student-teacher relationship and their daily game of Belli. Because of Daphnia's recent experiences, the board game of strategy, nation building, war, and peace meant something more than a way to pass time. By playing it, Daphnia was learning skills she may one day need to apply in actual life situations, which she now understood was Jarsus's intent all along.

The question of glass eye versus eye patch dominated the royal household for several days after Daphnia's return. At her mother's insistence, Daphnia wore the glass eye whenever she was in the palace or during formal state functions. But when she walked the streets of Saint Petersburg with Adimar, and whenever she was with Jarsus, she switched to the more comfortable eye patch.

Everyone in the Draugen Pesta capital, from the richest merchant to the poorest peasant, had heard what happened to the princess's eye. And while the pain of that experience sometimes reflected darkly upon Daphnia's countenance, it never interfered with the relationship she had with the people. There was always a ready smile on her face whenever she was among them, and smaller children were never refused a ride upon the back of her dearest friend, the massive and incredible Adimar, immortal son of the father of all wolves, the half-god Fenrisúlfr. Daphnia had become so popular with the people of Saint Petersburg, they lovingly began calling her Solnyshkuh, which means Sunshine in the old language of the giants.

With her daughter safely back in the fold, Sofia became a much easier queen to live with. Now if she could only get her husband back. The temptation to use the locket to call Michael was overwhelming. Indeed, there's no doubt she would have if she didn't have a kingdom to rule in her husband's place. There were many times she felt that was the only thing that kept her sane. But her northern heritage strengthened her determination. She knew how to endure the cold of a winter's night with blistering winds rushing through mountain passes. She knew how to eke out survival from a stony environment, and how to shelter both physically and mentally. She knew how to withstand anything that didn't kill her. It was that depth of character, that resolve, which ensured her kingdom… her family… would be safe and unthreatened when her husband returned. And if darkness should descend, no matter its form, Draugen Pesta would be ready.

CHAPTER TWENTY-FOUR

The Abyss

For the last several hours, demon officers had been whipping their charges into a frenzy as they prepared them for the invasion of Aster. They'd be the first to step upon mortal soil without being summoned, and each snarling demon considered themselves honored to be among the chosen. Kor, atop his splendid horse, rode back and forth through the legions of troops extolling their prowess as the fiendish beasts they were. The best of the best! Kor, once at the end of the long line of invading demons, nodded towards the army sorcerers to finish opening the doorway. It was going to be a glorious day! Kor closed his eyes and thought about the coming evening's pleasures—mortal females he'd rape and the succulent babies he'd feast upon. It was a great time to be alive.

With his eyes still closed, Kor took in the sounds of magical chanting along with the sizzle of powerful magic being drawn from the overhead ley lines. Thunder roared and lightning crackled as it flashed… followed by an overwhelming howl of the actual opened doorway. Everyone, including Kor, covered their ears. But the doorway quickly stabilized, and the howl died down to tolerable levels.

One of the army sorcerers rushed over to Kor. "It's ready, My Lord!"

Kor smiled and then gave his officers the signal to march the troops forward through the doorway.

Over the past few days, the *B'nai Elohim* and their Draugen Pesta allies had been coming out from behind their fortress walls and taking the battle directly to the demons. Braz'galar, along with his small crew, used the cover of the *B'nai Elohim* offensive to infiltrate the demon lines. A key assassination here and there of high-ranking officers or sorcerers, the fouling of food supplies and drink, the cutting off of key communications, and other types of sabotage brought about by Braz'galar caused as much damage and confusion to the demon armies as the frontal attacks of the *B'nai Elohim* did. The combined results of both efforts were killing demons at a horrific rate.

"It's working," Gabriella said. She, Michael, Lord Ternborg, and Belladonna, presumptive future overlord of the Abyss, were atop the wall overlooking the field of battle beneath them.

"Almost too well," Belladonna said. "You're cutting into what will be my army."

Michael nodded. "Indeed... but necessary if Aster's going to have any chance. You yourself said if Kor succeeds, the *Living Throne* will abandon its support for you and keep him in power. You can only succeed if Kor fails. And Kor can only fail if he has no armies to back him up on Aster."

"Besides, if you take the *Living Throne*, you won't need that large of an army anyway," Lord Ternborg added. "There will finally be peace in the Abyss... if you can keep it."

Belladonna nodded. "If it's within my power *to* keep it," she whispered to herself. Aloud: "I can... as long as I have Braz'galar and his resources on my side... and as long as those within the *Living Throne* don't betray me. Never forget just how brutal and power-hungry they themselves were during their time as leaders of the Prefecture. I may also have to cull a few city overlords who might not be so receptive to my rule... so civil war is a possibility."

Three Draugen Pesta warriors raced along the battlements and stopped next to Michael. The *B'nai Elohim* leader acknowledged their salutes and accepted the message scrolls they were carrying.

"Return to your posts," Lord Ternborg said as he looked at Michael, who was reading the first of the three scrolls.

"According to Braz'galar, Kor's sorcerers are opening the doorway to Aster," Michael said as he handed the scroll to Gabriella.

"That agrees with what he just messaged me," Belladonna added.

Lord Ternborg raised an eyebrow. Michael and Gabriella didn't seem to hear.

"I'll explain later," Belladonna whispered to the Draugan Pesta king.

"Interesting," Michael said while reading the second scroll. "It appears Father Goram did more than buy us some time. It looks like the orb is stabilizing, or at least that's what Jophiel writes from the orb building. She says the whining is quieting, and the wobble is leveling out."

"How can that be?" Gabriella asked as she read the scroll for herself. "Unless..."

"Unless the Johari is alive and back where she belongs," Lord Ternborg finished for her. "I wonder how that's going to impact Kor's doorway?"

"And the third message?" Gabriella asked Michael. "Michael?"

When Michael didn't answer, Gabriella looked over at him. He was standing with his arms at his side, the message scroll forgotten in his hand. Gabriella touched him on the arm and he came out of his self-induced stupor. He looked at his second-in-command as if recognizing her presence for the first time. Instead of speaking, he handed her the scroll and then walked a few feet away to be left alone with his thoughts.

"What's on the scroll?" Lord Ternborg asked.

"It's a casualty list," Gabriella replied. "These upset all of us, but nothing like... oh, no."

"I've seen that reaction before," Lord Ternborg said. "In fact, too many times. There's someone special to Michael on that list, isn't there?"

Gabriella nodded. "Sara… she's Michael's partner…"

"Like a wife?" Belladonna asked.

"Nothing that drab," Gabriella responded. Then she looked at the faces of Lord Ternborg and Belladonna. "Excuse me. I didn't mean to be so harsh. But the relationship between males and females of the *B'nai Elohim* is rather complicated. Anyway, Sara apparently saw the list before sending it along and made a more recent addition… Arioch."

"Who's Arioch?" Lord Ternborg asked.

"Michael's oldest and dearest friend," Gabriella replied. "He's also the one who introduced Michael to Sara. I've seen those two together. Michael's going to mourn this loss like no other. Only losing Sara would be worse."

Belladonna looked over at the dejected Michael. "Poor thing. Too bad Sara isn't here to comfort him."

"She can't leave her unit," Gabriella said. "She's too involved in the fight right now."

Michael rejoined the group. "Sorry… needed a few moments too myself. Gabriella, if the orb is returning to normal, that means the Juxtaposition Point will soon be back to full strength. This should block Kor's invasion if he hasn't already left. And even if it's too late, we've done everything we can. Recall the troops. Any objections, Viktor?"

Lord Ternborg looked out over the killing field. "The sooner the better. But there are risks even during a retreat. We have to extricate our warriors from the front without giving the demons any kind of back-stabbing or attacks of opportunity. I propose sending my Phalanx to cover the withdrawal. I'll lead them myself. I've been itching for some time now to wrangle with a few of those demons."

Michael nodded. "Gabriella, hold off the recall until

Lord Ternborg is ready. Belladonna, please communicate with Braz'galar our intentions. You need him alive for your coronation… and rule."

"I've already notified him," Belladonna said as she held up a magical scroll. "What I write here becomes simultaneously visible on the companion scroll he keeps. Though I have to warn you, he doesn't read his more than a few times a day."

"When he hears me coming, he'll know what to do," Lord Ternborg said.

"I hope you're right," Belladonna thought, fearing what would happen if they left Braz'galar all alone.

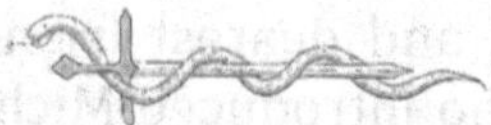

Though Trungren was a young demon, he was symbolic of all the demons Kor had selected to invade the mortal world of Aster—larger, stronger, and more ferocious than normal. His chitinous-protected outer body shivered in excitement as he waited with his brethren for the chance to march with his lord to victory. On the other side of the magic doorway he'd soon be marching through was treasure beyond his wildest desires… treasure just waiting to be pillaged.

The sound of magic crackled ahead. Trungren stared ahead as huge clouds abruptly appeared out of nowhere, merged, and swirled around in a counterclockwise direction. Faster and faster they circled until the only thing the young demon saw was a vast, angry mass of gray, spinning shadows. A dark pinprick of black appeared in the chaos, accompanied by a loud howl. Like most of his brethren, Trungren was forced to his knees by the noise. The black pinprick expanded until it became large enough to allow several columns of demons marching abreast to pass through. Horns sounded throughout the demon army and the first ranks of demons began the passage through the long tunnel of magic from the Abyss to Aster.

As Trungren approached the dimensional doorway, all his bravado and fearlessness melted away like ice over the heat of an open flame. A sense of foreboding overcame him as he entered the doorway. Each step forward became a struggle. If not for his fellow demons, he'd have bolted back to the safety of the Abyss without giving it a second thought.

Then came the sound of screams from ahead. Terrible, soul-wrenching screams of abject terror and agony. Everyone, including Trungren, stopped and listened. Within moments, the screaming of dying demons became louder. Trungren kept looking ahead, but couldn't see the cause of the horror coming his way. Suddenly, a demon came out of the darkness and shoved his way past Trungren. Then another, and another, until hundreds of demons were rushing past him.

Trungren, along with several others, held his ground as he continued to stare forward. When he finally understood what was happening, he realized no amount of running would save him or any of the others. The doorway was crumpling, disintegrating everything in its path in a blazing conflagration. He screamed just as loud as the others when touched by the full force of the collapse.

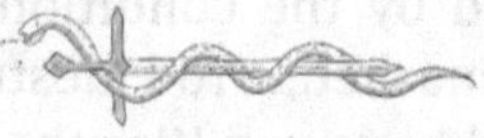

Kor was several hundred feet inside the tunnel before he realized what was happening. He turned his horse around and rode hard back towards the Abyss end of the doorway. Any running demon warrior he couldn't move around, he ran over. He made it out of the tunnel, but that wasn't enough. He had to get as far away from the spent doorway as possible. Kor whipped his horse to run faster as he looked over his shoulder.

An impossibly huge maw was rushing to devour him. He closed his eyes and screamed. A colossal explosion accompanied the end of the collapse and Kor was knocked from his horse and driven into the ground.

Sore and barely able to move, the Prefecture leader looked up from the grassy soil. Complete devastation was all around. Bits of floating ash and smoke filled the air. There was no sign of life for as far as he could see. He tried to reach out and touch the ley lines overhead to bring forth healing magic, but the ringing in his head prevented the concentration he needed to succeed.

"What happened?" Kor wondered out loud.

"You happened!" the voices from the *Living Throne* screamed in his head.

Kor covered his ears. "No!" he exclaimed before lapsing into unconsciousness.

Azazael and a few of his warriors found Kor, still unconscious, several hours later. The Prefecture leader was battered and bruised, but other than a nasty head wound, appeared to be none the worse for wear. Half of Kor's elaborate uniform had been blown or burned away. He looked weak and inconsequential. As warriors picked up the comatose Prefecture ruler, he woke and asked once again what had happened.

Azazael, disgusted by the condition of the Abyss's most powerful demon, remarked, "You destroyed everything we worked to achieve. I'd have you Kiss the *Pillar* if I didn't think the *Living Throne* had other plans for you." He then instructed his warriors to take the overlord back to the capital city.

"How dare your insolence!" Kor shouted as they carried him from the field of destruction. He didn't stop shouting until he lost consciousness once again.

Azazael shook his head as he watched Kor being hauled off like a sack of potatoes.

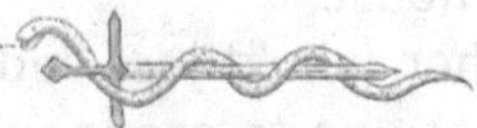

Landross veered his horse away from Drog'dronnan off in the distance in favor of one of the closer towns that dotted the landscape. He wasn't sure Nightshade would live long enough to make it to the city. Several field strider ranches surrounded the first town he approached. Herbie took off to make friends with the hounds of one such ranch. Landross, with Nightshade cradled in his arms, followed Herbie. Several ranchers met him at the main house. One came up and took the reins of Nightshade's horse from Landross's hand and tied it off to a hitching post. He did the same with Landross's horse as the former knight slide off, carefully holding the unconscious Nightshade.

"He's a mortal!" one rancher exclaimed.

"Shut up, Vagon," another said. "We got eyes." Then to Landross: "Looks as if you ran into some trouble, stranger."

Landross looked at his audience. Like all other ordinary demons, they each were humanoid with pale blue skin tones, long white hair, blue eyes, and small, antler-like horns growing from the top of the head. Landross knew from talking with Nightshade, as well as his own personal observations, that these demons were usually honest and decent folks.

"We got caught by a spiny hummeri spawning," Landross said. "My friend has suffered much to save my life. She's going to die if I don't get help for her soon."

All the ranchers shook their heads.

"Gotta watch those spiny hummeri," one said.

"Seems a bit early for a spawning, though," another said as he chomped on a tooth-pick like twig sticking out the side of his mouth.

"Mighty bad luck, stranger. I don't..."

"Get her in here this instant, Orran," a feminine voice called from inside the main house.

The demon rancher who'd just spoken, Orran, shrugged his shoulders. "I'm not one to argue with my Mattie. Follow me, stranger."

Landross wasn't sure what to expect when he carried Nightshade into the building. Whatever it was, it wasn't what he saw. The inside of the house was meticulously clean. Mattie, pretty in any universe, waited just on the other side of the door. Three little children, all females, stood in a large central room and watched with the curiosity of the young. From the kitchen area on the opposite side, the aroma of homemade strider stew and fresh biscuits waffled through the air, which made Landross's mouth water and his stomach growl.

Mattie directed Landross to a large sofa-type piece of furniture. "Put her over here. You said you were caught in a spiny hummeri spawning? How... not from around here, I guess."

"No ma'am," Landross replied. "I'd be grateful if you could help her."

Mattie looked up at the big mortal. "You care deeply for her."

"Well..."

"I can see it in your eyes," Mattie said as she striped away most of Nightshade's clothing. "There's seven sting marks. I'm surprised she's still alive."

"Can you help her?" Landross asked.

Mattie shook her head. "Maybe keep her alive for a few more hours."

Landross's heart dropped. The depth of his feelings for Nightshade surprised him.

"But I know someone who might," Mattie added. "Orran, get on our fastest horse... I think Lightning Blossom might be best... and get Isda."

"You don't really want that witch in this house, do you?"

Mattie's husband asked.

"She does things differently, but that doesn't make her a witch. Now go! There's not much time!"

Orran grumbled to himself as he and his fellow ranchers left the house.

"Naomi, take…I'm sorry, I didn't get a name."

"Landross, ma'am."

Mattie nodded. "Take Landross back to the kitchen and dish him a bowl of stew."

"Yes, mama."

Landross shook his head. "If it's all the same to you, I'd rather stay here with Nightshade."

Mattie suddenly stopped her ministrations to the injured overlord and backed away. "Nightshade?"

"You've heard of her?"

"Who in the Abyss hasn't?" Mattie replied. "Her father's one of Kor's principal advisors. She's as evil as he is."

"She helped to kill her father," Landross said. "On Aster."

Mattie stared at the knight but said nothing.

"Look, it's a long story, but madam, on my honor, she's not that person anymore," Landross assured Mattie. "Could a mortal love her as I do if she was?"

"What do I know about mortals? Except I've never heard of one in the Abyss. Maybe you're an overlord in disguise instead?"

Landross shook his head. "I'm who I say I am. But I don't know how to prove it to you other than to ask if an overlord would admit that was Nightshade?"

Mattie stood and grabbed Landross's shoulders by both arms and looked deeply into his eyes. "No… you're not an overlord. Neither are you charmed." The demon female considered, then nodded. "Alright, I'll trust you. Besides, Isda will know for sure. You look hungry. Get some of that stew. I'll keep Nightshade alive until Isda gets here."

Landross nodded and let Naomi lead him back to the kitchen.

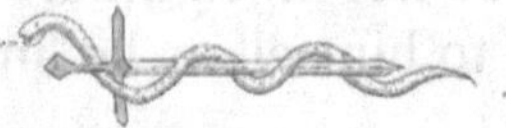

The force of the explosion knocked the dust off all the overhead rafters in the fortress. Everyone manning the battlements turned away as a bright flash of light threatened to rob them of their sight. When they could look, they saw a gigantic plume of smoke had risen thousands of feet into the air off in the distance. It knocked all the demons on the field below the fortress off their feet, where they lay stunned. Michael, Gabriella, Lord Ternborg, and Belladonna rushed up ramps leading to the ramparts to look for themselves. Next to Michael was Sara. He didn't want her out of his sight.

"Thank the old gods our people were safely back," Gabriella said.

"Braz'galar?" Michael inquired of Belladonna.

"He and his folks got in about an hour ago," Belladonna replied. "Believe it or not, he slept through the explosion."

"Anyone know what happened?" Lord Ternborg asked.

"It wasn't any of our doing," Gabriella said as she shook her head.

Michael continued to stare out at the plume. "The doorway to Aster collapsed. That's the only plausible explanation."

Then a faint cry rang out from the direction of the orb building. The cry gathered strength as more and more voices picked it up. "The orb's stable! The orb's stable!"

"We've got the Juxtaposition Point back," Michael said.

"Kor's failed," Belladonna remarked. "The *Living Throne* won't be happy with that."

"It's your time, Belladonna," Michael said. "I hope you're as real as you say you are."

The female overlord put a hand on one of Michael's arms. "You have my word."

Michael nodded, then turned to Gabriella. "Keep a close watch on the demons below... but I think it's time to get things back to normal."

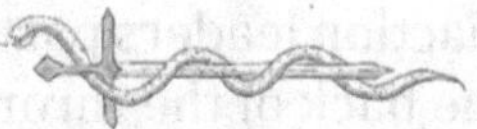

Kor regained consciousness in the palace throne room. He didn't remember how he'd gotten there. All he could recall were brief memories of Azazael's face and the laughter of unknown voices. He looked down. The luxurious clothes he'd worn for his triumphal march to Aster were torn and burned. His hands were dirty and the boots on his feet had holes in the front where his filthy toes stuck out. He crawled towards the throne for support, but two of several guards he hadn't noticed blocked his approach.

"Move or Kiss the *Pillar*!" he yelled, but to no avail.

Kor slowly stood and turned around. Except for Lilitu, the deceased Magic Faction leader, every other Faction leader stood and stared at him. He could see the contempt in their eyes.

"What are you'll looking at?" Kor screamed. "You there," he said as he pointed to one of the servants lining the throne room walls. "Draw my bath and get me new clothes. Gold with red borders, I should think... with a blue cloak. No! Not blue. Instead, I think I'll wear the black cloak. Yes... the black one! It matches my mood."

The servant looked at Azazael, who shook his head. "The palace servants are no longer yours to command," the military Faction leader said to Kor.

"No longer yours! No longer yours! No longer yours!" the voices from the *Living Throne* repeated in Kor's head.

"You've been replaced," Azazael added.

"You've been replaced! You've been replaced! You've been replaced!"

Kor shook his head. "Impossible! I'll burn you to a crisp, you little maggot!"

"Your predecessors have cut you off from the ley lines," a fresh voice said. The Faction leaders parted as Emprusa moved through them from the back of the throne room.

"Cut off! Cut off! Cut off!"

"I made a simple miscalculation," Kor said. Panic had entered his voice. "But even so, it still almost worked. I was so close! Next time will be different!"

Emprusa nodded to the guards standing next to the throne behind Kor. Two moved forward and grabbed the former leader while a third put fitted chains around his waist, wrists, and ankles. "The ancestors have given you to me."

"You can have him! You can have him! You can have him!"

Kor smiled. "Excellent, my love. You and me against everyone!"

"You still don't understand, do you?" Emprusa said.

Kor frowned.

The former First Consort nodded and the grip of the guards on Kor tightened. Another came up and held Kor's head still while a fourth forced Kor's lips together. Emprusa pulled out a needle and a length of glowing wire thread.

"I had this made especially for you," Emprusa said as she sewed Kor's lips together. "Blissful silence," she commented after she had finished.

"Agreed," Azazael said. "I'm only sorry it took this long to dispose of this… mongrel. I still don't know what I saw in him?"

Emprusa shook her head. "No one blames you. There was a time when we all thought Kor was the strongest and most capable. Oh, he was brutal enough… but, as it turns out, not very bright. By the way, Azazael, don't you think you should be high-tailing it out of the capital before Braz'galar gets here? I understand he's being re-employed as Belladonna's fixer."

"Don't worry about me, Emprusa. I've already accepted Belladonna as my leader. I think Braz'galar will let our little... disagreement... slide for the sake of her and the Abyss."

At the mention of Belladonna as the new Prefecture leader, Kor's eyes widened, and he tried to say something. Emprusa smacked him across the back of his horny head with a steel rod she'd been carrying for just that purpose.

"You better hope so, Azazael," Emprusa said. "You have few places to run to. No one but Braz'galar knows the extent of his reach. And you can't take him on in a fair fight. He'll dispose of you without breaking a sweat." She snapped her fingers at the guards holding Kor. "Come along, darling. We're going to have so much fun as I prepare you for the *Living Throne*."

Kor struggled as guards dragged out him of the throne room. Emprusa thrust the rod savagely into his groin to quiet him. "So much fun!"

"He's ours! He's ours! He's ours!"

"Belladonna! Belladonna! Belladonna!"

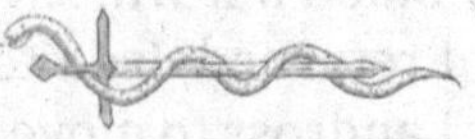

Isda finished her examination of Nightshade and stood. "Only a special kind of magic can heal her now," she said. "Blood magic."

Landross looked at the witch and frowned. "Blood magic?"

Isda nodded as she went to the large satchel she had brought with her and pulled out several bottles and a small cauldron. "Stoke the fire, child," she said to Mattie. Then to Naomi: "You girl! Go and fetch me your mother's sharpest knife."

"What are you going to do?" Landross asked Isda.

"Save your friend," Isda replied.

Landross shook his head. "No. I meant how."

The witch finished retrieving various other items from her satchel and, after placing them on the floor next to the bottles and the cauldron, grabbed a nearby wooden chair and pulled it over to sit in front of Landross. "Young mortal elf… do you know what the phrase 'cause and effect' implies?"

Landross nodded. "Something happens because of something else."

"Correct, my boy," Isda said as she pulled out a pipe and tobbakk, the Prefecture equivalent of tobacco on Aster, from a pocket on her skirt. She packed the tobbakk and lit the pipe. A pungent smelling smoke spread throughout the room. "Your friend needs a specific type of healing magic. Magic that I can summon only through a bloodletting. Yours, to be specific."

"Mine?"

Isda nodded. "You care for her, don't you?"

Landross hesitated, then shrugged. No point in denying it now. He'd already admitted his feelings for Nightshade to Mattie. Besides, she was willing to give up her life to save his. Shouldn't he be willing to do the same? "Yes… I love her. And I'm willing to give my blood if it will save her."

Mattie and Naomi returned. Isda took the knife from the girl and motioned for Landross to move closer to the cauldron. She then picked up a bottle and emptied its contents over the knife and into the cauldron.

"Give me your hand," Isda told Landross.

In an instant, the witch slashed deep into Landross's wrist. The bite of the knife forced a slight grunt from the former knight, but otherwise, he remained still and watched as his blood flowed into the cauldron to join the liquid just poured over the knife. He lapsed into unconsciousness a few seconds later.

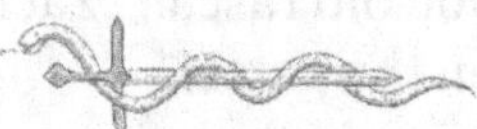

To the astonishment of everyone in the city of Zhaarmoth, a formation of seven *B'nai Elohim* appeared in the skies to the west. The city guard and its army scrambled to take up their battle stations while sorcerers prepared both defensive and offensive spells. The entire civilian population, as Braz'galar's underlords had trained them to do, took to underground shelters built for such occasions.

"Look at that," Lessien said to Laylah, Zachariah, and Yesper standing next to her. Zachariah had used his friendship with Braz'galar to barter his way up onto the battlements. "So those are *B'nai Elohim*. They're beautiful!"

"Not so to a sorcerer trying to escape the Abyss," Zachariah remarked.

"I guess everything we've heard regarding the *B'nai Elohim* now being vulnerable is wrong," Laylah said.

Yesper barked a short laugh. "Look around, Laylah. See how the entire city has responded to the appearance of just seven of the *B'nai Elohim*. Vulnerable or not, you think they'll ever be powerless?"

"Point taken," Laylah replied.

Several bolts of magical lightning, followed by the black signature of a plasma ray, streaked towards the circling *B'nai Elohim*. Magical wards blocked each attack. The *B'nai Elohim*, however, didn't reply with destructive magic of their own. Instead, they landed several hundred feet in front of Zhaarmoth's main gates. More than a dozen figures offloaded from the backs of the *B'nai Elohim*, including Braz'galar and Belladonna.

"Not exactly the welcome I was expecting for the Prefecture's new leader," Braz'galar scolded, though inwardly he was proud of the city's response to potential danger.

"Why Braz'galar, you old rascal!" Zachariah called out from the battlements. "Open the gates!"

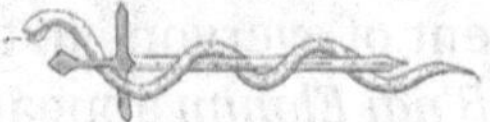

Landross awoke to the stares of Naomi and her two smaller sisters. He had a terrible headache. "Shouldn't I be dead?"

Isda's pipe smoking visage looked down at him. "Does it look like you're dead, stranger?"

Orran helped Landross up and over to a chair. "It feels like it," Landross said as he held his head.

"That'll go away... eventually," Isda said.

"How's Nightshade?" Landross asked.

"Come see for yourself," Mattie said.

Mattie and her three girls led Landross into a small bedroom. Nightshade was sleeping on the bed underneath a light blanket. The rise and fall of her breasts as she took in and exhaled breaths was steady and even, and her skin had regained its normal, healthy complexion.

"The wounds that marred her body are gone as well," Mattie said.

"I don't... I don't think I can ever thank you enough," Landross said. He was desperately trying to hold back tears of relief. They felt somewhat... unseemly... though he found he didn't really care.

"We were glad to help, weren't we, Isda," Mattie responded.

The witch grunted. "A few kronies would be welcome."

Landross smiled and fished out every Abyssian coin, plus a few Aster gold, he had. It was a substantial sum. "You can have it all."

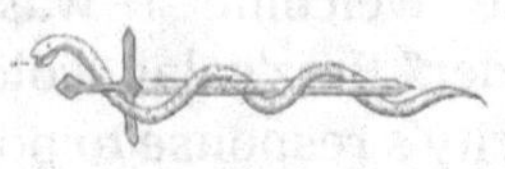

"I heard rumors of people looking for me," Lessien said.

Gabriella, one of the seven *B'nai Elohim* who traveled from their fortress to Zhaarmoth, nodded. "Father Goram, Nightshade, and the knight Landross."

"I knew Landross and Horatio would come," Lessien replied. "But I wasn't so sure about Nightshade. Are they back at your fortress?"

Gabriella, as was her way, didn't hold back when she answered the queen's question. "We lost Father Goram when he helped us revive the Juxtaposition Point."

"Lost?" Lessien could hardly believe her ears.

"Not dead," Braz'galar clarified. "He still breathes. But his mind is gone. The gorgon Abigail has him. She won't give up hope he'll regain consciousness someday."

"A gorgon has him?" the queen wondered. "But that's a creature of legend."

"We have one in the Abyss," Braz'galar answered. "I've seen her myself."

"She came with the priest to our fortress," Gabriella said.

"But how could you let a creature like that take Horatio? So she can turn him to stone?"

Belladonna briefly laid a hand on Lessien's shoulders. "It's not like that. Abigail's a gorgon, true enough. But the creature of your legend is nothing near reality. From what I… from what we've all observed… she genuinely appears to love Father Goram and, I suspect, he loves her."

"But Autumn…"

"He knows she's dead," Gabriella said. "He's mourned her loss, I'm sure."

Lessien was stunned. She wanted to take Father Goram home with her. Since she was a child, he'd been a fixture in her life. What would she do without his wisdom—his friendship? "And Landross? Nightshade?"

"They were traveling together and last seen in the city of

Drog'dronnan west of here," Braz'galar said.

"We went through there, Lessien," Laylah said. "Remember?"

The mortal queen nodded.

"According to my contacts in the city, that's the last time anyone saw them," Braz'galar said. "I presume they were heading here."

"They couldn't just disappear, could they?" Lessien asked.

There was a silence around the room.

"What aren't you telling me?"

"I'm sorry," Belladonna said, "but a short time after they were spotted leaving Drog'dronnan, there was a spawning of the spiny hummeri."

"A spawning of what?"

"Spiny hummeri... a kind of river creature," Zachariah said. "Twice a year they come out of the Arlinggamau Run after spawning to feed. The road Landross and Nightshade should have been following, the same road we used, runs through their feeding grounds. There are magical protections on the road itself, but if they strayed... well, nothing good would've come from it."

"They'd become food for these... these... spiny hummeri? Is that what you're saying?"

Zachariah nodded. "Yes. If they were caught too far off the road, only a miracle would have saved them." The overlord sighed. "They would've been here by now if they stayed on the road."

Lessien shook her head. "There're all kinds of things that might delay them. Maybe the Tamarau captured them? Or one of them got hurt, and they had to stop for a few days? Nightshade's from here. She'd know about the spawning, wouldn't she?"

"It only happens twice a year," Braz'galar said. "And after looking into it, I found this time it was early. And Nightshade's been away from the Abyss for quite some time, so it's possible she'd have forgotten."

"I refuse to believe they're dead!" Lessien was adamant.

"And you may be right," Braz'galar said. "The Tamarau aren't holding them. That much is certain. I have people looking. But nothing so far."

Lessien had to accept the truth, or at least what everyone thought was the truth, and because of it, she thought her heart was going to burst from the pain. The hurt from the possible loss of both Father Goram and Landross was soul-searing. It was almost as bad as when she had lost her mother and father. InnisRos's queen looked at her hands now folded in her lap. When Laylah draped an arm over her shoulders, Lessien couldn't take it anymore and broke down into tears as she leaned against her new friend's shoulder.

Somewhere in the depths of her grief, Lessien heard Gabriella say they needed to get her back to Aster. Truth! Undeniable truth! She sat up straight, blew her nose into a handkerchief offered by Zachariah, and looked at the *B'nai Elohim* female. "You're right. I've a kingdom to rule."

Laylah looked at Yesper, who nodded. "Mind if we tag along?"

Lessien smiled. "I was hoping you'd ask!"

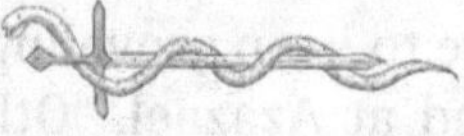

Belladonna, with Braz'galar at her side, marched into the capital city of Urthren, re-named from Kor after a long dead champion of the peasant class. This was the first of many changes Belladonna had in mind for the Prefecture. Behind Belladonna and Braz'galar were one thousand Taumaru warriors who would serve as her personal bodyguard. This was a gift from that tribe to the new Prefecture leader. It was a gift that not only established the Taumaru's connection to the *Living Throne,* but also guaranteed them a place in the Prefecture hierarchy. No longer would anyone consider them as outsiders.

Azazael, along with all the other Faction leaders, less the Magical Faction, met the new Prefecture leader at the palace gates. As Belladonna's party stopped before the overlords, everyone within sight of the spectacle dropped to a knee.

"All hail Belladonna, Overlord of the Belladonna Prefecture!" Azazael shouted. "Supreme Potentate of the Belladonna Prefecture, Warden of the *Living Throne,* Noble and Illustrious Purveyor to the *Pillar of Captured Souls,* Peer of the Realm..."

"That's enough for now, Azazael," Belladonna said.

The Military Faction leader nodded. "Yes, Your Grace. All hail!"

"All hail!" the crowd shouted.

"That doesn't have a very nice ring to it," Belladonna said to Braz'galar.

"I thought it sounded just fine," Braz'galar replied.

"We'll talk about it later," Belladonna said quietly. Louder: "Everyone, please get off your knees. I don't like it. Everyone that is except you, Azazael."

"Your Grace?" Azazael looked genuinely confused as he hurriedly knelt back down.

"She means you're to keep groveling," Braz'galar said.

Belladonna looked at Azazael. "Other than Kor, you and Lilitu are the Faction leaders most responsible for the war with the *B'nai Elohim* and the attempted invasion of the mortal world. Neither Kor nor Lilitu are here to answer for this. But you are."

"But, Your Grace!" Azazael pleaded. "I'm the one who captured and brought Kor back to the capital to face the *Living Throne* for his failure. I'm the one who turned him over to Emprusa for punishment before he was to join the *Living*

Throne."

"And we thank you, but..." Braz'galar shrugged. "We're wasting time, Belle?"

Belladonna nodded. She and Braz'galar had discussed strategy on several previous occasions and had decided the new Prefecture leader's safety was paramount. And while she appeared to have the support of everyone who mattered, particularly those in the *Living Throne*, old habits die hard.

"El'azar!" he called out.

A savage-looking Taumaru warrior with tattoos covering his bald head stepped forward and beat a hand against his chest. "Yours to command!"

"Gather three or four hundred of your warriors and take control of the palace," Braz'galar ordered. "If anyone resists... well, give them one warning. If they continue, kill them. This includes guards and all the servants. Afterwards, find a room large enough to hold all until we can properly vet them."

"Your Grace!" Azazael pleaded as El'azar walked back to his Taumaru. "Please don't allow those... those savages... to dirty up the palace. As your Military Faction leader, I can guarantee..."

Belladonna held up a hand. "You're to be replaced. I thought that would be obvious."

"But..."

"No buts, Azazael," Braz'galar said. "You're out. And so are your palace guards. Those 'savages,' as you call them, are a different breed of demon. With them at her back, Belladonna, unlike all her predecessors in the *Living Throne*, won't have to worry about overthrow attempts. To the Taumaru, their word is their bond... and they've pledged to protect our new Prefecture leader regardless of the cost. But don't think coming off their plateau to be here is a sign they've lost even a trace of their ferocity. That would be a grave miscalculation."

"Since I'm no longer to be the Military Faction leader, what do you have planned for me?" Azazael asked. "Emprusa was just as responsible. In fact, she encouraged the war every bit as much as I did... possibly more, considering how she uses her other... assets. Yet you let her go."

"That Emprusa had a hand to play in this, there's no question," Belladonna said. "And that she gave us Kor doesn't remove her from the responsibility she shares."

Braz'galar smiled. "The old boy wasn't in very good shape... but there was still enough left in him to Kiss the *Pillar* since the *Living Throne* didn't want him."

"Just one of several factors to consider," Belladonna continued. "She could have taken him and ran, but she didn't. She also expressed remorse and begged for mercy. I believe she was truly contrite, which is why I spared her life and sent her into exile."

"To the Taumaru," Braz'galar added. "They'll straighten her out. A few years of servitude will do her a lot of good, don't you think?"

Azazael looked first at Belladonna and then at Braz'galar. There was no mercy in their eyes. His whole body slumped. He'd already accepted his fate, whatever it was going to be.

"Who's your second-in-command?" Belladonna asked.

"I am, Your Grace," a female demon underlord called out and separated herself from the crowd of Faction leaders. "The name's Ciara," she said as she glowered at Braz'galar.

Belladonna looked over at her fixer. "You two know each other?"

"Indeed, Your Grace," Ciera answered instead. "Overlord Braz'galar tried to recruit me to spy on Azazael."

"What!" Azazael screamed.

"Don't worry, jackass," Braz'galar said. "She may not have told you about it, but she sure as hell let me know in no uncertain terms that she wasn't a sellout. Your secrets are safe. Isn't that right, Ciara?"

"I'm a warrior, not a spy!"

Braz'galar looked at Belladonna. "She'll do fine, Belle."

"Well, Ciara, you're my new Military Faction leader," Belladonna said. "Everyone, meet our newest overlord. Ciara, promote who you want to fill your staff... though I want you to reserve a spot for a young demon named Ashryn. She lost both her feet during the fighting, but she's got a sharp mind... especially for tactical and strategic planning. You won't be sorry."

"Yes, Your Grace."

Belladonna nodded. "Your first duty is to bury the dead resting in the fields before the *B'nai Elohim* fortress and then bring the armies back home. I'll want reports of unit strengths. Get whatever help you need from the city overlords who sent their armies on Kor's folly. Let me know if you run into problems... specifically with the overlords. And don't be afraid to ask for help. When that's done, come see me. There's going to be changes I want implemented and will need the military to handle any confrontations with Kor hangers-on."

Ciara saluted. "The Military Faction is yours to command, Your Grace!" she said before she left, followed by several lower-ranking officers.

"What are you going to do with me?" Azazael asked.

Belladonna looked at the disgraced overlord. "That's a good question. Some suggest the *Pillar* or Execution Hill... and Braz'galar wants you to die by his katanas. He's very proud of those two swords of his."

"I am," Braz'galar verified. "They're very sharp."

"But I'm not inclined to seek your death," Belladonna continued. "As you say, you delivered Kor for punishment from the destruction he wrought. That has to weight in your favor on the ledger, don't you think?"

Azazael feared an answer at this point might make things worse.

"Put this on," Belladonna ordered as she tossed a simply made open clasp bracelet to Azazael. "I asked *B'nai Elohim* sorcerers to make this with you in mind."

When the former Faction leader complied and snapped the clasp together, he felt faint and almost collapsed to the floor before regaining his balance. When he looked at his wrist, he saw the bracelet had fused with his skin.

"That bracelet cuts off your connection to all ley lines," Belladonna said. "You're no longer an overlord. I'm also stripping you of your possessions. No home, no belongings, no wealth… nothing except the clothes on your back. You're starting over, Azazael."

"But… but how am I to survive?"

"Maybe your family will take you in," Braz'galar said. "Or, if not, you'll find a peasant family willing to help. Most of them have kind hearts… even for a former overlord. But I warn you, you'll have to work to earn your keep."

"I'm used to working."

"Physical work, Azazael," Braz'galar mentioned with a smile. "And always remember. I'll have eyes on you. You try anything… anything at all… and I *will* know about it."

"Would you like to say something before you're removed?" Belladonna asked.

"Would it matter?"

"No," Belladonna replied. "Guards!"

Four Taumaru appeared and dragged the former Military Faction leader away.

"Why don't we take this to the throne room?" Braz'galar asked. "We're too exposed here in the open. And I suspect El'azar has the palace secured by now."

"An excellent suggestion," Belladonna replied.

The new Prefecture leader ascended the dais and sat on the *Living Throne*. All the previous Prefecture leaders, except for Kor, began to hoot and holler in Belladonna's mind. She shut them up with a thought after she warned them about doing it again. None of them were prepared for the first ever female Prefecture leader... or for the force of nature they themselves had unleashed.

Belladonna gazed out at the faces staring up at her. There wasn't a rebellious look in the bunch. "Pull up some chairs. I have a lot of changes I wish to discuss."

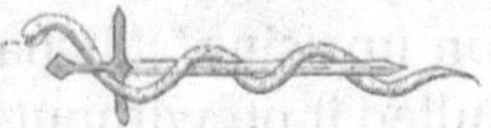

Michael rapped a couple of times on Lord Ternborg's room door and walked in.

"I was coming to see you later," Lord Ternborg said to Michael. The Draugen Pesta king was packing his away bag. He dismissed the adjutant who was helping.

"Thought I'd come to you instead," Michael replied. "Ready to go home?"

Lord Ternborg nodded. "Very much. I've been gone far too much lately and miss my family terribly. We're also having difficulties with our neighboring state..."

"The Hyrokkin."

"Right," Lord Ternborg agreed. "You know how warlike they are. The fighting between us has been going on for generations, and I'm tired of all the bloodshed. So, I'm working to barter a peace between us and them. But unfortunately, some decisions I've made in that regard haven't gone over well with Sofia. She's from the northern part of my kingdom, and they have a tendency to be more strong-willed than most others. A failing at times to be sure... but also a strength. This dichotomy is one of the many things I love about her. No better person to stand by your side. But the last time I was gone, Sofia killed one of my advisors. He deserved it, of course, and she had no other options. But still... maybe she could've handled it without using her knives and stuffing his body down a latrine.

That's the reason we have dungeons."

Michael laughed. "That does sound like her."

Lord Ternborg smiled as he continued packing. "Doesn't it, though? The gods only know how much she's trampled over the Hyrokkin since I left. And then there's my daughter... sorry, I'm rambling about things that are no concern of yours. What can I do for you?"

"I wanted to thank you again for everything you did to help with the... demon uprising," Michael said. "I'm not sure my people could've pulled it off without you."

Lord Ternborg looked up from his packing. "We still don't understand why the doorway collapsed and the Juxtaposition Point stabilized. I have to assume something happened to the Johari on my world... that someone, my guess the demons, or something neutralized her and somehow she returned. That's what saved us, and my people had nothing to do with it."

"Even so, as I said, the *B'nai Elohim* might not have survived if it wasn't for you and your warriors," Michael said.

"Don't sell yourself short," Lord Ternborg replied. "You were right to call upon us. And despite my problems, I was right to come. Everything we did here helped you... but it also helped to prevent Kor's invasion of my home world. By the way, are you still sure you need me to send a contingent of my warriors? The new Prefecture leader, Belladonna, seems to want genuine change."

Michael sighed. "I know that's true for now, but she's still a demon overlord and, as the Prefecture leader, the *Living Throne* is in her head. They may have supported her over Kor, but they're just as corrupt as he was. I can't afford to let my guard down... and I've around two hundred and fifty less *B'nai Elohim* to do it with."

Lord Ternborg nodded. "It's a cautious decision. As we agreed, I'll leave a thousand here and will let you know when I'm ready to send another thousand. It should be within a few days after getting back. I'll have my generals work out a deployment schedule for every six months."

Michael concurred. "At least until I can be sure Belladonna will keep her word... and stay in power."

Lord Ternborg offered a hand. It was the mortal way of saying they had settled upon a compact. It was also the mortal way of saying goodbye.

EPILOG

The robed and hooded figure blew on the hot vegetable pie he'd bought from a street merchant. He and his partner had just entered the Prefecture city of Zir Tachoss after a long night of traveling on horseback. They were in the city to visit an old friend. After stabling their horses, they headed for the food merchant's section of the city. The dog, who was constantly at their side, had already consumed his pie and was begging for another. The robed figure, who'd already eaten three, handed his to the dog.

"I'm full, anyway."

"What's that, dear?" the robed figure's companion asked.

"Oh, just talking to myself. Now that my belly's full, I ready for a soft bed and about ten hours of sleep."

His companion smiled. "Agreed. It's been a long night. We'll get that soft bed at Abigail's."

As the three walked the streets of the city, they observed a lightness in the air... a sense that all was well. Everyone still went about their business as usual, but they did so in high spirits. Changes the new Prefecture overlord had put into effect gave the common folks, for the first time, genuine hope for the future. The peasant attitudes reflected that.

The two clasped hands as they walked down the street. Here and there, merchants and ordinary citizens smiled at the couple and their dog. Those smiles were readily returned.

"I've never seen the peasants so... so..."

"Happy? Nightshade, it's the look of freedom! They've never had it before."

Nightshade nodded. "My sister's doing some rather amazing things, that's for sure. And if the looks on the faces we're seeing are any indication of her success, I hope she never stops!"

"Straight from the mouth of a onetime assassin who plotted to overthrow an entire world."

"I don't know that person," Nightshade replied. "Not anymore. And if I should ever..."

Landross laughed. "I know. I know. If you should ever turn into that person again, I'm to put you over my knee and slap your pretty little butt until you've learned your lesson. I'm looking forward to it."

Nightshade grinned. "I'm serious. Stop being so cavalier."

The two walked the streets of Zir Tachoss for another hour before they reached the street of their destination.

"Just down here a little way," Nightshade said.

Landross nodded. "I... whoa! Look at that!"

Both stopped and stared. Herbie, taking a cue from his master, stopped chasing a six-legged cat and rushed back to Landross's side. Abigail's shop had just come into view. Sitting at each corner of the shop were large crystal dragons. Four more were sitting on the corners of the roof. On the front porch under a large table of merchandise lay two large, four-legged dire wolves. Several pups were playing under the watchful eyes of both.

"I'd recognize those wolves anywhere," Landross said. "Ajax and Cassandra. And they're still having pups!" The former knight rushed over to the dire wolves and hugged the two adults. Then he sat and allowed himself to be deluged by puppy kisses. Herbie, though unsure of the spectacle at first, decided it looked as if it was great fun and added his slobbery tongue to the fray. Ajax and Cassandra watched with wolf-like amusement.

Nightshade knew there could only be one reason the dire wolves and the crystal dragon golems would be there—Father Goram. She rushed into the store.

"It's so good to see you again, Miss Nightshade," Tolves,

Abigail's shopkeeper, said. "We were wondering if the sightings of you and that knight fella were bogus."

Nightshade smiled. "Landross. He's outside playing with the puppies."

"The longer those little devils stay outside, the better," Tolves remarked. "Don't get me wrong. I love them to death… but they're constantly getting underfoot."

Nightshade became serious. "Tolves, how's Father Goram?"

The shopkeeper looked at Nightshade. "You heard what he did to help foil Kor's plans?"

Nightshade nodded. "I have. At least rumors. Nothing definitive. They say his mind's gone."

Tolves smiled. "Go upstairs and see for yourself."

Nightshade climbed the creaky stairs up to the first room on the second floor. Inside, she found Abigail looking over a ledger and making notes. The gorgon looked up and a huge grin crossed her face.

"Nightshade!"

The two crossed the distance between them and hugged.

"By the gods, it's good to see you!" Abigail exclaimed. "I've been so worried. Is Landross with you?"

Nightshade laughed. It was something she'd been doing more and more lately. "He is. Downstairs, playing with the puppies. Where's Horatio?"

"Right here," a smiling Father Goram said as he walked out of the adjoining room. "Back for some more instruction?"

The three most important people in her life were finally with her. For the second time, Nightshade hugged someone as if she'd never let them go.

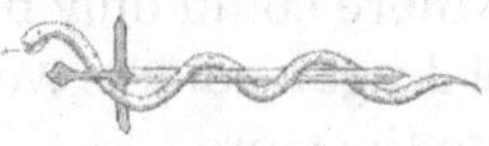

"There's two someone's here to see you," Sienna said. *"I put them in the parlor. One of them was rather... agitated... about being ordered around by a bear. The other is a child... but more than that."*

"We'll be richt out," Jarsus thought back.

The dwarf was in the middle of giving Daphnia a lesson in basic bookkeeping, accounting, and their importance to keeping the kingdom out of bankruptcy. It was one of the most boring lectures he'd ever given the princess and he wasn't sure about its value, at least in this stage of her education. But her parents insisted it was necessary. "Someone has to go over the books other than the chief exchequer," Lord Ternborg had said. "What if he's robbing us blind!" Jarsus believed the threat of decapitation was enough to keep the books balanced, but in this matter, his thoughts on the issue fell upon deaf ears. Daphnia was responding to the subject matter like most students—barely able to keep her eyes open. He stopped.

"Sienna says there's someone here tae see me," Jarsus said to the princess. "Let's tak' a break 'n' see wha it is."

Daphnia snapped to attention. "Thank the gods," she whispered.

The two left the library for the parlor. Inside, the two guests were sitting on overstuffed chairs. One was a golden-haired elvan girl who looked a little older than Daphnia. She had a ready smile which lit up her entire face. An aura of serenity surrounded her. The other was an older elvan female. The light complexion of her skin stood in deep contrast to her long, black hair. There was a scowl on her face. Two katanas, a bow, and a quiver of arrows lay across her lap. Jarsus knew she was the girl's guardian the moment he saw her. He appreciated that. He felt the same about Daphnia.

The black-haired female tensed as soon as Adimar entered the room. Her hands gripped the hilts of both katanas and her eyes narrowed. She looked ready to attack at the slightest provocation.

"Relax, Mariko," the younger of the two said. "I told you he was bigger than Romulus."

Mariko relaxed, but only a little.

Jarsus and Daphnia sat on a large sofa which faced the two visitors. The size difference between the dwarf and the Draugen Pesta princess was significant, yet it was the dwarf who commanded the attention of the newcomers. The fire in the large hearth that filled one complete side of the room was down to its last remaining embers, yet the room itself was warm and comfortable, in direct opposition to the windy chill in the air outside.

Jarsus poured a mug of ale from a decanter he always kept filled in the parlor. He never knew when someone was going to show up unexpectedly, and he always entertained best when he had a mug of ale in his hand.

"Care fur a mug o' pure tough, dwarven ale, lass?" Jarsus asked Mariko. "I kin ainlie offer water fur th' wee ones. Or ah kin gie ye a mug o' well-watered dwarven ale, if ye prefer."

"Believe me, you don't want any of that," Daphnia said. "Yuck!"

Jarsus looked at the princess. "Since when hae ye hud a chance tae sample dwarven ale?"

Daphnia's face turned red. "Uh..."

The youngest of the two visitors laughed. "No doubt a child's curiosity tempted by an unemptied mug you left behind."

The dwarf feigned indignation. "Ah ne'er lea guid dwarven ale behind! It's a sin against nature!"

The young elvan girl laughed. "Indeed! I've heard dwarves are most protective of what's in their mugs."

"Ye hear richt, lassie. 'N' Daphnia, we're nae dain wi' thes."

"You've been caught, Princess," Emmy said with a smile on her face. "We're fine, Master Blackmantle."

Jarsus nodded. "In 'at case, we kin git doon tae th' reason fur yer visit. Ye seem tae ken mair aboot us then we dae aboot ye. How aboot ye stairt by introducing yersel'."

"Of course. I'm Emmy DeRango and my companion is Mariko Takagi."

Daphnia's eyes widened. "You're not..."

"They ur, lassie," Jarsus said. "Ah see it noo. Tell me, Emmy, whit wid a goddess 'n' her pet assassin waant wi' us?"

Mariko bristled at being called a pet. "I'm no more her pet than you are to the Princess!"

"Calm down, dear," Emmy said. "He's a dwarf. They have a manner of speaking that's somewhat... direct and unfettered. Remember Azriel?"

Jarsus laughed. "A'd hae thought ye fur a stiffer backbone, girl."

Mariko heeded Emmy's advice and calmed down, though she wasn't going to let the dwarf go unchallenged. "My backbone's stiff enough, dwarf! On the other hand, yours, like everything about you, seems... small."

"Oh, dear," Daphnia said.

But the dwarf laughed again. "Ah lik' her!"

"Don't mind him," Daphnia said. "He's only baiting you. He does that to everyone. It's how he takes stock of their character. I'm the Princess Daphnia Ternborg and this is Jarsus Blackmantle, though you already knew that. Oh, and that living rug in front of the fireplace is Adimar. From what I understand, you've already met Sienna."

"Indeed!" Emmy said. "A most gracious bear."

"With manners," Mariko added.

Jarsus smiled. "Enough banter. Ye'r a lang wey fae Elanesse, goddess. How come urr ye here?"

"It's my understanding you're the nearest thing to an expert on what lies west of InnisRos," Emmy stated.

"The oblivion," Daphnia whispered.

Jarsus took a long pull from his mug of ale. "A've ne'er bin thare, if that's whit ye'r thinking. Bit thare wis an expedition sent lang ago. Na one returned… at least alive. Three captain's journals fae a ship cried th' *Florentina Kovalevsky* did mak' it back, 'n' a've studied thaim ferr thoroughly. It's th' journals ah know, nae th' place. 'N' that something oot there's gey dangerous."

"May I look at those journals?" Emmy asked.

Jarsus studied his two guests. "Ye think something's gaun oan oot thare, don't ye?"

Emmy nodded. "Yes. But what? I'm not sure. I'm hoping the ledgers can give me more information."

"Most o' it's as dry as an ogre's bathtub," Jarsus said. "Mostly day tae day recordings, ship supply tallies, atmospheric readings, star positions, 'n' th' lik'. A' helpful information if anither expedition wur tae be sent. A've tried tae decipher some o' th' ither hings th' captain wrote… hings that hae na real basis in fact. Incredible creatures, pure dead brilliant fauna oan th' islands thay encountered, 'n' streenge waither phenomena tae name a few. Bit it's a haun scribbled note at th' end o' th' third journal that's aye worried me."

"Beware the Oblivion… the end of all things!" Daphnia said with dread.

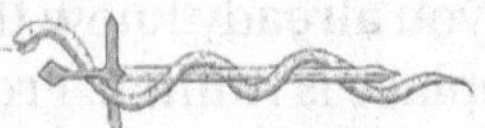

Sofia was in her office. Her husband, Lord Ternborg, was away again, but this time he wasn't conducting a war… just fulfilling normal kingly responsibilities—meeting with his generals, deciding squabbles between cities or major landowners, giving speeches, campaigning and raising money for pet projects, overseeing any other thing he felt required his personal attention, and so on. This time, he was making trips to Saint Dominic and Saint Martin, at their behest, to attend memorial services for all those who died during the Hyrokkin invasion. As much as Sofia wanted to go, it was still too soon after the attempted invasion of Aster by the Abyss. No one, including the *B'nai Elohim* leader, Michael, could be sure that the dimensional doorway collapse had killed all the demons. Considering what her husband described during his time in the Abyss, both felt one had to stay in the capital. Neither he nor Sofia wanted to take a chance of one or more surviving demons appearing unexpectedly without one of them available to take command.

The Draugen Pesta queen was reviewing financial accounts with the Chief Exchequer and one of his assistants. It was a yearly event, usually handled by the king, and, as usual, time, established by law, was running out.

"Where's the estimated operating budget for our embassy?" Sofia asked. "I see what we've spent to date, but there's nothing here regarding the yearly expense."

"As of right now, Your Grace, we can only surmise what those expenses might be," Chief Exchequer Vanya Stepanovich replied. "It's too soon for an accurate account. A breakdown of our nearest approximation is in Appendix A."

"Appendix A," Sofia whispered as she paged through the massive kingdom expenditure report. "Ah… here it is. Let's see… wait! How can that be? That's… that's…"

"That's the price for peace, Your Grace," Stepanovich's assistant said. "Begging your pardon."

"Pardon granted." Sofia sighed. "My husband warned me about this."

"Again, that number is our best guess," Stepanovich said. "We can't be certain how to budget for the embassy until after the first year."

Sofia nodded. "I understand that." The queen thought things over for a few seconds. "Okay… we'll shelve this for now. I'll discuss it with the king later. There was something I else noticed," Sofia said as she flipped through the report. "Ah, here it is. Let's turn our attention to infrastructure costs, specifically roads and grounds. Vanya, you have a costing evaluation report here for a new bridge across the Strukis River just north of here. Has the king approved this?"

"Your Grace..."

But before Stepanovich could answer fully, there was a knock on the door shortly before a servant walked in carrying a tray.

Sofia rubbed her eyes. "Actually, I could use a break. Let's pick this up tomorrow, gentlemen. I'll send someone to get you when I'm ready."

"Yes, Your Grace."

The servant stood next to the door as Stepanovich and his assistant left the room. She made sure the door was closed after their exit.

"Thanks, Tereza," Sofia said as the servant laid the tray on her desk. It contained wine and a few small, freshly baked pastries. "You're a lifesaver... in more ways than one."

The servant, Tereza Nikitina, was actually Sofia's new master spy. She poured two goblets of wine, handed one to the queen and took the other, as well as a pastry, and sat in a padded chair on the other side of Sofia's desk.

"I have news," Tereza said between bites of the pastry. "One of my operatives reports that Blackmantle had a couple of strange visitors earlier today."

Sofia sighed. "If these visitors saw Blackmantle, they saw Daphnia. Describe them to me."

"Two elves... one a blonde-haired child and the other a dark-haired adult," Tereza answered. "The adult is armed to the hilt with two swords, bow, arrows, and various knives. My operative believes the child is the one in charge, while the older elf is her guardian."

Sofia looked at Tereza with alarm. "And your operative didn't bother to consider these mysterious elves might be a threat to my daughter... particularly the armed one?"

"I realize there's not much history between us, Your Grace, but I've been in the spy business for almost as long as I've been alive… and certainly longer than anyone you presently have," Tereza said. "I earned Aleksei's confidence… which is no small thing. It's why he recommended me to you. I know how to do my job, as do my people."

Sofia had trust issues where Daphnia was concerned, particularly after the assassination attempt. And she hadn't warmed up to Tereza as much as Aleksei said she would. At the moment, Sofia didn't know if she wanted to fire the master spy, arrest her for treason, or show a knife, the ultimate signal of her displeasure.

"Since the Princess is our primary concern," Tereza continued, "and Jarsus Blackmantle's her teacher, I started frequenting the same café where he eats breakfast every morning. Aleksei briefed me about him, but I wanted to see for myself."

"And?" Sofia asked. Her knives were staying in their sheaths for the time being.

"I got caught by Sienna, his bear companion." Tereza smiled as she remembered the incident. It had been a comedy of errors on her part, and totally unexpected. "Did you know she can talk to you in your head?"

"Yes. What's your point?"

"Simple, Your Grace. Where Blackmantle goes, Sienna goes. I've introduced myself into her small number of acquaintances. We're not close friends, but we occasionally talk. I like her and I believe she likes me. And while she'd never betray Blackmantle, she's more than willing to give me innocuous information. So when I received the report of the elves, I asked Sienna. She assured me everything was fine."

Sofia stared. "How were you able to do that? It's my understanding that Blackmantle's bear is quite intelligent and not easily fooled. Very much like Adimar in that regard."

"I haven't fooled her… and she's not Blackmantle's bear, Your Grace," Tereza protested. "She's definitely her own person…"

"Person?" Sofia asked.

"Yes, person… as much as you or me, Your Grace. You yourself said she's intelligent. How can you be one without being the other? I've listened to her thoughts as she's listened to mine. She's smarter than plenty of people I deal with every day, present company excluded. How do you see the wolf? As Daphnia's loyal pet?"

"Of course not! But Adimar's the son of a half-god."

"Who's to say Sienna doesn't have the same pedigree?" Tereza replied. "She's certainly not your ordinary bear. And she loves Blackmantle like you'd love your best friend. She loves the Princess as well. I know you worry about your child. All mothers do. But I assure you the Princess couldn't be in better hands. She's as safe with the dwarf as she is in the palace."

Sofia sighed. "You're right. Between Blackmantle, the bear, the wolf, and the Lads… you've heard of the Lads?"

Tereza nodded. "I've never met them, but Aleksei briefed me."

Sofia nodded. "Pray that you never have to. Very well, Tereza… excellent job."

"Oh, I'm not done, Your Grace."

"Then please continue."

Tereza looked into her goblet. It was empty. She held it up to Sofia, who nodded. After she had refilled it and taken a drink, she nestled into her chair. "Apparently the child's name is Emmy…"

"You mean the new child goddess of the empaths?" Sofia exclaimed. "She's supposed to be across the Greater Boreskyre

Mountains in the ruined city of Elanesse. What would she want Blackmantle for?"

"Sienna wouldn't give me specifics, Your Grace. And I didn't press. I don't want to breach confidence with her. What she did say was they were looking at old ship ledgers…"

"Ship ledgers?" Sofia said. "Are you sure?"

"I speak the language pretty well, Your Grace."

Sofia pointedly ignored the sarcasm from the young master spy. Aleksei was much the same when he first began working for her. She'd bring Tereza to heel soon enough. "Those ship ledgers are from an expedition to the west of InnisRos that occurred long ago. Blackmantle wants my husband to fund another voyage there. It has something to do with comments about an unknown danger. I believe the ledger called it 'the Oblivion.' If a goddess is interested in the same thing…"

"Then the king is sure to fund it," Tereza concluded.

"And my daughter will want to go."

AUTHOR'S NOTES

[1] *"Father's blood, Stygian night.*
Mother's blood, burning bright."

"Joined together, renders child of the Abyss.
Merged with the earth, for bonded bliss."

[2] *The languages used in the Abyss for spells and incantations are closely guarded secrets and designed to be extremely difficult to learn and speak. There are reasons for this, such as the accidental release of dangerous magic. But the Magic* Faction of Kor also considers the widespread usage of it as a threat to their power and prestige. Only certain ceremonial phrases, such as those used in the naming ritual, are deemed safe for popular consumption.

[3] "Roses are red, Violets are blue.
Open the doorway, So I can go through."

[4] "B'nai Elohim, Guardians of fate.
Delay their awareness, so concern will abate."

[5] "Air, wind, water, and light.
Coalesce, harmonize, return, and ignite."

"Construct your silhouette, show your veneer.
Encircle me and all those who are near."

Beginning with this book, and the others to follow, dwarf-speak is in Scottish brogue. Standard fantasy dwarves speak with a Scottish or Northern European brogue. This is particularly true in the works of J. R. R. Tolkien who, in many opinions, including my own, is the father of modern fantasy. For example, "afraid" translates to "feart," or "but" translates to "bit." Though I believe the brogue accent adds to the depth and personality of the character, some of it's hard to translate. So I left some words in the dialog alone instead of using their brogue translation. Specifically, "trouble" translates to "fash" in Scottish brogue. For the sake of the reader, I left words that are so far off the English version alone.

ABOUT THE AUTHOR

Robert E. Balsley, Jr. (1954 -) was born in Sioux City, Iowa. At the age of four his parents moved their family to Cincinnati, Ohio. Upon graduation from high school in 1973, Robert joined the United States Air Force which sent him to Tinker Air Force Base, Oklahoma. Upon his discharge in 1979, he found employment as a civil servant on Tinker until his retirement in 2014. In 2018 Robert and his wife picked up roots and moved from Oklahoma to Burlington, Kentucky, which is just across the Ohio River from Cincinnati.

In 1990 he played his first game of Dungeons and Dragons and was soon writing his own games. From this sprang the ideas which ultimately led to his love of writing and the creation of his current novels. Many of the main characters in his novels are based upon actual people who played Dungeons and Dragons with him all those years. This includes personalities, idiosyncrasies, and all those other traits that make friends so endearing… and fictional characters so alive!

Throughout his life he's been an avid reader of science fiction and fantasy, with a little World War Two history thrown in. Isaac Asimov, James Bliss, David Eddings, George R.R. Martin, Terry Goodkind, and Robert Heinlein are among his favorite authors.

Robert's also a collector of figures and models such as Star Trek spaceships, WWII airplanes, Dungeons and Dragons miniatures, TV and movie monster figures (particularly Godzilla), and dragons to name a few. It's in this world of mankind's rich imagination that he develops his stories, plots, subplots, heroic and cowardly deeds, laughter, tears (and all reader—that makes the reader want to "turn the page."

www.ingramcontent.com/pod-product-compliance
Lightning Source LLC
Chambersburg PA
CBHW010141030826
48979CB00024B/1091

* 9 7 9 8 8 8 9 9 0 1 4 6 4 *